LEAVES MAY FALL

CARISSA HARDCASTLE

HARDCASTLE PUBLISHING HOUSE

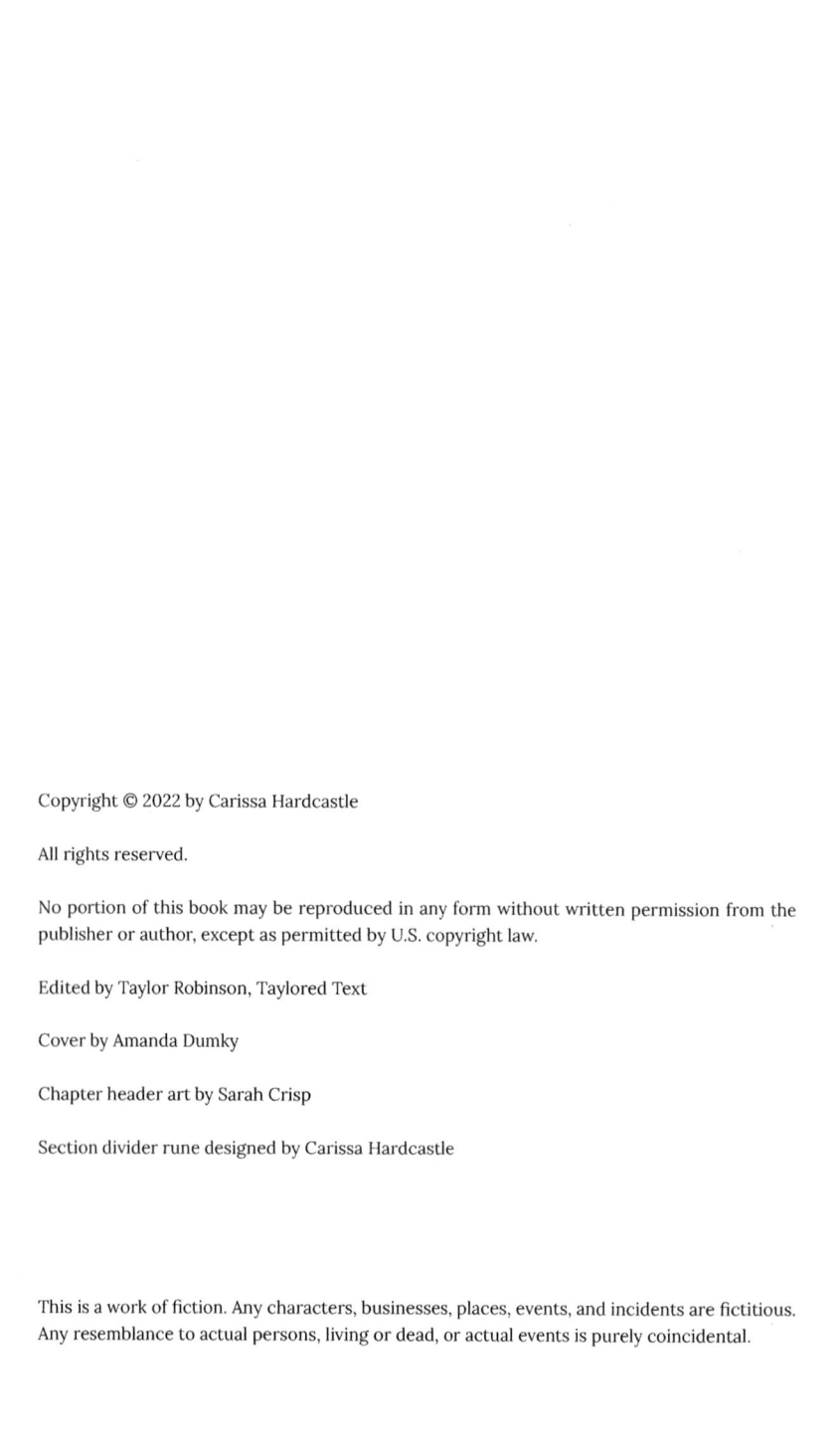

Copyright © 2022 by Carissa Hardcastle

All rights reserved.

No portion of this book may be reproduced in any form without written permission from the publisher or author, except as permitted by U.S. copyright law.

Edited by Taylor Robinson, Taylored Text

Cover by Amanda Dumky

Chapter header art by Sarah Crisp

Section divider rune designed by Carissa Hardcastle

This is a work of fiction. Any characters, businesses, places, events, and incidents are fictitious. Any resemblance to actual persons, living or dead, or actual events is purely coincidental.

Leaves May Fall is an epic fantasy with dark themes and depictions of violence, murder, strong language, sex, and drug and alcohol use.

Additionally, this story contains an occurrence of uninformed/non-consensual drug use and mentions of child abuse. No sexual assault takes place in the book.

Characters

The Stonebane Line

Regenya 413 Keeper
(reh-jehn-yuh)
Darius 370 high fae
(dair-ee-us)
Gressia 146 Keeper
(Grehs-ee-yuh)
Oren 29 Keeper
(Or-ehn)
Mollian 24 Keeper
(mahl-ee-ehn)

The Mercenaries

Jasper 34 fair folk (fae) 14yrs a merc
(jAs-per)
Aleah 22 half fae/human 9yrs a merc
(uh-lee-uh)
Leonidas 28 human 8yrs a merc
(lee-oh-nI-dihs)
Merriam 24 human 5yrs a merc
(mair-ee-uhm)
Campbell 24 fair folk (fae) 4yrs a merc
(kAm-behl)
Calysta 168 fair folk (nymph) 4yrs a merc
(kuh-lihs-tuh)

The Royal Guard

Pos Ferrick 320 Captain of the Guard high fae
(pahs Fair-ihck)
Kottor Dio 243 Ranger | Commander high fae
(kaht-or Dee-oh)
Ollivan 161 Ranger | Lieutenant high fae
(ahl-ih-vAn)
Eskar 127 Ranger | Lieutenant high fae
(ehsk-ar)
Rovin Arwood 27 Ranger | Lieutenant half-fae/human
(rah-vihn Ar-wUd)
Rillak 283 Guard | Sergeant high fae
(rihl-ehk)
Kodi 25 Ranger high fae
(koh-dee)
Bellamy 19 Ranger high fae
(behl-uh-mee)
Evangeline 19 Ranger high fae
(ee-vAn-jeh-leen)

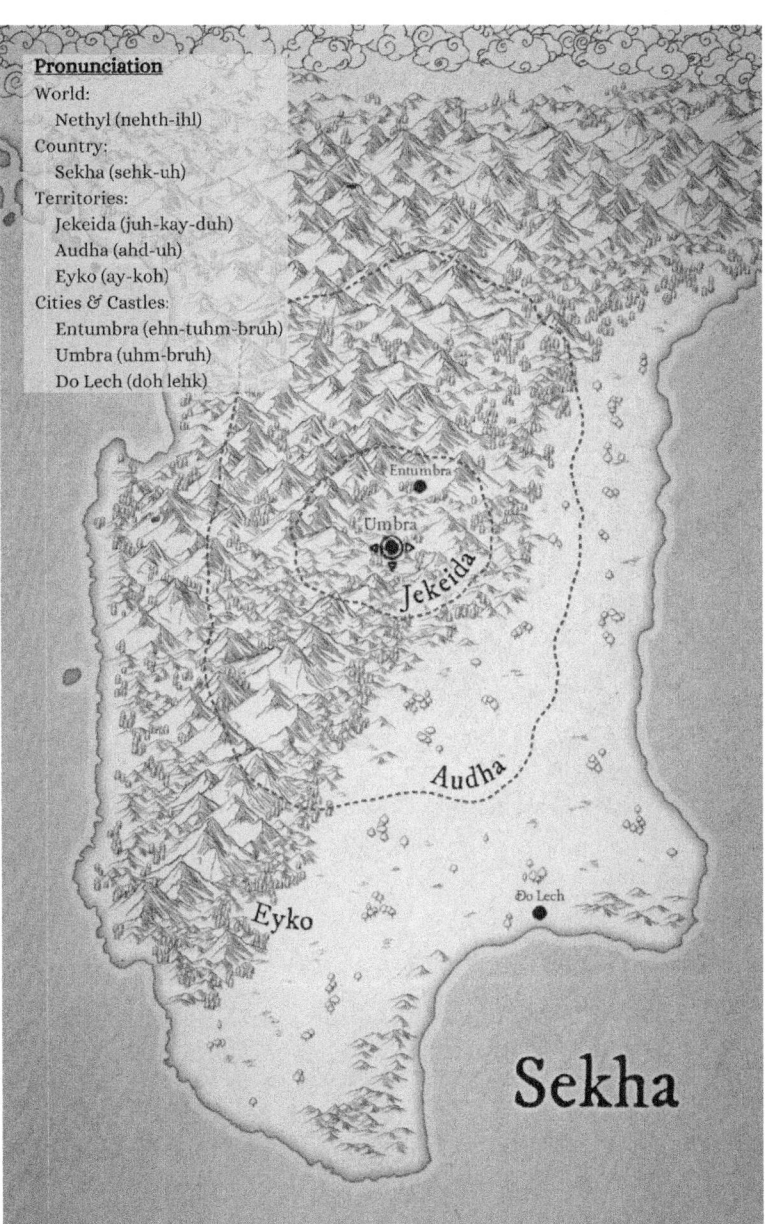

*If you've ever walked through a forest
and felt that maybe,
just past the edge of what you can see,
magic might exist ...
this is for you.*

Prologue

U viect oei

Sixteen years before ...

A LIGHT GRAY MIST shrouded the castle, softening the edges of the rough stones and sifting between the wrought iron catwalks and railings that lined the walls of the upper levels.

A man walked forward from the trees, feeling the slight, unnatural hum, usually imperceptible but trapped by the density of the humid air. His cloak flared out around him as he approached the castle, one narrow, steep stone staircase the only entrance. The railing was cold, beads of moisture speckling the iron. The chill bit into his hand as he gripped it, taking steps with a stride much more confident than he really felt. He resisted the urge to look behind him, knowing the ground sloping from the castle would appear far away already.

When his feet left stone and landed on a grated walkway, the tightness in his chest eased. He moved forward to a door set in the stone wall and pulled it open, the swollen wood sticking in the frame.

The room he entered was large and open. Stained glass windows depicting different forest and mountain scenes, all featuring dark-skinned fae with white hair, lined the walls, glowing in the weak light of the morning.

"My love," a soft voice greeted him in his native human tongue, and he turned, lips splaying in an eager smile.

"*Ruiko.*" He opened his arms as he stepped toward the fae female who had entered the room from one of the doors leading up to a tower, addressing her as he always did. Of the few words he knew in the Common language of the fae, beautiful was the one he used the most.

She smiled at him, her pale green eyes shining happily. "I was worried you wouldn't be able to make it." She allowed herself to be folded into his arms.

"You know nothing could keep me away." He ran a hand over the white curls spilling down her back. "Certainly not a few clouds."

"The roads are treacherous enough without the diminished visibility," she chastised, raising her head from his chest and placing a hand against his bearded cheek. She lightly brushed her fingers against the coarse sandy hairs. "If you'd gotten lost out there ..."

"I wouldn't have. I know this forest well, thanks to you." He smiled reassuringly, turning his head to kiss her palm.

She dipped her head, cheeks warming. Her light-brown skin was completely unblemished, showing nothing of her 130 years.

"So, what is on the agenda today?" he asked, releasing her. "Do you need me to do repairs? Upkeep?" he trailed off, sticking his hands in his pockets and keeping his shoulders relaxed and casual.

She waved her hand dismissively. "It's such a bleak day. How do you feel about an adventure?"

"I will follow wherever you lead, *Ruiko.*" He smiled, eyes glinting hungrily.

"Then let's go." She took his hand, leading him across the room and down a staircase. The chamber was lined with stone arch supports for the rest of the castle, giving the space the appearance of a maze. She brought him across the room and through a door leading to another set of stairs.

Further down she led him, the slight chill shifting to the sharp cool of air that had never seen the sun as dirt turned into cold granite beneath them. The tunnel led deep underneath the mountain, narrowing so that they had to travel one in front of the other until they broke out into a cavern.

In the middle of the room, a large arch was lit by thin strips of light lining the base of the walls. The light glinted faintly off the rough facets of the formation, a dark stone shot through with lines of transparent gold curved around a stone that shifted between violet and indigo. The hum of energy was deeper here, and his heartbeat quickened in anticipation, even as his body vibrated in a way that made his stomach turn.

"Show me everything," he whispered, stepping close behind the female as she reached toward the arch.

She smiled, leaning into his warmth as she pulled a small dagger from her belt, the hilt crudely carved with trees. "As you wish." She cut a shallow line across the middle of her fingers and swept them lightly over the stone, closing her eyes in concentration.

The air inside of the arch shivered, the hum emanating from within deepening and pulling. As she clasped his hand and stepped through, the very fabric of the world seemed to part and slide around them, almost like they were walking through water. When they had disappeared through the Gate, the air quickly settled back into a normal form, and the cavern was once again empty save for the infinite hum of the stones.

At almost the same time the fae and the human had stepped through the arch, a young girl stood at the edge of a forest in another reality, bottom lip tucked into her mouth as she contemplated the trees in front of her. She turned her head to look back at the house in the middle of the clearing, pale hair reminiscent of sunshine swinging against her shoulders from where it was gathered at the sides of her head in two pigtails.

Sensing no movement from the house, she turned forward and stepped into the trees.

The girl had explored the woods at the edge of her aunt's backyard in the mountains of Colorado hundreds of times before. She was eight years old, after all, and had been playing here since before she could walk. So, naturally, these woods held no mysteries save for those in her imagination.

But yesterday she had seen a boy in the forest, and he was certainly not in her imagination. He'd run off as soon as he'd seen her, darting behind a tree, and then ... she hadn't been able to find him. She'd rounded the wide trunk of the pine, but he'd seemingly vanished.

She was determined to find him again.

Still holding her bottom lip in her mouth, she quickly pushed through the trees, headed for the spot where she'd last seen him. When the aspens started to trickle into denser pine, she settled herself onto the ground, resting against the smooth trunk of a poplar tree.

An hour went by, and at this point she was leaning forward, chin propped in one hand and a small twig clasped in the other, idly doodling in the dirt as a soft mountain wind blew through the forest.

Then she felt it. A strange pull through the air, coming from inside and all around her, but just barely perceptible. Had she been engaged in any real activity, she wouldn't have noticed it at all. Just as she started to lift her head up, the pulling sensation flipped briskly into a rippling push.

It was all there and gone in less than a second. The soft scuffle of shoes against dirt came from her left, and she quickly turned her head, hands bracing against the ground on either side of her.

A boy appeared from between the trees, and she sat a little straighter, eyes lighting up. She wanted to wave, but was wary of frightening him off again.

He looked to be about her age, with skin the same color as the freckles that dusted her face and arms, but his hair was white. She'd never seen a boy with white hair before.

That hair hung in loose, shaggy curls over one side of his forehead, brushing just above two pale green eyes. The outer half of one of his irises was brown. His ears tapered to an elegant point, poking slightly from his curls. She'd never seen a boy with pointy ears before.

He slowly brought one hand up, flaring his fingers in a small, hesitant wave, tilting his head to the side with a smile, flashing canines that were sharp and slightly elongated. She'd never seen a boy with such sharp teeth before.

"What are you?" the girl whispered.

"*U viect oei,*" he whispered at the same time, smile growing.

She jumped back at the sounds coming from his mouth, eyebrows pulling together in confusion. She must not have heard right.

"*Ta oei fouj* Common?" he asked hopefully.

Her jaw dropped open, trying to decipher the words coming from his mouth.

"*U woujj xukt ej e 'ne.*" He swallowed, wiping his hands on his pants in a nervous way. He looked around slowly before gesturing forward with a questioning look and taking a small step towards her.

She waved vaguely at the ground and nodded, pushing herself to sit straight against the tree.

The boy closed most of the distance between them and sat down in front of her, leaving a few feet of space. He rested his hands on his knees, and she noticed a ring on each thumb glinting in the sunlight. Both rings were set with a stone: one dark purple, the other black shot through with thin veins of gold.

"Hello," she said, offering a tentative smile.

She felt pressure gather around her head, and she could have sworn something shifted in her mind. She brought a hand to her temple, her smile dropping in confusion.

"Hello, I'm Mollian Stonebane." The boy's smile exposed the ends of those two sharp teeth. "I'm sorry about the glamor. I just wanted us to understand each other."

The girl blinked. "What?"

The boy rubbed his forehead in frustration. "Did I do it wrong? Ugh, sorry, I've never done this before."

"Done what?"

"So you *can* understand me?"

"Yes, but you're not making much sense." She frowned in confusion.

"We don't speak the same language. I put a glamor on you so that you'd understand me. I'm no good at speaking most human dialects yet." He shrugged.

"A glamor." She tried out the word. "Like magic?"

"Yeah." He shrugged again, almost sheepishly.

"Wow." Her eyes widened, and she brought her hand up over her mouth. "This is way cool," she whispered.

The boy smiled, brushing white curls from his forehead.

She shook her head with a small laugh. "*Way* cool. What did you say your name was?"

"Mollian."

"Hi, Mollian. I'm Merriam." She smiled back, giddiness buzzing in her veins. This was by far the most exciting thing to have ever happened to her.

"I'm sorry I ran away yesterday. I promise I'm not usually that much of a scaredy-toad." He rubbed the back of his neck with a slight grimace.

Merriam shook her head, pigtails swinging lightly. She didn't even know what to think, much less say to him. Finally, she settled on, "Do you live here?"

He looked up, tilting his head to the side while he considered how to answer. "No, I don't. Do you?"

"My aunt does, but I'm here most days when there's no school. My parents work a lot." She looked down, fidgeting with the hem of her shirt.

"Mine, too," Mollian offered.

Merriam met his unique cracked gaze again. "Before the ... glamor, what language were you speaking?"

"Common."

"What country is that from?"

"Sekha. But most of Nethyl speaks it, thus the name 'Common,'" Mollian answered.

Merriam tilted her head. She was only in the third grade, but those certainly weren't the names of any countries she'd ever heard of. "You're not human, are you?"

Mollian smiled widely. "No, I'm fae. Faerie."

Merriam's eyes widened in surprised delight. "You're a faerie?!" she squealed, bringing her hands to her face. "Wait, don't you have wings?" Dozens of different fairytales ran through her mind.

Mollian laughed, shaking his head. "I don't have them. I'm high fae, not lesser. Well, a fair folk. My brother says it's rude to call them lesser faeries, even if I hear other people do it. Either way, only the fair folk have animal characteristics."

"Oh, but I bet it would be so cool to have them," Merriam mused.

Mollian shrugged. "Maybe, but I'd much rather have magic, and you can't have both."

"You can't?"

"Nope, not even the simple stuff. Though they are still immune to mind tricks."

"Mind tricks like glamors?" Merriam asked.

"Exactly like glamors." Mollian nodded. "Which, again, I'm sorry about. My brother is always going on about how I shouldn't use magic on humans without their consent. But it would have been hard to ask since you couldn't understand me," Mollian rambled.

"You have a brother?"

"And a sister, but I don't see her very often. And she's much older than me and Oren. She was already gone by the time we were born." Mollian again tried unsuccessfully to swipe the curls off his forehead and away from his eyes. "What about you?"

Merriam lifted her shoulders in a shrug. "Just me."

He looked thoughtful for a moment, then grinned. "Well, now you have me, too."

She couldn't help but grin back. And because it really is that simple at only eight years old, that was the moment they knew they were friends.

"Do you want to play a game?" Mollian offered hopefully.

"Like what?" Merriam asked.

Mollian tapped a finger to his chin, thinking.

"Do you know rock, paper, scissors?" Merriam suggested, scooting forward a bit. She held her hands out and demonstrated a quick run through of the game.

Mollian's eyes lit up. "Yes, we have something like that, too!" He closed the distance until their knees were touching, extending his own hands. "We call it shears."

They talked while they played, mostly about the mundane parts of life. Merriam talked about her favorite books and tv shows; Mollian told her about his favorite plays and hobbies. They compared notes on school, discussed which subjects were the best and worst, and talked about their favorite foods and animals and colors.

When they were bored with that game, they played tag around the trees. When they grew tired of that, they took turns drawing pictures in the dirt, talking all the while.

The sun started to drop lower in the sky, filtering through the trees and lighting Mollian's white hair into a halo of gold, contrasting against his light brown skin in a way that looked magical. That made sense to Merriam, because he *was* magical.

"It's getting late," she said reluctantly. "I have to go back." She pushed herself to her feet and dusted her hands off on her pants.

Mollian looked back, noticed the sun's position, and jumped up quickly. "I have to go, too." He frowned. "Will you be back here tomorrow?"

"I can meet you here right after breakfast!"

"I'll be here." Mollian smiled, holding his hand up in farewell.

Without really knowing why, Merriam placed her palm against his. When their hands were pressed together, a strange pulling sensation filled her, as if the essence of her was rushing through her hand and into Mollian. At the same time, the warmth of his touch rushed into her, moving up her arm, filling her, and finally settling somewhere in her chest.

She blinked in surprise, but the sensation was there and gone before she had a chance to fully acknowledge it. Only a heartbeat after, the excitement of meeting him was again overwhelming her.

"I'll see you then." With a final parting grin, she turned and ran back through the trees.

"Merriam, what were you doing out there? You're lucky your mother hasn't come by yet!" her aunt scolded as Merriam slid open the back door.

"I'm sorry. I lost track of time playing," she apologized, ducking her head dutifully.

"Go ahead and watch some tv, kiddo." Her aunt smoothed her fingers over one of Merriam's pigtails. "I'll give your momma a call and see where she's at."

Merriam sat on her aunt's couch, kicking her feet back and forth, teeth worrying lightly at her bottom lip as she flipped to the kids' channels.

"You're late again, Amanda." Her aunt's voice was soft, but still had a sharp edge that carried from the kitchen. "I'm not the one you need to apologize to … I know … Yeah, sure … bye."

She let her head fall back against the couch and clenched a fist to her chest, holding onto the magic of meeting the boy in the woods. The *faerie* boy.

It was okay if her mom was late to pick her up. She knew she'd be dropped off tomorrow on time. And she knew, with a strange confidence she couldn't identify, that Mollian would be there. She knew she could depend on him.

Back at the stone castle, the fae and the human had returned, sequestered away in a high tower room, bodies bare and slick with sweat, the sound of soft panting filling the air.

If the fae had been paying attention, she would have felt the shift echoing through her blood as the archway pulsed with a surge of energy when the two children placed their hands together just on the other side of her reality.

But she had been too focused on the man between her thighs and the waves of pleasure his tongue evoked from her to recognize it. She dug her fingers into that fine, sandy hair and tilted her hips up against his mouth, his beard scraping the delicate skin on the inside of her thighs as she gasped his name. Pleasure built and built in her core until release found her, and that thrum of power from the Gate deep beneath the mountain went completely unnoticed.

Chapter 1

Make them beg

MERRIAM CROUCHED ON THE branch of an oak, one hand resting lightly against the trunk for added balance, the other wrapped securely around the decoratively carved hilt of an axe. Rings glinted faintly in the dappled sunlight on the middle finger of each hand. Her long, pale hair was braided back from her face and twisted up into a coil at the back of her head, not a strand out of place. Not yet, at least.

She waited, taking deep, even breaths as she watched her surroundings, amber eyes scanning the forest floor and the trees around her. Her ears picked up the sound of horse hooves clopping along the packed dirt at an unhurried trot, and she caught movement through the trees only moments later.

A wood nymph stepped into the path carved through the forest by years of use. Her skin was a light olive green, and sunlight caught the length of her silky, petal-pink hair, highlighting it with gold.

The horses appeared on the trail, slowing as they noticed the female ambling along.

From her vantage point in the trees, Merriam watched the men look at each other before the lead came to a halt. There were eight of them; each carried a sword at his side, and three of them had additional knives at their belts. No other visible weapons.

The wood nymph tilted her head to the side, blinking inky black eyes at the men. "Hello," she said in a human dialect, her voice soft and melodic. "I mean you no harm. I will go about my way." She started to step to the side, a look of concern darkening her face.

The man in front chuckled, drawing his sword. "I'm sorry abou' that, little lady, but I don' think ya will be," he said in a thick North Eyko accent.

The female's skin paled, and she held up her hands, shaking fearfully. "I don't want trouble, please."

One of the men chuckled darkly. "Oh, but we do."

Just as the lead man snapped the reins, sending his horse running toward the nymph, Merriam dropped from the tree. As she fell, she swung her axe down into the head of a man underneath her with a sickening *thunk* that sounded over the noise of pursuit. She let go when she felt the blade sink deep into his skull, landing lightly next to the horse.

The man toppled over, and the remaining six all gaped at her. She braced her foot against his shoulder to wrench her axe free, visibly shivering at the sound of metal scraping bone. "I could go for some trouble myself, actually." She smiled brightly.

While this was happening, the nymph pulled a set of knives from the folds of her short dress, throwing one with practiced precision into the shoulder of the lead man's sword arm. He cried out, dropping the sword and pulling the knife free. "Fucking low-blood nymph *bitch!*"

Before the rest of the men could react, the other four of Merriam's troupe jumped down from the trees around them.

"I'm feeling rather generous today, boys. Which one of you would like to live to see sunset?" A male with dark skin and even darker wings asked, twirling a lance around in one hand.

"Oh, Jasper, don't take the fun out of it. I want to make them beg." Aleah's pale skin was scattered with even more freckles than usual, thanks to all the sun she'd gotten while hunting down this trafficking ring. Her flame-red hair bounced against her neck from a high ponytail, clearly showing off the clipped tip of one tapered ear that marked her as half-fae as she drew a sword from her belt.

Jasper's wings flared, glossy black feathers shining like ink in the sunlight. "Well, who am I to deny a lady?" He grinned, driving his lance forward.

The men exploded into action. The one closest to Jasper hadn't moved fast enough to completely dodge the lance, and it sank into one arm, poking out the other side. He screamed, raising his sword with the other to swing at Jasper, who lifted into the air and kicked the sword out of the man's hand before pulling his lance free and falling back to land on his feet.

Aleah danced around her own assailant, easily spinning out of the reach of his sword and then ducking back in to slash at his legs.

One of the other traffickers had been felled from his horse by Leonidas, the two men now locked in combat. Muscle rippled underneath the colorful tattoos of various birds that covered Leonidas' arms as he quickly overtook his opponent.

Campbell, a male with tan skin and antlers atop his head of short, dark curls was smoothly countering the attacks of another.

Merriam unsheathed a second axe from her belt as she swung the first into the thigh of one of the remaining traffickers, narrowly dodging his sword as she pulled him to the ground. She stomped down on his sword hand, feeling bones crack beneath her boot before wheeling away and attacking the man fighting with Campbell.

With the man distracted, Merriam cut through the straps of his saddle. The horse reared up when her blade nicked its skin, sending the man crashing to the ground before it ran off. As the trafficker scrambled to his feet, Campbell knocked the sword from him, ducking his head and ramming into the man's rib cage. The strong, sharp points of his antlers broke through bone in several places, and he roughly pushed the dying man free, blood dripping from his antlers to splatter onto his face and shoulders.

Merriam had already started running toward Calysta. The wood nymph had thrown the trunk of a fallen tree against her initial assailant, knocking him from his horse and crushing him against the ground.

The last man was riding toward the nymph, nimbly tossing a knife at her. She twirled away, bringing her hands up to manipulate the trees, but the knife caught her arm, and she hissed.

The nymph's black eyes shimmered in pain and anger as the iron of the blade reacted to the saturation of magic in her blood. She yanked the knife free, dropping into a crouch with a growl that bared pointed teeth as she summoned.

Brambles crawled out of the forest in answer to her call and tangled around the horse's legs, causing it to trip and topple over. The trafficker jumped from the saddle and rolled, trying to avoid the thorny branches.

Merriam jumped, sailing over the horse and folding onto her knees in the dirt, narrowly avoiding the brambles as she slid over to the man trying to scramble to his feet. She sliced across his thighs with an axe as he reached for his sword.

The brambles wrapped around his arm, tangling him up and holding him to the earth. Merriam nodded at the nymph before turning back to the others, not surprised to find only one other trafficker remaining, on his knees and glaring darkly at the redhead as she held the point of a dagger to his throat.

Jasper looked around, setting the butt of his lance on the ground and leaning his weight on it. "Well now, it looks like there's two of you, but I said only one, and I am a male of my word. What do you think, Aleah?"

"I still haven't heard anyone beg." Aleah frowned, twisting her knife against the man's throat.

He hissed, trying to tilt his head away from the weapon as blood beaded and trickled down his neck. Somehow, he managed to spit at Aleah's feet.

"Oh, boo. You're no fun." She rolled her eyes and plunged the blade into his throat.

His eyes went wide, and he made a garbled sound as she pulled her knife free, wiping the blade off on his shoulder before he fell forward and slowly bled out.

"Looks like we're keeping yours, Calysta," she said in the Common language, sheathing the knife at her hip, its handle carved with honey dripping over citrus.

"We always keep Calysta's," Merriam grumbled, sliding her own weapons back into her belt.

"You never keep yours alive long enough, Mer." Aleah shot her a pointed look.

"What can I say? I'm efficient." Merriam grinned, brushing an errant lock of hair from her face.

The trafficker caught in the brambles watched them with wide eyes, blood dribbling from his legs. It was clear from his expression that he wasn't fluent in Common.

"Legends, Cam. No need to go so deep next time," Leonidas muttered as he removed bits of bone and gore from the male's antlers, his short, dark curls matted with blood.

"That's not what you said last night," Campbell replied cheekily.

Aleah jokingly gagged as she walked by them, stepping up to Calysta and carefully inspected her arm. Slightly shimmery blood had dripped all the way down the nymph's fingers and off the points of her claws. "We could use some of that muslin, Leo," Aleah called over her shoulder. The blonde tossed her a wad of cloth, and she wiped away what blood she could before wrapping a strip of fabric tightly around the wound.

"Thank you." Calysta let the brambles escape back to the forest.

The trafficker was too scared to try to move now that he was free. Merriam watched his eyes flick to his sword, but his hand didn't even twitch.

A peregrine falcon came dive-bombing through the trees, knocking into the chest of the man and laying him flat. He screamed outright as the falcon pressed the talons of one foot into the base of his neck, staring him down for a second before turning its head to Leonidas and fluffing its feathers proudly.

"Oh, don't look so full of yourself. You're too late to be of any real help." Leonidas folded his arms over his chest.

The falcon let out a very defiant *kak*! and moved his talons from the trafficker's neck, shifting to face the blonde head on. He screeched again, stamping his feet. Each movement had the trafficker wincing, the tips of the falcon's talons piercing his skin.

"No, you weren't helpful at all. I'm not going to pretend you were just to make you feel better."

Watching the tall, muscular man argue with a bird while his face was spattered with blood was comical, and Merriam couldn't hold back her laugh. "I think you did great, Pan," she cooed.

The falcon screeched at Leonidas again before flying up to perch on Merriam's shoulder, mindful of his talons, and glare in the blonde man's direction.

"You're such a fucking traitor, Panic. I'll remember this the next time you're wanting a bit of meat off my plate," Leonidas told him.

Campbell laughed, walking up to Merriam and lightly stroking Panic's chest with a finger. "Don't worry, bud. We both know that's an idle threat."

Leonidas rolled his eyes, but held out a fist, and the falcon flew over to land on it, lightly smacking Merriam in the face with a wing as he took flight. "I'm going to make supper out of you one of these days," he grumbled, and the falcon puffed out his chest.

The trafficker watched all of this without a sound. Even if he had understood the words, he was more than likely in shock.

"Calysta, Campbell, round up the horses if you can. I'm sure they'll catch a fine price at the next town. We'll take care of this." Jasper gestured to the man at his feet.

The nymph and the antlered male headed off into the trees, and Jasper turned his attention to the trafficker. "Now, you're going to tell us all about your little operation, aren't you?" he asked in human tongue, crouching down next to the man. His wings were lifted slightly to keep them from brushing the dirt, and the dark flare of them looked downright threatening.

The trafficker swallowed, small patches of blood blooming on his shirt where the falcon had pierced his skin. "We were just earnin' a livin'," he sputtered. "There was a man. A human, like us. He wanted nymphs. Said he'd pay us fifteen silver per head."

"What did he want them for?"

"I don' know, honest! All he told us was tha' they had to be alive, otherwise he wasn' gonna pay us none."

"His name?"

The trafficker just shook his head. "We never knew it. We just called him *tohmzad*."

Demon.

"How did you get in contact with him?"

"We didn' do tha', neither. He sought us out from the beginning and said he'd find us. We was never to keep 'em in the same spot twice. He was adamant abou' it."

"How did he find you? Did you leave a sign?"

The man paused, then shook his head wildly.

Jasper narrowed his eyes, bringing the fatally sharp broadhead of his lance to the man's throat.

"You're jus' gonna kill me, anyway. And I'd rather tha' than what he'd do to me."

"Oh, I'm going to kill you. But I can make it slow. So *deliciously* slow. I'll cut you open and feed you to the falcon and his friends. My dear falconer will tell you how much his birds love fresh meat."

Leonidas nodded, a devilish grin curving his lips, and Panic gave a noisy flap of his wings, head tilting as he gazed at the trafficker.

"Or, you can tell me how you got in contact with this *tohmzad*, and we'll make it nice and clean. You have my word as a mercenary." Jasper placed his free hand against his chest and shot the man a winning smile, but his silver eyes glittered wickedly.

The man gulped. "Promise you'll kill me. Promise it."

"I swear it," Jasper said.

The trafficker swallowed again, looking shakily to each of the mercenaries before returning his gaze to Jasper. "He took our blood," he said, and Merriam felt a shiver run down her spine. "He took our blood an' told us to cut ourselves and the nymphs. Spill the mix of it into the ground outside of where we were stayin' an' he'd come to us."

Jasper glanced to Merriam, registering her reaction.

Ice ran in her veins. "Did he mark you? With ink or with his blood?" she asked, managing to keep the urgency from her voice.

The man shook his head wildly. "No, he jus' cut my arm open."

Merriam looked at Jasper and gave him a small nod, lifting a hand to brush the small iron aspen leaf at her neck.

Jasper swiftly drove his lance into the man's chest, Aleah flinching at the wet squelch of cracked ribs.

"What man is able to work blood magic?" Jasper asked as he yanked his weapon free, wiping the gore off on the man's shirt.

Merriam shook her head. "It shouldn't be possible. Not for a human." She rubbed the back of her neck, fighting the urge to reach for the tattoo between her shoulder blades. "We need to check him for tattoos," she said, crossing her arms. "Best not to take him at his word. He could have been glamored when it happened."

Jasper nodded. "I agree. But what if there are no marks?" His dark silver eyes held her gaze.

"I'll look into it," she promised, and knelt to start stripping the trafficker.

"Check them all," Jasper ordered, and they spread out among the bodies.

When a preliminary search revealed no suspect markings on any of the men, they rounded up the bodies to burn and collected any weapons and items of value to trade, sell, or keep.

Several hours later, sweaty and covered in ash, the six mercenaries loaded up the horses and headed for the nearest town, eager for food and a long night's rest. It would be at least a five-day journey back to Umbra, the royal city, and their home.

Merriam rolled her shoulders, stretching her neck as they rode through the forest. Hunting this trafficking ring had kept them away for the better part of a fortnight, and she was very much looking forward to being back in her own bed.

Chapter 2
Welcome back

MERRIAM WOKE TO THE gray light of dawn, the sun barely peeking over the horizon. She sat up with a yawn, rubbing the heel of her hand over an eye. Rolling off the mattress and onto the floor, she stood up and stretched her whole body out before walking quietly to the kitchen, careful not to wake the others still sleeping.

They each had their own room within the house, but it was tradition for them all to sleep together their first night back after a big job. Every mattress in the house had been brought to the floor of the mushroom (which Aleah had named as a joke, saying the only room without windows should be a mushroom; Jasper and Leonidas had denied her request to add a source of natural light, but had let the nickname stick) and they'd shared a few drinks before passing out, exhausted from travel.

Merriam stooped to pick up the few empty bottles of wine scattered about as she passed, setting them on the counter and walking over to the kitchen sink. She cupped her hand under the tap in lieu of finding a cup, taking a few sips before splashing the water over her face.

Jasper came in behind her, leaning against the opposite counter. "Have you decided what you're going to tell them?" he asked.

Merriam was the unofficial liaison between the mercs and the Crown, largely due to her connection with the younger Stonebane prince. She handled all of the negotiations for jobs and accepted payment on behalf of the group.

She dried off her face before turning to him. "I want to speak to Mollian about it first. I'm sure the queen will want the official debrief today, but I should be able to find him beforehand. I'm not sure what the implications are, and I don't want to go up in front of everyone blind."

Jasper nodded. "We'll stay close tonight so we can be here when you have information for us."

Merriam pulled her hair over her shoulders, gently working her fingers through it so she could braid it back. "I'll come by tonight to split the coin and pass along anything new, but I'm not staying the night again. We were gone for a while this time, and I'm sure there's a lot to catch up on with Molli."

"Of course." Jasper pushed from the counter, reaching to pull some ingredients from the cupboards. "Any interest in breakfast?"

Merriam tied up the end of her braid and tossed it over her shoulder. "No, I'm going to head out now so I can clean up and prepare before the debrief."

"See you later, then."

"Later." Merriam smiled, exiting the kitchen and bounding lightly up the stairs. She almost never used the main entrance, which was technically the back entrance, anyway. While her occupation as a mercenary certainly wasn't a secret, she got some form of pleasure from creeping out of windows and along rooftops, unseen and unnoticed by everyone below. Aside from that, she had worked hard to hone the skills she used in her job and took every opportunity to keep them sharp.

As she jumped down to the street and made her way up the sloping road to the castle, she noticed a buzz in the air and people milling about despite the early hour. Umbra was a diverse mix of high fae, humans, and fair folk of all shapes and sizes. She crept closer to a group of females on the street, whispering amongst themselves.

"Do you think he's changed much?" one asked, her hoofed feet shifting excitedly on the cobblestones.

"How long do you think they'll wait before throwing a return feast?" another speculated, long tail curling in anticipation.

Merriam blinked in confusion, continuing on before the pieces fell into place along with a flurry of butterflies in her stomach that were half anticipation and half anxiety.

The extra guards at the gates confirmed her suspicions. They gave off an antsy energy, and she didn't try to make conversation as they let her through.

The castle was already awake and moving, and Merriam found a servant to deliver news of her return to the queen before she let her mind stretch, searching for that prickle of awareness that let her know Mollian was close. She felt the familiar brush against her consciousness, his acknowledgment of her, and she hurried up the stairs and through the corridors toward the rooms they shared, eager to catch him before he disappeared for the day.

She rounded the corner just as he walked through the door. He stood about a head taller than she did now, and his unruly, white curls framed his face, just barely brushing his jawline and almost completely obscuring the leaves of the aspen branch tattoos at each temple. His face split into a grin as he saw her, cracked green eyes lighting up. "Ria!" He ran up to her, pulling her into a hug that lifted her off her feet. "You're back!"

Merriam looped her arms around her *mehhen*, both of them savoring the fullness they always felt in their souls after being separated for a period of time. "I got in last night," she told him as he set her down. "It was late, or I would have sent for you."

Mollian shook his head, a curl falling over his forehead in a way he'd never quite managed to prevent throughout the years. "I passed out pretty early. It's been crazy here the past few days with everyone preparing. Oren is coming back today." He held his hand up, and she pressed her palm to his.

"His return completely slipped my mind when I was gone. I didn't even realize it until I was on my way here. When does he get in?"

"Sometime this morning; it should be soon." Mollian bounced on his toes like an eager child, making Merriam laugh.

"Well, I won't keep you, but I really do need to bathe." Merriam smoothed her shirt, slightly crumpled from sleep. "I need to talk to you, though. Something about this last job."

"I'll make time," Mollian promised. He gave her a final hug before hurrying off.

The heir apparent had been gone for the past five years, studying and training in Entumbra in preparation to take the crown. Her first visit to Entumbra had been seven years prior, right after Mollian had brought her home to Nethyl. She'd felt the heaviness of the magic surrounding the castle almost instantly and been both completely captivated and wildly uneasy.

Since Oren had left, she'd stopped by Entumbra several times when it was on the way back from a job. Though the density of the magic still tugged at her, she'd eventually grown used to it and learned to ignore it. Plus, the promise of a hot meal had always been too good to pass up, and the company hadn't been half-bad, either.

Merriam ran the tap to her tub, stripping the clothes from her body and slipping into the steaming water. As she worked at pulling out her braid, she smiled, remembering some of the conversations she and Oren had during her visits. While he was nowhere near as talkative as Mollian—that was always a given—Oren still loved to tell stories of different worlds after he'd had a drink or two. They'd ended up spending a lot of time together; her cheeks heated as memories of her most recent visits flashed through her mind. She pushed them away, brushing off the nerves tangling in her stomach at the thought of seeing him again.

Finishing up quickly, Merriam dressed, braided her hair, and grabbed her weapons belt from where she'd dropped it on the floor. She headed out as she looped it around her waist, the weight of her axes a settling comfort.

She could feel Mollian close by and followed the soft ping of him against her mind, the rune on her back itching slightly.

Merriam exited the castle doors just as a group of horses trotted through the main gates.

Atop the first horse sat a male with light brown skin, his thick white hair shaved close to his scalp on the sides and back and longer on top, pulled into a bun at the back of his head. His temples were similarly adorned with aspen branch tattoos, but extended further than Mollian's, only the center of his forehead bare. A few stray hairs had fallen loose during the ride, framing his face.

He swung down from his mount gracefully, a huge grin lighting his face as he approached Mollian and embraced him, clapping his back a few times.

"Glad to see you've been able to keep things under control while I've been gone." Merriam heard him say as she walked closer. "I've missed you."

"I've missed you, too," Mollian replied, stepping back.

Oren's gaze finally traveled past his brother, spotting Merriam over Mollian's shoulder. "I think it's safe to say who's really been keeping you in check."

"Welcome back." Merriam curtsied, her heart skipping over a beat when she met his deep green eyes.

"This is a pleasant surprise." Oren pulled her into a hug as Mollian stepped to the side. "With your reputation, I didn't expect you would be home."

"I did try my hardest to be away," Merriam joked, returning the embrace.

"How lucky that your plans didn't work out." Oren released her, taking a step back to add polite distance between them. "I can't wait to hear about your latest adventures."

Merriam looked from him to Mollian, worrying at her lip. "Actually, I needed to talk to Molli, but you should be there, too. I know you just got back, but it's important."

"Let's talk over breakfast, then. A bath can wait, but I am famished." He gestured toward the castle, draping an arm over Mollian's shoulders. "I'll let you dominate this time as long as you promise to fill me in on everything the little prince has been up to the past five years." Oren ruffled Mollian's curls with one hand as they walked.

Mollian ducked out from under Oren's arm, shoving him in the side. "Act your age, fucker." He laughed, attempting to smooth down his unruly hair.

"Age isn't a matter of consequence among siblings, Mollian."

"I bet Gressia would deign to disagree," Mollian argued.

They ended up back in Merriam and Mollian's suite for breakfast. There was a decent spread of fruits, meats, and bread. Merriam's stomach rumbled as she piled food onto a plate, setting in on a strip of bacon as she went.

"Is it possible for a human to work blood magic?" she asked, slathering butter onto a roll.

Mollian's eyes shot to hers, the concern clear in his eyes before he

Cast the thought into her head. *Ria, what—*

Not me. She interrupted him.

Oren sat back, tearing a slice of ham with his teeth and chewing thoughtfully. "It is, but not if their blood is pure."

"Pure?" Merriam questioned.

"Blood magic can only be given by birth or by rite," Mollian clarified. "If you weren't born with the magic in your blood, it has to be given to you by someone who was. The only way to do that is through a Bond."

"And once a human is Bonded, their blood is no longer pure," Merriam connected.

"Correct, it's no longer purely human. Their blood is, in essence, fae." Oren picked another piece of ham off of the platter. "Though the potency of the magic is greatly diminished."

"Can any human get blood magic from any fae?"

"Yes, and no. A human cannot forcefully get blood magic, it has to be freely given by the fae. But there aren't many capable of blood magic," Oren clarified. While all High fae were gifted with the ability to work simple mind magic such as casting glamors and moving objects without touching them, Keeper magic like the princes' ran deeper. Their mind magic was more powerful, allowing them to Cast, and their blood also enabled them to control the Gate between worlds.

"Who outside of your family has blood magic?" Merriam asked.

"Aside from a few very rare instances, only nymphs and sprites, which manifests as some sort of nature element," Mollian answered. "They're the only fair folk with any magic at all, not counting the accelerated healing of the fae."

Merriam bit into a bright green apple, contemplating. "We think the traffickers we were sent after were working for a human. The man we talked to was a bit of an imbecile, but it sounded like this guy was using blood magic." She briefly relayed what the trafficker had said about the man taking his blood and keeping the nymphs alive.

Mollian and Oren exchanged a glance. "Well, that is concerning." Oren scratched the stubble along his jaw.

"Could he be using the nymphs for their magic? Bartering their freedom for their consent?"

Oren shook his head. "Magic knows the difference between coercion and consent."

"Why would he need the nymphs kept alive, then?" Merriam asked.

"That's a question that could certainly use an answer," Mollian said.

"Don't mention this during the debrief," Oren decided. "There will be too many people there, and this isn't the type of news that should go public until we have more knowledge. I'll talk to our mother about it later today." Oren stood, brushing his hands against his pants.

"Of course," Merriam agreed.

"I'll be at the meeting, but I should clean up first. I'm sure I smell like a horse." Oren excused himself, heading toward the door. "Let's catch up tonight, Mollian. Mer, you should come, too."

"I'll be debriefing the debrief with the mercs later, but thank you."

"We'll miss you, then," Oren said, opening the door to leave before adding, "Keep your fucking schedule open, Mollian." He shot them a parting grin.

Merriam leaned her head on Mollian's shoulder, his happiness almost palpable between them. "You missed him," she said teasingly.

"It'll be nice having him around to take the heat for everything again, that's for sure," Mollian joked, brushing a curl off of his forehead. "How late do you think you'll be out tonight?"

"It shouldn't be long. Everyone is still pretty tuckered out from traveling, so I doubt Jasper will even push training together tonight. I told him I'm staying here, though," she assured him.

"You'd better. I'll save you some of the good wine."

"So chivalrous and princely of you." Merriam exaggerated a swoon.

"We aim to please." Mollian flicked his fingers, and a grape lifted from the platter and lightly smacked into her cheek.

"Don't start things you don't want to finish, Prince."

"Who says I don't want to finish it?"

Merriam gave him a measured look. "Do you want to do this briefing with bacon in your hair?"

"Maybe." Mollian grinned, then fell back into the cushions. "It's good to have you back, too, Ria. I hate when you're gone so long."

"It must get incredibly boring without me to entertain you." She grabbed another handful of grapes and settled into the couch next to him. *I hate it, too,* she Cast to him.

Merriam told Mollian about her travels as they snacked on the leftover food until a knock sounded at the door, and a guard called through the wood. "You're needed in the war room, Prince Mollian. The mercenary, too, if she's with you."

Merriam snorted, standing up. "What's your bet? A newbie or one of Ferrick's sycophants." She rolled her eyes and opened the door. "The mercenary is here, thank you. Do I need to be escorted?" She batted her lashes.

The guard flushed, shaking his head and turning away.

"A newbie, then," Mollian said, coming up behind her.

Merriam sighed, slowly shaking her head. "I was hoping for more of a reaction."

"You don't need to get riled up anyway." Mollian led her out of the room, shutting the door behind him.

They made their way toward the front of the castle and into the war room, a small chamber carved out of stone and polished to a shine. In the middle of the room was a large table, the top overlaid with a map of Sekha: the interior mountainous territory of Jekeida, Umbra marked near its center; the middle territory of Audha wrapped around it, East Audha dropping into sprawling planes; and the perimeter ring of Eyko around them both, bordered by vast oceans on all sides but the North, where mountains gave way to a frozen wasteland.

A few courtesans and guards stood around, quietly conversing among themselves. Mollian walked shoulder-to-shoulder with Merriam through the room before leaving her at the end of the table and plopping down into a seat near the head.

Before long, a door across the room opened, and the Captain of the Guard entered, followed by Oren. They took their positions at either side of the head of the table before the Stonebane monarchs entered, and everyone stood as they took their seats.

The queen had the same light brown skin and white hair as her sons, twisted into many little braids, some piled on top of her head and the rest cascading over her shoulders. Her aspen tattoo was a full crown across her brow, and her pale green eyes were sharp and calculating, scanning the room with an almost cold indifference before speaking. "Sit."

Merriam straightened as everyone else took their seats around the table, bowing low to the queen and repeating the gesture to the king, a fae of olive complexion and short, dark hair. His tattoo was almost a twin to Oren's, extending across his forehead, but not meeting in the middle. He ran his fingers idly through his beard. Though Mollian and Oren had the complexion, hair, and eyes of a Keeper like their mother, their facial features—the high cheekbones, straight noses, and strong jawlines—were shared with their father.

"Merriam, last we spoke, I hired you to take care of some traffickers for us," Queen Regenya said.

"Yes, Your Majesty. My team and I were able to hunt them down. They will no longer be a problem for your people." Merriam met the queen's gaze evenly.

"No longer a problem?"

"They're dead, Your Majesty," she answered plainly, hands held placidly in front of her. She briefly explained how she and the others were able to find them and set up the ambush, leaving out most of the less palatable details.

"You're sure you've dispatched them all?" Captain Pos Ferrick narrowed his eyes. He was a burly fae, with brown hair cut close to his head and a neatly trimmed beard.

Merriam gave him a withering look. "Would I be here if I hadn't?"

The captain scoffed, shifting in his seat. "My Rangers have been hunting these traffickers down for months. Excuse me for finding it difficult to believe you've managed to complete the job in mere weeks."

Mollian caught Merriam's gaze from where he sat next to Ferrick and made a face in mockery of the captain. Merriam quickly averted her eyes, biting the inside of her cheek to keep from smiling. "Well, Captain, maybe you should have hired me months ago." She blinked innocently.

Mollian snorted, but quickly started coughing to cover it up.

"Enough." The queen lifted a hand, and Mollian's coughing silenced. "If the girl said they're all taken care of, then they are all taken care of."

The captain wanted to say more, but held his tongue as Regenya waved her hand to where Oren sat at her right. "Her payment."

The crown prince rose from his seat, gracefully stepping around the table to stand in front of her. "Eighty gold marks, ten for each." He handed her two bags.

"Thank you, Your Highness." She met his eyes, maintaining the contact while dipping her head.

Oren returned the nod, his lips twitching in a smile at the formality of her tone here compared to how he'd come to know her.

"Thank you, Your Majesties," she addressed the king and queen after Oren stepped back. She bowed at the waist, braid falling over her shoulder.

"I will call upon you when your services are required again," the queen said in dismissal.

Merriam nodded once and turned on her heel to head out the door. She tied the bags of coin to her belt and headed out of the castle into the city.

After walking through town for a few minutes, Merriam ducked into an alleyway and sprang onto a trash can, grabbing for a ladder anchored into the wall of a building. Climbing to the roof, she walked to the edge and leapt confidently to the neighboring building, even with the extra weight at her waist. She leaned over to grab hold of a drainage pipe and swung her body over the edge of the roof, lowering herself down until she was almost even with a window ledge. She stuck her foot out, transferring her balance from the pipe to the ledge. Slipping a small knife from her belt, she wedged it between the glass panes, unlatching them and swinging one out so she could slip inside.

"Welcome back. Didn't bring us any of your fancy breakfast yet again, I see," greeted a voice from across the room. A flap of wings accompanied the statement.

"Hello, Pan," Merriam cooed, ignoring the slight as she walked over to the falcon perched by the desk. Panic shifted his feet, flapping his wings again and dipping his head, which Merriam scratched with a finger.

"Go do something useful, you big softy," Leonidas grumbled, making shooing motions at the bird he'd raised from a hatchling.

Panic raised his head and *kak*'d once at Leonidas.

"I heard Prince Oren came back today." Leonidas stood from the desk, closing the ledger he'd been writing in and running his hands over his short, blonde hair.

"Yup, lots of bustle over at the castle," Merriam confirmed, following as he walked from the room.

"I wonder if Jasper will go by to catch up with his old friend." The dark-skinned mercenary was only a few years older than the prince, and they'd become close when Jasper briefly trained with the Guard before branching out on his own.

"Are you hoping he'll put in a good word for you?" Merriam teased as she followed him down the stairs.

Leonidas scoffed, "I don't need a good word, Mer. I'm the best falconer in all of Sekha and could be running the castle aviary in a heartbeat if I wanted."

"But instead, you'd rather live just on the wrong side of the law?"

Leonidas looked over his shoulder to toss her half a smile. "More excitement and fewer assholes."

Everyone else was already gathered in the mushroom, which had been cleared of the mattresses and blankets from the night before. Leonidas took a seat by Campbell, casually draping a colorfully tattooed arm over his shoulders.

Merriam unhooked the bags of gold and tossed them to Jasper before plopping down next to Calysta. "Eighty pieces."

Jasper caught the bag and set it on the table in front of him with a satisfied nod. "Let's hear it."

Merriam tossed her braid over the back of the couch. "Ferrick was a bit of an ass, as always, but other than that, there's not much to tell. I did talk to Molli and Oren before then, though."

"What did the princes have to say?" Jasper leaned forward, resting his chin on his clasped hands.

"Mostly what I already suspected. A human shouldn't be able to do blood magic without Bonding themselves to a fae, but it has to be consensual bondage."

Campbell and Aleah both snickered, turning into full on laughter when their eyes met across the room.

"Fucking children." Leonidas rolled his eyes at the two youngest mercs.

"Mer's the one who decided to bring kinks into this," Campbell defended.

Jasper was frowning, mouth pressed to his knuckles as he thought. His eyes finally flicked up to hers, the question in them plain.

"The only fae with blood magic should be Keepers, nymphs, and sprites," she confirmed, fidgeting with the aspen leaf at her throat. "It would be exceedingly rare for someone outside of them to be born with it."

"Rare, but possible?" Jasper raised an eyebrow.

"Yes. I'll have to look into it some more." Merriam sighed, dragging a hand down her face. "I'll do some deep dives in the castle library this week, see if I can find anything."

Chapter 3

There's a Gate in Entumbra

Fourteen years before...

MERRIAM HAD BEEN MEETING Mollian in the woods behind her aunt's house for almost three years when he showed up one day with a present.

"Hold out your hand," he instructed, grinning devilishly.

"You'd better not be about to hand me some sort of faerie worm, Molli." Merriam gave him a distrustful glare, but stuck out her palm.

Mollian opened his fist, dropping a metal chain into her hand before shoving his own into his pockets, watching her sheepishly.

Merriam plucked the chain between two fingers, inspecting the aspen leaf charm dangling on the end. It was about the size of a nickel and so ornately pressed with veins it looked almost life-like, despite its dark silver color. "It's so beautiful!" she whispered, running her thumb over the charm before looking up at Mollian. "Help me put it on?"

Mollian took the necklace from her and reached around to clasp it behind her neck as she held her short hair out of the way. "It's iron," he told her. "As long as you're wearing it, your mind won't be able to be manipulated by magic."

"Not even by you?"

"Not even by the most powerful fae alive," Mollian answered. "Now that you're fluent in Common, there's no reason for me to have to glamor you, and I don't want you to ever question whether I'm manipulating you or changing the way you see things." His young face was solemn as he dropped his gaze to the ground, brushing a curl off of his forehead with a frown. The movement exposed the short sprigs of aspen branches that had been tattooed on each temple on his tenth birthday, the leaves disappearing into his hairline. A symbol of his birthright and his bloodline. "I want you protected from other things, too, just in case."

Merriam fiddled with the leaf at her chest. "Like other fae who may cross over here?" she clarified.

Mollian pursed his lips. "Well, sure, but that would be highly unlikely."

"Do a lot of your kind come here?" Merriam asked.

Mollian shook his head. "My family has a specific kind of blood magic that lets us move between worlds. We're the only ones, at least in our universe, who possess it."

"How do you know?"

"Well, there are gateways that connect all the different dimensions to each other," Mollian explained. "Most gateways are minor, and can only access a parallel dimension."

"Like your world to mine."

"Exactly. Those gateways are small and more like flukes—little hiccups in reality—and never open for long. But there's a Gate in Entumbra that can access any dimension. It's a little confusing, but basically, Nethyl, my world, is the center of everything. The Gate connects every reality to the others, feeding energy to and keeping balance between all the different worlds and dimensions. But only Keepers—my family—can use it, because the magic in the Gate is the same as the magic in our blood."

Merriam sat down at the base of a boulder, pine needles and aspen leaves softening the ground. "Is it near here, then? Can I see it?"

Mollian sat next to her, their shoulders touching. "It's not here, no. It's about 250 klicks north." He did some quick math in his head, moving the fingers of one hand together as he counted. "Roughly 155 of your miles."

Merriam raised her brows in surprise. "How do you get here, then?"

The rings Mollian always wore had moved from his thumbs to his forefingers roughly a year before, and he slid them off now and held them out to her.

She took them, examining the tiny pillars of stone set into each. "Magic rings?"

"The stones are shards of the Gate: umbrite and orydite. In Entumbra, they wrap around and inside of each other, keeping the Gate constantly open, but it still has to be activated. Keepers long ago figured out that they could separate the stones to make them portable and create their own gateways at will. We call it Traveling."

Merriam held the rings gingerly in her palm, glancing up at Mollian.

"Don't worry, they're not going to eat you." Mollian laughed, plucking up the black and gold orydite ring. "Only Keepers can activate the stones. When we run them across each other, it creates something like a rip in the fabric of the universe, allowing us to pass through."

"How do you know where you'll end up?" Merriam questioned, twirling the remaining ring in her fingers and watching the sunlight dance through the dark purple umbrite.

"Earth is the parallel world to Nethyl, so it will always be here, and always in the matching place."

Merriam looked at him in confusion.

Mollian waved his hands through the air as he searched for the right words. "It's like ... it's like a piece of paper. Earth is on one side and Nethyl is on the other. If you're at the edge of the paper, you'll be in that exact same spot when you Travel to the other side. Traveling doesn't allow you to bend or fold the space, just lets you slip through to the flipped location."

Though her brow was still knit in thought, Merriam nodded, understanding the gist of it.

"The full spectrum of the universe is like millions and millions of papers, though. It's possible to jump through multiple layers, but you're still always in the same spot. Only it's not paper, because they're all connected and fed by the Gate. To open a full portal that could jump across different realities like that, I'd have to actually add my blood into the mix. At that point, it's just a matter of communicating with the stones about where I want to go."

"How do you do that?"

Mollian shrugged. "I don't know yet. That's not something I'll get taught until I'm older. Actually, a lot of this stuff I shouldn't even really know yet, but Oren tells me."

Merriam slipped the ring over her thumb, running a finger over the smooth stone. "Where'd you get the rings then if you're not supposed to know anything yet?"

Mollian placed the orydite ring back over his forefinger, holding it out in front of him proudly. "No one ever notices kids," he said simply.

"You *stole* them?" Merriam guessed.

Mollian tsked. "Stole is such a strong word, Ria. Technically, they're mine, anyway. I am a Keeper after all. A few years ago, when we went to Entumbra to visit my sister, I just wandered into a storage room and decided to put the poor things to use."

"They keep magic rings in a storage room?" Merriam gave him an unbelieving glance.

"Aren't all treasures really just storage rooms?" he asked, pulling the ring from her thumb.

"Wow. All this time together, and I didn't know you were a thief." Merriam knocked her shoulder into his.

"Again, is it really stealing if it belongs to me in a roundabout way?" Mollian grinned.

Merriam rolled her eyes. "Whatever you say, Prince," she teased.

He leaned his head against her shoulder and sighed. "I wish I could stay here sometimes. Things seem so much simpler without all the magic and responsibility."

Merriam leaned her head against his, breathing in his distinct Mollian smell that always made her think of spruce trees and plums, mixed with the light sweat of boy. "Does everyone on Nethyl know about the Gate?"

"Sorta. Everyone knows that dangerous stuff has come from Sekha in the past. They know that my family's bloodline can be traced back millennia and has always been not just Sekha's protectors, but the protectors of all of Nethyl. It's common knowledge that Jekeida, the inner territory, is home to a great power, but it's also known that we're the only ones who can wield it. Other than that, we try to keep the full extent of what the Gate is a secret. And the use of rings to Travel is even more guarded information. There are certain things that we don't want getting out in our world.

"We do share knowledge with Earth, though. Things like irrigation and hydropower came from Keepers. There was also one who fell in love with a human from Earth and shared a lot of our ideas with him—Lenardo Davinch or something like that—and he ended up becoming famous here. We do still try to learn from Earth, but we're very selective with what we allow to be brought over and who has access to that information."

Merriam smiled, looping her arm through Mollian's. She loved when he started rambling. His language had once sounded so harsh and unusual to her ears, but after years of his patient teaching and consistently using his words and phrases for things in her head, the Common language of Nethyl was warm and inviting. And Mollian could talk for hours. He was always learning new things and sharing them with her, cracked eyes alight with excitement. He'd told her about how dams worked and the purpose they served, and about the different rock formations in the mountains of Jekeida that were so similar to the mountains of her home. He'd once described to her in detail the intricate workings of plumbing systems as they'd been eating the small picnic of plums and cookies she'd brought into the woods. She'd thrown the pit of her plum at his face when he started talking about the toilets.

Mollian was so full of random facts that they'd hardly even talked about the differences between their worlds or what linked them. Which was fine by her. She knew, of course, that he didn't belong here. That he was intrinsically different. But she hated to think about it. She hated knowing that this boy who had become her closest companion, whose absence she felt like a pang in her soul, wasn't meant to be with her. She'd tried to bring a video game to play once, and it glitched constantly whenever he touched it. He'd just shrugged, saying it was probably some part of the magic in his blood that didn't agree with the technology. But she'd seen the hungry gleam in his eyes as he'd looked at the machine in her hands. She knew he wanted nothing more than to take it apart and figure out how it worked.

She had almost let him, too, her heart wanting nothing more than to watch the excitement and wonder and happiness in him as he worked out a new problem, but the device had been a gift from her aunt, and she knew if it somehow broke her mom would tear into her until she couldn't sit for a week, and she'd get an earful for far longer than that.

Merriam shook herself out of her thoughts, realizing she'd missed the tail end of Mollian discussing the intricacies of interdimensional politics among Keepers.

"So really it just depends, because it's not like there's a counsel for it or anyone else to vote or something like that," Mollian trailed off with a sigh, his deeply tan fingers picking a piece of dried leaf off of his pant leg. "Anyway, you would love Entumbra. It's the coolest place I've ever been, even if it does make me feel like my whole body is vibrating."

"Maybe one day," she said wistfully.

Mollian sat up, turning to face her. "Come with me, Ria."

"To Entumbra?" She tilted her head, hair falling over her shoulder. She'd just cut it a few months prior to the base of her neck. Her mom had been *furious*, and that was mild compared to what happened when her dad saw it.

But none of that had matched the cold fear in her veins when Mollian had seen the bruises on her. The righteous anger in his eyes had burned cold, the air thick and churning. He could have leveled the forest around them if she hadn't touched his hand, grounding him and pulling him from his rage in time for him to reel in the power that wanted so desperately to whip free.

"Yes." Mollian brushed a lock of blonde hair out of her face, dropping his hand into his lap. "Not just to Entumbra, but back to Jekeida. Stay with me." He blinked, the dappled sunlight streaming through the leaves catching in his eyes, lighting the brown shot through the pale green of his irises as he looked at her in earnest.

"Molli." She shook her head. "I can't."

Mollian just looked at her, lips pressed into a thin line.

"I have school. And ... and my parents. I can't just leave them," she said lamely.

Mollian's face hardened, unspoken words clear in his eyes. *They don't deserve you.*

"Molli ..." she trailed off, hugging her legs to her chest. "They do love me, in their own way. I can't just leave them. They're my parents. My family." She rested her chin on her knees.

"I could be your family," Mollian said quietly, not meeting her eyes.

"You *are* my family," she insisted, and he raised his gaze to hers again. "But they're still my parents. They do their best," she defended, too young to understand that they didn't.

Mollian sighed, giving in. "I know. And I'll still be here. Always."

Merriam heard the promise in his voice. They weren't able to meet all the time like they were that first summer, but it was still multiple times a month that Mollian managed to sneak away and find her. Whether that be at her aunt's house or at the park in her apartment complex. He glamored himself to look like a normal boy, rounding his ears, shortening his teeth, darkening his hair, hiding his tattoos. Merriam reached up to touch the aspen leaf around her neck. She'd be able to see through that glamor now.

Mollian stood, brushing his hands against his pants. "What should we do with the rest of the afternoon?" he said, forcing brightness into his voice.

Merriam held out her hand, letting him pull her to her feet. "Bet I can climb higher than you," she said, pointing to a cottonwood tree across the glen.

"Not a chance." Mollian grinned, breaking into a run.

Merriam shook off her somber mood, chasing after him and launching herself into the tree.

Neither of them knew it then, but that was the last time they would see each other for almost seven years.

Chapter 4

Ferrick is an ass

OREN HAD BEEN BACK in Umbra for only a week, not even enough time to fall back into a routine, and already felt like he was responsible for keeping everything moving. He knew a lot of this responsibility was in preparation for his coronation at the beginning of the next summer, the day after his thirtieth birthday. He felt he was in a limbo between having the power to make changes but not being able to step on toes, ruffle feathers, or upset the current balance of things.

His most recent meeting with Captain Ferrick had frustrated him to no end. The male was impossible to work with.

Oren stormed down the hall, flexing his fingers with vexed energy. He was due for another meeting in half an hour, or he would've taken off to the training courtyard for some physical activity. If he couldn't burn off the frustration, at least he could be alone to sort through his thoughts.

He all but threw open the doors to the library, stalking to the back and plopping down into an armchair with a frustrated sigh. He cracked the knuckles of one hand with his thumb, gaze fixed unseeing out the window.

Movement caught his attention, and he turned to see a head of pale blonde hair rise from the arm of the chaise lounge next to him. Soft amber eyes took him in, lighting with interest.

Merriam pushed up onto her elbows, rolling to her side and propping her head in one hand while the other marked the place in the book she'd been reading. "What's got you in a mood?"

Her presence had shocked him to the point that he missed the question. He tilted his head, regarding her as memories from their last encounter in Entumbra played through his mind.

Merriam gave him a look. "Okay, forget I asked. You're the one who stormed in here all dark and gloomy."

"I was expecting to be alone."

"That makes two of us," Merriam said wryly.

Something inside of him shifted, his anger starting to chip away. "I guess I am the one who interrupted you. Nothing too important, I hope?"

Merriam frowned down at the book. "The werewolf who's in hiding because she killed a high-born male has just joined leagues with a vampire, actually."

"Ah, so just some light fantasy, then."

"Do you realize how ironic that is, coming from a fae prince?" Merriam arched an eyebrow.

"Even the fae need tales with which to scare their children, my lady." Oren touched his chest in exaggerated graciousness.

Merriam snorted. "Okay, neckbeard. You know I'm no lady."

"Neckbeard?" Oren lifted a hand to his neck, but he already knew he was freshly shaven as of that morning.

Merriam sat up, folding her legs in front of her. "Sorry, it's a term from where I grew up. It's like weird, often slovenly guys who have never been with a girl talk to them that way to try to seem nice, but really it's just cringe-worthy and awkward." She waved her free hand about as she talked, nerves making her ramble.

"Did you just call me slovenly?" Oren asked, a smile dimpling one cheek.

Merriam rolled her eyes. "Calm down, Majesty." The title was clearly said in jest.

Oren shook his head at her, distracted for a moment as his eyes traveled over her customary braid, currently draped over her shoulder. He was almost overwhelmed with the compulsion to work it free. He knew she left her hair loose at night, and the image of her standing on an open parapet, flaxen tendrils blowing across her freckled cheeks, filled his head. What plagued him more was the feeling of his hands tangled in it as his tongue had swept into her mouth, feeling her press herself against him as one of her hands had dragged down his back to squeeze his ass.

"Captain Ferrick irritates me," he found himself admitting instead, running a hand over his mouth to shake off the thoughts that sent blood flowing to his cock.

Merriam blinked. "Huh?"

"My mood. Ferrick is an ass. He knows how to get under my skin, and he does it well."

"That fucker." Merriam pressed her lips together, her gaze full of empathy. "Is there anything I can do to help?"

"Probably not. Do you have a problem with him?"

"As a general rule, yes, but I'm always here for moral support. So if you think of anything ... well, you know where to find me."

"Glad to have you on my side, Mer." Oren smiled.

She shrugged a shoulder, eyes glittering with humor. "Figure it never hurts to have favor with the future king."

He laughed deeply and freely. "Have I told you before how much I enjoy your company?"

"Only once or twice." Merriam tossed her hair over her shoulder. "Hey, did you ever talk to the queen about what the trafficker said?" she asked.

"Yes, actually. She is going to tell the city guards and Rangers to keep their eyes and ears open, as well as send birds to the outposts in Audha and Eyko."

Merriam raised an eyebrow. "A human is supposedly using blood magic, and she's just going to have the Guard keep an eye out?"

Oren rubbed his hand over the back of his neck. "It goes deeper than that, but she wants to keep the investigation close to the Crown. There are things this could relate to that shouldn't become common knowledge. Stuff that could stir up fear and unrest in the other territories for no reason if the threat ends up amounting to nothing."

Merriam shook her head. "Whatever this is about, it's not going to amount to nothing, O. The guy was terrified." She met his gaze evenly. "He literally begged Jasper to kill him before he told us."

"Either way, this isn't your investigation. Not yet."

"Jasper has me looking into different possibilities. If there really is some maniac out there ..."

"Tell Jasper the Crown has decided not to involve you," Oren said.

"So what are we supposed to do about it? I've spent all week researching anything and everything this damn library has on blood magic and nymphs," she protested.

"For now, do nothing. It's not your responsibility." Oren shrugged. "If that changes, I'll personally bring you to the library in Entumbra. There is a much broader selection there for all of your wildest research fantasies."

"Oh, really." Merriam raised an eyebrow at his choice of words.

"More importantly," Oren quickly added, "I can't offer you payment to keep looking into it."

"Oof, yeah, that'll be a hard pass for the rest of the troupe, then." Merriam winced jokingly.

Oren stood. "It's truly been a pleasure, but I do have a meeting to prepare for, so I'll leave you to your reading."

"Have fun with that." Merriam untangled herself and collapsed back onto the chaise.

"What are you doing tomorrow?" he asked before he could overthink it.

Merriam tilted her head to more easily meet his gaze. "I don't think I have any solid plans yet."

"Have lunch with me," Oren invited. "Molli, too, if he's available."

Merriam hesitated for the slightest moment before smiling. "Okay, I'd like that. And I'll let him know."

"Until next time, Lady." Oren gave the smallest of bows before leaving the room.

As soon as the doors closed, he leaned against the wall. *I hope you know what you're doing*, he thought, running a hand over his hair, neatly smoothed into a bun at the back of his head. He'd always had a soft spot for Merriam because of the role she played in Mollian's life, and he admired the fire in her spirit. But the times he saw her during his five years in Entumbra had shown him a different side of her: stronger and more confident than the girl from the other side of reality who'd stumbled into his life almost eight years before, but also more wild, more free. Despite his best efforts, he'd become increasingly fond of her.

Chapter 5

Very into kidnapping

"Well, you look happy." Mollian looked up from his desk as Merriam swung open the door to their rooms. He had a variety of tools spread out and was working on laying gold leaf into the design he'd carved onto the handle of a dagger. While he had no interest in actual smithing, the younger prince spent much of his free time customizing weapons, an enjoyable art that kept both his mind and his hands busy.

"I was just doing some research in the library." Merriam shrugged, walking over and plucking a piece of paper and a pencil from the desktop.

"And?" Mollian watched her with a raised brow.

"I ran into Oren. He was having a bad day."

"Oh, really?" Mollian leaned back, a suggestive smile playing at his lips. "I'm assuming you made it better?"

Merriam wrinkled her nose, laughing. "It's not like that."

"What? Is my kin not good enough for you?" Mollian feigned hurt.

"Too good." Merriam sat on the couch, leaning over the table to draw. "Besides, your parents just stopped looking at me as if I were your pet. I'm not trying to rock that boat."

"They've known your worth for years now, Ria."

"A few years is hardly anything in your lifespan." Merriam waved her hand dismissively. "Regardless, it's not fair for you to tease me about this when I can't do the same to you."

Mollian, who'd never had a sexual inclination toward anyone in his life, flashed her a cheeky grin. *Don't hate a tree just because you're lost in the forest.*

Merriam laughed. *What the fuck is that supposed to mean?*

You know. It's a saying.

No, no, I don't think it is.

"Did you know he helped me find you?"

"He did?" Merriam perked up, turning to look at him.

"Yeah, he convinced our parents that I should be doing extra Keeper training. It's the reason I was able to search for you as much as I did. Of course, they didn't know I was wandering the country and not tucked away in Entumbra. How he kept that from being communicated between the Rangers assigned to guard me and our parents is still a mystery, especially because he's never been one to bend the rules."

"And yet he supported you in stealing a human girl from another world?" she joked, scribbling over the paper.

"Oh, yes, he's very into kidnapping." Mollian nodded solemnly.

"Why did he help you, though?"

Mollian shrugged. "I told him you belonged here, that I knew it in my soul. He told me that was a Keeper's intuition and to always trust it. But I think even back then he suspected our *mehhen* bond. He knew we needed each other."

Merriam brought her hand to the aspen leaf at her throat, sliding it back and forth on its dark iron chain. "I'm glad he listened to you."

Mollian winked his bi-colored eye, turning back to the dagger on the desktop. "I'm almost finished up here if you want me to train with you."

"Oh, I was actually going to meet up with the mercs and run some drills." Merriam pushed to her feet, folding the paper in half twice.

"Will you be back tonight?"

"Probably, but don't wait up."

"Be safe." Mollian held his hand up.

Merriam walked over and pressed her palm against his. She dropped the pencil back on the desk and affectionately brushed her fingers through his curls. "Always am," she replied, grabbing her axes from where they rested by the couch and slipping them into her belt as she left.

She ran quickly up the stairs, turning down a hallway and stopping in front of a door. She looked both ways to make sure no one was around before slipping the paper underneath, smiling to herself as she stood and scampered off.

$$\mathcal{\ell}$$

Merriam nimbly made her way through the back alleys of Umbra and up into the merc house. No one was in the little office at the top of the stairs, so she headed down to the ground floor.

Aleah was by herself, lying on her belly on the couch, feet swinging through the air above her as she read. "Hi, Mer," she greeted without looking up, tucking a lock of straight, flame-red hair back behind her cropped ear. She was the youngest of the group, but had also been around the longest. Jasper had picked her up off the streets of a small town in South Audha at only fourteen when she tried to steal from him. Eight years later, she still made a clumsy thief, but her merit as a mercenary was well-earned in other areas.

"Where is everyone?" Merriam descended the final step and glanced around.

Aleah shrugged. "Leo got called out on a job this morning. Jasper went to the market. Cam is around here somewhere, and Calysta is off doing her nymphy thing for a few days. She made us a fresh batch of meds before she left, though. They're in the cupboard across from the sink."

Calysta had an extensive knowledge of plants, and over the years had perfected a mixture of dried leaves, flowers, and roots that completely halted all phases of the menstrual cycle in both fae and humans. Merriam and Aleah took it monthly, as nothing was more inconvenient than bleeding or suffering from crippling cramps in the middle of a job. The nymph even made some money on the side selling capsules of the concoction to local apothecaries."

"Perfect. I'll grab some before I leave." Merriam sat down on the couch opposite Aleah, stretching her legs out in front of her and tipping her head back. "Maybe I have time for a power nap." She sighed contentedly, letting her eyes fall closed. "I feel like I've hardly slept all week running down this research."

Aleah slipped a strip of fabric into her book and closed it. "Did you at least find anything useful?"

"Nope. And His Majesty, the Crown Prince told me to let it rest earlier today."

"Really? They don't care that there could be a psycho running amuck out there?"

"On the contrary, the Crown doesn't want everyone else knowing that a psycho could be running amuck. I think something about the blood magic aspect of it is worrisome, but ..."

Aleah tipped her head to the side, absentmindedly running a finger over her clipped ear as her hazel eyes clouded with memories. "Will you ask Mollian about it?"

Merriam shrugged. "I'm sure he'll tell us what we need to know when we know it. But I don't want to pry when Oren said to let it rest."

The redhead nodded, hand dropping back to the couch. "I'm sorry, Mer. I know there's a separation. I didn't mean–"

Merriam moved to sit on the floor next to Aleah, tipping her head back against the couch cushion and grabbing Aleah's hand. "No explaining required, remember?" She squeezed lightly.

"Right." Aleah blinked, eyes clearing, as she let a smile tug at her lips. "Well, I guess it's not our problem, then. We should keep this in mind, though, and charge extra when they're desperate for us to hunt this guy down."

"Hunt who down?" Campbell came down the stairs, short curls mussed from sleep and rubbing the heels of his hands against his eyes. He scratched his head at the base of one antler with a yawn.

"The demon-man who hired those traffickers. The Crown isn't having us looking into it." Aleah dropped Merriam's hand, pushing up and swinging her legs to the floor.

"Their loss I guess." Campbell shuffled into the kitchen in search of a snack.

He returned to the mushroom with a plate of bread and butter, slathering a slice for himself before offering up the rest.

Merriam and Aleah both partook and were happily eating when Jasper came in the back door carrying a canvas bag. "We don't have to worry about that guy who hired the traffickers," Aleah told him around a mouthful.

Jasper looked to Merriam, who just nodded. "Was your research productive, at least?"

"I found nothing of any intrigue. It's been a painfully slow week," Merriam answered with a sigh.

"I can fix that." Jasper smiled at her, a wicked gleam in his silver eyes.

"Oh, you shouldn't have said that," Aleah whispered to her.

"When you're done with your bread, let's go into the training room. These two can put this stuff away." Jasper tossed the bag to Campbell.

Merriam stuffed the last bite of food into her mouth, brushing her hands on her pants and standing.

She followed Jasper into the large room set in the back of the building. There was a fighting ring in one corner, various weights in another, and along one entire wall were rungs, ropes, and little nooks and crannies that made up hand and footholds for climbing.

Jasper gestured for Merriam to lose her axes, so she unclipped her belt and set them aside.

They both went through a quick round of warm-ups, loosening their muscles. "Race to the top. First to five wins," Jasper said, pointing with his chin to the climbing wall as he tied back the twisted locs of his hair.

Merriam flexed her fingers and walked up to the wall.

He followed, tucking his wings in tight to his body. "Your call, Mer."

She watched, the muscles in his legs flexing visibly through the fitted fabric of his pants as he readied himself. She set her own legs into a slight squat, arms poised to reach. "Go!"

They sprang up simultaneously, Merriam kicking against the wall with one foot to propel herself higher before grabbing onto a handhold. Jasper's height and longer limbs had given him an early advantage, but she knew from experience that his bulk would also slow him down.

Keeping her body close against the wall, she tilted her head back and reached for the next handhold, using the muscles of her legs to propel her once she had a firm grip. She caught up with Jasper before long, glimpsing a glossy black wing out of the corner of her eye.

She pushed harder, and her foot slipped from a hold as she shifted her weight. Hissing through her teeth, she scrambled to regain purchase. She pulled herself upward, and her foot slid back into place.

Those few seconds had cost her, though, and Jasper loudly slapped the ceiling, grinning down at her. "There's one for me." He jumped down, opening his feathered wings with a snap and gliding to the floor.

Merriam took a breath before pushing away from the wall. Her stomach lurched into her throat as she free-fell, tucking her body loosely. She rolled on impact with practiced ease, unfolding onto her back after a couple rotations.

Jasper held out his hand, and she let him help her to her feet. "Grab some water and we'll go again."

She nodded, catching her breath and wiping at the sweat beading on her brow.

"Ooh, I want to play!" Aleah called as she and Campbell came into the room.

"Jaz has one. We're going to five." Merriam quickly caught them up, deftly catching the bottle of water Campbell tossed to her.

The four of them lined up against the wall, ready to go. Merriam had always loved climbing, even as a kid, but once she'd learned to free-climb virtually any surface with a hold and how to fall properly to avoid injury, her world had seemed so much bigger.

She was good at it, too, and had more natural inclination for it than any of the rest of them. Jasper had won when he was fresh, but her edge would grow as he tired. It was like her body was built for scaling walls, and it never ceased to thrill her.

Jasper called the next round, and she smiled as she threw herself easily into the movements.

In the end, she won by one. They were all tired and breathing heavily from the workout.

"Are you eating with us?" Campbell asked, wiping sweat from his face and body with a towel before sliding his shirt, which he'd discarded onto the floor five rounds ago, back over his shoulders.

Merriam nodded, taking a deep swill of water. "I'm starving. What's on the menu?"

"Venison and veggies." Campbell grinned. The quality of meals at the merc house had risen drastically when he'd joined them three years ago. "Leo grabbed a massive buck a couple days ago."

"Yeah, with a rack bigger than yours." Jasper knocked the tip of a wing against Campbell's antlers.

"Well, at least his brain wasn't bigger than mine, which is less than I can say for you." Campbell batted him away and ducked through the door.

"You planning to dine and ditch tonight?" Aleah asked, as they followed Campbell to the kitchen to wash up.

"Yeah, I have plans tomorrow," Merriam answered vaguely, drying off her hands before grabbing a knife and cutting into a head of broccoli.

"Plans," Campbell echoed, laying out a few venison steaks to season and trim.

"Plans," Aleah repeated, grinning deviously and wiggling her eyebrows at Campbell.

"Yes, plans to flay a couple of mercenaries who can't mind their business." Merriam sliced into the vegetable aggressively, but an amused smile curved her lips.

"Not with that, you're not. Would make for a sloppy flay-job." Aleah pointed to the large cook's knife Merriam held.

The loud flap of wings coming down the hallway announced Panic's flight into the mushroom. He landed on a perch set into the entry of the kitchen, head tilting back and forth as he surveyed the group.

The sound of the back door closing followed shortly after. "He already ate," Leonidas called. "Don't let him trick you into scraps."

The tall blonde made his way into the kitchen and stopped behind Campbell, hooking a finger over the point of one of his antlers and gently tilting his head back to brush a kiss against his lips. "I like watching you handle my meat," he murmured.

"We're going to have to eat that later." Merriam clicked her tongue against her teeth.

"That is not the image I wanted in my head over supper." Aleah gave an exaggerated grimace to the potato she was carving.

Leonidas ignored them, plunking a paper-wrapped package down on the far counter. "A gift from the wife of my client. I believe she said it was cinnamon sugar loaf cake."

Aleah's hazel eyes slid to the parcel before flicking up to Leonidas. "Transgression forgiven. You can make all the innuendos you want as long as you bring dessert."

"Did you just ask Leo to be your sugar daddy?" Campbell asked nonchalantly, sprinkling salt over the steaks.

Merriam snorted, slapping a hand over her mouth.

Before Aleah could respond, Leonidas interrupted. "And this is where I take my leave. You three are deranged." He shook his head, stepping back through the kitchen to the living room. "Where's Jasper?"

"I think he's still training. I never heard him come in." Campbell replied.

"Thanks." Leonidas turned to leave. "And no scraps!" he called over his shoulder.

Panic shifted his wings, his eyes trained on the slabs of deer in front of Campbell, who cut off a small chunk of meat and tossed it up to the falcon. Panic caught it, swallowing quickly before turning his focus to contentedly preening his feathers.

****

Oren pulled his hair free from its bun as he walked down the hallway, ready for a long bath and an even longer night's sleep. All of the meetings packed into today had completely drained him.

He pushed his fingers into the hair at the top of his head, massaging his scalp before shaking out the length, a few tendrils falling over the dark aspen leaves across his temples. He ran his palm from the closely shorn back of his head down to his neck, massaging the tense muscle.

Exhaustion flooded through him as soon as he opened the door to his suite and stepped over the threshold. He started peeling clothes off as he walked to the bathroom, dropping them as he went. After turning on the tap, he sat against the side of the tub while steam filled the room, stretching out his arms and legs.

After a bath that felt all-too short for the amount of tension that had been in his body, Oren pulled on a pair of shorts and toweled off his hair, returning to the main room to pick up his clothes from the floor.

As he stepped into the room, he summoned the clothing to him with a flick of his fingers and saw a slip of paper by the door. Tucking the pile under his arm, he walked over to snatch it up.

He looked at the door quizzically, as if it held an answer. When none came, he tossed his clothes into a basket before lowering onto his bed to unfold the note.

A smile spread across his face as he took in the crude drawing of a stick figure with a beard and exaggerated expression of surprise walking up the steps in the throne room and slipping on a small, roughly star-shaped object. Two words were written in a looping scrawl: "Ferrick" with an arrow pointing to the man and "banana peel" with an arrow pointing to the hazard. In the corner of the paper were two stick figures bent over in laughter, one with excessively long hair and one with a bun at the crown of his head and a squiggle of tattoos across his brow.

Oren shook his head and chuckled, setting the paper down on his bedside table and slipping under the blankets. Thoughts of the blonde mercenary with amber eyes that sparkled when she teased him filled his thoughts as his head hit the pillow, sleep taking him quickly and easily.

Chapter 6

An anomaly, actually

Seven years before ...

MERRIAM SAT IN A classroom, picking at her nail polish. Today, her father would come home from another trip on the road. Her mother would act happy, but she'd be jittery trying to stay sober. And then her father would take turns blaming her and her mother for the addiction before heading back out for a few more weeks, hauling whatever product his current contract required across the country in his eighteen-wheeler.

Only a few more months. She repeated the mantra to herself. *Only a few more months, and I can leave.*

Graduation was right around the corner, and her eighteenth birthday would be soon after that. There was no question as to where she would go. There was only one place she belonged, and she would find it or die trying.

She sighed and looked at the clock, wishing for once that the hands would stay still, dreading the evening ahead. Maybe she could find somewhere to hide all afternoon. The library was only open until six on weeknights, but at least it was better than nothing.

Too soon, the bell rang, and she slowly gathered up her books, released for the day. She pulled her lower lip into her mouth and bit down, trying to ignore the sour knot of anxiety in her stomach. Worrying wasn't going to help if her father was in a mood.

After stowing her books in her locker, she made her way off school grounds, heading toward sanctuary. At least, sanctuary for the next few hours. She made it to the library and settled down in one of her favorite spots along a side wall. The window here gave a marvelous view of the forest beyond.

Just as she was about to start reading, a flash of white caught her eye. She immediately sat up straight, heart pounding as she looked out the window, searching the trees.

Nothing.

Of course it's nothing. She reprimanded herself. It had been seven years since she'd last seen Mollian. Seven years since she'd last visited the forest at the back of her aunt's house.

But she knew he was real. Knew Nethyl was real. Even without the reminder of the iron chain around her throat, she had never, for one second, doubted her memories or their friendship. Their bond was much too strong for her to ever think she could have imagined it.

Their souls were the same. Two parts of a whole.

And hers had ached for his with every day that passed.

But the fact remained that she had moved fifteen hundred miles away from her aunt's forest backyard in the mountains. Fifteen hundred miles away from Mollian's home on whatever flipside of reality he was from.

Her parents had sprung the move on her without much warning. She hadn't been able to tell him where she was going. She hadn't even been able to tell him goodbye. That had been more painful than anything, if she was being honest.

Even seven years later, her heart still hurt when she thought about him. He had been her best friend, her only friend at times. She loved him more than she could put into words. And he had been ripped away as if he'd never even existed.

And what if he thought she'd gone away on purpose? They'd only been children, after all, and the chances of a faerie prince finding something else to catch his interest were probably high.

So, no, that flash of white couldn't have been Mollian. It was more than likely a dove or someone's cat wandering. It hadn't been Mollian the thousands of other times she'd seen movement out of the corner of her eye, and it wasn't Mollian now.

Settling into the chair, she swallowed down the lump in her throat and returned to her book. It was an easy-read thriller, perfect for the escapism she needed.

She wasn't ready to head home when the library closed, so she sat on a curb in the back of the parking lot until the sun set, waiting for the streetlights to flicker on before starting the walk home. Head down, she watched her feet move over the cracks in the sidewalk, focusing on her steps to keep from thinking about what waited for her.

Her father would be home by now, and she was mentally bracing herself for an awkward dinner, for her father's stilted conversation as he tried to hold back his temper and her mother's twitchiness as she tried to make it through the night unmedicated.

"Ria?"

Merriam's heart skipped a beat and then thundered in her chest. Her feet stopped so abruptly her momentum almost sent her falling onto her face.

Slowly, she raised her head.

There, standing under a streetlight, was a male, just over the cusp of boyhood. He was now several inches taller than she was, and his loose curls—white as fresh snow—hung just above his shoulders in choppy layers, falling over his forehead and into pale green eyes, one of which was shot through with brown.

He barely had time to smile, showing slightly too-pointed canines, and lift his hand, palm forward, before she started running, launching herself across the sidewalk as she choked on a sob.

Merriam threw herself onto him, arms looping around his shoulders as she buried her face in his neck. His scent hit her the same moment tears started to fall from her eyes, that scent that brought her back to spruce and plums.

"Molli," she whispered. The threads of her soul that had twined with his in childhood relaxed, the ever-present ache fading so suddenly she almost forgot how to breathe.

His arms had gone around her the moment she'd touched him, and they tightened now. "U *viect oei*," he whispered back, repeating the very first words he'd ever said to her. *I found you.*

Merriam just cried harder, her mind flooded with emotions. But the strongest and loudest was relief. Mollian was there.

"I'm so sorry," Mollian whispered in her human language, still holding her firmly. "I'm sorry it took me so long to find you. I never stopped looking, not once."

Merriam tried to breathe through her sobs. "You came for me," she answered in Common.

Mollian stilled at her use of the fae tongue, his throat tightening with tears as he affectionately ran a hand over her hair. "Always."

Merriam finally got her breathing under control and stepped back a bit, peering up at him. "You're tall now."

Mollian laughed. "Maybe you're short now."

Merriam just shook her head and clasped his arms. "I can't believe you're really here."

Mollian pulled her back to his chest. "Legends, I missed you."

"You have no fucking idea." She rested her head against him.

They stood like that for a while, glad just to be together again and knowing that they would have all the time in the world to catch up. They were both reeling slightly from the lightness in their souls, strangely settled after so long apart.

"My dad came back today," Merriam finally said.

Mollian immediately stiffened and stepped back. "Have you seen him?" He glanced over her face and then the rest of her exposed skin.

"No, I was just on the way ... home." The word didn't sound fitting, not now that Mollian was there.

Mollian let out a slow breath, weighing his next words. "Come with me."

"What?"

"Come to Jekeida and live with me, Ria." He grabbed her hands. "Every single day these past years I spent wishing I had asked you sooner, more often."

"Okay."

"I know this is the only life you've known, but I promise that—" Mollian stopped, looking down at her. "Wait ... you said 'okay'?"

"Not a day went by that I didn't wish I had just agreed back then. I'm not meant to be here, Molli. I don't think I was ever meant to be here."

Merriam met his gaze, her eyes reflecting the sincerity of the statement. "Take me with you."

"I'll stay with you until you're ready to leave. You can take your time, collect your things ... whatever you need. I'll stay. Even if you need a month."

"I'm ready now." Merriam dropped her backpack on the sidewalk. "There's nothing I need from here."

Mollian looked from her to the bag and back again. "There's nothing you want to grab? No one to say goodbye to?"

Merriam bit the inside of her cheek, looking up at him with fresh tears pooling in her eyes. "I don't want to go back there, Molli. There's nothing ..." She swallowed, shaking her head. "I'm ready now," she repeated.

"Let's go home, then," Mollian smiled, taking her hand as the word settled in her chest.

Merriam followed him into the woods without hesitation, leaving her old life behind without so much as a glance back toward the street.

"Hold on to me. The rip doesn't extend far," Mollian said when they were hidden from view of the street.

Merriam slid her arms around his waist, nestling her head to his chest. She heard the barely audible sound of two stones sliding together, and then she felt that familiar pull. This time, though, it started within her. She squeezed her eyes shut, overcome with vertigo as the world seemed to tip around her. Then, a strong push of gravity from her center, and she opened her eyes.

Merriam let go of Mollian and took a few steps back, looking around. The stars twinkled across a vast expanse of dark night sky in constellations she'd never seen before. The utter lack of light pollution made them seem unnaturally bright and almost close enough to touch. Two moons floated in the sky, one barely a sliver and the other half full, both reflecting pure white light. Tall, skinny cypress trees spread out on the horizon around her over soft rolling hills, the ground beneath her soft with fallen needles.

Mollian watched her with a questioning smile, adjusting the rings he now wore on each pinkie finger.

"Well, for the land of the fae, this doesn't look all too magical." Merriam nonchalantly crossed her arms over her chest as she surveyed the trees, but her voice betrayed her awe.

"So picky." Mollian poked her in the side. "Come on, camp is set up just over the hill. Are you hungry?"

"Starving." Merriam started walking in the direction he'd indicated. There was so much she wanted to tell him, but she wasn't sure she was ready for deep conversation. "So, they really just let a prince of the fae wander around hunting humans all by himself?"

"Prince of Sekha, not all fae," Mollian corrected with a wink. "But yes. Sort of. I have guards with me at camp, so I'm not really alone, and as far as they know, I'm doing Keeper training. Plus, I'm just *a* prince, not *the* prince, so it's not as big of a deal."

"Ah, yes, dear older brother is the heir apparent." Merriam nodded, remembering. "But he's not the eldest, right?"

"No, we have a sister. She's just under 150, so the eldest by a long shot."

"Wow, quite the age gap," Merriam commented.

Mollian shrugged. "It's not uncommon for high fae to live well over 500 years, though that is the average life expectancy for the fair folk."

"Oh, wow. And she was never in line for the throne?"

"No, she has a greater purpose." Mollian held out his hand to help Merriam over a felled tree.

"What do you mean?"

"The firstborn of every Keeper is sent to Entumbra. Their sole life purpose is to protect and tend the Gate. They have a stronger blood connection to it than the second-born. Their power is also magnified in proximity to the Gate. It calls to them in a different way than it calls to the rest of us."

"That sounds so lonely."

Mollian shrugged, pushing through some brush. "I would hate it, but she loves it. It's her own domain that she's in charge of, and because of the power in her, she's comfortable there."

"What's your purpose?"

Mollian glanced at her over his shoulder with a grin. "To rescue damsels in distress, of course."

Merriam rolled her eyes, pushing ahead of him through the trees, which were steadily growing denser.

"I'm an anomaly, actually."

"How so?"

"It's almost unheard of for a Keeper to bear more than two children. There's just no purpose. The magic in our blood also makes things more difficult. It's like ... it doesn't like to be multiplied," he explained.

"You were unplanned, then?" Merriam was fascinated with this bit of Keeper history she'd never heard before.

"Very. I just sort of happened. I didn't know all of this as a kid, though. My father thought it might go to my head or something. There hasn't been a third child in over a millennium."

"Did the last one have a purpose? The way the first and the second do?"

"Not according to any record I was able to find. From what I read, she lived a long, happy life, mostly splitting time living between Umbra and Entumbra, but also freely traveling around and exploring different worlds the same way the former kings and queens do."

Merriam let all of the new information settle, picking it apart and digesting it as she followed Mollian through the trees. "How many Keepers are there now?"

"Just us," Mollian answered. "My mother and my siblings, I mean. My aunt, who was the Keeper before Gressia, died roughly a century ago, and my grandfather died when I was just a baby."

By the time they crested the hill, Merriam's feet were aching. "I did not dress for a hike," she grumbled, leaning against a tree and rotating one soft pink converse out in front of her.

"Lesson learned, Ria, dress every day like a faerie prince is going to come steal you away," Mollian teased, tapping her nose with a finger.

Merriam pulled her hair over one shoulder, toying with the ends as she met his eyes. "I did. I wore nothing but pants and t-shirts and kept a bag with a jacket, knife, and a water bottle in it within arm's reach for so long my mom threatened to burn all my tennis shoes and backpacks if I didn't start acting like a normal child."

Mollian's smile fell. "I should never have left you after that last time."

"You had your own things to worry about, Molli," Merriam said softly. "It wasn't your responsibility."

"I promised to be there for you, and I let you down."

"You were a *child*. Same as I was," Merriam said with finality, pushing off of the trunk and continuing up the hill.

Moments later, she reached the top and saw firelight flickering through the trees. She stopped, looking at Mollian.

He grabbed her hand, giving it a comforting squeeze. "Let's go get into trouble." He grinned.

Merriam returned his smile, following him to the camp.

"Dio!" he called through the trees.

A few paces ahead, a blonde figure dropped from the canopy, landing softly and standing. "Welcome back, Your Highness." He bowed neatly.

"Merriam, this is Dio, a commander of the Rangers in Sekha's Royal Guard. Dio, this is Merriam, my dearest friend."

"A pleasure." Dio dipped his head in greeting. A question sparked in his eyes as he looked her over, but he said nothing.

"Likewise," Merriam replied, feeling a ball of nerves tangle in her stomach for the first time since seeing Mollian.

Mollian squeezed her hand again before dropping it. "I hope you've got supper ready. I'm famished!"

"Rillak should have something prepared," Dio said. "If that is all?"

"Yes, thank you." Mollian continued heading into camp.

Merriam watched as Dio nimbly swung back into the tree, quickly disappearing as he pulled himself higher through the boughs. *So that's one of the infamous Rangers*, she thought, impressed.

The camp was set up in a small clearing and consisted of two tents and a shallow fire pit. A large, grizzly male sat before the fire, turning what looked like rabbits on a spit. A single aspen leaf was tattooed on the back of each wrist, identifying him as a member of the Royal Guard.

"Smells amazing, Rillak!" Mollian greeted.

"It had better. Spent all day preparin' 'em, and you know Dio and Eskar are no help," the male grumbled in a light North Eyko accent. "I see ya found a girl."

"Indeed! Merriam, this is Rillak, one of the few resident cooks employed by the Guard."

Rillak snorted. "I ain't no cook, little human. I'm just one a the only ones smart enough to pull my head outta my ass and season the damn food." He shook his head in disdain. "I tell ya. Them Rangers like to think they're so high and mighty, but ain't one of 'em good for anythin' more than climbin' and trackin'. Hardly practical."

Merriam smiled, instantly warming to the gruff guard.

"If tracking weren't practical, then how'd those rabbits end up on your spit, Rillak?" A female stalked through the trees on the opposite side of camp. Her hair was sleek, black, and cropped short, giving Merriam a clear view of her elegantly tapered ears.

Rillak just huffed, pulling the meat from the fire to check the cook.

"Welcome back, Prince Mollian. I see you've brought a guest." She addressed Mollian, but her almond-shaped eyes traveled slowly over Merriam, judging her.

Merriam fought the urge to squirm under her gaze, biting down on her lip.

"Eskar, this is Merriam. We used to play together as children until her family moved to East Audha. She'll be accompanying us back to Umbra."

A flash of panic ran through Merriam at the thought of being asked details about this place she was supposed to have come from, but the worry was unwarranted.

Eskar had finished her assessment, and by the look on her face, she found Merriam rather underwhelming. "Back to Umbra? Does that mean we'll be moving out tomorrow?" She finally turned her gaze to the prince.

Mollian caught the appraisal but purposefully ignored it. "Yes, we can get an early start because I'll want to stop a bit earlier than usual. There's still some business I have to take care of in the next town, so we can stay there tomorrow evening."

"As you wish." She sat down on the ground next to Rillak, gracefully tucking her legs underneath her.

"Food's about ready," Rillak announced, laying the charred rabbits on a cloth next to him.

"Splendid, I'll grab some bread." Mollian turned and ducked into one of the tents.

Merriam stood where she was, unsure of what to do with herself. "Should I bring something to Dio?" she finally asked, wanting to be helpful.

"Rangers don't eat on watch," the female scoffed, looking at Merriam with unveiled distaste.

"It was kind of you to offer, Ria, but Eskar is right," Mollian said from behind her, holding a loaf. "He wouldn't accept it even if you did bring him anything." He sat on the ground and offered his hand to help her down.

Later that night, Merriam and Mollian lay on a bedroll in one of the tents, shoulder to shoulder, hands clasped together. They shared the same fear that if they let go, the other would somehow disappear.

"There's something I want to ask you ... something I want to do," Mollian broke the contented silence.

She waited, turning her head to look at him.

"I don't ever want you to feel like you don't have a choice in being here, in Jekeida or anywhere on Nethyl. I don't want you to feel trapped."

"This is my choice, Molli," she assured him, squeezing his hand.

"I know, but ..." He swallowed. "I want to be Bonded."

"Bonded?"

"There's a ritual, if you will."

"Are you asking me to sell my soul, Mollian Stonebane?"

"I'm asking you to take my blood."

She blinked in surprise, rolling over to face him fully. "What?"

"I want to give you my blood—and my rings—so you can go back if you want to. So you know you're never stuck in either world and don't feel dependent on me." Mollian turned onto his side, too.

"How does that work?"

"A tattoo. My blood would be combined with the ink in a rune that would make us ... one. For lack of a better word."

"What does that mean?" Merriam questioned.

"The Bond will be like a connection between us. We'll be able to communicate without speaking, and we'll be able to find one another. Always."

"We'll be able to read each other's minds?"

"Not quite like that. But you'll be able to have a sense of when I'm near and share your thoughts with me when you want to. It's called Casting."

"And you can only Cast to a person you're Bonded to?"

"Well, no. Keepers can Cast to anyone. It just gets more difficult and requires more concentration if the other person has no magic. It'll be different for you, though. Since you'll only have a little bit of Keeper blood, Casting to me will be easy, but Casting to other Keepers will require a lot of effort, and you won't be able to at all with other fae or humans."

"But we'll be able to talk to each other in our heads?"

Mollian nodded. "When we're in close enough proximity."

"That's cool as shit, Molli." Merriam smiled, her eyes sparkling in the darkness of the tent.

"Just, you need to understand that it's not reversible. Once you're Bonded to me, there's no going back. What's important to me is sharing my power with you, but since it's my blood that will be running through your veins, it won't protect you from me."

Merriam brought her hand up, tracing the aspen tattoo on his temple. "I've never needed to be protected from you, and part of me feels like we've been connected from the beginning."

"We have, I think. Not in this way, but our souls belong together," Mollian replied. "I can't explain how wild the odds are that we found each other, but I think—no, after today, I *know* we're *mehhen.*"

"Muh-hen?" Merriam repeated in question.

"It roughly means something like mirrored souls. That stretching we feel when we're apart? It's because we're two halves of the same. We may have never even known, but we awoke it when we were kids, and now we're tied together, in a way."

Merriam nodded, tucking her hands under her cheek. "Did you feel it slacken today, too? It's been taught for so long I almost didn't notice the ache anymore."

"My magic, too. It crawls under my skin sometimes, like it's pushing for a way out. I've learned to shove it down, but ... as soon as I was close to you, it quieted. You make it easy to control." With that statement he left unspoken the depth of how much he suspected he needed her. It wasn't her burden to carry, and he wanted her to always feel free to choose her own path.

They fell asleep curled up together—the first night either of them had felt truly whole since they'd met almost ten years earlier.

Eskar and Dio were standoffish the entire next day while they traveled. Mollian assured her that it was just a Ranger thing. They were intent on their jobs, but Merriam saw the way Eskar looked at her. Like she was a waste of space.

They entered a small town in the early evening, Merriam trying to keep from looking around in wonder at the mix of fae and humans bustling about everyday life. After booking a couple of rooms at an inn and eating a quick dinner, Mollian excused his guard for the night, promising he wouldn't stray far.

"Ready to go back Earth-side?" he asked with a grin, pulling Merriam out of the back door of the inn.

"Sick of me already?" she joked, wrapping her arms around his torso.

"Certainly." Mollian rotated his rings so the stones were against his palm before striking them together and pushing through the rift.

They came out of an alley, walking onto a sparsely populated street. "Now all we have to do is find a tattoo shop," he said, heading off down the sidewalk.

"Molli?" Merriam asked. "How are you going to convince a tattoo artist to add your blood to his inks?"

Mollian grinned. "Don't you remember, Ria? We fae can be very persuasive." When they made it to a tattoo parlor, he walked up to the counter and asked for a scrap of paper. He drew a tall, skinny loop bracketed by a curved line at the top of one side and the bottom of the other and dots on the opposite corners. "Can you fit us in tonight?" he asked, voice sickly sweet like honey. Merriam felt a pressure in the air and knew he was casting a glamor. She idly touched the iron aspen leaf around her neck, the only thing keeping the glamor from affecting her.

Before long, she lay on her stomach. Mollian nonchalantly slipped a knife from his belt, cutting a line up his wrist roughly an inch long. He plucked a small plastic cup off of the artist's prep desk and held it to the wound, and when it was full of his blood, he set it down.

"Got a spare paper towel?" he asked.

The tattoo artist ripped a sheet off of a roll and handed it over without even blinking. Mollian pressed it to the cut on his wrist and sat down.

Merriam fought off the shiver that ran up her spine at how easy it was for Mollian to get into a human's head. How easy it would be for him to get into her head if he wanted to. She started to touch her iron chain again, but caught herself, curling her fingers against her chest instead.

Mollian caught the action and correctly assumed her discomfort. "I only did it out of necessity. They have laws about cross-contamination and blood biohazards," he said sheepishly.

"I know." She smiled, holding out her hand.

Mollian took it in one of his, and the artist went to work.

Merriam winced as the needle dragged over her spine. "Explain to me how this works, exactly?" she asked, for distraction.

"The Bond will allow you to use the magic in my blood. Because I'm a Keeper, that includes Casting and being able to control the Gate, including using the rings to create smaller gateways. You'll also get some of the accelerated healing and immunity to glamors like all of the fair folk. But you only get a portion of the power I have, because it's diluted with your human blood."

Her brow pulled together in a frown. "Do you get a tattoo with my blood? Would that dilute your power?"

Mollian shook his head. "The rune works as a sort of binding agent, allowing someone with magic to share it with someone without. Only the one providing the magic gives blood, and only the person receiving the magic gets the rune."

"Will I be able to move things with my mind like you do?"

The prince tilted his head to the side as he considered his reply, a curl spilling over his forehead. "No, magic of the mind doesn't transfer with a Bond."

"What makes it different?"

Mollian shrugged, trying to play it off as nonchalant but bothered by the lack of knowledge. "Magic is fickle, and the laws are damn near impossible to dissect. I've read as much about it as I can and still only marginally understand it. My best guess is that the magic inherently in the blood is the only magic that's transferred."

"Will the necklace hinder anything?" Merriam asked, bringing his focus back from mysteries unknown.

"Nah, iron only blocks the mind stuff. To put it extremely simply, the iron in our blood keeps blood magic from being hindered by it."

"Good." She dropped his hand to tuck hers under her cheek. "I think it would feel weird to take it off after all this time."

His pale green eyes shone with concern, and he shook his head. "Never take it off. Like I said, it's my blood. You won't be protected from me, and I want you to know every step of the way that you have a choice in all of this."

"Okay," she agreed, smiling softly at his sincerity.

Mollian ran a hand through his hair, brow furrowing. "Don't tell anybody that we're Bonded, either. Not many people know about Traveling outside of the actual Gate in Entumbra, but I don't want to put a target on your back either way. Plus, it's also sort of a sacred ritual. We skipped over a Hel of a lot of procedure."

"Our secret then." Merriam fought back a laugh at the sudden abashed look that washed over his face, barely reminding herself that ink was being carved into her skin and to hold her body still.

It only took half an hour for the artist to tattoo the symbol between her shoulder blades. As soon as the symbol was finished, it was like some phantom tendon snapped into place inside of Merriam, running from her brain down to her core. She gasped, locking eyes with Mollian.

His eyes danced with mischief, and she could feel his presence like a soft ping reverberating through her consciousness. "Woah," she said, eyes wide.

Weird, huh? His voice swirled into her head.

"Very," she agreed. *But in the best way.* She formed the thought and pushed it over to him, an act that felt much more natural than she would have ever considered possible.

Chapter 7

Noted

MERRIAM STOOD IN MOLLIAN'S doorway, arms folded across her chest. "What do you mean, you have a meeting?" She glowered. "Who do you have a meeting with?"

"Just some delegates from other cities. Trivial stuff. Didn't I tell you?" Mollian pulled a shirt over his head and brushed his curls back from where they'd tumbled into his eyes.

"No, you didn't," Merriam huffed. "Oren invited us to lunch with him yesterday. I just assumed you'd be available."

"You know what happens when you assume, Ria." Mollian strapped a sword belt to his waist. "Wait, you're sure he meant lunch today?"

"Yeah, why?"

"He's the one that set up the meeting."

Merriam cocked her head to the side. "He definitely said you should come if you were available."

Mollian's face split into a wide grin, cracked green eyes sparkling. "He definitely knew I wouldn't be."

"He could have forgotten in his frustration with Ferrick," Merriam defended.

"Or—hear me out—*or* he wanted some alone time with you without making it obvious he wanted some alone time with you." Mollian sat down on his bed, slipping his feet into boots. "I doubt he even sees that dorky kid I dragged from her own dimension anymore."

"Me? Dorky?" Merriam gave him a withering look. "This coming from the male who hasn't figured out how to keep his hair out of his eyes for even a moment during his twenty-four years of life?"

Mollian ran both of his hands through his hair, holding it back with a small scowl that pulled at the branches tattooed on his temples. "Wow, I didn't know we were making this personal." He looked at a pillow, lifting it with his mind and tossing it at her.

She caught it before it hit her face. "Why would he invite you at all if he knew you weren't available? "

Mollian gave her a look, letting his hair fall free. "In case you haven't met you, you are a flighty little fucker when it comes to anything involving feelings. My brother has been around long enough to know that." He stood, walking to the door and sliding past her.

Merriam tossed the pillow back onto his bed and closed the door, following him into the main room with a frown. The truth in his words was uncomfortable to consider.

Mollian watched her, still smiling like a fool.

"I cannot be into your brother, Molli," she insisted, reeling in her emotions.

"Why's that, exactly?"

"For one thing, he's your *brother*. For another, he's less than a year away from becoming *king*."

Mollian just looked at her, shrugging his shoulders.

"Even if there was anything between me and Oren, I'm a *mercenary*. I can't be consort to the *king*. Not to mention, I have a reputation to uphold."

"I think you're being a little dramatic." Mollian laughed. "You've had years of kicking ass and taking names. I think your reputation is pretty solid around here now."

Merriam dropped her gaze, shaking her head. "There's still talk, though, Molli. Getting involved with another prince would only add fuel to that fire."

Mollian sighed, walking over to Merriam and putting his hands on her shoulders. "It doesn't matter what other people think. You've proven your right to be here a thousand times over. Proven that you belong here." He met her eyes intently. "No one is going to take that away. Certainly not some prick Rangers who never had a chance against you to begin with." He let her go, stepping back. "Besides, you're putting way too much pressure on yourself over this. Nobody said this was a date, remember? He just wants to have lunch."

Merriam sighed, rubbing her hands over her face. "Right, because I am *not* getting involved with the crown prince."

"Whatever you say." Mollian grinned again. "For real though, forget I said anything and just have fun. It's no different than when you would see him in Entumbra, right?" With that, he slipped out of the door, completely missing her eyes widening, freckled cheeks flushing with heat. He'd guessed that would be her reaction anyway, and smiled smugly to himself as he walked down the hall.

After finishing lacing up her boots, Merriam made her way up the stairs to Oren's rooms, repeating to herself that this was nothing more than a lunch between friends. Rillak stood outside on watch, eyeing her as she walked up.

"What do you want, little merc? The young prince isn't here."

Merriam smiled up at him. "Actually, I'm here for Prince Oren. We have an appointment."

"Well, ain't that somethin'." Rillak turned and knocked loudly at the door before cracking it open. "The little merc is here for you, Your Highness," he said.

Merriam shook her head. Seven years she'd lived in Jekeida, and she'd gone from being referred to as "the human girl" to "the little merc" but never by her name, as far as Rillak was concerned. She didn't mind, though. The burly guard was always kind to her in his own gruff way.

He was one of the few who had never referred to her as Mollian's pet or treated her with disdain.

"Go ahead and show her in, thank you." Oren's voice floated through the door.

Rillak stepped aside. "Don't be causin' any trouble now," he warned, eyeing the axes at her hips, but there was no bite to his words.

"I wouldn't dream of it, Rillak." She beamed, stepping by him.

Oren was sitting at a desk toward the back of the room, shuffling around some papers. He smiled broadly when she walked in. "I just have one last thing to finish up, but make yourself comfortable."

"Molli had a meeting to go to, so he won't be joining us," she offered, sitting down in an overstuffed chair close to the door, fingers twisting around the tail of her braid as she looked around.

"Oh, that's right. I'd completely forgotten." Oren waved a hand through the air, continuing to skim the page in front of him.

Merriam relaxed with that and let her eyes travel around the room, but she didn't get very far before she saw her crudely drawn picture of Ferrick tacked to the wall by Oren's desk.

Oren happened to glance up then and followed her gaze to the picture. "Truly, an amazing work of art." He chuckled.

"I'm glad you liked it," she said.

His green eyes, a deeper shade than Mollian's, turned back to her. "I'll treasure it as long as I live," he said, touching his hand to his chest in mirthful sincerity.

"Maybe if you're lucky, I'll add more to the collection," Merriam joked. "Just let me know the next time you're feeling vexed so I can be rightfully inspired."

"You'll be the first I seek out," Oren promised, returning to the page in front of him for a brief moment. He made a final notation before setting his pen down and standing up.

He strolled over to her and offered his hand to help her up. She felt suddenly shy as she took it, very aware of the warm strength of his fingers over hers. "How do you feel about taking some horses out?" he asked as she stood.

"I thought you said lunch?" she questioned with a frown. "Not that a ride doesn't sound fun," she quickly added. "I just ... well, I haven't eaten yet, and—"

Oren laughed, dropping her hand. "Forgive me, Mer. I did promise lunch, and I fully intend to follow through. I was more suggesting a picnic. Getting out of the castle for a bit."

"Oh?" Merriam looked at him warily.

"First and foremost, you and Molli are both so food motivated, I know better than to let you starve," Oren tutted with a shake of his head. "But I'm also suffocating. I haven't left the castle since I've been home." He opened the door and led her out.

"I'll be going out for lunch, Rillak." Oren addressed the guard, who stood a full head taller than he did.

"I'll keep a watch out, Your Highness." Rillak promised. "Little merc." He dipped his head to Merriam.

Oren led the way to the stables, stopping by the kitchen to pick up an already-prepared basket. He spoke briefly with a stable hand, who led out two horses, saddled and ready to go.

Merriam looked from the horses—the *two* horses—to the basket, to Oren.

Fucking Molli was right.

"You knew Molli had that meeting when you asked me to have lunch with you," she accused.

Oren gave her a sheepish smile, securing the basket to the back of his saddle. "I didn't know if you would agree to lunch with me if I made it sound like a date."

"Is it?" Merriam met his gaze evenly.

"Is what?" Oren didn't pull his eyes from hers.

"Is it a date?"

"Are friends not allowed to spend time together?" Oren at least had the good sense not to ask Merriam if she wanted help into her saddle, just pulled himself onto his horse.

She stood staring at him for a moment, then shook herself. This was nothing new. They'd hiked through the forest around Entumbra together countless times before anything physical had happened between them. That was when their friendship had really taken root, both of them escaping their responsibilities for a while and just enjoying each other's company.

Merriam easily boosted herself up, grabbing the reins with a shake of her head. "Well, lead the way, Majesty." She gestured toward the gates.

They headed south, away from the mountain town of Umbra and deeper into the forest. The horses climbed what was barely more than a small game trail, and Merriam recognized instantly where they were headed. She fought off the warmth that flooded her veins as she watched Oren, reminding herself that they were no longer in Entumbra. No longer separated from life and the responsibilities that came with it.

So this was not happening.

The crown prince had not asked her on a date.

She turned her gaze to the forest around them, needing to not focus on Oren.

They emerged from the trees at the top of the mountain, and Merriam swung down from the horse, dropping the reins and letting it graze as she walked to the rocky edge, looking out at the castle and the city sprawling below. The wind blew across her face, tugging a few strands of hair that had come loose from her braid across her cheek. She pushed them away, turning to find Oren spreading out a blanket over the ground.

"This used to be a favorite spot of mine when I was younger," he said.

"Molli showed it to me," she admitted. "I love it, too. We hike up here some nights to drink and get away from everything." She looked back over the mountainside again before stepping over and sinking down next to him.

"Can I let you in on a little secret?" Oren asked, pulling a decanter of wine from the basket and setting it down next to two wooden cups.

"Always." Merriam uncorked it and poured the pale golden liquid for them.

"He told me." His grin was almost fiendish.

"So this *is* a date." Merriam raised her cup to her lips, taking a sip.

"Still no. He also told me you're not into that sort of thing." Oren unwrapped a smoked turkey leg and handed it to her. "Glad to know your aversion isn't limited to me."

"When did you set up Molli's meeting?" She ignored his latter comment.

"Don't ask questions you don't want the answer to."

"You're unbelievable," Merriam told him, but amusement softened the words.

"I'm not sure what you're referring to, but I can assure you I had no nefarious intentions." Oren covered his heart.

Merriam rolled her eyes, letting it drop, and they ate in comfortable silence for a while before Oren slid a look her way. "So why no relationships?"

"I have plenty of relationships," she answered coyly.

Oren leveled his gaze at her, unamused.

She stared back innocently.

"Romantic relationships."

Merriam picked a strip of meat off the bone, popping it into her mouth with a shrug. "I just realized pretty early on that it wasn't worth the headache. With my life, I mean." She looked up at him briefly before turning her attention back to the turkey. "First, there's always a problem with my job. I only have so much control over my schedule, and I'm gone a lot. If they aren't intimidated by my job, then they're intimidated by my relationship with Molli. Even the ones who fully know he doesn't have romantic relationships are still bothered by how close we are. Besides, most of the males in Umbra find themselves far too self-important. They're not worth the time, anyway."

She bit into a bread roll before glancing up apologetically. "Molli's rambling ways must have brushed off on me over the years. Old suitors aren't usually the kind of thing you bring up during ... " Merriam trailed off.

Oren looked at her, amused. "During a friendly lunch?"

Merriam bit her lip, looking out over Umbra. "Yes, not quite appropriate conversation for lunch, is it?"

"Well, I guess it depends on the company, and as it happens, it's a conversation I don't mind having."

Merriam's stomach rolled, and she swallowed down the bread in her mouth with a big gulp of wine. "You're interested in conversing about all of my past lovers?" she joked, playing off her nervousness.

"No, that would be crass."

"Oh, I do excel in crassness."

"Strange feat for someone devoted to a life of unattachment," Oren commented.

Merriam took a sip of wine, peering at him over the rim of her cup with a wicked gleam in her amber eyes. "You know unattachment has never meant celibacy."

"I'm well aware." Oren matched her gaze, eyes smoldering. "Just so we're clear, I happen to have no issue with the mercenary lifestyle or with my little brother. And that, Lady, is the thread I'm interested in pulling."

The air between them had grown suddenly tense. Merriam was

half-convinced it would spark if a match was lit. Warmth flooded her body at the intensity of his gaze, and it took everything in her power to tear her eyes away from his. *Not a good idea.* She reminded herself, taking a deep breath to try to slow the beating of her heart.

She cleared her throat, unceremoniously wiping her hands on her pants. "I'm not sure I believe that, Majesty."

"What's not to believe?"

"That Oren Stonebane, the heir apparent of Sekha, soon to be one of the high rulers of Nethyl, known far and wide for his sound moral compass, has no qualms with a mercenary lifestyle." Merriam took another sip of wine, propping her arm up on a bent knee and resting her cheek in her palm to watch him.

Oren tipped his head back and laughed. Merriam tried not to watch the way the sun kissed his skin, the same light brown as her freckles, or shone on his hair, highlighting the snow white strands with golden light at the crown of his head and contrasting against the dark aspen branches on his brow. She tried not to think about the musical baritone of his free laughter, or the way the wind carried his scent to her, familiar in the way Mollian's was, but laced with something crisp and dark. She tried to ignore the butterflies that tumbled in her stomach and tightened her chest, making her heart trip over itself in a way that simply could not be healthy. But even as she fought her awareness of these things, she didn't look away from him as he opened eyes that sparkled with the green of new spring and met her gaze.

"You pose a fair point," he finally said with a grin. "Let me rephrase. While I cannot in good conscience condone a lifestyle of lawlessness and devilry, the odd hours and long jobs do not bother me in any unmanageable way."

Merriam shook her head slightly, a soft smile playing on her lips. "Noted."

"Just 'noted'?" Oren cocked an eyebrow.

Merriam finished the last of the wine from her cup, still not breaking eye contact. "Yep."

They sat watching each other for several long moments. The air once again was thick with memories of past times they'd sat together on the side of a mountain ... and of other things. He started to speak, and, scared of what might come out of his mouth, she blurted, "So why five years in Entumbra? What could you have done for that long?" A topic they'd somehow never broached during any of those visits.

Oren ran his tongue over one elongated canine, and the unbidden want to feel those teeth on her skin washed through her. "I studied the Gate, mostly," he finally answered.

"For five years?" She raised her brows.

"There are an innumerable amount of realities, Mer." Oren chuckled. "Communicating with the stones is a very intensive process. Learning how to tell them where you want to go, even when sometimes you don't even know exactly where that is."

"That doesn't even make sense."

"No, not really," Oren agreed. "It's like, there are all kinds of places out there. Some of them very similar to ours, some of them crazier and brighter with more vivid colors than you could possibly imagine, and some that are dark and acrid and can only support life that is vile to the utmost degree. And, of course, everything between." Oren ran a hand up the back of his head to where the close-cut hair met the base of his bun. "It's hard to explain. Impossible, really, without being shown what you're doing, but Keeper blood talks to the stones. It tells the Gate what you desire, to put it very simply."

Merriam shifted, turning to face him fully and crossing her legs in front of her. "So you think of a place you might want to go, and the Gate drops you there?"

"Sort of, but not quite. It's much more complicated than that." Oren struggled to find the words. His eyes dropped to her hands, resting on her knees, and Mollian's rings on each middle finger. "You know the way your blood sings when you Travel?" he asked.

Merriam's mouth dropped open, and she pulled her hands into her lap. "What?" she said lamely.

"Surely my overly talkative brother didn't give you the rings without telling you how to use them."

She opened her mouth, shut it, then opened it again because she knew no answer was as good as confirming his suspicion.

"I've seen the Bonding rune on your back."

"Ah, well." Merriam blushed, pulling her braid over her shoulder and forcing her focus on the conversation at hand. "We did it after he brought me here. He never wanted me to feel trapped or like I didn't have a choice." Her fingers found the iron aspen leaf dangling at the hollow of her throat.

"That's why he gave you the necklace, too, when you were children." Oren's eyes traveled down her face to the base of her neck.

"Yes." Merriam dropped her hand, smiling softly. "He's good. Like you." Her eyes met his.

Oren smiled at that. "Mollian has always been good, if a bit of a wild spirit," he agreed. "I helped him commission that for you." His gaze dropped back down to her throat.

Merriam tried not to fidget at the way her pulse jumped under his scrutiny. "He said you helped him find me."

"From the way he talked about you, I knew you belonged with him, that you were connected," Oren told her, reaching out to tuck a stray hair behind her ear.

It took everything in her power not to lean into his palm.

"The first time I met you, I knew I was right. Even outside of you and Mollian being *mehhen*, you've always belonged in this world," he said quietly.

Merriam dipped her head to hide the blush crawling up her cheeks. "Thanks, O. Especially in the beginning, when so many looked at me with open animosity, knowing that I had your support meant everything to me. Your friendship the last few years has been invaluable." She swallowed back the thought that followed: *losing that friendship terrifies me.*

"I will always be on your side," Oren said sincerely, catching the unspoken sentiment.

She looked at him, smiling impishly. "Even when I'm killing people for coin?"

Oren laughed that deep, free laugh again, making her stomach flip. "Yes, though I will never promise to always defend your actions." He matched her wicked smile. "You're much too volatile for that."

"And it would be wise of you not to forget it," Merriam ribbed, then brought her hands up, examining the stones glinting in the sunlight. "You said something about Keeper blood and Traveling, right?"

Oren nodded, leaning forward to take her hands and run the pad of his thumbs over the rings. "Do you use them often?"

She bit her lip, nodding. "Not every day, but they're useful tools for reconnaissance."

"You'll know what I mean, then. The way your blood almost vibrates?"

Merriam gave him a slow nod, forcing herself not to focus on the warmth of his touch.

"That's the blood communicating with the stones. Telling them to open a rift." Oren looked down at her hands for a moment more before dropping them.

"Molli told me once that the rings can only take you to a parallel dimension unless they actually touch your blood," she said, twisting the orydite around on her finger.

"He's right. They'll open a rift to whatever reality is parallel unless told otherwise, even with Keeper blood added. Jumping across multiple realities takes a lot of energy, too. The further away a universe is, the more draining it will be to Travel to it."

"How do you learn to do that?" Merriam asked curiously.

Oren's eyes narrowed a bit, and he smiled at her, shaking his head. "That's Keeper knowledge, Mer."

Merriam looked away. "Of course, sorry. Secrets of the sacred order and all that. I probably already know much more than I should." She fidgeted with her necklace.

Oren slipped a finger under her chin and forced her to look at him again. "You know exactly as much as you should. Like I said, you and my brother were connected long before you were ever Bonded." He dropped his fingers. *And this has always been your home.*

It rumbled through her head, and she smiled. Nobody aside from Mollian had ever Cast to her before, and it felt strangely intimate coming from Oren. Concentrating, she formed the thought and flung it to him. *Thank you for lunch, Majesty.*

Merriam's head ached lightly, and the tattoo between her shoulder blades burned with an itch. She rolled her shoulders in an attempt to shake off the feeling. Casting to him was not the same second-nature act as Casting to Mollian, but the fact that she could do it filled her with a sense of pride.

Anytime, Lady. Oren smiled at her, standing to pack up and head back to the castle.

Chapter 8

A code of conduct

A FEAST HAD BEEN scheduled in honor of Oren's return from Entumbra. It would be the last public celebration hosted at the castle until his coronation, and Umbra buzzed with energy and movement all week.

Merriam spent most of the days leading up to it running a small job for a local business owner and training with the mercs, but every time she went home to the castle, Oren would be with Mollian in the main room of their chambers. She would inevitably get roped into whatever conversation or game was going on between them, and as much as she hated to admit it, she very much looked forward to it.

Being around him was as easy as being around Mollian, though she made a conscious effort not to touch Oren, because every time she did, her stomach would flip and her blood would heat. Her body's traitorous reaction to his presence was of no consequence, though. She had made her decision long ago, and she repeated to herself often that no feelings were tied to the attraction. She merely needed a distraction, and he'd soon be pushed entirely from her mind.

The day of the feast, Merriam was finishing tidying up the training room at the merc house after running a couple of weapons drills.

"I hope there's going to be duck," Aleah jabbered, pulling the tie from her hair and shaking it out, red strands falling to brush her shoulders. "I haven't had duck in so long."

"There's not going to be duck." Leonidas sat on a bench with his sword and a whetting stone, honing his blade. The muscles in his forearms flexed with movement underneath the birds inked across his skin. "Do you know how many ducks would have had to be caught for a feast this size?" He raised the sword to eye level, giving it a thorough once-over.

Aleah glowered at him. "Well, do you know how many ducks it would take to feed all of us? Because I'll bet it's exponentially lower, yet we still never get any."

Leonidas lifted his clear blue gaze to her, raising a brow. "Are you not a perfectly capable hunter, Aleah? If you want duck, perhaps you should go kill one."

"Loan me Pan for a day, and maybe I will!" Aleah crossed her arms over her chest with a huff.

Campbell finished moving all the dummy targets back against the wall. "We all know you're never going to spend a day hunting." He rolled his indigo eyes in her direction.

"I might!"

"Or, you could just ask nicely," Campbell suggested.

Without looking up at them, Leonidas gave a shrug that was as good as confirmation.

"It's pig," Merriam spoke up, wiping her hands on her pants. "I heard some of the kitchen staff discussing it earlier this week."

Aleah sighed. "Well, I guess that will do." She gave a curt nod before heading into the main house. A few seconds later, they heard a loud shriek.

Leonidas jumped up, sword in hand, just as the cry was followed by, "Calysta!" He let out a long breath, shaking his head. "That fucking female," he muttered.

"Maybe you're just too tense," Campbell teased, nudging Leonidas in the ribs. "Come on, let's go say hi so we can get dressed."

They filed into the mushroom, where Aleah was just dropping her arms from around the nymph.

"It's so good to see you all!" Calysta smiled, showing the many points of her teeth.

"How was your trip?" Merriam asked.

"Tedious, but necessary." Calysta waved her hand. "Every time I go back, I'm reminded of why I left to begin with. But that's unimportant. Has any of the talk reached Umbra yet?"

"What talk?" Leonidas asked, fingers tightening around the sword he still held.

Calysta's ink-black eyes shimmered with concern. "Where's Jasper?"

"In the office." Aleah pointed her thumb over her shoulder toward the stairs.

"Can you bring him down? I'm going to grab something to eat, and then I'll tell you everything." She turned toward the kitchen.

"JASPER! CALYSTA IS BACK!" Aleah turned her head toward the stairs and hollered.

"Bold move," Calysta said, before disappearing into the root cellar.

Aleah gave a shrug, and Leonidas rolled his eyes.

Soon enough, Jasper came down the stairs and focused a dark silver glare on Aleah. "Scream at me again, and I will take your tongue."

They all knew it was an idle threat, of course, but Aleah had the good graces to at least lower her eyes and look abashed. "Sorry, Jaz."

Calysta came back up from the cellar with an apple, taking a bite and leaning her hip against the counter before beginning. "Did we ever finish looking into that man the trafficker was talking about?"

"The Crown wasn't concerned with us looking at it." Jasper folded his arms across his chest, wings flaring out slightly in vexation.

Calysta pursed her lips, a darker shade of green than her skin. "I think something bad is happening."

"Related to the traffickers?" Leonidas asked.

Calysta shook her head, the lengths of her long pink hair swinging slightly. "Possibly, but I'm not sure. I heard things. Disturbing things."

"What kind of disturbing things?" Merriam asked, propping her hands against the back of the couch.

"Deaths. Gruesome and unexplainable. There have also been several abductions of fae and humans, some of their bodies found days later, most still missing."

Leonidas took a subconscious step closer to Campbell. "How many?"

"A dozen murders, at least that all seem to have the same ... style." Calysta turned the apple idly in her claw-tipped fingers. "Bodies mutilated beyond recognition. Some have been speculating it's an animal attack, but that doesn't match up with other details. I don't know everything, but it sounded like the killing didn't happen where the bodies were found. And other strange things, too, like a heavy scent of sulfur around the abduction sites, and a few reports of thunder."

Jasper tilted his head to the side. "Thunder?"

Calysta nodded. "No rain or storm clouds, though. Just a single loud crack of thunder, sometimes two or three. Not in every instance, either."

Jasper flicked his eyes to Merriam in question.

She shook her head, chewing on her lip. "Sulfur ... could be demons? But they were all eradicated from Nethyl in the time of the First Keepers, according to legend."

"Where were these murders?" Leonidas asked.

"All over Jekeida, one or two just inside the borders of Audha. The earliest account I heard of was from just over a month ago, right before we killed the traffickers."

Jasper ran a hand over the twisted locs of his hair, frowning. "That's concerning. Regardless, there's not much we're going to do about it on our own. But keep your eyes and ears open, everyone. I have no doubts this job will end up falling into our hands, and I want to be as prepared as possible."

"Does that mean I'm back on research duty?" Merriam wrinkled her nose.

"Yes, it does."

"You're the one who lives in the same building as the biggest library in Sekha," Aleah pointed out.

"Well, it's not like any of you would struggle getting access, either," she grumbled.

"True, but you're the only one who won't be met with a sword if you're found there unattended," Campbell added.

"Like you'd ever let yourselves be discovered," Merriam replied wryly.

Aleah grinned, turning to head up the stairs. "I'm sure you'll live, Mer. Now go get ready for the party."

Calysta finished the last bit of her apple, licking the juice delicately from her claws. "I'm going to stay here tonight. I'm exhausted from travel."

"I'll see the rest of you in a bit, then," Merriam said before slipping out the back door and heading up to the castle.

Merriam tied the end of her braid and twisted it up, pinning it to the back of her head. The bottom half of her hair fell in loose waves, and she ran her fingers through it a few times before tossing it over her shoulder and turning from the mirror. "What do you think?" She gave a little twirl for Mollian, skirts flaring out around her feet.

She wore a sea green dress with a plunging neckline, the thinnest of straps looping over her shoulders. There was virtually no back, and the skirts were soft and layered, flowing lightly with every movement.

"You are gorgeous." Mollian offered her his arm. "And I'm sure you'll catch the attentions of a certain crown prince."

Merriam stuck her tongue out at him, tucking her hand into his elbow. He looked strapping in a well-tailored jacket of deep emerald with gold threading creating a garland of aspen leaves across the chest and lapels. The shirt underneath was as white as his hair, and his black pants were tucked into black boots cuffed with gold. "I told you, nothing is happening between me and Oren." She gave him a pointed look.

"Ria, he's my brother. And you're my best friend. Neither of you are particularly good at hiding things from me."

"There's nothing to hide." Merriam opened the door and pulled him into the hallway.

"Only because you're both so damn stubborn," Mollian scoffed.

"For good reason!" Merriam bumped her shoulder into him. "Now drop it, please."

The corner of his mouth lifted in an amused smirk. *Whatever you say,* he Cast before moving forward.

When they got to the entrance of the ballroom, Mollian excused himself, needing to meet up with his family before the meal. Though the queen had grown to respect Merriam over the years, she was regarded only as a mercenary and valuable ally and would not have a place at the head table.

While this irked Mollian, who'd explained time and again that she ought to be shown some level of consideration as his *mehhen*, Regenya had always refused. Fair folk and high-ranking human delegates had only just been given a seat at their table in recent years, and as much as the queen wasn't against abolishing the lines of classism, giving a low-born human a seat of respect would cause more uproar than it was worth.

Merriam grabbed a glass of sparkling wine off of a passing platter, sipping the human vintage as she glanced around the room. Long rows of tables took up the majority of the space, covered platters running the lengths. When the supper portion was over, the tables would be moved aside to open the floor for dancing and revelry.

Mollian had reached the front of the room, taking his place beside Oren at the head table on the dais. They leaned close in conversation, and Oren laughed. Captain Ferrick was sitting to their left, leaving two seats open at the center of the table for the king and queen. Oren's gaze lifted, feeling her stare, and met her eyes across the room.

Her traitorous little heart skipped a beat when he smiled at her before turning his attention back to Mollian.

"Whatcha' looking at?" The voice at her elbow made her jump, clinking the glass against her teeth.

"Legends, Aleah." Merriam turned around with a laugh. "You scared me."

"Because I look so devastatingly beautiful in this dress?" she asked, taking Merriam's free hand and twirling herself around. Her hair was twisted up into an elaborately braided bun on the top of her head, and a silky cream gown was tied around her neck, loose folds of fabric draped elegantly in the front and the cut tightening around her lower half, clearly showing off the definition of her backside and thighs.

"Yes, absolutely devastating," Merriam complimented.

"Come on, the others are grabbing our seats." Aleah slipped the glass from Merriam's hand, tipping it back and downing the rest. As they walked, she set down the empty flute and grabbed two more, handing one to Merriam and clinking hers against it.

Merriam shook her head in amusement at the flush already blossoming across the half-fae's freckled cheeks. "If you don't pace yourself, Jasper is going to take you home."

Aleah's hazel eyes shimmered as she glanced at Merriam. "He'll have to catch me first, and I'm pretty sure I can run faster than him."

Leonidas and Campbell were seated with their backs to the long balcony along one wall, Jasper across from them. They all had glasses of deep red wine, though Campbell's was almost gone. Leonidas and Jasper were both scanning the room warily, and Merriam laughed, pulling out a chair and plopping down next to Jasper.

"You two are ridiculous." She took another sip of her wine. "You do know that almost the entirety of the Royal Guard is on duty tonight?"

Jasper lifted a brow. "You trust them to watch out for you?"

Merriam snorted, setting her glass down on the table. "Of course not. But I trust them to watch out for the royal family, all of whom will be in attendance."

"Mmm," Jasper replied, still keeping an eye on the door.

"You know these two don't trust crowds." Campbell slid a jokingly exasperated look to the man next to him.

Aleah rolled her eyes. "Yeah, because last time we were in a crowd was during the spring festival, and you got so drunk you ran into the middle of the parade trying to chase down a food vendor and almost got trampled. Leo's got to keep his eyes out for any wandering platters trying to lure you away."

Campbell glowered at her, but Leonidas cracked a smile, running the fingers of one hand into the male's dark curls. "I can't have you chasing a poor waiter with a plate of finger foods across the room, can I?"

Campbell shook the hand from his head. "That was one time, and we hadn't eaten all day," he grumbled, bringing his glass to his lips. "And I came back, didn't I?" he added with a sly smile, flicking his indigo eyes up to Leonidas.

"Only after Leo damn near gave that poor dancer a heart attack going after you." Merriam giggled.

"Enough," Jasper finally said, turning his full attention to them. "Leonidas can't help it if his possessive gene makes him go a little stupid at times."

They all laughed at that, and Leonidas was about to speak before a gong sounded through the hall, and everyone quieted.

A Guard stood at the front of the room, loudly announcing the arrival of Queen Regenya and King Darius.

They stood together before their seats, and the queen raised her glass. "Welcome and thank you for joining us in celebration of Prince Oren's return. These past five years, he has been studying, learning, and crafting his magic in preparation to take the throne. Tonight, we drink to his final days as crown prince and my last few months as your regent."

"To Prince Oren," Darius called, raising his glass.

Everyone seated throughout the room raised their cups and repeated the cry. "To Prince Oren!"

Merriam watched Oren nod respectfully to his parents as she drank. His eyes slipped to hers as he brought his own glass to his lips, and she quickly glanced away.

"Now, we feast!" the king announced, and the two sat down.

Lids were lifted off of platters and away from the tables by high fae attendants lining the walls, using their magic to gracefully stack them all together in a coordinated movement, and the guests started piling their plates with food.

A few glasses of wine and several helpings later, the dishes were cleared away, and everyone stood so the tables could be moved. The mercs split up to mingle, Jasper and Aleah to find their different castle confidants, and Leonidas and Campbell to talk with the other hunters and falconers.

Merriam wandered through the crowd, only half looking for Mollian, mostly being lulled by the music and sipping on wine, until she caught sight of Oren. His hair was twisted into a knot at the back of his head, sides and back freshly shorn close to his scalp. He was laughing and brought a heavily ringed hand to his chest. Merriam's heart skipped a beat as her stomach erupted with butterflies. He looked downright regal in his jacket, forest green and gold, with white pants that fit snugly around powerful thighs. She dragged her eyes back up to his face and felt her cheeks immediately heat as her gaze met his, deep green eyes lit with merriment.

He said a few more words to the group he was with before excusing himself and walking past. To his credit, he didn't head straight for Merriam. He briefly greeted another party-goer and meandered to the drink table, picking up a glass of dark wine before walking up to her.

"You look even more stunning than usual," he said lowly so his voice didn't carry, eyes shining into hers.

Merriam looked down, the alcohol in her system doing nothing to help her blushing. "You're too kind, Majesty." She met his eyes again, taking another sip of wine.

Oren's gaze dropped to her mouth while she drank, watching hungrily as she lowered the glass and swiped her tongue over her lips. He caught himself then and looked elsewhere, taking a deep pull from his own glass.

"Is the selection pleasing for you tonight?" she asked cheekily, finishing her wine.

"Greatly," he answered. He tipped back his glass and offered her his hand, flicking the fingers of the other to float both of their empty cups onto a passing servant's tray. "May I have a dance, Lady?"

"Who am I to refuse the prince?" She took his hand and let him lead her to the floor, her eyes briefly meeting Mollian's across the hall.

Nothing happening, my ass.

Merriam looked away from him, biting back a smile. *Nothing at all.*

Oren pulled her close and drifted seamlessly into the dancing crowd. Merriam stumbled only slightly into the rhythm and made a mental note to cut back on the wine.

"So, how are things in the mercenary business?"

Merriam laughed. "Better than ever, thanks to the prince's glowing recommendation."

"I'll figure out some way for you to thank me."

"Thank you?" Merriam cringed. "Well, this is awkward. I was talking about Mollian."

Oren feigned a pained look before sending her spinning. "I don't know what you've heard about fae temperament," he whispered into her ear after pulling her back. "But we don't do well with bruised pride."

Merriam ignored the shiver that traveled down her spine as lips brushed her ear. "Damn, you must truly hate those post-sex conversations then, huh?" She innocently blinked up at him.

Oren raised his brows. "Am I to believe that you find me incapable of satisfying a partner?"

Merriam led herself into another twirl, spinning back into his arms with her back to his chest. "You said it, not me."

Oren dropped her into a low dip before pulling her back up and spinning her around to face him again. "I don't recall you having any complaints, but if you need a reminder, just say the words," he said huskily.

Heat flooded her at the wolfish gleam to his eyes. The song ended, saving her from a reply, and she curtsied gracefully before taking a step back. "Thank you for the dance, Majesty. I won't hoard your attentions all night."

Oren wanted to say more, but no less than three females had already stepped forward, hoping to be asked to dance.

Merriam smiled, turning away and grabbing another flute of sparkling wine. One more wouldn't kill her, and she desperately needed to calm her nerves. She stepped out onto the wide balcony, making her way around to an empty, mostly secluded corner and leaning on the railing. The cool night air swept along her skin, and she raised her face to the sky.

The once-unfamiliar constellations twinkled, shining brightly with the absence of added light from the new and half moons. She smiled to herself as she studied the stars and drank her wine.

She stood stargazing for longer than intended, her glass empty and forgotten next to her until another cup appeared in her peripheral vision. She glanced up to see Oren standing beside her. "I didn't hear you approach," she said, taking the offered beverage.

"You looked deep in thought." Oren lifted his own wooden cup to hers with a soft knock before drinking.

"I wasn't, really. Not about anything important." She tucked a stray strand of hair behind her ear, lifting the drink to her lips. Her eyes widened in surprise as the tangy-sweetness of lemon-lime soda flavored with artificial cherry hit her tongue. She almost choked on it, but swallowed it down and looked at Oren, soul bared in her amber eyes. "You brought me a Shirley Temple?"

His sole dimple appeared on his cheek. "I slipped out shortly after you left."

One of the few things from Earth that she ever craved, and he'd ditched his own party to Travel to another dimension and fetch it for her. They'd shared it once or twice in Entumbra with fast food, also retrieved from her former home. She swayed slightly, gripping the railing against the effects of what had probably been three-too-many glasses of wine. "This is amazing. You're amazing."

He shrugged, but was entirely pleased with her reaction, and they drank together in contented silence.

"Do you ever miss it?" Oren asked suddenly, glancing up toward the stars. "Your old sky?"

Merriam looked at him, starlight glimmering in his eyes and casting shadows along the strong planes of his face. She folded her hands together to keep from touching the aspen tattoos that marked him as a Stonebane prince and a servant of Sekha. "Only sometimes," she said finally. "I was never home there, not the way I am here. I did love the stars, though. They were some of the only reliable things in my world." She finished the last of her drink. "The stars and Molli were all I had."

Oren reached out to play with a lock of her hair. "I'm glad he found you." His eyes shone drunkenly, and he lightly dragged his fingers across her cheek, her neck, to her shoulder. "In case you haven't been reminded lately, you do belong here." His fingers made their way down her arm, finally taking her hand, bringing it up to his mouth and brushing the barest of kisses across her knuckles before releasing it.

Merriam's heartbeat quickened at his touch, and her breath caught in her throat as his lips made contact with her skin. She rested her hand lightly on the railing, trying to appear more calm than she was. "You told me just a few days ago, actually."

"Well, it warranted repeating." He leaned closer, and the breeze carried his scent around her—pine and plum laced with something dark, like the crisp night sky above them.

"You smell good," she whispered, and then brought a hand to her mouth. "I did not mean to say that out loud." She looked out across the garden, mortified.

Oren laughed, brushing her hair off her back and tracing the tattoo between her shoulder blades. "You're welcome to smell me anytime."

"Legends, how creepy am I?" She twirled the empty cup around, swallowing against the electricity racing down her spine and spreading through her limbs.

"If you were any creepier, I'd probably have to hire local mercenaries to take you away," Oren teased, leaning his folded arms against the railing.

Goosebumps covered her skin, and she wasn't sure if it was from the cool night air kissing her largely exposed back or a side effect from the fire-hot touch of Oren's fingers. "Is threatening to hire my own people to get rid of me some kind of power play?"

"I could show you a power play." Oren dipped his head lower to hers.

"Don't threaten me with a good time." Merriam lifted her face to blink innocently at him and found his mouth very near. Her own went dry as she noticed his gaze fixed on her lips.

"In regards to the last conversation we had in Entumbra," Oren started, not pulling away.

Merriam shook her head slightly, not wanting to talk about it with wine muddling her thoughts. She meant to pull away, knew she should pull away, but her eyes fell closed and she slanted her mouth over his. He leaned in without hesitation, seeking to deepen the kiss, and she let him, parting her lips and sweeping her tongue into his mouth. He tasted of rich faerie wine and overly sweet cherry, and she tightened her hold on the railing as he pulled her bottom lip into his mouth, dragging it through his teeth. A soft moan traveled up her throat, and she nipped him back. She let go of the rough stone to bring her hand to his face when she heard Mollian in her head.

MERRIAM!

The shout of her full name had her jerking her head back, Oren's eyes fluttering open dazedly. Before either of them could speak, Mollian came walking around the side of the balcony with Eskar and Ollivan, a dark-haired Ranger, in tow.

"Brother, we're needed in the war room," he said.

Merriam tried to catch his eyes. *Is something wrong?*

Maybe. I don't know. Follow us.

He was nervous, and every spark of desire faded from her. Something was definitely wrong, and the pit growing in her stomach chased the buzz of alcohol from her mind.

Oren nodded, also having sobered up plenty in the last few moments, and led the way back through the ballroom.

Merriam trailed behind Oren and the guards at Mollian's side.

Sure looked like a whole lot of nothing to me.

She bit back a smile, barely resisting the urge to elbow him in the side. *Mind your business.*

They reached the doors to the war room, the king and queen already seated inside.

"This does not concern you, Merriam," Regenya said coolly when she laid eyes on Merriam.

"I thought she should be present," Mollian said evenly. "Considering the circumstances."

"That is not for you to decide," the queen bristled. "She may be your friend, but she is a mercenary first and foremost when it comes to matters of the Crown. She will know only what I deem necessary *if* I decide to employ her." She turned her gaze back to Merriam. "Now leave us."

I'm sorry, Ria. I'll clue you in later.

Merriam dipped her head to the queen before backing out of the room. Eskar shut the door in her face with a thinly veiled sneer.

Merriam stood for a moment, debating whether or not to go find Jasper and fill him in. Calysta's information about the strange murders and disappearances surfaced from the back of her mind, and she chewed on her lip, trying to figure the odds of whether this could be connected.

"Looks like the puppy got left all alone."

Irritation flitted through Merriam at the cool voice, and she clenched her teeth. She turned to glare at the half-Fae male standing across the hall. He stood just taller than Mollian, with thick, brown hair falling in waves that framed his face, barely brushing his shoulders. His dark eyes regarded her with unbridled contempt, and his strong jaw ticked underneath the short scruff of his beard. His hands were tucked casually into his pockets, a short sword strapped to his side. His lithe body was held with perfect posture despite the arrogant tilt to his head, not a wrinkle or speck of lint on his deep green dress jacket. His silver lieutenant stripes cut across his biceps, and a Ranger badge flashed on his chest.

"Are you upset you weren't included, Rovin?" Her voice dripped with pique.

"Of course not. I'll get a full brief as soon as Eskar and Ollivan are done talking with Their Majesties," Rovin scoffed.

"How great for you." She started to head toward the ballroom, much too tired to deal with his bullshit tonight, and truthfully, she was still tipsy.

"You could've been part of that, too, you know. But you quit." Rovin folded his arms across his chest. The tips of aspen leaves peaked from the cuffs of his sleeves, tattoos that extended up his forearm, identifying him as a Ranger.

"How drunk are you, Rovin?" Merriam tilted her head to the side and took a step forward. "How many of *your* jobs have I been hired to complete?"

"Rangers have a code of conduct. We do things by the law." Rovin bristled, eyes narrowing dangerously.

"Mercs have a code of conduct, too. We get things done." She smiled, venomously sweet.

Rovin dropped his arms, fire lighting in his deep brown eyes. "You and your merry little band better watch yourselves."

"Or what, Lieutenant?" she said the word as though it were a slur. "What are you and your code of conduct going to do?" Her amber eyes flashed with a fire matching his, the alcohol in her blood cutting off all of her inhibitions. She took another step closer to him, feet shifting into a fighting stance.

"Mer! There you are!" Aleah called, skipping down the hall. She'd grabbed Merriam's hand before she felt the tension crackling between the merc and the Ranger. "Oh." She brought a hand to her chest, hazel eyes shining from too much wine. Leaning against Merriam, she spoke in a stage whisper, "Is this who your plans have been with?"

Merriam immediately stiffened, and Rovin's tense posture broke as a flicker of curiosity ran through his eyes. "Aleah, you're drunk." She stepped away from Rovin, tugging the smaller girl by her freckled arm down the hall. Merriam could feel Rovin's stare burning into her back until she turned the corner.

"I guess he wasn't the plans, then," Aleah hiccuped with a giggle. "Probably good I came along when I did, because you looked like you were about to take his sword and impale him with it."

Merriam sighed, the irritation itching under her skin from Rovin's confrontation dissipating in the bubbly presence of the redhead. "I would have done it, too, if it weren't for your horribly timed interruption." She looped Aleah's arm through hers.

"I suppose it would have made for an interesting night," Aleah considered before looking up at Merriam. "Who was he? I think I recognized him."

"An asshole whom I've yet to put in his place," Merriam replied with a shake of her head. "Where are the guys?"

"Leonidas is in the aviary, giving pointers." Aleah rolled her eyes. "Cam and Jasper have finally had their fill of treats and drink and gossip and are ready to head home for the night."

"What brought Leo to the aviary this time?" Merriam laughed. The falconer had a proclivity to birds that she would almost swear was magical despite his being human.

"A new brood of young owls." Aleah sighed. "They're cute, but pretty useless right now."

"A parliament," Merriam corrected automatically, catching sight of sleek black wings ahead.

"A who?" Aleah blinked in confusion.

"You should go get him before he ends up sleeping here," Jasper was saying to Campbell as they walked up. "Oh good, you found her." Jasper reached to take Aleah's arm from Merriam.

"Hey, I'm not a child!" Aleah protested, but tucked herself contentedly into Jasper's side.

"No, you're a stray cat, always running off." Jasper rested a dark arm over her shoulders.

"Yeah, and cats always find their way home." She folded her arms across her chest.

"Do you need help collecting Leo?" Merriam offered. "The aviary isn't that far out of my way."

Campbell's indigo eyes turned to Merriam with a knowing glimmer. "You just want to see him all soft over the birds, but I'll accept the company, anyway."

"Guilty." Merriam smiled. She gave a parting hug to Aleah and Jasper, whispering to him, "Something is happening. I'll let you know when I know more."

He nodded. "We'll wait outside for you, Cam."

Merriam and Campbell left the ballroom, heading down to the ground level and exiting through a side door to cross a courtyard, following the muffled cacophony of calls to the building that housed various birds for messages and hunting. They went through the outer doors and were stopped by a castle guard at the inner set. "No entry to guests, sorry. Party is back in the castle."

Merriam shook her head. He must be new. "I'm not a guest; I live here," she said, forcing the irritation from her voice. "My friend is inside, and—"

"Well, which is it, missy? Do you live here, or is your friend inside?" the guard interrupted, unamused and annoyed.

Merriam flexed her fingers, eyes turning to the ceiling. "Legends," she muttered.

"Look, it's both," Campbell tried to explain, stepping up to the guard.

"No, *you* look." The guard also moved forward, roughly pushing Campbell back by the base of his antlers.

Just as the guard's hand made contact with Campbell, the inner door swung open, and a tall, broad frame filled the doorway. Before Campbell's head even finished snapping back from the shove, the guard was slammed heavily into the wall, the breath leaving his lungs in an audible *whoosh* and his skull cracking against the stone.

"Lay your fucking hands on him again and you'll be having to ask your sister for help to jerk off," Leonidas snarled, his hands fisted in the guard's uniform.

The guard's eyes were wide with fear as he lifted a shaky hand to the back of his head, checking for blood. "I didn't—"

"I didn't ask." Leonidas released him, but kept him pinned with a deathly blue glare for a moment longer before turning from him, grabbing Campbell's hand and walking outside.

"I was hoping for cute-raptor Leo, but I guess possessive Leo is an okay substitute," Merriam joked.

Leonidas gave a short laugh, the tension leaving his shoulders as he raised Campbell's hand to his lips. "I may have had a few drinks." He shrugged apologetically.

Campbell shook his head, giving Leonidas a light shove in the chest. "You can't just throw into people like that, Leo. We'll never get invited back."

Leonidas opened his mouth, but Campbell cut him off. "I'm fine. Truly. It looked more aggressive than it was." He waved the encounter off, wrapping his arms loosely around the blonde's waist and looking up to meet his eyes. "You don't need to be my savior, you know. I'm a perfectly capable fighter."

A smile tugged at Leonidas's lips, and he pressed a swift kiss to Campbell's forehead. "I guess I should stop stealing all of the fun for myself."

"Thank you. Now let's go meet the others. We're all waiting for you."

"Sorry I got caught up, it's just these barn owls, only fledglings—"

"I know, I know." Campbell laughed. "I can't wait to hear all about them."

"Goodnight, Mer," Leonidas called as they parted ways, slipping his hand into Campbell's.

Mollian was still gone when Merriam reached their rooms, still in the meeting with the Rangers. She tried not to worry herself with the unknown as she slipped out of her gown and prepared for bed, exhausted after a night that had been a strange mixture of fantastical and frustrating.

Chapter 9

A thief and a murderer

MERRIAM WOKE TO THE sound of her door opening and soft footsteps crossing the floor. She didn't need to open her eyes to know it was Mollian. His presence was a balm to her soul, the same way hers was to him. They were twined together, each day spent in the other's presence adding another tether between them. *Mehhen* were rare, and the bond was impossible to replicate. Their souls were simultaneously mirrored and the same, feeding off of each other while they grew together and becoming stronger for it.

She felt the covers being pulled back and a warm body slip into bed beside her. Instinctively, she rolled over, pressing her forehead to his bicep and wrapping her arms around one of his.

His comforting spruce and plum scent wrapped around her like a warm blanket, settling in her soul with a familiar rightness that she could never even begin to explain to someone else.

Are you awake? His voice rolled softly through her.

She considered letting herself slip back into sleep, but curiosity pricked at the back of her mind. She slowly forced her eyes open, pulling away to look up at him. With full consciousness came an uncomfortable pressure in her head. Her tongue felt thick and heavy, and she could taste the sickly sweet remnants of wine at the back of her throat.

Merriam pressed her face back to Mollian's arm with a groan. "Water?" she croaked the question.

Mollian sat up, handing her the glass on her nightstand. She pushed up onto an elbow and drank deeply, still feeling a bit tipsy. When she'd finished, she fell back onto her pillow, Mollian stretching out beside her with one arm folded under his head.

Merriam rolled to her side, curling her knees up to her chest and studying the angles of his face. "Should I be worried?"

Mollian dropped his eyes from the open window across the room to meet her gaze, a smile tugging at the corner of his mouth. "You should always be worried. You're essentially a thief and a murderer by trade and, on top of that, the most important thing alive to the prince."

She rolled her eyes, nudging a knee into his hip. "As you once told me, not *the* prince, just *a* prince, so I think I'll be okay on that account," she teased.

"I wasn't talking about me." Mollian gave her a pointed look.

A hot blush rushed to her cheeks, and she fought the urge to drop her gaze. "I told you, there's nothing happening," she insisted. "He's the crown prince. He flirts with everybody."

Mollian raised an eyebrow. "Are we talking about the same Oren?"

Clicking her tongue against her teeth, Merriam shook her head. "We shouldn't be talking about him at all. If you're going to ask about silly infatuations instead of telling me what happened tonight, I'm going to go back to sleep."

"So you admit you like him?" Mollian grinned.

Merriam gave him a withering look and closed her eyes, nestling deeper into the pillow.

"Okay, okay. It's dropped."

Merriam peeked one eye open at him, waiting.

"There's something happening in Jekeida that we haven't seen before. Bad stuff."

Her other eye popped open, interest and excitement flashing through amber.

Mollian was thoroughly unamused. "I don't know when you started throwing yourself into danger like it was a field of flowers and kittens, but I don't think that I'm a fan."

Merriam laughed. "Meeting up with a strange boy from another dimension in the woods as a child wasn't your first indication that I have a low sense of self-preservation?"

"Point taken," Mollian conceded. "But this is serious, Ria. Not just a group of men trying to get paid. These murders are almost personal in their level of brutality. They're completely depraved."

Merriam wet her lips. "Calysta heard some things," she admitted.

Mollian gave her a questioning look.

"She didn't know much, just stuff she heard from villagers in her travels. Jasper told us to stay alert, just in case." She shrugged a shoulder. "It sounded like the sort of thing that might eventually become our problem."

Mollian sighed. "My mother wants to take care of it quietly. She wants the Rangers to look into it."

Merriam's mouth pulled into an instinctive frown.

"There are indicators here ... if things are happening the way my mother suspects, it can't become public knowledge," he said seriously.

Merriam let out a breath of frustration, giving Mollian a wilting look. "I know that, *Prince*. But they already know something is going on, plus everyone saw you guys go into the war room in the middle of a party."

"Yes, but the details—"

"Are privileged information of the crown, I know." She rolled onto her back. "Like I said, Jasper already has us looking into Calysta's intel. So, regardless, we'll be ready when you need us." She tried to fight back the irritation crawling over her skin. It wasn't Mollian she was upset with.

"Ria." Mollian turned to face her.

"Just so you know, I'm not going to be allowed to share any of the information we find with you, either." She folded her arms over her chest, flicking her eyes to meet his. "You're going to have to pay for it."

"I would never ask you to do otherwise." Mollian's brows pulled together.

"Exactly." Merriam stared pointedly at the ceiling. "Because there are boundaries between my life with you and my life with them. Boundaries that were established years ago."

Mollian scraped a pointed canine across his lip, contemplating his next words. "I wouldn't blame you if you did tell them everything I know, though. They've been better to you than my parents or anyone in the Guard ever has."

Merriam finally relented, facing him again. "But I could never do anything to hurt *you*, Molli."

Mischief sparked in his cracked eyes. "Just me?"

"The Rangers can all go to Hel," she replied sweetly.

Mollian laughed, propping up his elbow and resting his head on his hand. "Luckily for you, they're probably headed there." His gaze darkened, remembering the severity of what they were heading into.

"What is it, Molli? What are we hunting?" Merriam whispered, eyes wide.

"We don't know for sure," Mollian replied, pushing a curl off of his forehead. "But our suspicions are that it's not from Nethyl. The abductions add a completely different layer that further complicates the investigation."

"Calysta mentioned thunder," Merriam added, reaching out to pull the lock of hair back down over his brow, communicating in her own way that her frustration with him had passed. "Do we think it's some sort of nymph or other magic?"

Mollian frowned. "That's not something that the Rangers reported as a common occurrence. They only mentioned it off-hand. It could be just an elemental sprite going off or something similar."

Merriam pressed her lips together, considering. "That's possible, and if it's what the Rangers want to assume, that's fine."

"But you're still going to keep it in mind," Mollian guessed with a smirk.

Merriam tucked her hands daintily under her cheek. "That's privileged information, Your Highness."

"I don't know how much Calysta heard, but these bodies were completely ripped apart. A couple look like they may have been exsanguinated. They're all covered in strange bite marks that nobody can identify. Pieces of all of them are completely missing. And the smell ..."

"Like sulfur?"

"That's probably a much better way of describing it than Ollivan did," Mollian said with amusement.

Merriam chewed on her lip, digging through the exhaustion and light traces of alcohol still muddling her mind. "Could be a demon then."

Mollian dropped onto his back, hand tucked underneath his head. "Yep."

"What about that guy who hired the traffickers? Could this be linked to it?"

"Yes, but it's tricky."

"Meaning it involves information the public doesn't have access to." She shook her head.

Mollian dragged a hand over his face. "There are still so many unknowns. Nymphs have been trafficked for years for countless different purposes, but mostly for slavery. Since you guys took out the last ring, there haven't been any more reports of nymphs being taken. For now, the priority is on the disappearances of the fae and the humans. And where the thing that's hunting them broke through. Nothing should be able to just cross into our dimension at random, only through the Gate."

"Is it possible someone is creating a rift, like when we Travel?" Merriam's brow furrowed in thought. "That trafficker told us a man was using blood magic, and now there's half-chewed-up bodies smelling of sulfur. Something nefarious has come through somewhere."

Mollian sighed. "It's something we're looking into. Gressia would know if the Gate had been opened. If anything, with power pushed through unbidden, she'd have felt the tremor. My mother's been in contact with her, letting her know to increase the warding around Entumbra. It's also possible a small rift has opened on its own somewhere in the mountains as well, which happens every now and then. Whatever is doing this could have slipped through."

"What if someone purposefully pulled it onto Nethyl, though?" Merriam whispered.

He turned his head to look at her. "Then we might all be fucked."

She shuddered, reaching out to grab Mollian's hand. "I want to be prepared for the worst. I want to know everything."

Mollian nodded. "Most of the information about things from other dimensions won't be here. We'll have to go to Entumbra."

"We?"

"We."

"Let's go on an adventure, then." She smiled, a thrill rushing up her spine despite herself.

"We'll have to wait a week or so. Let the Rangers start doing their thing before we go running off in defiance of the queen."

"But then an adventure?"

"Then an adventure," Mollian promised, her excitement bleeding into him as well. The feeling that he'd been cooped up in Umbra too long was suddenly overwhelming.

Merriam settled back into the pillows, turning towards Mollian and resting her forehead against his shoulder. *Stay with me tonight?*

Mollian gave her hand a squeeze. *Always.*

Despite the nature of the conversation, it didn't take long before her breathing evened out and she slipped back into sleep.

Over the next week, Merriam spent most of her time at the castle. Jasper and Aleah were off gathering information from neighboring towns, and she was perusing the royal library for anything that might be of help. When she didn't have her nose stuck in a book, she was using the castle's training grounds to keep her skills sharp. Twice a day she ran drills alone, practicing not just with her axes, but also with knives and swords and a bow. She went on runs through the forest glen just outside of the courtyard, leaping into trees and moving through the canopy at different intervals.

She had learned the Royal Guard's training schedule over the years, but it was much more chaotic with the Rangers now preparing to leave on scouting missions. Others in the Guard were also doing extra training to bolster defenses around Umbra. As their routine shifted, Merriam did her best to work around it. She'd tried training with them before, and it had been a miserable experience, one that left her with nothing but feelings of disdain for the Guard, especially the elite unit of Rangers.

Avoiding them in the ring had completely upended her schedule, and she often found herself training in the middle of the night or during the heat of the day, visiting the library whenever another group showed up.

She woke before dawn one morning, stretching languidly before dropping her legs over the side of the bed and sitting up. She ran her hands over her eyes with a yawn, standing up to move to the bathroom and splash some water on her face before brushing her hair out and braiding it down her back.

She pulled on leggings and a loose shirt, still half asleep, before lacing up her boots and slipping into the hall. A breeze, still cool with night, filtered through the open windows of the castle, awakening her senses.

When she reached the training room, she pushed open the door and peeked inside. The room was dark and quiet; the moons shining dimly through the windows. She flipped a switch against the wall and rows of soft lights flickered on in the ceiling. While most technological advancements on Earth weren't possible on Nethyl, there was crude electricity fueled by wind and water.

She pulled two targets into the fighting ring on one side of the room, dropped two training axes into her belt, and grabbed a long staff before stepping into the ring. She shook out her arms, taking a few deep, measured breaths as she let herself slip into the steady, calculated calm of a fight.

After several warm-up exercises, Merriam was wide awake and ready to go. Her feet shifted into a fighting stance, light and balanced, before lashing out at the first target with the staff. She struck, dancing back in avoidance of a counterattack, and dipped forward again. She whirled and twirled around the two targets until sweat dripped down her back and her breathing came in harsh pants.

Merriam tossed the staff to the side, pulling out the axes and letting the handles slide through her hands until her fists gripped right underneath the dulled wooden blades.

Taking a deep breath, she launched herself at a target, ducking low and letting her hold fall to the center of the handles before springing up and swinging them with shocking momentum. One cracked into the neck of the target, the other slid across the torso in a way that would disembowel an enemy.

The door clicked shut, and she glanced over her shoulder, annoyance bubbling up that the Guard couldn't get their schedule under control.

But instead of the green rough-spun of a guard's training shirt, her eyes landed on a head of snow-white hair currently being pulled into a bun by light brown hands.

"That was an impressive move," Oren complimented, tying off his hair and walking to the wall to select a weapon.

"Thanks, it's worked well for me," Merriam answered cheekily, lifting an arm to wipe the sweat from her forehead.

"I'm going to pretend like you didn't just insinuate that you've spilled someone's guts and instead ask if I can join you." Oren twirled a sword in his hands.

Merriam tilted her head with amusement. "The prince is asking me permission to use his facilities? I'm honored."

Oren stepped up to her, close enough that she had to tilt her head to meet his gaze. "I hope you'll still feel honored when I lay you out on your ass."

The light of challenge blazed in Merriam's amber eyes. "Oh, I'm sure you'll try, Majesty." She whipped around, the end of her braid swiping across Oren's chest, and walked to the center of the ring, setting her feet and raising her axes.

Oren took a couple steps toward her before she exploded into action, leaping forward and raising an axe up to swipe at him. As he lifted his sword to block it, she swung her other axe from the side. He spun easily out of the way, pulling his sword back to launch his own attack on her.

They danced around each other in combat, the sharp cracks of wood against wood filling the air. Oren raised his arms for a swing, and Merriam ducked toward him, intending to slip inside his reach and throw him off balance.

As soon as she lunged, he dropped his arm, stepping into her advance. The movement confused her, but she didn't have time to halt her momentum. Before she realized what was happening, one axe was knocked from her hand and she was flipping into the air. She landed flat on her back, second axe skittering from her fingers as the impact forced the breath from her lungs.

Merriam panted heavily, the point of Oren's sword poised at her throat. "How did you do that?"

Oren dropped the weapon to his side and offered her a hand. "Simple physics." His dimple appeared with his smirk.

She let him pull her up. "Teach me?"

"It would be my pleasure, Lady." He stepped back and tossed her an axe.

She caught it, watching intently.

"A big part of it is momentum and knowing where your opponent is going to put their weight." He dropped into a fighting stance. "Here, I'm centered, but if I were to try to take a swing at you"-he leaned and extended his sword arm-"my weight moves onto my front foot. Then all you have to do is step into me, and use that momentum against me." He gestured for her to come forward, showing her how to position her body and knock the hilt of her axe into his hand to grab his sword. "Now, speed it up."

She did, and this time he ended up prone.

They practiced a few more times, adding in some extra fighting moves and simple counters.

"Water break," Oren panted after a few rounds, moving to fill two cups from a tap set in the wall. He brought them over to a table, turning to sit on it and patting the wood next to him. "You're not half bad, Mer."

"Not half bad?" Merriam brushed a few stray strands of hair from her face. "I definitely had the upper hand on more than a few occasions." She took the cup he offered before hopping up to sit by him.

"You can add 'humble' to the list of all of your best qualities." He laughed.

"I didn't know we were keeping a list, but I'd love to hear what's on it." Merriam smiled at him over the rim of her cup.

Oren finished his water, setting the cup aside and reaching to curl a lock of her hair around his finger. "Maybe one day I'll tell you. If you're lucky." He gave a gentle tug before releasing the strands.

"Who'd have thought the prince had such a rebellious streak?"

"How do I have a rebellious streak?" Oren asked with a laugh.

Merriam held her hand up, listing things off on her fingers. "Aiding and abetting the kidnapping of at least one human from another world, support and encouragement of a mercenary lifestyle, entering into a friends-with-benefits relationship, withholding information. Need I continue?"

"I'm not sure all of that counts as rebellious, or is even decidedly true."

"Oh? Enlighten me, Majesty." Merriam arched a brow.

"Your argument about the friends-with-benefits is invalid."

She laughed. "You're dumb."

His shoulder brushed hers, intensity replacing the amusement in his gaze. "I've always liked you, Mer, but I was never going to pressure you for more than you were ready to give."

Merriam's breath caught in her throat. "I'm sweaty," she whispered, gaze straying from those bright green eyes down his dark skin to his full lips. She was suddenly very aware of how close they were sitting.

"Likewise," Oren whispered back, hand still on her face. His eyes studied hers for a moment, gauging her reaction to his proximity.

"O, we should—"

He tilted his head down and slid his lips over hers.

Though he'd taken the risk of cutting her off, he was holding back, keeping the kiss soft for fear that she might run off without the courage of alcohol in her veins. But she raised a hand to the back of his head and pulled him further against her, heat tugging low in her abdomen.

"Merri," he whispered against her lips, the name full of restrained urgency and desire.

A clatter of something out in the hall had her jumping away from him and almost out of her skin.

"I'll find you later," he whispered, standing to remove his gear.

The door swung open, and a few guards came in, chattering amongst themselves. Oren gave her a quick wink before turning towards the door. The guards scrambled into a stiff salute, which he acknowledged with a nod as he left the room.

Merriam slid down from the table, turning away from the guards and putting all of her training weapons back in their place. She was buzzing with heat, her mind reeling with thoughts. She stopped to drink another cup of water before walking into the courtyard to go for a run. The sun was not yet over the mountains, but pink stained the few clouds in the lightening sky as she took off, losing herself in the monotonous movements and pushing all thoughts of Oren forcefully out of her mind.

When she returned, the training room was bustling with motion, so she rounded the courtyard to take a less populated route. She turned a blind corner and ran straight into a warm, muscled torso, her forehead knocking into a chin. She bounced back and brought her hand to her head, lifting her eyes to apologize before seeing who stood in front of her, rubbing his scruffy jaw and looking royally pissed.

"You'd better hurry inside before the sun finishes cresting the mountains. I heard trolls and sunlight don't mix." Merriam let a small smile play across her lips, taking a step away from the wall to walk past the two Rangers.

"Where are you off to in such a hurry?" Rovin moved out of her way, giving her a look of mild abhorrence.

Merriam rolled her eyes. "To fuck your sister."

The mohawked Ranger behind Rovin let out a bark of laughter.

"Shut up, Kodi." Rovin shot him a glare before turning his deep brown eyes back to Merriam. "Someone said you and the prince were using the training room this morning." He cocked his head to the side.

"What's your point?"

"Just interesting is all."

Merriam clenched her teeth, wanting to continue past, but knowing he wouldn't leave her alone until he'd said his piece.

"Interesting, isn't it, Kodi?" he continued, eyes locked on Merriam's. "That the little human has decided it's not enough to just be one prince's pet, but now she needs to be the whore of the other. Tell me, Merriam, what is it you hope to gain?"

Anger flashed in her amber eyes, and she struggled to rein her emotions in before she did something stupid.

She started to step away, but Rovin continued, "Who's next on your list of males you want in your back pocket, hmm? Maybe Captain Ferrick? Convince him to let you join us, after all?"

Merriam's lip lifted in a silent snarl as she turned and spit right in Rovin's face before pulling her arm back and punching him square across the jaw. Her knuckles rang, and she shook out her hand, taking a step back.

Rovin's hand slammed into her throat, pinning her to the wall of the castle. He watched her, eyes full of outrage and disgust, as he wiped his sleeve across his cheek. "Do that again, and I will kill you. I don't care whose bed you're sleeping in, *pet*."

Merriam clawed at his hand, gasping for air as he squeezed.

"Rov," Kodi warned, bi-colored eyes watching Merriam's face with mild concern.

Rovin released her, and Merriam sagged against the wall, coughing. "You don't have the fucking balls," she rasped, bringing her hand to her throat.

He scoffed at her, tossing his hair from his face and walking away.

When the Rangers had gone, she slowly slid to the ground, propping her elbows on her knees and resting her face in her hands. She knew the guards in the training room hadn't seen anything compromising, so it had been a baseless accusation on Rovin's part.

But the fact that the connection was made at all sent her stomach turning. She had worked so hard to build autonomy. To build a reputation. She had been right in assuming a relationship with Oren would send all of that down the drain.

It wasn't worth it.

It *couldn't* be worth it.

Taking a deep breath that burned going down her sore throat, she stood, resolving that she would not let whatever was happening with Oren develop further, and promising herself that she would make Rovin eat every single horrible thing he had ever said or done to her.

Shaking off the bitterness of the encounter, she continued back into the castle.

Mollian gave her a concerned look as she entered their common room. He was lacing his boots up, and she sat across from him unceremoniously to rip hers off.

"What's up with you?" he asked, watching her with his fingers around a half-looped knot.

Merriam tossed her boots aside and stood, shaking her head. She opened her mouth three separate times, trying to figure out what to say before finally flinging her arms out and spewing, "Your fucking brother kissed me, that's what." Before turning and stomping into her room.

A smile pulled at Mollian's lips as he stood up to follow her. She ignored him, moving into the bathroom and running the tap. He leaned in the doorway, still grinning.

"Can I help you?" She turned around to face him.

"I'm just waiting for more of the story."

"And I'm going to take a bath."

"Not the story I care about," Mollian said dismissively, and she stripped her shirt off and threw it at his face. He batted it away with a laugh, and she turned around to remove her bra and slide off her pants.

Sinking into the water with a sigh, she pulled her knees up to chest and rested her chin on them, waiting for Mollian to sit on the edge of the tub. "He knocked me on my ass, and then taught me how he did it," she eventually said.

"Very romantic."

Merriam splashed water at him. "I wish he didn't make me feel so seen," she murmured, glancing away.

"Since when is that a bad thing?" Mollian asked.

"I don't want to feel this way about him, Molli. Liking Oren is ... complicated and messy and only going to get us both in trouble," she said with resignation.

Mollian looked at her, eyes full of bottomless compassion and empathy. "You know I always have your back. Either way."

"I know." Merriam looked up at him with a small smile. "Now get out of here and let me bathe in peace."

Mollian held his hand out to her, and she pressed her palm to his before he stood and walked out, leaving her alone to wash away the stress of the barely started day.

Chapter 10

Pet

Six years before ...

MERRIAM TIED OFF THE end of her braid and shook out her arms, triceps aching from the effort of dealing with the lengths of her hair.

"You're sure you want to do this?" Mollian asked.

"Yes. I have to. For myself."

Mollian just nodded, leading her out into the courtyard. "Let's go, then."

"Prince Mollian, a pleasure to have you join us today." A male with close-cut brown hair who seemed to take up twice as much space as Mollian greeted the prince with a small bow. His jawline was obscured by a neatly trimmed beard, but if it was anything like the rest of him, it was probably strong, harsh lines.

"Thank you, Captain Ferrick. I'm pleased to have the time today," Mollian replied, inclining his head slightly.

"What do you think you're doing here?" The captain looked Merriam up and down disdainfully.

"She's with me." Mollian stepped in front of her slightly.

"She's human," Ferrick stated.

"Yes." Mollian met his gaze evenly.

Ferrick eventually sighed. "You're responsible for her, Prince."

Mollian nodded, turning back to Merriam, whose freckled face was flushed. Anger and embarrassment radiated from her, almost palpable. She was trying her best to bury the emotions beneath a layer of confidence, but she wasn't used to dealing with fae yet, and her feelings were plain in her face and her eyes.

Just breathe through it. You're doing great. Mollian Cast to her with as much confidence and comfort as he could lace into the words. She nodded grimly, and the two went to stand at the end of the line.

"We'll be starting with a run today," Ferrick called, strong voice carrying. "Three klicks to the well outside of town. Let's go." He turned and took off into the trees.

Mollian tried to catch Merriam's eye, but she'd already taken off with the guards.

As they ran through the grove in the courtyard, Mollian matched his stride to Merriam, who stayed toward the tail end of the group. They made it out the back gate, and the guards started spreading out. Merriam held her pace, breathing heavily but smoothly.

When they reached the well, Merriam walked to the far side, placing her hands on her head to try to settle her breathing. Mollian drew some water and offered her a sip. She smiled gratefully. *See? I can do this,* she Cast, and he smiled encouragingly.

"Push-ups, sit-ups, and squat-thrusts. Do fifty of each and then head back to the courtyard. Anyone who doesn't make it back before the door to the interior training room closes won't be training today." Ferrick turned and ran back.

"Of course he's not going to be doing them." Mollian rolled his eyes, dropping down to the ground.

Merriam dropped, too, alternating between the exercises.

Mollian finished before Merriam, who was clearly starting to lag.

"Go, I'm fine."

"I'm not going to leave you out here," Mollian insisted.

"Go, Molli," she hissed, jumping up from a squat thrust and planting her hands on her hips, breathing heavily.

Mollian pressed his lips together, swiping at the curls stuck to his sweaty forehead. Finally, he nodded before turning and beginning the run back.

When he made it to the training room, he sat in a crouch against the back wall, eyes on the door, waiting for Merriam to run through. He'd never tested the distance of the Bond between them, had never had a chance or a reason to. He and Merriam had hardly been out of each other's sight except to sleep for the past three months. But he reached out with his mind now, searching for the familiar brush of her consciousness against his.

After a moment, he felt her. While he couldn't tell her exact location, he could tell that she was close. Close, and irritated, because his reach was pushed peevishly back to him, as though she'd swatted him away. A smile pulled at the corners of his lips. He'd known she would be fine, but he was glad for the evidence that her spirit wasn't broken. The Guard would not take it easy on her, and he didn't want them to dampen the fire in her that had only grown the longer she'd been in Umbra.

Mollian stood, heading across the room to grab a training weapon.

Out in the courtyard, Merriam ran, feeling a trickle of sweat slide down her back as her breaths ripped from her lungs. She was close. She could see the edge of the trees, and she pushed herself harder.

Her lungs burned, and her legs felt like jelly, but a few strides further, she saw the outline of the door.

Closed.

Frustration bubbled through her, erupting from that place she'd shoved it into earlier that morning. She sprinted full tilt to the door, sliding to a stop just a few feet in front of it. She grit her teeth, wanting to scream, but instead plunged her fingers into her hair, cradling her head as she leaned over and caught her breath. Standing up and walking into the trees, she picked up a stone and tossed it with as much force as she could muster.

It ricocheted off a pine, skittering to a stop a few feet to the side.

She walked up and kicked it, sending it sailing further into the trees.

"Stupid fucking rock," she called after it, spinning around and slamming the side of her fist against a pine. Shaking her hand out with a hiss, she fell back against the tree with a huff. "Well, it looks like there won't be any combat training today," she mumbled.

Dappled sunlight warmed Merriam's face as she looked up through the canopy, still catching her breath. She'd known this was going to be difficult, hadn't expected it to be handed to her. So she swallowed back her frustration, steeling herself for the long haul, and turned around.

Maybe she couldn't learn combat today, but she could still grow her stamina. Her strength. Her skills. She reached up, grasping a branch of the pine, and clumsily pulled herself into the tree, climbing until the boughs sagged under her weight, then jumping back down, moving to another tree, and repeating.

Her hands were raw and her arms rubber by the time the door to the training room opened, Mollian nearly tripping over himself in his rush to get out.

His eyes found her, just inside the tree line, and relief and worry warred across his face, his brows pulling together.

Merriam shook her head, wiping sweat from her brow with the hem of her shirt. *They can't break me.*

Mollian's mouth quirked up in half a smile as he walked up to her, holding up his palm. "You didn't miss much, anyway." He told her as she pressed hers against it.

She leaned her shoulder against the rough trunk of a pine. "I'll make it next time," she promised.

"I know you will." Mollian grinned, leading her back around the side of the castle. "Let's go see what's for supper."

They entered through the kitchens, grabbing a platter of food to bring up to their rooms and eat.

Merriam lay sprawled on her stomach on the floor of their common room, nibbling on some chicken and reading. Mollian sat with his back against the couch next to her, legs stretched out in front of him. "Ria," he started, running a hand through his loose white curls.

She looked up, swinging her feet contentedly in the air behind her.

"I'll need to get back to my old routine soon. Fully, I mean. My mother is getting frustrated, and Oren's study in Entumbra is coming soon." He picked at a cuticle. "It's not that I don't want you hanging with me all the time, because I do. It's just she thinks I'm distracted from my duties or whatever, and—"

"Molli," Merriam interrupted with a smile, "it's fine. I'm a big girl, I can entertain myself. Besides, isn't that the whole point of my training with the Guard in the first place? I need something to do. And I want to be useful."

"I talked to Captain Ferrick after training today. He's going to allow you to keep training with them," Mollian offered. "But if you don't like it—"

"I'm going to love it, and you know it. Tell me you don't think I'd have marketable skills as a Ranger." Determination sparked in her amber eyes.

"I know you'd be great at it. I just don't want you to feel like you have to fight to fit in here. I know you belong here, job or not, and no one else will ever be able to convince me otherwise."

"It's not you I need to convince, Molli." Merriam leveled a gaze at him. "And before you say it doesn't matter what everyone else thinks, it matters to me that I have my own place in Sekha outside of being your friend. I love you, but I need purpose or I'll go crazy."

"As long as you're happy, I'm happy. Though I'm confused why you'd want to spend so much time with some of those assholes." Mollian shrugged.

"Scared they'll steal me away forever?" Merriam teased.

Mollian raised an eyebrow, feigning cockiness. "Are you forgetting you Bonded yourself to me? You've sealed your fate, human."

I guess I forgot all the warnings in fairy tales about selling my soul to a fae prince.

Tsk Tsk, Ria. Should have listened better.

She went to sleep that night feeling a contentment so deep in her bones she didn't think anything could shatter it.

Until, of course, she showed up to train with the Guard alone the next morning.

"Fhajdo'k fyht."

Merriam tensed at the words spat in her direction, clearly an insult. She wracked her brain. The first word, she knew, but the second was stuck just outside of her recall. She turned around to see a tall male, only a couple of years older than her at most, standing a few paces away. Muscles flexed underneath the newly inked aspen branch tattoos trailing up his forearms as he twisted a training sword in his fingers before sliding it through his belt. His chestnut hair was left in loose waves, brushing just above his shoulders, and his eyes were a deep, warm brown, but they glinted hard as flint as they took her in.

"Where's your master today?" he asked with a smirk, the tip of one pointed canine peeking out from under his lip.

Her brows knitted in confusion for a moment before that last word clicked into place. *Prince's pet*. Her eyes narrowed into a glare, and she was about to retort when a familiar, lithe female walked between them.

"Don't taunt the poor girl, Rovin, you might scare her off," Eskar said as she brushed past Merriam without a glance in her direction.

Rovin chuckled. "Probably for the best. This is no place for a lost puppy."

"Mmm, I suppose not." Eskar's gaze flicked to Merriam only briefly before she collected her weapons and walked away.

Merriam tried to breathe through the irritation that clawed its way through her veins, making her skin itch. She grabbed a sword from the wall, shooting Rovin one last glare before walking away.

After the initial warm-ups, the group was split between the normal Guard and the Rangers. Even though she'd clearly seen his tattoos, annoyance still churned through Merriam when she saw Rovin was with the latter group, learning the skills she so badly wanted to hone. Almost as if he felt her eyes on him, he turned to look at her, a venomous smirk stretching his lips. She turned away, trying to pay attention to the commander in front of her group who alternated between issuing commands for different fighting stances and sword strokes.

At the end of training, Merriam leaned against the outer wall of the castle, gulping water from a cup as sweat trickled down the side of her face. Rovin walked by her, knocking the cup from her hands as he passed without even looking at her.

"What is your problem?!" She pushed from the wall, anger flashing in her eyes.

Rovin ignored her, continuing inside.

Merriam lunged forward, shoving her hands against his back. "I'm talking to you, asshole."

Much to Merriam's satisfaction, Rovin stumbled a bit at the unexpected force before whipping around. His brown eyes were molten as he looked her over. "I'd keep my hands to myself if I were you, pet."

Merriam scoffed, her eyes slipping over the clipped tip of one ear that had become visible with his movement. A cruel smile pulled at her lips, and she blinked innocently, tilting her head to the side. "Or what, *halfling?*"

Rovin's eyes flashed angrily at the slur as he took a step toward her, leaning in until he was inches from her face. "Let me tell you how the hierarchy works around here. *You* are nothing. Nobody. You aren't one of us, and not a single person in this ring would come to your rescue if you picked a fight. So try me, human. Because I've *earned* the right to be here." His voice was low and dangerous, and the smell of him surrounded her. Sweat, but just underneath that was the musk of fallen leaves, the crisp bite of apple, and—barely perceptible—the sweet silk of caramel.

The invitation of his scent was chased away by her fury long before it ever had a chance to really register with her. Any sting she felt from his words was consumed by the anger flooding her veins, buzzing in her head until she saw red. "I don't need to be one of you. I'm going to be better."

Chapter 11

A reminder

Merriam spent the rest of the morning in the library until her head throbbed from the endless research. She grabbed a fiction book from a shelf–something light and graphically romantic–and trudged back to her rooms, where she sprawled across the couch and stayed until Mollian came back in from his day's meetings.

"Productive day, I see?" Mollian plucked the book from her hands and read a few lines before handing it back.

"Very, thank you." Merriam swung her legs over the side of the couch to sit up. "Do you have plans for supper?"

"Unfortunately, yes." Mollian frowned. "And I'm bound to be out until very late. Or early, depending on how you look at it." He wiped a hand over his face before pushing his curls back.

"Another dignitary to entertain?" Merriam asked sympathetically.

"Yes, his home is on the opposite side of Umbra, and he's notorious for his late nights and extensive wine collection. Which would be fine, except all he wants to talk about is roads. Roads into the city. Roads out of the city. How to better engineer the roads *inside of* the city."

"Sounds like a great time." Merriam laughed. "Don't have too much fun."

"I won't." Mollian smiled grimly, moving over to the desk on the far wall to work on the set of throwing knives he was customizing. "What about you? Will you go stay with the mercs?"

Merriam shook her head. "It's weirdly been a long day. I'd rather just eat supper up here and have an early night."

"Now that *does* sound like a great time." Mollian turned his full attention to the weapons and tools in front of him.

Merriam went back to her book, only realizing night had started to fall when her stomach growled unhappily and Mollian stood from his chair. "I'll have food sent up for you." He patted her on the head as he headed out the door.

"Ugh, you spoil me." She smiled.

Supper ended up being a duck breast, bread, and an assortment of fruits. Merriam hungrily tucked into the food, finishing everything except for a peach, which she left for later. She was just lying back down to finish the book when a knock sounded on the door.

She sat back up, eyeing it curiously. "Yes?" she called.

The doorknob turned, and Oren stepped inside.

I'll find you later. His whispered words from earlier floated back to her, and her heart fluttered. She ran her tongue across her lower lip as she watched him enter the room, taking a seat across from her.

Nothing can happen, nothing can happen, nothing can happen. The mantra ran on an endless loop in her mind, and she pushed herself up, grabbing the platter of supper remnants to set out in the hall so the kitchen staff could easily grab it. When she was done, she closed the door and leaned against the wall, forcing herself to breathe slowly. Oren's eyes had never left her, and her skin blazed under the heat of his gaze.

"Where's Mollian tonight?" Oren asked, grabbing the peach off of the table and tossing it into the air.

"He had plans. Some business about roads or something." Merriam propped one foot against the wall, crossing her arms casually and trying her best not to fidget. "He said not to expect him back until early tomorrow morning," she added, and then internally cursed herself for offering up the unnecessary information. Unnecessary because nothing was going to happen.

"Ah." Oren bit into the peach, eyes locking on Merriam's.

He looked at her like she was an anomaly. A beautiful, strange anomaly that he wanted to tear apart and explore every part of. The intensity of that gaze pulled at something low in her stomach, and her breathing hitched. "Legends help me," she breathed, barely audible. Oren's eyes drifted slowly down her body and back up. He hadn't even touched her, yet desire pulsed unbidden between her legs.

"I've been having trouble remembering what you told me."

Merriam raised a brow in question.

Another bite of peach, tongue flicking out to lick juice from his lips. "The last time you visited me in Entumbra."

Merriam's gaze had dropped to his mouth, but she pulled it back up to his eyes. "I didn't think it was that complicated of a statement. Do you need a reminder?"

"Do you?" His deep green eyes shone with unmasked desire.

Her mouth went dry, traitorous heart fluttering in response. "What?"

"Do you need a reminder of the times you came to me, seeking escape from whatever troubled you?"

Merriam bit her lip.

"Because the only reminder I want right now is how good you feel when you come around my cock."

Her breathing hitched, mantra slipping completely from her mind, and she pushed off the wall to step toward him.

His eyes stayed locked onto hers as he continued to eat the fruit, his gaze darkening with lust as she grew nearer.

She went around the table to stand in front of him, slowly taking the peach from his hand and bringing it to her mouth. She took one bite, a droplet of juice spilling down her chin. He lifted his hand to run a thumb across her skin to catch it, fire searing in his wake and making her blood rush. She swallowed and set the peach back down into his palm before turning around and walking to her bedroom.

The peach dropped to the table, and Oren's footsteps were no more than a scuffle against the carpet as he followed her.

She stood in the center of the room. Oren closed the door behind him and came up to her back, close enough for her to feel the heat of him, but not quite touching. He pulled her hair over one shoulder, and his fingers traced down her exposed neck.

Catching his hand, she turned to face him, fingers wrapped loosely around his wrist as she led his hand to the hem of her shirt. "I want you to take me, Oren."

His hand tightened against her hip. "The things I have missed doing to you, Merri," he said, voice low.

That name made her heart race, and an empty ache filled her. The only thought in her mind was that she desperately needed him to fill it. "Show me." Her eyes met his, dancing with challenge and desire.

Oren slid a hand into her hair and pulled her into him, lips crashing into hers. He sucked her bottom lip into his mouth and bit, dragging a moan from her throat. Sweeping his tongue against hers, he ran his hand under her shirt and up her back. His mouth tasted of peach, and she sucked on his tongue, blatant need burning away every last inhibition and rational thought.

She fisted his shirt in her fingers, rising up on her toes to meet him. Her hands slipped down the front of his chest and tugged the fabric up. He broke the kiss only long enough to help her take the shirt off, then pulled her back, relishing the feel of claiming her again.

Merriam dragged her fingers up his back, feeling the powerful muscles flexing underneath her touch. She moved her hands to the back of his head, pressing her body flush against him as her thumb stroked just behind his ear.

Oren grabbed her braid at the base of her neck and pulled, tilting her head back and exposing her throat. He nipped at the sensitive skin, and she gasped, rocking her hips against him in a response and silent plea.

He pulled away from her to tug her shirt over her head and untie her pants, pushing them over her hips. She shimmied them the rest of the way down her legs until they were pooled on the floor.

"I want to taste every Legends' damned inch of you," he whispered against her mouth, feathering kisses down her jaw, her neck, her collarbone. He dropped to his knees in front of her, brushing his lips over the base of her ribcage and across her belly.

He looked up at her as he hooked his fingers into the waist of her panties. "I want to taste how much you want me."

Watching him kneel before her did things to her body she could never even begin to describe. Blood rushed in her head, and she saw nothing but him, heard nothing but him. The heady lust in his eyes alone was almost enough to make her come. She put her hands over his and pushed them down, fabric sliding against her skin.

Oren pressed a knee between her legs to spread them apart, gripping her thighs and running his hands along her skin. He kissed the top of each thigh before pressing his mouth to her. He ran his tongue along her center with a groan. His hands slid around to the back of her thighs, holding her firm as he again flicked his tongue out, teasing along her entrance and then up over her clit.

Merriam grabbed his hair with a moan, throwing her head back as pleasure raced through her body and back to coil in her core. Her toes curled against the floor as he slipped his tongue inside of her. "You are exquisite," he whispered against her, bringing one hand around to slide in two fingers, sucking lightly at her clit.

"Fuck," she whimpered, tilting her hips up to meet mouth. "Fuck, Oren."

He answered with a groan, steadily pumping his fingers before curling them repeatedly against that spot inside of her.

Her whole body tightened with pleasure, and her breaths came in short pants. "O," she gasped as he pressed his tongue across her clit again. "Don't you dare fucking stop." She tightened her fingers in his hair and pulled, and he repeated the movement that had caused her to pant his name.

"Fuck, I can't," she hissed, leaning forward as she came, her whole body trembling with release.

Oren ran his tongue over her through the orgasm, letting her ride it out before slowly dragging his fingers out of her. Still catching her breath, Merriam untangled her fingers from his hair. She held his head between her hands, thumbs brushing the tattoos at his temples. He stared up at her, his own thumbs tracing slow circles on her thighs. She was again overwhelmed with the weight of his gaze, the adoration and wonder in his eyes. She had never felt seen the way she did when he looked at her.

What does that look mean? his voice rumbled in her head, eyes searching hers.

Maybe it was just because he was still on his knees in front of her, but Casting to him felt intimate on an entirely new level. She reached out for his mind and pushed the words to him, careful and deliberate. *Just trying to remember if you're half as good with your cock as you are with your mouth.*

Oren's face lit with a devious grin, and he slid his pants off as he stood. Merriam ran her eyes slowly down the planes of his torso to the cords of muscle over his thighs and the hardened length between them.

"My eyes are up here, Lady." He smirked, hooking a finger under her chin.

"It wasn't your eyes I wanted to see, Majesty," she replied, meeting his gaze.

Oren leaned in to kiss her, guiding her back to the bed. After lowering her down, he crawled over her and buried his face in her neck. His canines dragged below her ear, and she hissed, digging her fingernails into his shoulders and arching her back into him.

Oren pulled away from her neck and kissed her just long enough to swipe his tongue across hers and suck at her bottom lip. He brushed the pad of his thumb over a nipple before sucking it into his mouth, his other hand scraping down her side to grasp her hip.

The empty ache between her thighs throbbed in almost painful need, and she moaned, wrapping her legs around his waist and pulling his hair free of its bun so she could tangle her fingers in it. "Oren, please," she moaned, tilting her hips up, trying to get contact.

Oren chuckled huskily, warm breath sending a shiver through her as it brushed across her skin. "What, Merri?" He nipped at her breast, sliding his tongue possessively across her as his fingers dug harder into her hip. "What do you want?"

Merriam whimpered in frustration, trying to pull him down to her with her legs. "You," she gasped as he placed a kiss between her breasts.

"You have me." He flicked his eyes up to hers as he put his lips to her skin. The lust burning in his eyes pooled heavily in her abdomen, and she yanked hard on his hair.

"I want you," she ground out, "inside of me."

He continued his fervent worship of her body, memorizing every part of her.

"Please." The ache for him was insistent, and she felt as though her next breath was dependent on it being met. "Oren, please."

He dragged his tongue up her neck and nipped at her earlobe, sending another shiver through her. "I love hearing you beg for me," he whispered before reaching between them and grabbing his cock. He dragged it down her center, growling in satisfaction at her wetness. Her hands moved from his hair to his shoulders, and she glanced down between them as he pushed into her.

A low moan escaped her at the fullness that worked its way through her core, and she rolled her hips into his tortuously slow movement. He covered her mouth with his, swallowing the sound. He pulled back, thrusting in deep. She whimpered, dragging her nails across his shoulders and latching onto his biceps. He fucked her with a measured pace, each push strong and deliberate and so full of *control* that she tightened her legs around him, knowing she had lost all of hers.

His hair fell across her cheek as he pulled his mouth from hers. Reaching back, he unhooked one of her legs from around his waist and slid his hand up just underneath her knee. He angled her leg up by his shoulder and kissed it softly before pumping into her hard and fast.

She threw her hands out over her head, fisting them in the sheets for something to hold on to. He placed his palm flat against her lower abdomen, teasing her clit with his thumb.

Merriam tilted her head back, eyes fluttering shut, and almost choked on a breath at the intensity of the pleasure coursing through her. She tightened around his movements, rocking her hips to meet him as pressure built in her core.

"Look at me," Oren demanded, and when she opened her eyes to meet his, he nipped at the skin of her inner leg again. "I want you to look at me when I make you come."

The pure command in his voice ran straight through her, and she reached for him, her hand wrapping around the back of his thigh as he fucked her. "Oren." It felt like the only word she could remember, the pressure inside of her building higher and higher until it exploded. She cried out, eyes snapping shut as the orgasm ripped through her, and Oren dropped her leg, leaning forward to muffle her cries with his mouth as he ran a hand up the side of her neck and into her hair.

"Fuck, Merri," he whispered against her lips. "You're so fucking perfect."

Her hands traveled over his torso, his arms, his face. "Come inside me," she whispered. One hand dragged down his back and squeezed the powerful muscle of his ass, pushing him into her, and his hand tightened into her hair, pulling her head back. His teeth sank into her shoulder as he made a few final thrusts before holding himself in deep, spilling into her with a muffled moan.

Oren licked at the spot on her shoulder where his canines had pricked her skin, trailing kisses up her neck before pulling up to look at her. His hand slid from her hair to cup her cheek, thumb brushing softly across the freckled skin.

Merriam felt his gaze like a vise around her heart, squeezing and digging in until she knew it would never be free. *You're well and truly fucked, aren't you?* she thought, raising her hand to his face to brush his hair back behind his ear before placing her palm to his cheek, mimicking his caress.

Oren turned his face to kiss her palm, eyes staying locked to hers. After sliding out of her, he scooped her up, lifting her from the bed.

She let out a small yelp of surprise, throwing her arms around his neck.

He brought her into the bathroom, setting her down on the edge of the tub and wetting a washcloth. She watched as he wiped himself off, eyes straying from his muscled arms, to his toned ass, to his strong calves, and back up to his face.

His hair was still down, spilling over one side of his head.

She could count on one hand the number of times she'd seen him without his bun and had decided long ago that this was her favorite Oren-mussed up and less put together.

He rinsed the washcloth and wrung it out before walking over to kneel in front of her. She silently watched as he gently nudged her legs apart, wiping the damp cloth down her center. Her hands braced on the edge of the tub as he cleaned himself from her thighs. He had just been buried inside of her–had just had his *mouth* on her–but this felt far more intimate than any of that. She'd forgotten how attentive he was.

He tossed the washcloth into the laundry basket behind him with barely a glance over his shoulder before running his hands from her thighs up her body until he was clutching her face, tenderly brushing the few stray hairs back and watching her with those green eyes so full of emotion.

"I am extremely, entirely fond of you," he whispered before leaning in to kiss her. It was gentle and sweet, and she'd barely gotten her hands up to touch him before he picked her up again, walking her back to her bed.

Oren threw the covers back with his mind before laying her down and sitting beside her. He ran a hand over her hair, and she watched him as his eyes roved her body. "Like what you see, Majesty?" she said lightly.

Oren smiled. "I do." His eyes flicked to hers for only a moment.

Merriam bit her lip, fighting the blush that rose to her cheeks.

Then she realized he hadn't started getting dressed. *He wants to stay.* The knowledge settled like a cold stone in her gut, instantly sobering her. "Oren, you should leave." The words fell from her mouth before she had a chance to think them over.

Those eyes that had been shining the vulnerable green of spring since he'd walked through her door shuttered, and he pulled his hand from her hair.

"I just meant that if you stayed late, when Molli isn't even here ... " She sat up, tucking her knees to her chest as she watched him stand and grab his pants from the floor.

"I get it. The castle is full of gossips." He tied up his pants, lifting his shirt with a flick of his fingers.

Merriam shook her head, trying to backpedal. "It's not that I don't want you to–"

"Merriam, it's fine." Oren pulled his shirt over his head.

The sound of her name coming from his lips made her stomach plummet. Not *Mer*, certainly not the hungrily whispered *Merri*, but *Merriam*.

He quickly, roughly, pulled his hair back up into its customary bun, finally meeting her eyes again. He paused, conflicted, but swallowed down the words he wanted to say and gave her a small smile before turning to leave.

The muffled click of the outer door closing behind Oren seemed to echo through her head. She wanted to Cast to him, call him back, but she couldn't focus enough to form a coherent thought, much less summon the concentration it would take to Cast it. She dropped her face into her hands with a groan, pushing her fingers up into her hair as her forehead rested on her knees.

How had that gone so definitively wrong?

Merriam swung her legs from the bed, picking up her discarded clothing items and tossing them to the bed in frustration. *Your fucking brother, Mollian!* She Cast forcefully, knowing he was much too far to hear it, but it helped her feel better, regardless.

She walked back to the bed, tugging on her shirt and pants and throwing herself backwards onto the mattress with a huff. She hadn't meant to let anything happen. Hadn't wanted anything to happen.

Had she?

She bit her lip, recalling the heat of his gaze on her, full of unbridled adoration, and her heart constricted. Covering her face, she let out a frustrated sigh. "You fucking like him, shithead," she muttered, dropping her hands, eyes turning to the ceiling. "You weren't supposed to fucking like him."

Merriam moved into the common area to wait for Mollian, picking up her book to pass the time. When she'd read the same page at least ten times without any retention, she set it down, scrubbing her face.

In her head, she knew that a relationship with Oren would mean trouble for both of them, but every time she thought of the hurt and confusion radiating from him as he left, her chest tightened almost to the point of pain.

Entumbra was so empty and secluded, she'd often stay with Oren late into the night, swapping stories of adventure or just relaxing in each other's company, Oren putting together notes and research on various worlds and Merriam slowly working her way through the collection of fiction Entumbra's library had to offer. It had never felt weird, just hanging out together after they'd both found release. The physical aspect of it had always been an easy way to turn her mind off when she needed to stop thinking.

But this had been different.

Or had it, really?

"Legends, you're an idiot." She stood up, walking purposefully to her bathroom.

"You care about him. That's a fact." She worked free the mess her braid had become and ran a brush through her hair. "You fucked him. Fact. You don't care that it was here and not in Entumbra … Fact?"

She set the brush down and sectioned off the hair at her crown, letting the repetitive movements of braiding help settle her nerves. "You hurt him. Fact. He deserves an explanation. Fact." She tied off the end of her braid, bracing her hands on the edge of the sink and staring at her reflection in the mirror. "So, what are you going to do about it?"

She chewed on her lip, butterflies suddenly tumbling in her stomach as she made up her mind. "Legends, you're a wreck," she whispered to the mirror before walking to her window and throwing it open.

The summer night was cool, the mountain wind little more than a breeze. She took a deep breath to steal her nerves before tossing a leg over the ledge and swinging herself out over the wall.

The stones of the castle were rough and uneven, providing plenty of grip and holds for her hands and feet. Her stomach dropped a little with the dizziness she always felt free-climbing outside of the merc house, but she'd learned long ago that fear was a friend. Especially when it came to scaling, it was good to have a little sense of self-preservation.

She worked her way up the wall, bare toes easily finding purchase on the stone. She had a moment of unsettling realization that this was almost *too* easy. Anyone with half a brain would be able to make this climb. But it was there and gone within a second, and she concentrated on her movements.

Her hands finally slipped over a slim parapet, and she crawled on top, running across it to the next section of wall leading up to Oren's window.

Merriam's palms were sweaty with nerves, her heartbeat picking up. She almost laughed at how ridiculous it was. She was about to scale a wall probably fifty feet from the ground, but the thought of talking to a *male* is what made her hands shake.

Before she could second guess herself, she launched into the final climb.

It wasn't until she reached his window ledge that she realized she hadn't thought this through all the way. The window swung outward, and if he had it latched ...

Merriam rested her arms on the ledge, and she saw with relief that the window was cracked. She ducked her head as she pulled it open further and raised herself into a sitting position, turning her body so her legs were dangling over Oren's floor.

"What are you doing?"

Oren's voice made her jump so hard she almost lost her balance, and her heart leapt into her throat. "Legends, Oren. Are you trying to kill me?" She placed a hand over her chest and slid to the ground.

Oren pushed himself up onto an elbow, blanket pooling at his waist. "Are *you* trying to kill *me*?" he asked pointedly.

Merriam gave him a mirthless look. "Obviously." She leaned against the edge of the window and wiped her palms off on her pants. "Now will you shut up, please? I came to tell you something."

Oren tilted his head, his loose hair spilling over a shoulder. "You are an enigma, woman." His eyes were still closed off, but shone with mild amusement.

The glimmer in his gaze gave her hope, and she pushed off of the windowsill, moving so that the faint light from the night sky could shine through the window.

Nervously, she approached the end of his bed, perching on the edge of it.

Oren shook his head with a sigh. "Your ass is about to fall off the bed. I'm not going to bite," he told her, sitting up and motioning for her to come closer.

Merriam climbed onto the bed, sat cross-legged next to his legs, and looked down at her lap, biting her lip. Now that she was actually here, she had no idea where to begin. "I'm sorry for earlier," she finally blurted.

Oren tucked a finger under her chin, lifting her gaze to meet his. "Legends, Mer, did you scale the fucking castle because you were worried about my damaged ego?"

Merriam clicked her tongue against her teeth. "No, I mean ... " She grunted in frustration, pushing his hand away. Her body's elevated response to his touch was too distracting for this. "Just ... I like you, okay?"

Oren's eyes searched hers, those shutters beginning to crack open again.

"I like you a lot, and it scares me. It scares me because the paths our lives are on are so different. Like I told you in Entumbra, we shouldn't be able to work out." Merriam wiped a hand across her face and took a settling breath.

Over the years he'd been gone, they'd developed a close friendship during her infrequent visits. That friendship had grown into something ... deeper. Some jobs had taken more of a mental toll than others, and he'd been the perfect distraction to wipe the horror from her mind.

But it had just been sex. They'd agreed on that front.

Entumbra was so far separated from real life: no prying eyes to gossip, no weight of responsibility to consider. Even when feelings had started to develop, she'd always stood fast that whatever was going on between them wasn't something they could take out into the world when Oren finally returned to Umbra.

She was so sure of it that her trysts with the heir apparent were the one detail of her life she'd never shared with Mollian. And even if the younger prince had always suspected something, he'd never brought it up.

Oren sensed where her thoughts had drifted. "If I had a copper for every time you've told me that we wouldn't work, I could buy an entire tavern."

Merriam chuckled sardonically. "And yet somehow we still find ourselves here."

"I got to give you my reminders. I suppose it's only fair that you share yours." He pushed a hand through his hair, resting it at the top of his head as he waited for her to speak.

The difficulty of not staring at the flex of his arm and bare chest irked her, and she dropped her eyes to the space between them with a slight scowl. "I have a reputation ... no, that sounds cocky. I've earned a place for myself here, and finally–*finally*–I am seen as my own person, not just some burden Molli shoved onto everyone. I know you already know all of this in theory, but I need you to really fully understand how much effort it took for me to get to where I am." Merriam pulled at a loose string on Oren's blanket. "I'm past the point of denying that I want you, that a large part of me wants this, but I cannot give up my individuality. I just can't.

"You're going to become king next summer. Choosing a human to have at your side is one thing, but a mercenary?" Merriam shook her head, peeking up at him. "I just wanted you to know that I want for you to stay with me and touch me and hold me, but the only thing I want more than that is the respect I spent so many years chasing. It's unfortunate that it came in a way that's incompatible with your responsibilities, but I can't give it up, O."

Oren brushed a thumb across his lower lip before holding his hand out to her. "Come here."

She let him pull her closer to him, not quite on his lap, but close enough that if she leaned forward an inch, her shoulder would be against his chest. Every nerve in her body was aware of his proximity.

His eyes glistened a deep green in the near-darkness, his thumb caressing her cheek, and she suppressed the shiver that went through her at the warmth of his touch. "I won't ask you to give up your independence, Mer. If that is your one stipulation to being with me, you have it. It's done." He leaned forward, brushing a soft kiss against her lips. "If I can't claim you in front of the court-in front of my kingdom-fine. The only thing I care about is that from now on, I am the only one who touches you. The only one who kisses you. Agree to be mine as I have undoubtedly been yours since the first time you kissed me," he whispered the words against her mouth, resting his forehead against hers.

"Do you think it can really be that simple?"

"I admire you enough to try."

That vise clenched one notch tighter around Merriam's heart.

He pulled her into his chest, tucking her head under his chin and holding her there, arms wrapped around her. "Thank you," he said eventually, the words reverberating through her body, "for coming to me."

Merriam snuggled against him, relishing the warmth and the weight of his body. "I had to," she said simply, then pulled away to meet his gaze. "Climbing up here was actually pretty easy. I could do it all the time and no one would ever be the wiser." Heat flushed her face. "Not that I have to be up here all the time. That sounded presumptuous. I just meant-"

Oren laughed. "Mollian is rubbing off on you, Lady. You're rambling."

"It's hard to think straight around you sometimes," Merriam admitted, smiling softly.

Oren nipped at her lip, canines dragging across it. "I like having that effect on you, Merri," he said huskily.

That *name*. A wave of desire rolled through her, and she drew her tongue up his tapered ear, lightly taking the tip between her teeth.

Oren hissed, hands finding her sides and digging into her hips. "Fuck, Merri."

She grinned, straddling him and brushing her fingers up the short hair on the back of his head.

"For the record." He captured her hands in his, holding them to her sides. "I want you here, always. I know better than to caution you about climbing the walls, so I'll just leave it at fucking be careful, Mer. But I want you here." He let her hands go, and she dragged them down his chest.

"Noted, Majesty." She leaned forward to kiss him.

Oren wrapped her braid twice around his fist. "I have to be up with the sun tomorrow."

"Sucks to be you, doesn't it?" Merriam pouted, fingers dancing across his stomach.

Oren tensed, pulling her hair back and exposing her throat. "This is what's going to happen." He growled against the sensitive skin below her ear. "I am going to fuck you. Hard. And then you are going to sleep in my bed, and if you're wearing anything at all, it had better be something of mine."

She couldn't even nod because he still held onto her hair. So instead, she rolled her hips against his erection and ran her fingers into his hair.

The movement was enough to snap Oren's control, and he wrapped his arm around her waist, flipping her over so she was underneath him and doing exactly what he had promised.

Chapter 12

You are definitely insane

M<small>ERRIAM WOKE TO ARMS</small> tightening around her, and her whole body stiffened, preparing to fight. Her eyes flew open, and then she remembered.

She was in Oren's bed. The smell of pine and plum and clear night sky surrounded her, and she relaxed into the warmth of the body pressed against every inch of hers.

Fingers brushed against her neck before being replaced with the light touch of lips. Merriam's eyes fluttered closed, and she tilted her head compliantly, shifting against the hardened length pressed against her backside.

Oren moved a hand to her hip, holding her still as he nipped her neck. "I told you, I have obligations this morning." He pressed a kiss just below her ear before pulling away.

Merriam groaned in dismay at the loss of his warmth, burrowing deeper into the covers.

She had half a thought that she should get up, too. But she was just so *comfortable* and sated. The thought of getting out of bed and ruining this little bubble of serenity was thoroughly unappealing.

She felt a familiar wave of magic lap at her mind, sending the tattoo on her back tingling as she irritably pushed it away. But now she was awake, and she opened her eyes again with a sigh, rolling onto her back and stretching.

"Well, good morning, Lady." Oren came from the bathroom, grabbing a shirt from a drawer and slipping it over his head.

Merriam smiled at him, sitting up and sliding her fingers into the waves of her hair, wild from sleep. The braid had not lasted long last night. "No breakfast?" she asked with a pout.

Oren chuckled, bending down to kiss her. "I promise I'll be better prepared next time."

Merriam slipped from the bed, tucking her hands to her chest and leaning into Oren. She nuzzled her cheek against his shoulder as he pulled her closer, and she momentarily allowed happiness to freely bubble up inside of her, spilling over and warming every dark corner of her existence. "Can it really be this easy?" she whispered, pulling her head back to look up at him.

Oren traced a thumb over her cheek. "Waking up before dawn? Not always, but sometimes."

She clicked her tongue, rolling her eyes. "You're insufferable," she told him, pushing away and walking over to where her clothes were piled on a chair.

Oren sat on a bench to pull on his boots and watched her strip his shirt from over her head. A smile played at his lips, eyes never leaving her. His gaze stayed on her the entire time she dressed, and when she finally turned around, she felt if she looked into his eyes too long, she might fall into his soul.

"Come here." The bald order in his voice—so commanding and kingly it made her toes curl—mixed with the unbridled adoration of his gaze sent butterflies tumbling in her stomach, and her feet moved almost of their own accord.

When she reached him, he grabbed her hand and turned her around, pulling her down to sit on the edge of the bench between his legs. He began methodically working his fingers through her hair, gently pulling the tangles free. His breathing matched his movements, measured and confident, but a slight tension radiated from him, sparking through the air between them.

Oren was just as nervous as Merriam. He'd never wanted to hold on to a thing so badly in all of his life, afraid that the moment she was out of his sight, she would change her mind again. Their non-relationship had started budding over three years ago, but they'd always been aware of the different roles they had to play.

The fear of her shying away from her feelings again was like ice in his veins, and it was all he could do to swallow it down and try his best not to scare her off.

The fair gold of her hair shone against the tan of his fingers, sliding through his hands like silken rays of sunshine as he braided her hair.

"I meant what I said last night," Oren said. *Come back. Be with me.* The words formed in his head, and before he could second guess them, he Cast them to her.

They unfolded in her mind as soft as a whisper, and Merriam's heart tripped over a beat. The feel of his fingers in her hair and the vulnerability of his words were too overwhelming for her to concentrate enough to push a thought to him. She bit her lip, tracing a finger over his knee. "Okay."

He tied off her braid, moving his hands down to squeeze her hips before giving them a quick *tap tap*. She stood, and he finished putting on his boots before following.

"Have a productive day, Mer," he said against her lips, giving her a final kiss before walking out the door.

The sky was barely lightening over the mountains as Merriam climbed down from Oren's room, and she heard Mollian moving around in their common area.

"You're up early," she said as she entered, eyeing the breakfast tray hungrily.

"I'm up late, actually," Mollian grumbled, lifting a loaf of bread to his mouth. His eyes flicked up to her, gaze narrowing. "Where the Hel did you just come from?"

"My bedroom." Merriam sank onto the couch next to him and grabbed a link of sausage, still blessedly warm.

"Ass," Mollian said with his mouth full. "You weren't in there when I got back. Figured you were out running drills or in the library or something."

"Or something." Merriam slathered butter onto a piece of bread.

"I know you didn't Travel. I felt you here."

"Then I'm sure you also felt me shoo you away." Merriam took a large bite, propping her feet up on the table and leaning into the cushions.

Mollian narrowed his eyes suspiciously. *You're being obtuse.*

You're being nosy.

You're being dodgy.

You're being annoying.

You're fucking my brother.

Merriam choked on her bread, sitting up and coughing heavily.

Mollian pushed his hair off of his forehead, watching her with a smug smile.

"I hope you're enjoying my pain," Merriam coughed.

"Oh, very much so." Mollian bit into a sausage link.

Merriam grabbed the cup that was sitting in front of Mollian and took a long drink. "We need more milk," she said as she set the cup back down.

"Like I said, you were gone when I came in this morning."

"Yes, we've mentioned."

"Mmm." Mollian watched her, waiting.

"He came to see me last night, after you left," Merriam said eventually, taking one last sausage, relaxing into the couch and resting her head against the cushions. She chewed quietly for a moment before adding. "I kicked him out, after."

Mollian snorted. "That was probably a first for him."

"He got my head all messed up, Molli. I was so confused. I wanted him to stay more than anything, but the thought of anyone knowing about it also terrified me." Merriam rolled her head to the side to look at Mollian. "I climbed up to his room to talk to him about everything."

"You climbed up to his room?"

Merriam bit her lip with a shrug. "I didn't know what else to do."

"You might actually be insane."

"We're seeing each other now, though. Secretly."

"You are definitely insane," Mollian corrected.

Merriam glared up at the ceiling before letting out a sigh. "Yeah, I am. But it's like I lose the ability to think rationally where he's concerned. I quite literally cannot help myself." She fell to the side, head in Mollian's lap. "What am I going to do, Molli?"

Mollian placed a hand on her head, patting it in a mock-patronizing way. "I suppose you're going to keep climbing the castle walls until you're old and gray."

"I suppose."

"Or maybe Oren can grow his hair out like that one fairytale of yours. Then you can just grab on and have him pull you up instead of you doing all the work," Mollian offered.

Merriam laughed. "I'll have to suggest it to him." She bit her lip, flipping onto her back to look up at him. "Am I being stupid?"

Mollian met her gaze, running a thumb over her hair. "He's going to be king, Ria. You won't be able to hide in the shadows forever. But he cares about you, and he would never intentionally hurt you. You make him happy. As long as being with him also makes you happy, then pursue it."

"I just want to stay in this little bubble for a while and not think about the rest of it." Merriam sighed.

"Then do that. You've earned some happiness."

Shortly after Mollian went to get a few hours of sleep, Merriam decided to go for a run before tackling more research. She pulled the door open to find Eskar on the other side, fist raised to knock.

Slowly lowering her hand, Eskar looked Merriam up and down, the corner of her lips pulling in distaste. "Your presence is requested."

Merriam, unable to help herself, also gave the Ranger a once-over, wrinkling her nose slightly. "I'm actually busy at the moment, but thank you for the request. I'll pencil you in later." She stepped around the female, shutting the door.

"I'm afraid you'll have to clear your schedule, merc. Queen Regenya needs to speak with you," Eskar said, stopping Merriam's retreat.

Merriam turned to face her, a slow smile spreading across her face. "Oh, has she already given up hope that the Rangers will be able to fix this new problem? I'm sorry to hear it's too much for you, but I'm sure something less ... taxing will come along soon," she crooned, continuing back down the hall to the stairwell.

Eskar bristled, eyes shooting daggers. "You will come with me to the war room," she ground out.

Merriam didn't even turn around. "Where does it look like I'm going?"

"You're a fucking brat," Eskar spat, moving to follow her.

Merriam laughed. "Am I a brat, Eskar? Or are you and the rest of the Rangers just upset that I'm constantly finishing your jobs for you?"

"Someone is going to teach you some manners one of these days,"

Eskar hissed, roughly knocking into Merriam's shoulder as she passed her on the stairs.

"Just name a time and a place, Ranger," Merriam replied sweetly.

Eskar said nothing until they reached the war room, knocking twice before pushing open the door and escorting Merriam inside. "The mercenary, Your Majesty."

"Thank you, Lieutenant. You may leave us," the queen said in dismissal before turning to Merriam and motioning for her to come forward.

The queen sat at the head of the table overlaid with a map of Sekha. On one side sat Captain Ferrick and Commander Dio. On the other sat Oren, and Merriam swallowed past the feeling of her heart lodging in her throat, forcing her eyes not to linger on him. "Your Majesty." She bowed her head, holding her hands loosely behind her back.

"Thank you for agreeing to meet with us on such short notice, Merriam," the queen said. "Are you aware of the new terror that has struck Jekeida?"

"One of my comrades has heard reports of abductions and a few rather gruesome murders throughout the territory," Merriam answered.

"Gruesome, indeed," the queen agreed. "There have been developments to this situation, and it is now my belief that your troupe may be best-equipped to handle it."

Merriam looked first to Oren, the pull of his gaze almost undeniable. His eyes were guarded, but not worried or anxious. Then she looked at Ferrick, who was barely holding back a scowl as he stared at the table. Dio just watched it all with mild curiosity.

Turning her gaze back to the queen, Merriam answered, "I'm listening."

Later that night, Merriam sat on one of the couches in the mushroom of the merc house. The remnants of the strawberry tarts she'd snagged from the castle kitchens littered the table in the center.

Aleah dragged a hand over her mouth, unceremoniously wiping crumbs from her freckled face. "All right, then. Let's hear it."

"The short of it is that the chance is very high we are dealing with some sort of actual demon that has worked its way onto Nethyl." Merriam sat forward, leaning her elbows on her knees. "Nobody is sure how it got here. I was already planning a trip to Entumbra to do some research, but now it's also going to be recon. A demon shouldn't be capable of creating their own portals in the fabric of the universe. It had to have somehow found a temporary rift or slipped through the Gate. We just have to figure out which."

Jasper stretched an arm over the back of the couch in thought. "It's just one demon?"

"That's what some of the Rangers have reported. Nobody knows what kind or what it looks like, though. The Rangers are currently focusing their efforts on figuring out where it's making its lair."

"What's the payout?" Leonidas ran a hand over his hair, slightly longer than usual and in need of a trim.

"One hundred gold. Twenty-five now and seventy-five when we kill it." Merriam chewed on her lip. "The Rangers are going to keep working the case, too. We don't have to work with them, but if they get it before we do, then we only get the first half of the payment."

Calysta tilted her head in thought, hands folded placidly in her lap. "They don't know what kind of demon it is we're dealing with. There are many worlds, many demons. Some of them are brutal but easy to kill, but others can be toxic to the touch, shift into different creatures of different sizes, or even be capable of possession that consumes the soul of the host until nothing is left but a husk. The high fae have forgotten, but the nymphs remember." She turned her inky-black eyes to Jasper. "The challenge will be a fun one, but I have a feeling it will be very dangerous, regardless of whether or not it is just one creature."

Jasper nodded, running a thumb over his bottom lip as he considered. "Does anyone else have any qualms or questions?"

Aleah shook her head, looking to Leonidas and Campbell.

Campbell scratched the base of an antler. "Do you think we're getting stiffed? I mean, how long has it been since anyone has had to hunt down a demon? Calysta, were you even alive to remember it?"

Calysta shook her head. "Lesser demons have slipped through before, but they were taken care of shortly after passing the wards around Entumbra. It's been quite a while since one has crossed over and been able to avoid detection for so long." She was still young, only 180 years old, but her people knew much about the history of Nethyl."

Campbell pressed his lips together. "Exactly. If we're going to be risking our lives, it had better be worth it."

"Fair. What do you suggest?" Merriam asked.

"One fifty. Fifty now and a hundred after."

"Greedy bastard," Leonidas joked. "I agree, though. Like Calysta said, we don't know how dangerous this thing actually is. We need to make it worth our time."

"So 150 gold and we have a deal?" Merriam clarified, looking around the room.

"When will you go to Entumbra?" Jasper asked after everyone had agreed.

"I'll present our counteroffer in the morning and head out in the afternoon."

"Calysta, go with Merriam. See what you can get from the forest," Jasper said.

The nymph nodded.

"I'll work with my contacts in the castle to glean whatever information we can from the Rangers, since I'm sure they'll be none too forthcoming if the request comes from you." Jasper shot Merriam a look.

She grinned sheepishly, shrugging.

"In the meantime, Leo, prepare your birds. I want a couple of ravens sent with Mer and Calysta so we can get any pertinent information as quickly as possible."

"This is so exciting!" Aleah clapped, jumping up from the couch. "An actual demon. Who would have thought?"

Leonidas gave her a withering look, ice-blue eyes unamused. "I'm sure exciting isn't the word most people would use for that."

Aleah stuck her tongue out at him. "Don't be such a killjoy, Leo. This is definitely more exciting than hunting down some old thief or trafficker."

"I'll send a message after the briefing tomorrow morning when I know the exact time we're leaving," Merriam said to Calysta. "I'll include a written contract as well," she told Jasper, who nodded.

"Meeting adjourned, then?" Aleah scooped up the leftover strawberry tart mess and headed into the kitchen.

"Keep your eyes peeled, Mer," Jasper said, placing a hand on her arm.

"I will," she replied.

He gave her arm a gentle squeeze. "And don't do anything reckless."

"I'll try," she said with a grin.

The closer Merriam got to the castle, the more nervous anticipation began to buzz in her veins. Even though Oren had as good as told her to visit him again, she worried about being too presumptuous, especially since she was the one that always forced distance between them in Entumbra. She was deep in her head by the time she made it to her rooms and was almost second-guessing whether or not she should actually try to go see him as she slid off her boots by the door.

"Calysta is going to Entumbra with us," she told Mollian, who was going over papers at the desk in the back of the room.

Mollian sat back, rubbing a hand over his face. "If I have to read one more proposal about a road," he grumbled under his breath. Stretching his arms out behind his head, he gave her a lazy grin, eyes glinting with mischief.

"What did you do?" She asked, narrowing her eyes.

"Me? I didn't do anything. Why would you think I did something?" His canines dimpled into his bottom lip.

"Molli," she said in warning, crossing her arms over her chest.

"Ria." His posture stayed relaxed.

Look who's being obtuse now. She narrowed her eyes further.

I can see why you do it. It's quite amusing.

Merriam threw her hands up with a huff, turning to head to her room.

"Oren stopped by earlier."

Her feet stilled immediately.

"He's also going to Entumbra. I mean, I thought it was weird. He just spent five years there. Surely he's had his fill for a while, but he was very, *very* eager to be included when he found out we were planning to go. Must be he misses our dear sister, though that's another mystery, because I've always found her to be rather pompous and prickly."

Merriam turned around to meet Mollian's eyes. "And just how exactly did Oren know we were planning a trip to Entumbra?" she asked pointedly.

Mollian ran his fingers through his hair, raking the curls from his forehead. "Well, he was curious about your plans for the rest of the week. He seemed to be under the impression that you would be seeing him tonight, actually. Don't worry, I told him you would probably want to be in bed early to make sure you're well-rested for tomorrow. I also may have suggested that you looked a little worse for wear this morning and maybe his room was too uncomfortable for your standards." Mollian's grin grew wicked, amusement sparking in his cracked green eyes.

"I looked marvelous this morning, thank you." Merriam glowered.

"Ehhh, I'm not sure that's the word I would use." Mollian grimaced, then dodged the pillow thrown at his head.

Merriam was already disappearing into her room before he could retaliate, dipping into the bathroom and locking the door. She brushed out her hair, piling it on top of her head before running a bath and letting the heat of the water wash away the nerves knotting in her stomach. Moving into her bedroom, she dressed in leggings and a shirt before brushing her hair back and starting a loose braid at the nape of her neck.

"Should I expect you to be out all night?"

Merriam turned her head to see Mollian across the room, leaning in the doorway with his hands held casually in his pockets.

"Yes, Dad, no need to wait up." Merriam rolled her eyes, but smiled.

Mollian walked over to her, cupping her face in his hands and searching her eyes. *Let yourself be happy.*

His voice thrummed through her, and she felt that unexplainable completeness in her soul that always accompanied his proximity. *I love you, Molli.* She leaned into his palm.

He abruptly pulled her into his chest, resting his chin on her head. "If you plummet to your death, I swear on every Legend that I will go to Hel myself and rip you to shreds," he muttered.

Merriam pulled back, clicking her tongue. "I'm offended you have such little faith in me." She placed her palm to her chest.

Mollian shook his head, pushing her away. "Don't complain about having to wear the same set of clothes all week if you end up not having time to pack tomorrow."

"You'll be the one having to smell me," she quipped, walking towards the window.

The wind was coming in briskly off the mountains, and the bricks of the castle chilled Merriam's toes and fingers as she crawled up the side. Oren's window was wide open, and she smoothly pulled herself over the sill, rolling to the floor and closing her hands over her toes. "I guess I should have considered wearing boots." She smiled up at Oren, who was sitting on his bed with a book.

He laughed, walking over to shut the window before squatting in front of her and taking her feet in his hands. The warmth from his palm spread all the way up her calves, and she leaned back on her hands as she watched him.

"They were clean," she offered. "But I'm not sure when the last time the outside of the castle had a good washing."

"I'm sure it's a priority." Oren smiled, lifting one foot to press a chaste kiss to her instep before dropping her feet and offering her a hand up.

She moved to the bed, climbing on top and sitting cross-legged on the covers. Oren sat next to her, one knee shifted up while the other foot stayed on the floor. He cupped her cheek, sliding his thumb over her bottom lip before moving his hand into her hair. "What did the mercs say about the job?" he asked as he tugged the tie off of the end of her braid.

"Am I really here to talk business?" Merriam raised a brow, feeling the light pull on her hair as he methodically worked his fingers up her braid, unraveling the plait.

"Mmm, I suppose not." His eyes burned into her.

Her heart skipped a beat, and she tried to focus on her breathing as empty desire began to pool in her core. "How come all the merc jobs go through me still now that you're back? Don't you and Jasper have history?" Merriam asked, trying her best not to sound flustered as her hair finally fell loose, and Oren ran his fingers through it freely. Scalp to ends. Scalp to ends. Scalp to ends. Goosebumps raised across her arms, and her chest tightened.

"Are you really here to talk about another male?" Oren wrapped her hair around his fist once. Twice. Holding it right at the base of her neck.

She gulped, mouth dry. "I suppose not," she whispered.

Oren pulled her forward and tilted her head to the side, kissing just below her ear. "What did you come here for?" he whispered against her skin before moving lower and nipping her neck.

A moan rose from her throat, and she braced her hands on her knees.

"I'm not sure that was an answer." Oren's lips moved to her collarbone.

Her whole body ached for contact, but he wasn't touching her anywhere except with his lips and his hand in her hair, holding her firmly in place. Heat flared in her eyes as she jerked her head back.

He met her gaze lazily, unperturbed by her attitude. "Is there a problem?"

"I want to touch you." She glared at him.

Oren smirked, letting her hair unravel from his hand.

Heady desire buzzed in her veins as she pulled herself across the space that separated them. Her knees were on either side of his waist, and her hands wound up his shoulders and into his hair, tearing it free from its bun before she had time to process what she was doing.

Oren groaned, slanting his mouth over hers and kissing her slowly and thoroughly, fisting one hand in her hair while the other ran down her ribs to her hip and back up. "You're going to be the death of me, Lady."

Merriam smiled against his lips. "You don't sound too discomposed at the thought." She opened her eyes as he pulled back slightly, her soul bared in moonlit amber, and she could almost feel him look into every part of her as he met her gaze.

Something flickered under the surface of his eyes, and Merriam's chest tightened as she understood the broken parts he'd seen in her. The need in her belly cooled, still present, but dampered against the vulnerability that filled her at knowing he truly saw all of who she was. She opened her mouth to speak, but he was lowering his lips to hers again, collapsing onto his side before rolling onto his back, pulling her on top of him.

She lay against his chest, feeling his heartbeat. His fingers brushed down her back as he lazily ran a hand through her hair.

"You smell like rain and wildflowers." His voice eventually cut through the silence. "It's absolutely addictive."

Merriam laughed, fingers playing along the planes of his torso. "Glad I'm no longer the only creeper going around smelling people."

"I wouldn't say I'm smelling *people*," Oren protested. "Just you."

A smile crept across her face, and she nuzzled against him.

His touch grew more insistent, fingers dragging down her body possessively. *You see your brokenness as something to hide, but I see how it made you strong.*

Merriam shuddered beneath his fingers, just light enough not to bruise, desire rekindling heavily in her core.

Your strength—your fire and spirit—is intoxicating. He ground his hips against her, his cock creating blessed friction against her groin. "You are intoxicating," he breathed.

Chapter 13

We kill people for money

MERRIAM STOOD PLACIDLY BEFORE the king and queen, hands held behind her back. "Due to the unique and dangerous nature of this job, our requested fee is 150 gold. Fifty up front, one hundred once the job is completed," she said evenly.

Ferrick scoffed loudly from his position to the left of the regents. "One hundred and fifty pieces for one creature? That's absurd."

"Is it, Pos?" Oren leaned forward in his chair, elbow propped against his knee, and turned to look at the captain. "Because I seem to recall you specifically saying you didn't want to risk your men when there were still so many unknowns. Or am I mistaken?"

Ferrick's jaw ticked, and he radiated irritation at being addressed so informally, but he knew better than to correct the crown prince in public. He pursed his lips, focusing his anger on Merriam instead, blue eyes as cold and hard as chips of ice.

Flirt. Merriam focused her attention on Casting the word to Oren, but stared back at the captain, keeping her eyes soft and sweet, knowing her lack of reaction would just aggravate him further.

What Oren Cast back was less a word and more a satisfied, suggestive rumble she felt through her whole body.

Regenya waved her hand dismissively. "The crown will agree to your price. I'll have the contract drawn up shortly. It is my understanding that you and my son are planning a trip?"

Oh, her son definitely wishes to plan a trip with you.

Merriam fought the urge to shoot Oren a look. Her tattoo still itched slightly from Casting to him before, and she knew if she tried again her head would be throbbing. "Yes, Your Majesty. Mollian thought it might be prudent for me to research the archives of Entumbra before figuring out how best to handle the situation."

"Prudent of him, indeed," Regenya said thoughtfully. "It's been quite a while since he's visited. Captain, have a bird sent after we've adjourned. Let my daughter know Mollian will be there so she can prepare some studies for him."

Ferrick pulled his glare from Merriam to look at his queen. "Of course, Your Majesty."

"You depart soon?" Regenya asked Merriam.

"I think the plan is to leave after lunch," she replied to the queen.

"Very well. The contract and your payment will be ready before midday," Regenya said, standing from her chair.

"Oren, would you be willing to meet up with her before she leaves to get everything taken care of?" Darius asked, looking to his son.

"Yes, of course." Oren inclined his head.

Regenya nodded, turning to leave.

Darius gave Merriam an apologetic smile before following his wife.

"Always a pleasure, gentlemen." Merriam smiled brightly at Ferrick before turning to the prince, humor flashing in her amber eyes when they met his. She turned on her heel and left the room, heading up to pack.

A few hours later, she was back in the war room, sitting on the table and swinging her legs back and forth.

Oren came in, closing the door behind him. "I hope I haven't kept you waiting too long, Lady. I had to tell Her Majesty the Queen of my intentions to go back to Entumbra with you and Mollian."

"I was actually just debating whether or not I should go sell my services to another monarch with a demon ravaging their kingdom." Merriam held her hand out in front of her, casually examining her nails.

Oren walked up, setting a rolled parchment and bag of coin on the table next to her before grabbing her knees, pulling her abruptly to the edge of the table, and stepping between her legs. "So fickle, even after demanding a pay raise." He caught her chin between his thumb and forefinger, eyes like green flames.

"Well, I am a mercenary. It comes with the territory." Merriam dipped her tongue out to lick his thumb.

"Does it?" His eyes bore into hers, and her chest constricted, breath catching in her throat. He dragged his thumb across her bottom lip, the look in his eyes all but daring her to bite him.

Merriam let the full force of her desire burn hot in her eyes, but didn't move her hands from where they rested against the table over the map of West Eyko on either side of her. "You did say you were fine with my occupation."

Oren's dimple appeared with his smirk. "I did. And it still feels unreal that a mercenary would choose a prince."

A smile pulled at the corners of her lips. "Oh, I had a choice? I just figured with your impending coronation and all … who knows what would've happened to me if I refused you?" She dragged her foot up the back of his calf, and Oren dropped his hands from her face to her thighs, his thumbs tracing circles into her skin through the fabric of her leggings.

"How do you constantly test my control?"

Merriam shrugged, her stomach flipping. "Just add it to my list of talents." She wrapped her hands around the back of his neck, pulling his mouth to hers and kissing him, soft and sweet. "I believe we have business to discuss, Majesty."

Oren trailed his lips from her cheek down to her neck, nipping her just above the iron chain that rested against the base of her throat before pulling back. "Indeed, we do." He gave her thighs a final squeeze before grabbing the document to the side of her. Stepping out from between her legs, he unrolled the paper and set it on the table beside her.

Merriam hopped down, standing next to him as they went over the contract and signed it. "I'll go send this off and let Calysta know to head over. Tell Molli I'll meet him at the stables?"

"Just him?" Oren lifted a brow.

Merriam rolled her eyes. "You and your fragile male ego," she teased, raising up on her toes to kiss him. "Try to keep it under control while we're out, okay?"

"Bossy for a low-born human, aren't you?" Oren lightly whacked her on the butt with the contract as she turned to walk out.

"Someone has to keep you in check, Majesty," Merriam threw over her shoulder before leaving.

"We have an escort," Mollian said as Merriam and Calysta walked up to the stables, bags and two raven cages in hand.

"Why do we have an escort?" Merriam tilted her head in confusion.

"The crown prince is going on a trip with two known swords-for-hire," Mollian said wryly.

"Yes, swords-for-hire currently employed by this same prince. Honestly, it's like they think mercenaries have no honor."

"We kill people for money, Mer," Calysta pointed out. Even speaking flatly, her voice was soft and musical.

"You're not helping."

"Well, it's true. Better safe than sorry." Calysta's shoulders lifted in a shrug.

Merriam threw her hands up, "Fine, if the Guard wants to come, that just means less pulling watch and more sleep for me." She started walking again.

"Wait, you should know—"

"Well hello, *merc*." The smooth voice interrupted Mollian, who shot Merriam an apologetic glance.

Merriam barely suppressed the compulsion to roll her eyes. "Rovin. What a fucking pleasure." The expression on her face suggested it was anything but.

She knew it was only because of Mollian's presence that the Ranger didn't say anything more, but she still couldn't quite keep herself from groaning when she saw Eskar come out of the stables, stopping to secure her gear to a horse. *Really?* She Cast to Mollian.

Mollian shrugged, bringing a hand up to scratch the back of his head.

You didn't get to request the escort?

Ferrick assigned them.

Merriam pressed her lips together, shaking off her irritation as a few stable hands led horses out into the courtyard. She and Calysta loaded their gear as Mollian left to tell Oren they were ready to head out.

Rovin watched her swing up into the saddle, his brown eyes shining in the midday sun while a hand rested on the short sword at his hip.

"You can relax there, Lieutenant. The princes aren't even out here. I'm not going to disappear to go hunt them down," Merriam chided.

Rovin narrowed his eyes before looking away to get on his own horse. "Don't pride yourself, pet. I don't find you threatening at all."

"That's probably because you've never seen her sink one of those axes into someone's skull," Calysta intoned from where she stood in front of her horse, gently petting its nose.

Merriam choked back a laugh, and Rovin watched the nymph with a stunned expression.

Calysta's inky black gaze moved to him languidly. "What? You're not actually surprised at the prospect of murder?"

"Rangers are too prim to discuss such gruesome things so baldly." Merriam bit back a grin.

"Oh, apologies. I'll try to remember to censor anything gory from conversation. I'd hate to offend their delicate ears." Calysta blinked at Rovin, a mischievous smile flickering across her face, before she gave her horse a final pat and pulled herself into the saddle.

Rovin's mouth opened and closed, unsure how to reply.

"Close your mouth, Ranger. You look like a fish." Merriam turned away.

The nymph smoothed the lengths of her petal pink hair over one shoulder, smiling with a small shrug.

Rovin's mouth snapped shut with an audible click, and his brows lowered into a glare. Whatever he had finally decided to say was interrupted by the princes walking into the courtyard and Eskar joining their group.

"Thank you for waiting. I had something come up last minute that needed attending. I appreciate your patience," Oren addressed Merriam and Calysta.

"It was no problem at all. Allowed Calysta just enough time to traumatize your lieutenant, Majesty." Humor sparkled in Merriam's eyes as she smiled brightly at Oren.

A smile twitched at the ends of his lips, and he met her gaze with a look that was both an order to behave and a challenge not to. After situating himself in the saddle, he turned to Eskar. "If we're ready?"

Eskar gathered the reins in her hands, giving Merriam a distrustful glance before dipping her head respectfully to Oren. "I'll scout ahead, you take the rear," she told Rovin before trotting off.

"Make sure you keep your eyes peeled. She's got a quick wrist and good aim." Calysta said to the Ranger, miming throwing an axe.

"Am I to understand that you're planning to kill me?" Oren asked as they followed Calysta through the castle gate.

"Not until after I get the rest of my payment, of course." Merriam smiled sweetly.

"I guess I'm not even worth the effort of assassination," Mollian grumbled, pulling up next to Merriam's other side as the path widened.

"If I'd known it would make you feel better, I would have had one of the others ask around to see if there's a price on your head. I'm sure I could get at least fifteen gold pieces, even for the younger prince," Merriam joked.

"If you know of an actual intention of assassination of one of the royal family, you should be reporting that information to the Guard," Rovin called.

Merriam looked back to see his face set in a deep scowl, jaw clenched in irritation. "Yes, Rovin. Because my first instinct when hearing someone wants to kill my best friend would be to ask what the payout would be."

"They'd probably end up—" Calysta started before glancing to Rovin and stopping herself. She adjusted her shoulders, sitting up straighter, and continued. "They'd probably end up weighing at least a head less than they started and very much un-alive. I would hate to have to be the one to try to get *those* stains out of her clothes." She widened her eyes, pressing her lips together and looking away at the prospect.

Rovin's mouth dropped open again, still completely taken aback by the creature ahead of him. He recovered more quickly this time, though. "I'm surprised you wouldn't just capture them and hold off on the slaughter until you told someone who would pay you for it."

"Oh, of course I would," Merriam scoffed. "A girl's gotta eat, Lieutenant."

Mollian tipped his head back, laughing freely.

Oren's lips twitched. *Don't cause trouble, Lady.* He forced his horse into a faster stride, pulling to the front of the group.

Merriam focused on the back of his head, mustering up as much sass as she could and weaving it into the thought. *He started it.*

Rovin hung back further for the rest of the day, though Merriam could occasionally feel the prickle of his glare against the back of her neck.

As the sun sunk below the mountains, they stopped for the night and set up camp.

"I'll take first watch," Merriam volunteered, piling bread, meat, and fruit onto a cloth to carry off into the woods.

"Mer," Oren got her attention, tossing her a skin of water.

She caught it in her free hand, shooting him a thankful smile and tucking it under her arm. Before she left the clearing, she looked at Eskar. "Wouldn't want you guys to starve after a long day of riding." She winked before taking a large bite of the bread.

Eskar's eyes narrowed, mouth pressed into a thin, angry line.

Tucking the corners of the cloth together, Merriam held the bundle in her teeth as she found a cottonwood close by, climbing into the boughs and settling down against the trunk. She propped one leg up on the branch in front of her and let the other dangle freely, eating her supper in content silence as she listened to the sounds of the forest around her and the idle chatter from the camp.

Resting her head against the rough bark, Merriam peered through the leaves at the moons, both waxing, their light casting a bright glow over everything. A cool wind filtered through the boughs, caressing her skin and bringing with it the smell of a campfire. She pulled her cloak closer around her, folding her arms against her chest to ward off the chill of the mountain air, and let her eyes wander the forest below, not really focusing on anything, but watching for movement.

The sounds from the camp died down, and a few hours later, she saw Rovin walk to her tree. Merriam used the trunk as leverage to stretch her back, turning first one way and then the other, before dropping down to the ground in front of the Ranger.

"It's pretty quiet tonight," Merriam offered, stepping past him.

"Surprised you could tell over the sound of your smacking and chewing," Rovin retorted.

"As much as I'm sure you struggle with it, Rovin, it is in fact possible to eat in a quiet, civilized manner," Merriam threw over her shoulder.

"I'm surprised to hear you can do anything in a civilized manner." He leaned against the cottonwood trunk and crossed his arms.

Merriam turned back around with a sigh. "Is it exhausting? Being such a fucking prick all the time? Honestly, you've had a stick up your ass since the day I met you. Maybe take it out and relax every once in a while. Fuck."

Rovin bristled, the tick of his jaw barely visible under his scruff. "I relax plenty, just not on duty. Thank you for your concern though, pet."

"Look where that's gotten you. Running security on another one of your jobs that was hired out to me," Merriam scoffed, turning on her heels and walking off. "Have a horrid night, Ranger."

Exhaustion tugged at her bones as she stepped into the circle of camp. The Rangers' tent was off to one side, Mollian and Oren's near the center. Calysta was sleeping to the side of their tent underneath a small cave of brambles she'd grown over herself. The nymph always slept beneath the sky unless the weather was extremely bad, and even then Jasper was barely able to coax her under a roof.

Merriam slipped into the brothers' tent, unlacing her boots and leaving them by the entrance before tugging the tie off of the end of her braid and quickly running her fingers through her hair. A window flap on one wall was hanging open, allowing in just enough moonlight for Merriam to see.

Mollian was already asleep, stretched out underneath the window with his white curls spilling messily over the side of his face, eyelashes brushing against his cheeks. When he was like this, Merriam could still see that eager eight-year-old boy who had befriended her in the forest and kept her afloat through a childhood that may have otherwise killed her. Out of habit, she walked over to him, ready to slip under the covers and huddle against his familiar warmth while sleep took her.

She caught movement out of the corner of her eye and turned to see Oren, propped up on his elbows and watching her.

His hair fell loose down one side of his face, tucked partially behind a pointed ear. Moonlight shone in the deep green of his eyes, and Merriam felt her chest tighten at the implication in them.

Without taking his gaze from her, Oren leaned over and pulled back one side of his blanket.

Merriam lifted her fingers to the aspen leaf at her throat, walking over and lowering herself down beside him.

Oren smiled softly, lying back down and rolling onto his side, one arm looping around her waist to pull her to him.

She yielded easily, fitting her back against his chest and tucking her legs against his. Pine and plum and night sky wrapped around her, calming every one of her senses while at the same time lighting them on fire.

Oren buried his face into her hair, his chest expanding as he breathed deeply. "Everything feels right when you're with me," he murmured, pressing a kiss to the back of her head. He lifted his hand from her waist, pushing his fingers into her hair and gently massaging her scalp, every once in a while trailing his fingers down through the lengths before repeating.

Merriam's eyes drifted closed from the soothing, repetitive touch. She meant to reply, but sleep was already dragging her down.

Chapter 14

A dangerous occupation

Five years before ...

"Oh look, the prince's little pet wants to play again." Rovin strapped a practice sword into his belt.

"Too bad nobody wants to catch fleas." Kodi snickered, knocking his shoulder into Rovin's.

"Wow. Can't you even come up with an insult that's applicable? Or have you been knocked in the head one too many times?" Merriam gave them a withering look and reached past to grab a gear belt.

"Yeah, Kodi, get it right. She can't have fleas; even they have better taste than that." Rovin pushed a hand through his chestnut hair. He rarely, if ever, tied it up, always hiding the clipped tip of one tapered ear.

Merriam wanted nothing more than to grab a handful of those stupid, thick tresses and slam his head into the table. But she kept her hands to herself, buckling the belt around her waist.

"Why even bother with the weapons, pet? Nobody is going to spar with you." Rovin picked imaginary lint off of his shirt, leaning against the wall.

"Maybe if one of you had the balls to actually fight me, we could learn a thing or two from each other." Merriam shot him a sickly sweet smile.

Captain Ferrick came into the hall then, and Merriam swallowed down a groan. Today would be a long one if he was here to train them.

"Five klicks, go. Then form up in the ring for drills," he barked, and immediately the Guard were in motion.

Merriam quickly grabbed a sword from the wall, shoving it into her belt as she fell into a run towards the courtyard door. Once she was outside, she felt her body relax, slipping into a familiar rhythm as her legs stretched out. Her strides were strong and confident along the familiar path through the trees.

The run went by quickly, her lungs barely laboring as she neared the training ring back in the courtyard. Just before she breached the tree-line, something caught her foot, and she went hurtling to the ground. The skin of her palms tore as they skidded across the dirt, and her knee barked painfully where it made impact. She rolled over onto her back, winded.

"Poor, clumsy human." Rovin laughed, twirling his sword in his hand before slipping it back into his belt.

Merriam glared at his back as he ran off, anger boiling in her veins as she pushed herself off of the ground and limped back into a jog. Her hands burned, but she wiped them off on her pants and grit her teeth.

When she made it to the ring, the Guard were already paired up. She let out a sigh and moved to her usual spot to the side, where at least she had a good vantage point of everything so she could mimic the techniques properly.

"Damn, looks like no partner again, Mer. Tough luck." Kodi shook his head in mock sympathy, bi-colored eyes glittering with amusement.

"Despite your very best efforts, I've been doing just fine on my own," Merriam shot back.

"Would you like to test that theory?" Rovin's lips lifted in a feral grin, hand resting on the hilt of his sword.

Merriam drew her weapon, fire burning in her amber eyes as she challenged, "Fuck around and find out."

Rovin's eyes narrowed, and he took a step forward.

"Merriam!" The call was not a command, yet it commanded the attention of everyone in the ring. The Rangers turned toward where the heir apparent stood just outside of the door to the training hall. Oren raised his hand before they could kneel, his bright green gaze trained on Merriam. "My brother has need of you, if you'd please come with me," he said before turning his attention to Ferrick. "Pardon my interruption, Captain."

Ferrick bowed his head. "Whatever you need, Your Highness."

Merriam stepped through the ring, head held high.

"Yes, run along, pet. Your master calls," Rovin taunted under his breath as she passed.

Her hand tightened around the hilt of her sword, and it took all of her control not to turn toward him and spit in his face.

Oren held the door open for her, motioning for her to go inside. As soon as the door shut, he said, "It's not worth it."

Merriam whirled around, ready to retort.

Oren held up his hands placatingly. "Before you rip my head off, just listen."

Merriam pressed her lips together and crossed her arms, sword still hanging from one hand.

"I'm not saying he's not worth the effort. You want to put him in his place, and honestly, I'd love to witness it. But you need to cool your temper. Don't challenge him when you're high on emotions. If you're going to fight him, do it when you can hand him his ass on a platter. But you don't need to take that shit from them. It's not worth it."

"I won't just sit around here uselessly. Despite what everyone thinks, I am not Mollian's pet." Merriam's eyes didn't waver from Oren's.

"That's not what I'm saying. I know you want to prove your worth, but you don't have to kill yourself to be a slave of the Crown."

Merriam cocked her head to the side, confused.

"Why do you want to be a Ranger, Merriam?"

"I'd be good at it," she answered with conviction. It's what she'd been pushing for the entire year she'd spent training with the Guard.

"You don't have to be a Ranger to use your skills. You can hone them in an environment that isn't doing its damnedest to tear you down at every turn. You're already tied to Mollian, but that doesn't mean you have to tie yourself to the Crown." Oren walked up to her and took the sword from her hand. "There are plenty of people who can teach you things the Rangers never would. There are options that don't keep you under Sekha's thumb, Mer. If you want to prove yourself useful outside of Mollian's opinion, do it in a manner where a prince's assertion would hold no weight."

Merriam dropped her arms. "How would I even know where to start?" Oren held her gaze for a moment, as if considering, and she fought from squirming under the weight of those intelligent, powerful eyes. "There's a local mercenary, Jasper. He'll help you, if you're interested."

"A mercenary?" Merriam asked doubtfully.

Oren shrugged, his dimple appearing as a smile pulled at his lips. "Not much different from a Ranger, if you think about it. Only one answers to royalty and the other answers to whomever they choose."

Merriam chewed the inside of her cheek, dropping Oren's gaze as she thought. "I really do have a choice, then. I can have autonomy."

"You're going to do amazing things, Merriam." Oren handed her the sword. "But do them for yourself." Just before he exited, he tossed over his shoulder, "I'll talk to Jasper."

Merriam stared at his back as he left, not entirely sure of what had just happened. She hung the sword back in its place and removed the belt from her waist, dropping it into a basket under the training weapons.

She plodded through the castle, casting out for a sense of Mollian. When her head ached and the tattoo between her shoulder blades started to sting, she gave up and headed to their rooms.

Merriam stood at a window, staring past her faint reflection and contemplating Oren's words. Her eyes traveled to the rugged stone siding of the castle wall, and she pulled her lower lip into her mouth, tilting her head. She unlatched the window and pushed it open, leaning out slightly over the drop. Scaling a wall couldn't be that much more difficult than climbing a tree. She gripped the sill with one hand and hissed, pulling away.

Her palms were shredded from her earlier fall, and she frowned at them. "Well, that's not going to work."

"What's not going to work?" Mollian asked as the door clicked shut behind him.

Merriam jumped, turning to face him. "My hands are all beat up." She held her palms out to him.

"You must've been pretty deep in thought if you didn't hear me come in," Mollian said, taking her hands. His demeanor darkened when he looked at them. "What happened?" He raised his eyes to hers.

Merriam pulled her hands back. "I just tripped, Molli."

He narrowed his eyes. *Since when do you trip?*

"It happens to the best of us." Merriam gave him a pointed look. *Drop it.*

Mollian sighed, pursing his lips. He didn't need to Cast his thoughts for Merriam to know that he wanted to pommel Rovin.

"I'm done with Ranger training," she decided.

"Because of them? Ria–"

"No, not because of them," she interrupted. "Not really. Oren–"

"Oren talked to you? What did he say? Just because he's the crown prince doesn't mean–"

"Molli. Stop." Merriam grabbed his arms, laughing in mild exasperation. "Listen to me for a second before you jump out of your skin."

Mollian pressed his lips together pointedly, dipping his head for her to continue.

"Oren told me I could have other options. He said I could make a name for myself outside of all of this." She waved her hands, vaguely indicating the castle. "I have real potential to be something great, Molli. But the Rangers are never going to allow me to grow. It would be an uphill battle at every turn. Your brother just ... helped me see I don't need them. I can be better without them. He gave me the name of someone who might help. Jasper."

"Jasper? Wait, are you saying you're going to become a mercenary?" Mollian raised an eyebrow.

Merriam shrugged. "I might as well try it out."

"That's a dangerous occupation, Ria. I won't be able to protect you."

She scoffed, pinning him with a look. "That's kind of the point. I'll never prove my own merit if everything I do is connected to you."

Mollian frowned, brushing a curl back to expose the tattoo on his temple. "You have a point. And he's right, you know. Bastard usually is. Jasper is an old friend of his."

It was Merriam's turn to frown, shaking her head. "What's the point of leaving the shadow of one prince only to step into the longer shadow of another?"

"One, don't get so philosophical on me. It's weird. Two, Oren's association may be able to get you a meeting with Jasper, but he won't take you in unless you can prove your own merit. Don't have any misconceptions about that."

"Call me cocky, but I don't think I'll have a problem there." Merriam's eyes gleamed with confidence.

"I will call you cocky, though you're not wrong." Mollian smiled. "My *mehhen*, a mercenary. Are you really going to make me pay for your services?"

"You'll get the family and friends discount." Merriam poked him in the ribs.

Chapter 15

A snack

MERRIAM'S EYES FLUTTERED OPEN. She couldn't remember ever having slept so deeply while on the ground. Oren's arm was draped heavily over her waist, and she grabbed his hand, cuddling it to her chest as she snuggled deeper into his sleeping warmth.

Almost as soon as she moved, she felt the stiff resistance of his cock pressed against her backside. She stilled, but not before he tightened his arms around her, grinding his hips against her once as a low noise of satisfaction rolled through his chest. He pulled his hand free, smoothing her hair back from her cheek and running his nose over the shell of her ear, making her shiver. "Waking up like this could easily become my favorite thing," he whispered, his voice gruff with sleep.

Merriam turned her head to look at him, the slight stubble along his chin scratching her cheek. "Waking up on the ground?" Merriam clarified in a soft voice.

Oren nipped at her, anchoring his hand back at her waist. "Yes, Lady. My one wish is to never have to sleep in a bed again." He raised himself on an elbow, trailing his lips down her neck.

Merriam stiffened. "Molli~"

"Left several minutes ago," Oren murmured, brushing his thumb just underneath her ribcage.

Merriam's stomach flipped, and her head rolled back into Oren as she bit her lip. "Oren."

"Mmm?" He pulled the collar of her shirt over, pressing a kiss to her collarbone.

"We are in a tent." Merriam lifted a hand up, fingers splaying over the back of his head. She was acutely aware that every inch of their bodies were pressed together.

"Very observant of you." Oren snaked his hand under the bunched up fabric of her shirt, pressing his palm to her stomach and working it slowly up her body.

"If you don't stop, I'm going to scream." Merriam tightened her fingers around his hair and pulled.

Oren chuckled against her neck. "Wrong threat, Merri."

Merriam let out a frustrated noise, kicking him lightly in the shin. She hated how much her body wanted this to happen. Right now. In the middle of a damn camp.

Oren removed his hand from her ribs, rolling her over onto her back and dropping a kiss to her lips before pulling away with a wolfish grin. "Until later, then." He stood up, grabbing a shirt to pull over his head before leaving the tent.

Merriam sat up, pushing her hands into her hair and stretching. She quickly pulled her hair into a tight spiral at the top of her head and secured it before shoving on her boots and following.

"Good morning." Mollian smiled knowingly from across the clearing, picking apart a roll and popping the pieces into his mouth. It was all Merriam could do not to stick her tongue out at him.

Calysta sat next to him, hand propped on a chin and looking like she wanted nothing more than to crawl back into her bushes and sleep.

Merriam laughed, walking up to her and pulling a dried leaf from pink strands that were otherwise smooth and neat. "You have nature in your hair."

Calysta frowned, running her fingers through the lengths. "That'll happen I guess." She sighed, biting into an apple core.

"If we head out within an hour, we should make it to Entumbra just after nightfall," Eskar said as she came into the clearing, presumably having just finished her watch.

Rovin tossed her an apple, moving to start tearing down their tent.

Merriam sighed, still clearing the sleep from her mind and body. She sat down next to Mollian, taking the bread from his hand. "I think it's only fair you tear down the tent since you got to sleep all night." She gracelessly shoved the food in her mouth.

Mollian snorted. "Isn't pulling watch partially what you're being paid for?"

"Fair point, Prince. But I'll raise that you've got magic. I'm all muscle," Meriam said with a shrug, talking around the food.

"If you're trying to play the part of helpless lady, maybe don't refer to yourself as muscle while speaking with a mouth full of food."

"I'll keep that in mind next time." Merriam grinned, catching Rovin's annoyed shake of the head from the corner of her eye.

After they'd finished tearing down the camp, they set off, Merriam munching on an apple as the horses walked. The trail through the mountains grew gradually narrower until they had to travel single file. The sun had just dipped below the mountains as they rounded a curve, and Merriam saw a tall metal spire poking up through the trees a ways ahead.

She steadied her breathing, closing her eyes and focusing on the air caressing her skin as she moved through it.

There, barely perceptible, she could feel the familiar hum, and it echoed in her blood. As they continued closer, the tattoo between her shoulder blades lit with a slight tingle. She shivered, brushing off the feeling and focusing on the rhythmic clopping of horse hooves on the mountainside.

Merriam had never been to Entumbra prior to being Bonded, so she'd always been able to feel the way the air seemed to vibrate with the strange power of the stone gateway below the mountain. She was able to easily ignore the feeling, even forget that it was there, but it was an ever-present current running through her body.

The path soon widened, spitting them out just before the base of a castle built from rough stone and wrought iron. It was wide at the base, narrowing towards the top. A large dome was at one end, with a bridge connecting to a taller stone tower, ending in a narrow spire.

The base of the castle was solid rock, and a steep, narrow staircase leading to the second story was the only entrance. Merriam slid down from her horse, tilting her head back to take in the ominous-looking structure.

One of the stable hands, a young human boy, came out to collect their horses, and Oren thanked him before leading the way up the steps.

They entered an atrium, sunlight streaming through stained glass windows that depicted Keepers walking through various worlds. "Gressia!" Oren called. He'd already reached out to her with his mind and knew she was aware of their arrival.

A door to the left creaked open, and a beautiful fae waltzed into the room. Loose white curls spilled around her shoulders, the top braided back from her face. Her forehead was free of the aspen tattoo the rest of her family shared. Her duty was to the Gate, not Sekha. Pale green eyes narrowed pleasantly as she smiled. "Little brother!" she crooned, throwing her arms around Oren's neck and kissing his cheek. "I didn't expect to see you back so soon." She stepped back, catching sight of Mollian. "And the third!" She brought her hands to her cheeks before pulling Mollian to her and repeating the greeting. "It has been far too long, brother."

Mollian laughed a bit uncomfortably, brushing his curls back. "It's nice to see you again, Gressia."

She turned her eyes to Merriam, something unidentifiable flickering briefly behind her cheer. "And of course, you wouldn't be far, Merriam." Gressia smiled sweetly, grabbing Merriam's arms and planting a kiss on her cheek.

Merriam shoved back against the irritation that crawled through her chest at the Keeper's words.

"I suppose I have you to thank for getting dear Mollian to finally come for a visit." Gressia dropped her hands.

"In a way." Mollian scratched the back of his head. Awkward tension rolled from him in waves, but Gressia ignored it.

Merriam caught his eyes, giving him a sympathetic glance before turning back to Gressia. "Unfortunately, we're here on rather unpleasant business."

"Of course you are." Gressia sighed regrettably. "I've been in contact with our mother, but let's discuss things over supper." She headed across the room without even acknowledging the rest of the party, expecting them to follow.

Merriam bit back a smile at the clearly uncomfortable expression on Rovin's face as they walked down wrought iron stairs to the level below. A long, wooden table was being set by humans, just teenagers, by the look of them. They left a platter of meat, roasted vegetables, and thin rounds of bread before disappearing back into the kitchen.

"So, the business that brings you to my domain," Gressia prompted, scooping food onto a plate and using a fork to daintily place a chunk of beef into her mouth.

"There's some sort of demon loose in Jekeida, Gress," Oren said plainly.

Gressia looked at him evenly. "As I've told Regenya, that's not possible."

"I'm not saying you let it out. I'm just reiterating what's going on. We need to figure out what we might be dealing with, and we need to figure out how it got here in the first place."

Gressia blinked, squaring her shoulders as she took another measured bite of food. "You may be about to take over rule of Sekha, little brother, but Entumbra is *my* realm. If something were happening here, I would know it."

Oren wiped his hand over his mouth in frustration. "I'm not saying you wouldn't. I'm here to work *with* you, Gressia. We want your help."

She dropped her eyes to her food, shifting in her seat with prim posture. "Okay, we can do some digging tomorrow. You brought reports detailing everything?"

"Of course," Oren replied, shoulders dropping into a more relaxed posture.

They ate in silence for a while, Gressia eventually setting her fork down by her plate and turning to Oren. "I'll have your old room prepared. Mollian can stay across from you with his ... human." The corner of her lip twitched like she was trying not to smile at a joke. Her gaze washed briefly over the Rangers and Calysta. "The Ranger will need to sleep in the rooms above the stables, along with the halfling and the nymph." She added before standing up and leaving.

Rovin bristled openly, but Eskar placed a hand on his arm, shooting him a sharp look. "She can't just fucking say that and then walk away," he growled, fingers clenched into a fist.

Oren sighed, running a hand over his hair down to the nape of his neck. "I'm sorry about her, Rovin. Don't take it to heart. She's just annoyed that I'm back in her space, and she's taking it out on anyone she can. Regardless, she has no right to talk to you that way. I'll speak with her."

Rovin's jaw ticked, but he nodded, pushing up from the table. "If you're all right here, Your Highness, I think I'll go see to our sleeping situation."

"I'll be fine, thank you. Keep your eyes peeled out there," Oren dismissed him.

Eskar quickly finished her food, then left to follow him.

"Well, that was quite the reunion," Calysta piped up from her spot next to Oren. "I don't understand why you were always so excited to stop by." She gave Merriam a strange look.

"I wasn't." Merriam brought a cup of water to her lips, glaring over the rim at Calysta.

"You were excited to stop by?" Oren asked, folding his arms on the table and leaning forward, amusement dancing in his eyes.

"Oh, yes! Every single time a job would take us by this route, she'd say we should stop for a hot meal or quick read in the library," Calysta offered.

"You enjoy the food here that much, huh?" Oren raised an eyebrow, smiling as he lifted his own cup for a drink.

"Having access to food from other dimensions is a novelty, obviously." Merriam looked intently at the cubes of beef still on her plate.

"That's definitely logical." Mollian grinned.

"No, you never really seemed to rave about the food that much, though." Calysta rested her elbow on the table, propping her chin in her hands. "I always thought you just felt at home with the company, but now I'm seriously questioning your sanity."

"How many times did you visit over the last five years, Ria?" Mollian asked.

"It wasn't that much," Merriam mumbled at the same time Oren spoke.

"It must've been at least two or three times a year after your first year or so with Jasper."

"You never told me you were here that much."

"You didn't ask." Merriam glowered at Mollian.

"Is it something about the food I'm missing?" Calysta asked.

"Yes, Mer, please explain why you insisted on stopping in." Oren smiled.

Merriam shook her head in exasperation. "I don't understand why I'm being interrogated right now," she huffed. "And your head is starting to look a little inflated there, Majesty," she said pointedly to Oren.

Calysta's eyes moved from Merriam to Oren and back, sparkling as a grin spread across her face.

"No." Merriam shook her head. "Calysta, no."

Calysta's tongue peeked from between pointed teeth, and she turned her head to look at Oren. "Would you consider yourself a snack, Prince?" she purred. "Because that would certainly explain Mer's insistence on stopping in for a hot meal."

Oren tossed his head back and laughed, deep from his belly. The sound of it did strange things to Merriam's insides, and if she hadn't been blushing before, she knew she was bright red now.

Having composed himself, the heir apparent ran his thumb across his lower lip as he looked across the table at Merriam, his silence speaking volumes.

"You're all horrible." She grumbled to her plate.

"What did I do?" Mollian asked defensively.

"Don't act like you weren't just encouraging this." Merriam poked him in the side.

Calysta giggled. "This is the most delightful revelation. Though it will make evenings out less interesting," she sighed.

"Less interesting?" Oren asked, raising an eyebrow.

"Calysta—"

"Mer and Aleah and I usually play a game with the locals when we're out of Umbra." She grinned. "Nothing sinister—usually. But it is very entertaining to watch."

Oren's eyes flicked back to Merriam, the light in them dancing with humor and enjoyment at her obvious embarrassment. "What sort of game is this?"

"It's not even a game. More of a competition really, based around free drinks and invitations—*declined* invitations—home. Jasper plays, too, sometimes."

Calysta laughed. "He always wins when he does, the bastard."

Declined invitations? Oren's voice rumbled through her mind, dripping in a suggestive tone that filled her and made her curl her toes in her boots.

She carefully formed the words, eyes locked to Oren's as she Cast the thought to him. *Mostly. I don't make a habit of mixing business with pleasure.* She realized with a jolt that it didn't take quite so much concentration here. As if being by the Gate fed the Keeper blood in her veins. Her tattoo barely even itched.

Is that a fact?

Yes.

We'll see. Oren's eyes narrowed on hers, promising something far too primal for her to give name to while she sat with her friends. Her mouth went dry, and she broke eye contact, licking her lips and drinking more water. "As fun as this game of mild humiliation has been, it's getting late, and we have work to do tomorrow." She pushed up from the table.

After excusing herself, she went up to Mollian's room, taking a quick shower to wash the day's travel from her skin before falling into bed. She was asleep before Mollian even came up from supper.

Chapter 16

The Legend of Orym

BREAKFAST THE NEXT MORNING was a quiet, moderately more comfortable affair.

"Mollian and I will probably be down with the Gate for most of the day," Oren said, wiping his mouth and draining the last of the juice from his glass.

"And I'll be sequestered away in the library." Merriam sighed before glancing to Calysta. "Would you be able to help me browse for a bit today?"

"Yes, the ones I need to talk to around here won't be out until after dark anyway," she agreed.

"Have fun," Mollian said before he and Oren left.

Merriam led Calysta back up to the main floor, into a doorway that opened to a narrow spiral staircase, stone giving way to iron. The nymph made a face, avoiding any unnecessary contact with her skin.

While the magic in Keeper blood wasn't tampered by iron, nymph blood didn't contain the mineral and thus their magic was highly susceptible to its effects. Though iron still acted as a suppressant to magic of the mind, it had to be in direct contact with a fae's skin. Otherwise, the proximity was just an uncomfortable but manageable pressure.

"So you and the prince, then?" Calysta asked, a smile playing over her lips.

Merriam bit the inside of her cheek, shrugging. "Maybe."

"Is he good?"

Merriam looked back at the nymph with an impish grin. "Oh," was all she said before continuing up the stairs.

"Oh," Calysta repeated suggestively, "that's enticing."

Merriam opened the door at the next landing, moving directly into the library. "He has a thing for hair."

"Do tell." Calysta grinned, black eyes glimmering.

"He's just always touching it. Running his fingers through it. Pulling it. And fuck if I don't just lose all ability of rational thought when he does. I think he knows it, too, and uses it to control me. I'm sure of it." Merriam shook her head, eyes scanning the shelves for anything that looked promising.

Calysta's musical laugh filtered through the room. "If only we'd learned it was that easy years ago."

Merriam stuck her tongue out, pulling a book from the shelf and handing it to Calysta. "Do you know what you're looking for?"

"Demon things, I'd assume," Calysta answered, taking the book to a table and sinking gracefully into a seat.

Merriam pulled another down and joined her, opening the book in her lap and propping her booted feet on the table, crossed at the ankles. "Like you said, there are countless worlds with countless demons. We need to cross-reference the information we have with the information the Keepers have gathered from other worlds."

They spent the rest of the day in relative silence, speaking up when they found something interesting and jotting it down. Rovin and Eskar eventually joined them, but kept to an opposite corner of the library. One of the human servants brought them lunch, warning them in the human tongue not to spill anything on the books. Merriam replied in the language that now felt foreign to her that they would be extra careful.

As the sun dipped below the trees, Merriam turned on the soft overhead lighting, just about ready to call it a night.

Eskar let out a sigh, setting down the book she was reading and standing. "This has been entirely tiresome and unhelpful."

As much as it irritated her, Merriam couldn't help but agree.

"We should run some drills before supper, Rovin. Today has been too sedentary." Eskar started walking to the door before waiting for the younger Ranger's reply, but he stood and followed, shutting the door behind him softly.

Calysta was deep into a book of Keeper history, twirling a lock of hair around an olive green finger absentmindedly. "Did you know that Keepers were given their blood magic from nymphs?" she asked, running a claw down the page.

"Well now, that is interesting." Merriam dropped her feet from where they were propped on the table, leaning forward.

"Way back when, the Gate was completely unprotected. But Orym Stonebane, the first Keeper, built this place. Tried his best to keep things from other worlds from getting through. That's why there's so much iron, to keep try to help contain the magic that flows from the Gate. Anyway, different nymph clans from all over Nethyl heard of his bravery and each sent one delegate here. They carved out pieces of the gate, ground the stone into a powder, and each gave some of their blood. Their blood magic mixed with the magic of the Gate, and they gave it to Orym. They cycled it through him until it mixed with his, giving him the power to seal the Gate and control it. He was one of the first high fae to ever have blood magic, and it came from nymphs."

"Keeper magic comes from nymphs," Merriam repeated, running her tongue over her bottom lip in thought.

"It would seem so." Calysta folded her arms on the table.

Merriam slid the aspen charm across the chain on her neck, her mind combing through the events of the past month. "Could a human take blood magic from a nymph in the same way? Like the guy who hired those traffickers?"

"I've never heard of anything like it." Calysta frowned.

"Molli told me that blood magic can only be given consensually. At least, that's the way it works with Bonding."

"Magic is ... complex. It is, in a way, its own living thing." Calysta agreed. "It doesn't like to separate and multiply, so if the one it belongs to is trying to hold on to it, it won't leave them easily."

"Do you think ... would it have been possible that this guy could have been trying to mix his blood the way Orym's had been? Maybe it somehow accidentally opened a rift that let a demon through."

"It's possible he could have been trying to give himself magic, but whether or not it ever would have worked is another question completely." Calysta dropped her chin into a hand, tapping her dainty claws against her cheek. "I'll see what I can find out tonight from those that dwell in the forest before we send anything back to the others."

Merriam nodded in agreement, and they carefully put away all the books they'd strewn about throughout the day.

"Do you guys know the Legend of Orym?" Merriam asked the princes as they sat down for supper that night.

Oren raised an eyebrow, scooping a concoction of rice, meat, and vegetables into a bowl. "Of course we know of the first Keeper."

"His magic was given to him by nymphs. I had never heard that part before."

"While the Legend of Orym is known across Nethyl, especially in Sekha, parts of the story have changed throughout history. The direct origin of Orym's magic has been left out of the common folklore, specifically to hinder someone thinking they can round up a bunch of nymphs and turn themselves into a Keeper," Oren explained. "Different renditions are told in different territories and countries, of course, but it's a detail that largely remains unknown."

"What if the man who hired the traffickers had heard about it and tried to do the same thing?"

Mollian's brow furrowed. "Even if he tried and somehow succeeded in getting the nymph blood to combine with his, he'd still need the stones."

"Are they located anywhere else?"

Mollian glanced at Oren before nodding slowly. "There are small veins of umbrite and orydite located across Nethyl, but nowhere near each other. They're on opposite poles of the planet, with the exception of Entumbra. It's highly unlikely someone would know to seek them out and bring them together. That kind of expedition would take years."

Merriam ate quietly for a moment, mulling it over. "Well, a demon got here somehow. Maybe the rift that let it in was a fluke, maybe it was opened purposefully ... what about the humans that work here? They'd have access to the Gate."

"Technically, yes, but none of them would ever venture down there.

The density of magic in the air, especially the further down you go, is far too unsettling for them. The lack of magic in them and the heavy concentration of magic in the Gate acts as a natural deterrent," Oren said with a shake of his head.

"Not to mention none of these workers speak Common. There aren't fae villages for quite a while. The humans here have been kept separated through the years on purpose so that they could act as attendants here without worry of them perusing the library and selling our secrets," Mollian pointed out.

Merriam narrowed her eyes in thought. "There are just so many variables here. There's got to be a way to rule at least some of them out for good."

"You're right," Oren agreed. "I'll take a closer look at the duty logs tomorrow. The rotation keeps anyone from having too much constant access here, but we'll double check that nothing was missed and ask around after supper to see if anyone has noticed anything suspicious."

Eskar and Rovin came in then, sitting at the table and serving themselves.

"I'm going to head out for the night." Calysta stood.

"I'll walk you out," Merriam offered, following suit. "Keep me posted?" She gave Oren a parting glance.

"Of course," he replied with a nod.

Rovin looked between them, a mix of curiosity and suspicion sparking in his eyes, but Mollian started up a conversation, pulling the Ranger's attention away.

Merriam walked with Calysta out onto the iron catwalk that surrounded the castle, a soft wind buffeting her skin. "I hope your night is productive."

"I hope you enjoy your prince." Calysta grinned, olive green skin almost glowing in the moonlight. She headed down the stone steps and disappeared into the forest.

Merriam stayed out on the catwalk, watching the trees and enjoying the night air.

"It's always so peaceful out here." Gressia came up to stand beside her, arms crossed daintily over her chest. The wind blew the curls back from her face as she looked up to the moon.

"It is. I've always loved it here," Merriam murmured.

Gressia laughed quietly. "Most humans think differently. Even the staff tend to be uncomfortable with the feel of the place."

"The Gate is responsible for the magic in your blood," Merriam stated. "That means it's also in Molli's blood. Maybe that's why it doesn't bother me so much. This place feels like Molli. Molli feels like home."

Gressia turned her head to look at Merriam, her green eyes—so similar to Mollian's—regarding her thoughtfully. "You know, I do like you, Merriam. I have from the beginning, which is not usually the case." She took a few steps back, leaning against the rough stone of the castle wall. "I know I can come across as harsh, but I've been on my own here for such a long time. Social norms just ..." She wrinkled her nose, gesturing vaguely. "This is my own little kingdom, and I'm protective of it," she finished.

Merriam turned around, leaning on her elbows against the railing as she faced the fae. "I never meant to impose, all those other times."

Gressia waved her words away. "Trust me, I was happy for my brother to have someone else to talk to. It was hard sharing my space with him for five whole years."

"At least Oren is the calm one." Merriam smiled.

Gressia's eyes widened. "Oh, can you even imagine if Mollian had to be stuck here for so long? I love him, but I would go mad."

Merriam laughed, then frowned. "He would hate it. So much."

"He's lucky he doesn't have a designated role." Gressia sighed, rubbing her arms and looking out across the forest. "I love it here. Couldn't imagine doing anything else with my life, even though I know a part of that is how much of the Gate's power is in my blood. But Mollian ... he's different. The burden of purpose would have weighed him down too heavily. Stunted him." Her eyes turned back to Merriam. "It makes sense to me that if any of us were destined to have a *mehhen*, it would be him. You help settle him. He's lucky he has you."

"I'm the lucky one," she replied softly.

Gressia pulled a napkin from her pocket, unwrapping it to reveal two candied apricots. "Would you like a treat?" she asked with a smile, holding one out to Merriam.

"One of yours?" The mercenary raised her brow. "I didn't think you shared."

Gressia shrugged. "You seem stressed, and I happen to have an extra." While the mere proximity of iron didn't stifle fae magic, living around so much of it with hardly any reprieve did have effects on the Keeper.

The weight of iron in the air constantly pressed down on her, often manifesting in headaches. Gressia self-medicated with psychoactive plants to ward them off. Cannabis was her go-to, which she preferred to eat rather than smoke.

Though she functioned quite normally, aside from her few personality quirks, Gressia was very rarely sober.

"Thank you." Merriam took the fruit.

Gressia popped hers into her mouth, eyes sparkling.

Merriam followed suit. A strange musky flavor hit her tongue as she chewed, but it was well hidden by the tang of the fruit and the sugary coating. "So what's the deal with you and the Rangers?" Merriam asked.

A grin played across Gressia's lips, and she shrugged. "They're self-righteous assholes from my experience. I like to keep them humble when I can."

Merriam laughed at that, covering her mouth with her hand. "You're not wrong in that judgment."

"Oren already gave me shit about it, but honestly, he can't do anything more than scold me." She tossed her curls over her shoulder. "You'll all be gone soon, and his Rangers will be perfectly fine."

Merriam's mouth tugged thoughtfully to the side. "His Rangers. It's weird to think of them that way."

"He's going to be king soon, little human."

"I know, it's just weird to think that they all answer to him, especially because they ..." she trailed off, unsure of how to finish the sentence.

"They don't like you."

Merriam shook her head, bemused. "I don't even know what it is I did."

"You existed, and you had instantaneous status."

Merriam snorted. "That is decidedly not true. The only status I had was as Mollian's pet."

"Ah, but a well-cared for pet who didn't have to work for any of what she had." Gressia tipped her head.

"That's not fair. I didn't ask for any of it, and I wanted to earn my keep. I *have* earned my keep," Merriam defended.

"You didn't ask for it, but it was still given to you. You were still more important to Mollian than any of them ever will be."

"Mollian won't be king, though."

"No, but he and Oren are close. Mollian will always have a sway over his opinion. By being favored by Mollian, you are subsequently favored by Oren."

Merriam scowled, uncomfortable with the statement. "That still seems like a stupid reason to hate someone."

"Have you ever thought about it from their perspective?" Gressia laughed. "For one thing, you got to train with the Guard on your own whim with no testing when they all fought hard to even be considered. Some almost killed themselves for the chance to join the ranks of those that serve the Crown. It is a position of honor. And that's with high fae. Lesser fae have even more of a challenge depending on what animal characteristic they possess and how useful it is. And do you know how many halflings are in the Guard?"

Merriam shook her head.

"The smallest fraction. They weren't even allowed to join until my great-grandfather's rule. Due to their human blood and inability to wield magic, they have to work even harder to earn their place."

Merriam pulled her braid over her shoulder, fidgeting with her hair to distract from the uncomfortable nature of the conversation. She'd learned years ago that the half-fae had suffered great discrimination in years past. It used to be common practice to clip the ears of half-fae children once they were found to have no magic to create a visual distinction between them and the high fae. It wasn't until the rule of Regenya's father that the practice was outlawed. But it was harder to enforce things in the outer territories, and there were plenty of bigots that thought they could still get away with the act.

"A human?" Gressia continued, running her fingers through her hair. "Humans, weak and brittle as they are—no offense—are almost never accepted into the training program. But you ... you got instant access. On top of that, you just fell into your own room in the castle at Umbra. You had your own bed, your own bath, a full wardrobe, and the finest foods the realm has to offer. All for no reason except that the younger prince loves you. Surely you can understand how that would breed animosity for those that have shed their blood, sweat, and tears for far, far less."

Merriam bit her lip, turning her gaze to her feet. "But I've worked for what I have now. I made my own name."

"Sure," Gressia shrugged, "but are you still going to say that your ability to train with the Guard and the suite of rooms you share with my brother are not privileged? The skills you've mastered to prove your merit don't change the fact that you were given these things without them."

Merriam turned to peer out over the moonlit forest, considering the Keeper's words. "Why would Molli never explain this, though?" She knew she sounded petulant, but she couldn't stop the response from spilling from her lips.

"It's a matter of perspective," Gressia laughed. "How is he supposed to see how his love for you has caused others to dislike you?"

Merriam frowned, but didn't reply.

They were both quiet for a while until a thought pricked at Merriam's mind. "Is Basta still around?" she asked, remembering the human who had been helping out around the castle for most of her visits.

"Oh, he's here and there. Business takes him everywhere lately," Gressia said. "It's unfortunate, really. His is the only presence I actually tolerate for extended periods."

"And a human one at that," Merriam couldn't help but add, casting a glance over her shoulder.

Gressia met her gaze with a wicked smirk. "Merriam, little love, when you find a person who can make your body sing on command, it won't matter what they are. That is a power unmatched."

Merriam smiled, turning forward and biting her lip.

"Oh, you're aware," Gressia said with understanding. "I know it's not dear Mollian feeding your pleasures. But would it happen to be someone else I might know?"

"Do you know many people?" Merriam asked dryly, leaning hard on her elbows. Her head was starting to feel very heavy. At the same time, her body felt weightless. She could hear Gressia chuckle in the background, but her mind was floating off.

Unbidden, a memory of her father flooded her mind. She'd been twelve, and out wandering the forest when he'd gotten home from a trip. When she'd returned, the tension in the house was so thick she almost couldn't breathe. Her stomach had instantly filled with lead when she saw her mother sitting on the couch, hunched over, hands clasped between her knees.

"Oh, Merriam," she murmured, her eyes coming up to meet her daughter's. They were glassy, shaking.

Her father turned around. "Where have you been?" His voice was low and cold.

"Hi, Daddy." She swallowed, taking a few careful steps into the room.

"I was out playing in the woods."

His hand shot out, fisting in her shirt and shoving her against the wall. "Your mother was worried sick."

"I told her." Merriam grabbed at his hand, eyes wide.

"Then why was she driven to *drink*, Merriam?" He lowered his face to hers.

"Momma," Merriam whimpered, trying to peer around him to the practically catatonic woman on the couch.

"You're talking to me right now, little bitch." He slammed her into the wall again, and she bit her tongue painfully when her head smacked against the drywall.

Merriam cried out, holding the back of her head.

"Stop, she didn't—"

"Oh, you really want to get in the middle of this right now?" Her father dropped her to turn to her mother, and she sank to the floor, tucking her knees to her chest and covering her head with her arms as he turned aggressively toward her mother.

"Little human, are you well?" A hand reached out and shook her, chasing the memory from her mind like water spilling from a glass.

Merriam turned her eyes to the light brown fingers on her shoulder, trailing down the arm up to the face of the fae behind her. She giggled. "I just got lost in the most random memory." Gressia smiled, and Merriam giggled again, her teeth chattering slightly. "Gress ... your eyes." Her pupils were blown wide, only a thin green ring outlining them.

"No, yours," Gressia laughed musically.

Merriam brought a hand to her face. "Gressia ..." She trailed her fingers slowly down her cheek. "What did you give me?" Panic started to crawl over her as she struggled to center her train of thought. This was unlike any high she'd ever experienced.

Gressia laughed again, taking Merriam's hands and clasping them in hers. "Just a special treat. Have fun, little love." She winked before turning away.

"Gressia, wait!" Merriam called, but stopped after one step, watching the fleeing back of the female. Gressia's long white curls swayed as she moved, leaking a color reminiscent of moonlight in her wake. Merriam stumbled forward to the castle wall, laying a hand against it to steady herself.

Chapter 17

Two moons

HER EYES WIDENED AS she watched the stone swirl with an intricate pattern of whirls and dots. Slowly, she sank down onto the iron grate, breathing softly to try to collect her thoughts and let the panic slide away. "It's fine. You're fine," she whispered to herself, slowly moving her gaze down the stone wall.

The ground seemed to dance far below the grate, dipping down and then slowly rolling back up. She poked her fingers through the holes of the catwalk, wondering if she might be able to touch it. Her mind sank out of focus again, and she was back on Earth, sitting in her room.

Her father was home again, and the sound of shattering glass filled the house. "Why do you do this, Amanda?!" he shouted. "You can't even fucking stand right now. Do you think Merriam deserves this? Do you think I deserve this?!"

She blinked, and she was lying on her back, staring up at the stars.

The grate bit into her skin, cool and slightly painful. She shifted against the sensation. Abruptly, she sat up, pulling her hair free and running her fingers through it to smooth it out. The waves cascaded over her shoulders and down her front, tickling the skin of her arms as it blew in the wind.

Her eyes focused on the tall spire sprouting up from the side of the castle, and she imagined herself up there, wrapped in the starry night sky. "Oren smells like the night sky," she stated, standing to her feet and walking around the catwalk, slipping into the tower from a side entrance.

When the door closed behind her, Merriam shivered, the still air in the corridor making her hair stand on end. The moonlight shone just bright enough through the window for her to see the steps in front of her. Another giggle bubbled up through her as she grabbed the railing, the cool iron biting into her skin. "Nope, don't like that." She pulled her hand away, running it across the rough stone instead.

Slowly, she climbed, eyes wide and marveling as she took in the patterns and colors swirling in the stone around her. Her hair kept brushing against her elbows, and she stopped, mesmerized at the way the light shone on the long strands. She sat down abruptly on a step, passing her hair through her fingers and reveling in its softness.

It was so long now, brushing the base of her spine when it was down, and she hummed quietly to herself, mind slipping back to when she'd cut it short all those years ago.

"Fuck, Merriam, what did you do?!" Her mother stood in the doorway to the bathroom, hands poised over her mouth and eyes wide with horror as she surveyed the mass of fine blonde hair that littered the bathroom floor. "*What did you do?!*"

Merriam met her mother's eyes in the bathroom mirror, worrying her bottom lip between her teeth and still holding the scissors in hand. "I was tired of it being in the way all the time."

"Fuckfuckfuckfuckfuck." Her mother fell to her knees, scooping up the hair as if she might be able to find a way to reattach it to Merriam's head.

"Mama, it's okay." Merriam set the scissors on the counter.

"Nonono."

"I'm going to clean it up. There won't be a mess." Merriam's brows knit together, a knot of apprehension building in her gut.

"Oh, Merriam ..." She stared at the hair in her hands, eyes welling with tears. "Merriam, I can't. I'm so sorry." She sobbed, shaking her head and dropping the hair before standing up and walking from the bathroom.

Merriam soon heard the sound of a cabinet opening, the cap of a bottle of liquor being tossed to the counter.

Cold fear settled in her bones, and she quickly swept up the evidence of her haircut, depositing it in the bathroom trash. Her mother didn't speak to her the rest of the day, just sat on the couch, smoking joint after joint and curing her cottonmouth with tequila.

Merriam licked her lips, dropping the hair in her hands and flexing her fingers. She looked around in dazed confusion before remembering the spire with a delighted giggle. Bracing her hands on the step above her, she pushed herself to her feet and resumed her climb.

The stairs ended in a trapdoor in the ceiling, and she ran her fingers over the warm wood before tossing it open. It raised with less resistance than she'd expected, slamming loudly onto the floor on the other side. Merriam jumped at the noise, almost losing her footing, and laughed, covering her mouth with her hands as she moved up the final stone steps.

Wind ripped through the landing, the windows dotting the spire free of glass. The rest of the stairs were made from iron grates in an effort to keep traction in the winter when ice and snow would filter in. Merriam wiggled her fingers before gripping the cold railing, climbing the steps.

The stairs narrowed toward the top, the final one nothing more than a small platform in an iron cage. She sat down, wrapping her arms around one of the bars and leaning her cheek on it as the wind whipped her hair around her face. Her eyes turned up to the moons. "Two moons." She giggled, tightening her hold on the bar as she tipped her head back further to look at the stars.

They sparkled, pulsing and shedding glitter across the endless depths of the dark sky. She watched, entranced, as her mind slipped back to the past.

Her father had come home the day after she'd cut her hair. Her mother hadn't been sober since the incident. Merriam had made herself a bowl of EasyMac for dinner the night before and a couple of peanut butter sandwiches throughout the day. Every time she managed to get into her mother's line of sight, her mother's eyes would skip off of her as she took another pull from the bottle.

When her father came through the door, Merriam was lying on her stomach on her bed, reading. She heard the keys drop onto the entry table and a frustrated sigh. "You fucking kidding me, Amanda? It's not even five o'clock."

"I didn't know she was going to do it." Was her mother's immediate response, fear tightening her voice. "I didn't see."

There was silence, and Merriam could imagine the look of confusion and brewing anger on her father's face. She sat up, overwhelmed with the sudden urge to hide or flee. She looked around wildly for a safe escape.

"Her hair." Her mother's feeble voice floated up the stairs.

Fear lodged in her throat like a rock as her eyes finally landed on her window. She launched herself off her bed and ran to it. Her heart pounding in her ears must have masked her father's footsteps on the stairs, because she didn't know he'd come up until her door slammed open.

Her hands were on the window, and she froze, turning slowly.

"So it's true, then." Her father's voice was low, and a chill ran up her spine.

"It was a hassle. I didn't like dealing with it." She brought a hand up to smooth over her hair.

"You do not get to make those decisions, Merriam," her father ground out slowly.

"But I—" She bit back on the retort, but too late.

"And now you're going to backtalk me?" He laughed humorlessly. "You are in *my* house. You will follow *my* rules. You will live how *I* say."

"Yes, sir," Merriam agreed quietly, eyes wide.

He grabbed her shoulders, slamming her back into the wall, only narrowly missing the window.

"I'm sorry," she squeaked.

"I don't think you are," he growled, lowering his face to hers. "What are you sorry for?"

"Cutting my hair." Tears rolled down her cheeks.

"Wrong."

"For not asking first—I should have asked you first."

"It's like you never fucking learn. Do you think I want to do this?" He dropped her arms, and she squeezed her eyes shut as she fell to the floor.

Merriam tipped back, tightening her arms around the iron and pulling herself upright as she dropped her gaze from the sky, blinking heavily. "Legends, fuck," she mumbled. Swallowing down a wave of nausea, she pressed the back of her hand over her mouth and breathed through the urge to heave until it dissipated.

She wiped her hand over her eyes, giggling as she realized how far away the ground was. The treetops swayed in the wind, following the same rhythmic dance as her hair. Color bled from them, floating up into the air before disappearing into the world.

On the ground below, she noticed a figure standing still, head tilted up to look at her.

She waved, watching the tilt of his head, a hand pushing into thick brown waves. Merriam could just barely see his eyes narrow from this distance. On some base level, she knew she should feel annoyed, but she just felt gleeful as she watched him, wishing she knew what internal conflict was going on in his head.

He seemed to have come to a decision, because he started up those steep, narrow steps that led up the side of the castle. Merriam leaned forward as she watched him, still holding on to the iron bar as her torso was suspended over the ground far below.

"Are you coming up here, Ranger-man?" she asked him, knowing he couldn't hear her. "Hope you don't want to fight. I don't think there's room." She fell into a fit of laughter at that, sitting back fully into the cage.

Letting go of the bar, she attempted to run her fingers through her hair, pulling it away from her face. She snagged on knots multiple times, grimacing and feeling frustration bubble up through her euphoria. She let out a disgruntled sigh and decided to get out of the wind so she could do something with her hair.

As she stepped down the spire, she noticed Rovin had made it to the iron catwalk and was walking stiffly and purposefully around the side of the castle. "Gressia doesn't like you either, asshole," she said matter-of-factly before crawling backwards down the steps.

She relaxed as stone once again surrounded her, turning around and continuing down until she dropped to the small wooden landing. Wind whistled through the tower, but not with the same intensity as it had out in the open. It was an interesting sound, the wind, and she sat down next to the stairs, pressing her back against the cold stone wall as she looked up to the windows. Their edges swam with an intricate geometric pattern, the breeze coming through the narrow slots pulling it away from the stone.

"What the fuck, Merriam?" The words sent a cold shiver down her spine, and she brought her hands up over her ears, blinking furiously to keep from slipping into another memory. But as her eyes dropped, she realized the words hadn't come from her head at all, but the Ranger that watched her with an irritated detachment, half of his body sticking up from the hole in the floor.

A giggle spilled from her as she imagined he'd actually come through the floor instead of the trapdoor, and she did her best to smooth her tangled hair back from her face.

"Are you high right now?" Rovin asked incredulously.

Merriam giggled again, shrugging her shoulders helplessly.

"What the fuck were you doing up there alone?"

Merriam licked her lips, watching him, the amber of her irises only a thin ring around her wildly dilated pupils. "I wanted to see the stars. But, Rovin, were you worried?" Her eyes searched his face and she bit back a grin, moving her hands down to her lap as her teeth chattered together.

"You were swaying like a drunk, Mer. I thought you were going to fall." His words held an angry bite that made her uncomfortable, and she pulled her legs up into her chest. "What did you take?"

"I don't know. Gressia gave me something." She folded her arms to her chest, her skin suddenly feeling cold. "Why are you mad?"

"Fuck, Mer, why do you have to be so irresponsible? Why would you go off alone tripping out on Legends know what?"

"You keep calling me by my name. My nice name. Nickname?" Merriam blinked at him, fighting to hold back a laugh.

"Glad that's where your focus is right now." Rovin held his hand out angrily. "Come on, you shouldn't be up here."

Merriam shook her head, huddling closer to the wall. "I don't want to go anywhere with you. You hate me."

"I'm not going to kill you. I'd lose my job," he said, as if it would reassure her.

"You go. Then I'll come down." Merriam watched him carefully.

He regarded her the same way. Depthless brown eyes glittered warily, and Merriam had the fleeting thought that she might fall into them. Her breathing hitched when she realized he was beautiful. Her mouth had dropped open slightly as she stared at him, and she tilted her head, watching him with something akin to wonder.

Annoyance spilled from him in waves, but he eventually nodded, heading back down the stairs with a glance over his shoulder.

Merriam hummed, pushing herself to her feet to follow him. The air itself seemed to roll away from him as he wound down the staircase, and she slowly worked the knots out of a small section of hair as she followed, the repetitive motion comforting.

When they reached the last stair, Rovin turned down the corridor that led into the castle. Merriam stepped the opposite way, opening the door to the catwalk.

Rovin wrapped his hand around the top of her arm, pulling her back in. "You should stay inside."

She barely heard the words, her blood roaring in her ears as she registered his grip on her. Her mind slipped.

Her father stood in front of her, holding her, pulling her to him angrily. But no, this wasn't right. She wasn't a child. She was twenty-four. The blood drained from her face, and she shook her head violently. "Nonono." She pulled at her arm.

Words were coming from his mouth, but nothing registered. Her mind was wild with terror. She had gotten out. Mollian had saved her.

Mollian.

Her mind latched onto the name, and she tugged harder against the grip that held her, closing her eyes against her father's angry face. "Molli! Molli!" She screamed it. She Cast it out wildly into the world. Frantic terror had seized her, and she dropped to her knees, tears spilling down her face as she sobbed and called for the one solace she'd always had.

Her arm was free, and she scrambled back against the wall, panting heavily as she tried to catch her breath. Her father was gone, and Rovin was gesturing to her, facing down the hall. Her brain slowly started catching his words. "... started freaking out. I don't think she knows what she took."

Her eyes moved from him to the imposing presence down the hall. The tall fae with his deeply tan skin, white hair pulled back into a bun. Oren's eyes landed on her, and he picked up his pace, kneeling down in front of her. "Mer, breathe. You're okay." He brought a hand to her face slowly, running a thumb across her cheek as he watched her.

"Molli." Merriam gulped, trying to get her rapidly beating heart to settle. She blinked hard, choking on another sob.

"What happened? Talk to me."

Merriam shook her head. "He was here. I saw him." Her eyes drifted back to Rovin, and she shuddered. "I need ... I need Molli."

"Molli was here?"

Merriam shook her head violently, sobs subsiding, but her whole body shivered.

"What did you take, Mer?"

Merriam shook her head again, wrapping her arms around herself. "Gressia ... Gressia gave me something."

A low growl ripped from Oren's chest, and Merriam cowered back against the wall. He turned to Rovin. "Thank you for watching out. I've got it from here."

Rovin nodded uncomfortably, slipping past them and out onto the catwalk.

"Come on." Oren scooped her up, and she was too frozen to protest. She watched the angry tick of his jaw, could feel the unrelenting tension in his muscles as he held her, his steps swift and rigid.

He was mad.

Anger pulsed through him with every heartbeat, and the heat of him almost seared her skin.

He was mad. And she was scared.

Her breathing picked up, coming hard and fast as she started to struggle against him with a whimper.

Oren walked into the atrium, lamps along the wall bathing everything in a warm light. Setting Merriam on her feet, he walked to the middle of the room. "What the fuck were you thinking?!" His voice boomed through the space, and Merriam flinched, scrambling backwards against the wall.

The air around Oren was swirling, tugging the color from his skin and clothes in tendrils. Merriam could still feel the heat of his anger where her body had pressed against his, and her mind threatened to slip back again.

She wrapped her arms around her head, pulling her knees tight to her chest and squeezing her eyes shut with a whimper. She fisted her fingers at her scalp, tugging on her hair, letting the pain anchor her in reality.

Gressia was by the windows, drawing her fingers over the shapes in the stained glass with a look of pure enchantment on her face. "Ach, why are you yelling, Oren? Don't ruin the mood." She waved her hand at him dismissively.

Oren caught her hand in his fist, spinning her to look at him. "Gressia,

I am not putting up with your shit right now. What is she on?!" he demanded.

Gressia was completely unaffected by the livid fire in his green eyes, easily shaking off his hold with a laugh. "Calm down, little brother. It's just mushrooms. She's fine."

"She is decidedly *not* fine," Oren growled through clenched teeth, pointing behind him to where Merriam was curled against the wall, muttering assurances to herself.

Merriam hadn't even registered that Gressia was in the room. Shivers racked her body, all of her muscles tense as she repeated to herself, "He's not here. He's not here." She wasn't sure if she was reassuring herself that her father had never been here or worrying over the fact that Mollian wasn't.

"She's on the come up and just having a bad time. She'll get past it; it's fine." Gressia laughed.

"Did she know what she was taking?" Oren demanded.

Gressia rolled her eyes at him, thoroughly amused. "She knew she'd be high."

The only thing Merriam's mind would focus on was Oren's tone. She knew he was talking to someone else, but nothing truly registered except for the fact that he was enraged. Her fingers tightened in her hair as she slowly shook her head.

Then hands were on her shoulders, gentle, warm, applying just enough pressure to let her know they were there. "Ria, hey, you're okay."

Without even opening her eyes, Merriam tossed herself forward into Mollian, letting the comforting weight of his arms around her back ground her, his spruce and plum scent slowly calming her as she breathed it in.

"Deep breaths, okay?" Mollian whispered in her ear.

Merriam opened her eyes, pulling back to look at him.

He put his hands on either side of her face, holding her gaze gently. "You're okay, I promise. I'm here."

Merriam blinked against the weird pattern playing over his skin and the way the color seemed to shift and bleed from his irises. But her soul still recognized his, the tendrils knotting them together slack in his presence, and his voice and his touch and his smell were the same, were purely Mollian.

"Hey, there we go. Welcome back. See? You're okay." He smiled encouragingly.

Oren was still holding Gressia in a death glare, and she was not even slightly concerned. "Honestly, Oren, she's fine now. I told you she would be. You're ruining my time," she said grumpily, propping her hands on her hips.

"I'm ruining your time?" His eyes narrowed dangerously. "I'm ruining *your time*? Gressia, you fucking *drugged* her!"

"With *mushrooms*, Oren. Legends. I don't even know why you're so mad about it."

"Can you stand?" Mollian asked Merriam.

Her eyes flitted to Oren. "He's mad," she whispered.

Mollian chuckled softly. "He is. How about we head somewhere with some more pleasant energy?"

Merriam nodded, letting him help her to her feet.

"You don't know why I'm mad? That you fucking *drugged* someone?" Oren let out an incredulous bark of laughter.

Gressia sighed, her head lolling back as if the conversation were exhausting her. "It's a hallucinogen, not poison," she said pointedly. "I know you're a goody-goody, but I don't understand why you're so riled up about this. She's Mollian's problem."

Oren bared his teeth and snarled at her, taking a couple steps forward until he was right up in her face. "She is not *Mollian's problem*." His voice was low and menacing enough that a flicker of worry finally crossed Gressia's face, the depth of his anger breaking through her own drug-addled mind.

Mollian still held Merriam's eyes, keeping her focused on him so she was missing most of what was happening on the other side of the room. He grabbed her hand to lead her out.

"Why do you care so much?" Gressia asked with a huff.

"Why do I care?" Oren laughed mirthlessly. "Because she's clearly fucking traumatized, Gressia. And I love her."

Gressia's eyebrows shot up, a giggle falling from her lips.

Merriam was following Mollian from the room, but Oren's words wrapped around her like a vise. *I love her.* She replayed it over and over in her head, not quite convinced he'd actually said it.

Chapter 18

Watch the clouds

MOLLIAN LED HER INTO his room, guiding her to the bed before climbing up to sit cross-legged in front of her. "So, welcome to your first mushroom trip. I promise it can actually be a great time." He smiled reassuringly. His warmth and calmness broke through the terror that iced her veins, and she started to relax, eyes slowly traveling around the room. "It wasn't right for Gressia to spring it on you like this and then leave you alone. Pretty fucked up, actually, but Oren is dealing with her. And we're going to focus on happier things now."

Merriam's eyes abruptly flicked back to Mollian. "Oren was mad," she said, gaze floating up to the ceiling.

Mollian nodded knowingly. "He was very mad."

"I didn't mean to." Merriam watched the patterns of shapes and swirls dance across the plaster. "I didn't know."

"Oh, Ria." Mollian's brows knit together. "He is not mad at you. Not at all. He's angry with Gressia."

Merriam dropped her eyes to look at Mollian again. "He was yelling, and he didn't like that I was like ... this."

"Hey, no." Mollian pulled her into a hug, cradling her head to his chest. "I promise he is not upset with you at all. Not even a little bit."

"I just got so scared," she whispered.

"I know, but it's okay. And he would never, *never* hurt you, Ria. You're safe, and everything is going to be fine now." Mollian brushed a hand over her hair. "What in the world happened to you, woman?"

Merriam tried to run her own fingers through the wild tangles in her hair. "Oh, the wind." She giggled. "I went up to the spire to look at the sky."

Mollian laughed, shaking his head. "Of course you did." He let go of her, moving to lounge back against the pillows.

"Oren smells like it sometimes." She smiled, then it dropped. "You said he wasn't mad at me?"

"I promise you on our Bond that he is not mad at you," Mollian swore.

Merriam nodded, letting out a heavy sigh. "Okay, good." She focused on the velvet blanket for several moments, running her fingers against the grain of the fabric. "I think ... I think he said he loves me," she finally said, a smile playing on her lips.

"Oh, he definitely said he loves you." Mollian grinned, watching her watch the blanket.

Merriam bit her lip, a smile spreading across her face. "Okay."

"Okay?"

"Yup." She giggled, pushing herself off of the bed and walking over to a tapestry hanging from the wall. It depicted a few deer walking about through an aspen glade, and she traced the deer with her finger, still smiling to herself. "One time I stopped here with the mercs after a job away," she said slowly, eyes never leaving the tapestry. "It was the first time I ever killed someone, and I was struggling with it."

"I remember."

"That was the first time we fucked—me and Oren. I just needed a distraction, and he was ... very distracting." Merriam's eyes unfocused as the memory rushed to the forefront of her mind. Her fingers splayed over the fabric as she leaned into the wall, and she shook her head of the thoughts. "We spent a lot of time together after that. I think mostly from convenience at first, and maybe familiarity. But I liked him, and it scared me. We were so separated from everything here. It was easy."

"I know," Mollian said, and Merriam turned to face him with wide eyes. "Don't look so surprised. We're *mehhen*. I know you better than you know yourself."

"But you never said anything."

Mollian shrugged. "Neither did you. I figured there was a reason."

A heavy sigh pushed from her lungs as she turned her attention back to the deer. "Telling you would have made it real, would have made me deal with it one way or another, and I wasn't ready." Her fingers trailed slowly down the threads until her hand dropped to her side. "I'm sorry I kept it from you."

"You never have to explain yourself to me, Ria. You have nothing to apologize for."

Merriam nodded, a sense of security wrapping around her with his words and continued presence, and she grew distracted by the world around her.

Everything in the room was gorgeous. The tapestries with their beautiful and colorful imagery, the plush, red rug next to the surprisingly large bed, covered in a thick, velvet blanket. Mollian watched in amusement at her childlike wonder and the way everything made her laugh.

"We should trip together sometime. It's weird that we never have, and it doesn't usually start out bad like that." Mollian told her as she sat in front of the cold fireplace, staring at the dark bricks.

"It was so strange, Molli." Merriam tipped backwards until she was lying sprawled on the floor, arms flung out. "It was like I kept going back in time, but only to the bad stuff. With my dad. I haven't thought about any of it in years." She shook her head, then flipped onto her stomach to look up at him. "Why do you think it all came back now?"

Mollian shrugged. "Maybe it's the way your mind was open. Unguarded. Let all those memories surface again."

"Mmm." Merriam laid her cheek to the floor, running her hands over the carpet. "I have a lot of good memories from then, too, though. Memories of you." She smiled.

"Oh, yeah?"

"Yeah." She let her eyes roll around the room as she sifted through all the moments with Mollian from her childhood. "Like how I was always better at climbing trees than you. And I would always bring us plums to eat, and we would toss the pits at the tree trunks to see if they'd crack.

You always got yours to because you cheated with your magic to throw them harder." She giggled. "We were such weird kids."

"We? If I remember correctly, most of the stuff we did was your idea," he teased.

"Well, someone had to come up with something. What were we supposed to do? Sit on our backs and watch the clouds go by?"

"Precisely. You know how much I love the clouds."

"Mollian, you haven't sat still for more than five minutes at a time in your entire life."

Mollian laughed. "Why am I being attacked right now?"

"Why are you an easy target?" Merriam burst into a fit of giggles at her own retort.

They continued bantering comfortably, Merriam occasionally making high observations about the world around her and how beautiful everything was. "Even Rovin is beautiful," she admitted, once again on her back. "Did you ever notice that before?"

"Sure, I thought that was a given."

"And you never mentioned it to me?" Merriam squeaked in shock.

"You're high as a kite, Ria. How was that conversation supposed to go?" He made his voice an octave higher, "Molli, that dumb Ranger is being mean again." He continued an octave lower than his normal voice, "Well, have you noticed he's pretty? At least you don't get bullied by an ogre."

Merriam cackled, holding her stomach as she rolled to her side. "Legends, Molli, you don't even sound like that! And neither do I."

"Are you sure about that?"

"You're an ass." She smiled at him as the laughter subsided. She licked her lips, sitting up. "I think I might be thirsty. Do you think water still tastes good?"

"Water definitely still tastes good," Mollian assured her. "Are you okay by yourself?"

"Yeah, I'll be fine," she assured him. Her pupils were still blown wide, the drugs in the height of their hold on her.

"Okay, stay put. I'll be back."

Mollian slipped out the door, closing it noiselessly behind him, and Merriam sat alone in the silence. Her mind kept wandering from what she was looking at, but never to a bad memory, just flashes of warmth and sunlight and spruce and plum. She blamed Mollian for the latter. The whole room smelled like him.

He hadn't been here in years, so maybe she was just imagining his lingering scent. She laughed again, sitting up and leaning against the bed. When she closed her eyes, shapes and colors danced across her lids. It was an effort to keep her eyes shut, and she made a game of concentrating on it.

As she focused on the task, she became suddenly aware of the hum in her blood. It felt as though something were pulling at her, and she held her hands in front of her face, turning them about and watching intently.

She stood, moving slowly toward the door. Her tattoo pulsed between her shoulder blades, and she shimmied uncomfortably. She left Mollian's room without even noticing, completely entranced by the soft buzz in her blood.

Merriam's eyes were trained on her feet as she walked down the hall and onto an iron spiral staircase. She almost believed they belonged to someone else with how they seemed to move of their own volition, following that strange pull she couldn't quite identify. The staircase ended in a room at the belly of the castle, filled with a dizzying system of stone arch supports. She'd never been in this part of the castle before, and she looked around in wonder as she walked through the arches, brushing her fingers along the cold stone and humming softly to herself.

Eventually, she came to a door, opening it to find a staircase that led down into the mountain. She licked her lips, eyes staring into the darkness, before taking one step and then another. The stairs were dug straight out of the mountain, hard-packed dirt that crunched softly under her feet. The air got colder and damper the further down she went. The light from the door was just a small orb when she felt the ground underneath her shift from dirt to solid granite.

Her hair stood on end, goosebumps covering her arms. Her eyes were picking up swirls of color in the darkness, and her teeth chattered as she giggled nervously, running her hands up and down her arms to fight the chill air. Up ahead, she could see a very faint flickering light, and she quickened her steps down to reach it.

The staircase ended in a large cavern lined with soft light along the walls and ceiling. In the center stood a tall arch, the lights flickering off it and dancing all across the room in a way that almost made her dizzy. The arch was a dark stone shot through with lines of transparent gold curved around a stone that shifted between violet and indigo.

Merriam took another step closer, and her blood *sang*.

The magic in her blood—in Mollian's blood—vibrated with an undeniable intensity, making it difficult to breathe. Her head buzzed, and she wasn't sure it was just an effect of the drugs. She blinked and found herself standing in front of the arch.

Tentatively, she reached out a hand, lightly stroking her fingers over the smooth, cold surface. Light reflected off of the ring on her middle finger, and her eyes focused on it. The ring held a purple stone, the exact color fleeting in the dim light. She brought up her other hand, the ring on that finger set with a dark stone, slim veins of gold running through the length of it.

It finally clicked in her drug-muddled brain. *The Gate.*

She swallowed, her mouth gone dry, and pressed her hand against the stone, feeling the thrum of power running deep inside match the hum in her veins. "Whoa," she whispered, splaying her fingers over the arch.

Her mind slipped again, but this time, not into a memory. This time, she saw a world.

There were huge trees everywhere, larger even than the giant sequoias she'd seen in pictures as a child. Some were covered in an unnaturally bright green moss that seemed to almost writhe over the bark. A large stream spilled languidly through the forest floor, and at its bank sat a humanoid female. Her body looked like it was made of glass, and her hair drifted down into the water, blended *with* the water, and Merriam couldn't say where one ended and the other took over. Off in the distance were strange animals she couldn't begin to identify. One looked like a pink horse, but its head was just an elongated, furry trunk, like an anteater. Another was brown and yellow, with a face like a cat, but the mouth was too wide, and the teeth too blunt. It had six legs that ended in strange flat hooves. The flowers were larger than Merriam, all dizzyingly bright colors.

Her eyes were wide, staring blankly at the Gate in front of her. Her blood continued to sing, Mollian's magic rolling from her skin where it touched the arch. Merriam dragged her hand over the side of the stone until she felt a sharp edge. Quickly and forcefully, she raked her hand across it, the stone ripping shallowly into the skin of her palm.

The sting of pain almost brought Merriam's focus back to what was in front of her, but that strange land still swirled clearly in her mind. Blood welled from the wound on her palm, and she swept her hand over the arch, leaving a thin trail across the stone.

The air inside of the Gate shifted, and Merriam blinked as the world she'd seen in her mind slowly materialized in front of her.

She gasped, tentatively reaching her hand forward. There was no resistance, only a strange void feeling as the air seemed to completely move around her hand where it passed through the arch. Something between a laugh and a sob escaped her as she wiggled her fingers in the empty space, her fingertips just barely kissed with the warm, densely humid air of the world on the opposite side.

She smiled in awe, lifting her foot to step forward through the Gate.

"Merriam, no!"

Chapter 19

Say evergreen

MERRIAM LOOKED BACK, THE motion knocking her off balance and causing her to stumble forward. She let out a startled yelp as her whole arm passed through the Gate, the other grasping wildly for purchase against the slick stone.

Oren launched himself across the room, tackling her from the side with an arm wrapped around her waist, twisting his body in the air so that he landed on his back, Merriam pulled to his chest, and slid across the floor.

He sat up, Merriam tumbling from his lap onto the ground, visibly shaking. Her eyes turned up to him, wide and confused and worried.

"Wait here." Oren said briskly, brushing his knuckles across her cheek. He walked over to the Gate, closing his eyes and running both hands over the stone.

Merriam watched him, not so much paying attention to his actions as to his body language, looking for any sign of agitation in his movements. When he turned back to her, she dropped her eyes, suddenly afraid of what she would see there.

Oren crouched down in front of her, offering his hand. "Can you stand?"

Merriam nodded, letting him pull her to her feet. His thumb brushed the tops of her knuckles, and he pulled her into his chest, his other arm looping around her back as he held her. After a moment, he stepped back, holding up her injured palm and giving it a once-over.

"I cut it on the stone," she offered.

Oren chuckled, tension leaving his shoulders, despite the anxiety still rolling through him. "It would seem so. Let's get you back upstairs so we can patch you up."

"What happened?" she asked, finally looking up to meet his eyes.

A smile tugged at the corner of his lips, and Merriam's mouth dropped open as she really looked at him for the first time that night. She slowly brought her hand up to trace the tattoo at his temple, along a cheekbone, down to his jawline. Her fingers brushed over his lips, which he parted to ever-so-lightly nip the pads of her fingertips as he watched her with those eyes the fresh, bright green of spring. She forgot to breathe as she stared into them. "You opened the Gate," he answered her.

"I think you're the most gorgeous thing I've ever seen," she whispered.

Oren dropped a kiss to her forehead, taking her uninjured hand in his. "You flatter me, Lady," he said, leading her back to the staircase.

"I think the Gate brought me down here." She chewed on her lip. "My blood ... it was the strangest feeling." She peeked up at him again.

He met her gaze, nodding. "It'll do that. The effect of the mushrooms probably made the call of the Gate even more compelling than you would usually feel."

Merriam nodded, the hum still running through her body. "I saw that world in my mind, O. Before the Gate opened. I *saw* it."

Oren smiled. "That will happen," he said simply.

They made the long walk up the stairs in silence, Oren closing the door firmly behind them when they were back in the room with the maze of supports. He rested his forehead on the door for a moment, letting out a slow breath. "Please, please don't go back down there tonight. I'll go with you another time if you want, let you see it and answer any questions you have. But please, Mer, don't wander off again."

Merriam wrapped her arms around herself, looking at the floor as she nodded her agreement. "I'm sorry," she whispered quietly.

Oren pushed away from the door, gently grabbing her arm and pulling her back into him. "You don't have anything to be sorry for. I was just scared, that's all. If you'd have gone through on your own, not knowing how to get back ... I would have never forgiven myself."

"Thank the Legends for your timing, then."

Oren laughed, giving her a final squeeze before releasing her and leading her upstairs.

Mollian found them in the stairwell. "You found her!"

"She was with the Gate," Oren informed him.

"Shit, Ria. I was only gone for five minutes," Mollian chastised lightly.

When they reached Oren's room, he brought her into the bathroom, picking her up and setting her on the counter to clean and dress her wound.

"Do you know where that place was?" she asked.

"We call it Nessium."

"Why did I see it?"

"I'm not sure. My best guess would be you might have been wanting to be outside in the forest, but your mind is seeing everything differently right now, so it changed the makeup of the world you were picturing. Nessium isn't that far separated from Nethyl, so that could be what the Gate latched onto when it heard you."

"Heard me?" Merriam's brows knit together.

Oren seemed to consider his next words, searching for a simple way to explain. "The Gate can hear the Keeper magic in your blood. Talk to it."

"Oh," she said as he pulled her off the counter.

"Mer." Oren raised a hand to her cheek, tilting her face to meet his eyes. "I'm so sorry I frightened you earlier. I wasn't upset with you. At all."

Merriam leaned into Oren's touch. "You're warm. I like it."

"You're still tripping." Amusement glimmered in his eyes.

Merriam nodded with a giggle, teeth chattering as a shiver ran through her.

"Come on." He grabbed her hand, pulling her through his bedroom and out onto an open balcony.

Mollian followed with some blankets, handing Merriam a cup of water that she took a sip of before cradling to her chest.

After spreading one of the blankets out on the rough wooden planks, Oren sat down, leaning against the wall with his legs spread in front of him. He pulled Merriam down so that she was lying between his legs, her head resting at the base of his chest so she could watch the sky, still holding her water cup. He draped another blanket over her to ward off the chill of the mountain air.

Mollian sat in a chair, wrapped in his own blanket, with his feet propped up on the low balcony railing. "You gonna drink that, Ria?"

"Mmm." Merriam was focused on the stars, fully giving her mind over to the drug in her system. Oren was a warm, solid presence at her back, and the gentle rise and fall of his chest wrapped her in the comfortable knowledge that she was safe. Her fingers played over the smooth edge of the wooden cup, and she remembered suddenly what it was.

Sitting up, she brought the cup to her lips and drank deeply, staring out into the dark forest as the cool water slid down her throat. When the cup was empty, she set it down and settled back into Oren, grabbing his hands and wrapping his arms over her chest as she continued watching the stars.

"How many of those do you think are planets?" she asked.

Mollian tipped his face up, looking over the familiar constellations. "It's possible all of them are, I suppose."

"There are eight other planets in Earth's solar system. And people have only made it to one other one, I think. I can't remember if we actually ever got there, or if that was just a movie." She frowned.

Oren pulled one hand free from her grasp, drawing her hair out from behind her head and over her shoulder. Slowly, he worked his fingers through the tangles.

"Do you think there's a way to harness magic the way people harness electricity and, like, radio waves and stuff?" Merriam asked.

Oren shrugged, and Mollian tilted his head in thought. "There might be, but it would be tricky. Magic is much more unpredictable than electricity."

"Why don't they work in tandem?"

"Magic is fickle," Oren answered simply.

"That's hardly an explanation." Merriam rolled her eyes.

Mollian pushed a curl off of his forehead. "The best I can describe it, it's the wavelengths magic uses to move through the air. It's stronger and more powerful than things like radio waves. Magic uses a large range of different wavelengths, completely absorbing those frequencies and leaving no room for anything else."

Merriam listened to Mollian continue to ramble about the inner workings of magic and the things he'd gleaned about the Internet, phone signals, and other things seen as basic amenities on Earth. She sighed deeply with contentment, her head resting against Oren's chest and his fingers working gently through her hair.

Her heart clenched at how happy she was in the moment. She'd never taken for granted that Mollian had found her, had saved her, had shown her a life she'd always been meant for. She loved him and considered him almost an extension of herself. He was the other half of her heart and her soul. She'd felt it since the first time they'd met, even if she didn't quite have words for it back then.

And now there was Oren, who'd been on her side before they'd ever even met. And he *loved* her. This male, who would soon be the king of Sekha and one of the most powerful rulers on Nethyl, *loved her*. And even though she knew it should scare her, knew that her basal reaction would be to run from this, the knowledge settled deep in her bones and warmed her completely from the inside out.

She wrapped her arms tighter around Oren's that was still slung over her chest, pulling his knuckles up to her lips to brush a kiss against them. The ring on his finger was cool against her lips, and she pulled his hand away to look at the strange dark orydite. She stroked it with a finger, feeling the faintest echo of magic, and shivered a little.

Mollian's voice had trailed off, and Merriam looked over to him, still staring up at the stars. "Have I ever asked you how you know so much?"

Mollian laughed. "Once or twice. What do you think I did on Earth while I was searching for you?" he teased.

They sat for a while, Merriam occasionally making high observations and Mollian expounding on them, Oren adding in his thoughts every once in a while.

Mollian eventually stood up. "It's been lovely, but I think I'm ready to turn in."

Merriam scrambled up and threw her arms around him. "I love you, Molli," she whispered. "Thank you for my water."

Mollian laughed, lifting her in his embrace. "Any time." He set her down. "Stay out of trouble the rest of the night, okay?" He chucked her lightly under the chin and bade them both goodnight.

"How are you feeling?" Oren asked, head tilted back to look up at her.

Merriam sank down into his lap, her back against his chest. "Euphoric," she said softly, tilting her head back against his shoulder.

"Good." He ran his nose over the shell of her ear, circling his arms around her waist. "Are you still getting heavy visuals?"

Merriam shook her head. "No, it's definitely not as intense. I can tell I'm still not sober, though."

"Are you ready to lie down?"

"I don't think I'd be able to keep my eyes closed," she answered honestly. "You can go to bed, though, if you're tired."

"I'm perfectly content right here."

Merriam smiled, shifting a bit so her forehead rested against his neck. "Good, because I'm rather comfortable."

Oren moved a hand to stroke her hair, now mostly free of knots. She could feel the slight tension that had entered his body, and she waited for him to say something.

Several moments went by, and Merriam finally prompted, "What are you thinking about?"

"You."

Merriam scowled, pushing away and twisting so she could look into his face. "You're lying."

The corner of Oren's mouth pulled up, displaying his dimple. "I am not lying. I'm the straight-laced one, remember?"

"You are, too, lying. Straight out of that beautiful mouth of yours."

A smile played over Oren's lips as he watched her. "You seem pretty sure of yourself."

"You're so tense I could probably bounce a copper off your pec. If that's what thinking about me does to you, you'll end up having a heart attack within a year."

Oren brought a hand to her face, brushing his thumb across her cheek. "I won't be surprised if I do, given all the trouble you seem to get into," he joked.

"Tell me, O." Merriam insisted, unswayed.

Oren searched her eyes, her pupils now shrunken down to a more natural size, and seemed to come to the conclusion that she wouldn't relent. "I was thinking about earlier, when you were in a panic. You were terrified of something, and it made you scared of me. I should have kept my temper in check until I knew you were okay."

Merriam shook her head, pressing herself back into him, her cheek resting against his chest. "It's not your fault, Oren. Rationally, I know you would never hurt me."

Oren smoothed a hand over her hair, and his voice came out low and rough with barely restrained rage. "Somebody did though, before." It was not a question.

Merriam licked her lips and answered, "Yes."

He went rigid for a moment before continuing his gentle stroking. "Who?"

She debated telling him that it didn't matter now, but knew he wasn't likely to drop it. Not after that shit show tonight. "My dad had a temper. He was gone a lot for work, but when he was home, he'd blame me for my mom's drug use and blame my mom for anything I did wrong." Oren's hand stilled, just holding her head to his chest as she continued. "I cut my hair one time. I don't think that was the catalyst, but it was definitely the final straw on top of Legends only know what else, and he lost it. He grabbed me, held me so hard it left bruises on my arms, and slammed me into the wall. He'd hit me if I screamed, but sometimes I couldn't help it."

Oren's fingers curled into her hair, his whole body tense. "Mer," he whispered, his heart breaking for the scared child of her past.

Merriam swallowed heavily. "After we moved, I would spend all day out in the woods trying to leave signs for Molli. Trying to conjure him somehow. My mom never noticed I was missing. She was always too drunk or high. He had come home while I'd been out one time. He hated when my mom wasn't sober, and he attacked me for her drinking. I think because I still reacted to him back then, while my mom was already numb to him. That's ... that's what I was remembering earlier. I haven't thought about it in so long. It just all surfaced tonight, and when Rovin grabbed me—"

"Rovin grabbed you?" Oren growled.

"He was trying to keep me from going out onto the catwalk, trying to make sure I stayed safe," Merriam soothed, and felt Oren relax a little. "I stopped seeing Rovin and started seeing my dad, and it was terrifying. All I could think of was that Molli had saved me and my dad shouldn't be there. And then you came. And you were so, so angry. And all I could remember is my dad being angry with my mom and ..." she trailed off.

"I'll kill him for ever having laid a hand on you," Oren swore.

Merriam listened to his heart beat in his chest, steady and strong. She thought maybe she should defend her father or feel some sort of emotion at hearing the male she loved say he wanted to kill him, but she felt nothing. Nothing except for a strange spark of warmth in her chest at the realization that she *did* love Oren. It was a warmth that filled her with equal parts hope and terror; made her feel both eternally safe and entirely vulnerable. She burrowed in deeper against him, placing her palm against his chest as if to assure herself that he was here, that he was real.

"Mer, I am so, so sorry I hurt you."

"You've never hurt me," she murmured.

"You were in pain, and I only made it worse."

Merriam lifted her head from his chest, looking him in the eyes. "Maybe you didn't handle the situation with the most finesse, but I trust you, Oren. I trust you not to hurt me. I trust you to keep my best interest in mind to some capacity in all of your decisions. And I trust you not to be perfect, because I sure as Hel can't live up to that standard."

Oren leaned his head forward to rest his forehead against hers. "You're incredible. Do you know that?"

Merriam smiled. "Yes, but feel free to tell me whenever the mood strikes."

Oren chuckled softly, brushing her hair from her face. "When did this happen?" He let the strands slip between his fingers.

"Before I climbed the spire. It was very windy."

"That would explain why it was a rat's nest."

Merriam scoffed, tucking herself back against him. "Don't lie, Majesty, you know the best part of your night was spending an hour messing with it."

Smiling, Oren ran his hand over her hair again. "It does enchant me," he admitted.

Merriam grinned, leaning into his touch. She breathed in deeply, the chill of the night air warded off by the heat coming from Oren and the blanket draped over her lap. She sighed in contentment, lulled by the rise and fall of his chest and his fingers playing through her hair.

Her eyes eventually slipped closed, and just before sleep claimed her, she felt lips brush against the top of her head as Oren whispered, barely audible, "I love you, Mer."

𝓁

At some point in the night, Oren had carried her to bed, because she woke up curled against his side, her head tucked into his shoulder and one leg thrown over his. She let herself enjoy the feel of him pressed against her for a moment before sitting up, stretching languidly. She pushed her fingers into her hair, scratching at her scalp before swinging her legs out of bed.

Oren caught her wrist before she could get up, and she looked to see him lying on his back, one arm bent behind his head. He smirked before pulling her back to him, and she landed with one arm on either side of his chest. "Where do you have to be so early?"

"Breakfast, Majesty." Merriam rolled her eyes playfully. "If I may?"

"Mmm, I like when you ask for permission." He smiled, eyes falling back closed.

"Does it make you feel nice and kingly?" Merriam drew a finger down his bare chest.

"It might." He peeked one eye open at her.

"Well, don't get used to it. I typically do what I want when I want to." Merriam flipped her hair over her shoulder.

"I wouldn't dream of taming that wild spirit." Oren's eyes raked down her body in a suggestive way that made her stomach flip. His hand moved up her arm to the back of her head, wrapping around her hair and tugging. "I'm definitely a fan of it." He pulled her down to his mouth, brushing a kiss against her lips and down her neck before releasing her and sitting up.

Merriam kneeled in front of him, fire starting to kindle in her amber eyes. "You can't just keep doing that."

A corner of his mouth lifted as he turned to get out of bed. "Doing what?"

"Being such a tease!"

Oren stood, grasping her chin and running a thumb over her lips. "If I recall correctly, Lady, you're the one who threatened to scream if I kept touching you the last morning we were together. Forgive me for misreading your desire."

"We were in a *tent*, Oren," Merriam huffed, pushing his hand away.

"So I recall." He grinned. "Are you saying I make you incapable of being quiet?" He raised an eyebrow suggestively.

"Your ego is too big." Merriam pushed herself off the bed and stalked to the bathroom, peeling off her clothes from the day before as she went.

The shower here was a small box, sectioned off from the rest of the bathroom with just a curtain. She turned the faucet on to get the hot water running, then bent over to twist her hair up in a bun.

Slipping behind the shower curtain, she lathered up a bar of soap from a shelf as she stood under the water.

A light brown arm reached over her shoulder, plucking the soap from her hands. "Oren! I need to bathe." She turned to glare at him.

"That's usually why people get in the shower." He answered dryly. "Turn back around."

Merriam obeyed, heat flooding her veins as she felt his presence behind her in the small space. He ran his hands over her back and shoulders, massaging her muscles as he worked his way down her body. His touch sent sparks dancing across her skin.

He took a step closer, reaching around to wash her front. Carnal need tugged low in her abdomen.

"Oren," she hissed as his fingers brushed across her breasts.

"You said you wanted to bathe, Mer. Now hush." He pressed a kiss to her temple before dropping to one knee and washing her legs.

He stood, running his hands up along her inner thighs, and she splayed her fingers on the wall to keep her steady. "Oren, stop," she whined in frustration.

"Do you *want* me to?" He spoke into her ear, his voice low and husky.

"No."

"If you ever do, for any reason, say 'evergreen,' and it all stops."

Merriam nodded.

"You'll remember it? For anything. At any time."

"Say 'evergreen,' and it stops," Merriam said breathlessly.

"Good girl," Oren purred, running his canines against the back of her neck, sending shivers up her spine. "Now tell me what you want."

"You." She pressed back against him, looping her arms around his neck and tilting her head back to brush her lips across his jaw. "Always you."

"I'm yours, Merri," Oren replied, letting her hair down. "But I'm not going to fuck you right now."

Merriam turned around, eyes narrowed in a glare that was half confusion.

He gently tipped her head back into the water. "Everyone will be heading to breakfast soon. So, unless you're okay with us walking down late together ..."

Merriam frowned, closing her eyes as his fingers moved deftly against her scalp. "We can be quick."

"I'd rather savor you."

"So it's all about what you want, then?" Meriam peeked an eye open to look at him.

"I'm a prince, Mer. So, yes, that's exactly how that works." Oren smirked.

Merriam rolled her eyes, closing them as he washed her hair.

He watched her face as his fingers tenderly worked. She looked so serene, droplets of water sticking to her freckled cheeks. Her expression was relaxed, despite the intimacy and vulnerability of the situation, and it warmed Oren to the core of his being.

Being in this shower with her again was borderline intoxicating, though the times before had never been innocent like this. He wanted so badly to claim her, let everyone know that she was undoubtedly his, and words of possession lingered on the tip of his tongue.

But he knew that wasn't something she would welcome, and he couldn't even begrudge her the sentiment because he understood it. So he finished with her hair, kissing her temple and swatting her ass before he accidentally let something slip that would scare her off. "You're free to go, Lady," he joked.

"Thank you for your services," she replied playfully, stepping out of the shower.

Merriam dried herself quickly, toweling off her hair and loosely braiding it. She had just finished getting dressed when the water turned off. Pulling a fresh towel down, she held it out to Oren as he opened the curtain. "I'll see you at breakfast." She rose onto her toes to kiss him before exiting the room.

She slipped across the hall into Mollian's room to grab fresh clothes. He was sitting on the edge of the bed lacing up his boots, and a grin split his face as he looked up at her. "How are you feeling this morning?"

Merriam leaned against the door after shutting it. "Exhausted and confused." She rested her head against the solid wood, gaze going up to the ceiling as she sighed. "But if you're talking about the little mushroom trip, I'm all good."

Mollian turned his attention back to his shoes. *Care to elaborate?*

Do I really need to? She walked over to the bag on the floor by the bathroom door, pulling out a clean shirt and pants.

She felt Mollian's stare searing her back for a moment before he stood up and moved toward the door.

"Wait." She turned her head to catch his eyes, and he leaned against the wall, arms folded over his chest.

Merriam quickly changed into the clean clothes, dropping the dirty ones unceremoniously on the floor before flinging herself onto the bed. "How did this happen, Molli? He loves me. He loves me, and I want nothing more than to love him."

"I can only tell you so many times to let yourself be happy. You've more than earned it—not that you ever needed to."

"I wish it were that simple. How is a mercenary supposed to be …" She didn't even let herself finish the thought.

"Queen?" Mollian, on the other hand, had no issues doing so.

"Consort," Merriam offered instead.

"Either way, you could no longer be a free agent. But Oren would never ask you to give up your life."

"Being free *is* my life." Merriam sat up, shoving socks onto her feet and her feet into her boots. "I should break this off. Before he gets hurt."

Mollian sighed, running a hand over his hair. "This is your business, Ria. I won't tell you how to handle it."

"Not even if I ask for your opinion?" She pouted.

"I'm unable to remain impartial." He looked like he wanted to say more, but he shook his head and opened the door. *I love you both. You make each other happy. That's all I care about. The other details are clutter.*

Merriam stared after his back, biting her lip. Finally, she made her way downstairs and sat at the table next to Calysta, who was popping berries into her mouth one by one.

"I heard you had quite the night." The nymph grinned, dark juice staining her teeth.

"You could put it that way." Merriam grabbed a slice of bread from the loaf at the center of the table and slathered it with preserves. Her whole body felt tired, her brain completely drained.

"Well, if you're going to be stingy with your details, I'm going to be stingy with mine." Calysta said with a shrug.

"Can we talk about it later? It was kind of a lot to process."

"I took the liberty of sending a raven back to Leo already. I gathered you hadn't figured anything else super pertinent out after talking with Gressia this morning."

Merriam snorted, almost choking on the food in her mouth. "That bitch."

"Oh, don't tell me you didn't find it enjoyable at all." Gressia sank gracefully to the bench next to her. "You seemed to be doing just fine last I saw."

"You could have warned me."

"I didn't know you had so much trauma buried in you, Merriam. It was a very enlightening experience all around." Her eyes drifted across the table to Oren, who radiated irritation in such strong waves it was almost a surprise the cups on the table were still standing.

"I'd advise you to treat your guests with more respect in the future, sister," he said evenly, turning his attention back to the food in front of him.

Merriam glanced away uncomfortably, and her eyes met Rovin's across the room. His usually steely gaze was softened with amusement. A blush crawled up Merriam's cheeks as she remembered completely breaking down in front of him. That was a hit to her reputation she didn't need.

"We'll be out of your hair by this afternoon," Oren said.

"Well, what a shame." Gressia sighed, standing up. "I have business to attend to, but I do hope you come back soon." She bent to press a kiss to the top of Merriam's head, the merc stiffening. Then she gave a waggle of her fingers to her brothers before turning and heading up the steps.

"I know people find me weird, but she is just something else entirely." Calysta laughed softly, licking a few drops of berry juice from her claws.

Oren and Mollian exchanged a look. "I blame the solitary confinement," Mollian said with a shrug.

Chapter 20

Covered in blood

It had taken longer to pack everything up than expected, but they were finally back on the road, leaving the heavy pressure of Entumbra behind. Merriam was scouting ahead of the group, wanting the space to sort through all of her thoughts and emotions and feeling completely drained in every way as an after-effect of the drugs.

The uncertainty around her relationship with Oren aside, she hadn't thought of her parents in years. Their large presence in her mind last night worried her, and it was impossible to stop thinking of those memories and of all the times she'd been screamed at, pushed around, hit by the people who were supposed to have loved and protected her.

She was lost in thought when something dark flashed in the forest at the corner of her eye, and she snapped her head up, instantly alert.

The forest was quiet and still in a completely unnatural way.

Unease worked its way up her spine, wrapping around her lungs and settling like a stone in her gut. She slowed her horse, turning in the saddle to search for the others. But she'd pulled too far ahead, and couldn't see them through the trees.

Before she could reach out for Mollian, something dark and cold barreled into her, knocking her from the saddle. She barely managed to land into a practiced roll, hopping to her feet and snapping her axes free from her belt by the time she had settled on her heels.

The creature in front of her was a thing of nightmares, at least double the size of her horse. It had a wide, flat face and rows of razor-sharp teeth that jutted from its mouth. It was covered in black scales, its body long and lithe like a lizard, but its legs were structured like a cat's and tipped in three large, jointed talons. Merriam's mouth went dry as she watched a long, barbed tail whip around the creature's body and toward her legs.

She leaped back, narrowly avoiding being taken out for a second time. As soon as her toes touched the ground, she sprung at the creature, swinging an axe for its throat as it watched her with golden, serpentine eyes. It raised one limb to swipe at her, and she shifted, blocking it with her other axe while the first missed its mark and cut deep into the creature's shoulder. Hot black blood flowed from the wound, reeking of sulfur.

It shrieked at a pitch that made Merriam's ears ring, and she fought the urge to cover them with her hands as it launched itself at her again. She danced with it, twisting and turning to avoid its claws and gnashing teeth as she attacked with her axes.

Its claws caught her shoulder, and she screamed, knocked off balance and sent to a knee. It lashed its tail at her, and she barely blocked it with one axe while swinging the other up and cutting deep. Blood rained down on her, stinging her eyes. She dropped, rolling away and wiping an arm across her face to clear her mouth and nose of the ichor.

She panted hard, setting her feet as its eyes found her and it coiled itself for an attack. It sprung, maw wide, and belted another violent screech. Merriam screamed back, running to meet it, ducking low to draw the blade of an axe along its underbelly.

Almost mid-jump, the creature shifted around, howling in rage and agony and flinging itself at something behind it.

Merriam's heart clenched as she saw a head of wild white curls, Mollian's face set in a feral snarl as he raised a sword to meet the demon. The end of its barbed tail twitched in the dirt behind him, and black blood was splattered across his face. She moved to jump onto the creature's back, but then Rovin was there, dropping from a tree and straddling it. His short sword sunk deep into the muscle along the creature's spine, and he held on with both hands, his thighs gripping the slick scales as the demon bucked wildly, letting out another horrendous screech.

The demon swiped a nightmarish paw at Mollian, and he ducked out of the way, claws catching his calf. Arrows flew from the forest canopy, sinking shallowly into the flesh of the demon's flat face, and it screamed as it shook its head, raising a paw to brush the arrows away. Eskar crouched in a tree, nocking another arrow and letting it fly, aim landing true thanks to the help of her magic.

Merriam saw her opening, and just before she launched herself into a sprint, Oren was at her side.

The belly, he Cast to her, but she was already on it, nodding briskly as they both sprinted toward the creature. He split off at the tail, running to the other side. Mollian held its attention as Rovin slipped a knife free from his belt, using the sword as an anchor to pull himself up closer to its head. Brambles crawled from the forest, wrapping around the limbs of the creature. It threw them off in frustration, but more kept coming.

Merriam slid underneath, raising an axe to cut through the shiny scales of its belly. Oren came in from the other side, ramming his sword up into an armpit and pulling it sideways, tearing into the creature and showering himself in putrid blood.

A low tone vibrated through the air, and the demon whipped its head around with a shriek before collapsing in on itself, dissipating into a thick cloud of liquid smoke and rolling off through the trees so quickly it was impossible to track.

Rovin fell to the ground with a heavy thud, narrowly avoiding landing on his sword. Eskar jumped down from the tree as Calysta stepped forward, the brambles receding back into the forest.

"What the fuck?" Mollian panted, weapon dropping to his side. His pant leg was wet and dark with blood from the wound on his calf, shallow gashes visible through a rip in the fabric.

"Where did it go?" Merriam shifted her grip on her axes, decoratively carved handles slick with gore, and turned in a slow circle, eyes watching the forest around her. "What just happened?"

Oren tried to wipe the vile black blood from his eyes and mouth, but his hands were also covered, and he did nothing but draw dark streaks across his face. He spit some of the blood from his mouth, lip curling in disgust. "My educated guess is that it realized it was losing and decided to leave before we could finish it off." His hand shook with adrenaline as he ran it down his hair, slicking the dark liquid down the back of his neck in the process.

"Was that the demon we've been hunting?" Eskar asked as she helped Rovin to his feet. He leaned to pick up his short sword, wiping it clean against his pants before sheathing it.

"That's the only plausible explanation," Oren answered simply, turning to Merriam. "You're hurt."

She hissed as his fingers brushed the scratch across her shoulder. "I'm fine." But her voice held no bite. The sting of other shallow scrapes and scratches echoed across her arms and legs, but her shoulder throbbed, and she could feel blood trickling down her back.

"We need to go back to Entumbra," Mollian said.

Merriam walked to her *mehhen*, bending down to examine his leg. "You're going to need stitches. Are you ready for your first real battle scar, Prince?" she joked, smiling up at him.

"That would sound a lot less ominous if your face wasn't covered in demon blood."

"No, we have to continue on to Umbra," Oren spoke. "We don't know where that demon went, and we don't have the means to track it. We still have a bird left. We'll send it back so a team can start getting ready and give them a full brief when we return."

"This crow is Leo's. It'll go to the merc house, not to the castle." Calysta folded her arms over her chest. "But I'm assuming it's a team of Rangers you'll want to assemble."

"That was my initial thought, yes, and logistically, it makes sense. There's more of them to spread out," Oren answered, holding a hand out placatingly. "Who knows how far that thing has gotten? It could very well be a wild goose chase."

Calysta scoffed. "Nice save, Prince." But she left to collect the horses and prepare the final raven to be sent out.

Eskar bristled at her tone, but before she could chastise the nymph for how she talked to the heir apparent, Merriam stood. "We should warn Gressia, just in case it hasn't gone far."

"As a general rule, demons and iron don't mix. So she should be safe, but you're right, I'll go back and tell her so she can strengthen the warding around the Gate. I'll Travel and be able to meet up with you before nightfall." The fact that Oren was suggesting Travel at all proved the severity of the situation. Though Earth's means of transportation were much faster than those on Nethyl, Oren hated the fact that it required glamoring humans.

"I'll go with you." Merriam gently tested her shoulder, trying to gauge how deep the scratch went into her muscle. She knew taking large groups to Earth was a bad idea. The more people, the more attention would be drawn. But two people would still be inconspicuous.

"No."

"Excuse you?" Merriam scoffed. "You aren't about to run around alone while a *demon* is on the loose."

"Don't be ridiculous. I'm perfectly capable of holding my own, and it won't take long at all."

"Don't be ridiculous?" Merriam repeated incredulously.

"Your Highness." Eskar stepped forward. "The merc is right, you shouldn't go alone. That thing held its own against six of us. It's dangerous."

Oren considered her words, drawing his hand down his cheek. "You're right. Rovin, you'll come with me."

"Oren, no. I should go. I know Earth's territory," Merriam insisted.

"No, you're hurt. Your body doesn't need the added stress."

Merriam's mouth dropped open. "You don't need to protect me. It makes sense for me to—"

"No," Oren interrupted, his eyes meeting hers, as hard and cool as chips of emerald.

Merriam swallowed at the weight and order behind his gaze. That was not the look of a lover. That was the look of a king, and it sent a current buzzing through her veins. She closed her mouth and nodded.

His eyes softened a fraction. *Your wounds need tending. I can't very well ravage a body running hot with infection, can I?* He looked to Rovin. "Let's go, Lieutenant."

Rovin shot her a look somewhere between smug and irritated before stepping in front of Oren, who was carefully wiping blood from the stones set in his rings. Once he was satisfied, Oren loosely looped his arms around Rovin, striking the rings together and pushing them both through the rift in reality. Merriam felt the familiar yet almost indiscernible pull and push run through her as the universe swallowed them up and spit them back out again.

She barely had time to blink before Eskar was on top of her, fisting a hand in her shirt and yanking her forward. "You need to watch your mouth, *mercenary*. You may be filth with no morals, but that is no way to talk to your future king," Eskar spat in her face, lips lifted in a snarl that bared elongated canines.

Narrowing her eyes, Merriam shoved the Ranger back roughly with two hands to the chest. "Get in my face again and—"

Mollian was between them, holding a hand up to each.

"You'll what, merc?" Eskar taunted, a lock of straight black hair falling over her dark eyes.

Merriam's eyes flashed, but Mollian spoke. "Cool it. Both of you. Tensions are still high from the fight."

"Control your pet, Your Highness." Eskar's eyes didn't leave Merriam's until she abruptly spun on a heel and walked away.

"Yet you're going to lecture me about how to speak to royalty?" Merriam called after her, taking a step forward.

Mollian's forearm pressed against the top of her chest, halting her. "Ria, breathe."

Her eyes flicked to him, anger seething in the amber depths. "She can't talk to you like that."

Mollian laughed at the irony. "If I recall, that was her exact issue with you and my brother."

That's different.

Care to explain that to her?

That's not what I meant. Merriam let out a breath, relaxing her posture.

Calysta, who'd corralled the horses, walked up with a med kit. "All right then, who's first?"

After their wounds were cleaned, rough stitches tied in Mollian's calf, and the bird sent to Umbra, they mounted the horses and continued toward Umbra. Eskar rode in front, but they all stayed alert even with the Ranger scouting ahead. Conversation was kept to a minimum, and they finally made it to the clearing where they'd set up camp on the trip out.

There was a stream not too far off, and Merriam and Mollian waded into the cold water, scrubbing dried flakes of black blood from their bodies. "How long do you think the smell will linger?" Mollian asked miserably, bending forward to dunk his hair into the water and roughly scrub the loose curls.

"I'm hoping it will leave when we change clothes." Merriam stripped off her pants, agitating the fabric. "This was one of my favorite pairs."

"You might have to burn them." Mollian wrinkled his nose.

As clean as they could get, they quickly dried off and dressed, wringing the blood-stained clothes as best they could and carrying them back up to camp.

Just as they'd laid the clothes out by the fire to dry, Oren and Rovin stepped through the trees. The two were both wearing clean clothes, probably having showered at Entumbra. Merriam bit her lip to keep from making a sarcastic comment about it, eyes flicking to where Eskar sat on the other side of the fire.

"We brought food." Oren held up a paper sack, grease spots spreading along the bottom.

Merriam smiled, clasping her hands to her chest. "You didn't!"

Oren met her eyes. This was an apology for leaving her behind, and her reaction was exactly what he'd been hoping for. His pleasure at her happiness made her heart skip a beat.

She stood up, holding her palms out. The scent made her mouth water as Oren laid a paper-wrapped burger in her hands. "Oh, you're my hero." She sighed dramatically, sinking to a log to lay into the fast food.

Rovin gave her a weird look that she ignored as she happily ate, dancing a little in her seat.

You can thank me later. Oren's voice dripped with suggestion, and heat crawled up her neck. She ignored that, too, and continued munching away.

The moons shone brightly in the sky, one a thick crescent and the other past half full, as the group sat around the fire, tearing into the greasy goodness that Oren and Rovin had brought back with them from Merriam's former home. Calysta had been brought a fruit salad stored in a small, hollowed out melon, which she also ate with abandon.

After the meal, Eskar volunteered for the first watch, Rovin drew mid, and Calysta the last. Merriam's body instantly felt heavier with the knowledge of a full night's sleep, and she trudged into the tent, unceremoniously toeing off her low boots, kicking off her pants, and collapsing onto a bedroll. She hissed at the pressure against her bandaged shoulder, rolling onto her side.

When Oren came in, he neatly lined his boots up to the side of the entrance. Merriam smiled as she watched him step over her own and strip off his shirt, folding it and placing it on top of the bag at the side of the tent. "What?" He lifted a hand to pull his hair free, stretching the muscles that ran up the side of his body.

She licked her lips, fighting the tightness in her chest as he watched her. "Could we even be more opposite if we tried?"

Oren knelt to grab the blanket at her feet, unfolding it before lying beside her and draping it over them. "I like to think we're very much alike."

"Oh, really? Name three things."

"We both love the mountains."

"There's one."

"And braiding your hair."

"Nope, I do that out of necessity and practicality."

"Mmm." Oren was propped on an elbow, cheek against one hand while the other began working her plait free. "Well, we both enjoy when I braid your hair."

"I'm not sure that counts, Majesty."

"It's true though, is it not?"

"Fine." Merriam nestled further into the pillow, folding her hands beneath her chin.

"We both love the stars." Oren finished setting her hair free and ran his fingers through the strands, still damp from the creek.

"Two of those things can apply to multiple people."

"That doesn't mean they don't also apply to us."

Merriam's eyes drifted closed, her body exhausted and his hand in her hair soothing. "I'm sorry I challenged you," she said quietly.

Oren lowered his face to hers, brushing his nose across her cheek and pressing a kiss to her temple. "Never stop challenging me, Mer."

"Your Rangers are loyal, though. Eskar was ready to throw down for how Calysta and I were talking to you."

"Did she—"

"I'm fine, O. And I can hold my own against any of them." Merriam assured him, rolling her eyes beneath her lids. "So protective for a male who left me all alone with the possibility of a dangerous creature nearby," she teased.

"Someone had to surprise you with supper, Lady." Oren twirled a lock of hair around his finger.

Merriam smiled. "Thank you for that. It's been ages since I've been back for comfort food."

Oren nuzzled her neck, nipping her lightly. "The way you looked at me earlier, when I told you 'no'... I wanted to take you right then and there. Audience be damned."

The tickle of his teeth against her skin made her shiver. "Even covered in blood?"

"Especially covered in blood." Oren slid a hand to her hip and pulled her back against him.

Mollian came into the tent then, stumbling to kick off his boots and leaving them lying next to Merriam's. Oren fell back against the pillow, eyes lifting to the ceiling. "Your timing is impeccable, brother."

Mollian dropped his shirt to the floor and fell chest down onto his blankets. "You've stolen my personal heater. I think I'm more inconvenienced than you are."

Merriam giggled, turning her face into the pillow to stifle the sound.

Oren's arm slid around her waist, holding her close. "Fair enough. I'll let you win this one."

Mollian's eyes were already closed, and he waved a hand noncommittally.

Merriam's heart swelled with contentment at their banter. Feeling the heat of Oren at her back. Feeling Mollian's closeness in her soul, his magic flowing quietly in her veins. The muscles in her legs twitched slightly as she relaxed and slipped into sleep.

Chapter 21

I kneel for *no one*

THEY MADE IT BACK to Umbra the following night. Luckily, the demon didn't appear to have any kind of poison on its claws. Both Mollian's and Merriam's wounds were free of infection and healing quickly, thanks to Mollian's fae blood.

Calysta had split off upon reaching the city, heading toward the merc house to update them with details of the attack. Leonidas had sent the message on to the castle, the mercs deciding it would be more prudent to try to figure out a pattern than to try to chase the demon blindly through Jekeida. Oren had tasked Eskar with briefing the scouting group with information too sensitive or lengthy to include with the initial raven and called a meeting of all the advisors and generals for the following morning. Regenya had handed him jurisdiction of the case before they'd left for Entumbra, and he was relieved to have final authority over the matter.

When they got to the castle, Merriam walked straight to her room for a hot bath, washing off the lingering feel of ichor from her skin and hair. Her wounds were closed, and she gingerly ran her fingers over the thick scabs that crossed one shoulder. Smaller scratches dotted her arms and legs, but she knew from experience they would fade to nothing soon.

Her fingers were pruned by the time she got out, the water long turned tepid. She dried off, running a brush half-heartedly through her hair before throwing on a loose shirt and a pair of shorts.

Still not wanting to be alone after the attack in the forest, she padded through the common area and into Mollian's room. He was still in the bathroom, so she stretched out on his bed, wet hair strewn out behind her, and was asleep within moments.

Merriam woke with the sun the next morning, blinking into the soft light of dawn that came through the open window. She stretched, rolling over and almost on top of Mollian, who grumbled and pushed her away with an elbow.

She curled into his side, bringing her legs to her chest and pressing her face against his arm. "I'm hungry."

"Sounds like a personal problem," Mollian mumbled on a sigh.

"Come with me to the kitchens?"

"I'm not the one who fell asleep before supper last night."

Merriam frowned.

"Leftovers are on the table. Now let me sleep."

"You're the best." Merriam softly butted his shoulder with her forehead before rolling out of bed and padding into the common area.

She was tearing into her third biscuit, slathering it with butter and honey, two plum pits discarded onto the table in front of her, when Mollian finally came into the room, pushing his hair from his forehead sleepily. He sat down next to her, tipping over and resting his head against his shoulder. "How are you not exhausted?" He stretched his injured leg out gingerly, rotating his ankle to test the muscle.

"I slept for like half a day," Merriam said through a mouthful of biscuit.

"So ladylike."

"Bite me."

Mollian sat up, grabbing the last plum from the platter and taking a large bite. "I'm not going to the brief today. I want to look into what kind of demon that might have been. We have a few references here that could prove helpful."

"Of course you're going to leave me alone with those animals."

"I would say I wish I could attend, but I've actually no desire to sit and argue politics over action," Mollian said unapologetically, taking another bite of fruit.

"Thank you for your undying support." Merriam rolled her eyes, brushing her hands off over the table and standing up.

She walked into her room to change, donning a tunic, leggings, and her weapons belt, an axe sheathed on each hip.

Merriam entered the war room, picking a spot against the back wall and leaning against it. A few advisors and a couple of commanders were already seated around the table in the center, talking quietly. Captain Ferrick came in, eyes sliding to Merriam and narrowing in a churlish glare before taking a position near the head of the table.

She rolled her eyes, not caring if he saw, settling more comfortably against the wall and listening to the casual conversation around the table.

A door across the room opened, and Oren walked through. His eyes met Merriam's only briefly before scanning the people assembled as he pulled out the chair at the head of the table and sat. Everyone instantly quieted as he settled, stretching one arm out to rest in front of him, dark purple umbrite glinting on his ring finger. Everything about his posture and his presence projected the command of a king.

"There's a demon loose in Sekha," he said without preamble. "Most reports of its attacks have been in Jekeida, with a few along the border of West Audha. We had hoped to take care of it quickly and quietly, without having to involve anyone outside of the Guard, but it's time to alert the public."

"I'm sure you've all heard some reports of attacks and disappearances. We believe they're connected. It's also now our belief that this demon may have been summoned."

Ferrick ran a hand over his beard. "What reason do we have to suspect that? Demons have accidentally found their way into our world before."

Oren cracked his knuckles with a thumb. "There's a possibility that whoever was trafficking nymphs may have opened a rift into a different realm, whether purposefully or not, and pulled it through. The disappearances also suggest that a person is involved."

"Could the demon not be taking people away to ... eat or otherwise slaughter wherever it is making its home?" a delegate from West Audha asked.

"We were attacked by the demon on our way back from Entumbra. That creature didn't seem to be capable of strategy or forethought. If it had broken into homes, it would not have been stealthy."

"So you believe someone is controlling the demon?" Ferrick questioned.

"I believe someone might *think* they have control of it. But realities that produce this kind of creature don't typically come with magic that is easy to harness. We need to find who let it in, and just as importantly, find *where* it was let in. There are ley lines of magic throughout Nethyl and some pockets where the power of the Gate has settled over the years. If enough of the nymphs' blood was spilled over one of these pockets, that could be how a portal was opened. We need to find the area and ward it, chase the magic off, to prevent something like this from happening again."

Oren met Merriam's eyes across the room. "We have already struck a deal with you and your troupe, Merriam. Considering these new developments, I am offering to double the final payout."

Merriam's eyebrows shot up despite herself.

"But you will be required to work alongside my Rangers." Ferrick's head snapped to Oren, his eyes narrowing at the prince's claim on the special unit of the Guard. Oren ignored him, eyes focused on Merriam. "This is unlike anything we have had to deal with in hundreds of years. I want it taken care of swiftly. One of my commanders will be given charge of this operation and be equal head with whomever you and the other mercs decide. All information will need to be shared equally, decisions made jointly."

Merriam sawed her teeth over her bottom lip for a moment, considering everything. "We will accept," she decided, knowing the others would find the price to be well worth any headache of working directly with the Guard.

Oren dipped his head.

"Shouldn't we be finding out what this person wants? What his motivations are?" Ferrick spoke up, clearly irritated.

Oren leveled a cool gaze at him, running his thumb over his mouth before resting his hand on the table. "What does the motivation matter, Pos?"

Ferrick pressed his lips together, shifting uncomfortably, but he held the eye contact. "I was only suggesting that perhaps if we learned what they wanted—"

"I couldn't give a fuck what they want," Oren interrupted, his voice still cool and calm. "They are attacking *my* kingdom, terrorizing *my* people. There is only one answer to that, as far as I am concerned."

"Yes, your Majesty, but—"

Oren's eyes blazed, his tone laced with finality and an almost palpable power. "I kneel for *no one*. Whoever thinks they can wreak havoc where I rule will very quickly learn the opposite."

Ferrick finally dropped his eyes, conceding.

Oren turned his gaze to the rest of those in attendance. "Are there any questions?"

There was some discussion about whether the Crown would be sending reinforcements to the cities most affected, as well as how they could better protect themselves. Oren answered every question with grace, promising that any new information would be disseminated as it was received.

After all further deliberation had finished, Oren stood, leaning against the table as everyone filed out of the room.

Merriam stood in the back, hands tucked nonchalantly in her pockets as she watched him watch his advisors and leaders of his Guard. She didn't think she had ever been more attracted to him than she was in that moment. His command of the room, of these powerful fae, was intoxicating.

His eyes found hers, and she let them burn. She may as well have been Casting to him, the unbridled intensity shining in the liquid amber of her eyes made her thoughts that clear.

Oren's gaze slipped back to the people exiting, and Merriam looked away from him, casually stepping forward as the last of the advisors exited the room.

"If you have further concerns, Merriam, feel free to discuss them with me in my office," Oren addressed her formally, turning to walk through the door at the back of the room.

Merriam followed behind at a slight distance. Oren held the door for her to enter, then locked it behind him. Instead of going to the desk at the back wall, he sat down on a couch across from the door, picking up a pile of papers and shifting through them, stopping to examine one.

Merriam leaned against the wall, watching his movements with unveiled hunger.

"Do you have any qualms about how the others will respond to this job offer?" Oren asked, flipping a page.

Merriam pulled her braid over her shoulder, toying with the end of it. "No, I think they'll all be quite pleased, actually."

"Good." Oren continued his browsing, marking something down every so often. A few moments went by before he said flatly, without looking up. "If you're going to keep looking at me like that, I will drag you to that desk and fuck you on it."

Heat unfurled through her body, desire pounding in her blood. Merriam walked with measured steps to the front of the desk before turning around and leaning against it. When Oren lifted his head to look at her, she placed her palms against the desktop and boosted herself onto it. Slowly and deliberately, she spread one leg and then the other, trailing her fingers from her knee up her thigh, never taking her eyes off of him.

Oren watched her, gaze gradually moving from her legs up her body, eventually meeting her eyes. He set down the papers and stood, moving to stand in front of her. "Are you testing me, Merriam?" he asked, voice low and heavy with lust.

She cocked her head to the side, fluttering her lashes. "I'm calling your bluff," she answered sweetly.

A soft growl rumbled deep in his chest, and he grabbed one of her legs, holding it up and removing her boot. He let the shoe fall to the floor with a thud before grabbing her other leg and doing the same. Then he stepped between her knees and unbuckled her weapons belt, setting it to the side before snaking his hands up her shirt to grab the waistband of her leggings.

Her breath caught in her throat at the desire lighting his eyes, and she grabbed his arms, lifting herself slightly so he could jerk the fabric down past her thighs, stripping the pants from her.

"When you told Ferrick you wouldn't kneel, I couldn't stop picturing you on your knees in front of me with your face between my legs," she said breathlessly, digging into his biceps and dragging her fingers down his arms.

"Oh?" Oren crept his hands up her thighs, slipping his thumbs under the light cotton of her panties. "Have you thought about it often?" he asked, curling his fingers around the top of the garment.

"Yes," she whispered as he slipped the panties from underneath her, swiftly pulling them free. The desk was cool and smooth against her ass, and she wrapped her legs around Oren, trying to pull him closer, needing to feel him against her.

"Do you think about my mouth on you when you've got your hand between your thighs?" he asked, holding himself away from her body and grabbing her hands from his arms.

"Yes," she breathed, pleading with her eyes for contact where she desperately wanted it. "I whisper your name when I come." She tilted her face up to his, and he brushed the lightest of kisses against the corner of her mouth. "I have every time since you first took me on the catwalk in Entumbra."

"Fuck, Merri," he groaned, capturing her mouth in a brief but heated kiss, biting her lower lip as he pulled away and shifting her arms behind her back. He tied her wrists together tightly with her panties. She could feel the dampness of where the fabric had been pressed against her stretched taut against her pulse points.

Oren held her chin between his thumb and forefinger, tilting her face up to him to kiss her leisurely. "You are a damned drug." He kissed her again, still light and unhurried, and slipped one hand around her to tug the tie from the end of her braid.

He brushed his lips across her face and neck as his fingers methodically pulled through the braid, slowly working her hair free. When his mouth found hers again, she tried to deepen the kiss, but he pulled away, keeping his distance.

Merriam tugged at her restraint, squirming and trying to pull him closer with her legs, but with her hands tied, he was able to maintain full control, keeping their bodies from touching.

"Oren, please," she whimpered against his lips. Her hair now fell freely down her back, brushing against the soft skin of her forearms with a slight tickle.

"That's it, Lady," Oren purred. "Beg for me." He dragged his teeth across her ear, down her neck.

She arched into the touch. "Oren," she gasped. Her need for him was almost painful. Her heart beat heavily in her chest as she was helpless to do anything but feel his delicate assault on her body, the fingers of one hand skimming over her thigh. "Please. I need you."

He slipped one hand into her hair, holding the back of her head as he kissed her fully. She swept her tongue greedily into his mouth, running the tip over his sharp canines. His kiss swallowed her moan, and this time, when she tightened her legs around him, he yielded.

Oren dragged his other hand down her back, relishing the heat of her pressed against him. She rolled her hips against where his cock strained against his pants, and he groaned, tightening his hold and pushing back against her. He tore away from the kiss, pressing his lips to her neck as he tugged on her hair.

Merriam moved her hips against him again. "I need you, O." Her head fell to the side, granting him better access to her neck.

Oren bit the delicate skin before pressing another hungry kiss to her mouth. "I want you. So fucking bad," he growled.

Before she could reply, he pulled away. She let out a little cry of disapproval at the loss of contact, but he was already lifting her from the desk, turning her so that she was facing it. Gently, he pressed her forward, and she complied until she was lying flat on the desktop, head turned to one side.

Oren slipped one foot between hers and forced her legs apart, sending a shiver of anticipation down her spine as the cool air licked at her wetness. He leaned over her, brushing her hair aside and planting a soft kiss on her shoulder blade. His fingers brushed across the healing claw marks there before he trailed his hand down her back to her ass, which he gave a firm smack.

He untied his pants and pushed them down to his ankles, grabbing his cock and running the head over her clit and up her center. He growled in feral approval at how she was damn near dripping for him and repeated the motion one more time, her hips tilting expectantly.

She was about to scream at him; her need felt so insistent, and then he was pushing in, and she lifted up onto her toes, letting him angle deeper. She gasped as he sank into her, clenching around him. He paused for a moment, letting her adjust, and then pulled out, tortuously slow. His hands wrapped around her waist, dragging down to her hips, fingers digging into her skin. He thrust into her hard, her thighs smacking against the back of the desk. He kept his hold on her, fucking her with deep, forceful strokes.

Merriam clenched her hands into fists behind her back as she moaned, relishing the fullness of him inside her.

"This fucking view," Oren grunted. "Legends, Merri." He slipped one hand from her hip down the front of her, pressing the pads of two fingers against her clit and sliding them back and forth across it.

"Oren," she gasped, straining against her bonds. "Don't—don't fucking stop."

He kept the pressure moving across her clit as he thrust. Her whimpers grew more and more insistent, almost enough to undo him. Oren sucked in a breath, trying to rein in his control, and then Merriam was pulsing around him, calling out his name.

The fabric of her panties almost tore as he ripped them from her wrists, pulling out of her and flipping her around to set her on the desk. "You are fucking exquisite." Oren grabbed her leg, hoisting it high on his waist and pushing back into her.

She gasped, hands flying to his shoulders to steady herself as he continued to pump into her, crashing his lips against hers and fisting his free hand into her hair.

She moaned into his mouth, pulling herself closer to him, wrapping one hand around the back of his neck as the other slipped down the planes of his chest.

"Merri. Legends, fuck," he ground out, hands tightening against her as he came. He kissed her deeply again, the intensity slowly softening to a sweet intimacy until he pulled away to rest his forehead against hers.

Her heart thundered in her chest, still coming down from her own orgasm, and she clenched purposefully around his cock.

He hissed, pushing deeper into her. "Damn you, woman."

Laughing lightly, she wrapped her arms and legs around him and nuzzled her face against his neck, breathing in his pine and plum and night sky scent. He rested his chin on top of her head, stroking her hair while the other arm wrapped around her waist, holding her close.

After several moments, he pressed a kiss to her hair and pulled away, easing out of her.

Reluctantly, she dropped her arms from his shoulders and let her legs fall, dangling from the desk.

"Stay put." He brushed a kiss to her lips, refastened his pants, and walked across the room to a door that led to a small bathroom. Wetting a hand towel in the sink, he brought it over and cleaned himself from her before tossing the towel into a basket in the bathroom.

"Would you like me to braid your hair?" he asked softly, running his fingers through the pale golden waves.

Merriam peered up at him, his bright green eyes shining with an open vulnerability that melted her. "Nothing would make me happier," she answered, hopping down from the desk to dress while Oren moved to the couch. She pushed his legs apart before lowering to the cushion between them.

He deftly worked his fingers through her hair, taming it into a tight braid that trailed down her back. "You're good to go."

She turned, catching his lips with hers, hoping to convey how much she cherished these moments after. How intimate they felt. How scared she was to voice any of it. "I'll see you later then, Majesty." She stood up, heading to the door.

"I look forward to it, Lady," Oren replied with a smile.

Chapter 22

I'm looking for Jasper

Five years before ...

MERRIAM WALKED THROUGH UMBRA, heading toward the tavern indicated on the note Oren had left for her before departing to sequester away in Entumbra. She toyed with the aspen leaf at her throat, trying to keep her breathing even to counteract the way her heart raced nervously.

She stopped a few paces from the door of the tavern, cleverly dubbed "What Ales You?" A falcon was perched on the sign, and its head tipped to the side to watch as she brushed her palms against her pants, taking one last moment to steel herself before approaching the door.

A handful of patrons were scattered about, but none looked at her as she went up to the bar, ordering a mug of cider before taking it to a booth in the back and sitting on the side facing the room.

She sipped on her drink, trying to appear calm and unaffected.

A tall, broad-shouldered man with close-cropped blonde hair and piercing blue eyes stood from the bar, scooping up a short glass tumbler that looked even smaller in his large hands. The dark liquid within barely stirred as he walked over to her.

Merriam narrowed her eyes as she watched him near. She could have sworn she vaguely recognized him, but couldn't place him exactly.

He stopped at the edge of the table, and his own eyes lit as if he recognized her. "You're the young prince's pet," he said in human tongue.

Merriam grit her teeth, eyes tightening in a sharp glare. "Fuck off," she replied in Common.

The man chuckled, gesturing with his drink to the seat across from her. "Mind if I sit?" He also switched to Common.

"I'd prefer you didn't." Merriam held her glare.

The man sat, taking a slow drink before setting his glass on the table and giving her a half-appraising look. "What business brings you here this morning?" he finally asked.

"Not that it's any of your concern, but I'm meeting someone. So if you could leave me alone, I would appreciate it."

A smile curled up the corner of his mouth at her icy tone, and he raised two fingers over his shoulder, cocking them forward twice before grabbing his drink and swallowing the rest of the liquor.

Merriam watched as a girl materialized from somewhere on the other side of the bar, bouncing from the shadows in an energetic burst of flame-red hair and heavily freckled skin. She slid into the seat next to Merriam, smiling brightly.

Stunned into silence at the audacity, Merriam only scooted over as a dark-skinned male walked up to the booth and sat opposite the halfling girl. His huge black-feathered wings were tucked in tight against his back, and some of the long, tightly knotted locs of his black hair slid over his shoulder as he cocked his head to look at Merriam, silver eyes watching her every movement.

Merriam licked her lips, mouth dry as she pressed against the wall, trapped by these strangers.

The winged male smiled. "There's no reason to look so frightened, Merriam."

"I'm looking for Jasper," she said suspiciously.

"At your service." His hand reached across the table, and she tentatively shook it. "The sunshine next to you is Aleah, and this is Leonidas."

"Lovely to meet you, really," Aleah gushed.

Leonidas only nodded, humor gleaming in those ice-blue eyes.

"Wait, I know you." Hearing his name finally made it click in her mind. "You help out at the aviary sometimes."

"I keep them competent, yes." He smiled lazily, running a hand over his short hair.

"Prince Oren tells me you have some skills that may be useful to us." Jasper continued to watch her.

Merriam nodded. "I'm a good climber. A great climber, actually, and skilled at reconnaissance. I can fight some, too, though I haven't had much training."

Jasper ran his hand over his chin. "The recommendation of the prince goes a long way with me, but I don't run a charity, Merriam."

She bristled, straightening in her seat. "Listen, I know I'm just a human—"

Jasper waved his hand to interrupt her. "I couldn't give a fuck about your species. Leonidas is human. Aleah is half-human. All I care about is their ability to do the jobs required. So, if you'll let me finish ..."

Merriam nodded, taking a drink to calm her nerves.

"I'm not going to ask you to prove yourself every day. That's not my place, and it's not fair to expect you never to have an off day. Whatever else may be said about me, I am just in the way I treat people. But before you join us, just show us what you can do."

"What do you need?"

Jasper tilted his head to the side, "You know your abilities best, Merriam. You tell me, what would be the most optimal way for you to show me that you're invaluable?"

Merriam blinked, caught off guard. "I can steal something," the words came tumbling from her lips before she had a chance to really think about them.

Aleah clapped her hands gleefully. "Oh, pay up, Leo!"

Merriam watched in confusion as Leonidas groaned, digging into his pocket and tossing over a silver coin.

"I bet him you would choose something illegal, but he was confident there was no way the prin—" she stopped mid-sentence, picking back up smoothly, "someone with your affiliations would offer to break the law."

Merriam found herself instantly warming to the girl and was unable to keep the smile from spreading across her face. "So, what do I take?"

Jasper, who'd been watching the bartender, returned his attention to her. "Take a bottle from behind the bar."

"Now?"

Jasper shrugged, watching her reaction.

Merriam surveyed the bar, the bartender, and the other patrons. She brought her drink back up as she watched. "Any requests?"

Jasper raised a brow with a smirk. "You understand you're making this more difficult for yourself by asking for input, don't you?"

Merriam shrugged, meeting his gaze evenly. "I never back down from a challenge."

Jasper let out a soft, dark chuckle at that. "Oh, you'll learn to, I assure you of that, merc. Grab the top shelf rum."

Merriam suppressed the urge to grin like a fool that he had addressed her as a mercenary, implying he'd already accepted her. Aleah slid from the seat to let Merriam out, and she walked toward the end of the bar, where a hall extended out with a bathroom at the end.

Dipping into the hallway, she rested her back against the wall as she looked behind the bar. The area behind it was mostly filled with kegs, but there was plenty of space between two of them, and she carefully measured the distance with her eyes, focusing on the spot she needed to be.

Merriam twisted the rings on her middle fingers so that the stones faced her palms, swiping them across each other quickly.

Back on Earth, she was standing on a grassy hillside. Keeping her eyes trained on the spot she'd been looking at in the tavern, she walked the few paces across the hill, squatting down into a ball and taking a quick look at the bright blue sky above her before striking the stones together again.

She'd judged the distance right and was crouched between two kegs behind the bar. Her heart sped up at the thrill of the agility and grace the next movements would require. She listened. There had only been one person sitting at the bar before, and they'd been heavily concentrating on the drink in front of them. Only ambient noise could be heard, but no scuffling of boots against wood. Nothing to indicate to her that someone would be walking up to order a drink.

Leaning forward slightly, she watched the bartender's feet. He was facing the sink a little ways down from where she hid, but turned to walk to the far side of the bar. As soon as both of his feet turned away from her, she sprang forward, heart pounding in her chest as she stood on her tiptoes, fingers reaching for a bottle of rum from the shelf above her head.

She pulled it down, almost dropping it, but cradled it to her chest and shuffled quickly backward between the kegs. As soon as her shoulders were between them, she struck her rings back together. Flipped back onto Earth, she looked at the bottle in her lap and let out a triumphant laugh.

Scrambling to her feet, she walked a few steps back to the general area she'd come from, not having to be quite as specific with how long the hallway was. Composing herself, she Traveled back to Nethyl and headed to the table at a nondescript pace, shielding the bottle from view of the bar and sitting next to Aleah.

"Legends, she actually did it," the girl breathed.

Leonidas watched her set the bottle on the table and slide it over to Jasper, whose lips were raised in half a smile.

"Well done, Merriam," he said, pulling the bottle to him and popping the top off to raise it to his lips. "Welcome to the team." He wiped his mouth with the back of his hand and handed the bottle to Leonidas.

"How'd you do it?" the blonde asked after taking a sip of his own and passing the bottle to Aleah.

"Is that awe I hear from you, Leonidas?" Aleah teased, making a face and shivering as she took a swig.

Merriam smiled, meeting Leonidas's gaze. "I guess I failed to mention that when I said I was good at reconnaissance, what I really meant was that I'm good at stealth and staying undetected."

Jasper's eyes were on her fingers, and something like recognition shifted over his face. But it was there and gone before she clocked it, and he sat with a relaxed, friendly posture as he explained where to meet tomorrow so she could start training with them before delving into what sort of jobs she might expect at what sort of frequency.

As they shared the rum, Merriam felt a small flame of hope flicker to life in her chest. Hope that finding her own place here wouldn't be the constant battle she'd feared it would be.

A week later, Merriam sat on the floor of the training room in the merc house, legs stretched out in front of her and sweat making her clothes stick to her body. Training with the mercenaries was equal parts exhausting and rewarding. She'd already felt like she'd learned so much from them.

Though it was clear Jasper led the little troupe, everyone's opinion held equal weight, and no one was ashamed to defer to another when needed. Their dynamic was unlike anything Merriam had experienced or witnessed in the year she'd trained with the Guard.

Even still learning where she fit with this group, Merriam already felt more at home with them after seven days than she ever had with the Rangers.

Leonidas was out on a job, but Jasper and Aleah had both trained with her today. The majority of the afternoon had been spent on the climbing wall, the half-fae teaching Merriam how to properly fall and Jasper giving pointers on how to leverage her body to conserve energy when scaling.

They were all hydrating, Merriam getting ready to head back to the castle for the night.

"You could stay here, you know," Aleah offered.

Merriam smiled, shaking her head. "I would, but if jobs are already possibly going to be keeping me away for days on end, I want to stay with Molli as much as possible."

"Rumor's always been that the younger prince wouldn't ever marry or take a mate." Aleah slid a questioning look to the human.

"Oh, no, it's not like that," Merriam explained with a laugh. "I love him, but not in that way. We're *mehhen*."

Aleah's gaze shuttered, freckles standing out as the color drained from her face. "Did you know?" she asked Jasper.

"No, Aleah." His voice was soft and soothing, and he reached out a hand to the younger girl.

Aleah pushed to her feet, clenching her hands into fists to keep them from shaking and walking briskly from the room.

Merriam watched in confusion, mouth open but unsure of what words to speak. She stood to follow Aleah, but Jasper gently grabbed her wrist.

"Don't," he said with a sigh. "Give her space to sort this through."

"What did I do?" Merriam asked, anxiety lacing its way through her. Of course this had been too easy to last.

Jasper stroked his thumb over her pulse point before releasing her. "Aleah learned the hard way how strong a *mehhen* bond can be. She trusts easily and loves freely until given a reason to do otherwise, but her past has taught her to be wary of certain ties."

"What happened?"

"That's her story to tell, when she's ready." Jasper replied with a sad smile. "Just keep doing what you have been, she will learn that you have room in your heart for more than one friendship."

Chapter 23

Thunder

MERRIAM LEANED AGAINST THE back of the couch at the merc house, waiting for any questions that would undoubtedly arise.

"So, Jasper is joint-leading this with one of the Rangers?" Aleah clarified.

Merriam nodded.

"But we're still able to do our thing the way we do it?" the half-fae specified, suspicious.

"The only stipulation is to share any information we have with them. It doesn't matter who takes this guy out, we get paid."

"I'm sure they're going to love that." Calysta smirked. "Do we know who is going to be assigned with us?"

Merriam shook her head. "All those details will be worked out tomorrow when we meet."

"For now, let's figure out a plan of attack." Jasper sat forward, resting his elbows on his knees. "I want to go into tomorrow with at least a few ideas of how to tackle this. We need to look prepared."

"'Look' being the key word there." Leonidas ran a hand over his short hair. "From what Calysta told us, that thing meant business."

Merriam gave him a grim smile, shrugging her shoulders. "Let's also not discount that if one came through, others may have as well. The chance of that feels greater if a person opened a rift rather than the rift being a random flicker of magic."

"The only plan that makes sense is to attack fast and hard. Have teams set up to attack from multiple points. If they bleed, they can die." Leonidas folded his tattooed arms over his chest.

"How do you expect to find it, though?" Merriam asked.

"Whether or not it was intentional, our current assumption is that this rift is over a pocket of magic that may have leached from the Gate, right?" Campbell asked, twisting a dark curl at the base of an antler in thought.

"Right." Merriam watched him think.

"Would a Keeper be able to track that?" he suggested. "Maybe figure out where the power may have been collecting? If someone did use it to open a portal, I doubt they would leave it alone for long."

Merriam toyed with her necklace, contemplating. "I honestly don't know if the Keepers can track that. I could ask, though. They know ley lines of magic run deep beneath the surface, so it makes sense they'd have some sort of map of where they are."

"We need to plot out the places the attacks have happened, see if there's any pattern." Jasper said. "We can't discount that if the rift was a fluke, it's probably already closed. Those portals don't hold for long."

"Why didn't we have that information before? That would have been helpful," Leonidas muttered.

"It was the Ranger's hunt. We were more back up than anything. They're stingy with need-to-know information," Merriam said with a roll of her eyes.

"But we're supposedly on a team now?" Leonidas raised a brow.

"Supposedly, yes."

"I don't trust them." He shifted against the wall.

"Me neither." Merriam sighed. "If you guys want to back out, I understand."

"Are you calling us cowards?" Campbell jokingly accused.

"Of course not. But this is an unprecedented job."

"Unprecedented is what we do best." Aleah grinned.

Merriam smiled, jumping over the back of the couch and settling into the cushions. "So what's the plan?"

After discussing the details, Merriam headed back to the castle to work out a meeting between the mercenaries and the Rangers the next day, promising to send a bird with the information.

It had just turned full dark outside, and as she walked, she looked up to the sky. Something unidentifiable tugged inside her, and she left cobblestone streets to wander into the forest. Once safely hidden in the trees, she turned the rings on her middle fingers around so that the stones were aligned above her palms. Putting the pads of her hands together, she pulled the stones across each other and created a rift in the world.

She felt that familiar pull, the tattoo on her back tingling, and then the push outward as she settled into her environment. Merriam stood on a sparsely forested hillside, and when she tilted her head up, she was looking at the once-familiar band of the Milky Way stretching across the sky.

Sitting down, she held her knees to her chest as she gazed at the stars. She sat like that for a while, letting her mind shut off as she lost herself in the sounds of the night. It would be so simple to stay there, where there were no demons, no struggle to prove herself.

Merriam rested her chin on her knees and watched the long stretch of road in the distance, peppered with headlights and taillights. It wouldn't be but a thirty-minute walk from here and she'd be at her aunt's old house. She knew it was there, but hadn't visited since she'd left all those years ago. It wasn't home. And her aunt wasn't family. She was a different girl now. A girl who fought demons. A girl whose best friend was a prince. A girl whose lover was soon to be king.

A girl who didn't belong on Earth.

Merriam smiled, glancing up at the sky again, marveling at the constellations of her childhood and the single moon shining down in a tiny sliver. The stars were the only things from this world that gave her a pang of nostalgia.

Suddenly, a loud crack rent the air, making Merriam jump. She put one hand to her chest, laughing at herself as she remembered where she was. It was probably just a hunter or maybe a homeowner scaring off a bear or a coyote.

Then a few drifting pieces of information clicked in her mind, and her blood ran cold.

Merriam struck her rings together, falling into a run as soon as she felt the world materialize around her. She pelted through the city, barely even slowing at the gates of the castle to let the guards wave her through. She threw out the awareness of her Bond, searching for Mollian. He would be the fastest way to reach Oren. The familiar ping of him lit in her consciousness.

Mollian had felt her reach and pulled it to him, letting her know to head straight for their rooms. She burst through the door, eyes landing on Mollian sitting at the desk across the room, already looking up at her.

"It's not just a rift," she gasped.

Mollian opened his mouth to speak, but she cut him off. "Where's Oren?"

"Probably in his rooms, but what's going on?"

Merriam was still panting heavily, trying to catch her breath. "Whoever summoned the demon didn't just open a single rift. He found a way to Travel."

Mollian's eyes went wide, and he stood from the desk, grabbing her hand and pulling her from the room. They quickly made their way up the stairs and down the hall, where Rillak was standing guard outside Oren's room.

The burly male straightened at Mollian's approach, inclining his head respectfully. "Young Prince, little merc," he greeted, stepping aside.

"Evening, Rillak." Mollian smiled at him, rapping twice on the door before cracking it open. "Don't let anyone disturb us."

"Of course," Rillak replied as Mollian stepped into the common area, pulling Merriam in after him.

When the door closed behind them, Mollian finally dropped her hand. Oren was walking out of his bedroom, slipping on a shirt. His hair hung in damp waves over the side of his head, and he brushed it back from his face as he took them in.

Merriam stepped away from Mollian, sinking unsteadily down onto one of the couches and digging her fingers into the cushion on either side of her. "The person we're looking for didn't just accidentally open a portal to a demon realm. They've been to Earth, too. They can Travel."

Oren sat down across from her, eyes darkening with worry as he searched her face.

"I went back tonight," she started as Mollian sat next to her. "I don't even know why, but while I was there, I heard a gunshot. Do you know what a gunshot might sound like from a distance to someone who had never heard one before?"

Oren ran a hand over his mouth, sighing deeply. "Thunder."

Merriam nodded, toying with the aspen leaf on her throat. "The reports of the gunshots could be so sporadic because he only has to use the gun when whoever he was attacking managed to get the upper hand. They're loud and would draw too much attention. Even if he didn't get it from Earth, he got it from another world. Something tells me that demon we fought the other day wouldn't be capable of making a weapon of that caliber. And if this man is Traveling ... it's not nymph blood he used to open a portal. That might have been enough to tear into another realm under the right circumstances, but—"

"You need Keeper blood to Travel," Mollian interrupted.

Merriam nodded, glancing briefly at him before back to Oren, slowly sliding her pendent across the chain. "I mean ... unless you've Bonded yourself to someone, O ..." She dragged out, not wanting to be the first to speak the accusation.

"Gressia would never," Oren defended.

Mollian brushed a curl from his forehead with a sigh. "She might."

Oren shook his head. "She's a pain in the ass of a sister, yes, but she is the Keeper of the Gate. She takes that job seriously and is dedicated to it. There's no way she would put the realm in danger."

"Not knowingly, no." Merriam dropped her hand back down to the couch. "But what if she had been manipulated?"

"You know a Bond won't take if it's been forced."

"No, not forced, just tricked," Merriam clarified. "Basta would have had years to build Gressia's trust, gain her affections."

"Basta? He–" Oren stopped mid-sentence. His brow furrowed, and he pressed his lips together. Then he let out a groan, pushing his hands into his hair and tipping his head back against the couch. "Fuck, Gress, what did you do?"

"She loves him. He knew what power she had, and when he realized she was soft for him, it would have been so easy for him to grow that desire. All he had to do was make her fall in love with him, and he could have everything he wanted."

"But what is it that he wants?" Mollian asked.

"Does that even really matter? Even if all he wanted was to inflict a reign of terror on the people of Sekha, it's working," Merriam pointed out. "The real question is, does Gressia know what he's doing?"

Oren shook his head adamantly. "No, she would never stand for his bringing something like that to Nethyl."

"Then do we tell her? If she confronts him, would he hurt her?" Merriam asked.

Oren shook his head, wiping his hand over his face. "I don't know," he said simply. "I've met him a few times, and he always seemed completely enamored by her, but I never had a reason to pay him any close attention. Gressia is more than grown enough to look out for herself. I wouldn't want to think he'd harm her, but I also never would have thought him capable of using her power for destruction, either."

"So, it's safe to assume he would, then," Merriam finished.

"I'll send some of the Guard to Entumbra to keep an eye on things and help keep her safe," Oren offered.

"Don't you think that will make her mad? Encroaching on her territory?" Mollian interjected.

"We can't leave her defenseless, Molli," Oren insisted. "What if you went, too? Tried to get a read on Basta's location? We need to find out where he stays when he's not with her."

Mollian nodded his agreement. "I'll go down with a detachment of the Guard, explain to her what's going on and gather as much information about Basta as I can."

"We need to fill everyone else in." Merriam folded her hands between her knees. "We were already planning to have a meeting with the Rangers in the morning, but now you should probably be there to help us orchestrate how much information is given."

"We'll do it first thing tomorrow," Oren agreed.

Merriam stood. "I'll send a bird to the mercs."

Oren and Mollian also stood, Oren reaching to grab Merriam's hand before she could leave. He searched her eyes for a moment, debating whether or not to say something, but only pulled her to him, pressing a chaste kiss to her lips before stepping back. "I'll have a detachment ready to go at dawn. Be safe, brother."

Mollian nodded before turning to leave, Merriam following with a final look over her shoulder at the crown prince.

Chapter 24

The human has no wings

AFTER A QUICK TRIP to the aviary, Merriam walked into Mollian's room, twisting the purple umbrite ring on the finger of her left hand.

He walked out of his bathroom, shirtless and mussing up his wild curls. He dropped his hands and smiled when he saw her, his face tired. "I don't suppose you want to offer to go to Entumbra with me? I very much do not want to be the one to tell my sister there is an entirely real possibility her consort has been using her for her Keeper blood."

Mollian collapsed onto his bed, and Merriam sat down next to him, folding her legs in front of her. "Unfortunately, I do have to figure out how best to approach capturing and incapacitating said consort and will be needed here."

"Who told you to go around being useful to everyone? I'm the one who went through all the trouble to bring you here in the first place." Mollian rolled his head to the side to look at her beseechingly.

Merriam stuck her tongue out at him, pulling her rings off and holding them out. "Here, take these so you can come back the fast way."

Mollian slipped them onto his ring fingers. "Does this mean you're going to miss me?"

Merriam held her hand out so that he could press his palm to hers. "It means I'm worried about you wandering around in the forest by yourself without me there to keep you out of trouble."

He laughed at that, removing his hand from hers and shoving her knee. "I was wandering those woods long before you got here, and you'd be wise to remember that."

"Whatever you say, Prince," Merriam joked, unfolding her legs and rolling off the bed.

"Stay with me tonight?" Mollian turned onto his side, curls spilling over his forehead.

"Of course," she replied before slipping out to get ready for bed.

ℓ

Merriam woke just before dawn, one arm slung over her head, the other over her stomach. She tried to curl up and roll onto her side, but was met with a jarring resistance at her scalp.

"Molli," she grumbled, flinging an arm out to swat at him. "Molli, you're on my hair."

"Am not," came the sleepy reply, but he shifted, and she could move freely.

"Aren't you supposed to be up soon, anyway?" she asked, stretching out onto her side before pulling her knees up to her chest.

"Aren't you supposed to mind your own fucking business?"

"Who pissed in your porridge?" She settled further into her pillow.

"So crass." Mollian tugged at the blanket, pulling it out from under her chin.

Merriam huffed, rolling over onto her other side and into Mollian instead of fighting for the blanket. "I don't even like you," she mumbled to his back.

Mollian's lips lifted in a sleepy smile. "I'm sure."

They both dozed for a few more minutes before Mollian finally sat up and stretched, stumbling into the bathroom.

Merriam rose shortly after, knowing she should also prepare for the long day ahead, and went to her own room to get ready.

She had just finished pulling her hair up into a high ponytail when Mollian came in, pulling her to his chest. "I'm going to head down. I'll be back ... well, I wouldn't expect any sooner than three days, probably more though. If it's going to be any longer than a week, I'll send a bird if I can't manage to Travel to Earth for a few hours to come back myself."

"Okay, be safe." Merriam squeezed her arms around his waist.

"Always." He dropped a kiss to the top of her head before stepping back and holding his palm up for her to press hers against. "Love you, Ria," he tossed over his shoulder as he left her bathroom.

"Love you." She gave him a final wave before finishing her morning routine.

A few moments later, she was lacing up her boots and going down to grab some food from the kitchens. She ate a quick meal of meat and fruit before heading to the war room to make sure things were set up for the meeting.

She pulled a few extra chairs from a storage closet, situating them around the table. She wasn't sure how many Rangers would be attending, but she wanted all the mercs to have a designated seat.

Merriam jumped when she heard the door to the back office creak open and spun around to see Oren leaning against the doorway with one hand in his pocket. "That's a new hairstyle."

She shrugged, flicking her hair over her shoulder. "It's nice to change things up every once in a while."

His eyes burned with green fire as he pushed from the door frame and stepped closer to her. "It's sassy. I like it."

Merriam raised her eyebrows as he stopped in front of her, wrapping the trailing end of her ponytail in his hand. "My hair is sassy?"

"It moves with attitude, like all the energy you try to hide with your fluid grace is betrayed by the way your hair swings." His eyes traveled over her face, never meeting her gaze.

Merriam clicked her tongue. "Must be why I prefer the braid. Can't have my feelings being that easy to read." She stepped into him, tilting her head up.

His hand tightened in her hair, and he angled his head down, lips just barely grazing hers before they stopped at her ear. "Don't tempt me, Lady, or I will take you over that desk again."

Merriam brought a hand up to his chest, trailing slowly down his front. "You're the one who walked over here and put your hands on me, Majesty. So who is doing the tempting?" Her fingers brushed just above his belt, and the feeling of his muscles flexing under her touch sent a spark of pleasure coiling in her core.

He nipped at her ear before abruptly releasing her hair and stepping away, pulling out the seat at the head of the table and sitting down. He watched her, gaze still openly heated, and ran a thumb over his bottom lip.

A raised voice filtered through the closed door, the pitch elevated in irritation. "All I'm saying is that we shouldn't require an escort. We're working *for* these people." The door opened, and Ollivan came through, followed closely by Aleah, whose cheeks were almost as red as her hair as she glared at the Ranger's back.

Jasper entered next, placing a placating hand on Aleah's shoulder and steering her toward the table. "I'm sure he meant no disrespect, Aleah."

"Surely," she snorted, finally peeling her eyes from Ollivan and taking a seat facing the door.

Ollivan looked exceedingly uncomfortable, but said nothing.

Jasper sat next to Oren, a few locs of hair falling forward as he bowed his head respectfully before smiling at his old friend. "Good to see you again, brother."

"It's been too long, Jaz," Oren replied as the rest of the mercenaries sat along the table. "I only wish it were under better circumstances."

"Getting paid is always a good circumstance, Your Highness," Jasper said wryly.

"I suppose I can't argue with that," Oren chuckled.

A group of Rangers came in as Merriam slipped into a chair next to Campbell at the end. They silently filed along one side of the table, and Oren motioned for them to sit.

Dio was at the head of the table across from Jasper, followed by Ollivan, Rovin, Kodi, and three other Rangers.

There were a few moments of tense silence before Merriam set both forearms on the table, leaning forward. "I'm not sure how much your team has already discussed strategy, Commander Dio, but there's a good chance whatever you've already come up with will have to be tweaked."

Dio turned his head to look at her, straight blonde hair slicked back from his face. "Oh? Tell me more about why our plans won't work, human."

Merriam ignored the slight, but the posture of everyone seated on her side of the table stiffened. Oren brought a hand up to rub his jaw, and Merriam's lips twitched in a smile as he tried to hide a tic of irritation. The fact that, with the exception of Rovin, every person seated on the other side was high fae was not lost on her. She remembered Gressia's words about the privilege she held in Umbra being the cause of so much of the contention between her and the Rangers, but she couldn't stamp out the fire that burned through her at Dio's disdain.

"Your plans won't work, Commander," she continued, flicking the end of her ponytail over her shoulder, "because this wasn't a fluke rift that happened to let a demon in. It wasn't someone accidentally opening a portal. Whoever brought this demon—and, let's face it, probably others—onto Nethyl did so purposefully. And it wasn't just nymph blood over a rogue pocket of magic that let him open a portal. He can Travel."

Dio's shoulders tensed, eyes flicking to the mercenaries.

"Relax, they're on your side for now," Merriam clicked her tongue, waving her hand dismissively. "They understand the concept, which is lucky for you because trust me, you want our help." She relaxed back into her chair, smiling brightly at the seething fae.

She could feel Rovin glaring at her from across the table and slowly slid her eyes to him, raising a brow in question.

His lips were pressed together, and he just shook his head before averting his gaze.

Merriam turned her attention back to Dio, letting her face relax into a vague amusement.

"First, I don't know how you can talk of privileged information so plainly with no shame. Second, you speak out of turn, *mercenary*. Nobody put you in charge. Watch your cockiness; humility is a hard fall," Dio spat from across the table.

Oren opened his mouth to speak, but Jasper's dark laughter cut through the tension in the room, all eyes turning to him.

"Calm yourself, Commander, is it? I don't believe we've had the pleasure of meeting yet, but I assure you, Merriam does not speak out of turn." His wings flared, the soft rustle of feathers punctuating the silence, and he cocked his head, silver eyes flashing something quiet and dangerous as he stared down the Ranger in front of him. "We all carry an equal voice in our troupe and are not afraid to defer to one another when a situation falls under a specific expertise." Jasper folded his arms over his chest and leaned back in his chair with a wide grin. "As for humility, there is a difference between cocky and confident, Ranger. And nothing is a hard fall when you have wings at your back."

Dio bristled, jaw clenched with irritation. "The human has no wings."

"The human has me," Jasper replied coolly.

Merriam could have kissed him for the look on Dio's face.

"I appreciate your concern, Dio," Oren finally cut in, "but I have already talked with Merriam after some reconnaissance she did last night, and these are things you all need to know. Things no one else may have been able to connect."

Rovin again narrowed his eyes at Merriam, but she ignored him, butterflies exploding in her belly at disclosing this next bit of news. No one aside from Oren and Mollian knew she wasn't from Nethyl.

"I understand your hesitation, Commander, but listen to what Merriam has to say." Oren soothed his Ranger before meeting Merriam's eyes and nodding for her to continue.

Merriam took as much confidence as she could from those green eyes before leaning forward to look at the people beside her whose reactions were the only ones that mattered to her. "As you know, Prince Mollian and I are not only *mehhen* but also Bonded." Though she and Mollian had agreed to keep their Bonding a secret, the mercs had seen her hurt too many times not to know her injuries healed faster than a human's should. Once they knew about the Bond, it was only a matter of time before she disclosed her ability to Travel and the part it played in her ability to get in and out of places unseen.

The Rangers knew none of this outside of the *mehhen* bond, but they would know enough about a Keeper's abilities to be able to figure the rest out.

Merriam licked her lips before continuing. "The world that is parallel to ours is free of magic and ruled by humans. I, um, understand a lot about their world and the way things work there," Merriam explained. "It's the world I grew up in. The world I was born in."

Jasper just watched her with those intelligent silver eyes, Merriam only confirming something he had long ago suspected.

Aleah's features had softened with empathy, shadows of her own memories flickering behind her eyes. The two had bonded over familial trauma, and if anyone understood the need to forget all ties to a childhood home, it was the redheaded half-fae.

The other three mercs just listened neutrally, though Campbell's indigo eyes shone with wonder.

Dio looked at Eskar, who rolled her eyes with a scoff.

Rovin's head tilted, watching her thoughtfully as he took in this new information.

But she purposefully didn't look across to the Rangers.

"While in the other world last night, I heard a gunshot." She continued with a quick rundown of everything she'd told Oren and Mollian the night before about the possibility of mistaking the sound for thunder and the ability to overpower even the strongest fae.

"Explain a gunshot. Why would it sound like thunder?" Eskar demanded, watching Merriam with thinly veiled distrust.

Merriam let out a breath, pressing her hands to her temples as she searched for words to describe it. "There's a weapon on Earth called a gun. Basically, it's a small, controlled explosion that sends a piece of shrapnel flying very far at a very high speed. The forced propulsion of the explosion creates an extremely loud clap that reverberates through the air much the same way thunder does."

"And it is your belief that the man we are looking for has gone to Earth and acquired one of these guns?" Ollivan asked.

Merriam nodded.

Oren ran a hand up the short hair on the back of his head. "Keepers have had knowledge of these weapons since the humans of Earth first invented them, and we've worked hard to keep anything like it from making its way to Nethyl. From what we've seen, they can cause much more destruction than they're worth."

Jasper nodded thoughtfully. "But the gun isn't the biggest issue here. We can take down one measly man with a high-powered weapon. My greatest concern is this demon he seems to have at his command. Where is he keeping it? If he can Travel, is he moving between worlds? Clearly he knows he can access more than just our parallel. How do we find him to put an end to the terror he's been bringing to Sekha?"

"These are the questions that weigh heaviest on my mind as well," Oren agreed.

Leonidas leaned forward, resting his elbows on the table. "We came up with a preliminary plan yesterday. I think with a few tweaks it could still work."

"The first step is still to find his base of operations. We can't forget about all the disappearances. If he's taking people from Jekeida and West Audha, it wouldn't make sense for him to be hopping around other dimensions. Traveling is a single-passenger deal, right? So we should work off the assumption that he's somewhere in Sekha, but where?" Aleah's eyes roamed the map in the tabletop before flicking up to the Rangers. "You have the coordinates of all the attacks that have taken place, right?" She blinked expectantly.

"Yes, but—"

Dio was interrupted by Kodi, "Of course we have the coordinates, but there isn't much of a pattern to them." The Ranger's dark brown hair was a mohawk of short, loose curls.

Aleah met his light bi-colored eyes with a smile that suggested she might bite, the ends of her elongated canines flashing. "Maybe you just weren't using the right equation, Ranger."

Dio was glaring at Kodi, and Rovin was looking at his friend incredulously, but Kodi ignored them both. "Oh, please do share this magical equation, little merc."

"Gladly." She gestured toward the table.

Kodi looked at Ollivan expectantly. The older Ranger glanced at Dio, who just nodded, clearly having given up the prospect of being in control of this meeting.

Ollivan stood and began plotting points on the map, sliding over a copy of the reports to Aleah, who procured a separate sheet of paper to write down dates and times.

Kodi watched her with a bright fascination, and it made Merriam's stomach flip with unease.

Aleah nibbled on the end of a pencil, her eyes tracking back from the points on the map to the numbers she'd scrawled across the paper. She listed the dates and times of each incident and the distances between each, combining them in multiple different ways and marking down a change every once in a while. Eventually, she came to a conclusion, grabbing a wooden marker from the side of the table and leaning forward, placing it deep in the mountains west of Umbra.

Merriam felt a knot of worry she hadn't acknowledged untie itself in her chest. The marker was as far from Entumbra as it was from Umbra, meaning Mollian was likely safe.

"That's where he's at?" Kodi glanced from the marker to Aleah.

"Yes, probably sitting with a cup of hot tea, reminiscing about the sunrise," Aleah said dryly.

"What's the radius?" Jasper asked, keeping things on track before they had a chance to truly derail.

Aleah tucked a lock of hair behind her clipped ear. "Roughly twenty, maybe thirty klicks. But if he is operating out of a single location, it will be somewhere around there."

Dio glanced from Jasper to Aleah and back. "How much do we trust these calculations?"

Jasper glanced at Aleah, who shrugged, sitting back in her chair. "Numbers don't lie."

Ollivan was nearly leaning over the table to peer at what Aleah had written. Eventually, he cleared his throat and asked, "May I see?"

Aleah slid the paper across the table, picking at her nails nonchalantly as Ollivan scanned her work. "This is ..."

"Brilliant? Masterful? Ingenious?" Aleah offered, flashing that grin that was equal parts pleasant and predatory.

Kodi was glued to her, practically drooling like a dog staring at a meaty bone he couldn't wait to sink his teeth into.

"Highly probable," Ollivan finished. "The numbers are accurate. I don't know why I didn't think of this myself."

Aleah just raised her eyebrows, as if vaguely insulted he would expect to find an error.

"With a tentative location, we can send scouting parties to find his home base," Leonidas said. "Once we know where he stays, we can watch his movements, learn where he keeps his creatures, how many he has, how best to plan an attack."

"And what do you suggest we do in the meantime?" Dio asked peevishly.

"Train," Jasper replied with a shrug. "Merriam has fought one of these demons before, along with two of your own, if I heard correctly."

Rovin nodded, expression serious. "We should focus on group fighting techniques. Those things are a team effort."

"Mollian is out doing some last-minute recon as well," Oren added. "Go ahead and organize a scouting mission, but scouting only. Try to send a report back within a week or two. We'll debrief and make a solid plan from there."

Dio nodded. "Rovin, I want you to stay here to help run training. Ollivan can take the others."

Rovin dipped his head in acknowledgment.

Jasper looked down the line of mercenaries. "Thoughts?"

"I can cover a lot of ground," Campbell offered. "Leo could use his falcons to scout, and if they see something, you would be able to get there quickly, Jaz. Calysta could provide extra cover as well."

"Smart," Jasper agreed. "Aleah and Merriam can continue to work things from here. I assume you'll be able to keep yourselves occupied?"

"Of course," Aleah answered.

"We can help the Rangers train." Merriam turned to Rovin. "I have invaluable experience."

"I wouldn't call it invaluable." Rovin rolled his eyes.

Dio narrowed his eyes, looking like he was about to disagree with Merriam's suggestion before Oren interjected. "That's a generous offer that I'm sure the Rangers would love to take you up on, Merriam," he thanked her before turning to Dio. "She held off the demon on her own for a good while before we were able to catch up."

The pride in his voice stroked her ego, and Merriam fought the urge to sit straighter in her chair and raise her chin like a preening bird. She did cast a smirk in Rovin's direction, though, and his brows pulled low over his eyes as he glowered at her.

"Well, I think that settles everything then," Oren said, pushing up from the table. "The Crown will, of course, provide horses and supplies for the entire scouting party. Can you be ready to leave by midday?"

"Thank you, Your Grace, we will be prepared by then." Jasper stood, inclining his head in a bow.

"Do you want help packing?" Merriam asked as the sound of chairs scraping the stone floor filled the room, everyone standing to leave.

"Yes, that would be appreciated. We could use the extra hands bringing everything back here," Jasper replied.

And here I was thinking you might want to repeat what happened the last time we had a meeting here. Oren Cast to her.

Merriam didn't have the wherewithal to send a proper reply with everything going on around her, so she just met his eyes, letting a message burn in them briefly but clearly. *Later.*

She felt Oren's gaze on her as she followed the mercs and Rangers out of the war room, adding an extra bounce to her step to make her hair swing.

Chapter 25
Take the bastard down

MOLLIAN CRANED HIS NECK to look up at the top spire of the castle. His teeth were set against the buzzing in his blood, so much worse without the distraction of conversation. The way the Gate deep below Entumbra sung to every fiber of his being was off-putting. It's why he never visited if he could help it. He never did understand how Gressia could stand to live here and attributed her strange attitude to the fact that she put up with the feeling all the time.

Mollian dismounted his horse, passing the reins off to the stable hand that came up before turning to address Eskar. "You can probably start setting up camp. I'll talk to Gressia and let her know that you're being stationed here until we get all this demon business under control."

Eskar dipped her head in acknowledgment, and Mollian started up the steep narrow steps that would bring him to the main level of the castle.

It had felt like an even longer journey than usual due to the quick turnaround and lack of distractions. Go figure that not one of the Guard sent to protect Entumbra was particularly talkative. Mollian was almost out of his mind with pent-up energy and the need for action.

He brushed his hair out of his face as he reached the top, stepping into the atrium and tossing out with his mind for a sense of Gressia.

He felt her in the castle and knew she'd have registered the touch of his magic against her mind, so he settled himself on a wing-backed chair in the corner, looking at the stories artfully depicted in the stained glass windows that lined the room. Stories of Keeper history. His history.

It wasn't long before a door across the room opened, and Gressia came spilling from a stairwell, her soft curls mussed up and the bodice of her dress slightly askew.

Mollian's stomach plummeted at the implication. Of course this wasn't going to be an easy visit.

"Little brother." Gressia smoothed her hair back and held her hands over her stomach as she fought to keep her breathing even. "To what do I owe the pleasure?"

Mollian stood, running a hand over his hair. "Oren sent me with a detachment of the Guard—"

"He sent you with *what*?" Gressia interrupted, taking a few fast strides over to a window at the front of the room to peer outside.

"Did he not send a bird?"

"No, he didn't send a bird." She turned to glare at him.

"It must have slipped his mind with everything else going on. But you know we got attacked on our way back to Umbra. He just wants to make sure you're safe out here."

"I don't want them," Gressia said plainly, crossing her arms. "I don't need to be watched."

"Gress, they're not here to watch you. You didn't see the demon. You wouldn't be able to fight it by yourself, no one would." Mollian stepped toward her, hands held out placatingly. "They know you're in charge here. They know they answer to you. Please, let them be here to protect you if something happens."

"For how long?"

"Just until we've been able to hunt down whoever brought the demon into our world. The second we have him eradicated, we'll call them back," Mollian promised.

Gressia pursed her lips, assessing him, then she nodded, dropping her arms and looking around. "Where is your human?"

Mollian rolled his eyes. "I wish you wouldn't say it like that. She's not my pet."

Gressia gave him half a smile, tilting her head to the side. "Oh, lighten up, Mollian. You know I'm fond of her. And she *is* yours, whether you want to think of it that way or not. She did Bond herself to you."

Mollian was about to reply when the scuffle of footsteps sounded on the stairs, and Gressia brightened, slipping her arm through Mollian's. "Speaking of," she said before switching to a human tongue, "Basta, my love! Look who came for a visit!"

A sandy-haired man just a few fingers shorter than Mollian stepped into the atrium. "Hello there," he greeted with a smile. "It's been quite a long time."

Mollian stepped forward and clasped the man's hand, offering a warm smile that he'd perfected through his years at court. "It's good to see you again, Basta."

"Mollian was just bringing some of the Royal Guard to stay here for a little while." Gressia dropped Mollian's arm for Basta's, pulling him over to the window to see.

"There's been several demon attacks throughout Jekeida. We just want to make sure that Gressia and Entumbra are safe," Mollian added.

"How long are you staying?" Basta asked as he observed the Guard making camp on the mountainside.

"Not very long," the prince answered, tucking his hands into his pockets. "But a few nights, at least."

"It's a shame I didn't know you were coming. I would have loved the opportunity to get to know Gressia's youngest brother better, but I'll be leaving at first light tomorrow."

Mollian fought to keep his expression open and friendly as his mind reeled with options and possibilities and decisions to be made. "A shame indeed," he said lamely.

Gressia gave him a strange look, and he forced his muscles to relax as he brought a hand to the back of his neck. "I'm sorry if that came off as short. I would love to catch up with you, Basta. It was a long trip; all I want right now is food and a bath," he said with a light chuckle.

"Of course you must be completely travel-weary," Gressia tutted, releasing Basta's arm. "Supper should be almost ready. I'll have your room prepared while we're eating."

As they headed down to the dining room, Gressia pulled a few attendants aside, giving them instruction in human tongue.

Does Basta not speak Common? he Cast to her, just registering that she talked to him the same as the other humans.

I have always spoken to him in his own tongue. Why would I not? I can glamor him if necessary. Gressia again gave Mollian a weird look, questioning why he thought her consort would need to understand their language when she had other ways to communicate with him.

Mollian sat opposite his sister and Basta, filling a wooden cup with water from a pitcher and piling his plate with food from a central platter.

"So how is Merriam?" Basta asked, taking a casual sip of his drink.

Mollian met his seawater eyes, keeping his expression blank but trying to register the depth of the question. Her name on Basta's lips gave him an uneasy feeling. The thought that she had any of the man's attention made Mollian want to slide his knife across Basta's throat. The violent reaction surprised him so much he almost forgot to answer the question. "She's well."

"I'm glad to hear it. I've only met her a few times, but she's a marvelous girl. You're lucky to have her."

Mollian tipped his head to the side, telling himself Basta had no reason to imply a threat, no reason to think Mollian suspected him of anything nefarious. He kept his grip on the flatware loose as he cut a bite of beef and forced a polite smile. "She's definitely something more than marvelous. I've never seen someone more sure on their feet or adept with an axe," he bragged, not missing the chance to remind Basta who he'd be going up against in case he was trying to find a weak spot. "I am lucky to have her in my life, but I never understood why people make it seem like I have a claim on her. She is and has always been entirely her own person."

Basta's brow furrowed in confusion, and he glanced to Gressia. "I apologize if I offended. She always seemed so eager to return to you whenever she stopped by. It was clear she missed you terribly, so I just assumed ..."

"Merriam and I are not together," he explained with a shake of his head. "We've been best friends since childhood and are practically family."

"Mollian doesn't have romantic relationships regardless, my love," Gressia said, resting her hand over Basta's.

"Ah, you have taken vows?" Basta nodded his head lightly in understanding.

"What? No, I just don't have any interest," Mollian shrugged, everyone in his life had long ago understood that was just a part of him. His mother had briefly had doubts when he'd first brought Merriam home, but they'd quickly dissipated when the platonic nature of their friendship became clear. "That sort of relationship has never held any appeal to me."

"Oh, well, then I'm glad she's so understanding."

Mollian cocked his head to the side, about to ask what that meant when Gressia interrupted.

"So why are you staying here? Not that your company isn't always a pleasure, I just never thought that you enjoyed your time here in seclusion. Plus, you only just left not even a week ago."

"I want to make sure the Guard have a chance to settle in and learn the grounds. I also need to do a little research."

Gressia frowned at her plate, switching to Common. "When Oren came back after you all were attacked, he said he'd never seen anything like it before and wasn't sure where it had come from."

Mollian shifted his gaze to Basta, who was eating quietly and looking only vaguely curious and confused.

"He doesn't speak it, Molli." Gressia rolled her eyes.

Mollian trusted that about as much as he trusted Merriam to step down from a challenge, but he nodded, keeping his features relaxed. "Oren thinks he may know which realm the demon came from. He wants me to see if I can find enough to confirm his suspicion and learn how best to kill it." Oren had suggested no such thing, but if Basta could understand, Mollian wanted to set him on edge, hoping it would make him sloppy with his next move.

"Leave it to our dear brother to remember anything and everything," Gressia snorted good-naturedly.

After the meal, Mollian slipped back out of the castle and down to the Guard camp. He caught Eskar's eye from where she sat around a campfire, motioning with his head to summon her.

She stood, brushing her hands on her pants as she walked over. "Your Highness," she greeted.

"I need you to track someone for me," Mollian said quietly, shoving his hands in his pockets and leaning against a tree.

Eskar's dark eyes lit with interest, and she raised a brow.

"A man will leave here tomorrow morning. Follow him, but do not engage."

"How long should I follow this human?"

"Ideally until you know where it is he's staying. We'll need as much information as possible."

"Consider it done." Eskar nodded.

"No matter what you see, stay back and stay hidden. I'm serious, Eskar."

"Your concern for my safety is touching, Prince." Eskar's lips lifted in half a smile, her eyes searching his face. "You think this man has something to do with the demon attacks?"

Mollian pushed a hand through his hair and let out a heavy sigh. "I think he has *everything* to do with the demon attacks."

Eskar's smile fell, her eyes hardening. "We'll take the bastard down, then."

Mollian clasped her shoulder before walking back up to the castle, intent on finding his bed.

He slept fitfully, waking at every noise, paranoid that Basta knew he was close to being caught. He twisted the umbrite ring on his finger, wanting nothing more than to go back to Merriam.

Mollian sometimes thought it was strange how whole he felt in her presence. Her connection to him had sung in his blood even before she was Bonded to him, but ever since then it was even more intense. He had power as a fae and power as a Keeper, but it felt different around her. Stronger, more intense, but also calm and steady and sure.

Aside from that, he just missed her. He'd rarely had to deal with anything stressful on his own in the seven years she'd been with him in Umbra. Even the more mundane stresses of his role as a prince seemed to lessen when she was curled beside him, her scent of petrichor and wildflowers soothing every restless part of his soul.

Mollian sighed, rolling over and tucking an arm under his head. He could feel immense power buzzing in his veins, rolling and stretching against his skin. Even without the Gate's proximity amplifying everything, his magic always felt wilder and more insistent when he was away from his *mehhen*. But it felt volatile with his already heightened sense of unrest with Basta's presence. He took in a deep breath, reigning in control and forcing the magic in his blood to settle, wrapping it up and burying it underneath layers of everything else that was him.

Exhaustion finally took over, and he drifted into an uneasy sleep

Basta was gone when Mollian woke the next morning. Apprehension filled him as he rolled out of bed, knowing he couldn't put off the impending conversation with his sister. He trudged into the dining room in the clothes he'd slept in, sitting heavily at the table as a bowl of porridge was set in front of him.

"You look rough, little brother." Gressia laughed, further mussing his unkempt hair before settling onto the bench opposite him.

Mollian pushed the porridge away, resting his arms on the table and taking a deep breath. "Gress, I have to tell you something."

Gressia raised a well-manicured brow, waiting.

"We think Basta is responsible for the demon attacks," he said evenly

Gressia let out a sharp cackle, bringing her hand to her mouth. "You're not serious?"

Mollian lifted one shoulder in a shrug.

"Mollian, I've known him since you were a child."

Mollian explained what Merriam had discovered during her short trip back to Earth and the conclusions they'd consequently come to. "Whoever is doing this has the ability to Travel."

"And what of your *mehhen*, Mollian? She's profiting from this little skirmish, isn't she?" Gressia challenged.

A sardonic laugh pulled from Mollian's chest before he could stop himself. "You can't be serious, Gess. Other than the fact that the demon almost killed her, when would she have time to be off kidnapping people? When she's not with me, she's with the mercs."

Gressia's lips pressed together as she glared at her brother.

"Who broached the subject of the Bond, Gress?"

"I offered it to him," she hissed.

"He didn't mention it at all, plant the idea in your head that having him Bonded to you would be beneficial?"

A flicker of unease crossed her face.

"He's the only person alive who would have the means. Have you checked the armory? Do you even know if he's taken rings?"

Gressia seethed, shaking her head emphatically. "No, Mollian. Even if he has the means, what of his motives? He loves me."

"I'm not saying he doesn't. I'm just saying maybe he also loves what you can do for him."

"Get out." Gressia glared at him, her pale green eyes shimmering with anger.

"Gress—"

"GET OUT!" she screamed, his untouched bowl of porridge flying off of the table and hitting the wall behind him with a loud clatter.

Mollian stood and exited the room, climbing the steep iron staircase to the atrium. He sat heavily in a chair and pushed his fingers into his hair, massaging the heels of his hands against the aspen branch tattoos on his temples. "Go to Entumbra and tell your sister that her lover is terrorizing the kingdom. Yeah, sure, no problem at all. Nothing would give me greater pleasure," he muttered.

After waiting for several minutes with no sign of Gressia, he went outside to join the Guard in some training exercises, figuring he may as well keep busy.

The morning passed quickly with several rounds of weapons training, and Mollian reached out for Gressia, wanting to apologize for his lack of tact and help her handle the news. When he didn't feel her, he knew she'd left Nethyl. With the Gate at her disposal, he had no way of knowing where she'd gone.

So he spent the rest of the day among the Guard, playing card games and helping them further settle in.

Two more days passed, and the Guard had opened up more as they found a routine and became accustomed to Mollian's presence. He was actually enjoying his time with them and had built a solid camaraderie with several of the younger soldiers closer to his age. The sun had just disappeared behind the mountains, and they were in the middle of a card game they called Cheat when Mollian felt the brush of Keeper magic against his mind. He looked up to the castle and saw his sister standing on the catwalk, torchlight illuminating her long white curls as they danced in the wind.

"You'll have to excuse me," he apologized as he set his cards down on the stump in the center of the circle and stood. "Duty calls."

"Sure, it's definitely not that you realized you were about to lose atrociously," one of the Guard joked.

"We all know who the sore loser is in this circle," Mollian quipped in return before heading to the steep stone steps that led up to the castle.

Gressia was already inside waiting for him, and she gestured for him to follow as she slipped through a doorway to an iron spiral staircase. They climbed until the stairs opened up into a large glass and ironwork dome, a few panels pushed open to allow the fresh summer breeze to waft through.

"Listen, Gress, I'm sorry if I threw all of that out there without much tact," Mollian started.

Gressia held her hand up, looping her arm around an iron support as she faced him. "No, your reasons for suspecting him are valid." She took a deep breath, leaning her head against the support. "In a strange way, I think I love him. He's been visiting me for twenty years, and his presence here has become a sort of comfort. I've always known he was attracted to my power, but I liked it. I liked that he was enamored by my magic.

"But you're right. He has the means, and even if I don't know his motivation ... I may love him, but my responsibility is to the realm first and foremost. To the Gate and to protecting it no matter the cost." Her free hand smoothed down the front of her dress, and her pale green eyes shimmered with fear and sadness and a hurt so deep Mollian felt the pain tighten in his own chest.

"If what you've told me is true," Gressia continued, "then I will do whatever I can to help you stop him. But there's something you need to know."

The cold weight of apprehension spread through Mollian at his sister's tone, and he steadied himself for whatever would come next.

(ℓ)

Merriam's eyes fluttered open. The room was dark, only scant light coming in through the cracked window, carrying with it a cool wind and the faint sounds of night. Oren's arm was a comforting weight over her side, and the solid warmth of him at her back combined with the soft rise and fall of his chest was almost enough to lull her eyes closed and let her drift off again.

She snuggled into Oren, grabbing his hand and pulling his arm tighter over her.

Then she felt it again. That soft brush against her mind that had woken her in the first place.

She instantly sat up, throwing the blanket from her.

Oren woke at the abrupt shift, pushing up sleepily and looking around.

"Molli's back!" Merriam jumped from the bed, reaching for her clothes as Oren sat up fully and pushed his hair back from his face.

"Mer, it's the middle of the night."

Merriam tugged her shirt over her head, pulling her hair free from the neckline. "Yes, and if he came back before waiting until morning, don't you think something important has happened?"

"More than likely he was just tired of our sister and ready to be back home," Oren grumbled.

Merriam slid her legs into loose linen pants. "I'm sure one more night wouldn't have killed him." She gave Oren a pointed look.

"Fine, I'll get him up here. Don't throw yourself out the window." Oren stood, finding clothes for himself as he reached out with his mind, knowing Mollian would understand to come to them when he felt Oren. Especially if he had already been to his rooms and noticed Merriam's absence.

Merriam skipped toward the bedroom door, and Oren grabbed her hand as she passed him. "I don't know who's on guard tonight, but I do know they'll talk."

Merriam stopped. "Right, you should probably let him in."

Oren tugged her against his chest, planting a kiss on the top of her head. "You are very lucky I love you."

A soft knock had him releasing her, stepping out of the bedroom to the outer door.

Merriam bit her lip, heart swelling with unspoken and unnamed feelings. Oren had told her he'd loved her a few times since they'd been back from Entumbra, always when he knew there would be an excuse for her not to return the sentiment. She was thankful for it, because she wasn't sure she was ready to admit that level of feeling and devotion yet—not when she was still holding on to her life as a mercenary with so much fervor and not when she wasn't sure how her life would fit with his.

She was brought out of her thoughts by voices in the main room, followed by the sound of a door closing. Already, she felt that fullness of her soul that told her Mollian was near. She pelted from the room, jumping onto the younger prince and throwing her arms around his neck.

Mollian laughed, holding her tight for a moment before setting her down. "Well, that was quite the greeting."

Merriam pressed her palm to his after they'd separated, pushing an errant curl back from his face. "I was worried about you. Any number of things could have happened."

"And I would have been prepared for them." Mollian chucked her under the chin.

"Why did you come back so late at night? How did Gressia take the news? Did you find out where Basta is staying? Aleah might have figured it out, but the scouting party isn't back yet," Merriam said in a rush.

Mollian blinked at her, gesturing to the couches in the center of the room. "Have you ever known me to hold back details?"

Merriam grabbed his hand, pulling him around the couches and sitting with her back against the arm of one, facing Mollian with her legs folded in front of her. Oren walked around the back of the couch, brushing a hand over the top of Merriam's head. She leaned into the touch as he smoothed her hair, watching him sit on the couch opposite before turning her full attention to Mollian, sitting forward with her elbows on her knees.

"Basta was there when I arrived," Mollian started without preamble.

Merriam sat up straight, eyes going wide, but she held her tongue against the impulse to interrupt.

"I don't think he knew anything was amiss, and he left the next morning. I assigned Eskar to follow him and told her not to engage under any circumstance. She'll hopefully find where it is he's staying. Did you say Aleah had a location?"

Merriam nodded. "A decent idea of the rough area. I guess we'll know for sure when Eskar and the rest of them return."

"I may have also led him to believe that you knew where he was getting his demons from and how to kill them." Mollian looked at Oren with a sly smile. "I was hoping to make him a little nervous; maybe he'd be overly cautious and calm down with the killing for a while or get sloppy and make it easier for us to capture him. Either way would work in our favor."

Oren chuckled, running a hand through his hair and flipping it over to one side of his head. "I wish I had that sort of knowledge, but that was good thinking."

"Gressia had no problem believing you would have recalled something like that," Mollian said. Something dark flashed in his eyes, and he rubbed his hands over his face. "She didn't take the news well when I told her, but eventually came around. She's glad to have the Guard there, but doesn't want them to hinder Basta from returning to Entumbra. She thinks it would be smarter to pretend like she doesn't know anything."

Oren nodded. "I don't like the idea of her confronting him on her own. I have no doubts that he knows every one of her weaknesses and would exploit them without a second thought."

"He doesn't know all of her weaknesses," Mollian said quietly.

Oren leaned forward, waiting for him to continue.

"He doesn't know that she has a child."

"What the fuck?" Oren stood, pushing a hand into his hair as he looked at Mollian with utter disbelief.

"I know," Mollian ran his tongue over his teeth with a slow shake of his head, still processing the information himself.

"How old?"

"He's five. He was born just before you started your studies in Entumbra."

"What the fuck?" Oren repeated, beginning to pace. "How?"

Merriam looked from one brother to the other. "Wait, she has a kid that no one knows about? Why wouldn't she have said something?"

Mollian loosed a long breath. "She shouldn't have even been able to conceive," he explained. "Her proximity to the Gate for so many years ... That's a lot of magic to constantly have running through your body. She's been there for well over a hundred years, it's wildly strange that she's not infertile. Plus the fact that as Keeper of Entumbra, her first responsibility always has to be to the Gate. It's an unspoken rule that they aren't to have children in any capacity."

Merriam's brow furrowed in confusion. "So she kept the child from you because she's not allowed to have him?"

"Partially, yes, but I don't even know how he exists." Oren said.

"Maybe because Basta is human? He doesn't have any innate magic in his blood."

Oren shook his head, still pacing behind the couch. "No, human villages are the only ones close to Entumbra. It's not uncommon for a Keeper to take a human lover."

"And Basta doesn't know about the child?" Merriam looked to Mollian.

"She swears it. She told me she wasn't sure why she never told him, but she kept holding off and holding off, and then the child was born—"

"How did he not notice, though?" Merriam interrupted.

Mollian tapped his temple with a finger. "She glamored him early on.

And before you ask if he would feel the glamor, she told me she was very adept at distracting him, which is much more than I ever wanted to hear from my sister's mouth." Mollian made a slightly disgusted face, causing Oren to snicker, even with the heavy atmosphere. "When she got further along, she made sure never to be in Entumbra if he visited. Because of the Bond, she could feel when he was near and used the Gate to avoid him."

"Entumbra isn't that big, though. How did she hide a kid while Oren was there for five whole years?" Merriam questioned.

"If you would let me continue, I was about to get to that. After the child was born, she took him off-world to a sparsely populated reality similar to ours. No one has seen him except for a few trusted humans who she sent to live with him and care for him when she couldn't be there. That's why none of us knew of his existence. She hid him there because he's not ... he's not a halfling, not like he should be."

Oren stilled, looking at Mollian.

"His father is Basta. Gressia is certain of that. But ... he has magic. Magic that fae don't possess." Mollian paused, cracking his knuckles. "He can shape shift."

"How is that possible?" Oren ran a hand through his hair again, massaging the muscle at the base of his neck.

Mollian shrugged, at a rare loss for words.

Merriam frowned, twisting the ends of her hair around a finger. "What if ..." she trailed off, biting her lip.

Mollian looked at her. "What if what?" he prompted.

"Never mind, it was just a random thought from my childhood," Merriam dismissed with a shake of her head.

"Well, we've got nothing, so it's not going to be any less helpful than that," Mollian said with a shrug.

Oren snorted. "Very encouraging, brother."

"What, it's the truth," Mollian defended before turning back to Merriam, his eyes earnest as he waited.

Merriam swallowed, licking her lips. "There's a lot of lore on Earth—mostly regarded as fiction—about demons. The kind we fought in the woods is very rarely talked about. Demons that have a physical shape and move on their own were never the popular stories. On Earth, demons worked through possession, taking over a person's body in a sort of ... symbiotic relationship."

She tucked a lock of hair behind her ear, glancing at Oren, who stood stoically with his hands resting on the back of the couch. "That demon we fought ... when it was about to die, when it got called away by whatever tone that was ... it changed into something else. I know that's not a full shift, but it is shifting to some degree. What if Basta is possessed by something similar?"

"Well, if that isn't the most terrifying thought," Oren said quietly.

"Maybe your nephew isn't a traditional half-fae because he's half demon."

Mollian rubbed his cheek with a hand, considering. "It would explain how Basta controls the other demon. If he's possessed by a stronger one or one with more perceived authority, that could be how he gets the creature to do his bidding. I don't even know what to begin to think about what that means for the child."

"Would he be able to be glamored at that point, either? Maybe he knows about it." Merriam fidgeted with the aspen leaf at her throat.

"Gressia is sure he doesn't know." Mollian shrugged. "Her magic is stronger because of her continued proximity to the Gate. Add that to the fact that most demons we know of don't mix well with iron, and it's entirely plausible she would have been able to glamor it."

"Fuck," Oren dropped his head forward, leaning heavily on the couch. "If this is true, we're in some deep shit."

"Where do we go from here?" Merriam asked, drawing her legs up to her chest.

"We'll worry about the child later. As long as Basta doesn't know of his existence, we have time to figure out how to handle that situation. But for now? We need to look deeper into demons and possession, try to see what we have here that could give us an edge. And we train and wait for Eskar and Ollivan's group to come back with more intelligence. Then we kill a demon," Oren said with finality.

Chapter 26
Bleeding on the floor

Five years before ...

IN THE MONTHS MERRIAM had been with the mercenaries, a friendship was slowly building between her and Aleah. But every time Merriam felt that they were getting closer, Aleah would pull back, hazel eyes guarded.

Mollian's friendly demeanor helped Aleah's unease immensely, though. He'd spent multiple nights at the merc house, drinking and exchanging stories of mischief. One night, the prince gifted Aleah a set of wickedly curved knives that he'd customized for her, carving the handles with citrus fruit and honey.

Tears had lined Aleah's eyes, and she'd thrown her arms around Mollian as she squealed her thanks. Knowledge that she could trust him, that she wasn't threatened by him or his claim on Merriam, was finally pushing its way past the barrier of fear in her mind.

The next day, the half-fae found Merriam working in the training room.

"My mother was a twin," Aleah said, sitting down next to where Merriam honed a set of throwing knives. "She and her brother were also *mehhen*."

Merriam's hands stilled as she looked up from her task.

Aleah's gaze was trained on the whetting stone, distant with memory. "My mother met my father when she was very young. His family worked for mine, so he grew up playing with my mother and uncle, and served them when he got older.

"He loved her from the beginning, at least to hear it from my mother's perspective. But he was a human, and she always felt she was above him and was destined for a higher pairing. My family have sat as overseers of a large port in South Eyko for millenia, a position that comes with power and prestige. She still encouraged his fancy, though. She'd let him think that maybe he had a chance, and she used to use him to make my uncle mad whenever they'd get in a fight.

"He's a jealous and protective fae, my uncle. He had dreams of him and my mother ruling all of South Eyko, maybe even more. And he loved her more than anything. Would have set the whole world on fire without hesitation, if only to save her."

Merriam had continued working the stone down the blade in her hand, punctuating Aleah's words with the comforting shriek of stone against metal.

"Obviously, my mother ended up pregnant, though she never told my uncle who my father was. Maybe she didn't even know for sure. My uncle doted on her throughout the pregnancy, threatened to kill whatever low-life fae had soiled her and left her to fend for herself, but my mother also always suspected he was glad she was left to depend on him. He had always worried that he felt their bond stronger than she did, and the thought of her moving away to live with the father of her child was more than he could bear. She never would have gone far from him regardless, though. She hadn't thought she'd be able to."

Merriam bit her cheek to keep from commenting that she understood, not wanting to scare Aleah into silence.

"My mother died in childbirth. It destroyed my uncle, but he kept himself together for me. I was his last connection to her, and I think that was the only thing that kept him from completely breaking." Aleah paused, reaching out to palm one of the knives in front of Merriam. She pressed the point of it into the pad of her finger, depressing the skin as she twirled the knife in a slow circle. "My grandparents raised me—he wasn't in any way ready to be a parent—but he was a constant warmth those first few years."

A pinpoint of blood bloomed on Aleah's fingertip, and she pulled the knife away. "I was four when my family discovered I was a halfling." A smile split her lips, sad and cruel. "He had a hunting knife he was rather proud of. The hilt was encrusted with jewels, and what young child isn't enamored with things that sparkle in the sunlight? My uncle left the room, only for a moment, but it was long enough for me to have grabbed the knife. When he came back, he took it from me with his magic. He didn't see that I was holding the blade, and it cut through my fingers."

Aleah dropped the knife into her lap to squeeze the pad of her finger, and the droplet grew. "I bled. A lot. I screamed, and I bled, and I didn't heal as quickly as I should have." She popped her finger into her mouth, sucking off the blood. "That, paired with my magic having not come in yet …" She shrugged, picking the knife up and tossing it into the air.

"The shift once he realized what I was … It was almost instantaneous. One moment I was being cradled in his lap, and the next he left me. Scared and hurt and bleeding on the floor."

Merriam reached out, placing a hand on Aleah's knee. Sorrow flooded her heart, aching for the young, confused girl whose only crime had been her heritage.

"My uncle knew of my mother's trysts with their old friend," Aleah continued, twirling the knife. "He brought me to my father, pushed me down at his feet." She swallowed, her brow furrowing as she studied the blade in her hands. "'You created this abomination, and it killed my sister.' Weird, the things your mind holds onto, but that accusation is still crystal-clear, even after all these years." Aleah laughed sardonically, finally flicking her eyes up to meet Merriam's gaze.

Merriam opened her mouth to speak, but Aleah cut her off, continuing her story. "They got into an argument that I don't remember the details of, but my uncle killed him. Bludgeoned him to death in front of me. I wore my father's blood on my face for almost an entire day before my grandparents found me and cleaned me up. My uncle despised me from that point on. The fact that a halfling killed his *mehhen* brought his grief back full-force.

"He clipped my ear on my next birthday. The fifth anniversary of her death." Aleah traced over the puckered, flat tip of her ear before returning her fingers to the knife. "That was the first scar he left me with, and the only visible one. He got smart after that, leaving the marks where no one could see."

She slowly lifted her shirt, exposing her abdomen. The entire expanse of pale, freckled skin was littered with scars. Some were thin, white lines that were barely visible, but others were raised and pink, crisscrossing her body and wrapping around to her back. "I learned very early on to stay out of his way, but never quite managed to lose his attentions for long." Aleah dropped her shirt with a faint sigh.

"I found my mother's old journals when I was twelve. That's when I learned how close they were. How much she loved him. How strong the bond between them was. It made a lot of what he did to me—his hatred of me throughout the years—make sense." Aleah shrugged again, tucking her hair behind her tapered ear. "Something about it finally gave me the courage to leave. Like understanding his pain also unlocked an understanding in my childish brain that I didn't have to stay. Nothing was keeping me there.

"When you told me about you and Mollian, I was scared. There are so many things that can happen in this line of work, and if something were to happen to you ... he's a prince. I've seen what happens when someone loses a *mehhen*. I won't lie to you, Mer, I was terrified knowing what he could do to me. The things my uncle got away with ..."

"Oh, Aleah," Merriam breathed, anguish lodging in her throat.

Setting the knife down, Aleah slid closer to Merriam, resting her head against her shoulder and grabbing her hand. "I'm sorry I pulled away. Mollian is nothing like my uncle. He's good and kind, and I shouldn't have judged you both based on something you had no control over."

"You have nothing to apologize for," Merriam insisted, squeezing the other girl's hand. "And there is absolutely no justification for your uncle's actions. None."

"I know you and the prince are close, but I also know you're my friend, too. He's my friend. I don't want to feel threatened by your being *mehhen*, but it's like a knee-jerk reaction to assume that you'll always protect him first," Aleah said quietly.

Merriam bit her lip, sorting through her feelings as she tried to find the words to explain. "Molli is ... is my soul. But not my life. I've always had the want and drive to have a purpose outside of just my significance to him. That's why I wanted to be a Ranger, why I joined you. I know I haven't been around long, but training to be a mercenary and spending time with you all has felt so much like home. I may not feel you like I feel Molli, but I would still do everything in my power to protect any of you."

A small smile pulled at the corners of Aleah's mouth. "I'm glad you like being with us. I've been stuck alone with those broody boys for far too long," she laughed before lifting her head to meet Merriam's gaze, hazel eyes wide and uncharacteristically serious. "Thank you. For still trying to be my friend, even when I was pushing you away. I'll do my best not to let those fears creep back in."

"You never owe me an explanation when they do. I'll do my best to quell them, but you never have to justify yourself," Merriam assured her.

Aleah nodded, hopping to her feet and tugging Merriam up with her. "Forget the knives for now. The baker told me yesterday he was going to try out a new recipe for a trifle. We can go for a run through the mountains and stop by the bakery on the way home."

Chapter 27

To first blood

THE MORNING AFTER MOLLIAN'S return, Merriam stood in the training hall gearing up for the morning routine. She strapped a holster to her thigh and selected a few knives from the wall to fit into it before slipping a training axe through a loop on her belt; the head sheathed in leather. As she double-checked that the straps and buckles were secure, the door banged open.

There was pine and plum and dark night sky, the scent slowly becoming more familiar to her than Mollian's, and she turned just as Oren finished stepping into the room.

"Good morning, Lady." He crossed the space between them in a few long strides and cupped her face in his hands, turning it up to him and kissing her. "Molli's watching the door," he murmured against her lips.

Merriam smiled into the kiss, anchoring her hands on his hips and pulling her body against his. "As much as I enjoy this interruption, the others will be arriving soon," she said, pulling back only slightly.

His spring green eyes sparkled as they met hers. "Have anything fun planned for today's session?"

"Rovin is in charge of this one."

"Then I'm sure we're in for a treat." Oren brushed another kiss against her lips before dropping his hands and stepping back, grabbing a belt of his own and slinging it over his hips. "Is Aleah running late?"

"She picked up a small side job for the day." Merriam caught herself admiring the deft movements of his fingers as they fastened the buckle, the way his muscles flexed along his forearms, before she felt a soft push at her mind, alerting her moments before the door opened again and voices filled the hall.

"It's not going to be a fun time. I'll tell you that much."

Merriam instantly let out a breath as annoyance filled her chest. "Oh, I'm sure," she couldn't help but mutter as she turned, rolling her eyes at Mollian over Rovin's shoulder.

Mollian winked at her, grabbing a sword belt to strap across his chest.

Rovin pinned her with a withering glare. "Look at you, all dressed up and ready to play."

Merriam blinked sweetly at him. "What are you more jealous of, Rovin, my indisputable skills or my winning charisma?" She leaned one hip against the table and made a show of examining her fingernails. "I know it's not fair that you have neither, but I could try to teach you a trick or two if you asked nicely."

Rovin took a step toward her, brown eyes flashing angrily. "Cocky doesn't suit you, merc."

Merriam lifted a shoulder noncommittally, pushing away from the table.

The Ranger stepped fully into her path. "Don't forget, pet, that though you may have won your way into this castle through the heart of the prince, you are still *no one,*" he said low enough so only she could hear.

Merriam glared in response, amber eyes cold, and brushed past.

More of the Rangers were filing in, getting ready for the day's training, when Rovin spoke. "Why don't you take point with me today, Merriam?" His voice dropped again as he brushed by her toward the training ring. "Or are you scared His Majesty would lose interest if he saw you couldn't keep up?"

Merriam stopped in her tracks. There was no doubt as to which prince

Rovin was referring, and her eyes immediately found Oren's. His mouth twitched a bit in thinly veiled anger. He hadn't heard the conversation, but he could read body language just as well as anyone, and he was well aware of the trouble Rovin had caused her over the years.

Though he was willing to let her fight this battle, he would more than happily step in. But he would not deny his involvement with her, no matter who finished this.

Merriam's chest tightened, suddenly overwhelmed with the struggle of having to hide so much of her feelings because people like Rovin refused to see that she had earned the right to be here, regardless of how it may have started out. She knew Oren would claim her in a heartbeat, despite the prejudices they'd face. She was the one who wasn't ready to deal with it.

Mollian watched her with a slight tilt to his head. His posture was the essence of mild curiosity, but he'd be by her side in a heartbeat if she needed him.

When she faced Rovin, she didn't smile. "Find me in the woods, if you can. Catch me before I catch you. I'll leave you to gear up." Merriam whirled back around, unstrapping the training gear and dropping it to the floor. Grabbing her actual weapons belt from where it hung by the door and slinging it over her hips, she stalked toward the exit. "To first blood," she threw over her shoulder.

Mollian, weapons forgotten, hurried to her side.

She burst through the back door into a sunny afternoon, heading for the copse of trees at the back of the vast courtyard.

Mollian rubbed his hands over his face a couple of times, before pushing them through his hair. "Oren is going to kill him. Rovin is going to hurt you, and Oren is going to actually kill him."

"You really have such little faith in me, Molli?" Merriam laughed, shoving a shoulder into his before starting a shortened warm-up routine. She stretched her arms to the front, arching up before moving them to the back, and swung her torso from side to side a couple of times.

"Oh, I have every confidence in you. You'll win this."

"Then no one will have to die." She smiled up at him from where she bent toward one foot, stretching out her legs. "Oren knows I can handle myself."

"He doesn't like the way they challenge you all the time. I can tell he wants an excuse to put them in their place."

"For being mean to me?" Merriam laughed again. "He's going to have a long list, then. Luckily for Rovin, it's not a crime to be an insufferable prick. Besides, it's not like I don't also rile him up on purpose."

"You do like to ruffle his feathers," Mollian agreed.

"Maybe today I'll get to pluck a few," Merriam said hopefully before heading for the trees.

As she walked through the woods, she swung her arms to release the tension in her shoulders and prepare for the fight. She had the distinct advantage of knowing how Rovin was trained. All of his attacks, counters, dodges, feints—they were all things she'd both been taught at one point and had observed several times throughout her tenure at the castle.

Rovin, on the other hand, had never watched her fight. Had never seen her swiftly and ruthlessly dispatch an opponent without a moment of hesitation. She had learned fast not to crave combat, but how to be brutal enough to win and win quickly. The longer a fight lasted, the greater the chance for injury, and injury was bad for survival.

Merriam had also learned very early on in her mercenary career never to start something she couldn't finish.

And she was positive she could finish this.

Her fingers itched to unfasten the axes from the sheaths at her hips as she let all the repressed emotion from years of being tormented by the Rangers, by Rovin, bubble up and fill her blood with fire. She let her fingertips dance across the leather encasing the axe heads as she stalked through the trees.

She swung gracefully up into a cottonwood, climbing out onto a branch thick with foliage that extended over one of the well-worn paths through the woods.

Merriam unclipped the closure of the sheath at her right hip, then settled into the leaves, breathing soft and even as she watched and listened.

With delighted surprise at his stealth, she saw Rovin stalking predatorily through the trees before she heard him. The Ranger passed through the forest with confident, silent footsteps. His short sword was hanging loosely at his side, but she knew better than to think the lax posture meant he wouldn't be prepared to swing it up into an attack or counter in the span of a heartbeat.

Cupping one hand around the side of her mouth, she let out a slow whistle—low note, high note, low note—trusting the sound to bounce from her palm off into the trees.

Rovin stilled at the noise, slowly turning his head as he scanned the forest floor before roving up into the canopy of the trees. His eyes narrowed as he searched the area the whistle sounded from, and he took a tentative step forward, twisting his sword around a few times before raising it as he continued a slow pace forward.

Merriam waited, completely unmoving, for him to pass her and expose his back.

Rovin shook his head in annoyance. "I know you're out here, Merriam. Just come down and fight me so we can finish this."

Her lips split into a grin.

"Get out of whatever tree you're hiding in, pet. You called this duel. We have demons to hunt, if you don't remember. I don't have time for your stupid games." His voice was laced with irritation now.

Merriam waited, still silent and unmoving. Wind wafted through the trees, lifting Rovin's hair and brushing over Merriam, carrying with it his scent of apple, fallen leaves, and barely perceptible sweetness. She fought the urge to roll her eyes. Of course, not only was the pompous asshole pretty to look at, but he also had to smell like all the best parts of an orchard. It made sense that all the perfection on the outside was hiding a core rotten with hate.

Unbidden, Gressia's words floated back through her mind. *Are you still going to say that you are not privileged?*

Merriam clenched her teeth. Privileged or not, she was done being treated like a worthless outsider after all these years. It was time to put Rovin in his place. She had endured enough.

Rovin took another few steps forward, and Merriam set both of her hands around the branch beneath her. With only the soft rustle of leaves disguised by the breeze, she dropped her feet from beneath her and swung down, releasing one hand to grab an axe from her hip before dropping to the ground and running at Rovin.

The Ranger heard her land, and barely swung around in time to bring up his sword, deflecting the swing of her axe that would have swiped across the back of his arm.

She smiled at him, deftly freeing the second axe and pulling it in a powerful arc towards his abdomen.

Rovin leapt back and instantly ducked forward again in an attack.

They traded offense and defense almost every other strike, dancing around each other with the clash of metal on metal ringing through the air. Merriam kept her movements and demeanor light, a breathy laugh spilling from her lips every so often when Rovin blocked an attack.

Her mood was having the opposite effect on Rovin, who was growing more and more irritated with each swing. He grit his jaw, an angry fire lit in his deep brown eyes.

"What's the matter, Rov? Not having fun?" Merriam taunted as she twirled just out of reach.

The Ranger didn't reply, just grunted as he charged her.

Merriam brought up an axe to block, but he changed direction at the last second, the pommel of his sword slamming into the back of her hand.

Merriam yelped, dropping the axe as she reflexively pulled her hand to her chest.

Fight to win, and fight to win quickly. Jasper's instruction from her early days as a mercenary filtered through her mind, and she shook her head to clear it.

Enough taunting, then.

Merriam tightened her grip on the remaining axe, waiting for Rovin to swing again. When he did, she ducked into him, knocking the side of her blade into the bottom of his hilt, sending the sword up out of his hand. Dropping her body, she dug her shoulder into Rovin's abdomen before she sprung up, sending him flying over her.

She whirled around and jumped on top of him as soon as his back hit the ground, straddling his upper body with a knee resting just below each elbow.

Merriam held her axeblade against Rovin's throat, looking dead into his eyes as she sliced a thin, shallow line from his jaw down to his collarbone. "The next time you challenge me, I'll destroy you where your men can watch," she vowed, eyes flashing.

She leaned back on her heels, unpinning his arms. Rovin pushed up onto his elbows, glaring into her face with enough hate to boil an ocean. She matched his gaze for several heartbeats, then stood, a foot on either side of his hips. The heat guttered out of his eyes, replaced with something akin to shame, and he dropped her stare. A question rose to her lips for a fleeting moment, but she swallowed it down and stepped to the side, turning to pick up her fallen axe and slip both into the holsters at her belt.

Her hand stung where Rovin had hit it, and she could already feel it swelling with a bruise. She held it to her chest as she stepped toward a cottonwood.

"Wait–"

"Leave me alone," she interrupted. Merriam didn't want him to watch her depart. She didn't want him to see the unbidden emotions that warred within her, so, gingerly flexing the fingers of her injured hand, Merriam pulled herself up into a tree, hoping for a chance to catch her breath and sort her thoughts.

"You can't just run away," Rovin called, frustration lacing his voice.

Merriam ignored him. Just as she was climbing fully onto the branch, a hand wrapped around her ankle.

She'd barely had time to register the grasp when she was yanked backwards. Her hands flung out, but she was already tipping over. As she frantically adjusted her body to manage the fall, she felt the weight at her hips shift, having just enough time to register that one of her holsters hadn't been clipped before she hit the ground.

As she landed, arms and legs tucked to roll, she felt an immense pressure in her thigh. The pain hit her only a fraction of a second after she rolled onto her hand and knees.

Merriam bit down on a scream, collapsing and rolling onto her back as her hand went to the side of her thigh. The urge to vomit washed through her as her fingers met cold metal. She took in a shuddering gasp, blinking heavily against the blinding pain that pulsed from her thigh before leaning up to look at her leg.

The head of her axe was sunk deep just below her hip, blade running vertically along her leg. It had slipped free of her belt in the fall, and her instinct to roll had caused her to land on it at just the right angle.

The sharp, tearing pain that coursed through her entire body when she slowly, shakily extended her leg fully was more than enough to tell her the muscle was damaged. Her breath came in short, ragged bursts. She looked with wide eyes to Rovin. "What the fuck did you do?" she gasped, gritting her teeth.

The color had completely drained from his face, his eyes wide and full of fear.

"*What the fuck did you do?!*" It was half a scream and half a hiss.

Rovin shook his head dumbly. "I didn't mean ... I was ... I was just angry. I wanted to talk to you, but I wasn't thinking straight. I didn't mean for this to happen," he stammered.

Merriam pushed herself to her feet, leg held awkwardly out to the side. She tried to take a step and bit down on the scream that rose inside of her, the sound that escaped coming out as a strangled moan.

Rovin lunged to help support her, and she tore her arm away from him, almost falling from the movement and her awkward balance. "Don't you *dare* touch me," she seethed.

"Fuck. You're hurt. Let me help."

"You fucking pulled me out of a tree, *asswipe*." She stumbled forward a few steps, the movement sending a fresh wave of dizzying pain through her as blood dripped slowly past the block the blade provided. She clenched her jaw and leaned against a nearby tree for a few breaths.

Rovin took one faltering step toward her before turning and sprinting off toward the castle for help.

Merriam lumbered forward to the next tree, holding her injured hand against her chest and forcing out slow, deep breaths through the pain. Her head was feeling light and dizzy, but she had to make it back.

Just as she was able to drag herself to another tree, she felt a wave of power roll through the air. Through the fog of pain in her mind, she couldn't even tell if it had come from Oren or Mollian.

Pressing her back to her current support, she laboriously lowered herself to the ground, choking back a sob. Her injured leg stuck out in front of her, and she pressed a shaky hand against one side of the wound. Her groan of pain turned into a breathy laugh as she tipped her head back against the tree. All the years of her climbing and jumping with weapons, and she'd never once forgotten to mind them or secure them back into place.

And now here she was, after having just tried to prove her competency once and for all, with her own fucking axe sticking out of her leg.

The sound of people crashing through the forest brought her head up, and she spied two familiar heads of white hair.

Mollian dropped to his knees and slid to her side, immediately stripping off his shirt and pressing it to the wound, fully obscuring the blade. "Fuck, Ria," he murmured. "It's going to be okay now."

She pressed her uninjured hand to her eyes, forcing back the tears that finally filtered through the cloud of shock and pain.

Oren knelt slowly beside her, tension radiating from his body. He placed the backs of his fingers gently against her cheek. Merriam moved her hand from her eyes to grab his, lowering it from her face to hold in her lap. "Let's get you to the infirmary, Lady," he whispered softly.

Rovin stood a few paces away, face still pale and full of fear. She regarded him coldly, thinking he must be terrified she would sic her princes—as he'd so haughtily called them—on him for this stunt. She narrowed her eyes, conveying the message that while he might play dirty, she could fight her own battles.

He swallowed, looking even more uncomfortable, and took a step in their direction. "I didn't—"

"Stay away from her," Oren snarled.

Mollian tied the shirt to her leg by wrapping his weapons belt snuggly around her thigh, adding pressure that would hopefully keep the axe immobile.

Oren scooped her into his arms and stood, taking a deep breath to rein in his temper.

Merriam ducked into his chest, her teeth clenched at the fresh tearing sensation as her leg was jostled.

"Accidents happen in duels. We'll take her to see a medic. Your men still need to train, Lieutenant Arwood," Oren said evenly to Rovin before turning away.

Merriam focused on taking measured breaths, her body relaxing as the scent so reminiscent of pine and plum and crisp night sky washed over her senses. It didn't dull the pain, but it helped to calm her racing heart.

With her eyes screwed shut and her face pressed into Oren's chest, Merriam missed the vulnerable look of pain and defeat that flashed across Rovin's face as he brought a hand up to touch the wound on his throat, already clotted over.

Chapter 28

I am yours

MERRIAM'S RECOLLECTION OF THE trip to the infirmary came in broken flashes of memory.

Oren setting her on the table.

A sickeningly sweet herb being shoved into her mouth as she was instructed to chew.

A poultice being swathed around the blade.

Her pants being cut from her legs.

The feeling of an immense pressure being relieved as the axe was pulled free.

The sight of blood pouring from the wound in a thick red wave.

A wooden dowel being shoved between her teeth.

A dark brown liquid being poured into the wound, sending a searing wave of pain through her leg as she screamed, teeth sinking into the dowel and legs kicking out against the hands that tried to clean her wound.

Mollian sitting behind her, holding her back to his chest and pinning her arms to her sides as he filled her head with soothing words.

Oren holding her legs down as a long, threaded needle worked through her skin, pulling it back together.

A bandage being wrapped around her thigh.

Oren carrying her to her room, lying her on her bed as her eyes fluttered closed.

She had woken up alone, the soft light from her window indicating the sun had just set. Her mouth was dry and tasted of whatever plant had been forced upon her. She sat up, pushing a few stray strands of her hair from her face.

Low voices filtered through the slight crack in her bedroom door, and she went to swing her legs out of bed.

A deep, dull twinge of pain went through her whole body as the muscle in her injured thigh stretched with the movement.

She whimpered quietly, pressing her hand to the bandage. "Molli?" she called, a waver in her voice.

He was instantly walking through her door, Oren on his heels. "Ria, how are you feeling?"

"Thirsty, and my mouth tastes ... gross." She smacked her tongue a bit and wrinkled her nose.

Oren went into her bathroom and brought back a cup of water, which she drank greedily.

"That would be the ardorflower leaves. They're what made you a bit loopy and tired," Mollian explained as she drank. "That was a nasty wound you got. What happened?"

Merriam shook her head. She would finish this thing with Rovin on her own. They would both be beyond pissed if they knew he'd pulled her down. "It was just a dumb lapse in attention to detail on my part, okay?"

Mollian's lips twitched, and Oren narrowed his eyes, fully intending to push the matter further, so she abruptly changed the subject. "Have you heard anything from Ollivan and Jasper about how the search is going? Have they sent a bird? I could go to the aviary and check."

"You aren't going anywhere for at least a fortnight," Oren said gruffly.

Merriam looked up at him, brow furrowed. "The fuck does that mean?" she asked defensively.

"Mer, you just had an axe in your leg. You need to give the wound time to heal. The more you move the muscle, the longer that is going to take." Oren softened his tone, sitting beside her on the bed.

"I can't sit here and do nothing for two weeks," Merriam squeaked incredulously, glancing to Mollian. "Molli, tell him I'll be fine. I have your blood—I'll heal fast."

Mollian sighed, pushing a hand into his hair. "Your leg was pretty butchered, Ria. A cut that deep takes time to heal, even accelerated," he flicked a quick glance to Oren before continuing, "but the medic said you could be good to be up and moving around within a week."

"A *week*?!" Merriam fell back onto the bed with a groan. "But we have so much to do!"

"You can work the logistic side of things for now, but you have to let yourself heal properly, Mer. If you don't give your muscle time to fix itself ..." Oren trailed off, but Merriam knew that she needed full functionality of the muscles in her legs for the amount of agility her job required.

She swallowed a lump in her throat and blinked up at the ceiling. "Okay," she whispered.

"I can grab you some books from the library to keep you occupied," Mollian offered.

Merriam leaned up on her elbows. "Can I get a map of Jekeida, too? And all the information we've compiled so far about the demons and Basta? Maybe I'll see something we've missed."

"Of course," Mollian smiled at her brightened attitude. "I'll set you up a full investigation station."

"Thank you."

"Whatever keeps you in bed." Mollian backed out of the room.

Oren reached out to cover her hand with his. "Will you please tell me what happened, Mer?" His voice was soft as his eyes searched her face.

Merriam brought her free hand up to the aspen leaf at her throat. "I just forgot to clip an axe in. It slipped out of my belt when I fell out of a tree, and I landed on it."

"You fell out of a tree?"

"I was distracted, okay? I promise, it was just an unfortunate accident, but I'm fine."

Oren ran a thumb over her knuckles. "When Rovin came out of those trees ... he looked so, so scared. All he said is that you'd been hurt. Merri, I was terrified. I don't think I've ever been so scared in my life."

Merriam's heart clenched at the emotion lacing his words. She tugged on his hand, and he laid down on the bed next to her, head propped on a fist.

"I don't know what I would do without you anymore," he whispered, brushing a finger down her cheek.

Merriam swallowed, and before she could overthink it, she softly replied, "I love you."

Oren's eyes flashed with shock before quickly filling with heated green fire, and his mouth pulled into a smile as he lowered his face to hers. "I am yours, Merri. Fully and completely yours," he said against her lips before kissing her.

He brought a hand up to her throat, fingers sliding behind her ear as his thumb brushed across her cheek. He nipped her lower lip, pulling it into his mouth and running his tongue across it.

She moaned, heat pooling in her core as she wound her arms around his neck to draw him closer.

Oren released her, pulling back only slightly and brushing his nose across hers. "We can't start something right now, Lady."

"Close the door." Merriam lifted her head up to brush her lips across his. "Molli won't open it."

Oren groaned, leaning into her kiss. "I have things to take care of, Mer, and you're hurt."

"I'm sure you can be gentle." Merriam's eyes glittered suggestively.

"At least give the sutures a chance to close the wound before you rip it open again," Oren ordered softly, nipping her lip once more before pushing off of the bed and walking out of the room.

Merriam sat up, brushing her fingers over her lips with a smile. She nearly jumped out of her skin when Oren came back through the door, a stack of papers in his hands.

He gave her a funny look as he walked to the other side of her bed, depositing his things. "Would you like more water or anything?"

"What are you doing?" she asked bluntly.

"I told you, I have work that needs to get done. This country doesn't run itself, and my mother is slowly but surely handing it over piece by piece. I'm not holding my breath that she'll stick around long after my coronation. She'll probably be off with my father wandering the planet before the feast is over."

Merriam shook her head, a smile playing on the corners of her lips. "No, I meant what are you doing here, in my room?"

"Well, there's no way you'll be climbing to mine any time soon. Or possibly ever again if you fell out of a Legends-damned tree. So, I told my Guard that I'm helping Mollian with something important and not to be alarmed if I'm not in my rooms when expected." Oren shrugged as if it were all that simple.

Merriam smiled fully. "You're going to stay with me?"

"Try to send me away, Lady, and see what happens." Oren settled himself onto the bed next to her, grabbing a stack of papers to go over.

Merriam sat there, stupidly grinning at him as he worked.

"Can I help you?" he asked after a while, eyes glued to the documents.

Merriam bit her lip, shaking her head. She knew that it couldn't be as simple as him saying he needed to go over things with Mollian. Why would they not be working in the war room or in Oren's chambers? But she decided to take this moment of happiness and let it be as simplistic as it felt.

Minding the thick bandage on her leg, she curled onto her side and placed her head in Oren's lap.

Without hesitation, his hand smoothed over her hair. Her braid was horrendous from the day she'd had, and his fingers plucked the tie from the bottom before working her hair loose, every once in a while leaving to flip a page or grab a new document, but always returning.

Her fingers curled against his thigh as she drifted off, anchoring herself to him through her touch as he was anchoring himself to her through his.

Chapter 29

A token

MERRIAM SAT ON THE edge of her tub as Oren gently but thoroughly cleaned her wound before reapplying a bandage, wrapping it securely around her thigh. The stitches had been removed the night before, and everything appeared to be healing nicely.

He scooped her back up and laid her on her bed before sitting down at the foot of it. "I don't think you should train tomorrow," he said tentatively.

Merriam sighed heavily, resting her head against the headboard but keeping her eyes on his face. "Oren, I have to. I've sat here for a week and let you tend to my every need. I'm okay now. I know not to push it, but I have to get back into routine. I have to."

"You don't have to." Oren's eyebrows pulled together in frustration, and he still didn't meet her eyes. His fingers picked at a loose string on her blanket. "I don't understand why you can't let yourself finish healing.

Just for another week."

"I can't stay cooped up in here anymore. Not in this room, and I'd prefer not even in this castle. I need out."

Oren glanced up at her. "Do you feel I'm smothering you?"

Merriam pushed her fingers into her hair. "No, I just need to help the others. I need to learn the strategy and teach what I can. I have a job to do, O."

"I know. I hired you for it," he replied dryly.

"I'm going whether you like it or not." Merriam crossed her arms over her chest, searching his face. "You don't own me, regardless of whether or not you're footing the bill for this job."

Before she had a chance to react, Oren had pulled her down the bed so that she was flat on her back. He was on top of her in the next breath, an arm braced on either side of her head and his face low to hers as he glared at her, an almost volatile fire in his deep green eyes.

"You don't think I'm not fucking aware of that, Merri?" His voice was barely restrained. "You don't think I don't constantly obsess over how much I just want to possess you? How much I want to mark you as mine? How much I want to keep you all to myself every second of every day?"

He lowered his face even closer, running his nose along her jawline and up to her hair. Her breathing was shallow, and she raised her hands to his chest, fisting her fingers into his shirt in the scant space between them.

"I want nothing more than to lay claim to you so that everyone on this fucking planet knows you are *mine*," he growled into her ear before pulling back to look into her eyes. "But I know that's not what you need. I know you would never be happy without having the freedom to roam and live your life for you. I know that you're your own person, and that means more to me than any of my selfish desires. I love your strength and your independence, and I would die before I ever stripped you of your fire. But, Mer, I can't help feeling frustrated that you constantly throw yourself into danger. You're hurt. You were hurt so badly, and you're still pushing yourself to go right back into the thick of things." He reached one hand up to smooth her hair back, pressing a kiss to her forehead and pushing back up into a sitting position.

"You drive me crazy, you know that?" His dimple appeared with a half a smile as he looked at her. "I've never loved anyone or anything as much as I love you, and I've never felt so inept at being able to keep something safe."

"Oren." Merriam sat up, fighting back a wince as she moved her leg. "Worrying yourself over my safety is going to push you to an early grave. I can take care of myself, and I know my limits. I promise I won't push it." She grabbed his hand and pulled herself closer to him, resting her head on his shoulder. "I'm sorry about all the secrecy, too. I love you. I love you so much. I feel horrible for it, but I just ... I can't—"

Oren silenced her with a finger to her lips, wrapping an arm around her and pulling her closer. "I don't want you to ever feel like you have to explain yourself to me. Never feel pressured to do something you don't feel ready for," he whispered against her hair.

Merriam sighed, leaning her head against his chest. "I don't deserve you."

Oren pulled away from her, cupping her cheek and brushing his lips lightly over hers. "You deserve everything, Lady."

He abruptly slid from the bed, kneeling on the floor in front of her with a boyishly mischievous smile.

Merriam tilted her head to the side with a curious smile of her own. *What are you up to, Majesty?*

Oren gently grabbed her ankle and folded up the hem of her leggings. "Merriam, treasure of my heart and my life's greatest love, will you promise me honesty and transparency and exclusivity to your heart and body as long as you wish to be mine?"

Merriam laughed at the overly formal words. "Are you asking me not to sleep with anyone else as long as I'm with you?"

"And to be open and honest with your thoughts and feelings. I may be a male, but I'm not single-minded," Oren defended with a grin.

"Then yes, I promise all of those things," Merriam smiled.

Oren held up a length of string he'd pulled from her blanket, looping it around her ankle. "Then let this string be a token of my love for you, that every time you look at it, you might think of me and know that I too, promise you honesty and transparency and exclusivity." He tied the ends together in a tight knot before placing a kiss where the string rested against the front of her ankle and folding the hem of her pants back down.

Merriam laughed, leaning forward to grab his arms and pull him up. "What would Sekha think if they knew their future king was such a romantic softy?"

Oren dipped his head to hers. "In the name of the honesty that was just promised, I don't give a fuck what Sekha would think," he said before capturing her mouth in a deep and claiming kiss.

Merriam wrapped her hands around his neck, pulling herself closer to him as her tongue met with his. Her hands slid down his chest, fingers grabbing at the hem of his shirt to pull it over his head as he wrapped an arm around her, gently lowering her to the bed.

She heard the door to the common room open, and quickly tugged Oren's shirt back down as Mollian's footsteps approached her door. Oren untangled himself from her as a sharp knock sounded, and Merriam wiped the back of her hand across her mouth as she sat up and called out, "Come in."

Mollian opened the door, ignoring the obvious proximity between the two. "They're back!" he said breathlessly.

Oren straightened immediately. "All of them?"

Mollian nodded. "Eskar returned with Ollivan and Jasper and the others. They're waiting in the war room."

Oren grabbed Merriam's hand to help her off the bed. "You're sure you're okay?"

Merriam glared at him, but it held no bite. "I'm not missing this. I'll ask Molli for help if I need it." She tested the weight on her leg, and only a dull pain throbbed from her wound when she stretched the muscle.

Oren nodded. "Let's go."

Chapter 30
A cruel way of life

Three years before…

MERRIAM GRIPPED THE HANDLE of her axe, palm sweaty. She shifted, antsy, with nervous energy rolling through her body.

Her first assassination job.

Taking a deep breath, she followed Jasper and Leonidas through the forest, eyes watching the shadows for movement.

Aleah nudged her with an elbow, shooting her a grin.

Merriam almost laughed at the half-fae's excitement. Aleah was only nineteen, but had already seen more horrors than anyone, even three times her age, should have had to deal with.

Of course, the redhead had caused more than her fair share of horrors during the five years she'd been with Jasper. Maybe she hadn't always been made to be a mercenary, but the circumstances of her life had turned her into a formidable sword-for-hire.

This specific job had taken them outside of Jekeida, to the middle territory of East Audha, mostly used for farming. A gang had sprung up, looting wagons going to and from the market this town relied on for trade. The overseer of the town had hired the mercenaries, worried about commerce and not wanting to wait for the legal process of requesting the Crown's aid.

The moons shone brightly in the sky, one full, the other just past half, providing the only light aside from the stars. A large shipment was scheduled to arrive tonight, and they had been tracking the wagon for a couple klicks now, waiting for the bandits to strike.

Merriam shifted her grip on the axe handle, rolling her shoulders to relieve the tension there.

Then they heard it, the sound of men hollering and the disturbed whinnying of horses.

The group ran forward, rushing toward the men surrounding the carriage. There were six of them, one busy corralling the horses as the others pulled the merchant from his bench and unloaded crates from the carriage, tossing them to the ground.

With two strong beats of his wings, Jasper was up in the air and on them first, pulling one from the top of the wagon and flinging him to the side. The man hit the packed earth with a sickening thud, and then Jasper came down on him, driving his lance into the bandit's chest.

Aleah had jumped onto the back of another, quickly sliding a dagger over his throat before dropping to the ground and drawing a sword.

One of the bandits was locked in combat with Leonidas, the clashing of swords ringing through the night.

Merriam held her axe tightly, but kept her wrist loose. Her heart raced, and her stomach churned with a sudden onslaught of fear.

A man almost double her size charged at her, sword raised high.

Merriam choked on a scream, pulling a second axe from her belt and raising them both. When the man got close enough to swing, she lunged forward, falling to her knees and rolling underneath his attack. She sprung to her feet just behind him, burying a blade into the bicep of his sword arm. Blood flowed down his arm as she pulled the axe back, setting herself into a fighting stance.

Now he was the one screaming, turning to face her with an expression of pure, murderous rage. He swung the sword wildly, and she easily knocked it back with the flat of one axe while she stepped into his reach and sunk the other into the base of his neck, splitting his collarbone with a sickening crunch.

Merriam let go of the axe, stumbling back a step as bile rose up her throat.

The man let out a snarl that was half a shriek, falling to his knees and wrenching the axe from his body. As soon as the blade was free, blood gushed from the wound, and his scream turned into a garbled cry as he fell forward, his face turning white as he brought a hand up to his throat.

Merriam watched him bleed and struggle to staunch the flow. Her own blood rushed in her ears, and the second axe slipped from her fingers as her breathing became quick and shallow. The bandit reached a hand toward her, his fingers brushing against the toe of her boot.

She jerked back, losing her balance and falling to the ground. Her eyes never left the spot where he covered the gaping wound in his neck, blood seeping through his fingers at an alarming rate.

"Merriam!" she heard the shout, but it didn't register in her mind. Her fingers flexed into the dirt, hands locking up as her breathing turned into silent gasps, her vision blurring around the edges.

A shadow fell over her moments before a solid gust of air brushed her cheek. Jasper landed next to her, easily scooping her up and then launching back into the sky. He flew over the trees, setting down in a small clearing and lowering Merriam to the ground.

"Deep breaths," he ordered before taking off back to the carriage.

Merriam tucked her hands to her chest, legs splayed out in front of her. She tried to focus on steadying her breathing, but her gaze locked onto the toe of her boot where the man had touched her as he died.

He *died.*

She killed him.

The words swam in a slow circle through Merriam's mind. She had killed someone. Spilled his blood all over the earth, all over her axes.

Her axes.

Mollian had just made them for her a few months prior, knowing they'd become her weapon of choice. He'd carved the handles with vines of wildflowers, thinking himself comedic since something so beautiful would be used for destruction.

But she'd dropped them, left them lying on the ground next to a pool of blood. Next to the body of the man she'd *murdered.*

And her stream of consciousness looped around and around, from the kill to her lost weapons and back.

Her breathing had finally evened out, but her mind was still reeling when Jasper finally came back. He landed in a crouch, large black wings flared to slow him. He tucked them against his back as he looked at Merriam, his dark silver eyes looking less like hardened steel and more like a soft storm cloud.

He held her axes out to her, the blades wiped clean.

Merriam met his gaze, slowly taking the weapons from him and setting them in her lap. "Thank you." She ran the tip of a finger down one of the blades, watching as her finger skipped over a notch from where a sword had bitten into it. She lightly went back and forth over the imperfection. "I'm sorry," she finally whispered.

"Mer." Jasper was crouched on the balls of his feet, but her head still only came to his chin. He reached out, cupping her cheek in a large, dark hand.

She slowly raised her eyes to his.

"You have nothing to be sorry for."

"I froze."

"I would be worried if you hadn't." A half-smile tugged at his lips.

"But we've trained. I told you I was ready."

"You trained to fight. Taking a life isn't something you can be prepared for."

Merriam leaned into the warmth of his hand, fighting back the tears that suddenly pricked at her eyes.

"This is a cruel way of life, Mer. That's the full, hard truth of it. It was either him or you, and you won that round." Jasper smoothed his hand over her hair, dark brown skin contrasting against the pale golden braid.

"There was so much blood, Jaz." It came out like a whimper. "And the *sound* of his bones breaking ..."

Jasper just continued to run his hand over her hair, letting her piece it all out.

"I don't know why I didn't expect it to be so graphic," she said finally, lifting her head to face him fully. "It was so very brutal, and it was all ... me. That's something that I'm capable of."

Jasper nodded, pulling his hand back to rest on his knee.

"I'm the kind of person capable of taking a life."

"You're the kind of person who has the strength to do what is necessary."

Merriam laughed darkly. "The strength? Or the lack of morals?"

Jasper grinned, flashing pointed canines. "Not a lack of morals, just knowledge that lines blur and the world is full of gray."

Merriam set her axes to the side, pulling her legs to her chest. "I don't think I feel guilty. Is that bad?"

"Remember when I said it was him or you? He wouldn't have thought twice about ramming that sword straight through you. So, no, I would not say a lack of remorse here is bad." Jasper stood, offering his hand.

Merriam took it, grabbing her weapons with the other as she stood.

"Are you okay?" Jasper searched her face.

Merriam nodded. "I'll be fine."

"You can talk to any of us. At any time."

"I know."

"I mean that, not just in theory. We see a lot of horrors in this line of work. The strangest things hit at the strangest times. When they do, you talk it out with us, okay? Don't let that shit fester in your mind."

"I won't. I promise." Merriam slipped her weapons back into their holsters.

"Are you ready to go back?"

Merriam nodded, and Jasper picked her up again, taking off to meet up with Aleah and Leonidas. As they flew, his scent of oakmoss and sea salt surrounded her, along with the knowledge that he would always protect her, just as he would protect any of their band of mercenaries.

When Panic flew up to greet them with a loud *kak*, Merriam amended the thought in her head. This wasn't just a band of hired swords.

This was a family.

Chapter 31

Give us a moment

MERRIAM GINGERLY SAT IN a chair at the end of the table, biting back a groan at the throbbing in her leg. If Oren noticed her distress, he had the good sense not to mention it.

Ollivan was pacing up and down one side of the table, clenching and unclenching his fists. Eskar was leaning against the wall, finger tapping in a staccato rhythm against the plaster behind her. Jasper was seated calmly, arms folded across his chest, the tense set of his shoulders the only sign that he was agitated.

Aleah skipped into the room behind Rovin and Kodi, one of the mercenaries must have gone to collect her as soon as they returned. Or more than likely, Leonidas had sent Panic to the merc house to alert her.

Oren waited for the last three to sit before speaking. "Report."

Jasper's silver eyes flicked from Eskar to Ollivan, who turned to face Oren and clasped his hands behind his back. "We found it."

"And?" Aleah prompted with a grin. "It was right where I said it would be, wasn't it?"

Ollivan's eyes rolled upward. "You mercs are all much too egotistical."

"Maybe you Guard aren't egotistical enough," Campbell offered, tilting his head with a smirk.

And you thought it would be a good idea for us to work together. Merriam Cast to Oren, words laced with amusement.

Oren cleared his throat, and the Rangers' attention immediately snapped to him.

Impressive. Merriam fought back a smirk.

Behave.

Make me.

A smile played on the corners of Oren's lips as he leaned forward in his chair. "Your calculations were invaluable, Aleah. If I thought for a moment you would consider it, I would offer you a job at court. Legends know we can always use more mathematically inclined minds."

"If I ever tire of the merc life, I'll be sure to let you know, Your Highness." Aleah dipped her head respectfully, hazel eyes bright with smugness at being shown favor in front of the Guard.

Oren turned his attention to Ollivan. "What's your report, Lieutenant?"

"It took us a while to figure it out, but he's sequestering away in a cave. Commander Dio met us out there and stayed back to keep eyes on him." Some of the frustrated tension faded from the fae's shoulders as he spoke. "He has guards, Prince. Fae."

Oren's eyes widened in surprise. "Fae?"

"High fae and fair folk," Ollivan confirmed.

"But why would fae be working for Basta?" Mollian asked.

Eskar spoke up from the back. "They're not normal. Their eyes were ... wrong, and it was like something didn't fit right under their skin. It wasn't an obvious thing, just ..." Eskar shivered.

Oren raised his gaze to meet Mollian's, holding for a few long seconds before he ran a hand over his head, sighing. "That's not the best news," he said, dragging the hand back down his face. "I'm guessing you didn't get a look into the cave?"

Ollivan shook his head. "No, we watched it for a few days, but once Eskar tracked him in, he never came back out, and it was never left unguarded."

"What are the odds he's Traveling from inside?" Merriam asked. Even though the terrain of Nethyl and Earth tended to line up, there were still inconsistencies, especially with things like caves formed through erosion or purposefully dug out for mining.

"It's possible, but I was able to easily track him the entire way from Entumbra," Eskar said. "He left alone, and no one joined him."

Oren drummed his fingers against the table in thought. "So his guard stay with the cave even when he's not there? Do you have an estimate of how many people he might have?"

"I don't think there are that many," Jasper said. "It seemed to be the same six on rotation, though we'd be stupid not to assume he's hiding that demon and possibly others in the mountain."

"I agree with you there." Oren looked back to Mollian, considering his next words. "There's a very real chance these people are no longer actual people."

"They're possessed," Merriam whispered.

Rovin looked at her, brow raised doubtfully.

"Did you just say they're possessed?" Leonidas asked.

"Molli and Mer put in a little joint-effort research while you were out, and the most plausible conclusion we've come to is that the man in charge of these demon attacks is a human from a village near Entumbra named Basta. We believe he has let himself be possessed by some higher level of demon, where he is still able to act himself, but the power of the demon inside him gives him dominion and control over things like the beast we fought in the woods."

"Fuck," Kodi muttered, rubbing the back of his neck. "What does that mean for us, then? If we're fighting possessed humans?"

"There's no way to know," Merriam answered plainly. "We've been reading up as much as we can, but there are still so many unknowns. The best I've got is to work off the assumption that they'll be stronger and faster than expected. Probably less deterred by pain, too."

"But their bodies are still mortal," Mollian added. "They can bleed, and they can die. So just hit them where it counts."

"So how are we going to do this?" Ollivan asked.

"Basta has a clear advantage with knowing the cave. We have no idea how far it extends into the mountain, the layout, what he may be stockpiling—we'll need to draw him out into the open," Merriam suggested.

"And how do you propose we do that?" Eskar scoffed. "Walk up and ask nicely if he'd like to come out and play?"

Merriam glowered at the Ranger. "Obviously not—"

"That actually might work to get an audience with him, though," Kodi acknowledged with a shrug. "All we need is to draw him out in the open, give one person the vantage point to make a kill shot."

"That's a suicide mission if I've ever heard one," Aleah countered.

"Is that concern in your voice, little merc?" Kodi turned his gaze to her, running a thumb over his bottom lip.

"Hard to be concerned about some dumb Fae bastard whose name I don't even know," Aleah answered flippantly.

Kodi's eyes lit with something bordering on ravenous. "Do you have the bite to back up that bark?"

Jasper shot Aleah a sharp look before she could reply. "You're getting off track."

She gave him an innocent shrug.

"As I was saying," Merriam stated loudly, capturing everyone's attention. "I think I know how to get Basta on the move." She looked from Oren to Mollian, biting her lip. "Do you think Gressia would help us?"

Mollian tilted his head to the side, a curl spilling over his forehead. "What sort of help?"

"Just a letter," she assured him. "She just has to write to him, asking him to come to Entumbra. If we know when he's going, we can set up somewhere around the halfway point to ambush him."

"I thought he could Travel. How do we know he'll stay on Nethyl?" Leonidas asked.

"Obviously he *can* Travel, but there's a reason he doesn't. Eskar was able to track him last time, so it's worth the gamble that he'll take the same route. Besides, Entumbra's location on Earth is densely populated. Even if Basta is possessed, he still can't glamor. How is he supposed to keep from drawing attention to himself or procure any means of transportation? It would be extremely difficult for him there."

"But can't he go to another realm? What if he's returning to the world the demons came from?" Rovin ran a hand through his hair, brow furrowed in thought.

Mollian frowned. "I don't think he would be. There are too many variables, like how far separated is that realm? The further away from Nethyl the rings are used to portal, the more energy it takes, and his human blood muddies the magic. Plus, wherever this reality is, it's not our parallel. He'd have to be very well versed in the layout of both worlds to avoid accidentally opening a rift over a lake or off a cliff. Merriam's right, we should expect him to remain here."

Oren tapped two fingers against his chin, considering. "It's not a bad plan. I'll send word to Gressia, but it's fully her choice. There's still the risk that he could make it to Entumbra before we have a chance to stop him, and then she might be in danger." He was also thinking about the added risk of Basta finding out about the child if he discovered Gressia's shift in alliance and harmed her in some way.

"How long do you think the correspondence will take?" Ollivan asked.

"I can have an answer back from her in a few days, and we can build a solid battle plan after that," Oren answered. "In the meantime, we keep running drills and trying to find out more about these demons and where they may be from. Send units out into the towns and villages closest to where he's staying. Our people need to be protected. We'll also have a team on rotation monitoring the cave and surrounding area to keep an eye on him, but that is strictly a stealth mission. Observation only."

Jasper turned to Aleah and Merriam. "Any interest?"

"Yes, I'll man the watch party," Merriam volunteered before anyone could deny her the opportunity. Oren's gaze burned into her, but she purposefully kept her eyes on Jasper. "I can explore the Earth-side of the area and see if it's possible he's getting in or out of the mountain from there. Plus, it will be nice for us to stretch our legs, right, Aleah?"

Aleah nodded her agreement. "Absolutely!"

"I wouldn't mind going back out, either," Calysta offered. "Unless you need me here, Jaz."

Jasper waved a hand. "It's fully your call."

Aleah grinned, tongue poking out between her teeth. "Girls' mission!" she squeaked, doing a little dance in her chair.

Jasper rolled his eyes, a smile tugging at his lips. "Don't inspire too much confidence, Aleah. You might scare the Rangers."

Aleah stuck her tongue out at him.

Eskar and Ollivan had been conferring while all this happened, and Eskar finally spoke up. "We'll need to consult with Captain Ferrick about this new information before we assign any of ours to go out. What time would you like them to be ready to depart, Your Highness?"

"I'd like a team to leave as soon as possible. How far of a trek is it?"

"Two days by horse, Majesty," Ollivan answered. "Less, if we ride hard."

Oren nodded. "Tell Ferrick I'll want them to leave no later than first light. To reiterate, this is strictly reconnaissance. You're there to monitor. Do not engage him unless absolutely necessary," Oren ordered before meeting the eyes of Merriam, Aleah, and Calysta in turn.

"Why did that feel personally intended?" Merriam asked in amusement.

"Because it was," Oren replied evenly.

Merriam lifted a hand to her chest in mock indignation. "We're professionals, Majesty. The kingdom could be in no better hands."

Rovin scoffed, shooting her a look of exasperation.

"I'm counting on it," Oren said before looking around the table. "Does anyone have anything else before we finish?" He waited a moment before pushing up from his seat. "In that case, Eskar, please send word to the stables to have horses ready before dawn. Calysta, Aleah, I can have rooms prepared for you if you'd like to stay here, so you can be better prepared to leave in the morning."

"Thank you, Prince Oren. That would be lovely," Aleah accepted.

"You're very gracious, Your Highness, but if it's all the same to you, I'll make my bed elsewhere on the castle grounds." Calysta inclined her head.

"Of course, whatever suits you." With that, Oren turned and walked towards the door, the meeting concluded.

As the Rangers and mercs filed out, Merriam stayed behind with Mollian, testing her leg carefully. "So how pissed do you think he is?"

Mollian laughed, offering his arm for support. "He's probably pacing the hallway right now, trying to decide if he has the authority to forbid you to leave."

Merriam waved off the help, concentrating on walking evenly as they exited the war room. "I guess he could always fire me," she joked.

"I wouldn't give him any ideas if I were you," Mollian advised, his eyes traveling to the staircase where Oren stood, arms folded, as he leaned against the wall.

Merriam smiled sweetly at him as they walked up, grasping the banister and making her way up the stairs. The muscle in her thigh ached as it flexed each time she raised her leg, but she kept her expression clear.

Oren accompanied them up the stairs, and when they turned into the hallway that led to Mollian and Merriam's quarters, he finally spoke. "Would you give us a moment, brother?"

Mollian gave Merriam a helpless look before continuing down the hall and ducking into their rooms.

As soon as he was gone, Oren turned, pinning Merriam to the wall with a hand on either side of her head, standing an arm's length from her. "What sort of stunt are you trying to pull?"

Merriam blinked innocently.

"I swear on every Legend, Merriam, if you end up even more hurt," he ground out, leaning in close.

"What, you'll lock me away?" She turned her eyes up to meet his heated gaze.

"Don't fucking tempt me, woman." Oren dipped his head down to nip at her neck, drawing a sharp hiss from her before he brought a hand to her throat, thumb gently stroking the spot to soothe the pain. He tilted his head back up, looking into her eyes. "I only have so much restraint."

The brush of his thumb against her skin sent shivers down her spine, and she slowly raised a hand to cup his cheek, angling her head so that their lips were almost touching. "For you, and only you, I promise I'll be careful." She dragged her thumb over his bottom lip, fighting the urge to take it between her teeth. "Now take me to my bed and fuck me before I change my mind about whether or not I find your possessive behavior arousing."

Oren smirked wickedly. "If you wanted me to throw you over my shoulder, all you had to do was ask, Merri."

She matched his grin, dipping under his arm and slipping around him, leg twinging only slightly at the sudden movement. She sauntered to her door, not bothering to check if he was following.

Mollian poked his head out of his bedroom as she entered, toothbrush hanging from his mouth. *I take it you worked it out.*

Merriam flashed him a grin, giving a little shrug.

Stop in to say "bye" before you leave in the morning?

Of course. Merriam skipped over and kissed his cheek before twirling away into her room. Her thigh throbbed, but the ache was dissipating as the muscle warmed, which she took as a good sign.

Sitting on the edge of her bed, she pulled her uninjured leg up to untie the laces on her boots. Oren came in, shutting the door behind him and discarding his own boots by the wall. Merriam bit her lip, her fingers pausing as she watched him pull his shirt off, the muscles in his chest and arms flexing slightly as he balled it up and tossed it into the basket in the corner of the room.

He was clearly at ease being in her space, fitting so seamlessly into the only place she'd ever had completely to herself. And she wasn't mad about it. His presence as a constant in her life had so easily become normal. It didn't feel like he was taking up space in her life, but more like he was filling a space that had previously been empty.

"A copper for your thoughts?" Oren knelt on one knee in front of her, pulling her foot down and removing her boot.

Merriam shook her head, a flush crawling up her cheeks. "Just ... you look comfortable here."

Oren's lips lifted in a half-smile as he untied the laces of her other boot. "I am comfortable here." He lifted his eyes to hers as he removed the shoe. "It's about to be my castle. I should hope I look like I belong."

Merriam kicked weakly at his chest, clicking her tongue against her teeth.

Oren caught her foot easily, peeling off her sock and placing a kiss over the string at her ankle. "I believe you gave me a bit of an ultimatum." He ran his hand halfway up her calf, massaging the muscle.

"Mmh, yes. You were being rather aggressively possessive." Merriam watched him, fingers fisting into the blanket on either side of her as his hand drifted further up her leg.

Oren let go, pushing up and leaning over her, placing a hand over each of hers. "If I were any lesser a male, I would have taken you in that hallway," he whispered, face hovering over hers.

Merriam wet her lips as she tilted her head up to meet his eyes, chest rising as her breathing hitched. "If I were any lesser a mercenary, I would have half a mind to have let you."

"You have ruined me, Merri." Oren's voice was low and husky, and his eyes slid closed as he dropped his mouth to hers, hands still pinning hers to the bed as he took her breath away and chased every thought but him from her mind.

Chapter 32

It's how we stay alive

MOLLIAN HAD STILL BEEN sleeping when Merriam left, but she'd sat with him for a few minutes, brushing her fingers through his curls as their souls settled each other. Those invisible tethers between them sometimes felt like a transfer of magic, not in the way the rune on her back gave her Mollian's power, but more like she was a reserve for some of his excess magic, giving it a place to spill over into so he didn't overfill with it. It was such a strange thing when she let herself think about it, but it was also so entirely normal that she couldn't imagine not feeling it. It was just another part of being his *mehhen*, another way he needed her that was different from the way she'd needed him.

Mollian mumbled a half-intelligible goodbye before she'd closed his door and headed out into the dark of pre-dawn to meet Aleah and Calysta by the stables.

Aleah was blinking sleepily, leaning into Calysta as she fought back a yawn when the Rangers walked up.

Merriam turned to survey the group, her mood brightening when she failed to spy Rovin among them. Kodi was with three other Rangers Merriam didn't know. Two of them appeared to be newly minted, the tattoos on their arms dark and fresh. Kodi smoothed a hand over the short brown curls that ran over the top of his head and down to his neck, lifting his lips in something between a smile and a smirk as his bi-colored gaze passed Merriam and landed on Aleah.

Aleah rolled her eyes at him before turning her face to look towards the door to the stables, hiding the grin she struggled to hold back.

"Good morning, ladies," he said, flinging his riding cloak back from his arms as he placed his hands on his hips. "Ready to go spy on some demons?"

"Been waiting on you," Aleah quipped.

"I like the idea of you waiting on me, little merc." Kodi grinned.

Aleah snorted, folding her arms over her chest. "You have a very skewed view of how that would end up working out, Ranger."

Horses were led out of the stables, and Kodi walked up to her, offering a boost up. Aleah begrudgingly accepted, pushing off of his clasped fingers and swinging into the saddle.

"It's going to be a long, hard ride. I hope you're prepared," he told her as he mounted his own horse.

"I'm not sure I trust that you'd know what a long, hard ride would be," Aleah replied sweetly.

"I'd love to prove that thought wrong."

"I'm sure you'd love to try."

Merriam had just finished strapping her bag to her own horse when a voice spoke behind her.

"Sorry I'm late. Is everyone ready to go?"

She grit her teeth as she swung up into the saddle. Of course, Rovin would be the commanding officer on this excursion.

"Sir, yes sir," Kodi answered with a salute, his formal words clearly in jest.

Rovin shot him a warning look, his eyes darting to the other Rangers.

Kodi gave him an apologetic smile, and Merriam let herself feel some satisfaction that he was giving Rovin a hard time.

They let the horses' muscles warm up for a klick before pushing them into a gallop, thundering through the mountainside. Merriam's thigh throbbed with the effort of moving with the horse, but the fae blood in her veins had done a good job of knitting the muscle back together, and she didn't feel any tearing pains. She concentrated on the rhythmic thump of her braid against her spine to keep her mind off the discomfort.

When the sun was high in the sky, Rovin gave the signal to stop for lunch. They let the horses graze as they stretched their legs, pulling a portion of food out to pass around.

Merriam rested one arm against a tree, flexing her injured leg and swinging it around to relax the muscle. It had started to seize up during the last bit of the ride, and she was determined not to be the one to slow them down. She felt eyes on her from across the clearing and looked up to see Rovin watching her.

His eyes were narrowed, conflicting emotions warring across his features before he walked over to her.

"How's your leg?" he asked, holding out some bread and hard cheese.

Merriam took the food. "Would be a lot better if there hadn't been an axe lodged in it last week."

Rovin pushed a hand through his hair, averting his eyes. "I'm sorry, Mer. I shouldn't have lost my temper."

Merriam pressed her lips together, watching him. "Don't try to be a controlling prick while we're out here, and I'll call it good. As much as I'm sure you hate it, we are working together now, and I'd prefer not to have to kick your ass again."

Rovin gave her a weak smile, sticking his hand out. "Temporary truce?"

Merriam raised an eyebrow, looking from his hand to his deep brown eyes with a scoff. "I never wanted a war to begin with, Lieutenant. I'll work with you, but a truce will only happen if you can pull your head out of your ass long enough to see I was never a threat to you."

Rovin dropped his hand, eyes darkening. "You speak on things you know nothing about, pet," he ground out, turning and walking back to the Rangers.

Merriam watched his retreat, confused by his reaction and surprised by her confusion. Shaking her head, she limped over to Aleah and Calysta.

"Are you going to be able to keep riding at this pace?" Calysta asked, ink-black eyes trained on Merriam's thigh.

Merriam pressed against the mostly healed wound with her palm, biting into the bread. "I don't have a choice, but yes. I'll manage."

Calysta frowned, squatting down to the ground and closing her eyes. A few moments passed, and a thin tendril of a vine crawled from the forest behind them, stopping at the nymph's feet and sprouting a few leaves. Opening her eyes, she plucked them up, the vine disappearing back into the trees.

"Let me access the wound," Calysta instructed, ripping the leaves up and grinding them together in her palm.

Merriam turned so that her back was to the Rangers, her riding cloak covering her as she unstrapped her belt and handed it to Aleah before sliding the waistband of her leggings down. The nymph kneeled in front of her, smoothing the poultice over the wound.

"This should numb the area, but it won't make the muscle any stronger, so don't go pushing it."

"Thank you," Merriam said as she pulled her pants up, taking her weapons belt back from Aleah. The ache in her thigh was slowly beginning to fade.

Calysta smiled, standing. "If only I had something to help Aleah's taste in males."

Aleah turned from watching the Rangers, poking her tongue between her teeth with a mischievous grin. "Let me have my fun, Calysta. I'm only toying with him."

Merriam frowned, glancing over her shoulder at Kodi talking with his comrades, stealing glances towards the red-haired half-fae. "Be careful," she sighed. "He's trouble."

Aleah's grin widened. "Oh, I'm counting on it."

When they finished lunch, the group continued through the mountains, slowing as the sun sank, but not stopping until the moons were high in the sky. A small fire pit was built and bedrolls laid out around it. It was too dark to effectively hunt, so they ate more hardtack before drawing watch and lying down to sleep.

Aleah had placed her bedroll close to Merriam, curling up with her back against Merriam's side and easily falling asleep.

Merriam watched the stars for a while, one arm stretched underneath her head, before her eyes slowly slipped closed and her breathing evened out.

The sun rose all too early, and they had a breakfast of bread and berries that grew close enough for Calysta to beckon forth before continuing the ride.

Kodi gave the signal for them to slow when they got closer, not wanting to draw undue attention that may alert Basta's guards to venture out, and led the way to where Dio had set up camp.

They arrived just as the sun was dipping toward the mountains to the west, and Merriam dropped from her horse, exhausted from travel. Shaking her leg out, she walked up to Dio, holding her head high. "Good evening, Commander," she greeted.

Dio looked down at her, inclining his head. "Merc."

Rovin came up behind her with a salute that Dio returned. "We're here to relieve you, sir."

Nodding, Dio gestured toward the fire. "Thank you, Lieutenant Arwood. Settle in and have some food. I'll brief you later tonight."

Merriam held back the urge to roll her eyes at the obvious slight, instead darting her gaze to the fire, a thin column of smoke rising from it. She turned her attention back to Dio, pointing to the flames.

The fae raised a hand to stop her question. "I assure you, we aren't daft. We've been watching the cave for days. It's around a bend in the mountain. The guards never stray from the entrance, and we're fully out of sight. The fire is a calculated risk that was deemed acceptable."

Merriam just nodded, moving off to claim a spot in a tent before filling her belly with hot food.

After everyone had eaten, Dio briefed the newcomers, filling them in on the current strategy and watch rotation. "The cave entrance is around the mountain, as we discussed earlier. Kodi and the nymph should be familiar with the location," he paused, looking to the Ranger, who nodded. "You can come up with your own watch schedule, but I'm sure you know the importance of keeping eyes on the area at all times. The guards seem to switch out three times a day, always two. So far, the man has only left a couple of times to bathe in a stream nearby. The guards go out and hunt every other day or so, so make sure you're well-hidden and off the main paths through the forest." A look of concern crossed over Dio's face, and he passed a hand over his fair hair. "Those people aren't natural. We haven't seen anything out of the ordinary, but you can feel it."

Rovin glanced at Merriam, who narrowed her eyes as she tried to decide if he wanted her to explain at the risk of sounding mad. She looked back to Dio, drawing a finger down the intricately detailed handle of one of the axes that hung on her side. "They're more than likely possessed. By demons."

Dio's eyebrows raised, but he didn't scoff like she expected. "I'm not sure anything would surprise me at this point," he said.

Merriam's lips quirked up in a small smile. "Expect the unexpected, I suppose."

"It's how we stay alive, merc," Dio said with a sigh before turning to Rovin. "Do you have any questions?"

Rovin shook his head. "Our orders are strictly surveillance. If anything happens, we have enough people here that it won't be a problem to dispatch someone to bring news back to Umbra."

"Sounds like you've got a handle on it, Lieutenant. My group and I will leave in the morning." Dio stood, then looked back at Rovin with a proud gleam in his eye. "I'm glad to see Captain Ferrick has given you charge of a mission. It's about time, and I know you'll do us proud."

"Thank you, Commander." Rovin's chest puffed up at the praise as he stood, excusing himself to head off toward a tent.

Merriam followed, watching Rovin curiously, a small smile pulling on her lips. "First command then, huh?"

Rovin turned to face her, eyes already narrowed in a suspicious glare. "What of it?"

"Ol' Captain of the Guard is finally softening up enough to hand command over to one of the fair folk. And on such an important mission? Makes my insides all warm and toasty."

"Watch whose heritage you're pointing out, pet." The Ranger bristled.

"Oh, come on now, you know I'm always rooting for the little guy. Just because you're an insufferable dick doesn't mean I can't be happy that Ferrick is lightening his prejudice against those who aren't high fae."

"I swear, Merriam, if you're thinking of a way to fuck this up for me..." Rovin warned, letting the statement hang unfinished between them.

Merriam laughed darkly. "What would you do about it, Lieutenant? As you now know, I do have some fae blood in my system. So, if your little stunt pulling me out of a tree was meant to take me out of the game for a while, it didn't work." Merriam tossed her braid over her shoulder. "Fortunately, though, I am more invested in keeping this country safe and doing *my* job than I am in your demise."

Rovin pushed a hand into his hair, sighing heavily. "If you would let me apologize, I—I didn't mean for you to get hurt. I didn't even think through what I was doing. I just wanted to talk things through, but my temper got the best of me. You were so far under my skin I couldn't think straight, and I'm sorry."

Merriam rolled her eyes and scoffed, "What a fucking apology, Rov. I get it. You didn't mean for my axe to end up in my thigh, but like I told you earlier today, you can drop it."

Rovin dragged his hand down his face, gave a defeated shake of his head, and turned, stalking into the tent.

"What was that about?" Aleah asked, stepping up behind Merriam.

She turned around, waving the girl off. "You know Rangers always have a stick up their ass about something."

Aleah pressed her lips together, giving Merriam a look. "Okay, but that one seems to really get you fired up."

"He picked this fight with me a long time ago, Aleah. You know that."

"You've sure let it continue, though, haven't you?" Aleah suggested quietly.

Merriam shook her head, walking back into the ring by the fire. "Just drop it, okay? We need to work out a rotation for watch."

"Testy," Aleah said with a smile, twirling to sit on a log and wait for everyone else to gather and hash out details.

(ℓ)

Merriam stretched her upper body as she walked through the woods. The sky was lightening, but the sun had yet to peek over the mountains, leaving a crisp chill in the air. She closed her cloak more tightly around her before cupping her hands over her mouth and perfectly imitating the call of a magpie.

A few moments later, a returning call pealed through the forest, and Merriam continued forward, climbing up into a cottonwood several paces back from where the trees thinned out. Her thigh twinged with the movement, but she was able to easily ignore the pain.

Bellamy, one of the newer Rangers, was propped up against the trunk of the tree, just beginning to stretch out the joints of his legs from what was presumably a largely motionless night.

"Anything interesting?" Merriam asked quietly, draping her arms over a branch and glancing to where two fae were visible standing guard outside of a narrow slit in the side of the mountain. They were both fair folk, one tall and slender with iridescent wings like a bug, the other a stocky, blue-skinned troll, teeth poking out from his lower jaw in an underbite.

Bellamy shook his head. "Guard changed out once in the night, but all else has been quiet."

"They were just starting breakfast when I left. If you hurry, you can probably grab some while it's still warm," Merriam said as he started his descent.

Bellamy looked up at her before dropping to the ground, smiling almost shyly. "Thanks."

Merriam smiled back, watching him walk through the trees for a few heartbeats before turning her attention to the guards outside of the cave, pulling her knees to her chest to keep warm. Over the past few days that they'd been camped, she'd made it a point to try to be friendly with the newer Rangers. Just because Rovin and the rest of them that had been around for the past seven years were all pricks, didn't mean she couldn't try to turn some of the tides in her favor. In her line of work, it was always good to have friends in as many places as possible.

She'd spent the entire first day here exploring the mountain on Earth, but there hadn't been a single indication that it was also hollow. From sun up to sun down, Merriam had hiked around the mountain, but hadn't found any sign of a cave or any sign of Basta.

As the sun slowly made its way over the mountains, bringing with it the heat of a late summer day, she let a leg drop, swaying in a movement that mimicked the leaves in the gentle breeze running around the mountain.

The guards changed once, but neither pair even looked into the forest, just stared blankly into space. Their stillness was borderline unnatural, and the hair along Merriam's arms raised as she studied them more carefully, wondering what it truly meant to be possessed and how it might affect them should she have to fight.

Her fingers flicked over the handles of her axes at the thought, an instinctive reflex she'd picked up over the years and one that had probably saved her life on more than one occasion.

When the sun sat directly overhead, a magpie call sounded from behind her: two staccato chirps. She watched the guards for a moment more, but when they showed no signs of awareness, she returned the same call.

A few moments later, a young female Ranger climbed into the tree. Merriam knew this had to be her first mission away from Umbra. Her eyes were always wide, face drained of color, like she was ready for pandemonium to break at any moment. Merriam offered her an encouraging smile. "It's all quiet. I'll make sure to save you a good cut of meat from supper."

The female, no more than a year or two younger than Merriam, nodded, her fingers in a white knuckle grip around the rough bark of the cottonwood.

Merriam silently slipped to a lower branch, tilting her head up at the Ranger. "Between you and me, Evangeline, your lieutenant's bark is worse than his bite. But you'll be fine under him. He'll always protect his own."

Evangeline nodded stiffly, brushing a stray lock of hair behind her tapered ear before situating herself on the branch and setting her sights on the cave entrance.

Merriam dropped to the ground, landing with bended knees and barely a sound. She walked into the trees before stopping to stretch out her injured leg, swinging and flexing the muscle until the dull ache spread and quieted.

Her stomach rumbled once, and she set off toward camp, whetting her appetite for the cheese, bread, and fruit she knew awaited her.

Three sharp magpie cries cut through the forest, and Merriam stilled aside from her fingers loosening the toggle closures of her sheaths. Two more cries followed, and Merriam quickly ducked further into the trees, crouching low behind the brush and keeping her eyes trained on the narrow path she'd been walking on.

Three followed by two. Someone was headed her way. More than likely, it was just a guard going for water or possibly a hunt, and they'd branch off onto a wider path shortly.

It wasn't long before Merriam saw the two guards from earlier walking through the forest, movements fluid in a way that was unnatural even for a fae. She suppressed a shiver as she watched them, letting them get a little bit ahead before following from a distance.

The realization that they were headed in the direction of the camp sunk like a cold stone in her belly. The only thought in her mind was that she couldn't let them get that far.

Wrapping her cloak securely around her shoulders to hide the weapons at her hips, Merriam stepped onto the trail, stumbling over a brittle twig.

The guards whipped around, taking her in with eyes as fully black as Calysta's.

Merriam hunched her shoulders, shrinking into herself. "So sorry to disturb you. I was out riding with my younger brother, but I fell off the horse. Silky knows the woods, and I'm sure she took him home, but I seem to have gotten a little turned around. Do you, by chance, know which path to take to get back to Ferda?"

The guards narrowed their eyes.

Merriam gulped visibly. "Sorry to have disturbed you, sirs. I'll just keep the mountain at my back and I'm sure I'll find the main road eventually." She smiled weakly before stepping onto a game trail to the side and walking off, casting a few nervous glances over her shoulder.

The men walked off the path to follow her.

Merriam turned her head forward, and her heart rate sped up, knowing she hadn't fully thought this plan through. They were no longer headed toward camp, but now she had to lose them.

A soft snap of a twig sounded behind her moments before the first heavy footfall, and Merriam was sprinting before the next boot hit the forest floor. She dashed through the forest, not looking back but knowing she was losing ground from the sounds of pursuit.

Two to one weren't the worst odds if it came down to it, and her eyes scanned for a good place to cut into the brush and either lose them or confront them. Leaping from the game trail, she darted between dense trunks, never continuing in a straight line, before jumping off to the side and landing in a crouch.

She pressed her back against a tree, gritting her teeth against the ache in her leg. She peeked around the trunk as the men slowed and held her breath, hoping they'd turn around.

The troll tipped his face up and sniffed like a dog. "Bitch is close," he muttered.

Merriam unclasped her cloak and let it fall from her shoulders, running her tongue over her teeth as she stepped from her hiding place and pulled both axes from her belt. "Forgive me, Oren, I really tried," she breathed, a small smile tugging at her lips.

She raised one arm, poising to toss an axe into the skull of the winged fae when her eyes locked with his.

His face split into a grin before a wet rip filled the air and his body slid away, unveiling a creature the size of a bear, but with an almost reptilian appearance. Its jaws were long and narrow, filled with rows of jagged teeth.

Merriam's heart leapt into her throat, and she swung her arm with all the force she could muster.

Her axe sailed through the air, the blade sinking into the base of its snout with a solid *thunk*.

The demon roared, tinted spittle flying from its jaws as it swiped a massive, taloned paw over its face. It pushed the axe free, and Merriam's eyes followed the glint of the metal blade as it fell to the forest floor before trailing back up to the demon. A steady trickle of black blood oozed from the wound, dripping into its mouth and down its neck.

It blinked once, black eyes lit with a rage so deep Merriam felt her blood chill. The troll's skin started to split, and Merriam fled.

She leapt over brush and brambles, sailing through the forest with a practiced ease fueled by pure terror as she heard the beasts running behind her. She broke through the trees, and a short expanse of rock stretched in front of her before abruptly dropping off.

"Legends fucking kill me," she said on a ragged sob. The tops of trees poked up from below the cliff, and she risked one glance backward.

The demons were right at her heels, hot breath brushing across her arms and neck.

They screeched when they saw her face, and it was enough warning for her to decide what was the safer risk. Burrowing into herself, she found an extra burst of strength that was nothing more than undiluted adrenaline and pushed her sprint faster, racing toward the cliff edge without giving herself a chance to overthink it.

Clenching her teeth, Merriam leaped, pushing from the cliff's edge with her good leg. She sailed through the air, her stomach in her throat, one hand clasping the handle of her axe, the other reaching.

After the longest few heartbeats of her life, her body sank toward one of the treetops, and she smacked into it with a force that knocked her breath from her lungs. She fell back into a branch, feeling it snap under her weight, and tipped over it before she was able to get an arm around another, axeblade sinking into bark to help stop her momentum.

One of the beasts had gone over the edge with her, and she looked down just in time to see it land back-first on a boulder, a sharp yelp and sickening smack echoing through the mountainside before a pool of inky blood spread below him.

Merriam gasped, trying to catch her breath, and turned her head up to where the other demon paced the edge of the cliff, snarling and snapping.

Her scrabbling feet found purchase, and she shakily lowered herself onto the branch, pulling her axe free from the wood and securing it back into its sheath. Keeping a portion of her awareness trained at the cliff's edge, she carefully stretched her arms forward, first testing her range of motion before checking for surface injuries.

Luckily, it didn't feel like anything was broken, but the skin of one arm was nearly shredded, and the back of the other was already forming a deep purple bruise. She took a deep breath and instantly winced, letting out a strangled cry. "Fuck," she hissed, bringing one scraped palm gingerly to her side. Her ribs were definitely bruised, if not cracked.

After a quick glance up at the remaining creature, Merriam turned her attention to her legs, stretching them out and rotating her joints. Her thigh didn't seem to be any more agitated, but one of her ankles hurt to move, strained from her awkward landing in the tree. She couldn't see any skin through the fabric of her pants, but she knew her legs were covered in cuts and bruises as the adrenaline faded from her system and all the small pains started creeping in.

Movement at the cliff caught her eye, and she looked up to see the demon abruptly turn and run off. Deciding it best not to wait for it to potentially come find her, she started making her way slowly down to the ground, wincing every time she had to stretch out her right side or put pressure against her ribcage.

When she finally dropped down to the ground, she was breathing raggedly, tears pricking her eyes as her whole body seemed to throb with pain. She glanced around, trying to figure out how to get back to camp.

"Fuck. I'm in trouble," she muttered, limping along parallel to the cliffside.

Chapter 33

Don't take offense, Prince

Six months before ...

SNOW FELL SOFTLY FROM the sky, coating the top of the glass dome where Oren sat annotating a book about the distant world of Nessium.

"You have an unhealthy obsession, little brother," Gressia commented as she joined him.

A dimple appeared in Oren's cheek with a lopsided smile, his gaze never leaving the page as he wrote another note in the margin. "Some of the details here are inaccurate. I want to do a little more recon, but it looks like a natural disaster came through at some point in the last hundred years or so and altered the layout of these lakes."

"Have you visited its parallel to see if the event was shared?" Gressia peered over his shoulder to look at his notes.

"Not yet," Oren replied, leaning back to give her a better view. "I wanted to double-check some things first."

Gressia nodded, eyes scanning the page. "Oh, your fair folk are here. They were just stabling their horses while I was on my way up."

Oren looked up then, craning his neck to peer out the window into the courtyard. Nervous anticipation rolled through him when he saw the mercenaries, hoods of their cloaks pulled up against the chill of the winter air. "They aren't mine, Gress." He rolled his eyes as he stood, closing the book and placing it on an end table.

"Well, they certainly aren't here for me." Gressia settled into a chair with her own stack of books and notepads, pulling a blanket around her shoulders. "They're like stray cats. Feed them once and they'll just keep coming back."

"Please, like you won't continue to do so even after I return to Umbra."

Gressia shrugged, a smile playing over her lips. "I've already let the staff know to prepare extra for supper, but I'll probably take mine up here."

Oren hurried down the stairs, trying to convince himself the knot in his stomach was just excitement over having visitors in general and not directly related to his brother's *mehhen*. Grabbing a cloak from a rack by the door to throw around his shoulders, he descended the steep, narrow steps, boots crunching in the light dusting of snow.

Merriam tilted her face up to look at him and smiled, lifting a gloved hand in a little wave.

Fuck. His nerves were absolutely, in every way, related to the human. Oren gripped the iron railing, letting the cold bite into his skin and ground him as he returned her smile before looking at the others and throwing out his arms in greeting. "Well, if it isn't Sekha's finest."

Jasper, dressed in a hooded cut of fabric that wrapped around his torso in a way that kept his wings free, stepped forward to meet him, flaring his dark wings as they embraced. "It's good to see you again, brother."

"It's always a pleasure." Oren released him, stepping back to survey the others. "I'll have the extra rooms above the stables made up. How long will you be staying?"

"Just overnight. We're all ready to be back in Umbra," Jasper answered.

"Supper should be ready in a few hours, but you're welcome to relax inside the castle or in the stable rooms until then," the prince offered, sliding his eyes to Merriam for the briefest moment before looking off into the forest. "I was just about to go check some of the wards around the perimeter, but I'll join you for food after."

"Anywhere with a fireplace is where I want to be right now," Campbell grumbled, shaking snow from his hair. Earmuffs covered his ears, but his antlers made a hood impossible.

Merriam pulled her cloak tighter around her, lifting one shoulder in a casual shrug. "I wouldn't mind a little hike if you'd like some company," she said to Oren.

"Company would be lovely." Oren smiled, looking at the others. "Anyone else? The loop is only a few klicks."

"Don't take offense, Prince, when I say that I would rather gouge out my own eyeballs than go on a snowy hike." Aleah looped her arm through Campbell's, pulling him toward the stables. "But you two have fun. We'll see you at supper."

The mercenaries headed up the wooden staircase to the living quarters above the stables while Merriam and Oren headed into the forest. Oren tucked his hands under his arms, hiding his fingers from the cold.

"Kind of ill-prepared, aren't you?" Merriam asked cheekily.

"I didn't have much time to think of an excuse to get you alone," he replied shamelessly.

Merriam's face heated, and she turned her eyes to the trees.

Oren asked her about her recent jobs as they hiked through the forest, occasionally stopping for him to add some of his blood to various runes carved into tree trunks. Though the magic connecting all the worlds was centered in the Gate, it had a tendency to slip free, which is when the random short-term portals appeared in other places. The Keepers did their best to limit these instances by trapping the magic around Entumbra, but it was still able to seep through every now and then.

The two drifted closer together as they walked, slipping into a comfortable rhythm. They'd scaled up the mountainside, stopping underneath a pine to rest. Merriam looked down at Entumbra, her breath catching as she looked at the stone castle stretching above the trees, blanketed in snow. She chuckled suddenly, shaking her head.

"What's so funny?" Oren watched her.

"I was just thinking how magical it all looks ... but it is, quite literally, magical." Merriam smiled, glancing up at him.

Oren reached out to brush a stray lock of hair from her cheek, his fingers cold against her skin. "Never stop looking at the world with wonder. It's one of my favorite things about you."

"One of them?" She raised an eyebrow, amber eyes glittering. "What are the others?"

"Wouldn't you like to know?" Oren teased.

Merriam took a step closer to him, placing her palm against his chest as she tilted her face up to him. "You know I have a thing for praise."

Snaking an arm around her waist underneath her cloak, Oren pulled her flush against him. "So brazen, merc."

She lifted onto her toes, gaze dropping to his lips. "Take advantage of it while you can."

"Is that your professional advice?" He brushed his nose against hers.

"Professional? No. *Professionally*, Your Majesty should avoid all entanglements with a known mercenary."

He brushed his lips against hers. "Personally?"

Merriam slid her hand up the back of his neck, pulling him into a deep kiss. Heat flared through her belly, and she pressed herself to him, relishing his warmth against the cold in the air. "Personally," she whispered against his lips, "fucking a prince in the snow sounds like an entirely magical experience."

Oren smiled, dragging his hand down to squeeze her ass. "What was it you said? Take advantage of it while you can?"

"Snow could be long gone by the time I make my way back through here again," Merriam agreed, running her fingers along the waistband of his pants.

"I could be long gone by the time you make your way back through here again," he chuckled, nipping her lip.

Merriam stiffened, lowering back to her heels. "You're going back to Umbra soon."

"Fuck, Mer, I didn't mean to ruin the mood." He wiped a hand over his mouth, taking a step back.

"No, it's fine, I just ... part of me forgot that this was only temporary."

Oren looked off to the castle. "It doesn't have to be."

She shook her head with a scoff. "You know as well as I do that this only works because we're so far separated from everything out here."

"I was under the impression we worked quite well together." He turned back to her with a smirk.

Fighting back a smile, Merriam rolled her eyes and shoved him in the shoulder. "Not at all what I mean. I'm a mercenary. You need a queen."

"I'm not expected to marry for years to come," Oren argued.

"And I'll be long dead by then," she joked.

The prince tilted his head, running his teeth over his bottom lip as he watched her. "If you were Bonded to a fae, your lifespan would be lengthened."

Merriam flexed her fingers in her gloves, Mollian's rings hidden safely inside them. Not that he'd never seen them before, but surely he would have said something if he suspected she had the ability to use them. "You're being quite presumptuous there, O."

"Am I?"

She stepped back up to him, trailing her hands down this chest, observing their path thoughtfully. "My life is being a mercenary. Your dick may be good, but no dick is *that* good."

"So you've told me," Oren said, gaze burning into her as he watched her. "So, where does that leave us?"

"I'm still here," Merriam replied vaguely.

"Possibly for the last time." Oren kept his posture loose as she ran her hands around his waist and up his back, pulling herself closer.

"Professionally, I would advise you to finish with your warding and return to the castle." Merriam tilted her face up to him, blinking innocently.

Oren gripped her hips, closing the distance between them. "To Hel with professionalism."

Chapter 34

The mood strikes randomly

MERRIAM HOBBLED ALONG FOR a while, weighing her options. She knew her absence would be noticed soon, if it hadn't been already. Someone would be dispatched to go after her. How long it would take for them to find and follow her trail through the forest, though, was much less predictable of a time-frame.

The shallow scrapes on her arms had already clotted over, but her whole body ached, and a sharp pain ripped through her chest every time she breathed too deeply. The cliff tapered to a steep mountainside up ahead, and she braced a palm against the rock to catch her breath and ready herself for what was sure to be a hellacious hike.

The sun glinted off the orydite on her middle finger, thin veins of gold glittering against opaque black. Merriam choked out a laugh, gasping as her injured ribs protested at the movement. The laugh trickled out into a small sob as she raised her other hand, purple umbrite flashing against the silver band. "This would have been helpful as fuck to remember before you threw yourself off a cliff, dumbass."

With the exception of the area around Entumbra, the terrain of Nethyl and Earth almost always coincided—one of the perks of them being parallel worlds. But, sometimes, there were discrepancies, especially in the more developed places on Earth.

Merriam looked to the sky, gauging the sun's position and debating how long it might take before someone made it all the way out to her. If she had been leaving any sort of a trail for someone to track, it would end where she crossed over. That was assuming someone even found her trail, and if the terrain on Earth might be more manageable in her current state...

Deciding it was at least worth a look, Merriam slid the stones across each other. She still stood next to a cliff, but the acrid smell of asphalt wafted around her, and she turned to the left to see a road through the trees. She bit her lip, taking a tentative step forward. If the road curved up the mountain, she could easily follow it. The flat surface would be the biggest relief on her ankle, which she could feel swelling inside her boot.

She took another step forward when the thrum of an engine filled the air, and a car soon sped past. Merriam set her jaw, deciding the risk of being seen was worth the energy she'd save by not trying to blaze a trail, and walked out of the trees onto the shoulder of the road.

It wasn't very busy, and the few cars that passed probably assumed she was a hiker or a vagrant wandering to the next town. She'd moved her axe to her right side, shielding it from view. She looked through the trees as she walked, trying to find a clear, easy path up the mountain so she could Travel back to Nethyl.

Up ahead, a dirt road branched off in the direction she needed, and she almost sighed with relief at her luck before remembering her bruised ribs and catching herself.

She limped up the road, tears pricking behind her eyes as she forced herself to keep a steady pace and not tire herself out. The rush of fear from earlier had drained her emotionally and mentally, and she was having trouble not focusing on how parched she was. Her mind was also just finally starting to process that she had almost died. Should probably very well be dead. Who in their right mind jumped off of a *cliff*?

Tires crunched gravel behind her, and Merriam stepped further off the side of the road to let the vehicle pass.

"Are you okay?" a voice called out.

Merriam glanced to the side where a middle-aged man was leaning over his center console to speak to her through an open window.

"I'm fine, thank you," Merriam said, throwing in a half-hearted wave.

The man's face screwed up, as if debating. "You're sure? You look like you took a tumble."

Merriam laughed lightly, fully fighting back tears. "I did, but I'm fine. I'm meeting my friends just up ahead here."

"I can give you a ride. You're limping something fierce."

"I'm fine," Merriam grit her teeth and continued walking.

"Can I at least give you a bottle of water? It doesn't look like you have any gear with you."

Merriam stopped, peering warily at the man, who now held a plastic bottle over his passenger seat. She swallowed, realizing again how dry her mouth was, and took a step toward the vehicle. Keeping her eyes on the man, she reached out and took the bottle, retreating as fast as her ankle would let her. "Thank you," she said, forcing her lips into a smile.

The man just nodded before rolling up his window and driving away. Merriam had enough sense to check that the bottle was still factory sealed before uncapping it and drinking her fill. She drained half the water in a few gulps before she continued walking, sipping on what was left.

Finally, the road leveled out, and Merriam looked to the right — to the north — and Earth's version of the mountain they were guarding. She hated to litter, but wasn't about to bring the foreign object back to camp with her, so Merriam set the bottle by the side of the road before stepping into the trees and striking her rings together once more.

The tightness in her chest eased a little now that she knew she was back in Jekeida. Back home. Using the mountain as a reference, she was fairly confident in the location of the camp, and pushed down the exhaustion in her bones to continue the hike.

The sun was sinking towards the mountains when she heard soft hoof beats close by and she slipped behind a tree, crouching low to let the brush help hide her.

A horse soon came into view, the rider atop it unmistakable to her.

Irritation and embarrassment warred with the relief that flooded her veins, a combination that almost made her nauseous with confusion. She pushed the thought aside and stood up, wetting her lips and whistling one sharp note.

Rovin's head immediately whipped in her direction, and he slid from the horse as soon as he saw her, a look halfway between panic and frustration lighting his eyes as he ran to her.

Merriam turned her face, fighting with the exhaustion-fueled emotions bubbling up and threatening to spill. She bit her lip, blinking furiously to fight back tears. She'd been found. She wouldn't have to walk. She would get food. She would get treatment for her wounds.

She would have to explain what the fuck had happened.

"I never thought I'd be able to say I'm happy to see you," she forced through the lump in her throat as Rovin reached her.

"Legends, Merriam," Rovin said, just above a whisper.

Merriam let him slowly take her wrist, pulling her arm out to examine the wicked bruise that stretched across her entire tricep. "I'm okay, just bumps and bruises, mostly. A rib or two might be cracked, though, and my ankle could use some rest and elevation."

"I followed your trail through the forest. Those guards ... what the fuck happened to them?"

Merriam swallowed, pulling her arm back from Rovin and brushing strands of hair that had loosened from her braid away from her face. "I was right. They're possessed. *Were* possessed. They ... the demons that were wearing them just, like, ripped free." She couldn't keep the slight tremor of terror from her voice, amber eyes wide and shining with it.

Rovin's own face paled as he watched her. "Demons like the one we fought on the way back from Entumbra? Two of them?"

"Similar, but different. They were slightly smaller and more lizard-like."

"You took on two at once?" Rovin asked, awe tinging his voice.

Merriam shook her head, meeting his eyes. "I threw my axe at one. The blade landed in its skull, and it brushed it off like a bee sting, Rov. Like it was nothing." His eyes widened, but he let her continue. "I freaked and just started running. I wasn't even thinking at that point. I just knew I needed to get away."

"Why didn't you ..." Rovin drifted off, gesturing vaguely to her hands.

Merriam laughed morosely, cutting off into a sharp hiss when the movement jarred her ribs. "I didn't even remember Traveling was an option. Nothing was in my head but putting distance between myself and those demons."

"I saw one at the bottom of the cliff where I lost your trail. How did you manage to throw it over?"

Merriam blinked. "I didn't throw it over, I threw myself. He just followed."

Rovin shook his head, offering her a hand to help her to the horse. "I thought you weren't trying to sabotage my first command."

"Changed my mind," Merriam grunted as he looped her arm around his waist, taking some of her weight so she could better favor her injured ankle. She braced her free hand against her side below her injured ribs, trying to keep everything still as she limped along.

"You're fucking insane," Rovin sighed.

Merriam's lips lifted in a tired smile. "Probably the only reason I've lived this long."

The ride back to camp was torturous, but quick.

"You found her! What happened?" Bellamy ran up, helping Merriam down from the horse.

Merriam tried to smile through a grimace of pain. "Just your casual demon attack. It happens."

Evangeline stepped forward, face pale and eyes wide with fear. Merriam almost laughed at how frightened the fae was. How she'd made it all the way through Ranger training with the trepid nature of a mouse was confounding. "I'm so sorry!" She clasped her hands to her chest. "I tried to warn you."

Merriam waved her off, limping over to a log and sitting down as Calysta walked up to check her over. "You did good; I heard you."

Evangeline's eyes filled with relief, but a moment later replaced with confusion as she looked from Merriam to Rovin.

Rovin also gave Merriam a questioning look.

Merriam sighed, holding her arm out as Calysta ran her olive green fingers over the cuts and bruises, careful of her claws. "I got Evangeline's warning and hid, then decided to follow them for a bit. Just to try to get more knowledge of their activities and whereabouts. They were headed straight for camp, so I created a diversion to lure them away. It worked. A little too well."

Rovin pushed a hand into his hair. "Legends, Merriam. Where was your head? We had strict orders not to engage."

Merriam scoffed, taking bread and cheese from Aleah, who sat next to her and gingerly rested her head on her shoulder. "I think we would have had to do a lot more engaging if they'd walked into camp. At least this way there's still a chance they think I was a lost villager," Merriam defended before taking a large bite of bread, glaring at Rovin.

Evangeline and Bellamy watched the exchange with rapt attention, and Aleah rolled her eyes at the argument building between the Ranger and the mercenary. The redhead glanced to where Kodi sat across the fire, and he winked at her before casually standing, ready to step in and diffuse the situation if needed.

Rovin's jaw ticked underneath the short scruff of his beard. "Get patched up and then we'll talk," he ground out before walking off to care for the horse.

Merriam finished eating before standing up and following Calysta into a tent. She peeled off her shirt so the nymph could have a better look at her.

"Pants, too," Calysta ordered, arms full of an array of plants she'd coaxed from the woods.

Merriam obediently sat to unlace her boots before sliding her pants down her legs and lying back on a bedroll, while Calysta sat down next to her.

"You're already healing well. Nothing should scar except for this nasty gash on your arm, which is lucky. What concerns me are your ribs. The way you're wincing every time you take a deep breath isn't good." Calysta rested warm fingers against Merriam's chest, just below the band of her bra. The nymph's touch was light as she skimmed over the bruising from the impact of hitting the branches. She pressed down a little harder, sliding her fingers over the bruise, and Merriam flinched. Frowning, Calysta ran her fingers over the area again.

"Fucking Legends, Calysta," Merriam growled, smacking her hand away.

Calysta gave her an impatient look. "I was only trying to feel the extent of the damage, whiny-willow. Luckily, I think it's just bruised. You'll probably be good to go within a week or two."

Merriam nodded, fighting back a sigh of relief that she knew would hurt.

"Of course, I'm not a medic, so who truly knows the extent of the damage, but I couldn't feel anything, and the bruising isn't too bad."

Calysta made a quick salve to rub over the worst of the cuts and bruises, a topical pain relief and something that should keep the bruises from developing worse. She decided Merriam's ankle was likely strained and advised her to elevate it as soon as her talk with Rovin was over. "And thank Mollian for his blood next time you see him. You would be in a Hel of a lot worse shape without that kind of magic in your veins."

"Thanks, Calysta," Merriam said gratefully as she dressed. Her body was already starting to feel a little better from the salves, if not still exhausted.

Stepping from the tent, Merriam found Rovin sitting by the fire.

His eyes met hers, and he stood, gesturing with his head for her to follow him to the edge of camp. He folded his arms over his chest as Merriam came to stand in front of him. "Bellamy is going to go back to Umbra with you tomorrow."

"What?!" Merriam shouted, then immediately cursed herself for the lack of control, shooting a quick glance over at the fire before looking back at Rovin with a hot glare. "You don't get to make those decisions for me, *Ranger*," she hissed quietly.

Rovin looked skyward in a silent prayer. "This isn't me trying to order you around, Mer. It's logistical. You need to let your injuries heal properly, and a report of those demons you saw needs to be taken to the Crown."

Merriam pressed her mouth into a line, hating his logic, but knowing he was right.

"I found your axe and cloak, by the way. They're at the side of your tent."

Before she could thank him, he turned and headed back to the fire. Watching him for a moment longer, she returned to the tent, intending to follow Calysta's advice and elevate her ankle.

Merriam and Bellamy stepped through a rift just on the outskirts of Umbra. Bellamy's eyes were still wide from what he'd seen on Earth. Merriam had insisted that if she had to go back, they'd Travel. So at Merriam's instruction, Bellamy had glamored a human to drive them the distance, shortening the trip to mere hours.

"Remember," Merriam raised an eyebrow at him, "keep that stuff to yourself, okay? Even some of the most high-ranking Guard haven't ever Traveled. Much of the knowledge of that realm is kept under wraps for a reason."

"The secrets of the Crown are safe with me," Bellamy promised, eyes sincere.

Merriam smiled at him, giving a curt nod and heading up toward the castle.

Once inside the gates, she cast her mind out like a net, waiting for the familiar blip of Mollian. He pulled her in, and she followed that tug with Bellamy on her heels.

A spark of surprise and apprehension ran through her when she realized they were heading for the queen's chambers. Bellamy noticed at the same time, his steps faltering.

Merriam turned to look at him, sympathy in her eyes. "You don't want to be here for this, do you?"

Bellamy shifted his weight before standing straight and shaking his head. "It doesn't matter what I want. I'm a Ranger now, and I have a duty to fulfill."

Merriam raised her eyebrows. "I'm impressed with your dedication to the cause, Bell. And I'll let you in on a little insider secret," Merriam dropped her voice, leaning forward. Bellamy followed suit, also leaning in. "Queen Regenya is testy, but Prince Oren is the one you'll want on your side since he'll be crowned in a few months. He appreciates wit, so if you've got any fun comments to make ... don't hesitate."

Bellamy blinked at her, mouth dropping in surprise, but she'd already turned back around and resumed walking.

"I request an audience," Merriam said to the guards posted outside of the queen's doors.

"Her Majesty is dining with her sons at the moment. You'll have to come back later," one replied.

Merriam just blinked at him sweetly, waiting.

Only a few heartbeats later, the door was pulled open from the inside, revealing a mop of wild white curls and pale green eyes, one cracked with brown, that shimmered with a mix of worry and relief. "Merriam, come in, please," Mollian greeted.

Merriam smiled at him, stepping forward past the guards. "One of the Rangers, Bellamy, is with me, too."

"Of course, Bellamy." Mollian waved him in with one hand while holding his palm up with the other. "My father is busy conducting business with some dignitaries from East Audha, but you've got the rest of us."

Merriam pressed her palm to his as she passed, feeling the familiar swell inside her at being reunited. The older she got, the more she left, and the further her jobs took her, she felt more and more settled returning to Mollian. They'd always been connected, but it was moments like these that really enforced the notion that they weren't just two similar souls. When she felt the assurance of his presence after being separated, it was clear they were two beings who shared the same one.

Shaking out of her thoughts, she stepped up to the table where the queen sat with Oren, dropping into a curtsy with her weight concentrated on her good leg. She rose at the same time Bellamy did from his bow beside her. She could feel Oren's worried stare against her cheek and summoned the concentration to Cast to him. *School yourself, Majesty.*

He coughed, his attention briefly returning to his meal. *Demanding, aren't we?*

Later, she replied, lacing it with as much promise as possible.

"Merriam, I didn't think your team would be back so soon," Regenya said in greeting.

"I returned early to deliver a report." Merriam subtly shifted her weight onto one foot. The muscle in her thigh was barely bothering her, but her ankle was starting to throb against her boot.

Careful as she was, both Mollian and Oren caught the movement, exchanging a look.

Quit talking about me. She Cast to Mollian, who shrugged a shoulder, the corner of his mouth lifting.

"We have confirmation that the men we're watching are possessed by demons. It's possible they're the same as the one that attacked us on the way back from Entumbra, but they're a different ... breed."

"Confirmation?" Regenya questioned.

"I saw the demons split open the bodies of the men they possessed, Your Majesty."

Oren stiffened, and Mollian's head jerked up, eyes roaming her body for any visible injuries.

Merriam recounted her story, hoping the queen had heard from the Rangers that she was Bonded to Mollian and that part of the account wouldn't be cause for extra discussion. Bellamy added in details about what the watch had seen after her disappearance to help fill in some of the gaps.

After the report, Oren dragged a hand down his face. "This shouldn't change our game plan for now, though the knowledge of what lives inside of these men is useful for planning. And if he can't get into the mountain from the realm parallel, it further increases the chances that he spends most of his time on Nethyl. Do you think the fighting strategies will need to change, knowing the demons may all be somewhat different?"

Merriam contemplated for a moment before shaking her head. "No, the teams are still the best bet."

Oren nodded, looking at his mother for a few moments. Merriam didn't even have time to contemplate the exchange they might be having before Regenya turned to look at her. "Thank you for the report, Merriam. I'm sure you and ... Bellamy, was it? I'm sure you're both weary from travel. You're dismissed. And Bellamy, you're exempt from any taskings until tomorrow. I'll send word to Captain Ferrick."

Surprise flashed across Bellamy's face only for a moment before he reined in his emotions. "Thank you, Your Majesty," he bowed deeply at the waist.

Merriam gave another curtsy before leaving the room. She and Bellamy parted ways, and she headed for her chambers, intent on a long, hot bath to ease her muscles.

She was almost completely submerged in the tub, head resting against the rim with the water just brushing her chin and swollen ankle propped on a folded towel on the edge when Mollian came in, sitting down on the floor.

"You really do have a death wish, don't you?" he joked.

Merriam cracked an eye open, smiling at him. "That's not fair. I thought I made it clear I only showed myself to them out of concern for the rest of the camp. Everyone knows the hero always sacrifices themselves for the good of the people."

"Since when do you play the hero?"

"The mood strikes randomly," Merriam said, pulling her foot into the hot water and stifling a sigh. Her ribs still hurt tremendously.

"Are you okay, though, for real?" Mollian folded his arms on the edge of the tub and propped his chin on them as he searched her eyes.

Merriam lifted a hand to push a curl off his forehead, and his nose wrinkled as water dripped down his face. "I'm incredibly lucky things didn't end up worse, and I know I have you to thank for that."

Mollian smiled, but his eyes still shone with worry. "I've been training with the Guard every day. I'm going to help you defeat him. For what he did to Gress. For what he's doing to our home."

Merriam nodded, dropping her hand back into the water. "We'll take him down, Molli."

He left her to soak for a while longer before she got out, brushing through her wet hair with her head tilted sideways to avoid lifting her arms too much. A wave of pain radiated from her ribs every time she reached for the top of her head, so she left it trailing down her back as she dressed. She was about to sit down on the couch with a book when a knock sounded at the door.

Mollian walked over to open it, revealing one of the Guard. "Prince Oren requests an audience with Merriam."

Merriam set her book back down on the coffee table. "Of course, tell his Majesty I'll be there shortly. Where am I meeting him?"

"He's in his chambers," the guard replied before heading off.

Mollian shut the door, a grin pulling at his lips. "Good luck, Ria. He's not pleased."

"Best not keep him waiting, then." Merriam changed out of her sleepwear into something more suitable for what was to be seen as a professional meeting before heading up to Oren's rooms, where she was waved in almost immediately.

When the doors shut behind her, she walked further into the room, leaning against the back of an armchair and watching him work at his desk. He finished with whatever papers needed the attention of the future king before pushing his chair back and turning to look at her.

Merriam dug her fingers into the cushioned seatback on either side of her, biting her lip as she met his eyes. "Hi," she said, barely more than a whisper.

Oren's lips lifted in a small smile, and he tilted his head to the side as he looked at her. "Hi."

"You wanted to see me." It was a statement, not a question.

"Have you seen a medic?" Oren had not only noticed the way she favored one ankle throughout her recounting the interaction with the demons, but also the scrapes and bruises on her arms and the way she caught herself before breathing too deeply.

Merriam looked away. "No, but Calysta said my injuries should be fine. The worst is my ribs, but they're probably just bruised. And I was dirty and tired. I'll try to see one tomorrow."

Oren stood, taking a few long strides over to her before sliding his hand into her hair and dropping his lips to hers. The kiss took her breath away, his other hand gripping her waist and pulling her to him as he swept his tongue into her mouth. She rose onto her toes to meet him, releasing the chair to place her palms on his chest.

Oren broke the kiss, resting his forehead against hers. "You could have died."

"Yes."

Oren's grip tightened on her hip, his eyes darkening with something possessive and almost feral for a moment before he let her go, taking a half step back.

"Why can't you just be mine? Why must we sneak around this castle and make up bullshit meetings to get a moment alone together?"

Merriam shook her head, meeting his eyes with a pleading amber gaze. "You don't understand, Oren. I had to fight. So *hard* for everything. If you claim me, I'll have to prove myself all over again."

"Come on, Mer. You don't think you've done enough to make a name for yourself already? Everybody who matters knows you're invaluable." Oren cupped her cheek. "You have always been amazing. Anyone who took all this time to see that isn't worth yours."

Merriam gently brushed his hand away. "That's not the point. People talk. I've barely gotten out of Molli's shadow. Do you realize what you're asking of me? Some of the people who *matter* will also spread rumors. They'll do everything they can to undermine me. This would be like giving them a sword and then turning my back to them."

Oren sighed in frustration. "Rovin isn't that bad. He wouldn't do something like that."

"If you believe that, you're delusional," Merriam laughed bitterly, grimacing when the action jarred her ribs. "And it's not just him, either. It was one thing being the prince's pet. I can only imagine the field day the higher ranking Rangers would have spreading rumors about the crown prince's whore."

Oren caught both of her hands in his. "*It would not be like that,*" he growled. "And I would personally see to anyone who would dare even imply such a thing."

Merriam's gaze softened, and she locked her fingers with his. "You don't see how fighting my battles would only prove their point?"

"I love you, Mer. I've loved you for so long, and I just want you by my side."

Merriam's throat tightened. "Oren ..."

"Tell me you will never want me the way that I want you. Tell me that if I were just a male from the streets of Umbra, you would never give me a second look."

Merriam swallowed hard. "If you were just a male, I'd have agreed to marry you after you asked me to duel and then knocked me on my ass."

Oren's lips pulled into a closed smile. "That's when?"

Merriam glanced down at their clasped hands. "You saw me as an equal. You acknowledged my skill, but then followed through with your own."

"I could give up the crown. Let Mollian have it."

"Oren, I would never ask that of you." Merriam gave him a sharp look. "You would hate yourself for it, too."

"I want you more than I want anything, Mer. You see me. Just as I see you."

"Oren." Merriam shook her head again, fear at his admission crawling through her veins. Panic at his open vulnerability and the request for her to show the same crawled up her throat, making it difficult to breathe.

"Say it, Mer. Say you don't love me, you don't want to be with me."

Merriam only stared at him, sorrow filling her gaze.

"Say you don't want me in your life. Because having to watch you put yourself in danger and pretend like I don't care, pretend like you don't matter to me ... I don't think that's something I can do forever."

Tears pooled in Merriam's eyes as she shook her head. "I cannot give you what you want, Oren."

"*You* are what I want, you insufferable woman!" Oren dropped her hands to grasp her shoulders.

A soft sob fell from her, and she again shook her head. "You don't want *this*, though. You don't want me in the shadows." The first tear fell down her cheek. "I cannot ask you to be unhappy for me. I will not."

Oren rested his forehead against hers and closed his eyes. "I want all of you, Merriam. I don't want you to give up your freedom or your position or your independence. I just want you by my side when you can be. I want you to hold my heart whenever we're apart, and I want to hold yours."

Merriam's breath caught in her throat, tears falling down her cheeks as she stared at her feet. "You have my heart, Oren. Always."

He dropped his face into her neck, brushing his lips against her skin. "I want people to know it," he breathed.

Merriam tilted her head to the side, relishing the feel of his mouth on her even while her heart broke.

"Merri ..." Oren murmured.

Merriam did break, then. She threw her arms around his waist and cried into his chest, embracing the pain that pulsed from her side with every sob. "I can't," she cried bitterly, unable to voice any of the other frustrations and fears that warred through her. Being a mercenary was her life, yes, but outside of that, she didn't know how to explain to Oren how much even just telling him she loved him had terrified her. The fact remained that Oren was going to be king, and as such, would have his choice of high-born fae from all over the world to sit beside him and rule. When his infatuation with her ran dry, where would that leave her? It was one thing to be brokenhearted, having to watch the male she loved carry on with another, but it would be an entirely different thing to have to deal with the looks of pity and disdain from everyone who knew she'd thought herself good enough for a king. Having to build herself back up from that would destroy whatever bit of soft humanity Merriam had left.

Oren circled one arm around her waist, careful not to press on her ribs, and held her close as he stroked her hair with the other hand, resting his cheek on top of her head. "Merriam," he whispered softly. Her sobs subsided, and she pulled one arm free to wipe the tears from her face before tucking both against her chest and leaning into him, letting him take the full weight of her body and her sorrow.

Merriam was just plucking up the courage to tell him she needed to step away, to leave him before he could leave her, when he sucked in a breath and said, "Marry me."

Every coherent thought fled her mind. Placing her hands against his chest, she tilted her head up to look at him. "What?"

"Marry me, Merriam. If you were queen, you would have every right to lead your own troupe. To take whatever jobs you want. No one would question your reputation or mine."

"Oren …" Merriam searched his eyes before bringing her head back down to his chest, her mind reeling.

"I know you've worked hard to build yourself a name here. After my coronation, marry me. Let me give you the resources to do great things."

Merriam again tilted her head to blink up at him. She was half-convinced she was in shock.

"We can continue to do things your way until then. I won't jeopardize the life you've built. Just … when I have power … share it with me, please." He brought one hand to her chin, tilting it up and grazing his thumb over her lower lip.

Merriam bit into her lip, her teeth running over where he had just touched her. She looked into his eyes, and the magnitude of her love for him came spilling from that hidden place inside her. Fresh tears shimmered in her eyes again as she whispered, "I love you, O. I love you, and nothing has ever terrified me more."

Oren brushed his lips against hers. "I know, Merri," he said against her mouth. And because he did see every broken part of her, he added, "I will never leave you." Then he deepened the kiss before she could reply.

Chapter 35

Odds

Oren pulled back, brushing his thumbs across her cheeks to wipe away the tracks of her tears before pushing one hand into her hair, twisting the still-damp strands around his fingers.

Merriam tilted her head with the slight pull of her hair. "You're going to knot it," she chastised, looking up at him.

Oren scoffed in mock offense. "Lady, your lack of trust in my intentions and abilities wounds." He released her hair, dragging his fingers down her arm to grab her hand. "Sit with me for a bit?" he asked, brushing a kiss across her fingers.

Merriam nodded, relocating to the couch while Oren grabbed some papers from his desk. Her mind was still reeling with his proposal and his insistence that he couldn't hide their relationship forever. Her heart felt equal parts fractured and full to the brim between not being ready to face public scrutiny and his continued understanding, even though it hurt him.

The prince sat down next to her, and she lay on her back with her head in his lap so she could rest her ankle on the arm of the couch, her hair fanned out over his legs. Oren absentmindedly ran his fingers through it as he looked over the papers, and her eyes closed at the soothing sensation against her scalp.

Slowly, she peeked her eyes open, looking up at him and watching the look of concentration etched across his features. Without really thinking about it, she reached a hand up to smooth the furrow from between his eyebrows, the clear skin that would soon be marked, connecting the aspen branches that stretched across his brow. He smiled, not moving his eyes from the paper. Merriam pulled his hand from her hair, holding it above her face and tracing lines across his palm and along his fingers. She rotated it, studying the veins that stood out beneath the light brown skin, mapping their path with a finger before twisting the band of the orydite ring he wore, splaying his fingers so she could rotate the ring fully.

"Enjoying yourself?"

"Immensely." Merriam smiled, turning his hand to draw shapes on his palm. After a while, she cradled his hand against her chest, letting her eyes fall closed for a few moments.

"Mer." Oren's voice, accompanied by the soft brush of fingers against her temple, pulled her from a light sleep.

She blinked, running a hand over her eyes.

"It's getting late," Oren said, smoothing her hair.

Merriam opened her mouth to reply, but stopped. What was she supposed to say? That she wanted to stay? Her own wishes were the only reason she wasn't being carried to his bed right now. So she closed her mouth, sitting up carefully, so she didn't put any undue strain on her ribs. She rested her head against Oren's shoulder, breathing in his pine and plum and night sky scent for a few heartbeats before standing.

Oren followed her to the door, grabbing her hand and pulling her close before brushing a kiss against her lips. "I meant what I said. Think about it," he whispered before opening the door, saving her from a reply. "Thank you, Mer, have a good night," he said before poking his head out to address the guards. "I'm heading to bed. Only wake me if it's urgent."

"Yes, sir," the guard answered.

Merriam turned and gave a small wave, "Good night, Majesty."

Sleep well, Lady. Oren Cast as he closed the door.

Merriam changed back into comfy clothes immediately after returning to her rooms and slipped into bed with Mollian. "How is it possible to love someone so much but allow yourself to hurt them so deeply?" she asked, curling into his side.

Mollian, one arm stretched underneath his head, shrugged. "I suppose you stop, one way or another."

"He asked me to marry him."

Mollian lifted his head, peering down at her. "The future king of Sekha asked you to marry him, and you're sleeping in *my* bed?"

Merriam scowled, not meeting his eyes, and her throat tightened again with unshed tears. "I don't know," she choked out.

Mollian moved his arm, wrapping it around her shoulders in quiet comfort.

Merriam spent the next several days recouping. Her ankle healed fairly quickly, but she still had to be careful about putting pressure on her ribs. They didn't hurt anymore unless she forgot and bumped them or worked herself too hard during training, so she slipped into more of an instructor role, helping the Guard run drills and prepare for battle. Even though everything they'd learned led them to believe that Basta only had a handful of demons at his command, Oren had thought it prudent to add this training into the entire Guards' training regimen.

Oren was still spending his evenings with Merriam and Mollian in their chambers, though he hadn't spent the night at all. He also hadn't brought up that conversation again or pressed Merriam for an answer, knowing that the commitment he was offering her would be equally as panic-inducing as it was comforting and giving her the time and space to work through those emotions on her own.

Even so, the proposal was ever-present on Merriam's mind when she had nothing else to apply herself to, and the stress of it manifested as a constant knot in her stomach. Oren was still sweet with her, cuddling with her on the couch, combing his fingers through her hair while they read, kissing her whenever appropriate. He hadn't pulled back at all, and while part of her felt like that should have made her choice easier, it only doubled her anxiety over it.

Rovin's group had just returned from surveillance the night before, and Merriam was about to head out to the merc house when Mollian found her and informed her that a letter from Gressia had arrived.

"Oren has already sent for Jasper and everyone else. We're needed in the war room to start putting the final pieces together for this plan of attack."

Adrenaline flooded Merriam's veins at the prospect of battle, the thrill of a fight giving her a burst of energy as she followed Mollian through the castle.

No one had assembled yet, so they headed through the war room and into the office, finding Oren seated at the desk.

Merriam's cheeks heated with the memory of the last time she'd been in this room. How had things felt so complicated back then, but seemed so simple compared to now?

"Gressia's letter will reach Basta in about four days. Figuring time for him to prepare for the journey and leave, that gives us five or six days before we engage," Oren said.

"Do we have an intercept point plotted?" Merriam asked.

Oren nodded, waving them over to the desk and running his finger along where he had a map laid out. "Here, halfway between Basta's mountain and Entumbra. The closest known village is several klicks away, so there should be essentially no risk of casualties. It'll take us two days to reach the spot by foot, and we'll want to be there before him."

"How long will it take him to get there?" She toyed with the end of her braid as she looked over the map.

"Assuming he's going by horseback, we'll give him a day." Oren ran a hand over his hair, taking it down to retie in a neater knot. "We'll need to be ready to leave in two days' time to ensure we get to the battlefield first."

They discussed a few more details while waiting for the meeting to start.

When they exited the office, Merriam was surprised to see Regenya seated at the table, though with something this big happening, it made sense for the reigning monarch to attend, no matter how much control she'd been giving to her successor. Darius was standing in for her at the other appointments she'd already had scheduled for the day.

Jasper was the last to arrive, only Campbell in tow. Leonidas was out on a job, and Aleah and Calysta were resting from travel. Kodi had perked up when the mercenaries entered, but as soon as he'd seen only the two males, he sunk back into his chair, looking completely disinterested. Merriam watched him for a moment, curious, and sat next to her friends as Oren laid out their plan, explaining everything in detail before opening it up for discussion.

Captain Ferrick asked a few logistical questions, and Jasper spoke up to clarify and expand on the information, completely unphased by the captain's clear contempt for him. Strangely, it wasn't Jasper's occupation or status as one of the fair folk that caused the contention, but rather his history with Oren. It was clear the heir apparent trusted Jasper's judgment and always considered his advice.

Ferrick, who'd been scorned by the prince on more than one occasion—even if it was never blatant—seethed.

Not that his feelings or opinions about this attack on Basta held any real weight, though. The captain had handed off command of the situation to Dio as soon as the first bird had come back from the initial scouting party.

Jasper would never ask any of the mercs to put themselves in danger he wouldn't also volunteer for. Neither would Oren.

"The point of the Rangers, of the Guard, is so that you don't endanger yourself," Regenya was saying evenly. "Let them serve you."

Oren's brows pulled together, and he shook his head. "I can't sit out of this one. Not when he's dragged Gressia so far into it. This is personal."

The queen shook her head, Casting her reply to her son to keep from arguing in front of everyone present.

"We can continue this conversation later," Oren said with finality, turning to the rest of the table. "Anything else?"

When the meeting was over, Merriam flashed him a supportive smile.

Legends help me, he sent with a roll of his deep green eyes before following Regenya into the back office.

After saying a quick goodbye to Mollian, Merriam went back to the merc house with Jasper and Campbell, picking up some alcohol along the way. It had become tradition that they drank before leaving for a big job. Not the day before, because nobody wanted to travel with a hangover, but the night before that.

Aleah jumped up from the couch when they walked inside, running over to Merriam and throwing her arms around her. "I have so much to tell you!" she squealed as she pulled back.

"She fucked the Ranger," Campbell threw over his shoulder as he walked into the kitchen.

"Kodi?" Merriam clarified.

"Kodi," Aleah said suggestively, a grin spreading across her face.

Merriam shook her head with a laugh. "I love you, but I hope you know what you're doing."

"He sure does, but that's a conversation for later." Aleah followed Campbell into the kitchen. "What's with all the booze?"

Filtering out Campbell's answer, Merriam walked into the mushroom to sit next to Calysta, resting her head on the nymph's shoulder. "Shit's actually about to get real," she said.

Calysta leaned her head against Merriam's, her floral, woodsy scent filling the air. "My odds are on Jasper, I think."

Merriam sat up with a scoff. "Justification?"

Calysta shrugged. "He's got wings. Seems like a good extra for fighting demons. Plus, if he wanted to trick one off of a cliff, he wouldn't have to almost kill himself to do it."

"Low blow." Merriam laughed, tilting her head back.

"How are you holding up, anyway?"

"I'm practically back to full health. My ribs still bug me a bit, but only if I knock them. I have full movement and everything without pain."

Calysta nodded. "Probably just a bad bruise, then. Did you ever go see a medic?"

Merriam shook her head. "I could feel it getting better every day, so I didn't bother."

Calysta rolled her eyes. "Getting any of you dimwits to see a professional is more difficult than pulling a squirrel from a tree."

"Is that ... is that difficult?" Merriam asked, entirely unconvinced.

"Well, I would know, wouldn't I?" Calysta said haughtily, nose in the air.

"Didn't realize you had a lot of squirrel-wrangling days before Jaz picked you up."

"Who wrangled squirrels?" Campbell asked, walking in with a tray of snacks. Aleah followed with a bottle of wine and a stack of cups.

"Have we started odds yet?" she asked, sitting on the floor and pouring the wine.

"Calysta says Jasper," Merriam took the cup of wine Aleah offered, passing it to the nymph.

Aleah wrinkled her nose. "Well, that seems like a cop-out."

"Why? Because you know I'm the best?" Jasper walked in, plucking up the cup Aleah had just poured and taking a drink before sitting on Merriam's other side, tucking in his wings.

"Wings give you an edge, bird-boy." Aleah rolled her eyes.

Jasper cocked an eyebrow at her, taking another drink. "Insults already, hmm?"

Aleah shrugged, pouring wine for Merriam and handing it over. "Like I said, you have an edge, gotta keep you even with us somehow. Sadly, your ego's gotta take the hit."

"Keep talking, Red," Jasper threatened playfully, silver eyes lit with amusement.

Campbell grabbed the bottle from Aleah, taking a deep pull. "Mer's fought more demons than any of us. My odds are on her."

Merriam placed a hand on her chest. "Thank you, Cam. I'm practically an expert at this point."

"Does no one remember how that last demon fight ended?" Calysta interjected.

"Shush. I lived, didn't I? And not all of us have wings," Merriam defended.

The back door opened, and Leonidas strode through, Panic perched on his shoulder. His blue eyes immediately landed on the bottles lined up on the counter.

"What's the occasion?" He asked.

"Just preparing to do our best to make it out of another job alive." Merriam saluted him with the cup in her hand.

His brow raised as Panic lifted from his shoulder to move to the perch at the threshold to the kitchen. "Somehow, I expected the planning stage to take longer. Hold on and let me make a drink. Where are we at with Odds?"

Calysta counted off on her fingers as Leonidas opened a bottle of whiskey. "I said Jasper; Campbell said Mer."

Leonidas sat on the edge of the couch next to Campbell, idly running a hand down the male's back as he took a sip of his drink. "I'm calling Mer as well for this one."

Aleah grabbed the bottle of wine from Campbell, emptying it into her cup and saying, "I'll go Leo." Odds was a game they played before every big job. They all bet who they thought would have the highest body count by the end. It was completely morbid, but just one of the ways they'd come up with to help themselves cope with the less pleasant aspects of their lifestyle.

Merriam had gone with Aleah, and Jasper chose Merriam. By the end of everyone justifying their choices, they were all at least two drinks deep.

Merriam slid off the couch to sit next to Aleah, taking a sip of the clear liquor and juice concoction she'd filled her cup with. "So, Kodi?"

Aleah tilted her head back with a dramatic sigh. "Kodi."

"You would get her started," Calysta grumbled, taking a bunch of grapes from the platter of food. "I've heard of little but *Kodi* for the past week."

"Kodi? Is he that Ranger who looks like he likes to play with fire?" Leonidas asked.

Aleah nodded, hazel eyes sparkling over the rim of her cup. "I can't speak to fire, but I can confirm he's fond of knives." Her tongue peeked from between her teeth as she grinned.

Merriam burst out laughing at the look of horrified concern on Campbell's face, and Aleah covered her mouth as she giggled.

"Yeah, I'm not drunk enough for this." Jasper stood, moving to the kitchen to make a fresh drink.

They were all entirely inebriated as the night wore on, and Merriam felt a warmth in her blood that was probably mostly alcohol, but she couldn't help but to think it was also from the happiness she felt being with the people around her. She trusted each of them with her life and would lay down her own for them without a moment's hesitation. They'd been through so much together, seen the best and worst parts of each other, and none of them had even once made her feel less than or worthless.

Her heart swelled as she watched them. This was her family. A lump formed in her throat as her mind drifted toward the only other important people in her life. The mercs all knew and accepted Mollian; he'd even joined in on these drunken nights on several occasions. They understood without question that he was an irreplaceable part of her and welcomed him with open arms. Even Aleah, with her painful past, hadn't taken long to warm up to him. They loved her enough to let her choose who she wanted in her life without judgment. The same way they did with any one of the troupe. She had never once felt any need to hide a part of her life from them, and if they had her back ... couldn't she conquer anything?

Merriam's teeth sawed across her bottom lip as she made a decision before giving herself a chance to overthink it. She stood, swaying as the blood rushed from her head, and finished the rest of what was in her cup. Wiping the back of her hand across her mouth, she caught Calysta's eyes, the amber depths pleading and vulnerable. "I need to ... I'll be right back."

Calysta grinned, instantly understanding in the way that she always seemed to. "Go get your prince, Mer."

Jasper cocked an eyebrow. "You going to make it there okay on your own?"

Merriam nodded emphatically.

"Don't get yourself into trouble," he ordered, silver eyes sparkling in a way that made her wonder if he knew which prince to expect tonight.

"Wouldn't dream of it," Merriam promised, skipping over to where Panic was sleeping on his perch. She stopped to brush a finger over one of his toes, and his head flipped up, a shriek building in his throat. It cut off when he saw her, and he tilted his head to the side.

"Sorry, buddy," she cooed. "I didn't mean to wake you." She poked a finger through his feathers to scratch his chest. "In case meanie Leo hasn't told you yet today, you're the most handsome boy in all the land."

Panic let out a soft *kak*, looking at Leonidas with a glare before tucking his head back in to sleep.

"Leave the bird alone, Mer," Leonidas called from the couch.

"Someone's got to show him some love and affection."

"Between you and Cam, he's going to go soft and I'll have to train a new one to get any work done," Leonidas grumbled, but Merriam knew he loved how much she and Campbell adored Panic. He'd raised the falcon from a hatchling, and though he had several birds trained to hunt or deliver messages, his bond with Panic was something entirely different. Campbell's dynamic with the falcon was probably half the reason Leonidas initially fell for him so hard.

Merriam slipped out the back door, jogging down the street towards the castle. The cool night air brushed her cheeks and filled her lungs, an amazing contrast to the warm flush of alcohol on her skin. She slowed as she neared the gates, breathing heavy from the exertion and the uphill jog.

The guards let her pass after only a cursory glance, and she waved at them happily, hurrying up to the main door.

Once she was inside, nerves started to tumble around in her belly, and she pulled her braid over her shoulder to twist the end through her fingers. This was it. The point of no return. If she didn't turn back now, there would be no going back in the future.

Her mind went back to being in the mushroom with the mercenaries, how at home and happy she'd been, and she pushed any further doubt from her mind, marching up the stairs.

"I need to see the prince."

The guard posted outside of Oren's door narrowed her eyes at Merriam. "He's sleeping."

"It's urgent," Merriam hiccuped, slapping a palm over her mouth.

"Uh-huh," the guard gave her an unimpressed look. "Come back when you're sober, merc."

Merriam huffed, "No, listen." A frustrated sound bubbled from her throat, and she raised her voice, "Oren! Oren, I need to talk to you!"

"Legends, Merriam, are you insane? Quit fucking hollering or you'll wake the whole castle," the guard glared at her, taking a step forward and looking like she wanted to clamp a hand over Merriam's mouth.

Merriam stumbled backward, bumping into the wall. She might have been close enough to reach out to Oren, but she'd never attempted it, and in her drunken state, she couldn't pull together enough concentration to try. *Molli will help*, she thought, turning to go collect him.

Oren's door cracked open then. "Mer?" One eye was squeezed shut against the light from the hallway, his voice gravelly with sleep.

Merriam turned around again, stepping forward. "You're awake!"

The guard glanced from Oren to Merriam and back, but Oren just gave her a placating look before waving Merriam inside. She slipped past the guard, bouncing on her toes.

"What's wrong?" Oren asked as he closed the door, waking up enough to truly look at her. "Wait, are you drunk?"

"It's tradition!" Merriam said happily, taking a step forward and throwing her arms around him.

Oren stumbled half a step back at the unexpected full brunt of her weight, but he held her until she pushed back, looking into his eyes and taking one steadying breath before she dropped her gaze to her feet, the nervous anxiety in her belly spreading until every inch of her skin itched with it.

"I've been thinking about what you said," she finally started.

Oren's eyes widened, but he waited for her to continue.

"I'm not ready to be fully public, and I don't have a timeline for when I will be," she started, peeking up at him. "But I know that I will be, and I hope you can wait for that, because I need you. And I want you to come with me to the merc house. Drink with us, relax, and have fun before all this shit goes down." She waved a hand through the air as she talked. "But come with me as ... as mine."

Oren blinked, surprise shining in his deep green eyes. "As yours?"

Merriam nodded. "I want them to know. They're my family, and I don't want to hide us from them."

A slow smile lifted the corners of his lips as he looked at her, and he trailed his fingers down her arms to grab her hands, squeezing them. "Nothing would make me happier than to go to the merc house with you, Lady."

Merriam bit her lip as she gazed up at him, fighting the grin spreading across her face even as nervous anticipation tumbled low in her stomach. "Baby steps are okay?"

Oren pressed a kiss to her forehead before pulling her close and holding her to him. "Baby steps are okay."

She closed her eyes, leaning into him heavily, half from the alcohol buzzing in her veins and half to try to communicate to him how much she loved him. How willing she was to try to push through her fears for him. Pulling away, she blinked, tipping her head back to smile at him before grabbing his hand and pulling him toward the door. "Okay, enough lovey-dovey stuff, let's go!"

"I need to change first," Oren laughed, dropping her hand and heading into his bedroom. Merriam followed, watching unabashedly as he stripped and redressed.

Like what you see?

"Very much," Merriam answered, bouncing with energy and trying to rehearse in her head how to introduce Oren to her friends. The thought made her giggle, and she fell to lean against the wall as she covered her mouth.

"What's so funny?" Oren asked, finishing with his boots.

"Everything." Merriam tried to compose herself. "I was trying to think of how to introduce you, but not only have they already met you, they're also working for you. And that's even funnier: I'm about to bring the future king of Sekha into a den of hired swords."

Oren laughed at that, giving her a quick kiss before grabbing her hand and walking out of his bedroom. "Just know if you're planning to hold me for ransom, you won't be getting paid for any of this demon business."

"Duly noted, Majesty," Merriam smiled, dropping his hand as they walked out the door. "Official mercenary business," she stage-whispered to the guard as she passed.

Oren gave her a stern look before turning to the guard. "I'll be back later, and I won't require an escort."

Purely on drunken instinct, her mind reached out for Mollian as she walked down the hall, searching for that familiar ping in her consciousness. Even though he would be long asleep by now, just feeling that presence would soothe her nerves. Plus, on the off chance he was awake, she could invite him along. Spend the night with all of her favorite people.

Her brow furrowed, and she tapped her hand against her temple a couple of times before reaching out again. She was drunk, but she wasn't *that* drunk. Her tattoo itched uncomfortably, and a slow pounding rolled through her head.

She stopped walking, lifting her hand again and rubbing the heel of her palm against her forehead.

"What's wrong?" Oren asked.

"I can't ..." She shook her head, throwing her awareness out like a net once more. Faintly, she felt Oren, which she registered with surprise only briefly, before pushing the thought aside and putting a hand to the wall to steady herself. "I can't feel Molli."

Oren's eyes narrowed, shining with light concern and confusion, and his gaze slipped from her face as he reached out for his brother.

Merriam had already started walking again, hurrying down the corridor toward the stairs and her rooms. Oren caught up quickly. "Maybe he went out?"

She shook her head emphatically. "No, no, something is wrong." Her breathing took on a panicked rhythm as she fell into a run down the hall. She slipped on the stairs, barely catching herself, but didn't slow down.

"Mer, wait!" Oren called, reaching to grab her arm.

She slipped out of his grasp, throwing herself at the door to their rooms and knocking it open. "Molli!" she called.

The common room looked just as she'd left it. Her heart pounded painfully in her chest as she moved to his closed bedroom door. She reached out, hand shaking, to open it. "Molli?" her voice came out soft and strangled.

She took a step into his room and froze, a thin wail working its way up her throat from somewhere deep inside her as blood rushed in her ears and her vision narrowed to the drops of blood trailing from the mussed-up bed to the open window.

Somewhere, she felt Oren's hand at her shoulder, that touch anchoring her back to reality. She clapped her hands over her mouth, swallowing the sound and sinking to her knees as Oren's voice broke through the roaring in her ears.

"GUARDS," he was yelling. No one was typically stationed outside of their rooms, but they did patrol the floors all night. Two of the Royal Guard came running in, and Merriam tuned out their conversation as she crawled across the floor, dragging her finger through a drop of blood.

"Oren," her voice shook. "Oren, it's still wet." She turned her head to look up at him before looking at the guards. "Send a bird to Jasper."

The guards went silent as she spoke, regarding her.

"SEND A BIRD," she screamed at them, jumping to her feet.

They glanced to Oren, and he nodded. "One of you send word. Just say Merriam will be there soon and that it's urgent. Tell the aviary it's going to Leonidas. They'll handle it from there. The other of you get whichever commanding officer is on shift. Go."

They both turned, swiftly exiting the room.

Merriam was already running to the open window, leaning over the edge.

"Mer, stop, breathe." Oren grabbed her arm, pulling her back.

She struggled against him. "He's gone. He's gone! We have to find him!"

Oren forcefully tucked her against his chest, and her entire body trembled. "I know. We will, okay?"

Merriam whimpered, fisting her hands in his shirt, her breathing erratic.

"Look at me, Mer," Oren commanded calmly. When her eyes met his, he cupped her face, thumbs brushing her cheeks. "It's going to be okay.

He's going to be okay."

Merriam still clasped his shirt, holding his gaze with wide, fearful eyes, trying to speak but struggling to breathe. Squeezing her eyes shut, she counted her breaths until finally, she let out one last, long sigh, and her shaking subsided.

Oren dropped his hands to her shoulders. "We're going to find him, I promise."

Merriam released his shirt, holding up her hand. "Basta took him," she choked out.

A smear of black blood was on the tip of her finger, and Oren's eyes went wide as it registered.

"We have to go after him. Forget the other plan. We have to go now!"

Oren clasped her hand. "We need a strategy, Mer. If we go in blind, we risk getting Mollian killed as well as ourselves."

"Basta took him," Merriam whimpered, the depth of the statement sinking in and grabbing hold.

Oren grabbed her chin gently, forcing her eyes back to his. "We're going after him, but we need a plan first."

One of the Guards from earlier came back, knocking once on the main door before coming in with a commander. Oren dropped his hand, turning to meet them. He brought them both into Mollian's room, discussing quietly with them while Merriam waited in the common area. Anxiety wound its way deep in her core, squeezing her chest. She focused on keeping her breathing even, the only thought in her head a repeated chant of *I'll find you. I'll find you. I'll find you.*

As Merriam burrowed deeper into her consciousness, she clutched a hand to her chest. The strands of her soul that had woven so tightly with Mollian's over the years, that connection that was so natural she hardly ever noticed it, was now pulled taut, stretched and fraying. And it terrified her. She always felt a minor coldness and emptiness when they were separated for longer periods, but it had never felt anything like this.

A frigid calm settled over Merriam, sudden and whole. There was no longer any fear or anxiety, just a resolve that settled in her bones, clearing her mind of everything except for the tasks in front of her.

Find Mollian.

Kill the bastard that took him.

Chapter 36

Make me forget

OREN ESCORTED THE GUARDS out before moving to kneel in front of where Merriam sat, staring blankly at the space in front of her. Oren stroked a hand down her thigh, squeezing her knee. "Come back to me, Mer."

Merriam's eyes lifted, focusing on the male in front of her. "I have a plan, but I need you."

The words constricted like a vise around Oren's heart, and he tightened his grip on her knee to keep from pulling her to his chest. "I'm yours; tell me what you need."

Merriam wiped her palms on her pants, licking her lips. A small part of her wanted to throw herself into his arms and take whatever small comfort he could give, but she buried that urge deep inside of her, leaving nothing but the cold determination as she explained her plan.

Oren listened, once again in awe of the woman he loved. The fact that she'd been able to think through an entire strategy in the midst of everything happening was incredible. When she was done explaining, she just looked at him, and it took him a moment to snap out of his reverie. "Do you want me to go with you to talk to the mercs?"

Merriam shook her head, standing. "No, get the Rangers together and brief them on what's happening."

"Let me send someone with you. It could still be dangerous."

Merriam looked at him, eyes glinting like cool chips of amber. "I would like someone to try to fuck with me right now. They would not win that fight." With that, she turned and walked from the room.

The bird had reached the mercs before Merriam, and they were all slowly sobering up with the help of an herbal cocktail Calysta had whipped up by the time Merriam arrived.

"Molli's gone," she said without preamble, leaning against the wall. "Basta took him. I don't know how, and I don't know why. Frankly, I don't care about either of those things right now. I have a plan, but if you guys aren't okay with it, I can figure something else out."

"We're here for you, Mer, you know that," Aleah said, walking over to squeeze her hand reassuringly. Her palm was cold and sweaty from memories of her past, but she swallowed down the fear that rose within her. "We'll find him."

For the first time since she'd discovered Mollian's absence, Merriam's lips lifted in half a smile. "You say that, but you haven't heard the plan yet."

"Why do I feel like it's a good thing we're still drunk for this?" Campbell ran a hand through the curls at the back of his head.

"We can't wait for Basta to get Gressia's message now that he has Molli. We never even fucking figured out what he was collecting the nymph blood for, but I'm not going to wait around to find out what he wants with Molli or his blood. We have to bring the fight to him." Merriam took a breath, looking around the room before continuing, "Obviously, we have no knowledge of what sort of cave or tunnel system he has inside the mountain or how many demons he has. We need a diversion."

Jasper folded his arms across his chest, tipping his head to the side. "We're the diversion."

Merriam nodded. "Basta's not stupid. He knows the Guard. He'll be suspicious if he sees them. But you guys? You could be anybody. Just lure his people out, dispatch them before they can shed their skin for their demon forms if you can, and while you're distracting them, I'll slip inside the mountain with a small team to get Molli."

Campbell shook his head adamantly. "No offense, but that's a terrible idea. We're good, yes, but no one is *that* good. Look, even Pan is trembling with the screaming-meemies." He gestured with an open palm to the falcon, who tilted his head, clicking his beak as he tried to deduce whether or not he was being offered a snack.

"While I appreciate your confidence in us, Mer, Cam has a point. How are we supposed to face off multiple demons without one of us getting picked off in the process?" Leonidas asked, protectively shifting closer to Campbell.

"You'll have the Rangers behind you. They only have to stay back long enough for you guys to coax most of Basta's guard out, and then you'll have help. I know this is a huge risk, but I think we'll be able to stack the odds in our favor."

"And we'd be leaving tomorrow?" Aleah asked.

Merriam nodded. "As soon as possible, preferably."

"It's a solid plan, Mer. I'm in," Calysta said.

Aleah nodded, giving Merriam's hand a final squeeze before dropping it. "Let's go get your *mehhen*."

"Pan may be freaking out about it, but I'm in," Campbell shrugged.

Panic, hearing his name, bobbed his head.

Leonidas rolled his eyes. "Quit projecting onto my falcon, scaredy-toad," he said before turning to Merriam. "You know I'm in. Someone has to protect these fools."

Jasper nodded, standing up. "There you have it, Mer. We'll be there."

Merriam knew she should say something about how much she appreciated them, but she was still locked into that frozen stillness of plan and action. She didn't think she could let one emotion through without all of them spilling free, so she simply said, "Thank you."

Jasper walked over to her, speaking low. "I'm assuming you're going back to the castle tonight. I can take you; you must be exhausted."

"I appreciate the offer, but I could use the walk."

"Okay, be safe, Mer. We'll get him back."

Merriam nodded solemnly. "I won't allow for any other option."

Back inside the gate, Merriam headed straight for the Ranger barracks to the east of the castle, knowing that's where Oren would have gone to talk things over with them and hoping he was still there. She had a feeling his conversation with them would take longer, especially if they were trying to work out how and why Mollian had been taken. Her fingers played over the handles of her axes, their reassuring weight at her hips the only comfort she allowed herself to register.

Her assumption proved correct when she pushed open the door and immediately met his eyes, as if he'd sensed her presence. "Are we good to go?" she asked.

Oren nodded. "We'll be setting out in the morning. Did the mercs agree?"

"Yes, they'll be here."

"I was just finishing up. Let me walk you back to the castle."

"No, I'm going after Molli."

Oren paused, blinking in confusion. "What?"

"I'm leaving now. I have to know that he's there. I have to know that he's okay."

Oren ran a hand over his hair. "Can you at least wait until morning?"

"I can't." A small crack split down the wall of her defenses, and she closed her eyes, taking a few breaths to patch it back up before looking at Oren again. "I can't."

Searching her eyes for a moment, Oren nodded. "You're not going alone, though. You need someone with you."

"I can go. I have a good lay of the territory, and the knowledge is still fresh," Rovin spoke up from where he was leaning against a table behind Oren.

Merriam flicked her eyes to him. "You'd be useless. I don't need knowledge; I need someone who can glamor."

Rovin bristled at the slight, brown eyes hardening with resentment.

Merriam didn't even register his reaction, just turned her gaze back to Oren. "I'll take Bellamy. He's Traveled."

"If he agrees," Oren acquiesced, then pulled aside a Ranger and asked him to fetch the fae in question.

Bellamy walked into the room a few minutes later, hair hanging past his shoulders in damp brown curls, fresh from a shower. "Your Highness," he addressed Oren, flicking his curious gaze to Merriam briefly.

Oren gestured to Merriam, who spoke bluntly, "I'm leaving tonight and would like you to accompany me."

"Of course. I can be ready shortly," Bellamy answered without hesitation. "Where should I meet you?"

"I'll wait by the main gate," Merriam told him before he disappeared back down the hallway.

Oren walked Merriam out of the barracks, standing close but not touching her. "Are you okay?"

Merriam didn't look at him as she shook her head. "I'm not. I don't know why Basta took him. I don't know what his plans are. But all I can think about is that every second Mollian is gone is another second something horrible could be happening."

"Don't do anything reckless, Mer. I know I can't stop you from leaving—I wouldn't try—but don't go in there alone. Promise me."

Merriam met his eyes, no emotion in them, just that steady determination. "I'll stick to the plan. I just need to be close enough to let him know I'm there. Let him know we're coming."

Bellamy spotted them, hurrying over. The top half of his hair had been tied back from his face and a sword strapped to his belt, along with a few knives. He held a smaller axe in his hand, handing it to Merriam as he stepped up. "For throwing, if you need it."

Merriam blinked in surprise at the consideration. "Thank you, Bell." She tucked it into her belt next to the axe hanging on her left side and turned back to Oren. "Two days?"

"We'll be there," Oren promised.

Merriam dipped her head respectfully before turning to leave. "I'll see you then, Majesty."

I love you. Be safe.

Unable to gather the concentration needed to Cast to him, Merriam lifted her hand, middle and ring fingers held down. She had a fleeting thought that he had no way of knowing the sign language for "I love you," but hoped he would understand the crux of it, because it was all she could offer in that moment.

She left the castle grounds with Bellamy, both of them quiet as they walked down the mildly sloping mountainside away from Umbra. When they were at the edge of the forest, Merriam stopped, turning to the fae. "You ready?"

Bellamy nodded, and she stepped close, looping her arms around his waist before opening the rift back to Earth.

Umbra was opposite a small mountain town, almost nothing more than a rest stop and a few homes along a highway. Bellamy still looked at everything with awe, but reined in his curiosity to focus on the task in front of him.

The two of them approached a man filling up his truck at a gas pump. He looked up, a mixture of suspicion and shock on his face as he took in their attire and the weapons at their hips.

As soon as his eyes met Bellamy's, Merriam felt the pressure change in the air around them. "Mind giving us a ride?" Bellamy asked, the low timbre of his voice sickly sweet, stormy blue eyes almost glowing.

"Not at all. Hop in. I'm almost finished up here," the man answered.

Merriam stepped up into the back seat of the truck, but Bellamy leaned one arm against the hood, waiting for the man to finish pumping gas before sliding in next to Merriam as the man buckled up and started the engine. "Where to?"

"West," Merriam told him, unbuckling her weapons belt and settling in for the ride.

They rode in silence for a while, Bellamy holding the glamor with minimal concentration. "Can I ask you something? Feel free to tell me to fuck off if I'm overstepping." Merriam turned to him, so he continued, "Is there anything between you and the prince?"

She faced forward, leaning her head against the headrest. "Mollian? He's my best friend."

"No, uh ... I meant Prince Oren."

Merriam looked at Bellamy out of the corner of her eye. "Fuck off."

Bellamy snorted good-naturedly. "Fair enough." He struck up a conversation with the driver to pass the time. A couple of hours later, Bellamy asked the man to pull over and drop them off. Merriam secured her belt back around her waist as Bellamy gave the man one last instruction. "Start heading back where you needed to be. You took a wrong turn and got lost. Might be time to call it for the night."

Merriam and Bellamy were concealed by the trees by the time the truck pulled away, and Merriam brought them back to Nethyl. They soon found the path that would lead them to the Ranger camp and made their way silently through the forest.

"How sure are you that Mollian was brought here?" Bellamy asked.

"Nothing else would make sense. This is the only place it seems he's been operating from."

"But wouldn't it take them days to get here? We've been working off the assumption that Basta isn't Traveling. So why now?"

Merriam bit the inside of her cheek, shaking her head. "It would be risky to take Mollian through this realm, but if he did, then we'll be here and ready when they arrive. But it's possible he thought it worth the energy to go through another realm to get here faster. Maybe not Earth, but something further away where maybe everything doesn't line up as equally."

"Why waste the energy, though? I'm not questioning the fact that we have to rescue him, I'm just ... it feels like a trap." Bellamy gripped the hilt of his sword as they walked, eyes scanning the forest.

Merriam blew out a long breath, forcing back the tide of panic threatening to rise up within her. "It does. We just have to hope we're smart enough to play around it."

As they neared the camp, Bellamy let out a bird-like whistle to alert the Rangers that they were near and not dangerous.

"Let them know I'm here, will you? I'm going out to the watch point for a bit," Merriam told him before splitting off, heading around the mountain.

After making the magpie call and waiting for the all-clear reply to continue, Merriam climbed into a tree near the edge of the forest. The Ranger in the branches looked at her with surprise. "I hadn't realized any of the mercenaries would be joining us this round."

"We haven't. There's been a change of plans. How long have you been on watch?"

"Since just after dusk. I'm due for relief soon."

"Did you see anything unusual? Any activity from the guards?"

The Ranger's eyebrows pulled together. "There was a pair of them that wheeled in a cart. It looked like a pile of linens, probably from a nearby village."

Merriam's heart clenched in her chest, and she let her awareness stretch out, willing the depth of the mountain not to act as a blockade.

But no, she felt it—felt *him*. Mollian's presence pinged in her mind, and almost instantly she felt him shove her away. It felt frantic and fearful, and she knew he was trying to warn her off, but instead, the cold resolve settled further into her, chilling her to the bone. "That wasn't a pile of linens. That was Prince Mollian."

The Ranger whipped his head to her in shock.

"Keep a close watch on them. Every movement matters." Merriam dropped from the tree and hurried to camp.

She briefly explained the chain of events and plan of action to the commander in charge before finding a tent with a free bedroll and collapsing onto it. Her body was exhausted, but her mind couldn't turn off. She slipped into an uneasy sleep, repeating over and over: *save Mollian. Kill Basta.*

The next two days waiting for reinforcements were spent Traveling to Earth to scour the mountain for an alternate entrance or escape route that she may have missed and sitting at the edge of the forest in Jekeida, letting Mollian feel her presence. He'd stopped trying to push her away, and instead they sat in each other's heads, and she hoped that her being there brought him some level of comfort.

Oren and the others arrived that evening with just enough time to rest before making any final adjustments the next morning and starting the attack. Merriam had greeted him and the mercenaries, filling them in on everything she'd learned—which hadn't been much—over supper.

With nothing else to report, Merriam sat in front of the fire, feeling the heat of it lick at her legs through the fabric of her leggings. But she was cold. There was nothing inside of her, no warmth, no emotion, no thought other than the two that had looped through her mind without end for the past two days.

Save Mollian.

Kill Basta.

A slight tremor rolled through her body, the need for action pulling at her skin relentlessly. Setting her half-eaten supper on the ground next to her, she stood, walking away from the fire. She stepped into the trees and Traveled, walking through Earth down a path she'd worn through the forest herself with how much she'd walked it. Again, she walked up to the place where a slit had been broken into the granite slabs of the mountain on the other side of reality. Here, though, there was only solid rock.

Not a crevice in sight that would allow her into the mountain. Nor anything to suggest that this mountain was even hollow to begin with.

"Doesn't look like we'll be getting out the easy way tomorrow."

Merriam didn't even pause at the voice behind her, just shook her head, still staring at the mountain face that rose at a steep angle in front of her.

Oren stepped closer to her, hands in his pockets.

She turned her head to look at him. The moonlight shone on his white hair, making it glow the same way snow does on a dark night. He just watched her quietly. He'd seen her this way before in Entumbra after especially brutal jobs. As she looked at him, a small fissure split the defenses her mind had thrown up to keep the panic out.

Mollian needed her, and she would be there. But for now ... she let the crack spread, her terror and worry spilling out and filling her so quickly she started to tremble. "Tell me it's going to be okay."

"It's going to be okay."

"Promise?"

"I promise." He pulled one hand from his pocket and trailed his fingers down her braid.

She turned, grabbing his hand and stepping away from the mountain, pulling him into the trees.

"Make me forget. Just for a little while. I need you," she pleaded, looking up into his eyes and taking a step closer.

Oren took her face in his hands and kissed her, understanding her need for distraction without question. He swept his tongue into her mouth, and she rose onto her toes to meet him, sliding her hands underneath his shirt and raking her fingers down his back.

She broke the kiss, dropping to her knees in front of him and unbuckling his belt. His cock strained against the seam of his pants, and she looked up at him as she slid the fabric down his legs. Oren sucked in a sharp breath, one hand sliding into her hair.

Still holding eye contact, she wrapped her hand around him and licked from base to tip. She repeated the action on the other side before closing her eyes and sliding him slowly into her mouth. She swirled her tongue around the tip, sucking heavily and tightening her hand at the base of his cock. As she lowered her mouth over him, his fingers tightened in her hair, holding but not pushing.

She slid her lips over him, pumping her hand in coordination with her mouth, her free hand grasping the side of his thigh to hold her steady. She took him deep, hitting the back of her throat and eliciting a deep moan from him. Desire built in her core as she tasted him, and she sped up her movements.

He shifted his hips, thrusting to meet her, and she moaned in approval at him taking charge, squeezing her thighs together. She looked up at him, that ever-adoring, green gaze sending heat running down her spine and filling her whole body.

You look so good with my cock in your mouth.

Hearing his voice in her head while on her knees in front of him was more erotic than she'd ever thought possible, and she whimpered as she took more of him into her mouth. *Use me,* she replied, still looking into his eyes.

The sound that came from him was near-feral, and he held her head steady with one hand as he fucked her mouth, sliding between her lips and half down her throat. She gagged, tears squeezing from the corners of her eyes, but she kept eye contact, her fingers digging into his thigh.

Fuck, Merri. You take it so fucking good.

She was aching for him, and his praise was more than she could handle. Keeping one hand around his length, she dropped the other between her legs to add pressure where she needed it.

Oren's eyes darkened further when he caught her movement, and he pulled her away by the hand wrapped in her hair. "Do you want to touch yourself, Merri?"

She panted, catching her breath, and nodded, barely able to move her head in his grip. She stroked him with the hand that still held him while she pressed her fingers in a slow circle at the apex of her thighs.

Oren brushed the thumb of his free hand under her eye, clearing away the tears there before grabbing her by both shoulders and pulling her to her feet. He led her backward a few steps until her back was pressed against the smooth trunk of an aspen. "Take off your pants," he ordered, and she obediently lowered them, discarding her weapons belt on the ground beside her.

He stepped closer until his body completely pressed against hers, capturing her mouth in a kiss and forcing a knee between her legs. Her hands were threaded into his hair, her tongue sweeping hungrily into his mouth when he pushed fully inside of her in a single thrust.

She gasped at the fullness, biting his lip before he pulled away from the kiss. "Make yourself come for me," Oren commanded, resting one hand against the tree above her head, the other gripping her hip.

Merriam watched him indulge in the sight of her as she lowered one hand, letting her fingers brush across her clit. His eyes burned with hunger, and a low sound of approval rumbled from his throat.

She bit her lip, adding more pressure and tightening her movements. A whimper escaped her as he pulled out and thrust back in, still watching her touch herself with all of his attention. He moved one hand down her body and under her shirt, palming her breast through the fabric of her bra. "*Fuck*, you feel so good."

Merriam moaned, shifting her hips with his movements as she circled her clit. Her whole body started to tense up, and she tilted her head back against the tree, closing her eyes. "Oren, I'm so close," she whimpered.

"Look at me." And she opened her eyes. He thrust into her again, both hands gripping her hips. "Good girl."

Her hand tightened in his hair, pulling hard as she came undone around him, calling his name.

He quickened his movements inside of her as she orgasmed around him, swiftly following with his own release as he brought his head to her neck, biting her as he slowed.

"I love you," she panted against his shoulder, releasing her grip on his hair and sliding her hand down his chest, resting it over his still-pounding heart.

Oren kissed her neck, nuzzling it for a moment as he caught his breath. "You are everything."

Merriam slid her arms around his waist, holding him close as she let her heart feel the weight of his words, absorbing them and letting them warm her from the inside out.

Chapter 37

We are protectors

Oren had sat on the ground, pulling Merriam down in front of him, facing away. Her braid was messy and loose from his hands in it, and he methodically pulled it free, combing his fingers through her hair a few times before twisting it back together. When he was done, he leaned forward and kissed her neck.

Merriam let herself lean into him for a moment, taking whatever strength and assurance he could provide and locking it away for the events to come. Then she stood, gesturing for him to stay still. He watched her curiously as she walked around him, tilting his head back as she stood behind him. She smiled softly, bending down to kiss his forehead between the aspen tattoos before gently tipping his head forward until he was looking straight ahead.

She lowered to her knees behind him, pulling his hair free and smoothing everything back before tying it up into a neat bun. Out of all the times he'd offered to fix her hair, she'd never returned the gesture, and butterflies flitted through her stomach as she concentrated on the short task. The intimacy of the action, devoid of any sexual tension, tightened her throat, and she felt even more assured of her decision to slowly start letting others know of their relationship.

"When we get back to Umbra, I want you to come to the merc house for supper," she said softly as she stood.

Oren caught her hand, pulling her back in front of him. He pressed his lips to the backs of her fingers as he gazed up at her. "I'll have to check my schedule, but I'm sure I can move some things around," he said, lips lifting to the side in a cheeky grin.

Merriam smiled, clicking her tongue against her teeth. "So magnanimous of you, Majesty."

They walked back through the forest, hand in hand. As they got closer to camp, Merriam slowly slipped back into her cool focus, shoving aside all of her feelings and fears. She gave Oren's hand a final squeeze as the last bit of the dam inside her slid back into place, letting him go as they Traveled back to Nethyl.

Merriam approached the fire, where final taskings were being handed out. "I'll take first watch tonight," she volunteered.

The commander in charge nodded, and she sat next to Jasper while everything else was sorted through.

Jasper stretched a wing out behind her, letting his feathers brush her shoulders in silent reassurance.

Merriam looked at him with a grim smile and determination in her eyes. "Are you guys ready for tomorrow?"

Leonidas leaned forward. "Entirely. My odds are still on you and your axes, so don't let me down."

Merriam lifted a brow. "When have I ever?"

The night was quiet and went by quickly. When her relief came, she reached out to Mollian once more, trying to tell him to hold on, that she was coming. It was impossible to convey that kind of emotion without Casting, but she chose to hope he would understand, regardless. The twined cords of their souls still stretched inside her, as if someone were trying to pull them apart, and she rubbed at her chest as she walked back to camp.

She found an empty bedroll next to Jasper and lay down beside him. He stretched a wing over her, and his comforting, familiar oakmoss and sea salt scent lulled her to sleep along with the mantra once again repeating in her head.

Save Mollian.

Kill Basta.

𝓛

Merriam woke before the sun, dressing quietly and twisting her braid into a spiral at the nape of her neck, securing it with a few pins. She pulled her weapons belt on, the third axe Bellamy had supplied still tucked on the left side, and exited the tent.

She grabbed an apple from the supply tent and stood in front of the fire as she ate, staring blankly into the flames.

Oren came to stand beside her, arms folded over his chest. *Ferrick told me I should have stayed behind. Did I tell you that?*

Merriam stilled, tilting her head to the side. *No.*

He was adamant that this mission was no place for a prince. Said it was too dangerous.

The fuck? Is that why he's still hiding in Umbra?

Oren snorted. *Of course, he's not risking his hide. I was so angry I couldn't think straight. The audacity to try to tell me I couldn't rescue my brother and not even offer to go instead ...* Oren ran his thumb over his bottom lip. *I'm done with his entitled shit. He doesn't deserve to head the Guard.*

Merriam looked up at him, furrowing her brow against the headache blooming in her skull. *Can you make that change?*

If Molli has been hurt, I'd like to see someone tell me I can't.

Merriam turned back to the fire, tossing in her apple core and watching it sizzle. She knew that it wasn't Ferrick's fault that Mollian had been taken, but the fact that he hadn't offered to join the rescue when his entire job revolved around the royal family didn't sit right with her. She felt Oren's anger radiating from him, but it hit the walls of the dam inside her and fell into oblivion.

As the first gray light of dawn shone over the mountains, everyone in the camp assembled around the fire to go over the plan a final time.

"The mercenaries will create a distraction, pulling out the guards. Once they're in the open, a detachment of Rangers will come in from either side to help fight. Merriam and I will slip inside with a small team to grab Mollian," Oren briefly reiterated. "Strike to kill. You'll want to take out those guards before the demons inside have a chance to break free."

The Rangers split themselves into two groups, Oren pulling Ollivan and Eskar aside to join him and Merriam. When everyone was settled, they headed out, splitting up and taking alternate routes through the forest. Merriam and Oren trailed the mercenaries, using the more direct path to the front of the cave. Merriam reached out for Mollian again, letting the brush of his consciousness further ground her.

They waited silently in the forest until one bird call echoed from the north and another from the south. Leonidas stroked a finger down Panic's chest before pointing him to the trees. The falcon obediently flew up, perching high in a pine. Leonidas gave him a signal command to stay, and Panic tucked his wings in, waiting.

Leonidas brushed a swift kiss against Campbell's lips, meeting his eyes for a moment, the icy blue burning with devotion and a silent plea to the Legends for safety before squaring his shoulders and stepping forward.

The tall blonde broke through the trees in a stumble, placing his hand over his chest and waving at the guards. "Oh, thank the Legends," he panted in a human tongue. "I need help, please!"

The guards looked at him, narrowing their eyes in distrust.

Jasper walked out next, twirling the weight of his lance around in one hand with a wicked grin.

Leonidas lunged forward toward the guards. "You have to help me, please!"

One of the guards opened his mouth to speak just as Leonidas, now within arm's reach, drew his sword and swung it up in a powerful arc.

The guard barely dodged it, bringing up his own sword to block the next attack. Jasper had sprung into the air, landing in front of the next guard. The fight was like a well-rehearsed dance, Jasper and Leonidas provoking the guards while slowly retreating backwards, pulling them from the cave entrance while also creating enough noise to hopefully draw attention from whoever else was inside.

Sure enough, another guard poked his head out, turning to call out an alarm before running from the cave. Aleah ran from the trees then, stopping just on the outskirts and pulling two long, viciously curved daggers from her belt. "Hey, fuckface, want to play?" she called.

The guard smiled wolfishly before his skin split and a wolfish demon stepped free, instantly launching itself in Aleah's direction.

"Oh, fuck," she breathed, but Campbell was already there, running to drive his sword into its side, yanking the blade up the creature's ribcage with the momentum of his twisting body. He pulled his sword free, and the creature lunged forward again with a scream, ichor leaking from its side as it stumbled to its knees.

"Our turn, let's go," Oren said. Merriam nodded, closing one eye to block the sunlight and turning to Ollivan, who stepped closer to her. She grabbed him and opened the rift to Earth, the forest eerily quiet after the noise of fighting. Oren appeared with Eskar a heartbeat later, and the four of them ran to the mountain, climbing up the steep incline to rest just over where the entrance of the cave would be.

Once they were all settled, Oren gave Merriam a nod, and she wrapped her arms around Ollivan in a tight side hug, still keeping one eye closed in preparation for the dimness of the cave, and Traveled back. Her foot slipped as the terrain underneath her changed, sending a few small rocks tumbling down. She cringed, but none of the guards noticed, fully engaged in fighting the mercenaries.

One of the guards had been dispatched before shifting, but three demons now fought in the clearing, two more guards running from the cave entrance and immediately shedding their human skin.

The Rangers poured from the trees then, joining the fight. Merriam watched, itching to join the action, her fingers playing over the carved handles of her axes. They waited just a moment longer to see if more guards would come out, then Oren gave the signal to slide the short distance down the mountain.

They slipped into the entrance completely unnoticed, and as they walked further in, Merriam opened the eye she'd kept shut, granting her better vision in the lack of light. Merriam reached out for Mollian again, also trusting the entwined strands of their souls to guide her. She looked at Oren before drawing her axes and leading the way further into the cave.

The passage opened up into a more expansive cavern lit with crude lights, wires lining the walls and ceiling. A few tunnels branched off along the sides, and Ollivan and Eskar looked around warily, evaluating.

Merriam stepped forward with confidence, following the pull of Mollian's consciousness down the tunnel straight across from them. She thought she could see light up ahead when Mollian violently pushed her from his mind, and she stopped dead, the hair raising on her arms. "Something's not right," she whispered, shifting her grip on her axes and holding them ready.

"I felt it, too." Oren spoke from just behind her.

Merriam tentatively reached out again, only to be forcefully pushed away. Dread broke through the dam inside of her, sinking in her gut like a rock. "It's a trap," she breathed.

A demon slithered into the tunnel then, huge and serpentine, but with dozens of small limbs tipped in claws that clicked against the stone of the tunnel. The passage was only wide enough for them to stand two across, and that was without wielding weapons.

The demon snapped its jaws, lurching forward. The only way out was at the end of this tunnel, and even though Merriam knew it was herding them, they didn't have enough space to fight it.

"Run!" Oren pushed her into movement, and she sprinted forward, the rest of the group hot on her heels.

She broke through into another cavern, instantly launching into an attack at an oversized cat-like demon that waited by the entrance. She swung an axe, twisting the handle in her hand so that the dull back of the blade struck the lower jaw of the creature. The blunt force snapped its head to the side with a loud crack as its jaw shattered. It screamed, and she flipped the axe back around, blocking the paw it swiped for her. Her axe sunk into its pad, and she almost lost her grip on it as the creature pulled its paw free, splattering her front with black blood.

Merriam jumped forward, rolling underneath it and sliding her axe along its belly. Blood soaked her as the creature stumbled, falling over as its guts dropped to the floor with a sickening splat.

Oren and Ollivan were engaged with the demon from the tunnel, and Eskar was battling against two guards still in human skin. Merriam's eyes found Mollian at the back of the cave, arms chained to the wall on either side of him with iron, a gag in his mouth.

LEAVE! YOU NEED TO LEAVE! He shouted into her head, eyes wide and frantic.

Not without you, asshole, Merriam shot back, launching across the cave toward him.

Mollian struggled against his bonds, tossing his head wildly. STOP!

YOU NEED TO LEAVE. TAKE OREN AND LEAVE.

Merriam shook her head as a strange pressure filled it, almost like the feeling of being glamored, but that shouldn't be possible, not with the iron necklace around her throat.

Merriam took another few steps forward, trying to rein in control of her body, which so desperately wanted to obey Mollian's orders.

Several more guards rushed into the cavern, and she turned to meet them, raising her axes and launching into a brutal attack. She dodged and blocked their swords, barely registering the crunch of bone as she swung her weapons into arms and legs or the cuts across her own skin from attacks she hadn't been fast enough to dodge. One shoulder was leaking enough blood that her arm was soaked, but her focus was only on the fight before her.

She was locked in combat with one guard, narrowly avoiding the knife that slashed for her stomach as her axes hooked around the blade that had swung for her head moments earlier. Keeping the angle of her weapons tight, she twisted, disarming the guard, and kicked a foot out, hitting his gut and sending him falling backwards into a guard behind him.

She was panting heavily, barely able to catch sight of Oren fighting across the cave, white hair matted with black gore, before having to turn her full attention to another two guards that lunged forward to fight.

A deafening crack split the air, and Merriam reflexively dropped into a crouch, bringing her hands up to cover her ears. The gunshot echoed through the cave, and Merriam's ears rang as her eyes searched the space. Time seemed to slow as she caught sight of Ollivan stumbling a couple of steps forward as blood bloomed across his chest. He looked down, confusion spreading over his face before he fell to his knees and crumpled to the floor.

Merriam's eyes were wide, and she scarcely had time to register what had happened before the weight of a boot slammed into her side, directly into her mostly healed ribs. She screamed, though it was indiscernible over the roaring in her ears, and fell to the side, dropping her axes as she instinctively hugged her torso.

Rough hands grabbed her, and she instantly realized her mistake, kicking out and trying to pull her arms from the grasp that held her. Her ribs radiated blinding pain with the movement, and she screamed right along with it as her arms were wrenched roughly behind her back, forcing her to kneel on the blood-soaked floor.

She felt her shoulders straining and had enough clarity to still herself before she pulled one out of socket. She panted, gritting her teeth as tears of pain and frustration and terror streamed down her face.

Mollian pulled against his chains, but then stopped abruptly. Tears fell down his cheeks and soaked the fabric of the gag wrapped around his face, but when his eyes met Merriam's, they were resolute, not angry or frightened. *It's going to be okay; I'll get you out of here, I promise.*

Merriam shook her head helplessly, turning to find Oren similarly forced to the ground, kneeling in blood and ichor, his wrists looped together by an iron chain. His eyes were ablaze with emerald fire, focusing on the back of the cave.

Basta stepped from the shadows of another tunnel that Merriam hadn't had the chance to notice, running a hand through his sandy hair to push it back from his forehead before stroking his neatly trimmed beard thoughtfully. "Well, I wish I could say this was a surprise, but you did play right into my hand," he spoke in the Common tongue.

Oren spat a mouthful of blood to the ground, somehow still managing to glare down at Basta, even from his position on the floor. "Let my brother go. I will not ask again."

Basta regarded Oren with a raised brow. "So demanding, Prince." An amused smile played over his lips.

Merriam's eyes darted from Mollian to Basta to Oren, trying to take everything in. The ringing in her ears was slowly fading, and she vaguely noticed Eskar, also subdued, who was staring blankly at where Ollivan lay sprawled in a pool of blood. A trickle of her own blood dripped from her temple, and her face was pallid.

Oren just glared, and Basta smiled. "You're not going to control me, not chained in iron. I know better. And Merriam does, too, poor sweet girl." Basta walked up to her, running a finger down the side of her throat and over the chain that rested against her collarbone.

Merriam fought the urge to lean away from his touch, instead meeting his cool blue eyes with a steady glare. "I'm going to kill you," she promised.

Basta tilted his head back and laughed, delighted by her spunk. "Merriam, dear, don't you see how these fae use you? They don't care about you, only what you can do for them."

"Is that what you think of Gressia?" Oren interrupted. "That she doesn't love you?"

Basta turned to look at Oren. "Oh, I think she loves what I do for her, but I'm also not so enraptured that I'm not smart enough to realize I am easily replaceable in her eyes. She never even bothered to teach me your language or even gauge whether or not I knew it. Not even after I Bonded myself to her. But that is neither here nor there. You all have so much power at your fingertips, and you refuse to use it." Basta clicked his tongue against his teeth. "You could rule literal *worlds*, but you have no ambition."

Oren bristled. "Our duty is to protect and guard the Gate, not use it to our advantage. That is not our power to control."

Basta laughed again. "Do you not know the very power that runs through your veins is the same power that runs through the Gate? Tell me how that doesn't make it yours to control?"

"We are protectors, not conquerors," Oren spat.

Basta narrowed his eyes. "And this is why you shall fall."

"Quit talking and kill me, then."

"Oh, I have no intention of killing you, Prince. Did we not just have a conversation about the magic that runs through your blood? I *need* you."

A flicker of confusion darted through Oren's eyes as he glared at the man.

"Gressia taught me how your Keeper magic works. The eldest inherits the strongest connection to the Gate, thus their sentencing to guard it for the rest of their days. Gressia will already do whatever I ask. Your sweet sister is ... very pliant and willing to please when given the proper motivation. But you, the second-born, destined to inherit the kingdom, you get what's left. The existence of a third just made things easier for me, of course. I know you care for your brother. But more importantly, Gressia told me about your little anger-induced confession."

Oren went unnaturally still, his eyes still not leaving Basta.

The man cocked an eyebrow, lips lifting in a smirk as he flicked his eyes to Merriam.

"Touch her and you die." Oren's voice was low and dangerous.

"Mmm, I thought as much," Basta addressed Oren, but looked over Merriam's face with pity. "See, I knew she would come for the young prince. How could the valiant mercenary not run to the rescue of her *mehhen*? And after my most recent visit to your sister, I knew you wouldn't let her go off to face me alone."

"Why take Mollian at all, then? Why not just go after me, you fucking coward?! Too scared of what me and my team did to your traffickers? What I've done to your demons?" Somewhere inside of her mind, Merriam knew provoking him was a bad idea, but her rage and frustration bubbled over before she could think about what she was doing. She tugged against the hands holding her arms behind her back, even as she grimaced against the strain in her shoulders.

"Sweet girl, what motivation would I possibly have for taking you, a human? Wouldn't that be an obvious trap? At least the third prince has some blood magic, if not much." Basta laughed, reaching out to cup her cheek.

She whipped her head to the side to try to bite him. He pulled his hand back, giving her a strange look before slapping her across the face, her head rocking. She slowly turned back to face him, eyes molten pools of amber as she glared a fatal promise. "Not so sweet, then," he amended, stroking his beard.

"I fucking warned you," Oren growled, the repressed violence in his voice chilling Merriam to the bone.

"Oh, you do love her, don't you?" Basta turned his attention back to Oren with a delighted chuckle. "Or at the very least, you think you do. What is it about her that made her stick out to you? Would you say something noble, like the fire of her spirit, or would you be an honest male and admit that you just wanted a taste of her tight cunt?"

"*You will stop talking now.*" The order that came from Oren was the order of a king, and the air pressure in the cave dropped in the way it does before a storm.

Merriam felt her blood stir in her veins, and she physically jerked to the side as something in her soul pulled taught. Her breathing hitched at the feeling, and her gaze jumped to Mollian.

His eyes were closed, but through the twined threads of their souls, she could feel him burrowing into his power, gathering it close around him, unable to unleash it due to the iron at his wrists.

Molli?

I've got you. You're getting out of here.

Molli, what's happening? You feel—I feel—something's different.

The axe, Ria.

Merriam felt it, then, the handle of the small axe resting against her thigh, and she shook her head in confusion.

Free me.

She felt the pull of his power stronger in her veins, as though the magic in the blood he'd given her all those years ago was trying to return to him.

Basta was watching Oren with amusement glittering in his eyes. Oren looked at Mollian, his brow furrowing slightly before his features smoothed, and he turned back to the man in front of him. "You're still so entirely confused about what's happening, Prince. I must say, I expected more from you," Basta tutted.

Merriam's eyes widened in even further terror as black veins spread up from the collar of Basta's shirt, climbing over his neck and wrapping around his arms as his eyes shifted to a red so deep they almost looked black.

"You're so concerned about *me* hurting her when you should actually be worried about what you might do." Basta's voice was layered with another, deeper voice that echoed throughout the cavern.

Gooseflesh raised over Merriam's skin as Basta stepped closer to Oren, laying a hand on the top of his head. Apprehension rolled through her, and she pulled again at the hands that held her. "Oren," she whispered.

I love you. He Cast to her.

"Oren, no." Desperation filled her voice, but she couldn't have held it back if she wanted to. "Leave him alone, don't touch him!" she screamed at Basta.

A wicked smile spread over Basta's face. "I need you, Prince. Once you're king, I'll be able to rule every realm imaginable. Endless power at my fingertips. Until then, enjoy watching yourself hurt the people you love most."

Basta raised his free hand, and one of the guards threw his head back, a swirling shadow pouring from his mouth. It looked somehow both liquid and gaseous, rolling across the floor in answer to Basta's call. The guard fell to the floor in an empty heap, as though everything inside him—bones, muscles, mind, soul—had been consumed.

With a grin spreading across his face, Basta tipped Oren's head back, curling his fingers, and the shadow rolled forward, climbing Oren's knees.

"NO!" Merriam screamed, throwing her body forward despite the pain. "NO!"

Oren's jaw clenched tight, lips pressed together as he glared defiantly at Basta.

Basta flicked his fingers forward again, and the shadow crawled further. The smell of sulfur was almost suffocating as the inky darkness slithered up Oren's chest and neck, finally playing across his lips. "It'll be great to have you on our side, Prince," Basta's layered voice whispered as he pushed the shadows further, and they forced their way into Oren's mouth, wrenching his jaw wide as they flowed into him.

When the last of the shadow had filled him, Basta released Oren's head, motioning for the guard behind him to step away.

The guard unlooped the iron from around Oren's wrists, which had begun sizzling where the metal touched skin, dropping the chain to the cavern floor with a jarring clank.

Oren slowly rose to his feet, rolling his shoulders as if feeling out the limits of his body.

"Oren?" Merriam called, voice small. *Oren?* She Cast pleadingly.

He turned to her then, and her blood ran cold as she saw his face, dark veins crawling up his neck and extending from his eyes, green completely swallowed by a flat, dark black.

No. It was not his voice that filtered into her head.

Chapter 38

Don't make me

WITHOUT WARNING, THE HANDS that had been holding Merriam's arms behind her back released her, and she toppled forward, barely catching herself before she fell to the floor.

Ria, the axe!

In the same instant Mollian Cast to her, Merriam felt the power that had been stirring in her blood multiply tenfold, pushed into her through her Bond to Mollian.

Without thinking, she rose onto her knees, grabbing the axe from her belt and raising it over her shoulder. She felt the magic build up inside her as she sent the axe sailing through the air with more force and precision than humanly possible, flipping end over end so quickly it was a blur. A ring of fire lit around her neck where the iron chain of her necklace touched her skin, and she screamed.

The blade of the axe slammed into the welded edge of the manacle on

Mollian's wrist, cracking both axe head and seam.

The power that had surged through her rushed out so quickly it left her breathless, and she collapsed forward with a gasp.

Oren stooped to grab his sword from the ground, twirling it in his hand as he slowly approached her.

Merriam scrambled across the floor, grabbing for her discarded axes and jumping to her feet. She gasped at the pain in her side, choking back a sob as she shifted into a fighting stance. "Oren, stop," she pleaded, blinking back the tears that blurred her vision.

A wicked smile cut across his face, baring elongated canines. His tongue flicked across his teeth as though he were looking forward to sinking them into her, and he lunged forward in a strike.

Merriam leaped to the side, knocking the sword away with an axe and spinning around to face him again. "Oren, please," Merriam repeated, dancing back a few paces.

He didn't pause as he swung again, brutal and precise. Merriam blocked the attack, her arms reverberating with the momentum of his swing. She pushed him away, jumping to the side and flipping an axe around in her hand, slamming the blunt edge of it into his arm.

He roared at the impact, striking out again without even pausing to shake off the pain.

Merriam struggled to keep her feet from sliding on the blood-slick floor of the cavern as she blocked his attacks, trying her best to keep from causing too much injury as she countered. She had never seen this fighting style before; his movements were different from any she'd encountered in her years of training at the castle.

They weren't Oren's.

While Merriam fought, Mollian ripped the gag from his mouth, grabbing the axe from the ground and swinging it into the other shackle with a strangled cry as a surge of power rippled from him. Power he'd suppressed his entire life. Power he'd never let himself truly acknowledge the depth of. The blade shattered on impact, popping open the iron clasp. Mollian's wrist was an angry, welted red from where the iron had burned him as he forced his magic past the barrier the metal had created, but he paid no attention, running toward Oren. "Hey, shithead!"

Oren paused, turning to face Mollian.

Merriam slid on her knees, knocking the back of a blade into Oren's knee and causing it to collapse beneath him. She rolled from the slide, jumping to her feet at Mollian's side. Her teeth were clenched at the pain radiating from her ribs, and the wound on her shoulder was still slowly leaking blood, dripping down her arm and slickening her grip on the axe.

Mollian bent to grab a sword from the floor, raising it as Oren regained his footing and ran for them.

Merriam's eyes darted around the room, trying to track the guards, who were hanging back, waiting for the order to attack.

Eskar had also risen to her feet, swaying slightly but wielding a sword. She shook her head firmly once to clear it and threw herself at a guard with a feral cry.

Oren swung for Mollian, who blocked the blow, face set in a feral snarl as he concentrated on keeping from mortally wounding his brother. His pale eyes glowed, and Merriam could feel power swirling under his skin, her own blood reacting to the pull of it.

Ria, listen, you need to grab Oren and run.

Merriam quickly glanced at Mollian, confusion flashing in her eyes as she spun away from another attack, the ring of metal striking metal filling the cave.

I'm going to steal the demon from Oren. And I'm going to collapse the cavern. You need to run as soon as he's free.

Molli, no, don't be stupid. Merriam feinted an attack, grabbing Oren's attention and allowing for Mollian to come in and try to knock the sword from his hands.

Mollian laughed, a little manically. *The mistake that Basta made is assuming that being the youngest means I have the least power.* He stepped into Oren's swing, blocking his attack with an upward strike.

Oren angrily kicked out at Mollian, catching him in the stomach before whirling to swing the sword at Merriam.

I don't care how much power you have; you don't get to sacrifice yourself. Merriam blocked Oren's attack, pushing back with a restrained swipe towards his abdomen.

Go. Mollian's voice was laced with command, even as he fought from doubling over to catch his breath, and Merriam felt her body aching to obey the power that flowed from him.

Merriam shook her head, partially to clear it and partially to deny him, jumping back from Oren to try to give herself time to strategize how to disarm him.

Mollian advanced on Oren, the magic in his blood swirling tighter and wilder as he prepared to grab his brother. *I love you, Ria. Our souls will always find each other. So go with Oren. Be happy.*

"Molli, no!" Merriam screamed, turning her eyes to him.

The broadside of Oren's sword smacked into her chest, knocking her backwards, and her skull slammed against the hard-packed earth. Stars erupted from her vision as she raised her head, trying to get her feet back underneath her.

She whimpered as pain exploded from her skull, radiating down her spine as she pushed to her feet. Oren took a step towards her. She raised her axes, ready to meet him. "Oren, please. I can't hurt you. Don't make me hurt you." A sob broke her voice.

Oren watched everything with silent rage, ripping and tearing at the demon who'd taken control of his body. He felt himself take another step forward toward Merriam, her amber eyes wide and pleading and full of misery. Something resolute flashed in the depths of them, and he knew that she loved him enough to kill him. Would rather see him dead than locked away inside of his body, helpless to stop the destruction of his kingdom and the realms he was born to protect.

That single spark of stoicism slid through him like a bolt of lightning. This was not how his story would unfold.

Oren dug into the swirling black mass in his mind.

He was the Crown Prince of Sekha. Protector of Nethyl, the planet that connected and fed power to every world and universe imaginable.

Oren found purchase against the demon, and he gripped hard.

He was brother to Mollian, who had inherited more power than many of the Legends. Mollian, who had never even acknowledged the depth of that power, content to live in the shadow of those he loved.

Oren yanked at the demon, feeling its hold on his mind, on his body, slip as it turned its attention inward with an angry shriek.

He was a male irrevocably devoted to the woman in front of him. A thought flicked briefly through his mind that he had never thanked Mollian for bringing her into his life. Merriam had more tenacity, more fire than anyone he'd ever met—fae or otherwise. She was also not afraid to love fiercely despite the broken, twisted parts that she tried so desperately to hide from the world.

Oren tightened his hold on the demon as it fought him, lashing out to free itself and push him back from control.

He was Oren Stonebane, and he would not yield to the darkness being thrust upon him.

He violently ripped the demon from his mind, pulling it away just enough to let him slip back into himself. It raged in his head, clawing and fighting to regain control.

Oren's eyes flashed green for a heartbeat, there and gone so quickly Merriam almost thought she imagined it. He faced Mollian, throwing up a hand and pushing him back with enough force to send the younger prince flying to the ground, sword skittering from his grasp.

With unnatural speed, Oren turned to Basta, whose confident smile faltered.

"Kill them," Basta ordered, the inky tendrils across his skin flaring with the command as he pointed to Merriam and Mollian.

"I told you," Oren said, voice echoing with the eerie rasp of the demon that still fought him, "not to fucking touch her." He was upon Basta before the man had a chance to react, swinging the sword in a powerful arc, blade sinking into his wrist and trailing diagonally up his body.

Basta stumbled back with a roar of pain, holding his mangled hand to his chest as blood, darker than red wine, poured from his wounds.

Oren dropped the sword, wrapping both hands around Basta's neck and squeezing. He leaned in close. "My power will *never* be yours to control," he hissed into Basta's ear before closing his teeth over it. With a violent jerk of his head, Oren ripped the cartilage free and spat the flesh to the ground.

Basta's fingers clawed at Oren's hands, his skin rippling as the demon inside him tried to separate itself from the dying human.

Oren slammed Basta's skull against the wall with a feral growl, dark blood dripping down his chin.

Basta's good hand dropped, and he glared wickedly at the prince, who pulled him forward to deal a finishing blow. But Basta had already pulled a gun from the waist of his pants and squeezed the trigger.

The shot rang through the cavern. Confusion played over Oren's face, cold seeping through his body as his hands went slack. He coughed once, strangled and gurgling, and fell to the ground.

Merriam's heart stopped, and she lurched forward, hurling an axe at Basta with a scream she couldn't hear through the deafening roar in her ears, but that she felt rip from her throat just the same.

The axe sank into Basta's arm, and he tore it free, tossing it to the ground with a snarl. Merriam raised her other axe as she ran, but as she brought her arm down, flinging the weapon forward, Basta wiped his uninjured hand over the gash in his arm, coating his fingers in blood before sliding his hands together.

Merriam's eyes widened in realization at the same instant Basta disappeared, slipping into whatever reality he'd chosen, using the power of his Bonded blood. Her axe sailed through the air, striking the cave wall and ricocheting to the floor, where it skittered to a stop next to its companion.

As soon as Basta disappeared, the remaining guards jumped into action, running at Mollian and Eskar. One of the guards tore open as the demon inside him broke free, leaping toward Mollian with jaws spread wide.

Merriam, oblivious to the chaos around her, fell to her knees next to Oren, putting her hands over the bloody patch just underneath his ribcage. "Hey, it's okay. It's okay," she whispered, a tear slipping down her cheek.

Oren's eyes, once again a dazzling green, found hers. He raised his hand slowly, brushing the backs of his fingers against her face. Blood bubbled from his lips when he tried to speak, and his brow furrowed. His gaze went unfocused, the light fading from his eyes as his hand fell abruptly.

Merriam clasped at Oren's fingers, raising them back to her blood-spattered cheek. "O," she whispered, squeezing the deadweight that was his hand.

No response came from him.

"NO!" she screamed, over and over again, until it became one unintelligible sound.

Pain erupted from her scalp as she was lifted by the hair and thrown to the side. Her shoulder hit the ground with a sickening crack as all the air was forced from her lungs. She lay completely winded as a guard walked up, raising his sword to strike.

Merriam watched his movements with fascination as a quiet calm crept over her. Her axes were several feet away against the wall of the cave, her entire body hurt, and Oren was dead.

Oren was dead.

The thought echoed through her head, time slowing as she watched the blade swing for her.

Movement blurred in her peripheral vision, and Rovin leaped in front of her, short sword raised to block the attack. Her eyes tracked up his back as he struck a counterattack, pushing the guard back with precise movements. When her gaze reached Rovin's head, dark chestnut hair swinging wildly, dripping with black demon blood and sweat as he fought, her mind snapped into place, and she whipped her head to find Mollian.

He had found a second sword, attacking the demon in front of him with an almost unhinged ferocity. Now that she was attuned to him, she could feel the power radiating from him as he used the magic in his blood to fight.

Still strangely calm, Merriam closed her eyes and slid her rings together, Traveling to Earth.

"Would you fucking look at that," Merriam said with mild surprise as she glanced at the cave around her. It looked like Basta had used this space as some sort of middle ground. Crates and boxes of supplies lined the walls, the space lit by dim fluorescent bulbs lining the ceiling.

Merriam walked over to the side of the cave, rolling her shoulder to test out the injury. It didn't feel like anything was broken, thankfully, but she knew her back would have a hideous bruise and the muscle was likely damaged. Nothing she couldn't push through, though.

Bending down, she Traveled back.

On Nethyl, she scooped up her axes and surveyed the room. Rovin was closest to her, still fighting the guard. Merriam flipped back to Earth, running toward the spot Rovin had been and Traveling again. She was right on the guard, swinging an axe into his exposed side, blade catching just underneath his ribcage and tearing him open. Her eyes locked on the next nearest foe, and she pulled the axe free as she brought her hands back together.

She was moving before the ground had fully solidified underneath her, the quiet of this empty cave barely registering as she flipped back to the fight, dispatching the next guard with a blow to the back of the knee and another to the back of the neck when he fell, head hanging limply from his shoulders as she locked onto her next target and Traveled again.

She moved between the two worlds, quickly and seamlessly taking out the guards that had come up from the rest of the cave system. They'd never expected this many to be hidden, but it was almost like Basta was building an army of the possessed, hiding them here until they were needed.

Merriam quickly scaled a stack of crates, the adrenaline running through her body overshadowing any of the pain from her injuries. She leapt, Traveling back mid-air and landing on top of a reptilian demon. She slammed one axe deep into the back of its neck, using the weapon as an anchor as she swung down, ripping the edge of the other blade across the creature's neck.

Rank blood splashed across the floor as the demon fell forward, and Merriam pulled herself up onto its back, feet scrambling for purchase. She yanked her axe free just after it hit the ground, scraping her rings together and launching across the cave.

She reappeared just to the side of another demon, slamming an axe into one of its many spindly legs, snapping it in one swing before moving to another. The creature screeched, turning unsteadily to gnash at her. She ducked, Traveling as she rolled and Traveling again as she popped back to her feet, taking out a few more legs until it listed heavily on one side. Figuring the Rangers fighting it were no longer in immediate danger, she turned, searching for the next opponent.

Her eyes found Mollian, sword locked with a guard still in fae skin. His white curls were matted down with dark blood, and his pale eyes flicked to her for only a moment before returning to the male in front of him, launching a barrage of attacks before finding an opening and spearing the guard through the center. He pulled his sword free and whirled away, joining another fight before his last opponent fully hit the ground.

Merriam turned to see Bellamy lunge in front of a fallen Evangeline, another many-limbed demon raising a pointed leg to strike. It let out a shrieking hiss, and Merriam was moving through reality, again using the boxes as leverage and throwing herself off of them. She flipped back, landing on its thin, curved back and dropping to her knees. With one powerful strike, she severed its neck.

Merriam misjudged her balance as it tipped forward, and she spilled to the ground, landing on her back next to Bellamy with a thud that sent a loud bark of pain radiating from both her rib and shoulder, her head also echoing with discomfort from its earlier impact.

Bellamy reached a hand down to help her up, and she grasped his wrist as she pushed through the anguish.

"Thank you," he panted.

"Likewise," she replied before disappearing once again.

She reappeared a few moments later underneath another demon, slicing through its soft underbelly before she was gone again, moving across the cave in a deadly wave of bloodshed.

Her mind felt strangely, completely void of anything except taking down every demon she could sink an axeblade into. The need to kill—the instinct to kill—consumed her entire being. The only other thought that registered for her was keeping track of Mollian.

He, too, was fighting with a precise brutality, dispatching enemies with hardly a pause between them or any hesitation or missteps in his movements. His power flowed through him, completely unhampered for the first time he could remember. Every swing was backed with a force and precision fueled by his magic, and leapt from one fight to the next without faltering.

Merriam lost sight of him most of the time, but she felt him, felt the presence of his magic in her blood alerting her to him, and it was the only thing that grounded her in her blind rampage.

She continued moving between the two worlds, taking out demons and guards until the cavern was littered with bodies and blood.

Merriam pulled her axe from the lower spine of a guard, letting the Ranger in front of her run him through the heart as he fell. She was already turning to look for the next opponent.

The sound of her heartbeat in her ears started to fade as she turned a slow circle. The sounds of fighting had stopped, making the cavern seem eerily quiet. Her eyes caught on a head of white hair against the cold stone floor, and her heart lurched into her throat as reality came crashing back through the steady concentration of a fight.

Molli, she Cast wildly as her vision tunneled to the body across the cave. She felt herself move to the brink of collapse as her mind threatened to shut down. *Help,* she threw out again, tearing her eyes away from Oren to look for the one source of solace she'd always known.

Chapter 39

I can't breathe

MERRIAM STOOD IN THE center of the cavern, panting heavily, axes gripped in her fists as droplets of blood, both the black of demons and red of her own, slipped down her skin. Her amber eyes were wild, locking onto Mollian's with a silent, wordless plea.

"Leave us," Mollian said, flicking his eyes momentarily to Rovin. "Search the rest of the cave."

Rovin straightened, nodding in direct obedience and immediately rounding up the Rangers and ushering them down the tunnels. It struck Mollian then that he was now heir apparent. Rovin obeyed him without question because he was the future king. The knowledge settled, bitter and cold, in his gut, and he forced the thought from his mind.

He took a step closer to Merriam, but stopped when she walked toward Oren. The axes dropped from her hands with a clatter, and she stumbled forward, sinking to her knees in front of him. "Evergreen," she said quietly, reaching a hand to touch his shoulder. "Evergreen," she repeated, shaking him as her voice cracked and tears cut tracks down her blood-stained cheeks.

"Evergreen," she sobbed, shaking him harder. "Evergreen, evergreen, evergreen."

Mollian walked up behind her, placing a hand on her shoulder. "He's gone, Ria."

Merriam shook him off angrily, smacking Oren's chest with her fists. "Fucking evergreen, you bastard! Evergreen!"

Mollian knelt next to her, firmly grabbing her wrists and pulling her into his chest. She clung to him, tears streaming down her face and soaking his shirt. "He said it would all stop if I said it. He promised," she sobbed against his shoulder.

Mollian squeezed her to him, and she flinched at the pressure on her ribs, freshly bruised. He moved his hand to the back of her head, holding her as silent tears spilled down his cheeks, wetting her hair.

The sobs racking Merriam's body also made her ribs throb, but she couldn't breathe, couldn't stop. And the pain in her heart was so much worse than any physical wound.

Merriam pressed her face against Mollian's shoulder and screamed.

She screamed until she had no breath left, devolving again into heartbroken sobs.

Mollian's heart, already in tatters, broke anew for her, and he buried his face in her hair as a strangled cry clawed its way up his throat. He had no words of comfort to give. So he held her as they cried together, shielding her eyes from the sight of his dead brother even as he used her to shield his own.

When her sobs subsided, Merriam took a shuddering breath, trying to calm herself. "What do we do now, Molli?"

Mollian shook his head, chin brushing against her hair. "I don't know," he admitted.

"He's gone."

Mollian nodded, not trusting his voice.

He saved you. He saved us, she Cast to him, her throat closing with emotion.

Mollian bit his cheek hard enough to taste blood. Anger, bright and hot, cut through his grief. He'd had a plan. He could have saved Oren. He could have saved Oren and killed Basta. His life could have been worth something. Could have truly served a purpose the way his siblings did. Mollian swallowed down against the bile that rose up his throat. Why hadn't he acted faster? Why hadn't he tried harder? He should have thrown more of his magic into controlling the situation, but he'd been too afraid of hurting Merriam or Oren to let his power take control before they were safely away.

Merriam stroked his face, pulling him from his thoughts. Her amber eyes shimmered with something sharp and resolute. "Don't you dare blame yourself for this. Don't you even go down that path, Mollian," she choked out.

A bitter chuckle spilled from his lips, and he rested his forehead against hers.

They sat together on the floor for a while longer before Mollian lifted his head, brushing blood and tears from her cheeks with his thumb. "Do you think you'll be okay to talk to the others?"

Merriam looked into his eyes, running her own dirty thumbs over his cheeks to clear away the tear tracks on his light brown skin. "I'll make it work." She pulled away from Mollian, turning to Oren and slowly reaching to trail her fingers down his face. She leaned forward, brushing a final kiss to his lips before resting her forehead against his. *You are everything*, she Cast.

Pulling away, she wrangled all the emotions inside her and shoved them into a dark corner, forcing herself into that same numb state she'd slipped into when Mollian had disappeared.

She resheathed her axes as they walked into the main cavern. Mollian stopped to talk to a Ranger, discussing the arrangements for the bodies to be gathered and brought back to Umbra. Merriam kept moving, exiting the cave and blinking in the bright morning sun.

She choked back a laugh at the absurdity of it all. How had it only been hours since they'd first launched the attack? How had her world been completely and irreversibly flipped in such a short amount of time? There was still an entire day left, a realization that immediately exhausted her.

She was about to stumble over to a tree when Aleah came running up to her, throwing her arms around Merriam's middle. Hissing at the pain that erupted from her side and back, she returned the embrace.

"I'm so glad you're okay," Aleah whispered. "We all made it, too."

Merriam looked up, searching for Jasper's familiar dark form. He stepped forward when her eyes found him, and she shook her head, forcing back the lump in her throat. "He's dead," she whispered.

Aleah pulled back, shock and confusion on her face. "What do you mean? No one's come out to tell us anything yet, only that Basta is gone."

Jasper moved forward, shaking his head slowly as his silver eyes filled with pain. "No."

Merriam forced the tidal wave of despair back down, staring at him mournfully.

Jasper shook his head again, rushing past Merriam and into the cave, searching for his old friend.

Leonidas and Campbell walked from the woods. One of Campbell's antlers had snapped off at the base, but it would grow back. Leonidas absentmindedly kept touching the younger male, as if assuring himself that he was alive and mostly unhurt. Panic flew down, lighting on Leonidas's shoulder and surveying Merriam with a curious look.

"What happened in there?" Campbell asked softly.

"Basta ... he took Mollian to get to—" Merriam swallowed hard, unable to say his name.

Calysta walked up then, a poultice already prepared from helping the others. "Quit pestering her. I'm sure you'll get a brief later." She gave them a sharp look before turning her inky black eyes to Merriam. Somehow, she knew.

Relief flooded Merriam at knowing she didn't have to talk about it yet, stripping off her shirt to let the nymph have access to the numerous wounds across her torso.

Calysta used wet moss to wipe off Merriam's arms and chest, but even the fabric of the wide band of her bra was stained with dark blood. When as much of the gore had been cleaned from her skin as possible, Calysta smoothed a pungent green paste over the cuts. The nymph clicked her tongue at the deep gash over Merriam's shoulder, already clotting over. Finally, Calysta's fingers brushed Merriam's neck over the angry, red line burned into her skin. Calysta cocked her head, flicking her eyes to Merriam's. "This is from magic," she said definitively.

Merriam licked her lips, turning her head to the side as Calysta slipped the poultice under the chain of her necklace. The cool mixture was soothing against the burn, and she let out a small sigh. "I think I used magic to throw an axe."

Calysta's eyebrows shot up, and Campbell's indigo eyes went wide as he looked at her.

"How?" Leonidas asked.

Merriam turned her head to the other side as Calysta continued to work. "I think ... I think Molli pushed his magic into me for a moment. I think he shoved it down the Bond just long enough for me to free him before it snapped back into him."

"I didn't even know that was possible," Aleah breathed.

"Me neither," Merriam replied.

"He could give you his magic because you're *mehhen*, not just because you're Bonded." Calysta stepped back, surveying the bruise blooming over Merriam's ribs. "Again?"

Merriam winced away from the pressure of her touch. "Some fucker kicked me."

Calysta frowned, running her fingers over the area once more before dusting off her hands and placing them on her hips. "Again, I think it's just badly bruised, but it may be cracked. See a real fucking medic when we get back to Umbra, Mer," she demanded.

Merriam gave her a weak smile. "I'll do my best."

Calysta scoffed, throwing up her hands. "I swear on all the Legends." She stomped off to collect more herbs to patch up any of the Rangers who needed help.

Mollian came out of the cave then, and Merriam excused herself, slipping her shirt back on and walking over to him, just needing the comfort of his presence.

"We'll be heading back to Umbra soon. Are you okay to ride a horse? We can Travel if needed."

"I'm not leaving him," Merriam answered immediately.

Mollian reached down to squeeze her hand. "Let's get back to camp and prepare for the trip home, then."

A few Rangers were tasked to stay and keep an eye on the cave in case Basta returned. The rest prepared to leave, making quick work of packing everything up even with their injuries.

The majority of the Rangers were healing with the magical quickness of full fae blood, but some would still carry scars.

Bellamy had sustained a cut down the front of his face, across one eye. Though it would scar, his eye appeared to be unscathed. A thick, gnarly scab currently trailed down his face, and it pulled taught when he caught Merriam's eyes and smiled grimly, giving her a small wave.

Merriam waved back, thankful for the distance between them. She couldn't handle any of his well-meaning questions or admiration in that moment.

Merriam shared a horse with Mollian, resting her cheek against his back and letting the rhythmic movement of the animal lull her mind, helping the numbness to flow through her veins and keep everything else locked down.

When they stopped for the night, Mollian walked with her to a stream to wash off the ichor that remained on them both. She watched the black blood drip down her skin with mild fascination. How easy it was to wash it all away as though it had never happened, as though it could ever be just a distant, unpleasant memory.

She spent the night curled against Mollian's side, though sleep never truly claimed her. His presence was the only thing that kept her from drifting off completely into a pit of despair, and she was haunted by the irrational fear that if she closed her eyes for more than a moment, Mollian might disappear.

The next day and a half of travel back to Umbra, Merriam stayed glued to Mollian's side. If he was called away for any reason, she felt her heartbeat speed up and her breathing get shallow. The first time it happened, they had stopped to eat and Mollian had left briefly to talk with the Rangers who had been scouting ahead.

Merriam had been fine one moment, and the next she'd felt completely void. The weight of everything that had happened in the cave came crashing through her. She'd stumbled over to a tree, resting her palm against the rough bark as she tried to catch her breath. But her vision had started to blur around the edges, and she couldn't get herself under control.

Aleah had walked over, taking Merriam's face between her freckled hands and forcing her to meet her eyes. "Breathe, Mer, you're okay. Breathe."

Merriam shook her head, eyes frantic as she grasped Aleah's hands. "I can't—Aleah, I can't breathe," she'd panted, fingers digging into Aleah's skin.

Aleah quickly flicked her eyes to Jasper, signaling him to find Mollian before she looked back to Merriam, trying unsuccessfully to soothe her.

Jasper returned with Mollian a few moments later, and as soon as he got close, the tightness in her chest started to ease. Mollian placed his hand on Aleah's shoulder, thanking her before taking Merriam's hands and pulling her to his chest.

Breathe, Ria. I'm here.

When he Cast to her, her body recognized the lick of his magic against her mind, and it settled, remembering the power that had coursed through her the day before. She gradually caught her breath, her heartbeat slowing as she leaned back to meet his eyes, pale green cracked with brown. *Don't leave me, Molli. Don't leave.*

I'm not going anywhere. He pulled her back to him, pressing a kiss to the top of her head. The weight of her in his arms was grounding. He needed her presence as much as she needed his. The reality of what his life would now be mixed with the raw depth of his grief in a heady storm of emotion that made his magic spiral wildly inside him. Merriam's proximity was the only thing that calmed him, small streams of his magic trickling into her through the ties of their souls and giving him some form of respite, even if not from the pain of loss.

Merriam had had another panic attack the next time Mollian had gone more than a few feet from her, but she'd hidden it better, knowing what to expect. She had always felt connected to him, but ever since he'd given her his magic, her body was even more attuned to him, the magic in her blood from the Bond awake to the presence of its source. Maybe it had always stirred when he was near but she'd never had a reason to notice it.

But now the way his presence affected the magic in her blood allowed her to keep a stronger check on her emotions, holding everything at bay until she figured out how to process it.

If she figured out how to process it.

The numb state in which Merriam was existing was becoming more and more comfortable by the moment.

❦

When they were close to Umbra, Mollian sent two Rangers ahead to alert his parents of their arrival.

The mercenaries went back to the house to rest and recover, only

Jasper staying with Merriam as she and Mollian accompanied the Rangers that transported the bodies of the dead down to the catacombs. Five Rangers had been slain fighting in the mountain, and their bodies were brought to the area reserved for the honor of those who'd given their lives for the country.

The prince would be brought to Entumbra to be laid to rest, but until then, they set him on top of a stone slab, covered with a deep green blanket.

Merriam squeezed Mollian's hand, stepping forward and resting her fingers against the fabric-wrapped body. "We'll be back for you," she promised before turning to leave.

One of the Rangers Mollian sent ahead stopped them as they ascended the stairs. "The queen is in the throne room, Prince Mollian. She's requesting your presence immediately."

Mollian stiffened. "Does she know?"

The Ranger shifted uncomfortably. "I did not feel it was my place to tell her, Your Highness. But I did make the mistake of mentioning you were the one that sent me."

Mollian sighed, steeling himself for a conversation he was in no way ready to have.

Merriam squeezed his hand a final time before letting go, turning her head to talk to Jasper as they made their way to the throne room. "Thank you for staying, but you don't have to be a part of this if you don't want to. It's not going to be pleasant."

Jasper nodded. "I might head back to the merc house. I would assume the smaller the audience for this conversation, the better." He rested a dark hand on her shoulder for a moment. "If you need anything, you know where to find me," he said quietly before heading off.

A few other Rangers lined the walls, most of whom had just returned, still disheveled and travel-weary. Regenya and Darius were seated on the dais, Captain Ferrick standing to Regenya's left, uniform pristine and scabbard strapped to his belt sparkling with a fresh polish.

Merriam stood next to Mollian, trembling with rage that heated her blood, coursing through her veins with ferocity. It was the first true emotion she'd felt since locking them down, and she couldn't get a grasp on it. Tendrils of hair hung about her face; she hadn't touched it since Mollian had helped her rinse it of blood, and her braid after the fact had been loosely done, the effort of tying her hair back almost too much to deal with.

Mollian Cast to her, more a feeling than any actual words, trying to placate her.

She glared daggers at Captain Ferrick and his perfectly clean appearance, at his audacity to show up here when he had refused to risk his own life or well-being.

Regenya tried to appear stoic, but her death grip on the king's hand betrayed her emotions. "Mollian, where is your brother?"

Mollian swallowed, forcing down the emotion that lodged in his throat. "Mother," he started.

"Where is he?" she asked, voice cracking on the last word. Clearing her throat, she spoke again. "Where is my son?"

"We brought him to the catacombs until we can take him to Entumbra," Mollian answered quietly.

Regenya nodded, a wave of emotion crossing her face as she battled with the meaning behind Mollian's words. Her eyes filled with tears, but her voice was clear as she ordered, "Tell me."

"He saved us. He saved me," Mollian said thickly. "Basta killed him."

Regenya shook her head, tightening her death grip on Darius's fingers.

The king pulled his wife's hand to his chest, his eyes filling with tears as he looked at Mollian in disbelief.

Ferrick rested a hand on the queen's shoulder. "I can listen to the rest of the brief and fill you in later, Your Majesty," he offered. "I can only imagine what you must be feeling right now."

Merriam's hands curled into fists at her sides, and she physically bit her tongue to keep from asking him where he was when his future king was trying to save the realm, when his men gave their lives to help rescue Mollian.

Mollian wrapped his hand around her wrist, squeezing hard enough for her to notice through her anger.

"This is a tragedy unlike anything Sekha has seen in centuries. We will never forget Prince Oren's sacrifice."

Hearing his name come from Ferrick's mouth snapped whatever restraint Merriam had been able to hold. She blinked, and her vision tunneled until nothing existed except Ferrick. She launched herself at him with a snarl that didn't sound human, ripping her wrist from Mollian's grasp.

She was across the room in three bounds, leaping onto Ferrick and knocking him to the ground with her hands wrapped around his neck. His fingers clawed against her, breaking skin, but she didn't even register it. "You don't get to say his name, you fucking spineless coward," she hissed, spittle flying from her mouth.

Hands grabbed at her, but she tightened her grip around the male's throat, squeezing her knees around his torso to hold herself to him as she cut off both breath and blood flow.

Merriam, Mollian's voice in her head was calm, but firm. *Let him go.*

Blinking against the fog in her head, Merriam remembered where she was, releasing Ferrick and letting herself be dragged back across the room, panting heavily.

Regenya looked furious, her bright green eyes–*his* eyes–burning hot as she lifted a hand, throwing open the doors to the throne room. "Mollian, if she isn't out of my sight in the next moment, I will have her locked in a cell for assaulting an officer of the Royal Guard."

Mollian met Merriam's eyes only briefly, apology shining in his gaze before looking at whoever stood behind her. "Escort her to my rooms, please. I'll be there shortly."

Regenya's voice followed Merriam out the door as she was ushered out. "The only reason I am letting this slide is because of her loyalty to you and the asset she has proven to be for this country. But if you cannot control her, she will not be allowed in this castle."

Merriam was too far to hear Mollian's reply, or perhaps the doors had been closed.

"Are you composed now?" For the first time, Merriam registered that the hands on her arms belonged to people. "I'd prefer not to have to drag you the entire way to your room."

Merriam turned her head to see Bellamy, who was looking at her slightly abashed. "I'm ..." she paused, turning her eyes down. *Okay* was definitely not something she was, but she was at least in control of herself, so she repeated his words back. "I'm composed."

Bellamy nodded, releasing her.

Kodi, on her other side, did the same, touching a fist to her shoulder. "I'll deny the words ever left my mouth, but that was pretty badass, merc. I can't even count the amount of times I've wanted to throttle that asshole myself." Kodi cut a sharp look at Bellamy, narrowing his eyes. "You didn't hear any of this, kid."

Bellamy just nodded, facing forward and continuing down the hall, hands in his pockets.

The walk to her chambers was silent, and she tried not to panic as her blood stirred at the loss of Mollian's presence. She focused on keeping her breathing even. He was fine. He was safe.

She sat down on the couch once inside her rooms, pulling her knees up to her chest. "You don't have to stay. I'm not going anywhere."

Kodi leaned one shoulder against the wall, shaking his head. "Sorry, I'm sure you're not, but I think we'll wait for Prince Mollian to get back, all things considered."

Merriam rested her chin on her knees, closing her eyes and letting her mind go blank.

"So what's Aleah's story?" Kodi asked.

Merriam opened her eyes, looking at him in utter disbelief. After everything that had happened the last few days, how the fuck did he find a question like that appropriate? Of all the self-centered, untimely questions, the Ranger had some fucking gall. She opened her mouth to say as much, dropping her legs as she prepared to stand and tear into him when the realization suddenly hit her, and she froze.

Kodi had no way of knowing the turmoil she was in right now, was probably just trying to distract her or strike up idle conversation, if anything. He wouldn't know that her heart had been ripped from her chest two days ago, because she hadn't wanted to tell anyone.

She had wanted to run around in the shadows, and now she would have to suffer in them as well.

Shoving the hurt down, she cleared her features. "If she wanted you to know, she'd tell you," Merriam finally answered.

Bellamy tilted his head, watching her silently, a dark scab still running down one side of his face. She met his gaze evenly, wondering if he could see into the deeper parts of her, see that she was utterly destroyed and barely functioning. He glanced away, shifting slightly.

He could.

"How do I make her want to tell me?" Kodi asked.

Merriam glanced at him in surprise. "You're serious?"

"As a broken rib," he swore, placing a hand over his chest.

Merriam raised an eyebrow suspiciously.

"Look, I know we haven't always gotten along–"

Merriam interrupted with a snort.

Bellamy watched them both with blatant curiosity.

"*But* I think a lot of what's happened between us can be water under the bridge at this point. It doesn't matter that you get to live here because Mollian picked you up out of another world or that he talked Ferrick into letting you train with us without going through any of the proper channels—"

Merriam gave him an incredulous look. "If this is you trying to be friendly, you've got some skewed fucking perspective."

Kodi lifted his hands placatingly. "If you would let me finish: I've seen you fight. I've seen your skill. You're good, Mer. Fucking Legends, you're better than a lot of us, even. Clearly you're doing something right, and I'd rather not have to fight you if it ever came down to it. Rov's an ass, but there's nothing he can do about your place in this country. It'll be good for both of us to have connections."

"What makes you think I have connections?"

Kodi grinned wickedly, pulling a match from his pocket and flipping it over his knuckles. "Connections to a redhead with sharp knives and a sharper mouth."

Merriam shook her head, turning her eyes to the ceiling. "Sweets."

"Sweets?"

"Never met someone with a stronger sugar addiction." A small smile pulled at the corners of Merriam's lips for the first time in two days.

"Thanks, Mer. I think this will be the start of a beautiful friendship."

"Uh-huh," she answered skeptically.

The door swung open then, and Mollian entered. Bellamy straightened to stand at attention; Kodi lazily pushed away from the wall. "She's all yours, My Liege." He saluted before motioning for Bellamy to follow him out.

Mollian watched the door close before turning to Merriam in confusion.

She tilted her head to the side, eyes slowly meeting Mollian's. "That was ... the strangest conversation I've had in a long while."

Mollian sat next to her on the couch, searching her face for a second. "What about?" he asked, deciding to let her have this distraction for a while longer. Even if Bellamy hadn't seen the shattered depths of her, there was no hiding that anguish from Mollian, not when the tethers tying his soul to hers were also frayed with the pain of loss.

"He's got it for Aleah. Bad." Merriam chuckled softly.

Mollian sank into the cushions. "I'm not sure who I'm more scared for if that pairing becomes a thing."

"The rest of us, for sure," Merriam decided.

Mollian agreed, and they sat in silence for a while before he shifted to face her, once again searching her face. The bald concern there cracked something in her chest, and she bit her lip to fight off the emotion rising inside her. "We need to talk about what happened earlier, Ria."

Merriam shook her head, turning her eyes away. "I hate him, Molli. I hate him so much. He's a self-righteous prick, and it should have been *him*." Her voice broke on the last word.

Mollian gently grabbed her arm, pulling her closer. He held her, careful not to put pressure on her freshly bruised ribs, resting his cheek against her head. "Unfortunately, he's in one of the most powerful positions in the country. That probably won't change for a while. You cannot make an enemy of him, Ria. My protection can only extend so far. If anything were to happen to you ..."

Merriam burrowed into him, and before she could force them back down, all of her emotions from the past couple of days came rushing to the surface. "I just want to hurt him, Molli. I want to hurt him because he doesn't, and it's not fair. He should hurt, too," she sobbed half-unintelligibly into Mollian's shoulder.

Tears slipped from Mollian's eyes as he held her, providing solace even as he drew his own comfort from her. He didn't have words to placate her. He knew how deep the pain ran, felt it wrapped around every fiber of his own being. His brother. His first friend. His future king. Gone.

Bathing proved to be too much mental effort for either of them, but they managed to change into clean clothes and eat a bit of food that had been brought up for supper. They were lying in Mollian's bed on their backs, looking up at the ceiling, when Mollian spoke.

"My mother forbade me from bringing you with us."

Merriam sat up, looking down at him with confusion on her face.

"I tried, Ria. I did everything I could, but after you attacked Ferrick ... she won't let you go to Entumbra."

Merriam shook her head frantically, loose blonde waves sliding over her shoulders. "I'll talk to her. I can change her mind. I need to say goodbye, Molli," she blabbered, panic rising in her chest.

Mollian tugged her down, wrapping his arms around her to soothe the panic. "We have two days. We'll figure something out."

Chapter 40

It's warm there

REGENYA HAD BEEN RELENTLESS in her decision, refusing to see or speak to Merriam, and two days later, Mollian was gone.

Mollian was gone and Merriam was alone, lying on the floor of the common area, staring up at the ceiling.

She'd gotten up with him that morning. She'd needed to prove to him that he could leave her. He needed to be able to lay his brother to rest, but he would never have left her if he had known without a doubt of the fathomless hole that filled her heart and her mind and her body.

So she'd woken up with him, forced a few bites of bread and fruit at breakfast. Then he had held her tightly, pressing his lips to the top of her head.

I'll be back soon. I promise.

It had taken more effort than she'd thought possible to form the thought and send it to him. *I know.*

After Mollian had left, Merriam headed for her bedroom, the food she'd eaten sitting like a rock in her stomach. The effort of holding herself together for Mollian had sapped every bit of energy she'd had, and she made it all of three steps before she slowly lowered herself to the floor, lying on her side and resting for a moment.

That moment had turned into hours, and Merriam had finally rolled onto her back. Her mind was blessedly numb, but her tongue was thick and dry in her mouth. She vaguely wondered when she'd last had any water. Rolling her head, she looked to her bedroom door. It wasn't all that far away. Surely she could make it the few steps to the door.

And after that, the bathroom wasn't much further. It couldn't have been, for all the times Oren had carried her there and back without a single grunt of effort.

Oren had carried her there.

Oren.

A sharp prick of emotion poked through her consciousness, trying to work its way through the numbness that engulfed her.

"Nonononono," she whispered, rolling onto her side and pushing herself into a sitting position. She pulled her legs up to her chest, pressing her eyes to her knees until she saw spots.

The more she tried to concentrate on her breathing, the more shaky and uneven it became.

That prickle was starting to tear through the barriers in her mind, letting in waves of nauseating pain.

"No!" she shouted, lifting her head up and pressing her palms to her ears.

She only had to survive a few days. A few days, and Mollian would be back, and she could let herself feel. A few days. That's all she had to make it.

Because she could not feel all of it alone. She knew it was entirely codependent, but she could not carry the weight of these feelings by herself.

But Mollian would understand. He would know what to do, how to handle them.

She frantically threw the walls back up in her mind, pushing back against that dark wave of grief she could not yet acknowledge. She just had to wait.

Mollian would be back.

She pushed unsteadily to her feet, shuffling to her bathroom for a drink of water.

Dropping her face under the faucet, she let the water stream across her cheeks as she slowly drank. When she was done, she shut off the tap, wiping an arm across her mouth to dry it as she stumbled back a few steps until she hit the wall.

She let herself slide down, resting her head against the plaster.

It was unfair that she wasn't allowed to be there when they laid him to rest. She should be there. She should be the one to offer him his final farewell. She had loved him better than anyone else.

Did you, though? The voice rose unbidden in the back of her mind.

"Yes," she whispered.

You didn't even want to tell anyone.

"No," she pleaded.

You wanted to keep him a secret.

"It wasn't like that." Her whimper was barely audible.

Is that really love?

Anger flared up inside of her, hot and bright and completely irrational. "I love him!" she screamed at the wall, slamming her palms against the floor. Tears filled her eyes and fell down her cheeks before she even had a breath to acknowledge them. "He was *mine!*"

A shuddering sob racked her body, and she pressed the heels of her hands to her eyes. "I should be there," she cried softly.

But Regenya had wanted her to have no part in her son's burial. Had wanted to deny any importance Merriam had in his life.

Merriam shook with anger. It wasn't right for her to be denied like that, even after Mollian had stood up for her, fought for her to be a part of it. He was the crown prince now, after all. His words should carry some weight.

A painful thought came hurtling through Merriam's anger, sliding into the front of her mind and blooming into an illogical but undeniable fear.

What if they came and took all of his things while Mollian was gone? What if she was left without a single thing to remember him by?

Cold fear replaced the anger running in her veins, and it was enough motivation to push herself from the bathroom floor. She grabbed an empty duffel from the bottom of her armoire and slung it across her back before tossing the window open and sitting on the ledge.

She flexed her fingers and started the all-too-familiar climb to his room. The injuries in her shoulder and ribs sent waves of pain through her each time she moved, but she welcomed the discomfort. Physical pain she was familiar with. She understood it. Knew how to handle it. So she leaned into it, letting it drown out the emotional pain that she was unequipped to deal with.

Merriam slipped through the window and stood in his bedroom, time seeming to slow heartbeat by heartbeat as she looked around the familiar space, every inch of it so very *him*.

Taking a deep breath that expanded her lungs, putting pressure against her ribs that chased away the cloud of grief, she went to work. She stripped the sheets from his bed and emptied his drawers of shirts and pants, shoving them all into her bag. When it was full, she climbed back down to her room, dumped everything onto the floor, and climbed back up.

She grabbed papers and books, tearing open the drawer of his desk to find a neatly wrapped box.

The pulse of her heart seemed to slow.

Merriam.

His elegant scrawl went across the top of the package.

Her heart dropped into her stomach, and she held the box in her hands, staring at it blankly.

Merriam traced the letters of her name, mentally adding another layer to the levee against the emotions swirling around in her head. Then she tossed the box into her duffel and climbed back down.

After making one more trip to grab a few more clothes, blankets, and towels, Merriam stood in her room, surveying her spoils and resting a hand over her ribs, which throbbed painfully in time with the beat of her heart. She let the physical pain wash through her, happy for the distraction from emotions.

Merriam bunched all the linens into a pile in the corner of her room and stacked all the papers neatly beside it. The box she set just to the side of the papers.

With her little nest made, she used the last of her manic energy to grab the platter of fruit and bread from the common room and fill up an entire vase of water from the bathroom.

When that was done, she replaced the clothes she was wearing with a pair of his pants and one of his shirts and sank into the pile on the floor. She knew if she even thought his name, that dam against the grief in her mind would break, so she sat staring at the food in front of her, trying to build the will to eat.

Eventually, Merriam grabbed a cracker and nibbled, washing it down with a sip of water from the vase before lying down and burrowing deep into the pile of sheets on the floor. She bunched a section beneath her head and curled into a tight ball on her side. Lack of food and the exertion of scaling the walls had her eyelids slipping shut.

A soft brush against her arm drew her slowly to consciousness. The backs of her eyelids were red, barely blocking the light from the sun shining unhindered through the open window. Her skin was warm, but she couldn't muster the will to kick off the sheets or brush them aside. She breathed deeply, pine and plum and clear night sky surrounding her, warming her from the inside out, and her lips lifted in a small smile.

Another brush against her arm, followed by a light pressure, and her heart hummed with the steady happiness of utter contentment. She couldn't for the life of her remember why she had ever tried to fight it before. She was still too sleepy to figure out how to get the words past her lips, so she carefully formed them in her mind, wrapping them in all the love that threatened to spill over the brim of her heart. With a placid sigh, she Cast the thought.

I cannot wait to be your wife.

A low chuckle sounded across from her, working its way through to her core and settling inside of her in an almost possessive way. *His.* Her body, her heart, her soul seemed to reverberate with it. For the first time, that claim—the way her entire being seemed to crave it—didn't scare her. She leaned into it, fully giving herself over to it. And it felt wholly *right.*

She peeked one eye open, her breath catching in her throat at the depth of vulnerable emotion in the eyes looking back at her. The deep, fresh green of spring sparkled with amusement and adoration and awe, somehow still looking at her as though she were the most wondrous thing in all the worlds he'd seen. Her chest felt tight as her heart swelled, tears pinching in the back of her throat with the knowledge that she did nothing to deserve this.

"I cannot wait to make you my wife." He smiled, running his hand up her arm to caress her cheek.

They were covered completely by a sheet, bright white surrounding them in an ethereal glow. Slowly, Merriam slid her hand up the sheet below her, finally raising it to lightly brush a finger across his lips. He took it between his teeth before releasing it, letting her trail the pad of her finger over the soft brown skin of his cheek, up the tapered point of his ear. She splayed her fingers out when she reached the cropped white hair on the side of his head, relishing the slight tickle against her palm as her hand slipped to the nape of his neck and up to the crown of his head, threading through the longer silky waves that fell freely.

He tilted his head into her hand, green eyes still locked with amber, and brushed the pad of his thumb over her lips. "You are exquisite," he breathed, pulling her face to his even as he dipped his own to meet her lips.

His kiss was soft and sweet and languid, like he knew he had his entire life to taste her and would enjoy every moment of it. He swept his tongue over her bottom lip, and she sighed into his kiss, bliss unfurling slowly down her spine and throbbing between her legs. As his tongue slid across hers, her fingers fisted in his hair, her other hand moving to wrap around the back of his neck and anchor herself to him.

A sense of urgency suddenly flooded her, buzzing in her veins. Something bubbled up from inside her, and she felt the overwhelming need to tell him how much she loved him. How much she needed him. How much she missed—

"Oren," Merriam gasped against his lips, cutting off the thought. "Oren, I—"

As though his name had broken some sort of spell, she had the sudden, intense feeling she was falling, and her whole body thrashed once.

Her eyes flew open, and she could see nothing except bright, empty white. Frantically, Merriam clawed the sheet from over her head, gasping as her heart raced wildly. She sat up, and her eyes scanned the room - *her* room - finally dropping to the pile of sheets and blankets and clothes beneath her. Her fingers bunched up the loose fabric of his shirt that hung from her shoulders as she brought her hand to her chest.

Merriam's throat tightened to the point of pain, tears pricking the backs of her eyes. "I love you," she whispered, almost choking on the next words. "I want to be your wife." Tears blurred her vision and spilled down her cheeks as she spoke the words she'd never before said out loud.

"I want to be your wife," she said again before a sob racked her body, her free hand digging into the blankets around her.

She repeated it, the words half unintelligible as she wept, her shoulders shaking and her chest feeling as though it would crack in half.

She repeated it, knowing it wouldn't make a difference. She was alone. Alone.

Alone.

The word echoed in her head, chilling her blood as the dam she'd so carefully constructed inside her cracked, unleashing a despair so dark and deep she was sure she would drown in it. Pulling her knees to her chest in an effort to staunch the flood crashing through her, she threw her head back and screamed.

Merriam woke from a daze. Or was it sleep? She couldn't tell anymore. She'd lived in her nest of Oren's blankets with no real sense of time passing, just slowly patching the dam of emotions that constantly threatened to spill free again.

The sun had gone down and come back up twice; at least she was pretty sure it had been twice. She'd heard a light knock on the outer door at some point, Calysta's soft voice floating through the wood. Merriam had been too tired, too numb to decipher the words, much less speak up. Eventually, the nymph had left, a flowering vine blooming through her window shortly after. Merriam had managed a small smile at her friend's gesture and burrowed down deeper into the smell of Oren before closing her eyes and letting sleep take her again.

The next time she'd awoken, it had been to the flap of wings as Panic lighted on her windowsill, a prairie dog grasped in one set of talons. He'd tilted his head as he surveyed her lying on the floor. With a soft chirrup, he'd hopped down on one foot and dropped the rodent beside her.

Merriam held out her hand, and he stepped forward to brush his head against her fingers before taking off out the window. Her eyes stayed on the dead animal for a long moment, and she cried. She cried because she felt so alone, and she cried because she knew there were still people who loved her and wanted to be there for her. She cried because none of those people were the one she wanted more than anything in that moment.

Eventually, she'd exhausted herself and dozed off again. When she woke, she grabbed Panic's offering by the tail and gently tossed it from the window. Calysta's vine had faded back by that time, and Merriam closed her window to only a small crack before curling up in her pile of linens.

At this point, she knew Mollian would be back soon. Her eyebrows pulled together as she thought of how she must look: disheveled braid, Oren's shirt falling off one shoulder, wrapped up in a nest on the floor. She knew he would understand, but she also knew if he saw her like this, he would feel even more guilty for leaving her alone. She loved him too much to add to his grief.

With much effort, she pushed herself up from the floor, giving her body time to adjust as she stood. She braced a hand against the wall as her vision darkened momentarily, then stumbled into the bathroom. She removed her braid and brushed through her hair before stepping into the tub.

She stripped her clothes and turned on the tap, sitting and drinking from the stream that slowly filled the basin with tepid water. She shivered, but the cooler water had a sharpening effect on her mind, and it woke her up enough to scrub down.

After drying off, she padded back into her room, sifting through her pile of linen for a clean set of his clothes. She donned a shirt, which again slipped low over one shoulder, and cinched a pair of cotton pants tight around her waist to keep them from sliding down. She left her hair free, but sorted through her nest, reorganizing the clothes, towels, and blankets into something slightly more orderly and hopefully less traumatizing for Mollian.

Her eyes traveled to that small box adorned with her name, and she brushed a finger over the letters before turning to the tray of fruit and crackers that had been her only source of nutrition for the past few days. Her stomach let out a low growl as she looked at what remained, and she selected a plum before settling back down on the now neatly folded palette of blankets.

She picked up one of the piles of paper from his desk as she bit into the plum, careful not to drop any of the juice onto the pages. The smell of the fruit filled the air around her, simultaneously comforting with the sense of Mollian and painful with the reminder of *him*.

Merriam smiled to herself, resting the papers in her lap and tracing a finger over his neatly scrawled notes in the margins of the page.

The document was something budget-related, and she had a fleeting thought that it might be important to whoever would be taking over, but she pushed the worry aside and flipped the page, contenting herself with feeling close to him by getting lost in whatever work he'd been doing last.

The sun slipped below the horizon, and she'd moved from budget papers to notes about possible changes in military policy. This had actually truly caught her interest, and she glared at the lamp by her bed, wishing she had the fae magic that would allow her to turn the light on without moving.

She settled for pushing her window open further, letting the light from the moons spill over the floor. Rolling onto her stomach, she pushed the papers into the beam of light and continued reading.

Merriam was asleep, her head pillowed on one arm while the other was stretched over the papers. She didn't wake when the outer door creaked open and Mollian walked in, quickly catching sight of her curled on the floor of her bedroom.

"Oh, Ria." His heart clenched. She looked so small in his brother's clothes, and the moonlight shining on her pale hair and freckled cheeks gave her an almost angelic appearance. A small smile tugged at the corner of his mouth at the thought. The number of times he'd seen the heat of violence glow in her amber eyes, face streaked with blood, was such a stark contrast to what he saw now.

Mollian walked over to her, carefully sliding the pages from underneath her and stroking her cheek with the back of his hand. "Ria, do you want to go to bed?"

Merriam blinked, her eyes clouded with the confusion of sleep for a few moments before clearing. She launched herself from the floor, flinging her arms around his neck and burying her face against him. "You're back!" Her voice was strangled with unchecked emotion, and his own throat tightened with unshed tears.

He pulled her close, tucking her head under his chin as he held her. It wasn't long before her tears wet the skin of his neck, and his own vision blurred as he shared her grief. *He loved you. So much.*

Merriam held him tighter. "It's not fair, Molli. I just want him back."

"Me, too," Mollian agreed quietly.

After a while, Merriam's tears dried, and she pulled away, sitting back in her nest and grabbing Mollian's hand to pull him next to her. "You …

the rings?" Her thumb brushed across the orydite on his ring finger.

"They're his. Usually they would have been returned to the treasury, but I think he would have been happier knowing I took them. Used them to get back to you faster." Mollian didn't finish the thought. Didn't voice that his brother had always understood that Mollian needed Merriam more than she had ever needed him.

"Is he at rest?"

Mollian nodded. "He's safe and at peace," he paused, leaning his head against Merriam's. "I've never seen a Keeper's last rite before. My grandparents died long before I was born. It was strange seeing what will happen to me one day. And it was strange seeing him ... well, it wasn't him. Not how it mattered, but it all felt very final."

"What happened?" Merriam asked quietly.

"We brought him down to the Gate. There's a tunnel that branches off to the side. When you follow it, it leads deeper into the mountain until it opens up into a large cave. It's warm there, comforting. There are bioluminescent moths, so many that the entire space is cast in a perpetual blue glow. One whole wall is made up of graves of past Keepers. My mother said the magic leftover in them trickles through the stone and back to the Gate, keeping it alive and all the different realms connected and letting the souls of the Keepers Travel wherever they want before they settle in the realm of the dead."

"Where do you think he went?"

Mollian frowned, contemplating. "He did always talk fondly of Nessium, so it's possible he's exploring there or relaxing by the water. But I also like to think he went to Earth, because it reminded him of you."

Merriam snorted. "Bad choice on his part. Earth is a fucking mess of a planet."

Mollian smiled. "You're not wrong, but it is the sort of romantic thing his doting soul would do."

"If we're lucky, maybe he'll find my parents and terrorize them a little. Make them think they're going crazy, thinking there's a ghost in their house." A hint of a wicked smile pulled at her lips.

"If he went to your parents, an actual ghost *would* be in their house," Mollian pointed out.

"Here's to hoping, then," Merriam sighed.

They sat quietly for several long moments, both pulling strength from the other as they let the cold weight of their grief settle over them.

"I need to bathe. Then maybe we can find food and settle in for the night," Mollian said.

Merriam nodded, standing up with him and following him to his bathroom. He didn't question her need to stay close to him, not after he'd been gone for so long with her being in such a fragile state.

She sat with her back to the tub, pulling her knees to her chest and closing her eyes as she absentmindedly toyed with the string around her ankle.

Mollian ran the tap and quickly undressed, slipping into the warm water.

"It's weird to think about," Merriam said when the tap turned off, still keeping her eyes closed and her fingers at her ankle.

"What's that?"

"When he gave me this string ... it was like his first proposal. We hadn't even been together that long. But I didn't question it. At all. Shouldn't I have questioned how much I wanted to throw my life away for someone I had just started seeing?" Merriam opened her eyes, tilting her head back to look at Mollian.

"You knew him for longer than that, though. Even when he was gone, you still saw him."

"Yeah, but still not a large accumulated amount of time."

Mollian shrugged. "Okay, but even outside of that, sometimes things just happen in a way that's not explainable. Love isn't something that's definable by science. It happens both on a cosmic level and also on a smaller scale, inside each person's soul. Think about it, when we first met, did you ever even once question the depth of our friendship?"

Merriam shook her head.

"When it had been seven years since we'd seen each other, did you even, for a moment, hesitate in coming to live with me in Umbra?"

Merriam again shook her head.

"You just knew. And you were right. This is where you belong."

"We're *mehhen*, Molli, doesn't that make our circumstance different?"

"We're *mehhen*, but does the cosmos really limit you to one great connection? We found each other, but maybe that was just a catalyst for you to find him. Maybe you were the soul he needed in this life."

"Seems rather fucked up for the universe to bring us together for only a short time and then strip him away." Merriam glared at the wall.

"It wasn't the universe that took him," Mollian said quietly.

"No, it wasn't." The dull sorrow filling Merriam quickly heated, sharpening to something deadly. "It was Basta. And he *will* pay."

Mollian rested his hand on the top of her head. "He will."

Merriam jolted suddenly, whipping around to face him as worry filled her eyes. "Molli, will you have to go away?"

Mollian tilted his head in confusion. "Why would I go away?"

"We're almost twenty-five, and you're now the heir apparent. Won't you have to go to Entumbra? To prepare to take the crown?"

Mollian frowned and ran a hand through his hair, slicking back his curls. "I ... I suppose I will."

Merriam's eyes filled with tears, her already broken heart shattering again at the thought of being without him for five years in the wake of her grief.

Mollian brushed her hair back from her face. "Hey, don't think about that right now. That's a problem for the future, and we have time."

Merriam blinked rapidly, only a single tear slipping down her cheek before she got them under control. "Molli ... you're going to be king."

Mollian quirked half a smile, pulling a towel from the rack on the opposite wall with a flick of his fingers and catching it in his outstretched hand. "Yes, I suppose I am. And you'd better come visit me while I'm sequestered away in that Hel-hole."

Merriam had leaned to the side to dodge the linen as it flew through the air. "Nothing could keep me away, Prince," she promised.

After dressing, Mollian poked his head out the door to ask for food to be sent. Two of the Guard were stationed on either side, another indicator of Mollian's new status in the world.

"Does this have a story?" he asked, tilting his chin toward the slightly organized mess visible through the open door to her room.

Merriam's cheeks heated, and she toyed with the ends of her hair with a shrug. "I, um ... I didn't want someone to take all of his stuff ... so I took all of his stuff. Or a good portion of it. Only the things that would fit in my bag so I could climb with it."

"Tell me you did not scale the wall of the castle with an entire wardrobe on your back and your ribs still injured!" Mollian's mouth dropped open.

"I didn't scale the wall of the castle with an entire wardrobe on my back," Merriam repeated. "And my ribs are healing."

Mollian shook his head, grabbing her shoulder and pulling her to his chest. "I shouldn't have left you, not with everything so raw."

"You had to, you know that." Merriam held him, letting his solid presence further ground her.

"Fucking Legends, Ria, just don't ... don't be so reckless. I can't lose you." His voice cracked at the end.

Merriam nodded against him. "You won't."

Their food arrived, and Merriam was able to eat half of her portion, more than she'd eaten in one sitting since his death. She supposed that was a step in the right direction.

"Do you want to sleep in your bed or mine?" Mollian asked, standing from the couch and offering his hand to help her up. "I love you, but I refuse to sleep on the floor, and I think an actual mattress would be good for you."

Merriam let him pull her to her feet. "Mine, then."

As they walked into her room, Merriam's eyes landed on the small box on the floor next to the pile of sheets and blankets. She bent to pick it up, holding it gingerly in her hand and looking at Mollian. "I found this in his desk, but I've been scared to open it."

Mollian sat on the edge of her bed and patted the space beside him.

Merriam gave him a strange look, but climbed up, folding her legs in front of her. "Do you know what it is?"

Mollian looked at the small box in her hand for a long moment before finally nodding, brushing a curl from his face. "He talked to me about it," he said vaguely.

Merriam pulled away the string tying the box shut. Her mouth popped open as she opened it. The lid fell from her fingers as she lifted her hand to the aspen leaf charm at her throat. "This is blood," she whispered.

Mollian nodded silently.

Licking her lips, Merriam plucked a small vial from the bed of loose cotton in the box. It was just bigger than half the length of her pinkie, and even though it was a tinted brown glass, the liquid inside was unmistakable. Her eyes flicked to Mollian, who was watching her carefully. "If this was for me ... would that even be possible? I'm already Bonded to you."

"That's why he talked to me about it first," Mollian rubbed the back of his neck. "He hadn't ever heard of it happening, and he knew I'd probably have a better understanding of the logistics behind it, or at least know where to look to find how a second Bond might affect you."

Merriam closed her fist around the vial. "I'm assuming since this exists, you decided it was plausible?"

"It's ... possible, yes. At the very least, I don't think it will hurt you. Our *mehhen* bond muddies the science a little, but in the way that since we're already tied together, if anyone's body could handle it, it would be yours."

"Can I ... can I Bond myself to him now, though?"

"The magic is still in his blood, same as it was when he drew it," Mollian said softly.

Merriam gently placed the vial back in the box, replacing the lid. "Is there even a point to it now?" Her voice wavered.

Mollian tucked her hair behind her ear, offering an empathetic smile. "That's up to you."

Over a week had gone by, and Merriam hadn't once touched the box that now sat on her nightstand, waiting for her decision. Mollian was slowly slipping into his brother's prior roles, and she was slowly slipping away.

She tried her best to get back to a routine, but her mind wouldn't focus. She'd wander up to the library and end up spending hours just staring at the bookshelf. She'd go to the training room and lean against the wall in the back, watching everything blankly. She had half a memory of Rovin trying to provoke her at some point, but she'd only looked at him blankly, not even registering the words.

Spending the evenings with Mollian was the only thing that brought her back to life for a little bit. He was her tether to the world, keeping her from fully floating away in her grief. She knew that he was in contact with the mercenaries, but she couldn't find the mental energy to try to visit them or even write a note. Whenever she thought about them, she was consumed with guilt at being away in the middle of such a big job. So Merriam didn't think about them.

Most of her time was spent tempering down the despair and anguish that rolled through her almost constantly. If it weren't for Mollian, she didn't know how she would have survived the pain.

She was lying on the couch, trying her best to read a book, when

Mollian came in one evening.

"I have to go out tonight," he said in greeting, resting a hand on her head as he walked by.

Merriam sat up straight, blinking at him in confusion. "What do you mean?"

"I have to have supper with some dignitaries. It's completely unavoidable. I've already declined twice."

Merriam stood, following him to his room as he changed into something more fitting for formal dining. "But, Molli–"

"I'm sorry, Ria. You know I want nothing more than to stay here with you, but I have obligations now ... and I can't neglect them forever."

Merriam frowned. "I'm not talking about forever, just ... just for now."

"I can't," Mollian said more firmly.

Merriam bit her lip, and the depth of her selfishness slammed into her, making her throat ache with the effort of holding back tears. "I'm sorry, Molli. I promise I'm going to be here for whatever you need. You're going through so much, and I've been—"

"Hey, we're okay. Always." Mollian pulled her into a hug, holding her tightly. "We both need time to adjust to what this life is. But *we* are always okay. We'll always have each other."

"Always," Merriam agreed, taking a deep breath. "Maybe I'll go out tonight. Just take a walk or something to get me out of the castle."

"That sounds marvelous. Do you think you'll visit the mercs?"

Merriam shrugged. "Maybe, but ... I don't know."

"Well, be safe, okay?"

"Of course," Merriam promised.

Soon after Mollian left, Merriam went to her room to put on a fresh pair of clothes. She'd slowly transitioned to wearing most of her own things, but she hadn't left her rooms today and was still in a shirt of *his* that she'd slept in.

As she was about to leave the room, Merriam's eyes landed on the box on her nightstand, and she walked over to open it.

The vial rested in her palm, the glass cool against her skin, a harsh contrast to the heat of anger that welled up inside of her. Anger at herself and her concern with the thoughts of other people. The dull ache she'd been living with since his death spread through her, alive and fresh.

She returned the vial to the box, clumsily lacing up her boots and stalking from the door, barely remembering to attach a small coin purse to her belt as she left.

Merriam walked briskly through the castle, emotions rolling under her skin in intolerable waves. Stepping into the first tavern she crossed, she ordered a glass of dark liquor, drinking it down swiftly before ordering another. And another.

The warmth of the alcohol subdued the heat of her hurt, and she leaned into the feeling, letting out a breath of relief at how good it was to feel nothing at all.

Merriam signaled for another drink, and soon enough her whole body felt numb and weightless, and she smiled.

Chapter 41

You're drunk, Mer

Rovin was about to follow some of the other Rangers into a tavern when he saw a flash of pale blonde hair across the street. "You guys go ahead. I'll catch up with you later," he called to his friends. They nodded non-committally, slipping inside.

He stepped into the road, watching as Merriam tripped over her feet, catching herself against a building. Annoyance bubbled up inside of him. She was drunk. She was drunk to the point where she was going to get herself hurt.

"Whoa there, sweet thing. Do you need a hand?" A husky male walked up to her, grabbing her elbow.

Rovin stiffened, hand going to the hilt of the short sword at his hip.

Merriam shook off the male's grip. "No, I'm fine."

Rovin started walking over to them.

"You don't look fine. Let me give you a hand. I can take you home." The male reached out to touch her shoulder.

Merriam's body tensed, and she shrunk against the wall, trying to get out of his reach. "Leave me alone," she slurred as he took a step closer.

"She's going home with me," Rovin called, closing the distance between them.

The male looked back in surprise at being confronted, and Merriam brought her knee up sharply into his groin.

He groaned and bent double. "You little bitch." He seethed, moving to grab Merriam.

Rovin stepped between them, partly unsheathing his sword. "I'd take a moment to think through your actions," he warned coolly.

"Prick," the male grunted, turning and limping away.

"Come on," Rovin turned to Merriam. "Let's get you home."

Merriam's eyes burned hot as she glared at Rovin. "I'm not going anywhere with you. Who do you even think you are, interfering in my business like that?"

Rovin scoffed, "The appropriate response for my saving your ass would be 'thank you.'"

"I was *fine*," she hissed through her teeth.

"Okay, fine." Rovin allowed, not in the mood to argue. "Now, will you just come with me?"

"No." Merriam pushed off the wall and stalked down the road.

"Mer." Rovin's fingers brushed her arm.

"Don't *touch* me!" She whirled on him, and for a moment he was sure she was going to strike him.

"I'm sorry, I won't. Will you come back to the castle?"

"No, I told you, I'm not going anywhere with you." She hiccuped and started to walk away again.

Rovin grit his teeth and followed a pace behind. "Where are you going, then?"

"Anywhere I damn well please," she huffed.

A frustrated sigh blew from Rovin's lips as he steeled himself for a long night.

They walked in silence for a few paces. She stumbled once, catching herself on a lamppost. She shot a glare over her shoulder as though his presence were the cause of her clumsiness. "Why are you stalking me, creep?"

"Mollian would have my ass if I didn't make sure you got home safely."

Merriam rolled her eyes. "Molli doesn't own me." She faced him and folded her arms across her chest. "And I don't report to him, either. I can take care of myself." She looked like a stubborn child, blonde waves falling wildly instead of tied in her customary braid.

Rovin pushed a hand through his hair in frustration, trying to reason with her. "I don't mean he owns you; I mean he'd be worried about you out by yourself when you're clearly intoxicated."

"His worry isn't my responsibility," she said with finality, but a flash of guilt crossed her face with the words. She whirled around so quickly Rovin was surprised she didn't fall flat on her ass, her long hair fanning out and smacking him across the chest.

"You're insufferable." He matched her pace this time. "If you won't go back to the castle with me, I'll just stay with you all night."

"Have I ever told you you're an enormous pain in the ass?" The smile she shot him was almost sickeningly sweet, but the look in her eyes might have been lethal if she were fae.

"Actually, no. At least, not to my face," he answered.

"Legends, you're actually the most annoying person on this planet."

"That's comical, coming from you." He rolled his eyes.

She bristled, picking up the pace. "You're killing off my innerbration. Inebridation. Interbation," she grumbled.

"I'm sure." Rovin rolled his eyes as he followed her into a bar.

She slid onto a barstool and called to the bartender, "Three shots, surprise us."

Rovin sat down beside her, leaning one elbow against the counter. "Three?"

"Don't worry, one's for you." She didn't even look at him as she accepted the glasses from the bartender and said, "It's on him."

Rovin glared at her, but dug into his pocket to toss the man a few coppers. "If I'm paying, why do you get two?" He dragged a glass across the bar to rest in front of him.

"Because if you insist on subjecting me to your presence all night, I'm going to need to be a Hel of a lot more drunk." She clinked her glass against his and tossed it down.

"That makes two of us," he replied, and let the fiery liquid slide down his throat.

"Why are you here, anyway?" Merriam asked, twirling the last shot around in her fingers for a moment before drinking it down. "How did you find me, I mean?" She peeked up at him, amber eyes glistening with drunkenness and searching his.

Drunk or not, he wasn't sure she'd ever made this much eye contact with him, and it almost made him lose his train of thought. "I was out with some of the Rangers after work."

Merriam looked him up and down before meeting his gaze again. "You really ditched your friends to get berated all night?"

Rovin snorted. "I guess I did."

"Fucking psycho." Merriam shook her head and signaled to the bartender again.

This time, she ordered them each a stein of blackberry mead. Rovin wanted to caution her about mixing alcohols, but bit his tongue against it, figuring it was probably too late for that snippet of advice, anyway.

Merriam chugged the drink and wiped the back of her hand across her mouth as she set the cup back on the bar. She slid down from her stool, pushing her hair out of her face. When Rovin turned to follow, she held her hand up. "Steady there, Ranger-man. I'm just going to go dance."

Rovin arched an eyebrow. "Ranger-man?"

Merriam waved vaguely. "Ranger-male. Does that make your half-fae ego feel better?" Then she turned and pranced off.

Rovin leaned back against the bar, sipping on his mead. He watched as she twirled around in front of the musicians, weaving between other dancers in a way that might have been graceful three or four drinks ago. A man approached her, offering his hand. Rovin watched closely, ready to intervene, but Merriam just wrinkled her nose at him and spun away.

Rovin ordered a cup of water and left it sitting on the counter, nursing his drink as he continued to survey the bar. His eyes kept straying to the mercenary, who was lost in the lively music. His own morals demanded that he make sure she made it back to the castle safely, regardless of the annoyance he felt at giving up his only free night this rotation to mind her drunken antics.

But that frustration was accompanied by guilt. He'd been conditioned to despise her from the beginning. Ferrick had met with Rovin and the other younger Rangers the night after Mollian had first brought Merriam to train with the Guard and told them she thought she could do what she pleased because the young prince was enamored by her. Rovin had idolized the captain back then, and the Hel he'd pushed through to earn his place among Sekha's best warriors was still fresh in his mind. It had been embarrassingly easy for Ferrick to sway him against Merriam, and his disdain for her had only snowballed from there.

It had been so effortless to hate her, to believe the picture he'd been painted of a girl who wanted nothing but to take the easiest route to a life of luxury. He'd been so thick-headed and, he could now admit to himself, obtuse, he never thought to question that view until he'd learned she wasn't even from this world. His initial thought was to hate her more for it, but he couldn't imagine being pulled from everything he'd ever known and having to figure out a new life for himself.

And then she'd challenged him. And she'd won.

She'd beaten him, and then a flurry of emotions had crossed her face. He wanted to talk to her, force her to have it out with him verbally so they could figure out their differences and put all the childish shit aside. Clearly, she'd done something right. Skill recognized skill, and he knew on some basal level it would be better to have her as an ally than an enemy. But she was already disappearing into a tree.

That hadn't gone well, obviously.

The mercenary continued to get under his skin and push him at every opportunity, it seemed. Tonight was slowly turning the tide back in his mind, pushing away thoughts of wanting to work with her. The entire kingdom was under attack by a demon from another realm, her whole troupe still helping the Guard search for Basta, and what was she doing? Out getting shitfaced without a care in the world.

On the dance floor, Merriam bumped into a male, stumbling back a few steps with an apologetic smile. The male returned the apology, offering his hand, which Merriam accepted. She danced with him for the rest of the song, and he bowed away from her as it ended.

Rovin watched warily, breathing a sigh of relief when the male left on his own. He could be having a couple of beers with his friends, relaxing after a long week so he could jump into the next rotation refreshed, but he was here instead. *Pet-sitting for the prince.* "You're a fucking prick," he muttered to himself, unamused by the irony of the guilt that washed over him with his thoughts.

Merriam made her way back to the bar when the musicians took a break. Her face was flushed, freckles almost blending into the red on her cheeks, and she gathered her hair up off her neck for a few moments, holding it on top of her head.

Rovin pushed the water closer to her.

Merriam rolled her eyes, letting her hair fall as she drank. "I want another mead, too." She hiccuped loudly and slapped her hand to her mouth.

"I don't think you need one."

Her eyes narrowed into that deathly glare. "I could give a fuck what you think. I'm still not even sure why you're here." She leaned heavily against the bar. "I'm going to the bathroom. Don't bother with the drink. I'll order it myself after." She spun on her heel and stumbled off towards the doors at the back.

With a frustrated sigh, Rovin motioned to the bartender. "Another mead, please. But cut it with water. Heavily." He slid an extra copper across the bar.

"Glad I'm not the one looking after her. She seems like a handful."

Rovin pushed a hand through his hair. "You have no idea," he breathed.

Merriam came back and eyed the mead for a moment before taking a few long gulps. Rovin steeled himself, ready for her to go off on him for watering it down. But she just gave him that sarcastically saccharine smile. "Look at you being so accommodating."

Rovin finished his drink and set the stein on the bar. "You're a brat," he told her.

She stuck her tongue out at him and took another sip. When she hiccuped again, he reached over to take the cup from her. "Stop!" She jerked it back, sloshing a little over her shirt. "Get your own."

"You're drunk, Mer. Give me the cup and let's go home."

"I'm at a bar, Rovin. That's the fucking point." She wavered a little on her feet, bringing the cup to her lips again.

Rovin felt the heat of anger rush through his veins. "You're acting like a fucking child. There's no reason for you to be out here making a damn fool of yourself. Get your shit together. Go home and sleep it off so you can do your fucking job." It took all of his restraint to keep from shouting it at her.

Merriam's eyes were a molten amber, simmering with rage and a pain buried so deep he hadn't seen it before. Her mouth narrowed to a thin line, and she tossed the rest of the mead into his face before slamming the cup on the counter and stalking out of the bar.

"For fuck's sake." Rovin groaned, wiping his sleeve across his cheeks before standing up and storming after her.

"Merriam!" he called when he hit the street, quickly spotting her stomping along.

"Leave me alone, Rovin!" she screamed over her shoulder.

Rovin quickly caught up to her in her drunken state.

"I don't want to fucking look at you!" Her voice was angry and tight.

"Then don't. But I'm still going to make sure you get home in one piece. Regardless of that fucking stunt you just pulled."

Merriam laughed bitterly. "Fuck you, Rovin." She cut into a side alley and launched herself up to grab the base of a ladder that hung on the side of the building.

Rovin was almost too impressed with her ability to swing her feet up to the first rung in her current state to be mad, but he followed her, grabbing for her ankle.

"What are you going to do? Pull me down and rip my fucking leg open again?" Her voice wavered, dangerously close to tears.

Rovin immediately let go, stepping back. An emotion he either couldn't or wouldn't name settled like a cold stone in his stomach. He let her get about halfway up before reaching to pull himself onto the ladder and climb after her.

When he got to the top, he found her sitting with her legs over the edge of the flat rooftop. He dragged his boots noisily as he came up beside her, not wanting to scare her. She was way too drunk to catch herself or land properly if she fell.

Tears streamed silently down her cheeks, and she hugged her arms around herself miserably as he sat next to her. He didn't know what to say, and he sure as Hel knew she didn't want *him* touching her right now, so he just sat there in silence, close enough to feel the heat rolling off of her in the cool night air.

"I just wanted to forget for a little while," she whispered, wiping a hand across her eyes and sniffling. "I hurt. I hurt all the time and I just wanted to forget that I hurt."

Rovin turned to look at her. Her face was turned up to the sky now, starlight shimmering in her tear-filled eyes. She fell back heavily onto the roof, but she didn't make a sound as she continued staring up at the stars, tears slipping down her face and wetting her hair.

Settling down beside her, Rovin rested his hands on his chest, watching the constellations in silence.

Her breathing evened out, and she finally relaxed her arms, letting them fall to her sides. "He asked me to marry him," she said plainly.

Rovin turned toward her, rising up on an elbow. His mind connected all the dots at once, and remorse tightened painfully in his chest. "I'm so sorry. I didn't know."

Merriam gave a little shrug. "Nobody did. I wanted it that way." She reached up to fiddle with the aspen leaf at her throat. "I told him that I'd already dealt with enough earning a place here outside of my relationship with Molli. I told him it would've been too frustrating trying to reinforce my reputation if we went public. And now he's dead. He's dead, and no one knows we ever claimed each other. He's dead, and I wasn't even given the right to lay him to rest." Her voice was soft as she spilled her heart out to the sky.

"I loved him so much. But he loved me more - loved me enough to put my wants over his. And now I don't get to love him at all." She covered her face with her hands as fresh tears spilled down her cheeks. "He's dead, and he died thinking I wouldn't marry him. I never got to tell him ..." her voice broke on a sob, "tell him I wanted to be his wife ... tell him I wanted the world to know I loved him."

Rovin's whole body went cold. How could he not have noticed her pain? He'd seen her on the ground, screaming mindlessly after Oren had been killed. He'd seen her brutally and mercilessly assassinate every demon left in that cave. He'd seen her wandering the halls of the castle, a phantom of her former self. And tonight he'd chastised her for being drunk. Her heart had shattered, and he'd been too annoyed and calloused to even try to see it.

What hurt him the most was knowing it was his fault she'd felt the need to hide. Regardless of what Ferrick may have told him all those years ago, he was the one who chose to constantly berate her and forced her to prove herself over and over and over again. He's the one who chose to rally the rest of the Guard against her in the beginning and force her out. For no reason other than that her existence had been forced to merge with his. He couldn't blame her for hating him. He hated himself.

She would have been his queen.

The realization hit sudden and hard, sinking like a stone in his gut. She would have been his queen, and he had tormented her relentlessly since the moment he'd met her. His frustration at the opportunity she'd been given—the opportunity he had fought tooth and nail for—cracked down the middle, and he saw it for the jealousy that it truly was. He'd first let himself glimpse it after they'd fought in the courtyard: after she'd bested him. But he'd been afraid to examine it too closely.

Like an idiot with too large an ego, he'd pushed back against recognizing her strength and determination, too caught up in appearances and his own standing in the Guard. He shook his head, pushing his disgust with his actions down. This wasn't about him.

"Mer, I am so, so sorry." He couldn't even bring himself to ask for forgiveness. He had no right.

"It doesn't matter now," she murmured, eyes closed. "None of it matters now." She folded her arms tight across her middle as her voice trailed off.

Rovin's heart cracked seeing her like this—so empty of her usual fire, so broken. He wanted to hold her, to comfort her somehow, but he didn't dare.

Her eyes fluttered open, and she sat up abruptly, freckles in stark contrast against her now pale-as-snow skin. "I think I'm going to—" Merriam barely had time to turn to the side before vomiting, heaving up the copious amount of liquid she'd consumed.

Rovin kneeled next to her and gathered her hair in his hands, holding it back from her face as she continued to empty her stomach. Slowly, he brought his hand up to her back, rubbing in soothing circles. "Atta girl," he said softly. "Get it all out."

When she had nothing left to bring up, she sagged limply against him. He pulled up the hem of his shirt, wiping off her mouth.

"I want to go home," she whimpered, eyes closed.

"Okay, come on." He slipped one arm around her shoulders and one under her knees, hoisting her up. She was a dead weight in his arms, head lolling against his chest. "I need your help to get off the roof, Mer." He shook her gently.

Her eyelids fluttered, and she shook her head, shifting to wrap her arms around his neck.

"Do you think you can hold on to me while I climb down?" he asked, her hair brushing against his lips.

She nodded, and he shifted his hold so that her legs could wrap around his waist.

He carefully reached his foot to the top rung of the ladder, keeping one arm tucked underneath her to help support her weight. When he was sure she could hold on with her own strength, he painstakingly made his way down to the ground.

His feet hit the cobblestones of the alley, and he rubbed her back to rouse her. "Do you think you can walk?"

Merriam shook her head against his neck, arms tightening around his shoulders.

"Okay, I need to set you down for just a second so I can get a better grip." He pushed at her waist, and she dropped her legs from him. Her arms stayed loosely wrapped around him, and he swept her up again, legs dangling to one side.

She burrowed against his neck. "You smell like ... like dead leaves ..." she mumbled against his skin.

"Sorry to offend, pet," he grunted, shifting her weight slightly.

"Leaves and ... apples," she sighed, and her fingers curled into the hair at the nape of his neck.

Rovin stiffened at the touch, tossing his head to dislodge her.

His entire body ached by the time he made it into the castle. The guards at the gate had given him strange looks, but let him through without a word.

Rovin stared miserably at the staircase, gritting his teeth before starting the ascent. The guards outside of her chambers watched him curiously as he walked up. "Mind opening the door for me?"

"Yes, Lieutenant," one of them scrambled into movement.

Mollian looked up as Rovin crossed the threshold, immediately setting down the weapon he was working on and rushing over. "What happened? Is she okay?" He held out his arms to take Merriam.

Rovin stepped past him. "Where's her bed?" When Mollian pointed to a door, Rovin walked as he explained. "She's an incompetent drunk." He waited for Mollian to open the door for him before continuing. "I saw her stumbling around and wanted to make sure she got home safely. She puked her guts up, so she probably won't be feeling too hot in the morning."

Mollian slipped into the bathroom, returning with a glass of water as Rovin set Merriam down on the unmade bed. Rovin slipped an arm underneath her, propping her up as he took the glass of water from Mollian. "Mer, you need to drink." He held the glass to her lips.

Merriam's eyes fluttered open, and she glared weakly at Rovin before obeying.

"Atta girl." Rovin let her lie back down.

Mollian removed her boots and socks, dropping them to the floor.

"Can you help me with her clothes?"

Rovin nodded, though a little taken aback.

"We're going to get you into something clean, okay, Ria?" Mollian smoothed her hair, and she nodded weakly.

Mollian grabbed a shirt from an armoire across the room and pulled her upright, peeling her top off and discarding it next to her boots on the floor. Rovin helped get her into the new shirt.

"You seem like you've done this before," the Ranger remarked as Mollian untied her pants and pulled them from her legs, leaving her in only a shirt and underwear before tucking a blanket around her. Merriam sighed, rolling onto her side and curling into a ball.

Mollian shrugged, offering a small smile. "You should have seen the first few times she got drunk off of faerie wine. Makes this look like nothing." Mollian fondly rubbed her back through the blanket. "Of course, she's done the same thing for me at least as many times, if not more."

For the second time that night, Rovin was struck with guilt so powerful his chest ached. Here was yet another male who clearly cared about Merriam more than Rovin had ever cared about anything in his entire life. "I'm sorry. For everything," he said lamely, but his eyes were sincere as he met Mollian's cracked brown and green gaze.

The prince waved him off. "It's in the past," he said simply. "Thank you for looking out for her."

Rovin just nodded, turning his attention to Merriam and brushing a few strands of hair from her cheek. "You're still insufferable," he said gently, and her lips twitched into a semblance of a smile.

Mollian watched him, gauging the softness of the encounter. "Do you know?"

Rovin awkwardly pushed his hand through his hair, stepping back. "I didn't before tonight. I mean, I knew they were close. I used it to rile her up ... but I didn't know, not the full extent of it."

Mollian sat on the bed next to Merriam, watching her sleep as he nodded.

Rovin shoved his hands into his pockets. "I feel terrible."

"Don't. It was her choice, so don't punish yourself." He smoothed her hair from her face. "I wish she'd stop punishing herself for it." He sighed. "He knew. Even if she never got the chance to say it out loud, he knew how she felt."

Rovin swallowed hard. "I had no idea how badly she was hurting ..."

Mollian looked up, white curls slipping over his forehead. "I don't know how much of this she's going to remember tomorrow."

Rovin held his hands up. "Don't worry, I won't say anything to her unless she approaches me first. I won't push her so hard anymore, though. I don't think I could stomach it."

"Who knew you were such an empath, Arwood?"

"You'd better keep it to yourself if you know what's good for you, Stonebane." Rovin's threat was undermined with a tentatively friendly smile. It faltered as he remembered his future king now sat in front of him, and he straightened. "I'll get out of your hair."

He turned to leave, and as he shut the door, he saw Mollian lie on his back next to Merriam. She uncurled from her ball to stretch out alongside him, hands tucked daintily under her chin and forehead nestled comfortably against his arm. She visibly relaxed as she breathed him in, knowing she was somewhere safe and familiar.

Rovin softly closed the door, watching the beam of lamplight wink out underneath.

That emotion—the one that he wouldn't allow himself to decipher—bloomed in his chest as he left their suite to head back to his own shared barracks.

Chapter 42

Back to square one

MERRIAM SLIPPED INTO CONSCIOUSNESS with confusion. She felt like she was slowly spinning, and she blinked in the darkness, trying to orient herself. Mollian was beside her, that much she knew, and his presence calmed her slightly.

"Molli, where are we?" she mumbled, pushing herself into a sitting position. A splitting headache bloomed behind her temples, and she groaned, rubbing the heel of her hand against her eye. As her vision adjusted to the darkness, she began to recognize her room. "Molli," she shook his shoulder.

"I'm sleeping," he shifted, dislodging her hand.

"How did I get here?" She wrapped her arms around her stomach, which felt horribly queasy, and fell to the side, her head resting on the base of Mollian's chest and moving with the gentle rise and fall of his breathing.

Mollian rested a hand on her head. "Rovin brought you home."

Merriam's whole body stiffened, and she gingerly sat back up, trying not to aggravate her headache. "What?"

"Rovin, you know, the Ranger who hates you? He saw you out drunk off your ass and made sure you got back safely." Mollian finally peeled open one eye, blinking up at her.

"The last thing I remember is ..." Merriam's brow furrowed, "walking outside and looking at the stars. And maybe climbing a ladder?" She ran a hand down her face. "Is there water?"

Mollian grabbed the glass from the nightstand and handed it over. "I don't know anything about a ladder, but I got the impression you gave our favorite lieutenant quite the run for his money tonight before he carried you home," he explained as she drank.

Merriam grimaced. "He *carried* me?"

"Hard to walk when you're passed out, so ..."

"Shit," she said with a small shake of her head before finishing the last of the water in the glass.

"Possibly not your finest moment."

"I'm surprised he didn't just leave me to my own stupidity."

Mollian rolled onto his side, propping up on one elbow to look at her. "I know he's never been your biggest fan, but he's not a monster. Plus, he rightly assumed that if anything had happened to you and he'd knowingly left you out there alone, he would have been in some deep shit."

"Look at you getting all protective and kingly," Merriam joked, turning to set the empty glass on the other nightstand before settling down onto her pillow.

"I've got a role to fill now."

Merriam pushed back the wave of grief that rolled through her. "You do."

Sadness washed over Mollian's features, barely discernible in the dark. "He would have been so much better," he whispered. "I just want to make him proud, to be good for Sekha the way he would have been."

Merriam reached out to clasp his hand, squeezing tightly. "He would be so proud of you and everything you've been doing to take care of his country," she told him, eyes welling with tears. "And I promise not to let you do a shit job of it."

Mollian laughed quietly, squeezing back. "Good, because I'm going to need all the help I can get."

Merriam let her eyes flutter closed, sinking back into sleep. "You underestimate yourself, Prince. You have always been amazing at whatever you put your mind to."

ℓ

A bright beam of sunlight woke Merriam the next morning, shining through the small gap in her curtains and falling across her eyes. She rolled over with a groan, head pounding.

Her bed was empty, but she heard Mollian moving around in their common room before she had a chance to panic. Slowly, she dropped her legs over the side of the bed, screwing her eyes shut and pressing her hands to her temples before standing and stumbling from her room.

"Good morning, sunshine," Mollian grinned, taking a bite from a slice of toast piled high with scrambled eggs.

Merriam scowled, plucking some toast from the platter on the table before sitting down next to him and leaning into the couch cushions. "You're dropping eggs everywhere."

"And you're going to get crumbs all over," he replied pleasantly. Leaning forward, he grabbed a couple of small capsules from the side of the tray and held them out to Merriam.

She let him drop them into her palm, leaning forward just long enough to take a swig from a glass of juice to wash them down before reclining again, resting her head on Mollian's shoulder. She ripped a chunk from the bread in her hand. "I feel like shit," she said around the mouthful.

Mollian dropped his head to rest on top of hers. "The medicine should help with the headache soon," he offered.

Merriam just grunted in response, taking another bite.

Several slices of toast and a handful of bacon later, Merriam was filling up a glass of water from the bathroom sink as Mollian dressed.

"You gonna live?" he asked.

"Yeah, I'll be fine." She leaned against the sink, brow furrowing as she took a long sip. "Well, possibly. There are things I need to do today that I'm not looking forward to."

Mollian ruffled her hair, offering a sympathetic smile. "I've got faith it will all work out."

Merriam swatted his hand away, leaving him to finish getting ready.

⟨ℓ⟩

The streets were busy, the market in full swing by the time Merriam ventured out. Her fingers nervously danced across the decorated handles of her axes as she walked. Their weight at her hips was a comfort, and she weaved her way through the shoppers, absorbing the energy and life that surrounded her.

She realized with a pang that this was probably one of the first markets since the mountain. All of Umbra would have been in mourning after losing their future king, but life had to go on. Vendors had wares to sell, and people still needed to buy food and other necessities. The knowledge that what would have been *his* people could pick up their lives with such apparent ease while she felt like her entire heart had been shattered tightened her chest, and she pressed a fist against her sternum as she slipped into an alley and away from the bustle of the market.

Merriam was soon staring up at the merc house, her heartbeat quick with anxiety. She licked her lips before slipping quietly through the back door.

She heard sounds coming from the training room, but also the creak of the floor as someone shifted in the office upstairs. Taking a deep breath, she made her way up and knocked before nudging the door open with a foot.

Jasper sat at the desk, his eyes flicking up as she walked in.

Merriam stilled, her throat unexpectedly closing as tears blurred her vision.

Before she could say anything, Jasper stood from his chair and crossed the room to her. He pulled her to his chest, his arms and wings wrapping around her and one hand holding the back of her head.

Merriam couldn't hold back the tears, crying as she clung to him. The smell of oakmoss and sea salt surrounded her, and the heat of him seeped into her bones, long cold and weary with grief.

"I'm sorry I disappeared," she said when she'd composed herself enough to talk.

Jasper's arms tightened around her. "You don't get to apologize right now, Mer. You don't have anything to apologize *for*."

"We're in the middle of a job—"

"You just lost someone very important to you in an extremely traumatic way," Jasper interrupted. "No one has the right to tell you how you should deal with that, just as no one has the right to expect you to handle your grief in a specific way. You needed time to process it. We were always going to be here when you needed us."

Merriam pulled away to wipe the heel of her hand underneath her eyes, sniffling. "I feel like I abandoned you all."

"Not one of us feels that way, Mer," Jasper reassured her. "I know you never officially told us about your relationship with him, but Calysta informed the others after what happened in the mountain. I had my suspicions for a little while, just based on the differences in you both. Deductive reasoning did the rest."

Merriam gave a watery smile. "I was going to tell you all. That last night when we drank together, I was going to bring him here so you all could know him like I knew him. But then Molli was gone ... and everything just happened so quickly after that." She wrapped her arms around her torso, and Jasper pulled her to him again.

"I know, and I cannot tell you how sorry I am for your loss and for the grief you're experiencing. Sekha lost a king, I lost a friend, but you lost something much more important than any of that."

Merriam let him hold her for a while longer, soaking up his steady strength. "Nobody is angry with me for disappearing?"

"Not at all," Jasper promised.

Merriam sighed. "I came here half-expecting to grovel."

Jasper held her at arm's length, giving her a sharp look. "If you weren't dumb with grief, I'd shake you for thinking that we care so little."

Merriam shrugged, dropping her eyes. "I left without a word to any of you; your anger would be understandable."

Jasper shook his head, silver eyes soft with compassion. "Nonsense. Do you feel ready to see the others?"

Merriam nodded, wiping the last of the tears from her cheeks. "I'm ready to get back into things. I *need* to get back into things. I have to have something to focus on or I don't think I'll ever be okay."

"Let's go get you caught up, then," Jasper said with a smile, gesturing with one hand for her to lead the way downstairs.

Merriam went to the kitchen for some water, still nursing her hangover, while Jasper ducked into the training room to collect everyone.

"Mer!" Aleah ran up behind her, jumping onto her back.

Merriam laughed, water sloshing onto the floor before she had a chance to set the cup down. Aleah dropped, giving Merriam a chance to turn around and throw her arms around the redhead.

"I'm so happy you're back!" Aleah's arms tightened around Merriam, and she dropped her voice. "And I'm so, so sorry. I can't even imagine what Hel you've been in."

Merriam squeezed her back. "I'll be okay," she replied.

Campbell and Calysta joined the two in a large embrace, and Merriam's heart swelled with love for these people.

When the four finally split up, her eyes found Leonidas leaning casually against the entrance to the kitchen. He smiled at her, spreading out an arm, and she walked over, sliding her arms around his waist. "It's good to have you back, Mer," he said, giving her a squeeze.

Panic screeched from the perch above them, and Merriam held her arm out to him as Leonidas pulled away. "Thank you for coming to see me, buddy," she cooed as he lighted on her forearm. Turning her attention from the bird, she looked at the group gathered in the kitchen. "Tell me what's been going on."

"We've been staying in touch with the Rangers, who are keeping an eye out for Basta, but he's been suspiciously quiet. No new reports of demon activity in Jekeida. We've also heard from Gressia that he hasn't been back to Entumbra," Jasper explained.

"So basically, we're back to square one," Merriam sighed.

"Except this time we know what to look for. We know what to prepare for," Leonidas amended.

(ℓ)

Merriam walked back to the castle with her heart lighter than it had been in weeks, despite the weight of the conversation. Being around her friends had done her so much good, and she resigned herself to keep busy from now on. If she was moving or focusing, she wouldn't have time to be lost in despair.

The sun had just set, and she decided to cut through the courtyard and run a few rounds with her axes before supper, since it had been a while.

As she rounded a blind corner, she almost ran straight into Rovin. She jumped back, a sharp retort ready on the tip of her tongue.

The Ranger raised an eyebrow at her, but his deep brown eyes were soft and ... playful? "Look who's alive."

Merriam cocked her head to the side. "What, no smart comment about watching where I'm going? Staying out of your big important lieutenant way?"

Rovin snorted, running a hand through his hair. "I'm too tired from chasing you all over Umbra last night to come up with anything with enough bite to make it worth it."

"Mmm, well, no one told you you had to." Merriam folded her arms across her chest.

"Mmm, well, no one told you how to handle your liquor, so ..." Rovin shrugged. "As a Ranger of the Royal Guard, it's my job to serve and protect the Crown and its assets."

Rolling her eyes, Merriam dropped her hands to her hips. "Well, serve and protect where you're wanted in the future, thank you."

Rovin matched her stance, the mimicry lighting a spark of irritation in her chest. "Seemed pretty wanted when I carried you home, which you're welcome for, by the way."

Merriam wanted to shove him against the wall and wipe the smug grin off his face. His actions were so confusing, she could find no response but to glare at him.

"Killed my arms. And back. And chest, in case you were wondering. I could hardly swing a sword today. Wasn't expecting the upper-body workout last night. Too bad you missed it; would've given you some great material to throw at me in future arguments."

"I think you've actually lost your mind," Merriam stated.

"Don't hurt yourself thinking too hard. I've met my good deed quota for the week and won't be coming to your rescue this time, pet." Rovin gave her a mock salute before turning and continuing on his way.

Merriam stared after him, mouth agape at the bizarre interaction. *What the fuck happened last night?*

Chapter 43

You'd remember

ALMOST A WEEK HAD passed, and Merriam had thrown herself completely back into training and hunting for Basta. All of her time was spent running drills with the mercs, rounding up any information from their contacts, and honing skills by herself at the castle when she left her friends. She fell into bed exhausted every night and was thankful for it. She didn't have time to feel grief when she was constantly on the move.

Merriam stood in the courtyard, breathing heavily as she reached behind her for another arrow and found her quiver empty. Dropping the bow and quiver, she pulled training axes from her belt and whirled toward the nearest target, dipping and turning in fluid, practiced movements as she struck. Her mind was blessedly empty; nothing except for her weapons and the target existed.

"The Rangers have the ring reserved soon."

The voice broke her concentration, and she whirled around, pale braid swinging over her shoulders. She panted, face glistening with sweat. "I'm busy," she said coolly, tucking one axe underneath her arm and wiping her forehead against a shirtsleeve.

Rovin tossed her a skin of water. "I wasn't trying to interrupt, but it didn't look like you were going to be taking a breather any time soon."

Merriam caught the water, begrudgingly taking a few long pulls. "I wasn't," she replied when she drank her fill, tossing the skin back to him and then turning to the wooden dummy, shifting her feet into a fighting stance.

"Really, it's reserved," Rovin said before she could swing an axe. Merriam faced him in exasperation, amber eyes burning with a fight. "But you're more than welcome to join us if you want," he continued.

Merriam's mouth popped open, her arms dropping to her sides. "What?"

"You've led enough sessions teaching them demon-fighting strategy. No one would begrudge your joining in on a normal round if you're not opposed to the company." Rovin shrugged, pushing a hand casually through his hair.

"Did I ... did we ... did we fuck?"

"When in this Legends-blessed world was that supposed to have happened?" He snorted.

"I don't remember much from the other night ... and it's weird that you're being so ... nice." Merriam eyed him suspiciously.

"You were drunk off your ass. I most certainly did not take advantage of you, but thank you for your confidence in my morals." Rovin gave her a withering look, stepping into the ring. "And just for the record, pet, if we had fucked, you'd remember," he said lowly as he passed her.

Merriam scoffed, but he'd already moved across the ring to warm up.

"Mer! Are we doing more demon training?" Evangeline asked, walking up with a timid but friendly smile.

"No, I was actually just—"

"Hey, stranger," Kodi interrupted as he entered the courtyard. "You trying to get your ass beat?" He smiled cheekily, twirling a practice sword in his hand.

Merriam raised a brow. "Well, I guess I can't back down from that challenge."

As more Rangers filtered into the courtyard, Rovin shifted into a full lieutenant persona, answering questions and issuing instructions to keep everyone organized as they prepared to train.

Evangeline had struck up a conversation with a couple of Rangers close by as she stretched, making sure to include Merriam. The mercenary was feeling oddly relaxed, laughing with the Rangers and enjoying running through exercises with them.

Rovin had complete command of the courtyard, and Merriam made a conscious effort not to stare at him. Despite how he'd treated her in the past, he was a good leader who clearly had the respect of the lower-ranking Rangers. Her lips pulled into a frown as she watched him interact with his comrades. He was encouraging, even in critique, and something bitter turned in her stomach as she wondered why his treatment of her had been so drastically different.

Trying to push the thought from her mind, she looked away just as Bellamy entered the courtyard. "Sorry I'm late, Lieutenant," he called to Rovin, who acknowledged him with a wave. His eyes landed on Merriam, and he smiled, walking over.

Merriam's face paled as her eyes trailed down the rugged scar that crossed Bellamy's face from brow to mouth. "Bell, I—" Her hands started to shake, and she clenched them into fists. Flashes of his wound fresh from the fight filled her mind, and with them, other memories from that day. Panic tightened her chest, and she blinked against the blur at the edges of her vision. "I'm sorry. I have to go."

Bellamy's head tipped to the side, his brow furrowing with concern. "Mer, are you okay?"

"I can't," she whispered, walking off without a backward glance.

Trying to force even breaths, she quickly made her way up to her rooms and cast out for a sense of Mollian.

She brought her hand to her mouth, stomach turning, and ran through the castle. As soon as the door to the antechamber was closed, she collapsed against the wall and slid down to the floor. "Fucking Hel," she whispered, and then completely broke down, sobs wracking her body and hands clasped over her mouth.

Guilt rolled through her, and she fell over onto her side, curling into a ball.

Mollian walked in a few moments later and fell to his knees as soon as he saw her. "Ria." He folded his legs in front of him and then gathered her into his lap. She clutched at his shirt, burying her face in his chest. His smell of spruce and plum wafted around her, but instead of calming her, it only made her cry harder, body shaking as she wished he smelled of deeper pine and clear night sky. As she wished he was his brother. "You're safe," Mollian soothed, running a hand in circles against her back. "Are you okay? What happened?"

Merriam shook her head against his chest.

"Breathe." He tucked her head under his chin and rocked her, arms circling her as if he could block out all of her pain or absorb it into himself. "Breathe."

When her sobs had subsided into a more gentle crying, he asked, "What happened?"

Merriam let out a shuddering sigh. "I miss him, Molli," her voice cracked. "I miss him all the time. Every second of every day. It's like I'm drowning."

Mollian hugged her tighter, knowing no words would offer the comfort she needed.

"The only time I feel like my head is above water is when I'm in motion. When I'm doing something that only requires muscle memory and I don't have to think. I can just shut my brain off." She sniffed, rubbing the heel of her hand across her eyes. "Lately, it's nice to feel nothing. Because nothing is better than the misery of knowing I'll never see him again."

"He loved you. More than I think he ever expected to love anybody," Mollian murmured against her hair.

A fresh wave of guilt hit her, and she pushed out of Mollian's lap and rested against the wall. She set her chin on her knees, brushing away the fresh tears slipping down her cheeks. "I was in the courtyard, running through some routines," she whispered, looking at a spot in the room over Mollian's shoulder. "Rovin interrupted me, but he invited me to join the Rangers. I watched him with them ... and I was jealous. Jealous that they never had to fight for the respect that I did. But then I saw Bellamy ... and his scar brought me back to that day, and I realized that I gave up a real relationship with ... with him for nothing. For whose approval? Why did I care so much, Molli?" She turned her gaze back to him.

There was no judgment in his eyes, just understanding. She sighed heavily, and he reached to brush away the last few tears that leaked from her eyes. "He never held that against you."

Merriam leaned her cheek into his palm. "It hurt him, though. I never got the chance to fix it."

"Do *not* punish yourself," Mollian replied, gently but firmly. "And don't you dare, even for a moment, think that you didn't make him happier than I'd ever seen him."

Merriam nodded, gently pushing his hand away and standing. "It was the strangest thing ... for a moment, I was actually having fun being with the Rangers. I didn't feel out of my element. Is that weird?"

"I don't think it should have to be," he answered simply.

Merriam moved to her bathroom, stripping her sweat-dampened clothes off as the tub filled with water. She knew she needed to get her emotions under control, that the constant need for movement was just a coping mechanism, but she wasn't ready to sit with her feelings yet. It was easier to repress and ignore and push through the pain that constantly flowed through her.

When she was chin deep in the tub, fragrant bubbles floating around her, Mollian rapped a knuckle on the door frame, popping his head in. "I, uh ... have some news."

Merriam gestured for him to come in, and he sat on the floor across from her, leaning against the wall with his head tilted back. "I'm going to Entumbra."

Merriam instantly sat up straight, water sloshing over the side of the tub with the abrupt movement. "You mean ..." she drifted off, her heart lurching into her throat at the thought of being here without him. "We haven't found Basta yet. It's too dangerous. What if he goes back for Gressia?"

"There are still Guard posted at Entumbra. We'll be protected, but I have to go ... If I'm to take the crown at thirty, I already have catching up to do." He ran a hand through his wild white curls.

Merriam gripped the edge of the tub, body turned to face him. "I still need you. I can't do this alone."

Mollian looked at her, sadness in his eyes. "I need you, too. But I have a duty to Sekha now. And I owe it to him to do everything I can to be the kind of king he would have been."

Tears filled Merriam's eyes, and she smiled softly. "He would be so proud of you. Always."

Mollian smiled, but his brow was furrowed. He was now heir to more responsibility than he'd ever wanted. His entire life had changed in a single moment, and one of the people he'd always depended on most wasn't even there to help him navigate it.

"When do you leave?"

"In a few days."

Merriam nodded, pressing her lips together. "I guess I'll be moving out, too. There's no reason for me to be here if you're gone. I also get the feeling I wouldn't be welcome."

"This is your home. Don't be ridiculous."

Merriam leveled him with a look. "You're my home, Molli, not this castle. And either way, I don't think I want to be here without you, anyway. I already have a room at the merc house. It'll be good for me to be around them instead of sequestered away here with a whole group of people who aren't my biggest fans."

"Sounds like they're warming up to you," Mollian pointed out.

"I probably traumatized poor Bell," Merriam groaned, wiping her hands over her face. "I took one look at his scar and dipped out."

"He seems like the understanding type," Mollian offered.

"I'll find him later to apologize. Pass me a towel?" Merriam held her hand out.

Mollian reached behind him, pulling one down from the rod on the wall and tossing it over. "Will you come with me? On the way there, I mean. You could also visit him ... say the goodbye you were denied ..."

Merriam wrapped the towel around herself, stepping from the tub. She stood for a moment, dripping water onto the mat beneath her feet.

Mollian rose from the ground, lifting her chin with a finger so that her eyes met his. "You deserve to say goodbye, Ria. It doesn't matter what's happened since he's been gone. He would want you to continue to live."

"I still love him so much. How do I even acknowledge that there's a part of me that wants to move on? That doesn't want to live in constant misery thinking of the things I should have done differently?"

Pale green eyes looked back into hers, reflecting a pain slightly different, but just as deep. "Come to Entumbra with me. Tell him all of these things yourself. The magic that flowed in his blood is the same as the magic that flows in the Gate. You'll feel him there," Mollian said softly, leaving her to finish getting dressed.

Merriam chewed on her bottom lip as she brushed through her hair, leaving the waves to tumble freely down her back. She slipped into an oversized shirt—one of his, which she tied into a knot at her waist—and a pair of leggings. Sitting cross-legged on her bed, she reached over and pulled the box containing the vial of his blood from her nightstand drawer. She lifted the lid and ran a finger down the dark glass.

She closed the box with a sigh, setting it back in the drawer and moving into the common area where Mollian was seated at the desk in the corner. Perched on the arm of a couch, Merriam watched him work for a moment before speaking. "Is it more harmful or helpful for the grieving process to Bond yourself eternally to the one you lost?"

Mollian slowly turned to look at her. "I think that's one of those questions only you know the answer to."

"Well, if you had to say definitively one way or the other, which would it be? You know me. How would I feel with either outcome?" Merriam pressed.

Mollian pursed his lips, thinking how to best word his reply. "What's your biggest regret?"

Merriam's heart dropped into her stomach, guilt flooding her as she met Mollian's eyes. *You know it's that I never claimed him.* She couldn't bring herself to say the words out loud.

"What is a Bond other than a fancy name for a claim?" Mollian asked with a shrug.

Merriam tilted her head to the side as she let the words sink in. "Possibly more helpful than harmful, then?"

Mollian shrugged, refusing to answer outright, knowing this was a conclusion Merriam would have to come to on her own.

"I'll go to Entumbra with you, Prince. One last adventure as you fully slip into the role of heir apparent," Merriam said, dropping from the couch. "Any interest in supper?"

Chapter 44

Until then, live

THE NEXT FEW DAYS were spent packing. Mollian was deciding which of his possessions he may want or need during his five-year stay, and Merriam was sorting her entire room into trunks and boxes to be brought to the merc house. It had been decided that she would move out after escorting Mollian to Entumbra. The mercs would help her load everything onto a cart the day she returned.

They were all excited to have her with them full time, Aleah and Campbell especially, but while Merriam was looking forward to their company and falling back into a routine with them, she wasn't looking forward to the ache she'd feel in her soul at Mollian's absence.

Ever since he'd given her his magic, she felt his proximity even more deeply, her blood awake to the source of the magical properties it carried through her body.

The night before they were to leave for Entumbra, they lay in Mollian's bed, Merriam on her side with her arms wrapped around one of his and her head resting against his shoulder. "I want to be Bonded to him. Will you go with me? During the trip."

Mollian's lips lifted in a small smile, his eyes closed. "I would be hurt if you asked to do it without me."

"I'm about to do a lot of things without you. This isn't something I want to add to that list."

The smile fell from Mollian's face, and he opened his eyes, staring at the ceiling. "I don't even really want this," he whispered quietly.

Merriam squeezed his arm, offering silent support.

"I never wanted to be king. But now ... I have a life here. I have you. The thought of living in that harrowing castle for five whole years ..."

"I promise I'll come visit. Often. You can show me all the things you've discovered and we'll go on adventures."

"I'll hold you to it."

Merriam looked up at him after several quiet moments. *Are you still awake?*

A heavy sigh that was as good as a yes.

Where do the dead go?

A realm we can never visit.

"Why not?" she asked, barely audible.

Mollian's brow furrowed as he tried to think of the easiest way to explain. "Every world has different laws that govern it. This world, for example, has gravity, plants that feed off the sun, and fire that requires heat and kindling and air to burn. Those are simple laws, easy to understand. The realm of the dead is different. Nothing living can go there. The very make-up of it won't allow it."

Merriam nodded, though she didn't quite understand.

"If we were able to see those we miss, we'd never get back to life. We'd live forever in a state of grief and waiting for the next time we were reunited."

"Is it bad if I say that would be worth it? To see him again?"

"He'll be waiting for you. His soul won't move on into the next life until he knows yours will be there waiting for him," Mollian comforted. "But until then, live."

Merriam drifted off to sleep, letting Mollian's words and familiarity settle her soul while he still could.

The next day, they were out at the stables at dawn. A team of Rangers would escort Mollian to Entumbra along with a fresh detachment of the Guard to relieve those currently posted at the castle. There was still no word on Basta, but the threat of him and his demons loomed constantly.

Regenya was there to see them off, reaching up to smooth the curls from Mollian's face, her fingers lingering over the tattoos at his temples. "Stay safe, my sweet boy."

"I will, Mother," Mollian promised, patting her hand on his cheek before pulling her into a hug.

Regenya looked to Merriam, worry battling the coolness of her deep green eyes. "Protect him," she said.

"With my life," Merriam answered, swallowing down the bitterness she felt towards the queen. This was the first they'd spoken since before Mollian had been taken.

Regenya nodded, turning back to the castle, and the group set off.

When they'd set up camp for the night, Merriam wandered a little ways off into the trees, sitting on a grassy hillside and looking out over the mountains while Mollian pulled Rovin aside to let him know of their plans to Travel to Earth.

Merriam rolled the vial in her fingers, watching the liquid swirl around inside as Mollian found her. "Isn't blood supposed to have a shelf life?"

Mollian shrugged, looking up at the stars. "Keeper blood is a carrier for powerful magic. I've always just assumed that whatever properties allow the blood to carry the magic through us also changes the way it acts in other instances. As long as it's still ... wet, it seems to be active."

Merriam nodded, closing her fist around the vial before slipping it back into the pouch on her weapons belt. "I'm ready to go if you are."

"Rovin's pissed," Mollian remarked mildly, offering her a hand to pull her up.

"Rovin can suck a dick," Merriam replied, a smile tugging at her lips as she stood. Then she frowned. "Weirdly, I feel better knowing he'll be here to keep an eye on things. As much of an ass as he is, at least I know he's loyal to you and will do what it takes to keep you safe."

"You going soft in your old age, merc?" Mollian teased, elbowing her in the side.

"Of course not. I also feel better taking Bellamy with us, considering he's never tried to choke me or threatened to kill me," Merriam added.

"Give it time, pet." Rovin walked up to them with a smirk, Bellamy at his heels. "I still don't like this," he said, crossing his arms over his chest. "How are we supposed to know if anything goes wrong?"

"I've thought it through. You know I would never knowingly put Mollian in danger. It would be highly improbable for Basta to try anything. We'll be in a populated area, and he'd bring too much attention to himself. At the very least, he has some idea of the kind of weapons Earth has and what kind of destruction they're capable of." Merriam tossed her braid over her shoulder, gesturing for Bellamy to step forward.

Rovin shifted, shoving his hands in his pockets as he glanced at Mollian. He knew better than to challenge the future king on why his presence was needed, but it didn't mean he agreed. Finally, he nodded stiffly, turning and walking back toward camp.

Mollian Traveled with Bellamy, and Merriam followed a heartbeat later, opening her eyes to a dimly lit alley and the sound of a busy street nearby.

Bellamy was bouncing on his toes, already poking his head out of the alley to look around.

Mollian looked at Merriam, raising an eyebrow. *Quite the protection detail you chose.*

Merriam shrugged, pushing past Bellamy and onto the street. "Glamor," she reminded him.

Bellamy nodded, closing his scarred eye in concentration as he wrapped a glamor around himself, slightly altering the appearance of his clothing and his less-human features.

Merriam felt the pressure around her change as Mollian glamored her clothing, too, mostly to hide the axes that hung from her hips as well as his own appearance for their walk down the street.

When they found a smaller tattoo shop, Mollian and Bellamy worked to clear everyone but one artist out, convincing patrons and artists alike to go home for the night and get some sleep. Merriam played with the aspen leaf at her throat, the air around her heavy with glamor.

"What can I do for you all?" the remaining artist asked.

"There's a tattoo on my back; I'd like you to repeat that design, but offset. And add some aspen branches trailing down my arm," Merriam answered, fingers running down the arm in question as she spoke.

"Sounds dope, let's get started."

Merriam pulled the vial from her pouch, passing it to Mollian before unbuckling her weapons belt and setting it to the side. She stripped off her shirt and lay on the table.

Mollian periodically added blood to the ink as the time passed. Her back didn't take long, but the intricate aspen branch and leaves wrapping around her arm would take several hours.

Merriam had felt the shift as soon as the second Bond symbol was complete. A surge of power rolled through her body with an almost sickening pressure. Her fingers dug into the leather of the tattoo table as new magic spilled into her bloodstream, assessing and stretching and figuring out where to fit. For one sickening moment, she worried her human body wouldn't be able to withstand the additional magic.

You okay?

Merriam's eyes darted to Mollian's, and the pressure inside her started to ease as the magic settled. The rush of power left her feeling equal parts dizzy and antsy, like she needed to expend energy. *I forgot how strong the connection comes on.*

The artist finished the aspen detailing on her back, and she moved into a sitting position for the rest of her arm.

Bellamy had flipped through every bit of flash in the shop, lamenting that he hadn't kept a spare artist back to get his own ink and was practically bouncing out of his seat with energy.

"Why don't you go find us something to eat?" Mollian suggested.

Bellamy pressed his lips together, shaking his head. "Rovin would slaughter me if he'd heard I left you here alone."

"I'm hardly alone. I've got Sekha's most bad-ass mercenary on protection duty. And luckily, she's still under contract with the Crown."

Bellamy glanced at the door, uncertain. "With full respect, Your Highness, I'm positive I'm not supposed to leave you."

"I appreciate your sense of duty, Bell, but I do outrank Lieutenant Arwood. Please find us food and maybe a deck of cards or something to help pass the time."

"Yes, sir," Bellamy finally agreed, slipping out the door.

"I like him," Merriam smiled, wincing slightly as a leaf was outlined on the inside of her upper arm. "He's going to make a good Ranger."

"Speaking of," Mollian sat next to her, leaning forward and resting his chin on a hand.

Merriam watched him skeptically. "Why do I feel like you wanted to have this conversation where you knew I couldn't run away?"

"Because you know me better than I know my own self," Mollian answered.

Merriam dipped her head in concurrence, waiting.

"I know I'm about to ask you for a lot—for everything—but when I come back from Entumbra ... I'll need you, Ria. I don't think I'll be able to rule on my own. I don't think I'll be able to take that weight every day without breaking from the pressure."

Merriam reached out and took his hand, her already-broken heart splintering again at his misery.

"You have time to think about it, and I'll understand if you refuse, but when I'm king, be my chief advisor. Help me rule the way my brother would have ruled."

Tears filled Merriam's eyes, and she squeezed Mollian's hand as one slipped down her cheek. "I would be honored to be your advisor, Molli."

"Just like that?" Surprise flashed in Mollian's eyes, a smile playing on his lips.

Merriam turned her gaze down, shrugging. "I have five years to continue building my reputation and changing the way the Guard views me. That's also five years I won't constantly be under their noses and in their space. I love being a mercenary, but ... I was almost ready to give it up ... for him. I wasn't completely there, but I know I would have done it, eventually. And now I don't even have that option. That choice was taken from me. I won't let it be taken again. Regardless of what else is going on in the kingdom, I choose you, Molli. Come five years from now, I will be here for whatever you need." She raised her eyes back to his as she finished. "I've decided I'm done living my life for anyone but myself. I will regret not making that decision sooner until the day I die, but I won't spend a moment longer letting anything step in front of my happiness."

"Being a merc makes you happy, though," Mollian pointed out.

Merriam's eyes screwed shut for a second as the needle dragged over the inside of her elbow. "How much more fun might it be to be chief advisor to the king?" She grinned. "Who's to say I can't also be a spy for the Crown?"

"My mother would have a conniption if she knew the chaos I'm inviting into my court."

After Bellamy came back with food, the three ate in companionable silence, Merriam with one arm outstretched as the artist continued to work, shading in the leaves on her arm. The young Ranger had also managed to track down a deck of cards, and they passed the rest of the time playing games.

When the tattoo was finally finished, Merriam hopped up from the chair, moving in front of a mirror to see the full piece. Two Bonding symbols lie between her shoulder blades, tucked into a bed of aspen leaves that ranged in color from deep green to vibrant red. A similarly colorful leafy branch crawled across her shoulder blade, wrapping over one shoulder and down her arm, ending midway between her elbow and wrist. She rotated her arm, getting a good look at it, and smiled at Mollian's reflection in the mirror. "It's beautiful."

She slipped her shirt on and re-fastened her weapons around her waist. The fabric of her shirt stuck to the ointment over the fresh ink, but with the extra fae blood now coursing through her veins, she'd already stopped bleeding.

Merriam left a few pieces of gold on the counter before they Traveled back home and made their way back to the camp.

Rovin stood from where he'd been sitting by the fire as they approached, eyes scanning first Mollian and then Merriam briefly for any signs of attack. Even though it was now early in the morning, he'd refused to sleep until Mollian was back safely. "All quiet?"

"Everything went smoothly," Mollian assured him.

Rovin opened his mouth to reply, but his eyes caught on the design running down Merriam's arm.

"Go ahead and make your jokes, Lieutenant." Merriam held her arm out, rotating it so he could see the full design. "I have officially marked myself as property of the Crown."

Rovin's eyes trailed from her arm up to her face. "It looks good," he said before walking away.

Merriam blinked, unsure how to respond. *Has he been acting weird lately?*

Weird like how?

Merriam turned to Mollian, narrowing her eyes suspiciously. *You know something.*

I know I'm very tired, and I know we have a long day of travel tomorrow, Mollian Cast before looking at Bellamy. "Thank you for accompanying us," he told him, clapping him on the shoulder before walking to his tent.

Merriam stared after him, mouth slightly agape. *This isn't over, Prince.*

"Why do I feel I've missed something?" Bellamy asked, mostly speaking to himself.

"Because you're very astute," Merriam answered regardless, following Mollian.

The prince had just pulled his shirt over his head, tossing it to the side and dropping to a bedroll.

"Tell me," Merriam demanded, bending to unlace her boots and discard her weapons.

"What would you like to know?"

"Don't be coy, Molli," she sighed, kicking off her boots and folding her arms over her chest.

"You told him. The night you blacked out and he had to carry you home, you told him."

Merriam's eyes widened with surprise, and she lowered herself onto the ground next to Mollian. "How much?"

"Everything, as far as I can tell. At least enough for him to know about the marriage proposal."

Merriam groaned, sliding her hands down her face. "Lovely. So lovely. He pities me. That's why he's trying to be more inclusive."

Mollian choked on a laugh, swallowing it down. "For someone who's so smart and perceptive, you are the most daft, willfully ignorant person I've ever met."

"The fuck is that supposed to mean?"

"First of all, have you ever known Rovin to show pity? Second, you're really going to lie there and tell me you don't think the weeks you've spent training with the Rangers have impacted the way they view you? You don't think they've spread stories about the way you slaughtered all those demons that day in the cave? They admire you, Ria."

"I'm not dissecting this right now," Merriam grumbled, turning away from him.

Mollian put a hand on her shoulder, rolling her back over. "Don't pout, it's unseemly. Also, very poor taste to turn your back on your future king."

Merriam rolled her eyes. "Spare me, Your Highness."

"I think he is truly sorry for the way he's treated you in the past. I'm just not sure he knows how to say it or thinks you'll be receptive to an apology."

Merriam pulled her braid out from under her back, curling the end around a finger. "We have so much history, I'm not sure an apology would even matter. It's not that I want to fight with him for the rest of my existence—I'm tired of the contention, it's exhausting—but I also feel like so much has happened for so long ... It's all water under the bridge. But the bridge is next to a waterfall, and the spray is constantly soaking everything. Our habit is just to taunt and provoke each other whenever possible."

"Wow, that's ... deep."

Merriam prodded him in the ribs with her elbow. "You're an unhelpful ass."

"Just know he's trying to turn over a new leaf. Keep that in mind while I'm gone. You're going to be on the same side in five years, so it'll help if I don't have to worry about constant infighting and bloodshed."

Merriam sighed, rolling to face Mollian and resting her head against his shoulder. "We wouldn't want things to get boring though, would we?"

"You're nothing but trouble."

A smile played at the corners of Merriam's lips. "You've already invited me into your court. No take-backs. I'll be putting in my five years' notice with the mercenaries as soon as I'm back in Umbra."

"Do you think that will give them enough time to find a replacement?" Mollian asked, feigning concern.

"Probably not," Merriam said, sleep starting to claim her. "Maybe I'll have to stay on part-time for a year or two."

I might be able to fit that into your contract.

A contract? I didn't know chief advisor was a salaried position.

Room and board included.

Dental and vision as well, I hope, Merriam added, slightly delirious in her half-asleep state.

Mollian gave her a strange look, but didn't question her, letting her drift off next to him instead. The familiarity of it all made his heart clench, and he dreaded the thought of being without her for five years. She was the only one who'd always made him feel completely at ease, never judging his random observations or showing annoyance at his long and detailed explanations of things. Merriam had always let him be him, as though she understood.

Which she did, he knew. Their souls were too interconnected for anything else to be true.

Chapter 45

I'll follow your lead

MERRIAM WOKE A FEW hours later, anxious energy weaving knots in her stomach. She dressed and slipped from the tent before Mollian woke, heading out into the forest. With a brief wave at the Ranger on watch, she broke into a light jog.

Her body was still adjusting to the new magic that flowed through her veins, and she attributed her nerves and general feeling of unsettledness to the fresh Bond. She also knew that today she would truly say goodbye. Her heart ached with the thought, tears springing to her eyes.

Merriam pushed into a faster pace, refusing to let the feelings consume her. She shoved them back down into that hidden place inside her, promising herself she would let them out and sort through them when she was with him. When she could tell him everything that was in her heart.

She slowed her run as she came to a drop in the mountainside, climbing onto a rocky outcropping and perching on the edge, feet dangling off the side. Merriam held her arm in front of her, umbrite ring flashing in the light of the rising sun as she admired the tattoo over her arm. A strange peace settled over her as she looked at it, and she smiled. It was strange how her anxiety dissipated, knowing she was marked with the symbol of Sekha. His symbol. Mollian's symbol.

It felt right.

Her stomach grumbled, breaking the mood, and she stood, taking one last admiring look at the forested mountainside in front of her before running back to camp.

Strips of pork belly were being roasted over the fire, fat sizzling and hissing as it dropped into the flames. Her mouth watered at the smell, and she sat down next to Bellamy to wait for it to finish cooking.

"Good run?"

"Enjoyable enough," Merriam replied, grabbing a skin of water from the side of the boulder and taking a long drink.

"I'm not trying to tell you what to do," Rovin spoke up from across the fire, "but it's probably not the best idea to be going places alone right now. We don't have any knowledge of where Basta is or what he's planning, but he knows Prince Mollian is now heir apparent, and he knows of your closeness."

Merriam opened her mouth to retort, but she switched courses before she said something sarcastic. "I hadn't even considered that. I'll grab someone next time," she conceded. Her own surprise at her words was reflected back at her in Rovin's eyes, the light of the fire dancing in the brown depths.

"That smells divine," Mollian said as he walked up, breaking the awkward tension. He sat down on the ground next to Merriam. "Where'd you run off to this morning?"

"Just had some energy to burn," she replied as he took her arm and looked it over.

You're healing up nicely.

Quickly, too, which is a much-appreciated perk.

Mollian let her pull her arm back into her lap as a Ranger passed around bread and Bellamy pulled the pork from the fire. They ate their breakfast mostly in cordial silence and tore down camp before continuing through the mountains.

As they neared Entumbra, Merriam noticed the vibrations of the Gate felt slightly more disruptive than before. It was harder to push away the sensation of her blood tingling in response and recognition from the forefront of her mind.

I feel itchy. She Cast to Mollian.

If you have a rash, you'd better not infect me with it.

If I have a rash, you're probably the one who gave it to me.

I'm not the one who's constantly tumbling around in the woods, though, am I?

Tumbling?

Tumbling.

I'll have you know, Prince, that I am widely regarded as one of the most skilled mercenaries Sekha has ever seen.

Skilled at tumbling, from what I've seen. An image of her falling from a tree flashed into her mind.

Merriam jumped, almost slipping out of the saddle. She turned to look at Mollian, riding behind her on the narrow trail.

You good? He raised a brow.

Merriam blinked, turning back around. *What the fuck was that, Molli?*

What was what?

Since when can you Cast images?

What?

Merriam turned to look at him again, but he shook his head, entirely confused. *That wasn't on purpose, then?*

Clearly. Now would you care to elaborate?

Merriam tilted her head to the side, imagining Mollian toppling from his horse and throwing the image at him.

A bark of laughter behind her was confirmation that it had worked.

Since when is this a thing? she asked again.

I don't remember ever trying to Cast anything but words before, but I can say with certainty that I have never experienced nor heard of it being possible.

Merriam was silent, her mind reeling with this new information.

It could be because of our proximity to the Gate. Or maybe our mehhen bond has changed with the added magic in your blood. Either way, an interesting development.

Merriam snorted. *That's one way to put it.*

I'll have to try it with Gressia. Maybe that'll help narrow it down for us.

Merriam didn't reply, her mind again drifting to Entumbra and what today would mean. The thought of saying goodbye to *him* was a constant weight at the back of her mind, her stomach still a knot of anxiety. Not far off from that was the knowledge that today would be her last full day with Mollian for a long while, and the thought made her want to physically cling to him like a child.

What am I going to do without you? She Cast on blind instinct.

Enjoy your last five years being lawless, of course. And visit me so that I can share all the secrets of the universe with you.

When they looped around the mountain, the tallest spire of Entumbra visible in the distance, Merriam felt the anxiety in her stomach spread throughout her body.

Dozens upon dozens of crows circled the castle, dipping down below the tree line periodically. A few larger condors were also present, trying to chase off the crows.

Molli...

Fuck.

She sped up as the trail widened out, and Rovin came riding up beside her, reaching over to grab the reins and slow her.

"Let me go," she glared at him.

Rovin forced her to a slow walk, her horse shaking its head with a disgruntled whinny at the confusing directions. "You don't know what you're rushing into. Take a second to think."

Her amber eyes burned with fire as she looked at him, but as much as she hated it, he was right. She took a deep breath, nodding, and he let go of her reins, pulling his horse back from hers.

"Hold everyone back. I'll sneak ahead and send a signal if all is clear."

"I'm going with you. You might need back up before everyone else is able to get there," Rovin insisted.

"I'm going, too; Gressia could be in danger." Mollian pulled his horse up beside them.

"No," Merriam and Rovin said at the same time. She shot him a glare before looking at Mollian. "If something bad has happened, you need to be away from it. We can't risk anything happening to you."

Mollian pressed his lips together, but conceded, knowing she was right. "Be careful, both of you."

"Always am," Merriam replied, slipping from her horse.

Rovin hopped down next to her, adjusting the short sword at his side. "I'll follow your lead."

Merriam nodded, heading into the forest, away from the road and on a direct path to the castle. She had half a mind to Travel for the sake of approaching unseen, but was nervous about not knowing what they would be walking into.

The only sound that echoed through the forest was the harsh chatter of scavenger birds. There was a stark lack of ambient camp noise as Merriam and Rovin approached the courtyard, and she swallowed, pulling her axes free and gripping them tightly. She rolled her shoulders to loosen the muscles, glancing nervously at Rovin as she stepped quietly through the trees.

He'd unsheathed his sword, holding it at the ready. Giving her a brisk nod, he dropped back a bit, letting her take point.

Merriam pressed her back to a tree as the courtyard became visible, taking a few deep, calming breaths before moving quietly toward the stable. She hugged the stone wall as she made her way around the building, Rovin close behind.

The stench of death and sulfur permeated the air, raising the hair on Merriam's arms. The noise of the birds was raucous from this close, drowning out any sound their approach would have made.

Merriam listened closely for any sign of danger as she reached the corner of the stable. The wet rip of flesh sounded from close by, and her stomach churned. Carefully, she peeked around the side of the stable, and bile crawled up her throat.

Choking it back, she stumbled from the cover of the stable.

Carnage.

That was the only word that would accurately describe the state of the clearing.

The detachment of the Guard that had been stationed at Entumbra had been entirely slaughtered. Broken bodies littered the courtyard, the ground soaked with blood. Several corpses of demons lay among them, but it was clear the Guard had been caught unprepared.

By the state of the bodies, stomachs and limbs torn open and dragged across the clearing as the birds fought over the carrion, they'd been dead at least a day, if not more. Blood rushed in Merriam's ears as she walked through the open graveyard.

Dead. Every one of them dead.

"What the fuck happened?" Rovin breathed, stepping carefully over the gore scattered across the ground.

"Basta," Merriam answered with the obvious. She jerked her head up to the castle, taking off at a run toward the stairs. She threw her consciousness out, searching for Gressia, but felt nothing. Fear coursed through Merriam's veins as she leapt up the steep stone steps. The lack of Gressia's presence didn't have to mean anything. She could have heard the attack and Traveled to safety.

She heard Rovin's footfalls behind her as he followed, and she ran down the catwalk and into the atrium.

The humans who had been on duty had suffered the same fate as the Guard, their bodies ripped open and resting in dark, rust-colored pools of dried blood. Merriam halted, panting heavily as she again searched for the feeling of the Keeper. She'd never felt for anyone other than Mollian; it was possible she'd missed Gressia's magic.

Rovin stood at her side, scanning the room. "What the fuck?" he breathed again, eyes wide.

Merriam's breath caught as she felt a slight brush against her consciousness. "Gressia is alive." She closed her eyes, concentrating on the faint ping in her mind and trying to pinpoint a location. Her tattoos itched madly with the effort. The feel of Gressia was so faint, but the fae had felt her, and was pulling her in.

Merriam followed the pull up a spiral staircase and down the hallway that led to Gressia's bedchamber.

"Wait, Mer, we need to clear the castle!" Rovin hissed, hurrying after her.

"Then clear it," she snapped, tightening her grip on her axes.

"We shouldn't split up." Rovin scowled at the back of her head.

Merriam grit her teeth in irritation, not stopping to face him. "Then stay with me. I'm going to Gressia. If Basta and his demons are still here, we have no hope of fighting them off, regardless. He took out that entire detachment. We may be good, but we're not *that* good."

Before Rovin could reply, she pushed open Gressia's door, surveying the space. Everything looked mostly unaffected, but the sheets were pulled from the bed, listing to one side.

Merriam stepped into the room, moving silently around the bed until she heard a wet, feeble cough. "Gressia," she hurried to the side of the bed, where the Keeper was sprawled on the floor, holding a blood-soaked sheet to her abdomen.

Gressia's pale green eyes fluttered open, filling with relief as Merriam swam into focus.

Merriam sank to her knees next to the Keeper, setting her hands over the sheet to add pressure. "We're here. It's going to be okay."

"Mollian," Gressia forced out, coughing again.

"He held back. He's safe," Merriam assured her.

Gressia shook her head weakly, blood leaking from the side of her mouth. "I need him."

Merriam nodded, closing her eyes. Mollian was roughly a klick away. He should be close enough to feel, especially with the amplified power of the Gate's proximity. Merriam flung out her mind and immediately felt him there. When she felt him reach out in return, she pulled him further in, letting him know it was safe to head in. "He'll be here, hold on," she told Gressia.

"We don't know that it's safe yet. He needs to hold back," Rovin said, frustration and fear lacing his words.

Gressia's gaze flitted up to the Ranger. "Basta is gone. He went—" Gressia broke off, coughing up more blood.

"Save your strength, Molli is coming," Merriam moved one hand to smooth white curls back from Gressia's face.

Her eyes had fluttered closed, but she opened them again at Merriam's touch. The light in them was faint, and Gressia weakly grasped at Merriam's hand. "He doesn't know."

Merriam shook her head, confused. "You can tell him when he gets here, save your strength."

Gressia coughed again, clutching at Merriam more firmly. "Basta," she forced out, taking a few shuddering breaths. "He doesn't know ... about my—" another cough, and her eyes slid closed. She forced them open again with great effort, looking at Merriam pleadingly. "Keep him safe."

Merriam tilted her head, not understanding. "Gressia, just hold—" she broke off, eyes going wide with realization.

Gressia saw the look, relief again flooding her gaze. "Protect him." Her eyes slipped closed again and did not re-open.

"Gressia, no, hold on!" Panic swept through Merriam as she applied more pressure to the sheet over the fae's stomach. "Just a little longer, please," she pleaded, tears filling her eyes.

Rovin dropped to the floor next to her, touching her shoulder. "She's lost too much blood, Mer," he said softly.

Merriam shook her head frantically. "No, no, she has to be okay. He cannot lose another, not like this!" Her voice wavered with emotion as she fought back the tears.

Rovin pressed his fingers to Gressia's neck, feeling for a pulse. "She's gone," he said gently.

Merriam looked at him, again shaking her head. "No, she can't be." She moved her hands from the bloody sheet to Gressia's chest, locking the fingers of one hand over the other and throwing her full weight into compressions. "He can't lose her!"

"Merriam, we were already too late." Rovin tried to console her, but she kept pumping the Keeper's chest, feeling her ribs bend under the pressure.

"I have to try," Merriam panted, a tear slipping down her cheek. "I have to try."

Rovin nodded, moving to the window to watch for Mollian and the other Rangers.

The horses thundered into the clearing, scattering the crows. "He's here," Rovin said.

Merriam stopped compressions, wiping the tears from her cheeks before grabbing her axes from where they'd been discarded on the floor and standing. "I need to be the one to tell him," she said, amber eyes resolute. She slipped her weapons back into her belt and headed down the stairs.

Mollian met her in the atrium. "Where's my sister?"

Merriam swallowed back tears as she looked at him, opening her mouth to speak.

But Mollian read it in her gaze before she had a chance to form the words. "Take me to her," he said softly, pain filling his eyes.

Merriam silently led the way back up to Gressia's room. "I'm so sorry, Molli. I tried to bring her back. I tried," she whispered as Mollian walked around the bed.

He knelt beside her, taking her hand in his. "Gress …" his voice broke, head dropping forward as he pressed her hand to his cheek.

Merriam turned her back, letting him mourn the sister he'd never truly had a chance to be close to. Letting him mourn the loss of his entire line.

No, not the entire line.

"Molli, the child," she said, turning back to face him. "He needs protection."

Mollian's head jerked up. "What if Basta went after him?"

"She said he didn't know. He never found out."

Mollian dropped his eyes back down to Gressia, smoothing the hair back from her face. "I'll keep him safe, Gress. I promise I will keep him safe."

Mollian stood, reaching a hand out to Merriam as he walked toward the door. "Will you come with me?"

Merriam squeezed his hand, trying to push as much comfort into the gesture as possible. "She didn't say where he was, Molli. How are we supposed to find him?"

"She took me to see him after telling me. She didn't introduce us, but she brought me to the world." He swallowed hard, leading her from the room. "I think she did it in case something like this ever happened. She wanted me to be able to find him."

Rovin met them in the stairwell. "We've cleared the rest of the castle, Your Higness."

Mollian nodded his thanks. "We're going down to the Gate."

Rovin's brow furrowed as he tried to figure out what questions were appropriate from a lieutenant to a prince in this situation, not wanting to be disrespectful.

"There's something I have to do." Mollian answered before the Ranger could ask. "Merriam is coming with me, but I can't take anyone else. Not for this." Mollian led the way down to the belly of the castle.

Rovin followed. "What if Basta is there? What if you get into trouble? None of us will be able to follow."

Mollian pressed his lips together, moving through the room with the maze of arches. "Then I'll have to hope Merriam is crafty enough to get us back to the Gate," he answered simply.

They headed down the tunnel, Merriam's blood prickling in her veins the lower they went, the magic in her blood buzzing in proximity to its true source.

When the tunnel opened up into the cave, light glinting off the stone of the Gate, Merriam clasped Mollian's hand tightly. She forced back the apprehension that rolled through her as they approached, stopping to stand in front of the many-faceted umbrite and orydite arch.

Rovin stood at the entrance to the cave, sword hanging at his side, but everything about his posture suggested he was alert and ready for any threat. The set of his jaw made it clear he wasn't happy with the situation.

Mollian pricked his finger on the stone, sliding his hand across the arch. The air around them crackled almost imperceptibly as a small lakeside cottage appeared in front of them.

They stepped through the Gate together, the sensation similar to Traveling with the rings, but more external. An absence of everything brushed across Merriam's skin before warm, humid air caressed her face in a gentle breeze.

She looked behind her; the Gate was completely overgrown with vines and moss, easily blending into the surrounding forest.

Mollian pulled her forward, walking down a timeworn path to the cottage. He knocked on the door before swinging it open and stepping inside. A small fire was lit in the hearth, and Merriam's eyebrows raised in shock to see a human woman standing at a counter, slicing vegetables.

The woman startled, brandishing the knife and backing up against the counter.

Mollian held his hands up. "We're not here to harm you," he spoke in a human tongue. "My name is Mollian. I'm Gressia's brother."

The woman shifted her grip on the knife, eyes flicking to Merriam for a moment before studying Mollian. Her posture relaxed as she recognized his Keeper traits. "What do you want?"

"We're here for the child."

The woman narrowed her eyes. "There is no child here."

A black cat walked into the kitchen then, winding around the woman's legs before sitting down. It looked at Mollian with eyes a heartbreakingly familiar shade of green, tilting its head to the side.

Merriam stepped closer to Mollian. "You said the kid was a shifter, right?" she whispered in Common. Licking her lips, she squatted down and folded her arms over her knees. *Hello,* she Cast. *I'm Merriam. What's your name?*

The cat looked at her, blinking slowly.

I know you've never met him, but this is your uncle, Mollian. He's your mother's brother. Do you know about brothers and sisters?

The cat glared at her. *I'm not stupid.*

Merriam bit her lip against the near-hysterical laughter that tried to bubble up her throat as the small, childish voice filtered through her head. *I'm sorry, I didn't mean to offend.*

Is Momma with you?

Merriam's heart, broken as it was, splintered yet again at the question. She swallowed hard, looking up at Mollian for only a moment before looking back at the cat. *She's not here, but she sent us to find you.*

Why? She says I'm safe here.

You were, but not anymore.

The cat stood, taking a tentative step across the kitchen toward her. The woman stiffened, leaning down to scoop it up.

As soon as she got her hands on it, the cat shifted into a gray jay and flew up to the exposed rafters, chirping angrily. Its eyes were still slit like a cat's and vivid green.

Mollian looked up at the bird, smiling cordially. "That was an impressive move, kid."

The bird watched him, ruffling its feathers.

He looks like Momma.

Merriam smiled softly even as her heart clenched, flicking her gaze to Mollian for a moment. *Maybe just a little less pretty, but yes.*

Where is she?

She sent us to come get you.

The jay's head tilted to the side. *You already said that.*

Merriam licked her lips again, trying to think of how to respond.

Is she dead? The small voice was even smaller, buried under fear.

Merriam looked at Mollian helplessly, unsure how to respond, but not wanting to lie. Wrenching her eyes back to the bird, she nodded.

The bird dropped from the rafters, lighting on the ground before shifting into a fae child. His skin was the same light brown as Mollian's. As his mother's. A shock of straight white hair fell over deep green eyes, pupils slit vertically. Tears filled them, and he wrapped his arms around his knees, lip trembling.

Mollian stepped forward, dropping to one knee in front of the boy.

"Is she really dead?" the child asked Mollian sorrowfully.

Mollian nodded. "I'm so sorry," he said softly. "She loved you so very much."

The child watched Mollian for a moment, eyes searching his face. Suddenly, he jumped from the ground, throwing his small arms around Mollian's neck as he started to cry.

Mollian's eyes widened in shock for a moment before he wrapped his arms around the child's body, brushing one hand in soothing circles over his back.

The child's face was pressed against Mollian's shirt, muffling his cries, but his whole body shook.

Merriam's throat clogged with emotion as she dropped to her knees in front of the pair, placing a hand compassionately on the back of the child's head and meeting Mollian's eyes.

We can't let anyone know about him, not while Basta is still alive. Mollian Cast to her.

I don't think we should leave him here, though. It'll be easier to keep him safe if he's close. Merriam pulled her hand back, running it over her mouth as an idea blossomed in her mind. *We should take him to the merc house. I'd argue there's nowhere safer in all of Jekeida.*

Mollian blinked, considering. *Do you think they'd be okay with it?*

All we need is for him to shift into a bird in front of Leo, and he'll have a bodyguard for life.

The woman had been watching all of this warily, but hadn't moved from her position in the kitchen, unsure what to do and thinking she wasn't paid enough to deal with this.

The child peeled away from Mollian, swiping the backs of his hands over his eyes and sniffling as he peered into Mollian's face. "You're Momma's brother?"

"My name is Mollian. I'm glad to officially meet you."

"She told me about you. You and Oren."

A sharp pang cut through Merriam's chest hearing his name, and she pressed the heel of her hand over her heart. She rapidly blinked back the tears that sprung to her eyes, forcing the emotion back down with great effort.

"I can only imagine the stories she had to tell," Mollian said, letting the child step back.

"She told me that I would be safe with you. She said I couldn't trust anybody who came here except for you and him. Is he coming, too?" He peered around Mollian's shoulder to the door.

Mollian's throat bobbed as he swallowed down his pain. "No. No, he's with your mother. They're keeping each other company now."

"Oh," the child's face fell, eyes filling with a deep empathy as he looked back at Mollian.

"Listen, I need you to come with me, and I promise you'll be safe, but there's a lot of danger right now. We have to be very careful about how many people know who you are—who your mother is. Do you think you can stay in an animal form for a little bit?"

The child nodded. "What kind of animal? I can do a lot."

"Preferably something easy to carry."

"I can be a gecko," the child offered.

"Maybe not so easy to lose or kill," Mollian amended.

"I can go back to a cat?"

"That will work." Mollian stood, turning to the woman and switching back to her language. "Your services aren't needed anymore. Are you from around Entumbra?"

The woman nodded. "Gressia hired me to stay here with him."

"Gressia is dead. If you come with us, I can have someone take you back to your village. I assume you know the importance of keeping the child's existence to yourself?"

The woman nodded gravely, her face ashen.

Mollian turned back to the child, who'd already shifted back into a black cat, and scooped him up before walking out of the cottage and back towards the forest, Merriam and the woman following. "What's your name?"

The cat settled on Mollian's shoulder, tail curling around his neck. *Ryddan.*

Chapter 46

Everybody calm down

Rovin pushed off of the wall of the cave as they walked back through the Gate, eyes immediately locking onto the woman who followed them.

"Who is she?"

"Just someone who was doing a favor for my sister," Mollian answered. "She'll require an escort back to her village."

Rovin's eyes were filled with confusion, but he nodded. "I'll have—" he broke off, blinking dumbly when he noticed the cat perched on Mollian's shoulder.

Mollian pulled Ryddan down, handing him off to Merriam. "Let's go upstairs, Lieutenant. There's much to be done and little time to do it."

Rovin led the way back up through the castle. He called over a couple of Rangers who were in the atrium cleaning blood from the floor. The bodies had already been removed, thankfully, as the woman looked like she was just barely holding in a scream at the sight of the gore that remained.

After the Rangers left to take the woman home, Mollian walked over to a wingback chair in the corner, sitting down heavily and dropping his head into his hands.

Ryddan struggled in Merriam's arms, jumping free and padding over to Mollian. He propped his front paws against Mollian's knee and rubbed his furry little cheek against Mollian's hands.

Mollian sat up, laughing sorrowfully and pulling the cat into his lap as he wiped a tear from his cheek. "We need to take this news to Umbra. I don't know where we go from here, but my mother needs to know. It's her decision to make. Merriam, you need to Travel back." *Drop Ryddan with the mercs on the way to the castle.*

Merriam nodded. *Cute name.* "I'll need a Ranger." *Bellamy won't ask questions.*

"Of course, take Bellamy. I'll stay here; I can't leave the Gate unguarded."

"What about Basta?" Rovin asked, pulling his curious gaze from the cat, who was watching him just as curiously.

"Basta is gone, and he has no reason to believe that he'll come back to anything other than an empty castle. We just have to hope that he decides it's unnecessary to bring a full force."

"Why did he attack Gressia at all?" Merriam wondered.

"Killing my brother was a pretty obvious way of outing himself as using her. If she wasn't going to allow him unhindered access to the Gate, she'd outlived her usefulness to him. Honestly, as secluded as Entumbra is, it makes sense he wouldn't camp out here. He knows where the Gate is and how to use it, but it's in an inconvenient location to stage for war." Mollian idly stroked Ryddan's back, tilting his head in thought. "The demons don't like iron, either. When they were locking me up, they wouldn't even touch it with their bare skin. This castle is half-composed of the stuff. Even though Gressia had iron in her blood, she was still high most of the time to alleviate the pressure of being surrounded by it for years on end."

"If that's true about the demons, whatever is living inside Basta probably isn't comfortable in this environment. Could explain why he conquered and moved on. As far as he knows, the Gate is unguarded, at his disposal when he next needs it." Rovin scratched the stubble on his cheek, still trying to puzzle everything out.

"Whatever his current motives, don't let your guard down." Merriam reflexively touched the axes at her hips. "I should go find Bellamy."

Don't tell my mother about Ryddan. I need to figure out how to break the news.

I won't.

Ryddan jumped from Mollian's lap just as he stood. Merriam embraced her *mehhen*, wishing she could absorb some of his pain. "I love you," she whispered against his chest, feeling the burn of tears in her throat.

"I love you," he replied before she stepped back. "I'll be fine. Go."

Merriam nodded, looking at the cat. *Come on, kid, you're coming with me.*

I'm not a goat.

Merriam choked back a laugh, bending down to scoop him up. *No, not at all.*

Rovin gave her a weird look, but quickly turned his attention to Mollian as they started discussing details of preparing the castle for the queen's arrival.

I can walk.

Fine, but stay close. Merriam gently dropped the cat from her arms. She hurried down the steps, searching the courtyard for Bellamy's long, brown curls.

Who were these people?

Merriam stumbled to a stop, looking from Ryddan to the mutilated bodies that still littered the clearing. She bent to pick him back up, thinking he probably shouldn't be stepping through the gore. *They were Guard, sent here to protect the castle.*

What happened?

Merriam bit her lip, trying unsuccessfully to keep his head tucked under her arms. He kept stretching his neck out to look around, eyes wide and ears angled back. *I don't know.* She finally told him.

Bellamy was helping another Ranger relocate a body to where they were building a make-shift funeral pyre in the back of the castle. Merriam caught his eye, motioning with her head for him to join her. He nodded, finishing the job before excusing himself.

"We need to go back to Umbra to talk to the queen. The princess ..." Merriam hesitated, remembering who she held in her arms. "The princess is dead," she said plainly, deciding the child had already heard and seen as much already.

Bellamy's eyes went wide, filling with sympathy. "Is Prince Mollian—"

"Molli's holding up for now, but we need to go."

"Yes, of course," Bellamy nodded, stepping closer. He noticed the cat then, tilting his head in question.

"We're bringing him to the mercenaries first."

Bellamy gave her a quizzical look, but asked nothing else as he loosely wrapped his arms around her, careful not to squish the cat between them.

Merriam shifted Ryddan so that his front paws were on her shoulder, making it so that she could twist her rings around and strike them together.

Just as the stones slid across one another, she had the fleeting thought that she'd never seen the rings portal more than two people at once, and her stomach dropped in fear.

But all three of them had made it to Earth, Ryddan crawling onto her shoulder and hopping lightly to the dusty concrete floor, tail-tip twitching curiously. Merriam watched him, wondering if his Keeper blood made it easier for the rings to transport him. Or maybe his smaller form was easier on the magic.

Either way, they'd all made it safely. They were in a long-abandoned warehouse, dust coating every surface in varying layers. Unlike the vast mountains of Entumbra, this region of Earth was mostly flat plains, one of the only places between the two worlds that so drastically differed geographically.

Bellamy, as was becoming standard, looked around in awe.

Despite the weight of everything, Merriam shook her head at him, a warm spark of affection blooming in her chest. "Come on, Bell, we've got a job to do."

"Right, yes," he replied, following her to the door but still looking around.

Ryddan was right on their heels, little pink cat nose twitching as he took everything in.

They stepped outside, blinking in the harsh sunlight, and a loud, rumbling whine filled the air overhead.

Bellamy jumped, looking up to the sky. Ryddan's fur was fluffed out, and he crouched low behind the Ranger.

Merriam laughed, waving them along. "It's just an airplane. I'll tell you about them once we find a ride."

Bellamy's eyes found the object in the sky and widened even more. "How the fuck ..."

"Car, Bell. Car." Merriam grabbed his arm, pulling him down an alley and onto a road. "A glamor might be nice, too," she prompted.

"Right." He cast his magic around them, altering their appearance to any human who might glimpse them.

Ryddan could feel the magic pressing against him, and made a game of weaving in and out of it as he walked.

They were next to a large airport, moving along several warehouses where semi-trucks were backed up against buildings. A plethora of questions bombarded Bellamy's mind, but he kept on task.

It wasn't long before they reached a pedestrian parking lot and found a person heading into work. Bellamy jogged to catch up to her, and after only a brief conversation, she walked back to her car, waving Merriam over.

They filed into the back seat. "Head south, toward the Springs," Merriam instructed.

The woman punched the city into her car's navigation system, but the glamor Bellamy held interfered too heavily for it to work. The woman shook her head in annoyance at the technology as she backed out of the parking spot and headed toward the freeway.

Almost as soon as they were moving, Bellamy turned to Merriam, a million questions warring for priority in his mind. "An airplane?" The words came tumbling out.

Ryddan sat facing the window, front paws propped against the edge of it as he watched everything streaming past.

"They're a mode of transportation used for traveling long distances. They fly similar to how a bird glides. I don't know the exact science behind it, but it's got to do with the way the air moves over the wings. We're in Denver; it's a pretty large hub almost in the center of the country," Merriam explained.

This gave more questions than answers, and Bellamy pestered Merriam with inquiries about air travel, semi-trucks, and Earth's cities the entire drive.

Merriam was happy for the distraction, unable to stress about what the rest of the day would entail.

As they got closer, Merriam threw out driving instructions, directing the woman into the mountains in between explaining things as best she could to Bellamy.

"Mollian knows more about a lot of this stuff than I do. You'll have to talk to him about it sometime," Merriam stroked her fingers over Ryddan's side. He'd curled up in her lap at some point and was now asleep.

Bellamy blinked, looking awkwardly out the window. "I wouldn't bother His Majesty with this stuff. That would be highly inappropriate."

Merriam was once again hit with the strange realization that her best friend—the strange, spirited boy she'd met all those years ago—was going to be king. Not only were his responsibilities going to drastically change, but also his relationships with almost everyone in his life. "A king still needs friends, Bellamy."

"Friends who are newly appointed Rangers with no rank or status?" Bellamy raised an eyebrow.

"Friends who will share his passions and engage him in conversation about things that he's excited about. Friends who want to talk to him because he's Mollian, not because he's king."

Bellamy's steel-blue eyes again filled with empathy as he met Merriam's gaze, and he nodded his understanding.

Once they were deep in the mountains, Merriam directed the woman to pull over to the side of the road, and Bellamy leaned forward to thank her for the ride, giving her a few final instructions to get her back down the road before the glamor wore off.

Merriam cradled the still-sleeping Ryddan in her arms as she and Bellamy waited for the car to drive off before Traveling back to Nethyl.

They were just on the outskirts of Umbra, and Merriam led the way to the merc house.

"Stay here; I'll be out shortly," she said when they reached the alley. She walked around back, pulling a key from a small pocket on her belt and letting herself in.

Ryddan slowly blinked awake, yawning hugely and squirming in her arms. She let him drop to the ground, and he sat, looking around curiously.

Merriam heard sounds from the kitchen and walked further down the hallway. "Hey, it's me," she called.

Ryddan followed her, cautiously at first, raising his nose and sniffing at the air. The smells from the kitchen had him perking his ears, pausing for only a moment before darting forward and around the corner.

"Mer?" Campbell's voice floated down the hall. "I thought you weren't coming back for another—what the fuck?"

Merriam rushed forward, hearing a loud flap of wings followed by a startled yowl that changed abruptly into a deep, menacing growl.

"Fuck! Leo!"

"No, shit!" Merriam swung around the corner. She slid to a stop in front of a large gray wolf, hackles raised and teeth bared at Panic, who'd been spooked back up to his perch and was screeching angrily.

Merriam raised one palm in front of Ryddan and the other in front of Campbell, who stood ready to fight with a large butcher's knife in his hand, indigo eyes wide.

The door to the training room swung open, bouncing against the wall with a clatter, and Leonidas came bounding in, sword drawn. He stopped dead when he saw the wolf, eyes tracking from its large form to Merriam's pacifying stance to Campbell.

It's okay. I promise they won't hurt you. Merriam Cast to Ryddan.

The wolf let out another growl, shifting his gaze from Panic to the tall human across the room.

"Everybody calm down," Merriam looked from Campbell to Leonidas. "Leo, please, for the love of fuck, quiet Panic."

Leonidas gave a sharp whistle and clicked his tongue, and Panic obediently flew over, letting out one final shriek before settling onto Leonidas's shoulder. "What the fuck is going on?" he demanded, sword still raised.

"That was a fucking *cat*," Campbell pointed the knife at Ryddan.

"Cam, calm down. I can explain." Merriam took a step closer to the wolf, slowly lowering her hand to its head. *It's okay. They're friends.*

It attacked me! The wolf glared at Panic.

He didn't mean it; you probably scared him. He's nice, I promise.

Ryddan looked at her, green eyes suspicious.

"Well, go on, then," Campbell prompted.

Merriam slowly stroked the wolf's neck in what she hoped was a calming manner. "This is Ryddan. He's in danger, and I need your help to protect him. This is the safest place I know of, and there's nobody I can trust as much as you."

"You want us to watch a wolf?" Leonidas asked incredulously.

"He's not a wolf, he's … he's a shifter. A youngling."

Ryddan cocked his head, watching Panic, and in the blink of an eye shifted into a peregrine falcon—the perfect twin to Panic, aside from his deep green cat's eyes.

Panic's feathers fluffed out momentarily, and he stretched his neck, tilting his head as he looked at the falcon that now stood on the floor. He shifted his feet on Leonidas's shoulder before hopping down, taking a few steps forward and spreading his wings wide.

Ryddan stretched out his own wings, flapping them a few times and letting out a small chirrup.

"Legends, Mer." Leonidas lowered his sword, watching the two birds on the floor.

"I can't explain a lot, and I know that's not fair, but he has to be protected. Just until we get this Basta situation figured out. No one can know that he's here."

Campbell set the knife down and walked around Merriam, squatting down and tilting his head to the side. The antler that had broken in battle was half grown back already, but still a harsh reminder to Merriam of everything they'd already done for her in this fight. And yet still she was asking for more.

Ryddan turned his head to look at Campbell, but when Panic flew over, stamping his feet happily and pushing his head against Campbell's shin, Ryddan followed suit.

Campbell looked up at Merriam. "What does he eat?"

"Fuck if I know," Merriam wiped a hand down her face.

Campbell stood, walking back into the kitchen.

Panic flew up to his perch, looking down at Ryddan with a *kak*.

What do you eat? Merriam asked as Ryddan lighted next to Panic, who'd shifted over to make room.

Whatever my animal wants. He answered in the simplistically matter-of-fact way children had of taking things at face value and not digging for anything deeper.

Campbell cut off a couple of small slices of the pork shoulder he'd been preparing when they walked in, tossing one first to Panic and then to Ryddan.

Leonidas sighed, watching the birds. "Does he understand us?"

"Yes." Merriam leaned back against the counter.

Leonidas ran a hand over his short hair. "What do we do with him when we find Basta? We can't leave him alone."

Merriam chewed her lip. "I hadn't thought that far ahead, to be honest. But I'll figure something out."

"The others are out tracking down information, but they should be back soon." Leonidas walked past her into the kitchen, filling a cup with water.

Merriam rubbed the back of her neck. "I can't stay."

Leonidas's head jerked up, icy blue eyes meeting hers in a glare. "You're going to bring us a *youngling* and then dip out?"

Merriam held her hands up placatingly. "I don't have a choice, Leo." She swallowed against the lump in her throat. "I have to go tell the queen that her daughter is dead. Molli is alone in Entumbra with his dead sister, and I have to go back for him. I have to make sure he's okay. But the youngling, Leo, you have to protect him. Tell Jasper I'm sorry I couldn't stay and explain, but please, protect him. You're the only people I trust." The words tumbled from Merriam in one continuous string, emotion spilling free from behind the dam she'd so heavily fortified over the past few weeks.

"Legends, Mer. Why wouldn't you lead with that?" Campbell asked. "Go, we'll keep Ryddan safe."

Leonidas nodded. "Is there anything else you need from us?"

Merriam shook her head, forcing back the despair that was rising within her. "Just keep looking for Basta. I'll be back when I can, or at least send word once I know something."

"Likewise," Leonidas promised.

Merriam nodded, turning to Ryddan. "These are good people. You can trust them. Stay with them. I'll be back for you, okay?"

Okay. Mollian, too?

Mollian, too. With that, Merriam said a final thank you to Campbell and Leonidas before walking out the back door, collecting Bellamy and heading to the castle.

Chapter 47

The living must eat

MERRIAM HAD GONE TO see the queen by herself, Bellamy more than happy to wait outside the chambers.

The queen shook her head the moment Merriam walked into the room, standing from where she'd been having dinner at a small table and walking over, the light brown skin of her face ashen. "Why are you not with Mollian?" she asked fearfully, reaching briefly for Merriam's hands before pulling back, wrapping one arm around her waist and bringing the other to her mouth.

Darius came up behind her, resting a comforting hand on her shoulder.

Merriam found herself suddenly unable to speak, tears lodging in her throat. She fought the urge to pull her braid over her shoulder or slide the aspen leaf charm across its chain against her throat, forcing her hands to stay still at her sides. "Basta attacked Entumbra. We're not sure when, but probably at least a day ago. Gressia died defending the Gate."

"No, NO!" Regenya wailed. There was no other word for the sound that came from her mouth. She turned, burying her face in her husband's chest.

Darius held her tightly, tears streaming down his own face as he looked at Merriam. "Mollian—is Mollian okay?"

Merriam nodded, managing to push back her own emotions while the regents fought with the reality of losing yet another child. "He stayed in Entumbra to protect the Gate. There's a group of Rangers and a full detachment of the Guard with him, but no one ... no one was left from before."

Regenya pulled herself together, steeling her features as she wiped underneath her eyes with delicate fingers. "We must go to him. Now."

"Do you know where Basta went? What his plans are?" Darius asked as Regenya walked to the door to issue orders to the guards on duty.

"We don't, but the mercenaries are keeping a constant watch for any information or news. As soon as we hear something, we'll be ready to strike. Our best hope at this point is to catch him off-guard. We can't let him bring the fight to us."

Darius let out a long breath, nodding his agreement. "I fear for the safety of us all if he is able to amass his army."

"Nethyl won't be the only realm in danger if Basta succeeds," Merriam said quietly.

The king nodded, squeezing Merriam's shoulder as Regenya moved past them into their bedroom. "Give us a moment, please."

"Of course," Merriam dipped her head and slipped into the hall.

When he saw her, Bellamy pushed off of the wall he'd been leaning against. "How did it go?"

"As expected." Merriam ran a hand over her hair. "I'm Traveling back to Entumbra with them tonight, but I don't think you're needed."

His eyes darted to the guards positioned outside the queen's chambers, and he lowered his voice. "What's going to happen?"

Merriam shook her head with a shrug. "I don't know where we go from here. The Gate can't be left unprotected, but Mollian has had no real training. He's never even spent an extended amount of time in Entumbra." She dragged her hands down her face. "I have no clue what the protocol is for this. To be quite honest, that scares me more than anything."

Bellamy awkwardly patted her on the shoulder. "I know I can only promise so much, and there's also the whole Ranger thing that I've previously committed myself to, but you can trust me. I don't know everything that's going on, but I want to help where I can. No matter what Captain Ferrick or Commander Dio or any of the others think about you, our priority is the Crown. I know yours is Prince Mollian, and that's as good as the same in my eyes, which means we're on the same team. Anything I can do, let me know. Even if it's watching out for that weird cat."

Merriam choked out a laugh, a stray bubble of emotion floating over the dam inside her and popping in her chest. "Thanks, Bell."

Regenya stepped from her chambers then, Darius behind her with a bag across his back.

Bellamy nodded at Merriam before bowing deeply to the monarchs. "Your Majesties," he said before making his leave.

Regenya barely even registered the Ranger's presence or departure, her haunted eyes only briefly focusing on Merriam before she motioned for the girl to follow as she walked down the hall.

They Traveled to Earth as soon as they'd left the castle gates, and Darius secured a vehicle for them. "North," he instructed.

"We're going to DIA," Merriam amended.

The drive felt entirely too long. Merriam sat in the front seat, as far away as possible from the heavy cloud of grief that filled the back of the vehicle. Merriam directed the driver to the proper area, and they walked the rest of the way to the warehouse.

Night had fully fallen when they arrived in the courtyard of Entumbra.

Rovin noticed them from the catwalk and headed down. "Your Majesties, Prince Mollian is waiting for you outside of the tunnel," he said after a bow.

"We will go alone," Regenya said, meeting Merriam's eyes for the first time since leaving Umbra.

Merriam nodded, letting them move forward alone. She reached out for Mollian, alerting him to her presence if he needed her.

"What do you think happens now?" Rovin asked.

Merriam looked at him blankly. "I don't know why anyone would think I'd have even the slightest clue."

Rovin shrugged, pushing his hair back from his forehead. "You know a lot more than most people, and more than anyone would expect. You and the prince both, actually."

Merriam turned to survey the courtyard, now clear of bodies, though blood still stained the ground. A thick pillar of smoke rose up behind the castle from the mass pyre. A shiver ran down her spine as she barely suppressed a deep breath. "I'm sure a Keeper has died before another has been trained up in the past, but it's never even crossed my mind to look it up."

"What if Mollian is tasked with the Gate?"

Merriam bit the inside of her cheek, fighting back against the small fissure growing in her heart. "He will do what is needed for this world," she finally said. "But he would not be happy." The words were a quiet afterthought. She had the urge to go to him, but knew this was a time Regenya and Darius would need with him alone.

"Come on, someone cooked up some rabbit." Rovin turned toward the stables.

"Food?" Merriam asked.

"It's been a long day, Mer. The living must eat."

Merriam's stomach rumbled, reminding her that she was, indeed, alive, and she followed Rovin over to the circle of Rangers around a small campfire, taking turns pulling meat from a spit.

She sat on the edge of a log, leaning in towards the warmth of the fire as the chill of the night air swept across her skin.

Merriam ate with the Rangers, but didn't join in the conversation. She had a fleeting thought that in a different life, these could have been her friends and comrades. It wasn't something she dwelled on, though. She was very quickly wrapped up in her own head, wondering what the next move would be. What would happen with Mollian. Where Basta was hiding. How the mercs were fairing with Ryddan. Were they upset with the added burden she'd thrown on them?

Rovin's shoulder brushed against her as he angled his body slightly in conversation. His skin was warm against hers, and she instinctively leaned into the contact. He stiffened, shifting away, and it snapped her out of her thoughts.

She abruptly stood, walking back toward the castle and up the stone steps to the catwalk. Merriam stood at the top of the stairs for a moment, but memories of the last time she'd stood and watched the stars there slipped into her mind, and she moved inside instead.

She headed for the library, figuring she may as well try to look up some history, when she felt the brush of Mollian's magic against her mind. She immediately turned around, stopping by his bedroom—where she'd correctly assumed her things had been placed—and grabbed a cloak before hurrying down the stairs.

Merriam secured the garment around her shoulders, fabric billowing out behind her as she hurried through the belly of the castle toward the tunnel. The pull of the Gate sang in her blood, a magnetic force that pulled her down and under the mountain.

When she reached the cavern, she saw Mollian leaning against the opposite wall, hands in his pockets. She raised her palm in greeting, and he pressed his against it, sadness radiating from him.

Are you ready to say goodbye?

A fissure opened up inside of her, and her heart dropped into her stomach. *I don't know*, she answered truthfully, but followed Mollian into a tunnel nevertheless.

The cave was just as he'd described it, a bioluminescent blue glow cast by thousands of moths on the ceiling and walls, bathing everything in an eerie yet calming light.

Regenya looked up from where she stood with Darius in front of an alcove. Her eyes shimmered with tears as she gave a shallow nod.

Merriam slowly moved forward, feeling Mollian's presence at her back and thankful for it. She stopped in front of a nook; the thick swaddling wrapping the body inside was still clean and untouched by age.

She bit her lip hard enough to draw blood as she stepped forward, reaching out a hand and resting it gently on top of the wrappings.

Feelings started clawing their way to the surface and her eyes filled with tears, but she didn't let them fall. "I miss you," she whispered quietly, voice wavering. "I miss you so much it's all-consuming. I forget I'm alive sometimes." She took a deep breath, reigning in control of her emotions. "I hate it, too. I hate that I'm constantly trying to fight how much I miss you and how much I hate you for being such a self-sacrificing, protective asshat. We could have figured something out. But no, you found a way to get yourself shot in a reality that hasn't even invented guns."

Mollian touched her shoulder as bitter laughter fell from her lips. She shrugged him off, folding her arms across her chest and leaning against the wall next to the open grave. "I hate myself for not being able to love you as fully as I should have. It's my own fault, and it will forever be my biggest regret." She let out a long breath, head falling against the cold stone. "More than any of that, I guess I just need to tell you that I love you. I would give anything to have you back. But I can't hurt forever. Just … please, please forgive me when that day finally comes when I wake up and my first thought isn't of you."

Merriam lightly stroked her fingers down the side of his head, taking a shuddering breath. "Even when that day comes, know I still love you. I'm just selfish enough to choose life."

Mollian touched her again, concern shining in his eyes. *Ria—*

Merriam held her hand up, shaking her head. A moth flitted over, lighting on Mollian's cheek. *I'll be okay*, she Cast, reaching up to brush it away.

Regenya approached her. As the queen's eyes traveled up the tattoo on Merriam's arm, a sad smile stretched her lips. "Come. It's late, and we have much to discuss."

Merriam looked at Mollian in question, but he just tucked his hands into his pockets with a small, reassuring smile. Exhaustion flickered in his eyes as he followed his parents back to the Gate. An image of Mollian's bed flashed through her mind, blankets turned down invitingly.

It's only us, by the way.

What?

I tried Casting an image to my mother. Nothing.

Oh. Merriam frowned. *Have you asked her why we're able to?*

No, I haven't told her that we could.

The group entered the large cavern that held the Gate, and the queen stopped, turning to Merriam. "The Gate must be protected." She turned her eyes to Mollian, love shining through the depths of her grief before focusing back on the mercenary. "The duty of watching Entumbra now falls to me."

Merriam blinked, letting the words sink in. "What about Molli?"

"He is to be king, Merriam."

Merriam's breath caught in her chest. There had never been a king so young before. A king who hadn't spent years studying in Entumbra, learning about the Gate and the worlds it connected. She could feel unease rolling from Mollian, and the queen spoke again just as Merriam's eyes met his.

"I know we've never quite seen eye to eye, but I hope you are at least secure in the knowledge that I see how hard you have worked to get to where you are. I respect your drive and determination. But more so,

I have always seen the love you have for my son. The connection you share is rare and powerful. He will need you, Merriam."

Merriam pulled her eyes away from Mollian to look at Regenya, layers of emotion swimming in her pale green eyes. "I don't understand."

"Please, protect him. And protect my—" her voice broke, "my grandchild."

Merriam was at a loss for words, and she struggled to pull all of her thoughts together. She again looked at Mollian. "You're going back to Umbra?"

He nodded.

"As ... as king."

He nodded again.

"There won't be a formal coronation, at least not for a while. Certainly not until the threat of Basta has been wiped out," Regenya said, resuming control of the conversation. "Sekha needs a ruler. But today my family will sit vigil for Gressia. Mollian will take the last shift, and at dawn tomorrow, I will pass on the crown. You will bear witness to it, as his Bonded and his *mehhen*."

Everything seemed to be happening very fast, but Merriam just nodded, biting her lip as she tried to sort through all the thoughts running through her mind. She followed Mollian and Darius up the stairs, everyone silent. When they split off at Mollian's room, the king embraced his son, and Merriam slipped through the door to give the two a moment alone.

Mollian joined her in the bathroom only long enough to brush his teeth, and by the time she exited, he was already fast asleep. Dawn wasn't yet peeking over the mountains, but it wasn't far off, and Merriam felt exhaustion deep in her bones as she climbed in next to the prince.

He rolled, pressing his forehead to hers, and they slept.

The next day, Merriam stayed close to Mollian until night had fallen, and he went below to wait out his remaining hours as a prince. Too anxious to sleep, Merriam held her own vigil sitting atop the spire, cloak wrapped tightly around her against the chill wind of the night.

Darius signaled for her, and she climbed down, following him underneath the mountain where Regenya and Mollian waited.

"It's time," Regenya said.

Darius put a reassuring hand on Merriam's shoulder as she watched Mollian lower to one knee before Regenya and recite vows to the kingdom.

Using a long needle, the old regent joined the aspen branch tattoos that extended from Mollian's temples, creating a full crown across his brow. Crushed stone from the Gate was mixed into the ink, further connecting him to its power and to the realm.

When Mollian stood, Merriam could feel the depth of his power stirring in her blood. Her breath caught in her throat as his cracked green eyes met hers. Without even really understanding what she was doing, she took a step toward him. He still felt like Mollian, his presence and the threads of his soul wound with hers, setting every part of her at ease.

But there was something else, as if a well of power he'd always possessed, but had never fully acknowledged, had been uncovered. She felt his full admission and acceptance of it reverberate through her as she fell to her knees in front of him, bowing her head.

He was still Mollian.

But he was wholly and irrefutably her king.

Chapter 48

Never you

Tears pricked Mollian's eyes as he looked at the girl in front of him. He had the undeniable sense that everything had changed in the hours he'd spent deep below Entumbra. But when Merriam raised her head, amber eyes meeting his, he knew that in some ways, nothing had changed. He held his hands out, pulling her up and hugging her to his chest with his face pressed against her hair. Neither of them said anything, the moment too big for words.

When they finally parted, Merriam smiled at him, mischief flashing in her eyes. "Let's go introduce your Rangers to their king."

"Why do I get the feeling you're going to enjoy this much more than I will?"

"Because you know me," she replied simply, leading the way up the long tunnel back to the castle.

Regenya gathered all of the Royal Guard to the courtyard, formally proclaiming Mollian as king. Throughout the day, they came individually or in small groups to swear fealty to him and renew their oaths to the Crown.

"He seems to be taking this all in stride," Rovin said, coming to stand next to Merriam.

She sat in the back of the atrium with a book, Mollian conversing with a few Rangers across the hall. "He may not have been born to it, but I think he was somehow always destined for regency," Merriam admitted quietly. She flicked her eyes up to Rovin, his gaze on the king. "Is it wrong for me to feel that so strongly?"

Rovin shrugged, running a hand through his hair. "I don't know," he finally replied, looking down at her. He pressed his lips together, emotions warring through his eyes as he searched her face, finally coming to a conclusion. "Will you come outside with me for a moment?"

Merriam nodded, concern darkening her features as she set the book down and stood to follow the lieutenant out onto the catwalk.

He stood leaning against the railing, staring off into the forest. "Be careful when you go back to Umbra."

Merriam stiffened, eyes narrowing. "Are you threatening me?"

The corner of Rovin's lip twitched, and he shook his head, turning to face her so she could fully see the distress in his eyes. "Not this time, pet. I just ... there's a reason things were made to be so hard for you in the beginning. Some people in power don't like the sway you hold over Mollian—*King* Mollian. You've earned your spot in Sekha ten times over as far as I'm concerned, and every Ranger who's fought beside you respects you more than you probably realize. But we're just pawns of those in power."

Merriam let out a soft, bitter chuckle. "Has anyone ever told Ferrick it's ironic he felt so threatened by a human child?"

Rovin shrugged. "Even more ironic that if he'd played his hand differently, he could have had you as deep in his back pocket as the rest of us."

"The captain sure fucked up there, didn't he?"

"Indeed, he did," Rovin agreed.

Later that night, Merriam lay across from Mollian, hands tucked under her cheek as they talked. "What did you tell your mother about Ryddan?"

"Only that I'd hidden him and he was safe. No one should suspect that he's with the mercenaries for now."

"She didn't ask?"

Mollian shook his head. "She knows the fewer people that know of him, the fewer people who know where he is, the safer he'll be. Her only request was that you bring him to meet her when it's safe."

"Me?" Merriam cocked a brow.

"I'll be busy running a country, Ria."

"I hadn't realized I had such a big fan in your mother, is all."

"She saw the tattoo on your arm when you brought her here … she asked me about it."

Merriam bit her lip, looking away. "Ah, well."

"I told her it wasn't my story to tell, but she's smart enough to have pieced it together. Your attack on Ferrick was a pretty glaring clue."

Merriam fought back a grin. "Not my finest moment. I should've smacked his head into the ground a couple times. Maybe it would have knocked some sense into him."

"So feral, merc," Mollian teased.

A frown furrowed Merriam's brow. "He hates me."

"If he doesn't wish to work with you, he can resign," Mollian said firmly. "There will be no room in my court for open disdain, not when you've done so much for Sekha."

"I can fight my own battles, Prince," Merriam said lightly, pushing Rovin's warning to the back of her mind.

"Your battles shouldn't be with your allies," he reiterated. "And I'm no longer a prince."

"Deepest apologies, Lord King. I won't make the mistake again."

"See that you don't. I'd hate to have to make an example of you in court," Mollian chastised playfully.

Merriam sighed. "So much for a five years' notice."

"Neither of us could have predicted this. If you need more time, I understand."

Merriam's frown deepened, and she raised a hand to trace the aspen leaves across Mollian's forehead. "I don't think I have a choice anymore, Molli. We're too deeply connected. My place is with you."

Mollian's eyes filled with apology, glistening in the bright white light of the moons. "I never wanted you to feel obligated. You should always have a choice."

Merriam brushed a curl from his face before dropping her hand. "I didn't mean it like that. We've always been connected, and it's always felt obvious to me that I belonged with you. But now ... it's nothing you did, not fully. It's the *mehhen* bond. It changed when you became king. Like whatever is weaving us together was somehow strengthened. You must feel it, too, right?"

"It feels almost like you're an extension of me. Not in a way that I can control you, more in a way that I'm aware of you. Aware of my magic in your blood—his, too, from the Bond."

"That feeling has steadily gotten stronger, even before tonight." Merriam rolled onto her back, twirling a strand of pale blonde hair through her fingers. "I've felt it more and more this year, but I think it's been happening since you brought me to Nethyl. Like the longer we're around each other, the more tightly we're bound."

Mollian also shifted to his back and reached down to grab Merriam's hand, lightly grasping palm to palm. "Why does this feel so much bigger than the two of us?"

"I think because it is. But I know—with every fiber of my soul, I *know*—that my place is with you."

They lay in silence for a moment before Merriam spoke again. "I need to finish out this last job with them. But once Basta is dead, I'll tell them I'm leaving."

Mollian turned to look at her. "It's okay to be sad, you know. This has been your life for five years."

Merriam blinked up at the ceiling, examining the few emotions that she allowed to slip past her mental block. "I don't think I am sad. I love them, and for better or worse, they're my family. Somehow I know my leaving won't change that. I've always had a foot in both worlds—being with them and being with you. Besides, it's not like I can't still work with them. Chief advisor can double as head spy master, can't it? Maybe throw in king's assassin for good measure." Merriam gave him a wicked smile.

Mollian laughed. "I guess we'll have to come up with a new title for you if you'll be wearing so many hats."

"Maybe we will. Something so that everyone knows to be scared when they hear it. So they know not to fuck around because I will deliver the full wrath of the king."

"Calm down, power-hungry." Mollian rolled his eyes. "You'll still be held accountable to the law."

Merriam raised her eyebrows, a mischievous smirk playing on her lips. "I was under the impression I would *be* the law."

"We're going to have to have a very real conversation about your official duties." Mollian ran a hand down his face.

"The official ones, yes, and the unofficial." Merriam grinned.

"Has anyone ever told you you're more trouble than you're worth?"

"Never you." Merriam's smile softened.

"No, never me," Mollian agreed.

They left for Umbra the next morning.

Regenya and Darius said goodbye to Mollian on the wrought iron catwalk as the Rangers prepared everything for the trip.

After releasing Mollian from an uncharacteristically long hug, Regenya dabbed tears from the corners of her eyes with a knuckle and turned to Merriam. "Thank you."

Merriam blinked, cocking her head to the side.

"For loving my sons," Regenya clarified softly.

"Your sons are easy to love," Merriam replied quietly, fidgeting with the umbrite ring on her finger.

"Mollian is going to need you. He's young, and there are some who will try to take advantage of that. If anything, I know that you will keep his best interest at heart. The future of Sekha lies with him."

Mollian rolled his eyes. "Mother, you don't have to be so dramatic. First and foremost, I'll be fine. Your lack of faith is disheartening. Second, Merriam has already agreed to act as my advisor, so you don't have to try to guilt her into anything."

Regenya's eyes widened as she looked at Merriam, and she clasped her hands to her chest. "You're leaving the mercenaries?"

Merriam regarded her warily. "Yes."

"Is it because ..." Regenya glanced at Merriam's stomach, bringing a hand to her mouth.

Mollian choked on a laugh, breaking into a cough. "Legends, Mother," he wheezed.

Merriam's face flushed, and she looked off to the side, rubbing her neck. "Uh, no. No."

"I'm sorry, I didn't mean to offend."

"Not offended, just extremely uncomfortable." Merriam still didn't meet the former queen's eyes.

"This is entirely awkward, and I would like to promptly forget any of it ever happened. Mother, Father, I love you. Be safe; I'll be in touch." Mollian gave each of his parents a final hug before ushering Merriam down the stairs.

"Can't ever just have a normal goodbye, can we?" Mollian sighed.

"Is everything all right?" Rovin asked, handing over a set of reins to Mollian.

"Yes, it's fine. My mother somehow got it into her head that Merriam might be carrying the next heir to the throne."

"Molli!" Merriam threw her hands out. *What the fuck.*

"I'm sorry. But you have to admit it's a little hilarious."

"Mortifying, more like. And if you say things like that, rumors are going to spread." Merriam scowled, pulling herself up into the saddle of an unclaimed horse. She hadn't even had a cycle in the past three years, thanks to Calysta and her plant magic.

"Forget I asked." Rovin stiffly turned and walked away.

"I'm sorry, Ria," Mollian patted her leg. "The knowledge of Ryddan probably just made her a little too imaginative. But even if you are technically barren-by-choice, I do think she's still come around to you." Mollian assured her before swinging onto his own horse.

Just because you're king doesn't mean I can't still knock you on your ass. Merriam Cast at his back as they headed into the forest.

Oh, I think it does. That could be treason.

I'm the law now, remember? Doesn't apply.

I'm not sure that's what we agreed on.

I'm quite sure it was never outright denied.

The trip back was fast and blessedly uneventful. The Rangers were on high alert and extra respectful. Though the crown of aspen leaves was a powerful symbol, they could feel the change in him the way Merriam had, though not quite as intensely.

When they reached the city, Merriam split off from the others, heading to the merc house on foot to check in on Ryddan and see if they'd been able to get a location on Basta while she'd been gone.

She slipped in through the upstairs window, Jasper sifting through papers at the desk. "Welcome home."

The word cut through Merriam, and she forgot to breathe for a moment. "There's been a slight change of plans, actually."

Jasper stood, stretching out his back with a luxurious crack, wings flaring wide. "So I learned when I came home to two falcons in the kitchen."

Merriam smiled sheepishly. "I hope he hasn't been too much trouble."

"Trouble? That child is nothing but trouble, but he's able to play off of everyone's energy. We're all somehow more enamored than we are annoyed. Surprisingly enough, Leo has the biggest soft spot for him, but I do think he honestly just sees Ryddan as a bird in his mind."

Merriam's smile faltered slightly as Jasper spoke. "The child?"

Two falcons flew through the door then, Panic playfully chasing after one that was slightly smaller with bright green eyes.

When the smaller falcon saw her, it shifted mid-air into a fae, landing in a heap at Merriam's feet before springing up and flinging his arms around her waist.

Jasper just raised an eyebrow at her.

"You came back!" Ryddan said, tipping his head back to smile up at her.

"I thought we agreed you were going to stay an animal?" She ran a hand through his silky white hair, brushing it to one side of his head.

"You told me I could trust them."

"Right." Merriam resisted the urge to wipe her hands down her face.

Ryddan released her and ran from the room, shifting into a small blue bird and chirping delightedly as Panic tried to pluck him from the air.

"Mer." Jasper's silver eyes narrowed slightly as he searched her face. "Whose child is that?"

"Gressia's." Merriam knew there was no point in trying to hide anything from him. It was impossible to deny Ryddan's Keeper heritage.

"And his father?"

"Is whatever is hiding inside of Basta, as my educated guess."

"Does he know? Are we likely to be targeted?"

Merriam shook her head vehemently. "Basta never learned of the child's existence, and nobody has any reason to believe he's here. I would never have asked you guys to take on that risk unknowingly. You know that."

"In theory, but with everything that's been going on, it's possible there could have been an oversight."

"That would have been a Hel of an oversight, Jaz."

Jasper shrugged, not disagreeing. "How are you handling everything?"

"I'm not. Not really. But avoidance is working for me for now." Merriam slumped against the wall. "I know I'll have to deal with everything, eventually. I just can't right now. I need to focus on finding Basta. And on Mollian. He's king now."

Jasper blinked, eyebrows shooting up. "That seems fast. Without even a proper mourning period?"

Merriam tilted her head in agreement, folding her arms across her chest. "Something is happening, Jasper. Molli—" Merriam broke off, pushing her fingers into her hair to rub at her scalp. "We know Basta wants the Keepers for their access to the other worlds. We need to find him. Soon. Before he learns about Molli being king."

"We're working on it, but wherever he's gone to lick his wounds, he's done so quietly."

Merriam scrubbed her hands over her face with a groan. "What do we do? We can't just sit around and wait for him to regroup. He cannot get his hands on Molli. Legends know why the dumb fuck didn't have a demon possess Mollian last time, but he can't be given the opportunity again. Not now."

Jasper leveled his gaze at Merriam, silver eyes lit with intuition. "You're not talking about his being king, are you? Something else has changed."

"It has." Merriam met his look evenly.

"It would be helpful to have as much information as possible," he prompted.

Merriam shook her head, lips pressed together. "I can't—" before she could finish the thought, memories ran unbidden through her mind. Memories of her first meeting with Jasper and Leonidas and Aleah. Memories of how quickly they'd accepted her. Memories of Calysta and

Campbell joining, of them drinking together and fighting together and using inappropriate humor to cope together. Fresher memories of how they'd all been there, understanding of her grief.

Never once had they ever questioned her loyalties to them, even fully knowing the bond she shared with Mollian. Childhood had taught her that love didn't mean safety. Family didn't mean acceptance.

But the past five years had shown her the opposite.

They're my family, she'd told Mollian.

You can trust them, she'd told Ryddan.

She swallowed against the sudden lump in her throat, not trusting herself yet to process one emotion without having to process them all. Blinking back tears, she met Jasper's eyes.

Unsurprisingly, he understood exactly where her mind was. His hands were tucked casually into his pockets, and he shrugged lightly. "I was wondering when you would stop trying to figure everything out on your own and realize we're in this together," he said. "He's a part of you, Mer. We would never knowingly do anything that might endanger him any more than you would knowingly endanger Panic."

Merriam laughed. "A sane person may question equating the importance of the king of Sekha to a bird, but that definitely gets the point across."

"As if I don't know you, Mer," Jasper smirked. "Now what's going on?"

"Molli was never the weakest," Merriam admitted. "I think he's always known it, even if he never truly let himself admit it. I don't know if it was always that way or if something changed when he met me, like the *mehhen* bond altered or amplified his magic. But now that he's king ... Jasper, it's like nothing I've ever felt from him before." Merriam licked her lips, dropping his gaze as she searched for the right words. "And I *can* feel it. When I'm close to him, I feel him in my blood like a call to action. It's like ... like an antsy feeling, and energized. Like I just need him to tell me what to do and I'd be able to do it."

Jasper watched her, calculating.

Merriam bit the inside of her cheek, saying the words before she could second-guess them. "I think he was always meant to be king. It was always supposed to be him."

Jasper cocked his head to the side. "If Basta were to take him again ..."

"If Basta were able to control him, it could very well mean the end of everything."

"Do you think one of his demons is powerful enough to overtake him?"

Merriam shrugged. "I don't know. When ... when um ..." Merriam shook her head hard to clear it.

"How did he fight it?" Jasper asked gently, correctly guessing the cause of her distress.

"I don't know. He knocked me to the ground and then, before he could deliver a killing blow, he turned and attacked Basta instead. I think when it came down to life or death, the thought of hurting me or Molli was powerful enough for him to take back control, at least for a little while."

Jasper walked over to Merriam, pulling her against his chest with one dark arm. "We'll figure it out, okay? We'll find the bastard."

Merriam nodded, leaning into Jasper's embrace for a moment before stepping back. "I need to go check on things at the castle. Do you mind talking to the others?"

"Go, I'll fill them in."

Merriam nodded, moving back to the window and slipping out, silently making her way through the city to the castle on the mountainside. She reached out for Mollian, following his ping to their old chambers.

Two of the Guard were posted outside the door, but they didn't stop her as she passed.

Mollian was leaning one shoulder against the door to his room, arms folded across his chest. "It feels weird to have to leave it. This space has been mine as long as I can remember."

Merriam walked up and rested her head against his shoulder. "You're king, Molli. Tell them you want to stay."

Mollian sighed heavily, shaking his head. "The royal chambers are more interior to the castle and easier to guard. These rooms are easy to breach, as you've proven time and time again." He cut her a glance.

"They were able to take you from here," Merriam remembered, completely missing his attempt to lighten the conversation.

"If it helps, I don't really remember much of it." Mollian draped an arm over her shoulders.

"Mmm, well, in that case." Merriam rolled her eyes.

"How's Ryddan?"

"He's fine. Seems like a happy, content kid, all things considered."

"Good. And the mercs are okay watching him?"

"From what Jasper tells me, yes. But they know."

Mollian stiffened, glancing down at her, a white curl falling across the black aspen leaves on his brow.

"He's just a kid. And how old? Six, maybe? He's been in his fae form, and in case you missed it, you Keepers are pretty easy to identify."

"Well, fuck."

"They'll protect him, though. He's in the safest place he could be."

"There's a lot I'm unsure of right now, but not of that."

"What do you need from me?" Merriam looked up at him.

"Be okay with some of the servants moving all of your stuff into our new rooms?"

"*Our* new rooms?"

"What, like being king is supposed to change the codependency of this relationship? Please." Mollian rolled his eyes, pushing off the door frame. "Come scope it out with me. We can pick out new wallpaper or whatever."

Mollian grabbed her hand, pulling her down the hall. The guards followed as they made their way across the castle and up to the suite of rooms that would now belong to Mollian.

Sensing his need for distraction, Merriam humored him, enthusiastically suggesting color schemes and design plans for the common room and bedrooms, writing everything down on a sheet of paper taken from the desk at the back of the large antechamber.

All of Regenya and Darius's personal effects had been removed in the days they'd been gone, some sent off to Entumbra and others held in storage. The large space felt cold and empty.

They had just sat down to eat, side by side on the large couch rather than at the formal dining table, when a commotion sounded from the hall.

"I need to see Merriam!" Bellamy's voice was muffled through the solid wood of the door.

Merriam dropped the chicken she'd been about to bite into, wiping her hands on her pants as she stood.

The blood in her veins turned to ice as she walked across the room to the door, opening it to invite him in.

Bellamy's stormy blue eyes were lit wildly, long brown curls in disarray. "Calysta is hurt," he panted.

Chapter 49

They were demons

Merriam whirled around, eyes landing on Mollian just long enough for him to give her a quick nod. *Go, be safe*, he Cast to her as she grabbed her weapons belt from where she'd hung it by the door, swinging it around her waist and buckling it as she walked.

"Where is she?" Merriam asked, following Bellamy down the hall.

"The merc house," Bellamy replied. "I've been stopping by most nights to exchange any information and saw her stumbling down the alleyway. It's bad." His scarred face was drained of color.

"Do you know what happened?"

Bellamy shook his head. "It looked like she'd been attacked."

Unease washed through Merriam, constricting her chest. She turned to Bellamy, grasping his upper arms as she looked up at him, demand cold and clear in her eyes. "Stay with Mollian. Don't leave him alone, not until you hear from me."

"You think Basta could be involved?"

"I think we'd be stupid not to assume so, and I'm not taking any risks," Merriam said. "Stay with the king." She waited for him to nod his agreement before continuing down the hall at an urgent pace.

The mountain air was cool against her skin as she hurried through the city, the sky darkening with dusk. Every one of her senses was on high alert as she headed for the merc house, barely keeping herself from breaking out into a run.

Drops of bright, shimmery blood led her down the alley to the back door, and she did let herself run then, skidding to a halt in front of the door and fumbling for the key in her belt. She let herself in, hearing hushed voices from the mushroom, and ran down the hall.

Calysta lay on one of the couches, a sheet spread underneath her. Her long pink hair draped down the side of the couch and pooled on the floor, messy and matted, and her olive skin had a pallid gray tint. Aleah also sat on the couch, holding the nymph's head in her lap and smoothing her hair back from her face. Jasper knelt on the floor next to them, a pile of bloody rags and a bowl of water beside him.

"What happened?" Merriam asked, sinking to her knees on the floor at Jasper's side and taking Calysta's hand.

"She was attacked in the forest. Leo went to look; Campbell is finding a medic."

Calysta laughed weakly, her eyes closed. "The first time a medic will grace these halls. Apparently, I can patch up all of you, but I can't be trusted to patch up myself."

"Tell me the last time one of us came home practically gutted and then maybe I'll let you argue your point," Jasper said calmly, pressing a fresh cloth to the gash that ran across her entire abdomen.

A black cat sidled up to Merriam, leaning heavily into her side before tentatively sniffing at Calysta's hand. *Is she okay?*

She will be. Merriam stroked his back.

"Ryddan, can you get me some fresh water, please?" Jasper asked.

Shifting into his fae form, the child picked up the bowl in his small hands and brought it carefully into the kitchen.

Merriam leaned back, watching him raise the bowl over his head and slide it onto the counter before climbing up to access the sink. She turned to Jasper with a look of concern. "Should he be seeing this?"

Jasper shrugged, eyes moving from Calysta to the kitchen. "I have an unfortunate feeling that child will see a lot worse than this before he's grown. If he's going to need to learn to process death and fighting, I think it's better for him to learn so when he's surrounded by people who can help him navigate it all."

Calysta groaned, eyes fluttering open. "Wait, there was something important."

"You've lost a lot of blood, but you'll be okay now. Cam should be back soon with a medic," Aleah soothed.

"Don't patronize me. I'm injured, not an idiot," Calysta ground out, groaning as she suppressed a cough that would jar her ravaged abdomen. "They wanted my blood."

"What?" Merriam tightened her hold on Calysta's hand.

"They were demons," Calysta pushed out with labored breath, meeting Merriam's gaze. "Two of them. They took my blood."

Merriam's vision narrowed to a pinpoint, the world seeming to slow around her as she struggled to breathe. Her blood rushed loud in her ears, drowning out the noise around her as she processed the words.

"Mer, hey, are you okay?" Jasper grabbed her arm just as she was about to sway backward.

She blinked, clearing her vision, and was finally able to pull in a full breath. "No, I need to go. He's going after Molli."

"Hold on, take a second to think." Jasper released her.

"He doesn't know that Molli is king. He's taken him once before; he could think it's an easy target. And even if he doesn't think Molli has a lot of magic, he's still got a stronger blood magic than the nymphs as well as a direct connection to the Gate." Merriam stood, dropping Calysta's hand. "He needs a Keeper. The only thing that makes sense right now is that he'd go for Mollian. Why else would he have come back to Umbra?"

"We need a plan," Aleah said. "We know he has at least two demons with him; you can't take them on by yourself."

"He needs stealth on his side to infiltrate the castle. He won't have brought a lot of backup."

"We can't go with you, Mer. We can't leave Calysta." Aleah's voice was tight with indecision.

"Like Hel you can't," Calysta muttered. "Cam and Leo will be back soon. I'll survive at least that long."

Merriam shook her head, clenching her hands into fists to keep them from trembling. "No, if Basta wants Molli, he'll make it quick. He should wait for full dark to fall. I can get there first, wait for him, and take him out before he knows I'm there. I can end this."

Ryddan came back with a fresh bowl of water, sloshing some over the rim as he took clumsy steps with the weight of it. Jasper took it from his outstretched hands as he turned his deep green cat eyes up to Merriam. "Can I come? You said when you came back, Mollian would come too, but he hasn't."

Merriam placed a hand on his head. "Soon, but not now. Stay here. And if anything happens—if people show up you don't know—you hide, okay?"

Ryddan glowered, petulantly pushing her hand from his hair. "I don't have to hide. I can be a dragon and fight them off."

"A dragon won't fit in the house, Rydd," Aleah said placatingly, patting the couch next to her.

"Go," Jasper told Merriam. "Be smart. We'll follow as soon as we can."

Merriam nodded, leaning down to squeeze Calysta's hand once more before heading back out into the alley. As soon as the door was closed and locked behind her, she Traveled.

She took half a second to glance up at the cloudless sky, the thick band of the Milky Way starting to show in the fading light, and ran. She sprinted through the mountainside, dodging trees and leaping over bushes as she beelined toward the familiar area that paralleled the courtyard outside of her chambers—her *old* chambers.

The automatic amendment pulled a manic chuckle from her chest, and she pushed the hysteria down. The terror in her veins was too bright, too wild, and she knew she needed to slip into a calmer mindset before instigating anything.

It was a struggle, though. Merriam was having trouble shaking the debilitating fear that accompanied the thought of anything happening to Mollian. The harder she tried to push the thought from her mind, the more firmly it seemed to sink in. It didn't even matter that Basta could destroy the entire world and countless others if he had access to Mollian's power. It didn't matter because she couldn't lose him. She wouldn't survive it.

She skidded to a halt in an aspen glade, bending over and putting her head in her hands as she took deep breaths, trying to settle herself. The familiar grip of panic tightened around her, and she pressed a fist to her chest as she fought to push it back. "Fucking asshole, NOT NOW," she growled from between clenched teeth.

Closing her eyes, she forced even breaths from her nose, and slowly the wave of panic receded. Standing up, she shook her hands out and rolled her head over her shoulders as, finally, the cool, calculating calm required for a fight sank over her. Striking her rings together, she slipped back to Nethyl, just on the inside of the tall stone wall of the castle. Keeping to the shadows, Merriam crept around until she was opposite Mollian's old window.

The trees weren't very thick here, and she could clearly see the side of the castle and the darkened window. Half-hidden behind a slim aspen trunk, Merriam leaned against the wall and waited, watching.

Before long, Basta materialized in front of her, just inside the tree line, a demon on either side of him.

Merriam silently unclipped her axes.

Basta sent the two demons forward with a wave of his hand. They looked like giant, humpbacked wolves, but their joints moved unnaturally as they ran for the castle wall. Their long flexible fingers gripped easily to the stone, and they began to climb.

The soft slither of wood against leather whispered through the air as Merriam pulled her axes free, blending into the rustle of the leaves in the breeze.

She stepped from behind the tree, silent and sure-footed, raising an axe over her shoulder as she gained a clear line of sight.

A few things happened all at once.

Merriam threw her axe, sending it sailing toward the base of Basta's skull.

Rovin and a group of Rangers came around the corner of the castle, a couple of them bursting into loud laughter at something another had said.

Basta, alerted by the noise, turned toward the Rangers and took a step back further into the trees.

The blow that should have been precise and lethal ended up hitting Basta's arm at an angle, the blade of the axe sinking into muscle before falling to the ground, covered in blood that glistened too darkly in the moonlight.

Basta roared in pain and anger, turning to face Merriam and alerting the Rangers to his presence. He glanced quickly from Merriam to the Rangers now behind him, calculating his odds.

"NO!" Merriam screamed, breaking into a run and pulling the other axe from her belt.

Blood streamed down Basta's arm, coating his hand. He struck his rings together and was gone.

"No!" she cried again, sliding to her knees in the place where Basta had last been. Her gaze landed on her axe, the blade wet with his blood. "Fuck." It fell from her lips in a whisper, fear chilling her blood as she let herself acknowledge what she was about to do. Twisting the orydite ring around on her finger, she wiped her hand over the flat of the blade, coating the stone in Basta's blood.

She slipped the axe into its sheath, holding the other tightly.

"Merriam, no!" Rovin shouted, sprinting across the clearing.

Merriam paid him no attention, keeping her mind completely blank of every thought except the blood on her hands before swiping one stone against the other.

Rovin dove, his arms wrapping around her just as she slipped from the realm.

His weight drove her into solid, rocky ground, pushing the breath from her lungs. He scrambled up, eyes wide as he looked around.

Merriam was staring up at a dark sky, bolts of lightning jumping from cloud to cloud in flashes of indigo. "Where the fuck?" she muttered, trying to catch her breath in the dense air.

Rovin offered her a hand, and she let him help her to her feet. Before he could say anything, Basta was running at them, sword in hand. Rovin spun Merriam out of the way, drawing his short sword with a practiced ease and bringing it up to block the attack.

"I don't know how you followed me here, but you're going to regret it," Basta growled, pushing away from Rovin. His voice was once again doubled, echoing with something dark and powerful and deep. "This is *my* realm."

The arm that had been wounded in their last fight was now dark, trailing wisps of shadows and tipped in long claws that gleamed in a flash of lightning as Basta again swung for Rovin.

Merriam pulled her second axe from her belt, launching herself at Basta with a wild scream. He spun, blocking her attack and swiping towards her torso with an inhuman speed. She was able to leap back, knocking his weapon down, and the tip scraped across her hip. She grit her teeth against the pain, spreading her feet to rebalance.

Basta was already attacking again, slamming the pommel of his sword into her hand, and she cried out at the impact, dropping one axe. He immediately spun to attack Rovin, who blocked, face set in a feral snarl.

Rovin and Basta locked in combat, a brutal dance of attacks and parries. Merriam flexed the fingers of her hand, quickly testing for broken bones before running at Basta, sliding on her knees and swinging her axe at the back of Basta's leg.

Basta turned with preternatural speed, kicking her to the side. She hit the ground with a thud that knocked the breath from her and rolled, arm outstretched and still managing to hold on to her axe.

Rovin leaped at him, sword angled in a deadly arc for Basta's neck. But Basta turned, slamming his sword against Rovin's blade, knocking it from his hand and grabbing the Ranger by the throat with his demon hand, lifting him from the ground. Rovin struggled for breath, feet kicked in the air and fingers scrabbling against Basta's hand as a small blood vessel in one of his eyes burst.

Merriam scrambled to her feet, gasping for breath. "Rovin!" She launched her axe through the air. Rovin's eyes focused on her, and he reached one arm out, catching the axe and slamming the blade into Basta's side.

The sound that came from the man's chest thundered loud and unnatural as the demon inside him raged. He tightened his grip around Rovin's throat, pulling the axe from his side and tossing it to the ground before throwing Rovin down next to it. The Ranger landed on his shoulder with a sickening pop, and his face went white as he rolled onto his back.

The second Merriam had released the weapon, she'd started sprinting, crouching to pick up Rovin's discarded short sword. Her feet slid against the smooth dark stone as she switched direction, altering her momentum to race at the demon stalking toward Rovin with murderous intent.

Merriam flipped the sword in her grip, lifting it over her head before she jumped. Basta turned, raising his sword to meet her, but she was already driving down with both hands. The blade plunged into his side, just below his arm.

She screamed, rage lighting her amber eyes as she pulled the sword down, throwing all of her body weight into the jerky movements as the blade cracked through bone. Basta stuttered a step, blood bubbling from his mouth as his weapon dropped. She ripped the sword from him, a gaping gash down his side, clearly showing where the blade had cut through lungs and intestines.

Merriam panted, ready to strike again, but the life was filtering from Basta's eyes, and he crumpled to the ground with a solid thud. His gaze locked onto hers, and then his jaws were wrenched open as an oily black cloud rolled from his body. It sailed up into the air before crashing down, swirling into a hulking, massive form of a demon.

He had dark gray flesh and wore only black leather pants. His feet and hands both ended in three long claws that glinted in the flashes of lightning, and his back was lined with sharp spines, the shortest longer than Merriam's arm. "You killed my fucking meat suit," the demon spoke in the Common language he'd learned while sharing Basta's body, his voice deep and reverberating through Merriam.

She shifted her grip on the sword and swallowed as she looked up at him. Even Rovin would only come to his chest. "Oh, my bad," she said, taking a couple steps back. "I meant to kill *you*."

The demon chuckled darkly before dropping to all fours and launching himself at Merriam. She barely had time to raise the sword before he was on her, one hand wrapping around her throat and lifting her from the ground.

She grabbed onto his claws, dropping the sword as she strained to relieve the pressure on her neck. He leaned in and sniffed her, drawing a breath deep into his lungs. "You've got portal magic, little human."

His grip wasn't quite tight enough to cut off her breathing, but the force against her throat was still uncomfortable, and she fought back a cough. "Why don't you possess me then, dickweed?"

He drew his forked tongue up her cheek. "Gladly, just invite me in."

"Fuck off," she ground out, arms straining with the effort of holding herself up.

The demon threw her, and she hit the ground with a force that knocked the breath from her lungs as she rolled, her knee striking painfully into a rock. "You'll consent, little human."

Merriam gasped for breath, pushing up onto her hands and knees as she looked around for a weapon.

The demon turned to where Rovin lay prone and unmoving, blood trickling slowly down one temple. "Let me in or I kill the male."

"Fine, kill him."

The demon turned his attention back to Merriam, curiosity lighting his dark red eyes, pupil slit like a cat's. "Not the sentimental type?"

"He's made my life Hel for as long as I've known him. Take him out, and you're doing me a favor," Merriam said cooly, her gaze not leaving the demon.

"Then I'll let *you* kill him," the demon said, grabbing Merriam again and dragging her to her feet, his hand wrapped around her throat.

She kicked out, fear icing her veins as he raised his free hand, beckoning forth a black mass from behind a rocky outcropping. "I'll never agree. You won't break me."

"I'm bored of this, and don't care to try. I only need your permission because I would *share* your skin. A lesser demon, however, will just consume you from the inside until you're nothing but a husk. I only need you long enough to take me back to that marvelous little world of yours. Your pretty little prince will let me in without a fight if he thinks he can save you."

"No!" Merriam choked out, clawing at his skin.

"I rule here, human, and soon, I will rule everywhere," the demon hissed as the shadow rolled forward to Merriam's feet.

Its touch was damp and sticky and cold, and she choked back a scream as it crawled up her legs. Merriam wrenched her mouth closed as she saw Rovin peek an eye open, rolling over to his uninjured side and slowly crawling across the ground to where one of her axes lay.

She pulled her eyes back to the demon, glaring in heated defiance even as despair washed through her. It was too late. "I would rather die than help you," she hissed through her teeth, hoping Rovin would know to kill her before she could be used to transport the demon back to Nethyl.

In her peripheral vision, she saw the Ranger clasp the axe and stand.

The inky form of the lesser demon had rolled up and over her chest, making it hard to breathe. She tipped her head back, keeping her lips pressed firmly together as she seared the demon with her gaze.

The demon's red eyes danced with amusement as he watched her angry resignation, savoring her knowledge that she was helpless to stop this. He slid his hand up her throat until it clasped her jaw, his claws piercing the skin of her cheeks as he squeezed.

The shadow crawled over her neck, recoiling as it slid over the chain of her necklace. It touched her lips, and she almost gagged at the overwhelming scent of sulfur that engulfed her.

Kill me, Rovin. Kill me. The Cast was useless, she knew, but tears pricked her eyes as she held her breath, wondering what he was waiting for. She kept her glare on the demon that held her, cold resolution filling her along with a strange peace. If she died here, Mollian would be safe. Mollian would be safe, and ... *I'm coming, O.*

She let her eyes fall closed, waiting for Rovin's death blow as the formless lesser demon forced its way past her lips, prying her jaws wide as it surged down her throat.

As it *tried* to surge down her throat.

It recoiled with an unnatural hiss, peeling away from her.

The demon's eyes narrowed as he watched, surprise evident on his face. His lips pulled back in a sneer as his gaze landed on the chain at her throat, and he growled in frustration.

Merriam's eyes locked with Rovin's just as the Ranger sent the axe flying. She reached out, and the handle hit her palm with a smack that echoed up her arm. Merriam immediately swung it sideways, catching the demon in the ribs with a sickening crunch.

He roared, dropping her, but she kept her grip on the axe, gritting her teeth against the sound of blade against bone as it wrenched from his side.

No longer being controlled, the lesser demon swirled off with a piercing shriek.

The greater demon raised a hand to swipe at Merriam, but she dropped to her knees, pain shrieking up her thigh as the injured one struck the ground. Adrenaline blocked it from her mind, her only focus slamming the axeblade into the back of the demon's leg, snapping tendons in a gruesome spray of vile, black blood.

As the demon fell onto one knee, Merriam sprang up, raising the axe over her head. His eyes locked with hers, and cold hatred seethed in the dark depths of them as he raked his claws across her abdomen.

Merriam screamed, her arms already pulling her weapon in a downward strike that slammed just below the demon's temple, splitting his skull and bursting one eye on the way. She fell next to the demon, letting out a mindless cry as she clutched her stomach.

The demon made a sound that was half a growl and half maniacal laughter as he reached up and yanked the axe from his face. When the blade pulled free, a dark sludge spilled from his skull, and the sound abruptly stopped as he toppled to the side.

Merriam stared at him, panting heavily as she bent over her wounds. It was over.

She suddenly felt very tired. The pain of Oren's death spilled over from that place inside of her, filling her bones with the heavy weight of dull grief. She let it flood her, finally ready to accept it and let it run its course. Let herself acknowledge that, though there had been a moment when she'd been prepared for death—to be reunited with him—she was ready to choose life instead.

Rovin stumbled over to her, concern shining in his brown eyes, his chest still heaving as he caught his breath and came down from the adrenaline rush of the fight. "That shadow slid off, back over those rocks." He crouched down next to her, one arm hanging limply at his side.

Merriam turned her eyes up to meet his, and he slowly brought his hand up to her face, running a thumb across her cheek to clear it of blood splatter.

"Are you okay?" he asked, letting his hand drop.

Merriam hesitated. "I will be," she finally said, amber eyes flashing with the reflection of lightning.

Rovin nodded, holding her other axe out to her. "Thanks for lending it to me."

Merriam took it, her eyes never leaving his, searching and appraising what she saw there. "Thanks for having my back."

One side of Rovin's mouth pulled up in half a smile, then his eyes focused on something behind her, and the color drained from his face. "Unless you haven't had enough action today, I think it's time for us to leave."

Merriam turned to see several dark shapes running across the expanse of rock, and her stomach lurched. "Shit." She slipped her axes into her belt and brushed one of the stones across a still-bleeding cut on her arm, unsure of where they were or how far from Nethyl it was. Standing on her knees, she leaned forward to throw her arms around Rovin, striking her rings together with a single thought running through her entire being: *home.*

"Fucking Hel," Rovin hissed when she let go, biting onto a fist as his dislocated shoulder was jostled.

"Sorry," Merriam grimaced, pushing herself into a standing position with a hiss. She offered Rovin a hand, and he pulled himself up with his good arm.

They surveyed the courtyard, the two demons dead, but no fatalities suffered by the Rangers.

Jasper and Aleah were there, too, the latter running up to hug her. "Where the fuck did you go? We got here and you were gone."

Merriam hugged her back with a wince, emotion clogging her throat as her blood-spattered cheek rested against warm, red hair. "He's dead. I killed him." Her eyes locked with Jasper's, filling with tears. "It's over."

She felt the brush of Mollian against her mind, and she pulled him in as she stepped back from Aleah.

"You need a medic," Jasper said, placing a hand on her shoulder as he looked her over.

Merriam waved her hand, but wasn't quite able to stand up straight. "It's not as bad as it looks; I'll be okay. Rov needs help, though." She looked around for the Ranger in question.

Her blood stirred, responding to Mollian's presence even before she turned to see him running into the courtyard, Bellamy at his heels, a couple of the Guard further behind.

"We heard the fighting," Bellamy panted as they neared.

Mollian slammed into her, wrapping her in a tight embrace. Her legs buckled, and they both sank to the ground. The full weight of his power echoed in her soul, unfamiliar in its intensity, but the feel of it the same comfort it had been since she'd met him. "I couldn't feel you. I heard fighting, and I couldn't feel you," he whispered against her hair, his voice rough with the remnants of his terror.

"I'm okay," she promised.

His hold on her tightened briefly before relaxing, and he pulled back, grabbing her face in both hands and looking into her eyes. "What the fuck happened?"

Merriam tugged his hands down, shaking her head. "Demons attacked Calysta, and I just ... I knew he was coming for you."

"Where were you? When we got to the grounds, I Traveled to Earth, but you weren't there either."

Merriam let out a shaky breath. "We went to whatever world the demons came from."

"We?"

"Rovin hitched a ride, the idiot."

"The idiot ended up saving your life, in case you've already forgotten,"

Rovin called, stepping over and rotating his arm carefully. Someone had slipped his shoulder back into socket.

"You might want that in a sling," Merriam pointed out. "And you wouldn't have had to save my life if you hadn't startled Basta and made him move out of the way. That throw was perfect."

Mollian looped an arm over her shoulders, waving over a medic as his eyes landed on her bleeding abdomen. His face paled a little as he pulled her back to his chest. "You can brief us all later. For now, I'm just glad you're okay."

Merriam leaned into him slightly. *I'm not. But I know I will be. I'm ready to let myself be.*

Chapter 50

Today, you go home

IT TOOK SEVERAL DAYS for things to settle down in Umbra with Mollian officially taking over as king. The formal coronation still hadn't been planned, but all of the governors, officers, and courtiers had been met with, and individual meetings had been scheduled to go over anything that would need Mollian's eyes on it immediately. He'd accepted his new role with grace and dignity, and was already proving to be a just ruler.

Captain Ferrick had stood close by almost the entire time, which grated on Mollian's nerves, but the young king knew better than to make waves so early on in his reign when things were so fragile.

Merriam also hovered nearby while all of this was taking place, not because she thought Mollian incapable, but because she was still coming down from everything that had happened with Basta. She was constantly reminding herself that he was actually dead and wasn't coming back. The tender pink scars across her stomach were a reminder of the demon she'd fought. The demon she'd only survived due to a necklace gifted by a young boy who didn't want dominion over her.

Additionally, she was letting herself feel the emptiness Oren's death had left in her heart, and being close to Mollian helped remind her that she was alive. That she had the strength to move on while also holding Oren's memory close.

Merriam was brushing her hair, getting ready for bed, when Mollian slipped into her room. He dropped onto her bed, tucking one arm underneath his head and crossing his ankles while he waited for her.

She flopped down next to him, lying on her belly with her cheek propped on a hand. "What troubles the mind of the high king of Sekha?"

Mollian turned his head to look at her. "Why does something have to be troubling me?"

Merriam reached out and smoothed the furrow between his brows, giving him a look.

"I'm king. Everything troubles me," Mollian sighed.

"You've been too busy. Let me clear you off a day or two to just breathe."

"You'll clear off a day? Just that simply?" Mollian asked with a laugh.

Merriam shrugged. "Why shouldn't it be? I'll just tell all of your appointments that you're otherwise occupied. I've slayed demons; I'd like to see someone refuse me."

"I guess we'll have to add threatening the courtesans to your list of responsibilities."

"Someone's got to do it." Merriam smiled, blinking innocently.

"Thank you," Mollian said seriously, "for sticking nearby. I know it's not fun for you, but feeling you close through all of this has kept me sane."

Merriam reached across the space between them to grab his hand. "I told you, I'm here. For whatever you need. Hopefully that includes a lot of kick-ass secret missions and maybe some fun assassination taskings. But, regardless, this is my place now."

"I'm sure we'll be able to find ways to keep you entertained," Mollian assured her. "Though we never did find you a title, did we?"

"You've been understandably busy, Lord King. I can forgive the oversight."

Mollian brought his hand to his chin, making a show of appearing deep in thought. "Let's see. What duties have you been assigned? Chief advisor, king's assassin, spymaster."

"Enforcer, schedule-keeper, party-planner, best friend, personal space heater," Merriam listed.

"Such an invaluable member of the court," Mollian acquiesced. "Keeping more with the theme of advisor and spymaster and enforcer ..." He drifted off, eyes searching the ceiling as he thought. "How would you feel about marshal?"

"Marshal," Merriam tested, straightening her shoulders as much as possible while lying mostly prone.

"Commands respect, I think. Though, like you've said, if someone doesn't already know not to fuck with you, they'll learn soon enough."

Merriam crossed her arms under her pillow, dropping her head down. "Marshal of Sekha. I think that's worth leaving behind the title of mercenary." Her smile fell from her lips as she finished the sentence. "I suppose that's a conversation I should have with them sooner than later."

"I think it's time for Ryddan to stay in the castle as well. We haven't seen or heard of anything from the demon realm since you defeated Basta. He is a prince of Sekha and a Keeper. He needs to grow up in the castle."

"He's also half demon, Molli. We won't be able to hide it, and there are some who may not like it."

Mollian dragged a hand down his face. "He'll need protection, but I don't want him to feel caged. Especially with his entire life up to this point being sequestered and hidden."

Merriam chewed on her lip in thought, rolling onto her side and pulling her knees to her chest. "He'll need a personal guard, headed by someone we can trust to give him a long enough leash without him being endangered."

"Either way, bring him home tomorrow. Let him start getting settled. We'll put him in Oren's old room, I think."

"Oren would have liked him." Merriam smiled softly, an ache wrapping around her heart. She closed her eyes briefly, accepting the pain, letting it consume her, and then letting it drift off. "Ryddan reminds me a little bit of you when you were young. I think Oren would have been soft toward him because of it."

Mollian smiled. "Legends save Umbra if he's even half as adventurous and troublesome as I was. Oren would have known how to handle it, though. He was always more patient than either of us."

"Yes, he was," Merriam agreed, scooting closer so she could rest her forehead against Mollian's arm, letting his touch be a comfort and a balm to the grief that squeezed at her heart.

The next morning, Merriam and Mollian shared a light breakfast before heading their separate ways. Mollian had several meetings lined up with advisors and courtesans, and Merriam was off to the mercenaries. She had one stop to make before that though, and made her way to the Ranger's barracks by the castle gates.

She slipped inside, nodding to the few Rangers sitting around eating breakfast and getting ready for their various shifts. "Is Bellamy here?" she asked one who was just finishing lacing her boots.

"He's still asleep, in Bay Three." The Ranger nodded her head toward the long hallway that housed the Ranger's sleeping quarters. "You'll have to wake him up if you want him. I'm not going to incur that wrath."

"Thanks," Merriam replied, stepping down the hall. She pushed open the door to the third bay, three bunk beds against the walls on either side of her.

One Ranger, just pulling a shirt over his head, gave her a strange look, and she gave what she hoped was a pleasant smile as she scanned the room. She spied Bellamy's long curls splayed over a pillow on the bottom bunk across the room and walked over, gently shaking his shoulder. "Bell, I need to talk to you," she whispered.

"Fuck off," he shook her off, pulling the wool blanket over his head.

"I could, but I won't," Merriam quipped, shaking him again.

Bellamy groaned, pulling the blanket down as he rolled onto his back and opened his eyes. He shot upright when he saw Merriam. "What are you doing here? What's wrong?" He swung his legs out of bed, pushing hair from his face.

"Woah, relax, everything is fine. I just need to talk to you."

"Legends, Mer. You can't scare me like that." He dragged a hand down his face. "Let me get dressed. I'll meet you outside."

Merriam nodded, turning to leave. She ran into Rovin in the hall, instinctively jumping back a little out of his way.

He turned to look at her, brown eyes still cloudy with sleep. "Fuck are you doing here?" he asked, not unkindly.

"Looking for Bellamy. I've got a tasking for him," Merriam answered, leading the way down the hall.

"Since when do you hand out taskings?"

"Since I became marshal." Merriam smiled brilliantly.

Rovin scowled in tired confusion, waving her off. "Whatever you say, pet. It's too early for this." He stalked off to grab food from a long table against one wall.

Merriam waited outside the barracks, wrapping her cloak around her in the chill of the morning air. The leaves on the trees were just starting to turn from green to brilliant reds and oranges, and she let herself soak up the beauty of her mountain home, making a mental note to drag Mollian out within the next couple of days so they could relax and take it all in for a while.

Bellamy walked up, still blinking sleep from his eyes, half of his hair pulled back from his face, the rest spilling freely over powerful shoulders. He crossed his arms over his chest, the aspen branch tattoo on his forearm contrasted against his fair skin.

"I have an unusual request," Merriam started. "I want you to know straight up that you have no obligation to agree."

Bellamy narrowed his eyes suspiciously, skin pulling around his scar. "Okay."

Merriam licked her lips, grabbing his arm and pulling him a few steps further from the barracks. "That cat we brought back from Entumbra? He's actually a shifter. And a prince, Gressia's son."

Bellamy's eyes widened, mouth popping open. "A prince?"

"A prince of Sekha," Merriam confirmed. "But he's half-demon, and that fact could put him in danger."

"A demon?" Bellamy's eyes widened even further.

"*Half*," Merriam stressed. "He's just a kid, and he could very well be the only heir of the Stonebane line. His safety is imperative."

Bellamy tilted his head to the side. "What do you need from me?"

"I'm bringing him to the castle today. We've kept his existence quiet until now because the last thing we needed was Basta or the demon inside of him to learn he had an heir. But even with that threat past, there's still a possibility that some people might not take kindly to a prince with demon blood in his veins. I know it's technically outside of your realm of responsibilities, but Ryddan needs a bodyguard."

"You want me to be personal guard to a Stonebane prince?" Bellamy asked, surprise raising his voice slightly.

"You and a small team of others. But there's not a warrior in this castle I trust more than you to be in charge of this," Merriam said honestly.

"Mer, I don't even have any rank." Bellamy dropped his arms, shoving his hands into his pockets.

"First of all, you don't need rank to be a good Ranger. Second, that's something that can easily be fixed. The role of bodyguard would already come with a pay raise, of course. But, again, no pressure. It's a big ask."

"I'd be honored to serve the kingdom in such a way," Bellamy said.

Merriam let out a breath, a weight she hadn't acknowledged lifting from her shoulders. "Thank you, Bell. I'll schedule a meeting with Captain Ferrick to get all the details ironed out, but after that, you'll report directly to me or to Molli."

Bellamy nodded, a little dazed.

"And I'll work on that rank promotion, too," Merriam added before heading toward the gates.

She stopped at a bakery to pick up a tray of sweet rolls drizzled with a cinnamon icing, the tantalizing smell making her mouth water as she walked through the streets. She slipped in the back door of the merc house, heading to the kitchen to deposit her offering. Noise filtered in from the training room, and a knot of anxiety twisted in her stomach. After five years of being here and making this her life, she was actually going to leave.

Tears sprang to her eyes, and she blinked them back, forcing herself to breathe evenly as she entered the training room.

Jasper and Leonidas were fighting, Calysta and Campbell were throwing knives at a target, and Aleah was lying on her back at the base of the climbing wall.

Panic was perched above the door and screamed happily at her, alerting the others to her presence.

Ryddan, who'd been scaling the climbing wall as a squirrel, turned his head to look at her, fluffy tail twitching. He flipped around, dashing down and leaping from the wall over Aleah.

He shifted into his fae form as he hit the ground, running up to hug her.

"Hey, Rydd." Merriam smoothed his hair to the side. "I brought breakfast. It's in the kitchen."

Aleah sat up. "Breakfast?" When Merriam nodded, the redhead jumped up, skipping over. "There's a reason you're my favorite." She blew Merriam a kiss, grabbing Ryddan's hand and pulling him through the door.

Jasper and Leonidas had set their weapons to the side, while Calysta and Campbell were pulling the knives from targets. Calysta's exposed stomach was bandaged over the still-healing wound, but she was on the way to a full recovery.

"Breakfast? Why does that feel like a bribe?" Jasper asked.

"Because you're entirely too suspicious," Merriam told him, turning to walk back into the mushroom.

They sat on the couches, eating and talking about prospective jobs and poking fun at one another. Merriam chewed her lip, feeling her heart break a little at leaving this. At leaving them.

"What's wrong, Mer?" Campbell asked, catching the flash of misery that crossed her face.

Merriam swallowed back the emotion clogging her throat. *Just spit it out.* But when she opened her mouth, no sound came out. Tears blurred her vision, and she bit the inside of her cheek, shaking her head with a laugh. "Legends, why does this hurt so much?"

All eyes were now on her, and Ryddan shifted into his black cat, jumping up to curl in her lap. Merriam gently stroked his fur, letting the motion calm her as she collected her thoughts. "Molli has asked me to be his marshal, and I can't refuse him. I can't explain it, not fully, but I feel it in my soul that my place is now with him. I won't be a mercenary anymore."

"He is your *mehhen*, Mer, of course you belong with him." Calysta's inky black eyes swam with emotion.

"Mollian has been your king for longer than just the time he's been crowned with the aspen leaves," Jasper said, tilting his head. "You have always belonged to him, and I think you know that. Just as he has always belonged to you. He will need you to rule."

Merriam nodded, tears slipping down her cheeks. "I love you all, though. You have made Umbra my home. You helped me find myself."

"Just because you have a fancy title now doesn't change anything," Aleah said, tears also falling down her freckled cheeks, hazel eyes bright. "You're one of us, Mer."

"Yeah, you don't get to drop us that easily," Campbell agreed, leaning forward to squeeze her knee. "We're here, always."

"Titles mean nothing when you're family. Mercenary or marshal, we are yours." Jasper met her gaze evenly, silver eyes shining with sincerity and something akin to pride. "You will do great things for this country, Merriam."

Wiping the tears from her face, Merriam moved Ryddan from her lap and stood, the others following suit and embracing her in turn. "I'll still be here so often you'll be sick of me," she joked. "And I'll make sure you get offered all the best contracts."

"Oren would be proud of you," Jasper whispered, pulling her to his chest again. His oakmoss and sea salt scent swam around her, and, for the first time since his death, now over a month ago, her heart swelled at Oren's name. There was still pain, but also a warmth that accompanied his memory.

She nodded, squeezing tight the fae that had become something akin to an older brother, a protector, an advocate to her over the years. "Thank you," she whispered back.

Merriam turned to Ryddan, who'd shifted back into a fae and was sitting on the couch, watching them with wide green eyes. "Today's a big day for you, too. You're going to live in the castle with me and Mollian. Today, you go home."

"Home?" Ryddan tipped his head to the side.

"Home," Merriam repeated, a word that now meant so much more to her than just a place to rest her head. Home was Jekeida. Home was Mollian and the people around her. Home had been Oren and was now his memory. Home was this life she'd carved for herself and was determined to protect at all costs.

As the sun rose higher into the sky, Merriam walked through the streets of Umbra toward the castle, the prince of Sekha perched on her shoulder as a kestrel. Her steps were light, even with the weight of grief still in her heart. She knew she was where she needed to be. Where she belonged.

Epilogue

keep it a secret

LIGHTNING FLASHED ACROSS THE sky, unaccompanied by thunder. Small flickers of light popped through dark indigo clouds as other lightning bolts skittered through the atmosphere. The air was thick with humidity and completely still. A large palace jutted out over a cliff, made of blocks carved from dark, matte stone that matched the rocky landscape sprawling off into the distance. At the base of the cliff was a vast sea, dense with sulfur that caused the dark water to glow yellow when lightning flashed above.

On the balcony overlooking the sea stood a large being. His feet ended in three thick, viciously curved claws. Slick leather pants hung from his hips and ended at his calves, hugging heavily muscled legs. The material was a gray only a few shades lighter than the dark charcoal tone of his skin. His broad chest was bare, and huge leathery wings were folded loosely behind him, the webbing connecting from his shoulders down to the small of his back. Three sharp horns jutted forward from his forehead, straight black hair slicked back behind them. His face was beautiful and fully human save for the dark gray skin tone and eyes that were a red so deep they were almost black, pupils vertically slit.

He slowly drummed the three black claws of his hand—almost perfect matches to the claws on his feet—against the stone banister. They gleamed in the light that danced through the sky, smooth and strong and utterly deadly. He rolled his head over massive shoulders, cracking his neck before turning around. "Speak."

"His Eminence, Djuhl Charn, is dead," a lesser creature, smaller in stature but still muscled and bred to kill, said, bowing low as he spoke to the demon before him.

"Dead?"

"His host was killed by a female human. She possesses the same magic as the portals."

The greater demon stroked his chin in thought. "My brother was a fool to have joined himself to that sniveling beast," he said, lips curling back in a sneer to reveal long, sharp fangs in both his upper and lower jaws. "All that time wasted playing by that *human's* rules. I told the fool if he wanted another realm, he should have taken it. Instead, he wanted to learn and observe and *strategize*."

"There is something else, Your Eminence," the lesser demon interrupted, shifting nervously on his feet, claws scraping against the stone.

The demon folded his arms across the wide expanse of his chest, waiting.

"Djuhl Charn left a spawn."

The demon's wings flared in surprise. "Charn has offspring?"

"It would appear so, Your Eminence. The one who birthed it was somehow able to keep it a secret from him."

"A Djuhlin," the demon breathed, a smile splitting his face as he ran his thumb over his bottom lip. "What is she? The one who birthed it?"

"She was of magic, your eminence. Powerful magic."

"Portal magic?"

"Yes."

"Prepare my warriors." The greater demon spread his wings wide as another bolt of lightning cracked across the sky. "No one rests until the Djuhlin is found."

Acknowledgments

Josh - thank you. For everything. You have been my biggest champion and supporter through this entire process. Thank you for always being willing to listen to me talk through ideas and plot holes. Thank you for listening to my excited, mostly unintelligible babble when I'd finally figured something out. Most importantly, thank you for keeping our lives running while I threw myself into this book. Thank you for keeping me fed, minding the dogs, and being so understanding of the massive amount of time I was putting into this. I have accomplished one of my life's greatest dreams, and you helped me make it happen. I love you forever, and I promise if this goes to film I'll make sure the contract states you get to play a bartender.

The hive - Murs, Cass, Tay, and Sarah, I am eternally grateful the internet brought us together! Thank you for all of the encouragement from the very beginning, for being the very first people to fall in love with my characters and forcing me to tell their stories. Thank you for filling my life with chaos and being there to choose violence with me when the days (more often than not) called for it. You people are my soul, and going though this manic ride with you made it all the more enjoyable! I can't imagine sharing a brain with anyone else.

My beta team - thank you for your excitement and for asking all of the hard-hitting questions, forcing me to dig deeper into this plot. You all helped *Leaves* become *Leaves* in such a big way. You're all amazing, and I'm so glad I had you!

The heathens - you are the most bad-ass, uplifting humans I've ever encountered. Thank you for all the sprinting, all the encouragement, and all the unhinged conversation. I can't tell you how happy I am that my existence has overlapped with yours! Thank you for being such a great hype group—the first people to ever see snippets of this book back in the earliest stages of its creation. Seeing your love for the world

I was creating pushed me to keep going! You guys fill me with the screaming-meemies in the best way.

My family - thank you for the endless support. From the first "book" I wrote back in middle school (*Mace and the Arrow*, a tale about a couple of cats that saved a girl from an ex-con) to my every-story-is-a-tragedy phase in high school, you've always encouraged me to chase my dreams and never give them up. I really, really lucked out having you all in my life. I love you.

Kira, Heidi, and Erika - y'all were my first ever critique partners. My first hype crew. My first co-writers. You helped me start perfecting my craft and really call myself a writer from the very beginning. I wouldn't be where I am today without that friendship and creative support. Even after all these years, it still means the world to me.

DIA - thank you for fueling weird conspiracies for as long as you've been around. I hope you (and the Illuminati) don't mind me throwing an interdimensional gate deep below that system of tunnels you've got running around down there. I mean, hey, the lizard people have got to get here somehow!

Bishop Castle - this magnificent building inspired Entumbra. Thank you for sharing a little bit of magic with the world!

You, the reader - thank you for being here. Thank you for giving me a shot. Thank you for spending time in my world. I hope you enjoyed it. <3

About the Author

Carissa is a lifelong adventurer and bookworm who will never turn down fast food, still listens to 2000s pop punk, and always greets wildlife that crosses her path. Though fiction has been her passion since she was young, she also spent seven years as an air traffic controller in the Air Force, where she cultivated a love for all things aviation. Carissa grew up exploring the Sierra Nevadas of California, but now lives in Colorado with her husband. Mountains are her happy place, and much of her writing pulls inspiration from the grandeur and magic of the Rockies. When not writing or out finding adventure, she enjoys consuming horror and fantasy in any medium available.

Printed in Great Britain
by Amazon